DEATH

★ AND ★

HONOR

ALSO BY W. E. B. GRIFFIN

DEATH
★ AND ★
HONOR

W.E.B.
GRIFFIN

AND WILLIAM E. BUTTERWORTH IV

G. P. PUTNAM'S SONS

NEW YORK

G. P. PUTNAM'S SONS
Publishers Since 1838
Published by the Penguin Group
Penguin Group (USA) Inc., 375 Hudson Street, New York, New York 10014, USA • Penguin
Group (Canada), 90 Eglinton Avenue East, Suite 700, Toronto, Ontario M4P 2Y3, Canada (a division
of Pearson Canada Inc.) • Penguin Books Ltd, 80 Strand, London WC2R 0RL, England •
Penguin Ireland, 25 St Stephen's Green, Dublin 2, Ireland (a division of Penguin Books Ltd) •
Penguin Group (Australia), 250 Camberwell Road, Camberwell, Victoria 3124, Australia (a division
of Pearson Australia Group Pty Ltd) • Penguin Books India Pvt Ltd, 11 Community Centre,
Panchsheel Park, New Delhi–110 017, India • Penguin Group (NZ), 67 Apollo Drive, Rosedale,
North Shore 0632, New Zealand (a division of Pearson New Zealand Ltd) • Penguin Books
(South Africa) (Pty) Ltd, 24 Sturdee Avenue, Rosebank, Johannesburg 2196, South Africa

Penguin Books Ltd, Registered Offices: 80 Strand, London WC2R 0RL, England

Copyright © 2008 by W.E.B. Griffin
All rights reserved. No part of this book may be reproduced, scanned, or distributed in any printed or
electronic form without permission. Please do not participate in or encourage piracy of copyrighted
materials in violation of the authors' rights. Purchase only authorized editions.
Published simultaneously in Canada

Library of Congress Cataloging-in-Publication Data

Griffin, W.E.B.
Death and honor / W.E.B. Griffin and William E. Butterworth IV.
p.   cm.
ISBN 978-0-399-15498-0
1. United States. Marine Corps—Fiction.   2. World War, 1939–1945—Fiction.
I. Butterworth, William E. (William Edmund).   II. Title.
PS3557.R489137D43   2008   2008012656
813'.54—dc22

Printed in the United States of America
1 3 5 7 9 10 8 6 4 2

This is a work of fiction. Names, characters, places, and incidents either are the product of the authors'
imagination or are used fictitiously, and any resemblance to actual persons, living or dead, businesses,
companies, events, or locales is entirely coincidental.

While the authors have made every effort to provide accurate telephone numbers and Internet addresses at
the time of publication, neither the publisher nor the authors assume any responsibility for errors, or for
changes that occur after publication. Further, the publisher does not have any control over and does not
assume any responsibility for author or third-party websites or their content.

★

IN LOVING MEMORY OF

Colonel José Manuel Menéndez,
Cavalry, Argentine Army, Retired

He spent his life fighting Communism and Juan Domingo Perón.

★

DEATH

★ AND ★

HONOR

PROLOGUE

Historians now generally agree that the tides of war had begun to turn against the German-Japanese-Italian alliance, "The Axis," in the spring and summer of 1943.

From the American perspective, the war had begun with a series of humiliating defeats. The Japanese attack on Pearl Harbor on 7 December 1941 saw most of the battleships of the U.S. Pacific Fleet either lying on the bottom or so seriously damaged as to be out of action for the foreseeable future. The next day, the Japanese attack on the Philippine Islands destroyed half of General Douglas MacArthur's air force.

Before the month was out, MacArthur was forced to declare Manila an open city and retreat to the Bataan Peninsula and the island fortress of Corregidor. On 23 December, Wake Island fell to the Japanese. Two days later, the British forces in Hong Kong surrendered.

President Franklin Delano Roosevelt ordered MacArthur to Australia. MacArthur arrived 20 March 1942, delivered his famous "I Shall Return" speech, then learned there were only thirty-four thousand soldiers in Australia and very little supplies.

On 18 April 1942, Lieutenant Colonel Jimmy Doolittle led a small flight of B-25 "Mitchell" medium bombers in a raid on Tokyo. They took off from an aircraft carrier on what most of them considered a suicide mission, knowing the actual damage they could do was minimal, but that some victory—almost any victory—against the Japanese was necessary to prevent despair among the American people.

The exultation of the American people when they learned of the raid was short-lived. Just over two weeks later, on 6 May 1942, Lieutenant General Jonathan Wainwright was forced to surrender all U.S. forces in the Philippines. It was the largest surrender in American history.

In early July, MacArthur learned that the Japanese were about to build an air base on Guadalcanal, in the Solomon Islands. If the base was built, the Japanese could both attack Australia and interdict supply of Australia by sea.

Less than a month later, on 7 August 1942, the just-formed, ill-prepared First Marine Division, which had not planned to go into combat for another year, landed on Guadalcanal. The desperate action almost failed. On 9 August, after losing the cruisers USS Vincennes *and* USS Quincy *and the Australian cruiser* HMAS

Canberra *at the Battle of Savo Island, the invasion fleet was withdrawn. It took with it the Marines' heavy artillery, most of the supplies it had planned to put ashore, and even a large number of Marines.*

The Marines who remained ashore were on their own. Firing ammunition made for World War I and living off of captured Japanese rations, they not only held on but began to clear the island of Japanese. The airfield the Japanese had been building was captured, finished, and named Henderson Field to honor a heroic Marine pilot. Australia was now safe.

On 17 August, a small group of Marines—one of whom was a son of President Roosevelt—of the Marine Second Raider Battalion staged an attack on Makin Island. The short-lived raid was a success not so much for what it accomplished in destroying Japanese supplies, but because it meant the Japanese, fearful of other submarine-launched Marine raids, would have to divert large numbers of troops to protect the islands they had captured.

America, having licked its wounds, was now slowly starting to fight successfully, even in the Japanese-occupied Philippines: On 1 October 1942, a reserve lieutenant colonel named Wendell W. Fertig, who could not bring himself to obey Wainwright's order to surrender, pinned homemade stars to his collar points and nailed a proclamation to a tree announcing that Brigadier General Fertig was assuming command of U.S. forces in the Philippines. Large numbers of similarly minded Americans and Filipinos quickly joined him.

On the other side of the world, in the early fall of 1942, the German army was locked in an enormous battle with the Soviet Union at Stalingrad, and the English were fighting the Afrikakorps under General Erwin Rommel, who threatened to overrun Egypt and with it the critically needed Suez Canal.

The American contribution to that part of the war initially was trying to supply its allies, especially the Soviet Union, which could not win at Stalingrad without a massive infusion of American supplies—everything from aircraft, tanks, and ammunition to food.

The German navy fought this effort by intercepting the supply convoys with hunter packs of submarines. They operated in the North Atlantic near Europe, in the North Atlantic off the coast of the United States, in the Gulf of Mexico, and in the South Atlantic near Argentina and Brazil.

New York and other cities on our eastern seaboard were blacked out primarily so that cargo ships would not be silhouetted against bright lights, making them easier targets for the submarines. This had a further, unexpected result. The citizens of these blacked-out cities could see red glows on the horizon as American cargo ships bound for Europe were either torpedoed or shelled, set afire, and sent to the bottom.

The Americans got into combat in North Africa in November 1942. The original action—heavy combat—was not, however, against the Germans. It was against the French.

Although many Americans believed—and the Office of War Information tried to convince them—that the U.S. Army would be welcomed in French North Africa, others were far from sure about that.

They remembered that in 1940 many French had cried "Better Hitler Than Blum," making reference to a French socialist politician. They knew there were large numbers of French who believed Germany was probably going to win the war, and that the Germans were having little trouble in finding Frenchmen to volunteer for the Charlemagne Legion of the SS.

The Germans had permitted most of the French fleet—a potentially formidable force—to sail to the then-French protectorate of Casablanca, Morocco, where it and French army and air forces in North Africa remained armed and under French command, subject only to the supervision of a small number of Germans in the Armistice Commission. The French fleet, if so inclined, or pressured by the Germans, could hamper—or even deny—British and American passage from the Atlantic Ocean to the Mediterranean.

Agents of the United States Office of Strategic Services (OSS) sent to North Africa undercover as consular officers reported that while they had had some success in establishing contact with French officers and convincing many of them that France and the United States had a common interest in defeating Nazi Germany, they had by no means convinced all of them.

The Americans, under the command of Major General George S. Patton, hoped of course to put the troops of Operation Torch ashore in Morocco without having to fight to do so. The plan called for a force of nine thousand men to land north of Port Lyautry, north of Casablanca, to take the airport. Simultaneously, an eighteen-thousand-man force with eighty tanks would land at Fedela, and a third force of six thousand men and one hundred tanks would land at Safi and march on Casablanca from the south.

The invasion began at midnight 8 November 1942. It took the French several hours to mobilize their forces—OSS agents had some success in having various French units respond very slowly, or not at all, to their orders to do battle—but by 0600 it was apparent the French were not only not going to welcome the Americans as liberators, but had already begun to cause casualties in the landing force.

At 0617, Patton issued the shoot-back order: "Play Ball."

At 0700, U.S. Navy aircraft from the carrier USS Ranger *reached Casablanca harbor as five French submarines sailed out to battle the American fleet. There was a dogfight. Seven French aircraft went down in flames, as did five U.S. Navy Wildcats.*

At 0804, as surface vessels of the French fleet prepared to leave the Casablanca harbor, the battleship USS Massachusetts *opened fire with her massive sixteen-inch cannon. In ten minutes, thirteen French vessels—submarines, freighters, and passenger ships—were on the bottom of Casablanca's harbor, and many French warships had been damaged. The commanding officer of the French cruiser* Albatross *was killed by U.S. Navy gunfire.*

In the next thirty-six hours, with negligible damage to themselves, the USS Massachusetts, *the cruisers* USS Augusta, USS Brooklyn, USS Tuscaloosa, *and* USS Wichita, *and aircraft from the carrier* USS Ranger *either sank or knocked out of action most of the French fleet, including the battleship* Jean Bart *and the cruisers* Primaguet, Fougueux, Boulonnais, Brestois, *and* Frondeur.

At this point, French army and naval officers who were still willing—if not entirely able—to resist the invasion were convinced by French officers who had been dealing with American OSS agents that raising the white flag was really in the best interests of France.

U.S. forces, including those landed elsewhere in North Africa, began a march toward Egypt to join the British fighting Rommel's Afrikakorps.

In Russia meanwhile—on 23 November 1942, two weeks after the American landings in North Africa—the quarter-million-man German Sixth Army, which had been trying to take Stalingrad since August, was surrounded by Soviet forces. Two weeks later, General Friedrich von Paulus informed Hitler he had received an ultimatum from the Russian commander, Marshal Rokossovsky, calling for his surrender. Von Paulus reported that his forces, ill-equipped to fight in weather thirty degrees below zero Fahrenheit, were exhausted, just about out of ammunition, and reduced to eating their horses.

Hitler forbade surrender.

On 31 January 1943, Hitler promoted von Paulus to field marshal and suggested to him that if he did wish to become the first German field marshal ever to surrender, there was the option of suicide. Von Paulus declined, and within hours was captured by the Red Army. The very last of his troops surrendered on 2 February.

Not two weeks later, on 14 February 1943, the German army, under General Eric Rommel, fought U.S. forces for the first time. The Germans proved a far tougher adversary than the French. The German counterattack to stop the American drive across North Africa lasted six days, ending 20 February in a bloody defeat of the U.S. II Corps's Fourth Infantry Division and its supporting forces at a two-mile gap in the Dorsal Atlas Mountains in central Tunisia called the Kasserine Pass.

German Tiger and Mark IV tanks mounting 88mm cannon were far superior to the U.S. M3 and its 75mm weapon, which was nontransversing and, moreover, riveted rather than welded. When hit, the rivets came loose and ricocheted around the tank interior, usually killing all of the crew.

German battlefield discipline proved far superior to American.

One thousand Americans died and hundreds more were taken prisoner, and most of their artillery and heavy equipment was lost.

General Dwight D. Eisenhower, the overall commander, took drastic action. The II Corps commander was relieved, and George S. Patton, promoted to lieutenant general, was rushed to Tunisia to replace him and turn the situation around. He began to do so by ordering the immediate application of the cavalry tactic that officers lead from the front.

Patton also understood the tactical use of aviation. On 23 February, a massive U.S. bombing attack on Rommel's forces drove him back through the Kasserine Pass, on a retreat that ended only when he reached prepared positions on the Mareth Line.

There was no longer any question whether the Americans could successfully fight the Germans.

Or that they could stay in North Africa.

The war was going on, too, near the southern tip of the South American continent, in Argentina and Uruguay. Cities were not being bombed into rubble, cannons were not roaring, and no one was going hungry or freezing to death. But both the Axis and the Allies realized the importance of these "neutral countries" both to the war effort and, as importantly, to what would happen when victory and defeat came.

Buenos Aires ("nice breezes"), the capital of Argentina, was a large European-looking city one-hundred-odd miles across the Río de la Plata ("silver river") from

Montevideo, Uruguay. Both cities were a very long way from the battles raging at Guadalcanal (8,500 miles), Stalingrad (8,200 miles), and the Kasserine Pass (6,500 miles); and from Berlin (7,400 miles), London (6,900 miles), and Washington, D.C. (5,200 miles).

By comparison, it was only 577 miles from London to Berlin, 829 miles from Berlin to Stalingrad, and 1,100 miles from Berlin to the Kasserine Pass.

The war had actually come to Uruguay and Argentina in December 1939. The pocket battleship Graf Spee—*the pride of the German navy, named after a World War I naval hero, Admiral Graf (Count) Maximilian von Spee—had sailed from Wilhelmshafen on 21 August 1939, with orders to head for the South Atlantic and there to interdict Allied shipping heading for England.*

Wool, leather, and—especially—meat and other foodstuffs from Argentina and Uruguay had been of enormous value to the British in World War I, and the Germans were determined to shut off that supply in this war. The British were equally determined to keep the supply lines open, and dispatched the cruisers HMS Ajax, HMS Achilles, *and* HMS Exeter *to find the* Graf Spee *and sink her.*

They found the German ship off the coast of Uruguay, close enough to shore so that the roar and concussion of the naval cannon caused the sea lions on the rocks near Punta del Este to leap to their deaths.

The Graf Spee *suffered serious damage but managed to limp up the River Plate into the harbor at Montevideo. International law required that a warship of a belligerent power could claim the protection of a neutral harbor for only seventy-two hours.*

The captain of the Graf Spee, *Hans Langsdorff, one of the most respected officers in the German navy, radioed Berlin explaining his plight: There was serious damage to the* Graf Spee *that could not be repaired in the time he had. He had lost more than one hundred sailors in the battle off Punta del Este, and had as many more seriously wounded crewmen who required immediate treatment not available on the* Graf Spee, *whose onboard hospital had been destroyed in the sea battle.*

And there were three British cruisers waiting for him in the South Atlantic Ocean.

Under these circumstances, he could see no alternative to letting the seventy-two hours run out, then allow himself and his ship to be interned by the Uruguayan government.

The reply from Grand Admiral Eric Raeder, commander in chief of the German navy, came immediately: Loss of life was not a consideration when the honor of Germany and the German navy was at stake. The Führer, Adolf Hitler, ordered that the Graf Spee go down fighting.

Captain Langsdorff understood honor.

Thus, he arranged for his wounded to be taken ashore and interned so they would receive medical attention. He put his dead ashore and arranged for their burial in Montevideo. He arranged for most of his physically fit crew to board small vessels hastily sent from Buenos Aires by Argentine Axis sympathizers. On arrival, they would be interned.

When the seventy-two hours was almost up, he hoisted anchor and sailed the Graf Spee out of Montevideo's harbor. When she was far enough into the River Plate so that her wreck would not interfere with shipping, he scuttled her. He made sure he was the last man to leave her, then took her battle ensign, boarded a small vessel, and made for Buenos Aires.

In Buenos Aires two days later, after ensuring that his officers and men would be treated well in internment, Captain Langsdorff put on his dress uniform, positioned himself so that his body would fall on the Graf Spee's battle ensign, and shot himself in the temple. That, he believed, would prove he had scuttled his ship because he saw that as his duty as an honorable officer, not because he was afraid of losing his life.

Captain Langsdorff was buried by the Argentine military with full military honors in Buenos Aires's North Cemetery. Most of his crew, in dress uniform, attended. His pallbearers were Graf Spee seamen. They then marched off into internment.

Vice Admiral Wilhelm Canaris, the senior German intelligence officer, who in World War I had been interned in—and escaped from—Argentina, immediately dispatched German intelligence officers to Buenos Aires to arrange for escape of the interned crew of the Graf Spee.

With the Graf Spee gone, there was no longer a chance for the Germans to shut off the supply of matériel to the British using a sea raider or other surface navy warships. German Admiral Erich Raeder turned to submarines. Because of the distance from the submarine pens in France, this was an enormously difficult task.

Neutral Uruguay was sympathetic to the British chiefly because of a large English colony and the enormously popular Brit ambassador, Sir Eugene Millington-Drake. But neutral Argentina was predominantly—though by no means entirely—pro-Axis.

The Argentine army was armed with Mauser rifles, wore German helmets, sent their senior officers to the Kriegschule in Germany, and had their headquarters in *a handsome, enormous building—the Edificio Libertador—built by the Germans as a manifestation of their solidarity with the Argentines.*

Its navy, however, largely British- and (to some degree) U.S.-trained, was sympathetic to England.

Moreover, there was a large Jewish colony in Argentina—including forty thousand Jewish gauchos—that was by no means sympathetic to Hitler, and there were large numbers of other European refugees who were decidedly anti-Axis.

The practical result of all this was that while pro-Axis Argentines did their best to see that German submarines not only managed to get fuel and supplies but were advised of departing British merchant ships so they could be intercepted and sunk, there were anti-Axis Argentines who did their best to keep the supplies flowing to England.

Things changed soon after the Japanese attack on the United States at Pearl Harbor. Brazil declared war on the German-Italian-Japanese axis in January 1942. That gave the U.S. Army Air Corps immediate access to Brazilian airfields, and the U.S. Navy to Brazilian ports and fuel.

B-24 bombers were soon prowling the South Atlantic just outside the Argentine and Uruguayan territorial limits. These aircraft had most of their machine-gun turrets removed—to increase range by reducing weight and drag—and their bomb bays loaded with special antisubmarine bombs.

This was not entirely a heartwarming manifestation of Brazilian–U.S. cooperation to fight a common enemy. American intelligence agents reported their strong suspicions that the artillery, tanks, and ammunition requested by Brazil of the "Arsenal of Democracy" were as likely to be used by the Brazilians against the Argentines as they were against the Axis.

A war between Argentina and Brazil, the two largest countries on the South American continent, was not going to contribute much to a war against Germany, Italy, and Japan. The flood of supplies to Brazil dwindled to a trickle.

And then American intelligence agents in Europe began to hear whispers of two secret German operations, which sometimes overlapped.

One was that it was possible for German Jews outside Germany to purchase the freedom of their relatives from Nazi concentration/extermination camps, followed by transport to Argentina and Uruguay.

The second secret German plan, called Operation Phoenix, was to establish in

Argentina, Brazil, and Paraguay safe havens for senior Nazi officials—possibly in-cluding Hitler himself—to which they could flee when the Thousand-Year Reich went down to defeat.

The overlap between the two plans, intelligence officers reported, was that Op-eration Phoenix would be funded at least partially—and possibly substantially—by the ransom paid to get Jews out of Nazi death camps.

In something of an understatement, United States intelligence activities in neu-tral Argentina increased considerably about the time of the Soviet victory at Stal-ingrad and the second battle of Kasserine Pass.

I

[ONE]
Estancia San Pedro y San Pablo
Near Pila
Buenos Aires Province, Argentina
1130 22 June 1943

The Fieseler Storch, a small, high-wing, single-engine aircraft, flew at one thousand feet over the verdant Argentine pampas.

The pampas—from the Indian word for "level plain"—runs from the Atlantic Ocean just south of Buenos Aires to the Andes Mountains. The flat, fertile plains cover 300,000 square miles, an area roughly half the size of Alaska, a little larger than Texas, and just about twice as big as California. The pampas has been accurately described as incredibly vast, incredibly fertile, and incredibly silent.

The Storch was freshly painted in the Luftwaffe "Spring and Summer Camouflage Scheme." The two sergeants who had accompanied the plane to Argentina had dutifully complied with the appropriate Luftwaffe maintenance regulation, even though June in Argentina was winter.

The original idea the Wehrmacht and the Foreign Office had had was to send the airplane to Argentina and, after demonstrating its extraordinary capabilities to as many Argentine officers as possible, to give it to the Ejército Argentino as a gesture of friendship and solidarity.

Manfred Alois Graf von Lutzenberger, the slight, very thin, career diplomat who was ambassador extraordinary and plenipotentiary of the German Reich to the Republic of Argentina, had seen how useful the airplane had been in moving around the country—and especially between Buenos Aires and Montevideo, Uruguay—and somehow the gift had never been made.

The sergeants had done a good job. The random shaped patches in three shades of green and two of brown had been faultlessly applied. The black crosses identifying a German military aircraft had been painted flawlessly on both sides of the fuselage aft of the cockpit, and the red *Hakenkruez* of Nazi Germany had been painted in white circles on the vertical stabilizer.

———

There were two men in the Storch, both wearing Luftwaffe flight suits, a sort of brown coverall with many pockets. The pilot, Major Freiherr Hans-Peter von Wachtstein, was serving as the acting military attaché of the embassy until an officer of suitable rank for the position could be selected and sent to Buenos Aires to replace the attaché who had been killed.

The passenger, sitting behind von Wachtstein in the narrow fuselage, was Korvettenkapitän Karl Boltitz. Korvettenkapitän is the German naval rank equivalent to a Luftwaffe major—and to that of a U.S. Navy lieutenant commander and Army/Marine Corps major.

Both officers were tall, blond, well-set-up young men. Under their flight suits they wore nearly brand-new well-tailored woolen suits. Clothing was strictly rationed in Germany, but there was no clothing ration in Argentina—for that matter, no rationing at all—and both had taken the opportunity immediately on their arrival to buy complete wardrobes, from fine fur felt hats down to finely crafted shoes of the best Argentine leather.

On the endless rolling grass plain beneath the aircraft, von Wachtstein scanned the literally countless cattle spread as far as the eye could see. He thought their low-level flight over the pampas could have turned into a chasing of the cattle—except not one of the cows paid the slightest attention to the airplane.

Von Wachtstein switched his left hand to the stick of the Storch and gestured at the ground with his right.

Boltitz, who had been carefully studying the ground from the left window, now directed his look out the right side. He saw a sprawling, white-painted stone mansion sitting with its outbuildings in an enormous manicured garden, all set within a windbreak of a triple row of tall cedars. He nodded.

He saw, too, that there was an airstrip. He corrected himself. It was a small *airfield*. There was a fairly large curved-roof hangar. The tail of a light airplane protruded from the hangar's door, and there were three more small airplanes—after a moment, he identified them as American-made Piper Cubs—parked on a paved tarmac. There was even a fuel truck.

Parked with its nose into the hangar was a large, sleek, twin-engine passenger aircraft painted a brilliant high-gloss red. It took Boltitz a moment to identify it as an American Lockheed Lodestar transport, and then another moment to call from his memory something about it. It was smaller than the standard American airliner, the Douglas DC-3, which carried twenty-one passengers—the Lodestar carried fourteen—but it was considerably faster and had a longer range.

That Lodestar, Boltitz thought, *is as out of place in this setting as is the Storch. The Storch belongs on a battlefield and the Lodestar on an airport.*

Von Wachtstein took the stick in his right hand again and picked up the intercom microphone.

"This is Estancia San Pedro y San Pablo," he announced. "It takes in a few more than eight hundred eighty square kilometers."

Boltitz had trouble believing that.

"That's the size of Berlin," he challenged.

"Yes, it is," von Wachtstein said. "And more than twice the size of Vienna, and more than three times the size of Munich. I checked it in the embassy library."

"Fantastic!"

"And my mother-in-law's estancia, Santa Catalina," von Wachtstein went on, "which starts a couple of kilometers to our right, is nearly as big, eight hundred and five square kilometers, more or less."

"Mein Gott!" Boltitz exclaimed dutifully. He thought: *Why the hell is he so cheerful?*

Boltitz now noticed something else. There was a large open convertible—he couldn't be sure, but it looked like a Horch—parked in the shade of the hangar. A blond young woman was sitting on the hood, looking up at them.

Boltitz found his microphone.

"There's a blond woman looking up at us," he said, then asked, "Is that a Horch?"

"Señora Dorotea Mallín de Frade," von Wachtstein replied. "Mistress of all she can see. That is indeed a Horch. A 930V. One of the last to leave the factory. It belonged to Oberst Frade."

As von Wachtstein banked the plane, Boltitz got a better look at the car. It was enormous but graceful. It had black fenders and hood, and the body was painted in red nearly as bright as the airliner.

Boltitz remembered his father, in one of the rare times he said anything that could be in any way interpreted as critical of Adolf Hitler, telling him that *Der Führer* had really "killed the Horch."

"It's actually a better car than the Mercedes," Vizeadmiral Kurt Boltitz had said. "But since the Führer and his entourage ride around in Mercedeses, everyone with enough money to buy a car of that class naturally wants to be like our Führer."

Boltitz thought: *My God, I should have paid attention to what my father wasn't saying. He told me to pay attention not to what Admiral Canaris was saying, but what he was not saying. I should have been smart enough to apply that to my father, too.*

"And where Doña Dorotea is," von Wachtstein went on cheerfully, "one can usually find Don Cletus. We got lucky."

Fully aware that both his office and apartment telephones were tapped by the Sicherheitsdienst—the "security" branch of the SS—attached to the German embassy, von Wachtstein had not telephoned to tell either Doña Dorotea or her husband they were coming, or even to ascertain that either was at the estancia. He had to take the chance that one or the other was.

"Did we, von Wachtstein?" Boltitz asked sarcastically. "Did we 'get lucky'?"

Von Wachtstein didn't reply. He was concentrating on setting the Storch down on the four-thousand-foot-long gravel landing strip.

Not that he was going to need much of the runway. The Storch—its long, fixed, landing gear and large, high wing made it look like a stork; hence the name—could land practically anywhere and do it so slowly that it could come to a stop within a hundred feet of touchdown. Large slats fixed to the leading edge of the wing and enormous flaps gave it that ability, and the ability to take off at twenty-five miles per hour in about two hundred feet.

Without thinking of the circumstances of their coming to the estancia, von Wachtstein was showing off the flight characteristics of the Luftwaffe's "ground cooperation" airplane and his own skill to Cletus Frade, himself a pilot.

He realized this when he was on the ground and taxiing the Storch to park it beside the three Piper Cubs.

That wasn't too smart, he thought. *But under the circumstances, I'm entitled to be a little crazy.*

He considered that, then corrected himself: *Crazy, but not careless.*

The young blond woman slid off the enormous hood of the Horch, exposing more leg than she realized, and started walking toward the Storch.

On her heels came a large and burly middle-aged man with an enormous mustache. He was wearing a business suit that didn't quite fit. He cradled a 12-gauge Remington Model 11 semiautomatic shotgun in his arms. Around his neck was a leather bandolier of brass-cased double-aught buckshot shells.

"Sergeant Major Enrico Rodríguez, Retired," von Wachtstein said against the noise of the shutting-down Argus 10C engine. "Where Don Cletus is, Enrico can *always* be found. I think I should tell you Enrico's not fond of

Germans. He suspects, correctly, that people we hired wound up slitting his sister's throat while they were trying to assassinate Don Cletus, and ambushed Don Cletus's father, Oberst Frade, in that Horch. El Coronel died. The assassins thought Enrico was dead, too. He was full of buckshot, but he wasn't dead."

"*Mein Gott!*" Boltitz muttered.

Von Wachtstein waved at Doña Dorotea, loosened his seat belt, then started to unfasten the fold-down doors on the Storch.

Boltitz saw someone jump down from the fuselage door of the Lodestar and start to walk toward them. He was a tall, lanky, dark-haired young man wearing khaki trousers, cowboy boots, and a fur-collared leather zipper jacket.

That looks, Boltitz thought, *like some kind of a flier's jacket.*

When the young man came closer, he saw that it was: Sewn to the breast was a gold-stamped identification badge. It carried the wings of a Naval Aviator and the legend C.H. Frade, 1LT USMCR.

"*Hola,* Peter," Señora Frade greeted him with a wave and a smile as he crawled out of the airplane. "An unexpected pleasure."

"Dorotea, may I present Korvettenkapitän Boltitz?" von Wachtstein said. "Dorotea is my wife's oldest friend."

Boltitz clicked his heels and bowed.

"Enchanted," he said in Spanish.

"What can we do for you, von Wachtstein?" Cletus Frade asked in Spanish. His hostile tone of voice made it clear that he was displeased as well as surprised to see the German.

The surprise was genuine. The hostility was feigned. It was difficult to dislike someone who had saved your life. More than that: Frade was both genuinely fond of von Wachtstein and admired him. Maybe even loved him.

Cletus H. Frade had given his relationship with Hans-Peter von Wachtstein a good deal of thought.

We're pawns on this crazy chessboard, he had originally thought, *and the people moving us around are perfectly willing to sacrifice either of us to advance their game.*

He'd changed that original assessment slightly: *Well, maybe not pawns, maybe knights. But certainly not bishops, who by definition are supposed to promote good works and practice decency and honesty.*

They had met six months before, in December of 1942, as the result of what he had politely thought of at the time as an almost funny misunderstanding between his father and his aunt—his father's sister, Beatrice Frade de Duarte—but what he now thought of, far less kindly, as a typical Argentine fuckup.

Two months before they met, both had been serving officers. Frade had been flying a Grumman F4F Wildcat of Marine Fighter Squadron VMF-211 off Fighter One on Guadalcanal, and von Wachtstein a Focke-Wulf 190 of Jagdstaffel 232 defending Berlin against what was becoming a daily bombardment by the Allied heavy bombers.

That had a lot to do with what happened, Cletus Frade had decided, perhaps immodestly. *We're both fighter pilots. Fighter pilots are special people. Only another fighter pilot knows what being a fighter pilot is all about. It has nothing to do with what side of the war you're on.*

Cletus Frade had been returned to the United States from Guadalcanal to perform two duties the brass considered more important than his shooting down any more Japanese aircraft or strafing Japanese infantry.

The first was to be exhibited—with half a dozen other pilots with five or more kills—on various platforms and theater stages on the West Coast. Seeing real-life aces, the brass reasoned, was almost certain to encourage people to buy war bonds.

The second purpose—for the combat-experienced pilots to serve as instructor pilots to pass on the lessons they had learned to new pilots—Frade thought was probably going to be more dangerous than taking on some Japanese pilot. A new Navy or Marine aviator trying to prove he was worthy of being sent off to do aerial battle was very likely to be as dangerous to his instructor pilot as a fourteen-year-old riding his first motorcycle in front of his girlfriend.

Frade therefore had been very receptive to the offer made to him in a San Francisco hotel room as he reluctantly was getting dressed to go on display again.

It had come from a stocky, well-dressed, mustachioed, middle-aged man who said his name was Graham. He had shown Frade his identification card, that of a Marine Corps colonel, and then said that if Frade would volunteer to undertake an unspecified "mission outside the United States involving great risk to his life" he could get off the war bond tour—right then, that night—and would not be assigned as an IP when the war bond tour was over.

Frade had already decided to do something outrageous to get himself relieved of his instructor pilot duties, but that almost certainly would have meant getting shipped back to the Pacific, which would also certainly involve great risk to his life. So, figuring that he didn't have much to lose, he signed a vow-of-secrecy document promising all sorts of punishments for even talking about his new duties.

It was only after he had signed that Colonel Graham told him he was now in the Office of Strategic Services, and what the OSS expected of him was to go to Argentina and attempt to establish a relationship with his father.

Not sure if he was embarrassed or amused, Frade had explained to the colonel that that was probably going to be a little difficult, as he could not remember ever having seen his father, and had it on good authority that his father had absolutely no interest in seeing him.

"I know," Graham said. "Your grandfather told me."

"My grandfather?" Clete had blurted.

Graham nodded. "I saw him just before I flew out here to see you. The kindest words he used to describe el Coronel Jorge Guillermo Frade—"

"My father is a colonel?" Cletus Frade asked, astonished.

Graham nodded again, and handed him a photograph. It showed a large, tall, dark-skinned man with a full mustache. He wore a rather ornate, somewhat Germanic uniform, and was getting into the backseat of an open Mercedes-Benz sedan. In the background, against a row of Doric columns, was a rank of soldiers armed with rifles standing at what the Marine Corps would call Parade Rest. Their uniforms, too, looked Germanic, and they were wearing German helmets.

"That was taken several months ago," Graham said. "The day he retired from command of the Húsares de Pueyrredón, Argentina's most prestigious cavalry regiment."

"Jesus Christ!"

"You're the product of an unfortunate infatuation, and a hasty, equally unfortunate marriage, right?"

Frade had looked at him but said nothing.

"I'll take your silence as agreement," Graham went on. "If I go wrong, stop me."

Frade nodded at Graham coldly but said nothing.

"Your mother converted to Roman Catholicism in order to marry your father," Graham continued. "Which ceremony was conducted in New Orleans, Louisiana, in the Cathedral of Saint Louis in Jackson Square, officiated by the

Cardinal Archbishop of New Orleans. Your Aunt Martha was your mother's matron of honor. Captain Juan Perón was your father's best man."

"You seem to know more about this than I do," Frade had replied, more than a little sarcastically.

" '*Sir, with respect,* you seem to know more about this than I do, *sir,*' " Graham said coldly. "Don't let my charming smile and warm manner fool you. I'm a Marine colonel and you're a first lieutenant. You have that straight in your mind, mister?"

"Yes, sir."

Graham nodded.

"Yeah, now that you mention it, I probably do know more about this than you," Graham went on conversationally. "Anyway, after a three-month honeymoon slash grand tour of Europe, during the last month of which your mother came to be with child, the newlywed couple went to Argentina, where a healthy boy—you—came into the world in the German Hospital in Buenos Aires. How'm I doing, Cletus?"

"Sir, from what I have heard before, that's correct."

"Shortly thereafter, your mother found herself in the family way again. There was some medical problem, and at her father's insistence, she came home, so to speak, for better medical attention. She died in childbirth, as did the baby. Your father then returned to Argentina, leaving you in the care of your Aunt Martha and Uncle James Howell. You were raised on a ranch near Midland, Texas, then were a member of the Corps of Cadets at Texas A&M—as was I, coincidentally— but you resigned from the Corps so that you could become a tennis-playing jock at Tulane. You went from Tulane into the Marines, where you flew F4Fs, shot down seven Japanese, and then were returned to the States to sell war bonds and teach new pilots how to stay alive. That about it, Cletus?"

"Yes, sir."

"And you cannot remember ever having seen your father?"

"No, sir, I cannot."

"Do you know how your grandfather feels about your father?"

"Yes, sir. He thinks he's an unmitigated bastard and the less said about the no-good sonofabitch the better."

Graham nodded.

"Maybe being an unmitigated bastard is the reason your father got to be a colonel. In the Ejército Argentino, that's like being a major general in the Marine Corps."

Frade looked at him but didn't say anything.

"And—if the coup d'état he's setting up works, and we think it probably will—he's probably going to be the next president of Argentina."

"Jesus Christ!" Frade had blurted.

"It would be in the interest of the United States, obviously, if the president of Argentina leaned toward the United States. Right now, the Argentines, including your father, are leaning the other way. You getting the picture, Lieutenant?"

"What makes you think I can change his mind? For that matter, that he won't be annoyed, really annoyed, rather than pleased, when I suddenly show up out of nowhere?"

"We don't know," Graham admitted. "All we know for sure is that it's worth a try."

Colonel Graham had been as good as his word. Frade never had to step on a stage again. Three hours after meeting Graham, he was sitting beside him in a Trans-Continental & Western Airlines DC-3 on his way to Washington, D.C.

Shortly after that, he was on a Pan American Grace Sikorsky four-engine seaplane on his way to Buenos Aires.

The day after meeting his father for the first time, and learning that he wasn't quite the unmitigated sonofabitch Cletus Howell had taught Cletus Frade to believe, El Coronel turned over to his only son the Frade family's guesthouse—a mansion overlooking the racetrack in Buenos Aires—for his use as long as he was in Buenos Aires.

Frade "went home" one evening to find another Spanish-speaking young man in the library. He was listening to Beethoven's Third Symphony on the phonograph and was well into a bottle of the excellent Argentine brandy.

By the time that bottle was empty and the level in a second bottle pretty well lowered, Lieutenant Cletus Howell Frade and Major Freiherr Hans-Peter von Wachtstein had learned a good deal about each other.

It had quickly come out that both were fighter pilots, which had immediately established a bond between them, even though they were technically enemies.

And the reasons both were in Buenos Aires rather than in fighter cockpits were actually quite similar. The German government had decided they had something more important for von Wachtstein to do than trying to shoot down the enemies' airplanes.

Von Wachtstein told him the German foreign ministry had decided that properly honoring Captain Jorge Alejandro Duarte, a socially prominent young Argentine officer who had died nobly in the Battle of Stalingrad, would be a marvelous way of reminding the Argentines that Adolf Hitler was at war with godless communism.

The young Argentine officer's body had been flown out of Stalingrad just before von Paulus's army fell to the Red Army. It would be returned to Argentina—in a lead-lined coffin—with a suitable escort, and then, after the posthumous award of the Knight's Cross of the Iron Cross at a suitable ceremony, Captain Duarte's body would be interred in the family tomb in Buenos Aires's Recoleta Cemetery.

The "suitable escort" is where von Wachtstein came in. He came from a distinguished military family and he himself had been personally decorated by Adolf Hitler with the Knight's Cross of the Iron Cross for his prowess as a fighter pilot. He had been ordered to Berlin from his fighter squadron to meet an Argentine officer, a Colonel Juan Domingo Perón, in order to see if Perón approved of him. Perón had found him suitable, and von Wachtstein had brought the body, by ship, to Buenos Aires.

The dead hero's mother—Cletus's aunt, and El Coronel's sister—had graciously offered the family guesthouse to the young German officer for as long as he was in Argentina—either unaware or not caring that her brother had turned it over to Cletus Frade.

By the time both young fighter pilots had staggered off to bed, they had agreed that (a) fighter pilots are special people; (b) Captain Duarte's flying around in a Storch directing artillery was a pretty dumb fucking thing for a neutral observer to be doing; (c) fighter pilots understand things beyond the ken of bomber and transport drivers; (d) getting shot down doing something really dumb doesn't deserve a medal, especially one of the better ones, like the Knight's Cross of the Iron Cross, even if (e) just about every medal on a fighter pilot's chest really should have gone to some other fighter pilot who really deserved it; (f) fighter pilots are special people, and after this dumb fucking war is over, we'll have to get together and do this again.

The bureaucrats at the German embassy, who had finally learned that von Wachtstein had been sent to the Frade guesthouse even though El Coronel

Frade's American son was already resident there, sent an officer to retrieve von Wachtstein early the next morning.

Both thought that they would probably never see the other again.

That didn't happen, either.

When Major Freiherr Hans-Peter von Wachtstein learned that it was intended to have Cletus Frade assassinated as a lesson to Cletus's father, to the officer corps of the Ejército Argentino—and, incidentally, also because it was suspected that young Frade was a secret agent of the Office of Strategic Services—von Wachtstein decided that his officer's honor would not permit him to look the other way. He warned him what was coming.

Thus Cletus Frade was prepared for the assassins when they came after him. He killed both of them, but not before they had cut the throat of Señora Mariana María Dolores Rodríguez de Pellano, the guesthouse housekeeper and the sister of Enrico Rodríguez, sergeant major retired.

"We were headed for Santa Catalina," Hans-Peter von Wachtstein lied to Cletus Frade. "The hydraulic pressure warning light came on. I thought I'd better sit it down and check it out."

Frade nodded but said nothing.

"Don Cletus, may I present Korvettenkapitän Boltitz? Herr Korvettenkapitän, this is Don Cletus Frade."

Frade examined Boltitz coldly, said *"Mucho gusto"* with absolutely no gusto, and did not offer his hand.

Boltitz clicked his heels and bowed. "Señor Frade."

"I'll have a mechanic look at your aircraft," Frade said. "And now, if you'll excuse me . . ."

"Cletus," von Wachtstein said. "He knows."

"I beg your pardon?"

"He knows, Cletus. Just about everything. That's why I brought him here."

"Oh, my God!" Dorotea said, horrified, and looked at her husband.

What the hell does that mean? Boltitz thought. *That she knows what "just about everything" means?*

And if she knows, how many other people know what von Wachtstein has been up to?

"Shit!" Frade said bitterly, and met Boltitz's eyes. "Do you speak English, Captain?"

"Yes, I do," Boltitz replied in English.

"Then you just heard how I feel about Peter's announcement," Frade said. Then anger overwhelmed him. "Jesus H. Fucking Christ, Peter! What did you do, lose your mind? Why the hell did you tell him anything, much less everything?"

"Clete!" Dorotea said warningly.

"Señor Frade," Boltitz said. "Major von Wachtstein did not betray your confidence. I was sent here to uncover the traitor in our embassy, and I did so."

Frade examined him, his eyes revealing his incredulity.

"I don't pretend to understand you Germans," he said. "But do you have any idea at all how close I am to telling Enrico to take you out on the pampas and make really sure you can't tell anyone what Wachtstein has told you about anything?"

"Clete, my God!" Dorotea exclaimed. "You can't mean that!"

"Put a round in the chamber, Enrico," Frade ordered. "And don't take your eyes off him."

Enrico said, *"Sí, señor,"* and pushed the button on the side of the shotgun's receiver. There was a metallic clacking as a shell was fed to the chamber.

Boltitz had two chilling thoughts:

If Frade tells that tough old soldier to shoot me, he will.

Frade is entirely capable of giving that order.

"I suggest we go into the study," Dorotea said. She inclined her head toward the Lodestar. A man wearing mechanic's coveralls was examining something in the right engine nacelle. This placed him in a position where he could overhear the conversation.

Yes, she knows, Boltitz thought.

What the hell is the matter with Frade, making his wife party to business like this? His five-months-or-so pregnant wife?

Boltitz felt Frade's unfriendly eyes on him.

"Does the name El Coronel Alejandro Martín mean anything to you, Captain?" Frade asked.

Boltitz nodded.

Martín was chief of the Ethical Standards Office of the Bureau of Internal Security of the Argentine Ministry of Defense. He was the most powerful man in Argentine intelligence and counterintelligence.

"Just as soon as that guy with his head in my engine can get to a phone," Frade went on, "good ol' Alejandro will be wondering what the two of you were doing here."

He raised his voice. "Carlos!"

He had to call three times before Carlos admitted to having heard him and came trotting over to them.

"Carlos, this is Major von Wachtstein of the German embassy," Frade said. "He has some trouble with his hydraulic pressure. Would you please do what you can to make it right?"

"Yes, sir. Of course."

"May I offer you gentlemen a coffee?" Frade said. "Carlos will come to the house when he knows something."

"That's very kind of you, Señor Frade," von Wachtstein said.

Frade gestured toward the Horch.

Boltitz was surprised when Dorotea Frade got behind the wheel. Her husband got in beside her and turned on the seat as von Wachtstein, Boltitz, and Enrico got in. He looked at Boltitz.

"Captain, I don't like to kill people unless I have to," he said, almost conversationally. "Don't push your luck by doing something stupid."

"I fully understood that I would be putting my life in your hands when I came here, Major Frade," Boltitz said.

" *'Major'?"* Frade parroted, disgustedly. "Jesus Christ, Peter, you really had diarrhea of the mouth, didn't you?"

He turned away from the backseat as the Horch began to move slowly, first making a wide turn on the tarmac, then turning onto a road lined with eucalyptus trees. There was grass between the trees. It was being patiently mowed by workmen swinging scythes. As the car passed them, they stopped and took off their hats in deference to Don Cletus, his lady, and their guests.

Frade replied with a casual wave of his hand and sometimes by calling out a workman's name, as if greeting a friend.

The tree-lined road was almost a kilometer long. Then it opened onto the manicured garden surrounding the house Boltitz had seen from the air. From the ground, the house was larger than it appeared from above.

As Señora Frade pulled the Horch up before the door of the house—beside a Buick convertible—the door opened and a middle-aged man in a crisp white jacket came out. He walked quickly—but too late—to open Señora Frade's door.

"Antonio," Frade ordered. "Have coffee brought to the study, then see that we're not disturbed."

"*Sí, señor.*"

Frade added: "And when the mechanic comes here, keep him waiting on the porch."

He waved his wife ahead of him into the house, and started to follow her, gesturing for Boltitz and von Wachtstein to follow them.

[TWO]

There was first a large reception foyer with a fountain in the center. Corridors radiated from the foyer. The Frades led the way down one of them, to a set of double doors Boltitz decided must be just about in the center of the house. He was surprised to see the doors were locked; Frade took a key from his pocket and unlocked them.

A real key, Boltitz thought, *one for a pins-and-tumbler lock, not the large key one would expect.*

He doesn't want anyone—servants included—in that room.

Frade waved his wife ahead of him again, and again signaled for Boltitz and von Wachtstein to follow them inside. Señora Frade sat down in a dark red leather armchair.

Boltitz glanced around the room. *It is in fact a study. Or maybe a library.*

There were no windows. Two of the walls were lined with bookcases. There was a large rather ornate desk, with a high-backed leather chair to one side. An Underwood typewriter sat on an extension shelf.

Two maids scurried into the room with a coffee service as Frade sat down at the desk.

God, that was quick! What do they do, keep coffee ready at all times in case the-master-of-all-he-surveys has a sudden urge for a cup?

Frade pointed somewhat imperiously to two chairs facing a low table, and Boltitz and von Wachtstein sat down. The maids put the service on the low table and Señora Frade began to serve the coffee.

Well, that makes it pretty clear that she's staying. Which means she does know everything, except what we're about to tell them.

Boltitz surveyed the room. The walls not covered with books were mostly covered with photographs and framed newspaper clippings, all of them of Cletus Frade. One was most of the front page of a newspaper, *The Midland Advertiser*. There was a picture of Frade, in a flight suit, being decorated. The headline read:

MIDLAND MARINE CLETUS FRADE
BECOMES ACE ON GUADALCANAL.
GETS DISTINGUISHED FLYING CROSS.

I shall have to keep in mind that Senor Frade has a very large ego.

Then Boltitz took a closer look at a large oil portrait. It showed a blond woman holding an infant in her arms.

What next? A statue? Maybe a painted ceiling, like the Sistine Chapel? Showing him being taken bodily into heaven?

Wait a minute . . .

That's not Señora Frade. At least not the one in here now.

My God, that's Frade's mother! He's the babe in arms.

Which means—why the hell didn't I figure this out sooner?—this is not his study.

This is—was—Oberst Frade's study. His father made this—this what? shrine?—to his son!

"That'll do it. Thank you very much," Frade said, and the maids quickly left the room. Frade got very quickly out of his chair, went to the door, and threw a dead-bolt lock. Then he went back behind his desk.

"Okay, Peter," he said, not at all pleasantly. "Take it from the top."

"Excuse me?"

"From the beginning," Frade clarified.

"I don't know where . . ." von Wachtstein said.

"Perhaps, Major Frade, I might be able . . ."

"Okay. Let's hear what *you've* got to say, Captain," Frade said.

Boltitz nodded. "I went to Major von Wachtstein's apartment two days ago—"

"That would be the twentieth?" Frade interrupted.

"Correct," Boltitz said. "I had determined that Major von Wachtstein had informed someone—I surmised, correctly, I was to learn, that he informed you, Major Frade—of the time and place where the *Océano Pacífico* would attempt to land certain matériel near Puerto Magdalena on Samborombón Bay."

Frade's face remained expressionless. His wife's eyes showed concern, even pain.

"As you know, when the *Océano Pacífico*'s longboats came ashore, they were brought under fire, which resulted in the deaths of two senior German officers, Standartenführer Goltz of the SS and Oberst Karl-Heinz Grüner, the military attaché of the German embassy here."

Again there was no expression on Frade's face. His wife's face was now pale.

"I thought you were going to tell me why you went to Wachtstein's apartment," Frade said evenly.

"It was a matter of honor among officers," Boltitz said.

"Honor among officers?" Frade asked. There was a faint but unmistakable tone of incredulity in his voice.

"Certainly, as an officer, the son of an officer . . ."

"I'm supposed to understand, is that what you're suggesting?" Frade said.

"Yes, sir. It is."

Frade shook his head in disbelief.

"Go on, Captain," he said.

"Clete," von Wachtstein said, "what he did, what he came to offer, was what he thought was an honorable solution to the problem."

Frade looked sharply at him but said nothing for a moment.

Then, his voice dripping with sarcasm, he said, "Let me guess. He was going to confront you with your sins against your officer's honor, and then leave you alone in a room with a pistol and one cartridge, right? So you could put a bullet up your nose, then get on a white horse, and ride off to Valhalla?"

"I had hoped you would understand," Boltitz said.

"It wasn't a pistol the korvettenkapitän offered, Clete," von Wachtstein said. "My suicide would have implicated my father. He would have been sent to a concentration camp, if not hung with piano wire from a butcher's hook."

"So what did he offer?" Frade asked.

"I was to crash on landing when I came back from Montevideo," von Wachtstein said.

Frade looked at Boltitz.

"And if he flew into the ground, you were going to keep your mouth shut about your suspicions about him?" he asked.

Boltitz nodded.

"So why aren't we scraping you off the runway at El Palomar, Peter?"

"Clete!" Dorotea Frade said, either in shock or as warning.

"I reported the korvettenkapitän's visit to Ambassador Lutzenberger," von Wachtstein said.

"How much had you told Lutzenberger about what you thought Wachtstein had done?" Frade asked Boltitz. "Before you went to his apartment, I mean?"

"Nothing."

"Why not?"

"I considered it possible that the ambassador was—"

"The traitor the Sicherheitsdienst was looking for?" Frade interrupted.

Well, Boltitz thought, *he knows enough about his enemy to make that distinction. Most people would have simply said "SS," thinking there was no difference between the SS and the SD; that all in the SS were Secret Police.*

Why am I surprised? Von Wachtstein told me he was good, and that the happy Texas cowboy image he presents masks a very professional intelligence officer.

"And I presume still are," Boltitz said. "I'm not SS-SD, Major Frade."

"You're not? Then who do you work for?"

"Admiral Canaris," Boltitz said.

"For him personally? Or you're assigned to the Abwehr?"

The Amt Auslandsnachrichten und Abwehr—Abwehr—was the foreign espionage and domestic counterintelligence organization for the Oberkommando der Wehrmacht, the supreme headquarters of the armed forces. Its head was Vice Admiral Wilhelm Canaris.

The question is insulting, Boltitz thought, *suggesting I am trying to make myself out as more important than I am.*

And the anger Frade experienced when von Wachtstein told him that he had admitted his treason, had told me everything, has had more than enough time to dissipate. He is being insulting with the purpose of making me lose my temper and say things I would not ordinarily say.

This happy Texas cowboy is a very dangerous man.

"I have the honor of working directly under Admiral Canaris's direction, Major Frade."

"There's that word again, *honor,*" Frade said, and shook his head and chuckled. "Okay. What about Major General von Deitzberg? He's from the OKW. Where does he fit into your chain of command? You're telling me you don't work for him?"

"Von Deitzberg is an SS officer," Boltitz replied, "an SS-brigadeführer, seconded to the army for this mission. No, I don't—"

"Define 'mission,' " Frade interrupted, and then before Boltitz could open his mouth, added, "You and the deputy adjutant to Reichsführer-SS Heinrich Himmler didn't come here just to find out who's the traitor in your embassy, did you?"

Boltitz locked eyes with Frade and thought, *He's letting me know he knows who von Deitzberg actually is. That's to impress me.*

But how does he know? Did von Wachtstein tell him that, too?

I don't think von Wachtstein knows any more about von Deitzberg than that he is SS; not that he works for Himmler.

"No," Boltitz said, looking at his coffee cup and taking a sip. "Of course we did not."

"Then define your mission in terms of the priorities, one, two, three, et cetera," Frade ordered.

"You will understand, Major Frade, that this is my assessment of the situation. It was never spelled out, one, two, three, et cetera."

"Okay, then let's have *your* assessment."

"I would say that Operation Phoenix is of the greatest interest to the senior officers involved," Boltitz said. "Von Deitzberg, I suspect, but can't prove, is involved in the ransoming operation of the concentration camp inmates. I have never heard any suggestion there is a Wehrmacht involvement in that. That would be your one and two. Three, which of course has impact on the success of one and two, is discovering the traitor in the embassy."

"Operation Phoenix can be defined as setting up places where the big shots—maybe even Hitler himself—can hide here when the war is lost?" Frade asked.

"Yes," Boltitz said simply.

"Did you share any of your suspicions of Peter with von Deitzberg?"

"No."

"Why not?"

"As I told you, I serve Admiral Canaris," Boltitz said.

"But you *were* going to tell him after Peter here committed suicide by airplane?"

"No. I thought I had made that clear. Once Peter had done the honorable thing, I would have done what I could to divert any suspicion from him."

" 'The honorable thing'?" Frade parroted sarcastically. "Jesus H. Christ!" Then he asked, "Did you share your suspicions, even hint at them, with anyone else? *Anyone?*"

"No," Boltitz said simply, meeting Frade's eyes.

"Let me turn the question around," Frade said. "Did anyone, von Deitzberg, what's that fairy SS guy's name in Montevideo? Oh, yeah, *Sturmbannführer Werner von Tresmarck.* Or that fat Austrian diplomat, looks like somebody stuffed him? *Gradny-Sawz?* Did anyone confide in you their thoughts that Peter was the fox in the chicken coop?"

Despite himself, Boltitz had to smile at the happy Texas cowboy's characterizations of von Tresmarck and First Secretary of the German Embassy Anton von Gradny-Sawz.

And he knows them, not only by name, but also by their sexual preferences and appearance.

The Americans have really penetrated not only the embassy but Operation Phoenix, and that filthy SS operation ransoming Jews from the concentration camps.

"Both von Tresmarck and Gradny-Sawz, Major Frade," Boltitz said, "came to me and suggested that since they were not the traitor, it had to be one of the other two. But neither was able to provide anything concrete."

Frade, obviously in deep thought, said nothing for a long moment.

"Okay," he said, finally. "Now let's get to the heart of this. What happened, Captain, to change your mind about all this? When Peter failed to do the *honorable* thing and kill himself, why didn't you turn him in?"

"Ambassador Lutzenberger sent for me and showed me two letters," Boltitz said. "They had been smuggled to him on the last Condor flight. One was from my father and the other from Admiral Canaris. My father said he knew I would follow, without question, whatever orders I received from Admiral Canaris."

"Why should he bother to tell you that?" Frade asked. "You're an officer. You obey the orders you're given, right?"

"My father knew what those orders probably would be. He wanted me to know he knew."

"Who is your father? Where does he fit in here?"

"My father, Major Frade, is a navy officer. Vizeadmiral Kurt Boltitz."

"And what were the orders your father the admiral was talking about? Were they in Canaris's letter?"

"Yes, sir," Boltitz replied, and heard himself.

I just called him "sir." And for a second time.

What does that mean? That I have subconsciously recognized his authority over me?

"And they were?" Frade pursued.

"Admiral Canaris's letter ordered me to accept any order from Ambassador Lutzenberger as if they had come from him," Boltitz said.

"And then what?"

"Excuse me?"

"What were Lutzenberger's orders? 'Leave Wachtstein alone'?"

"He told me he knew I had been to see von Wachtstein, and then that von Wachtstein was then in Montevideo, that he had told him to be careful, and that I should make an effort to know him better, as we had more in common than I might have previously realized."

"That's all?"

"Yes, sir"—Christ, I did it again—"but his meaning was clear."

"What happened to the letters?" Frade asked.

"Ambassador Lutzenberger burned them."

"You saw that?"

Boltitz nodded.

"And then you went to see Wachtstein and he really let his mouth run?" Frade replied, and then turned to von Wachtstein. "What did you tell him, motormouth? And why?"

"The korvettenkapitän told me he had seen the ambassador, Cletus," von Wachtstein said, "and what had been said—"

"According to him," Frade said, pointing at Boltitz, "the ambassador didn't say very much, just implied that he didn't think you nose-diving onto the runway was a very good idea."

Boltitz said: "We both interpreted his remark that I should make an effort to know him better, that we had a good deal in common, to mean that we should confide in each other."

Frade didn't reply for a moment.

"What you're asking me to believe, Captain, is that all it took to get you to change sides, to become a traitor to Germany, to turn your back on that code of honor you keep throwing at me, was a quick look at the letters Lutzenberger showed you. That's a hell of lot to ask me to swallow. Even if you believe, right now, what you're telling me, how do I know that you won't change your mind again tomorrow? Or, more likely, when you get back to Germany? You are going back to Germany?"

"Yes, of course, I'm going back—"

"Clete," von Wachtstein interrupted, "as embarrassing as it is for me to bring this up, you have benefited from the code of honor the korvettenkapitän and I believe in."

Frade glared at him for a moment, then shrugged, and smiled, and said, "Touché, Peter. I guess you told him about that, too?"

"He asked me how I had come to be close to you," von Wachtstein said.

"Look at me, Captain," Frade ordered. When his eyes were locked with Boltitz's, he asked: "In that circumstance, knowing that it was the intention of your military attaché to . . . hell, the word is assassinate . . . to *assassinate* an enemy officer—this one—would you have done what Peter did? Warn me?"

"I'd like to think I would have," Boltitz said. "Assassination is not something to which an honorable officer can be a party."

Frade shrugged.

He looked at his wife. "I'm probably losing my mind, but I'm tempted to believe him."

"Peter does," Dorotea Frade said. "I guess I do, too."

Frade exhaled audibly.

"I'm going to have to think this over," he said, and looked at Boltitz. "In other words, the jury is still out, Captain Boltitz." He moved his look to von Wachtstein. "I was about to say watch your back, Peter. But since you already trust this guy, I don't suppose that's necessary, is it?"

"The korvettenkapitän is a brother officer, Clete," von Wachtstein said. "And we have decided that what our fathers have decided, that our code of honor dictates that our duty is to Germany, not to Hitler and National Socialism. So, yes, Clete, I trust the korvettenkapitän."

Frade was silent again for a long moment.

"Okay," he said. "You were headed for Santa Catalina, right?"

Von Wachtstein nodded.

"How long had you planned on staying there?"

"I'd hoped to spend the night," von Wachtstein said.

"Spoken like a true newlywed," Frade replied. "Okay. Whatever is wrong with that ugly little airplane of yours is fixed. Get in it, go there, and tell either your mother-in-law or your bride that Dorotea and I accept their kind invitation for cocktails and dinner."

Boltitz wondered what that was all about when Frade, as if reading his mind, went on: "That may—but probably won't—explain your presence here to El Coronel Martín. It's worth a shot."

"I'll take you to the airstrip," Dorotea said.

"No," Frade said flatly. "Have Antonio take them in one of the Model A's. And while Carlos is being helpful, one of you say something—in German— about not liking me and/or how unfortunate it was that you had to stop here."

"In German?" Boltitz blurted.

"Good ol' Carlos speaks German, but thinks I don't know," Frade said.

He walked to the study door, unlocked its dead bolt, and held it open.

Von Wachtstein offered him his hand as he walked past.

"Keep your goddamn mouth shut, Peter," Frade said, but he took the hand and touched von Wachtstein's shoulder affectionately.

Boltitz offered Frade his hand.

Frade took it, and held on to it longer than Boltitz expected. When he looked curiously at Frade, Frade said, "Am I going to have to count my fingers when I let go, Captain?"

"No," Boltitz said. "But I think you will anyway."

Frade nodded at him. There was the hint of a smile on his lips.

Both men had just about the same thought: *Under other circumstances, we probably would become friends.*

After his wife passed through the door, Frade threw the dead bolt again.

He went to the desk, took a sheet of paper, and rolled it into the Underwood.

He patted his hands together for a moment, mentally composing the message, and then typed it rapidly.

```
URGENT


TOP SECRET LINDBERGH


DUPLICATION FORBIDDEN


FROM TEX


TO AGGIE


IN POSSESSION OF NEW INFORMATION REGARDING GALAHAD
CONNECTIONS. I AM UNWILLING TO TRANSMIT EXCEPT
PERSONALLY TO YOU. SITUATION HERE PRECLUDES MY
LEAVING HERE. ACKNOWLEDGE. ADVISE.


TEX
```

Aggie was United States Marine Corps Reserve Colonel A. F. Graham, deputy director of the Office of Strategic Services for Western Hemisphere Operations. Like Marine Corps Major Cletus H. Frade, Graham was a former member of the Corps of Cadets at the Texas Agricultural and Mechanical College at College Station, Texas, and thus an Aggie.

When he finished typing, Frade went to the door, unbolted and opened it, and handed the sheet of paper to Enrico, who was sitting in an armchair with his Remington in his lap.

"Take this out to El Jefe right away," Frade ordered. "Tell him to encrypt it and get it out as soon as possible."

El Jefe—"the chief"—was Chief Radioman Oscar J. Schultz, USN, who had been drafted into the OSS off the destroyer *USS Alfred Thomas,* DD-107, when she had called at Buenos Aires three months before. Schultz had been her chief radioman and cryptographer. He now operated a radio and radar station in a clump of trees on the monte of Estancia San Pedro y San Pablo several miles from the main house.

"I will send Rodrigo," Enrico protested.

"You will take it," Frade said firmly, and then smiled. "I won't leave the house, Enrico. I promise. I give you my word of honor as an officer and gentleman, and you know how important that is to me."

The sarcasm went over Enrico's head.

"I will send Rodrigo here, then I will go," he said. And then he asked a question. "Am I going to be permitted to kill the other young German bastard?"

"Not just yet," Frade said.

II

[ONE]
The Reich Chancellery
Berlin, Germany
1230 23 June 1943

Parteileiter Martin Bormann—a short, stocky forty-three-year-old who wore his hair closely cropped—pulled open the left of the huge double doors to his private office and smiled apologetically at the waiting Vizeadmiral Wilhelm Canaris, who was short, trim, and fifty-five years old.

Compared to just about everybody else in the senior hierarchy of Nazi Germany but the Führer himself, both men were simply uniformed. Bormann was wearing a brown shirt and trousers, and he had on shoes rather than boots. His right sleeve bore a red Hakenkruez armband with the black swastika in the center of a white circle. Canaris was wearing a naval uniform, but without the flag officer's silver belt to which he was entitled, and which almost every other admiral wore. Neither was either man wearing a holstered pistol, another item of fashion among most senior officers.

"I'm really sorry to have kept you waiting, Canaris, but you know how it gets in here sometimes," Bormann greeted the vizeadmiral.

"It's not a problem, Herr Reichsleiter," Canaris replied.

He thought: *I knew very well that you would keep me waiting. Not to do so would have been an admission that you were not working your fingers to the bone for the party. It is important to you that you appear important. That's why I called you "Herr Reichsleiter."*

Bormann's official title—he was second only to Hitler himself in the Nazi party—was Parteileiter, "party leader." But on several occasions Hitler had referred to him as "Reichsleiter"—a leader of the Reich. Canaris was convinced Hitler had simply misspoke, but the sycophants around Hitler, who were convinced the Führer never made a mistake, had begun to call Bormann "Reichsleiter" and Bormann liked it.

"I'll try to make amends with a good lunch," Bormann said, waving Canaris into his office. "With your permission, of course, I thought we would eat here. Just the two of us. That way we won't be interrupted."

"That sounds wonderful. But I can't believe we won't be interrupted."

"Trust me, we won't be," Bormann said.

Bormann took his arm and led him through another set of enormous doors into his private dining room, where a table large enough for twenty had two place settings on it.

A pair of waiters in white jackets, nice-looking young men in their late teens or early twenties, stood ready to serve them.

They were interns, Canaris knew, "studying the operations" of the Nationalsozialistische Deutsche Arbeiterpartei so that they would be able to later assume roles of responsibility in the Thousand-Year Reich. This was important enough for them to be given "temporary" exemption from military service.

There were more than two dozen of them working for Bormann. Every one of them, Canaris knew, was either the son or the nephew of a high-ranking Nazi Party official.

Which is corrupt and immoral, Canaris thought.

He believed that sort of favoritism was the basic flaw in the Nazi party and its leadership.

The SS, especially, is riddled through with thieves and sociopaths.

"May I offer you a glass of wine, Canaris? Or champagne, perhaps?" Bormann asked as he sat down and gestured for Canaris to take the chair at the side of the table.

"Thank you, no, Herr Reichsleiter. If there is any, I'll have a glass of beer."

Bormann snapped his fingers and one of the interns hurried to produce a bottle of beer, the proper glass for it, and to set it before Canaris.

Bormann lifted the silver covers on the plates on the tables, and nodded approvingly at what they had been keeping warm.

"That will be all, thank you," he said to the waiters. "The admiral and I will serve ourselves."

Both young men clicked their heels, bowed crisply, and walked out of the dining room, closing the door after themselves.

Canaris wondered if Bormann had his wire recorder running and was recording this meeting. It was an idle thought, as Canaris always acted as if he knew whatever he was saying was being recorded, and said nothing that could possibly be used against him.

Wordlessly, the two served themselves. First, a consommé, then roast pork with mashed potatoes, green beans, applesauce, and red sauerkraut.

"Very nice," Canaris said.

"Truth to tell, Canaris," Bormann said. "I suspected getting people out of the office and my desk clear was going to take more time than I would have liked, and that I would be forced to ask you to wait. So a special lunch was in order, by way of apology. And if I proved to be wrong, and I could have received you on time, you would have been impressed by both my efficiency and the lunch."

Canaris smiled and chuckled dutifully.

"I wanted to talk to you about Argentina, about Operation Phoenix," Bormann then said. "That's becoming a problem, wouldn't you agree?"

"I would."

"And with everything else the Führer has to deal with, I really hate to bother him with it."

"I understand," Canaris said. "It hasn't gone well, has it?"

"The only good news was that we didn't lose the special shipment on the shore of . . . what was it? Bonbon Bay? Something like that?"

"Samborombón Bay," Canaris furnished.

"Why do you suppose that was, Canaris? Why didn't the people who shot Standartenführer Goltz and Oberst Whatsisname, the military attaché?"

"Grüner," Canaris furnished.

". . . and *Oberst Grüner* grab the special shipment?"

"There are several possibilities," Canaris said. "The story Korvettenkapitän

Boltitz got from the captain of the *Océano Pacífico* suggests that they didn't have time to even begin unloading the special cargo from the *Océano Pacífico's* lifeboat when the shooting started. The Luftwaffe officer, von Wachtstein, then put the bodies into the boat and they went back to the ship."

"You believe that story? I've always thought it was odd that the other two were killed and von Whatsisname wasn't hurt."

"Von Wachtstein," Canaris furnished. "May I go on, Herr Reichsleiter?"

"Of course. Excuse me, Canaris."

"What I was about to say was that that suggests the possibility that the Argentines accomplished what they may have set out to do. That is, get revenge for the killing of Oberst Frade by killing two German officers. Once that was done, they had no further interest in the boat or its crew. And von Wachtstein was in civilian clothing, which suggests the possibility they thought he was just another seaman. And, of course, they had no idea what was in the crates."

"You think, then, that it was an act of revenge? By Argentine army officers?"

"Excuse me, Herr Reichsleiter, but what I said was that it *suggests* the possibility. We have no facts to go on. But, having said that, the fact that they showed no interest in the crates suggests they didn't have any idea what they contained, and didn't care. Robbery was not the motive, ergo sum. And robbery would offend the Argentine officer's code of honor."

"They can murder in cold blood but not steal?"

"In a sense. They consider revenge to be one thing, theft another."

"How do you think they knew when and where the landing would be attempted?"

"Again, several possibilities. They have a man in their Bureau of Internal Security, an Oberst Martín, who is far more competent than one would expect. One possible scenario is that he maintained aerial surveillance of the *Océano Pacífico* once she entered the River Plate. They have the capability to do that. And once the *Océano Pacífico* left the normal channel to the Buenos Aires harbor, and moved toward Samborombón Bay, he sent up a watch on the shore in that area. He also has that capability."

"What you're saying is that you don't think we have a traitor in the embassy in Buenos Aires?"

"I'm not saying that at all, Herr Reichsleiter," Canaris replied. "There very well may be. If there is, I'm sure Brigadeführer von Deitzberg will find that out. If indeed he hasn't already. Has anyone heard from him?"

"Not that I know of," Bormann said. "You didn't mention your man just now, Korvettenkapitän Whatsisname?"

"Boltitz, Herr Reichsleiter. He's a junior officer and he's taking his orders from, and will make his report through, von Deitzberg. He's not really an intelligence officer . . . an intelligence officer for something like this."

"I don't think I understand."

"Don't misunderstand me, Herr Reichsleiter. Boltitz is a good man. Very smart. If you want an assessment of the Royal Navy, of the probable course and speed of a convoy crossing the North Atlantic in January, that sort of thing, he's quite useful. He was a submarine officer—many successful patrols—but he doesn't have much experience—any at all, actually—in counterintelligence, which is what von Deitzberg is dealing with here."

"I suppose that's true," Bormann said.

"When von Deitzberg came to me asking if I had someone who could talk, as a seaman and in Portuguese, to the captain of the *Océano Pacífico* about what happened at Samborombón Bay, I assigned Boltitz to him. And Boltitz apparently impressed von Deitzberg, because he asked me if he could have him to go with him to Argentina."

"He speaks Portuguese?"

"Yes. And Spanish. And English. Many naval officers are multilingual."

"I suppose that would be useful to a naval officer."

"Yes. But, frankly, Herr Reichsleiter, I wondered if Boltitz wouldn't be more useful here in Berlin. I deferred to von Deitzberg."

"Huh," Bormann grunted. "It is sometimes hard, is it not, not to defer to a high-ranking SS officer?"

"Sometimes, as I suspect you well know, to do one's duty it is necessary. But we have a saying in the navy, Herr Reichsleiter, that it is always wise to conserve one's ammunition until you really need it."

Bormann chuckled.

I think the Herr Reichsleiter swallowed that whole.

Boltitz is not a counterintelligence officer. And he's in Argentina not because I wanted him there, but because von Deitzberg asked for him, and I didn't think objecting was worth the trouble it would cause.

"We're getting a little off track here, Herr Vizeadmiral," Bormann said. "What I wanted to talk to you about is making Operation Phoenix a success, not about the problems we're having with it at the moment."

"I'm not sure I follow you, Herr Reichsleiter."

"I'm sure, one way or another, we can get the special shipment into Argentina. What I'm concerned about is what we do with it when we get it there. What I'm saying, I suppose, is that I've been thinking we need a good Argentine ally."

Canaris nodded but said nothing.

"Someone of influence," Bormann went on, "someone who can make sure Operation Phoenix becomes a reality and, most importantly, remains a secret."

"I see what you mean."

"Someone we can trust," Bormann added. "I have learned over the years that one can usually trust people who have something to gain personally from the success of the enterprise in which one has an interest, more than you can people simply doing something as a duty, or for altruistic philosophical reasons."

Canaris nodded.

"That has also been my experience, Herr Reichsleiter."

"I thought perhaps you might know someone who would be suitable."

"I'll have to give it some thought, Herr Reichsleiter, but off the top of my head, no one comes to mind."

"But you do have friends in Argentina?"

"None that I would entrust with knowledge of Operation Phoenix," Canaris said. "We simply cannot afford any risk of having the Argentine government learn what we plan to do, and what friends I have there are officers of the Armada Argentina."

"So?"

"They might feel honor bound to inform their government what we are planning."

"Well, we can't have that, can we?" Bormann said. "Does the name Perón mean anything to you, Canaris?"

"He's one of the colonels around General Ramírez. According to the late Oberst Grüner, he was instrumental in the coup which deposed President Ramón Castillo a couple of weeks ago—on June seventh, to be precise."

"You didn't meet him when he was here?"' Bormann asked, as if surprised.

"I knew of him," Canaris said. "But I don't think I ever met him."

Of course I knew of him.

Despite what Bormann and his ilk like to believe, all Argentines are not two steps away from embracing Der Führer and National Socialism. There are God only knows how many refugees from the Thousand-Year Reich down there.

It was my duty to learn something about an Argentine officer attached to their embassy here and being fawned over by the elite. It was possible—unlikely but entirely possible—that he was working for the British.

I've often thought that the same Germano-Argentines who helped me escape from internment so I could return to serve the Fatherland would now go out of their way to ensure that Germans interned there now stay there, rather than return here to serve Hitler, proof of that being Oberst Grüner having absolutely no success getting any of the Graf Spee *crew out of internment and back here.*

Oberst Juan Domingo Perón is not a very interesting man, except for his unusual, if rather disgusting, sexual proclivities.

What's Bormann's interest in Perón?

"I made an effort to get to know him while he was here," Bormann said. "And, as a result, learned there are several very interesting things about him."

Well, one probably is that he likes young girls.

I wonder what Bormann thinks the others are?

"And they are?"

"He believes in National Socialism," Bormann said. "The philosophy, Canaris, not the party. That distinction is important. He came to Europe first to study Mussolini's fascism. He was impressed that our friend Benito has made the trains run on time. Efficiency, in other words, impresses him. Then he came here and—I think surprising him—learned that we Germans are somewhat more efficient than the Italians. He was particularly impressed with the autobahn. And with our social programs."

He's waiting for my response.

What I would like to say is, "So what?"

"That doesn't surprise you, does it, Herr Reichsleiter?" Canaris asked.

"He sees how Germany is doing things as something Argentina should emulate is my point, Canaris."

"I see."

"And he is very impressed with our Führer, Canaris, the man and the leader."

"Well, of course, he should be."

I daresay Roosevelt and Churchill are also impressed with the Bavarian corporal. Again, "So what?"

What the hell is he talking about?

"You're a clever man, Canaris," Bormann said, smiling. "You know where I'm going, don't you?"

"I'm not clever enough to understand where you're going, Herr Reichsleiter."

"And a cautious man, too," Bormann said, approvingly. "All right, let me give you another hint or two. Colonel Perón is ambitious. He sees himself as a future leader of Argentina, perhaps even as a future leader of more than just Argentina."

"That is a weakness of many South American officers," Canaris said. "They dream of glory."

"And wealth. Their officer corps does not come from the aristocracy, the landed gentry, so to speak. They have to live on what they're paid."

"Excuse me, Herr Reichsleiter, but that's not always the case," Canaris said. "The late Oberst Frade came from the landed gentry."

"Indeed?"

"Oberst Grüner told me that he had—in addition to other business interests—farmlands in excess of eighty-four thousand hectares."

"I wasn't aware of that," Bormann said.

"He was also a close friend of your Colonel Perón," Canaris said. "I wondered then, and wonder now, if eliminating Frade was really a wise thing to do. The message it was supposed to have sent to the Argentine officer corps— if the deaths of Grüner and Goltz were in fact an act of revenge—seems to have backfired."

"Perhaps," Bormann said somewhat impatiently. "But you will of course agree that we no longer have to worry about having a president of Argentina whose son is an American OSS agent."

"That's inarguable, Herr Reichsleiter."

"What we need is a president of Argentina who admires the Führer, National Socialism, believes in the final victory, and is interested in both his political future and feathering his own nest, wouldn't you agree?"

"And, ideally, who could be trusted with the Phoenix secret," Canaris said. "And you think Colonel Perón would fit the bill?"

"I've thought so for some time, actually. Which brings us to the point of this very private conversation."

Canaris didn't reply.

"I've actually taken some steps to recruit Colonel Perón's cooperation in this enterprise," Bormann said. "Are you familiar with Anton von Gradny-Sawz, Herr Vizeadmiral?"

"The first secretary of the Buenos Aires embassy," Canaris said. "When the question of a traitor in the embassy came up, I collected and read his dossiers."

" 'Collected and read his dossiers'?" Bormann parroted. "Plural?"

"We had one—just the basic facts—and the Sicherheitsdienst had a somewhat more comprehensive one, and then after the Anschluss, I took over the personnel records of the former Austrian government."

"And the party had one. Did you ask for that?"

"No. I presumed you had one, and that if there was anything in it that would be of interest to me, you would have passed that on."

"And what is your opinion of the Herr Baron?"

"Are you asking if I think he may be our traitor?"

"That would be included in your opinion, wouldn't it? What I was asking was what you think of him."

"He is a dedicated National Socialist who early on decided that it was his patriotic duty to bring Austria into Greater Germany, and was very helpful in doing so."

"And for being helpful was rewarded when Austria became Ostmark?"

"Yes."

"In other words, he was an opportunist?"

"I would be reluctant to use that term, but I can see where others might come to that conclusion."

"In your opinion, is it possible Gradny-Sawz is the traitor in Buenos Aires?"

"Anything is possible, Herr Reichsleiter, but I think that's unlikely."

"Why?"

"What would he have to gain?"

Bormann nodded and smiled.

"On the other hand," Bormann said, "he might decide that if Colonel Perón were to prosper, some of that might accrue to him?"

"I don't know the man well, Herr Reichsleiter, so this is not in the order of a judgment, but a question: Could you trust this man, knowing of his opportunistic tendencies?"

"I decided some time ago, Canaris, that because of his opportunistic tendencies, he probably could be trusted, up to a point. He would have to be watched, of course."

"At the risk of repeating myself, I don't know the man well enough to make a decision like that."

"The decision was not yours to make, Canaris, but mine. Gradny-Sawz has already begun to make approaches to Perón. The problem is that Grüner is no longer available to watch Gradny-Sawz." He paused to let that sink in, and then went on. "That's what we're really talking about here."

"I'm afraid I don't understand."

"We need a replacement for Grüner. Von Deitzberg has suggested Boltitz."

"Why not the ambassador?" Canaris asked. "Wouldn't that be the obvious choice?"

"I'm sure von Deitzberg has considered Graf von Lutzenberger," Bormann said, "and concluded Boltitz would be preferable."

"Is there an implication in that that von Deitzberg has less than full faith in von Lutzenberger?"

"The traitor in the embassy has not yet been detected," Bormann said. "Until he has been, everyone is therefore under suspicion."

"Even so, while I am reluctant to question SS-Brigadeführer von Deitzberg, I'm not at all sure that Boltitz is a wise choice."

"Why not?"

"For one thing, Boltitz has no experience—absolutely none at all—in these areas—"

"And, for another, you'd like him back here in Berlin?" Bormann interrupted.

"Frankly, yes, I would. I would like him doing work for which he is qualified. And he's not qualified for this."

"He has two very important qualifications for this. He enjoys the full confidence of SS-Brigadeführer von Deitzberg and Vizeadmiral Canaris."

"He does not have my full confidence to perform in a role like this," Canaris said.

"The decision has been made, Canaris. Frankly, von Deitzberg said that he thought you would be unhappy with it. I understand. But we must think of what is best for Operation Phoenix, Operation Perón, and the Führer."

"Those are also my priorities, Herr Reichsleiter. I can propose to you the names of half a dozen—"

He stopped when Bormann held up both hands, palms outward.

"Perhaps you didn't understand me when I said the decision has been made, Herr Vizeadmiral," Bormann said with a cold smile.

Canaris didn't reply.

"Korvettenkapitän Boltitz will be assigned to the embassy as naval attaché," Bormann went on, "where he will be in a position to keep an eye not only on Gradny-Sawz but on the ambassador and von Wachtstein as well. He will—von Deitzberg will set up the details of how before he returns—report directly to me. I will, of course, furnish you with the pertinent details of his reports."

Canaris nodded his understanding.

"A word of advice, Canaris, in case you were thinking of appealing this decision."

"I know full well how much faith the Führer has in you, Herr Reichsleiter. And I try hard to avoid fighting battles I know I cannot win."

"Don't think of it as a battle, Canaris. But rather as an accommodation—even a sacrifice—on your part for the common good."

Canaris nodded.

"And now, Herr Reichsleiter, may I plead the press of duties and ask to be excused?"

"I understand," Bormann said.

"Thank you for a splendid luncheon," Canaris said.

"It's always a pleasure to see you, Canaris."

Canaris laid his napkin on the table, came to attention, thrust his right arm out, and barked, "Heil Hitler!"

Bormann returned the salute with an almost casual wave of his arm.

Canaris's car, an Opel Kapitän, was the least pretentious on the row of official cars lined up outside the Reich Chancellery. All the others were either a Mercedes-Benz or a Maybach; there even was an American Packard. The vizeadmiral walked to his Opel and got in before the SS trooper in charge of what was the parking lot for very senior officers could have it waved to meet him at the steps.

Canaris thought about the exchange with Bormann all the way to his office. It had gone well, far better than he had hoped it would, and thinking that raised caution flags.

When things are obviously going very well, they almost surely are not.

He opened the door for himself when he got to his office building, and returned the salutes of the navy petty officers on guard with a military—not the Nazi—salute.

He went into his office and told his secretary to get him a cup of coffee, then leave him undisturbed.

He waited until the coffee—black, and in a heavy navy-issue china mug—was delivered. Then he got from behind his desk and went to his private toilet.

After a moment, without having used the facility, he flushed the toilet and turned the water on in the sink.

And then, very softly, almost in a whisper, he said, "I will be goddamned. The swine not only let my fox into his chicken coop, but practically pushed him in."

[TWO]
Office of the Director
Office of Strategic Services
National Institutes of Health Building
Washington, D.C.
0930 29 June 1943

Every once in a great while, there is not much going on that requires me to make an immediate major decision, Brigadier General William J. Donovan, the director of the United States Office of Strategic Services, mused, *so it therefore logically follows that when that happens—as now—I am presented with idiotic suggestions, off-the-wall analysis, and problems I really don't want to—shouldn't have to—deal with.*

There were several such suggestions, analyses, and problems on the desk of the stocky, well-tailored, sixty-year-old Wall Street lawyer who had been chosen by his Columbia Law School classmate and close personal friend, President Franklin Delano Roosevelt, to coordinate the flow of "war information." That meant both intelligence and propaganda.

Donovan had learned—or maybe brought with him from the practice of law—that idiot suggestions, on closer examination, sometimes proved really not to be so idiotic after all. And that off-wall-analysis sometimes contained information that was quite useful. And that problems he was reluctant to deal with were really the ones that deserved his full attention.

Reminding himself of this, he unwound the string holding together an accordion folder. He peered inside, then dumped the contents onto his desk.

He shook his head in disbelief. A thirty-second glance at what was being proposed showed him that this really was an idiotic suggestion: Someone wanted to give OSS agents badges and credentials, as if they were policemen, or agents of the Bureau of Internal Revenue.

Sample credentials had been prepared. Donovan picked up one of them, examined it carefully, and shook his head again.

The original organization—the Office of the Coordinator of Information— had given William J. Donovan the responsibility for coordinating both propaganda and intelligence generated by all the agencies of the federal government. It was created on 11 July 1941 by Executive Order of the President.

It had immediately become apparent that that idea wasn't going to work.

For one thing, Donovan knew little—and admitted it—about influencing public opinion. More important, the Army's and Navy's intelligence organizations didn't like the idea of anyone else coordinating, reviewing or having anything else to do with their intelligence data. Even more important, neither did J. Edgar Hoover, the powerful director of the Federal Bureau of Investigation, who had quickly made it clear that he wasn't going to willingly share FBI files with anyone.

Shortly after war came to the United States, on 7 December 1941, the Joint Chiefs of Staff, which was to control all the armed forces, was formed. Donovan, believing that there was a place in the military organization of the United States for a covert intelligence-gathering and sabotage organization serving all the armed forces, struck a deal with the new Joint Chiefs under which the COI—less the propaganda function, which would become the Office of War Information—would be placed under the Joint Chiefs.

The Joint Chiefs—underestimating "Wild Bill" Donovan—believed this would give them control of the intelligence-gathering and sabotage operations of what would be known as the Office of Strategic Services. President Roosevelt issued another Executive Order on 13 June 1942, establishing the OSS and naming Donovan, still a civilian, as director. Very importantly, the OSS would have access to the President's virtually unlimited "unvouchered funds" provided by Congress to be spent as the President wished, and not subject to public scrutiny. The JCS thought this was a fine idea, too, as it would relieve them of the responsibility of paying for Donovan's operations, which they considered useful and important mainly because the President said they would be.

Donovan immediately began a relatively massive recruitment of all sorts of people for the OSS. They came from business and academia, as well as from the armed forces. He set up a training camp at the Congressional Country Club and began to dispatch agents around the world.

It took about a month for the JCS and the FBI to realize that Donovan's OSS was about to give the phrase "loose cannon" a new meaning. Subtle, and then not-so-subtle, suggestions to the President that maybe the OSS wasn't such a good idea after all and should be sharply reined in—or, better yet, disbanded—fell on deaf ears. Donovan had told President Roosevelt what he intended to try to do, and the President had liked what he heard.

So did Mrs. Eleanor Roosevelt, the President's formidable wife, who had been present at many of these private dinner conversations. Moreover, Mrs. Roosevelt was very sympathetic to Donovan's concerns that he would be thwarted in carrying out his mission by the military establishment. She had had her own problems with them. They had trouble accepting her firm belief, for example, that there was absolutely no reason Negroes could not be taught to fly military aircraft. It had taken the personal intervention of her husband—who was, after all, commander in chief of the nation's armed forces—to overcome the military establishment's foot-dragging and get them to set up a pilot-training program for Negroes at Tuskegee University in Alabama.

When he was still the Coordinator of Information, Donovan had made a quiet deal with the State Department—which then had a very limited intelligence-gathering capability, and was getting little intelligence from either the Office of Naval Intelligence or the Army's G-2—to send a dozen intelligence officers to North Africa. Working undercover as vice consuls, they were able to keep an eye both on the French fleet, which had been sent to Morocco when the French surrendered, and on the Germans who had sent "Armistice Commissions" to North Africa to make sure the French fleet stayed there.

Donovan's "vice consuls" were also able to establish contact with French officers unhappy with their new, German-controlled government in Vichy, and smarting under the humiliating defeat France had suffered in 1940.

These contacts, and the intelligence developed, had been of enormous importance when the U.S. Army invaded North Africa in November 1942. The invasion—America's first victory in World War II—had been relatively bloodless and had done a great deal to restore morale in America, which had sagged when the Japanese had wiped out Battleship Row in Pearl Harbor, Territory of Hawaii, on 7 December 1941, and gone on to conquer the Philippine Islands, and a good deal else, in the months that followed.

This had been enough to squelch the suggestions that the OSS be disbanded, but the OSS—now derogatorily dubbed the "Oh, So Social" because of the prominence of many of Donovan's well-connected recruits—was still a thorn in the sides of the JCS and the FBI, and they counterattacked. They were now joined by the State Department, which had been somewhat shocked to learn that Donovan's "vice consuls" had considered their primary loyalty to be to Donovan, and had shown an alarming propensity to take action on their own, without waiting for an opinion—much less permission—from the ambassadors for whom they were theoretically working, or from the State Department itself.

Donovan was not on the short list of government agency heads given access to intercepted Axis communications. He had no access at all to MAGIC intercepts of Japanese messages, and only limited access to ULTRA-intercepted German messages. The OSS was told that the FBI, G-2, and ONI would handle counterintelligence within the United States, and that J. Edgar Hoover was assured by Roosevelt that the FBI was still responsible for intelligence gathering and counterintelligence in the entire Western Hemisphere.

In the latter case, however, Roosevelt did not tell Donovan he could not conduct operations in South America. The result of that omission was that in just about every South American country—particularly Argentina and Mexico— there were detachments of FBI agents competing with—and usually not talking to—Donovan's OSS agents.

And in the Pacific, General Douglas MacArthur had made it clear that he didn't want the OSS operating on his turf. Period.

The JCS and the FBI suspected—with more than a little justification—that Donovan was, perhaps with the tacit approval of the President, ignoring any and all edicts and directives that he thought were getting in the way of what he considered to be his mission.

The military tried one more thing to rein in Wild Bill. He was recalled to active duty as a colonel and promoted to brigadier general. They somewhat naively thought this would point out to him that he was only one—a very junior one—of the platoon of one-star generals attached to the Joint Chiefs of Staff, and should conduct himself accordingly.

Donovan chose to believe that putting on a uniform had not changed what the commander in chief had told him when he'd signed on at an annual stipend of one dollar as Coordinator of Information: that he worked directly under the President and was answerable only to him.

And there was a psychological advantage to wearing the uniform when dealing with other senior officers. He had been awarded the nation's highest award for valor in action in France in the First World War. Although he rarely actually pinned the blue-starred ribbon of the Medal of Honor to his tunic, everyone seemed to look for it, and were aware that he could have pinned the ribbon on had he wished to. It reminded every professional soldier that this civilian-in-a-general's-uniform was in fact a soldier who had not only performed superbly in combat, but had seen much more of it than had most of his professional soldier critics.

The idiotic suggestion to give OSS agents badges and identification cards would have been funny, Donovan thought, had it not represented the expenditure of a lot of time and effort, and revealed an appalling ignorance of how OSS agents were supposed to work, which was, of course, in absolute secrecy.

Some nitwit—probably a half-dozen nitwits—on a lower floor of the building had come up with an absolutely nonsensical idea, then spent much of their own—and other OSS personnel's—time in getting it ready to submit to the boss for his approval.

A mental image came to him, and he smiled:

"Guten tag, *Herr Oberburgermeister, my name is John Smith. I'm a spy for the OSS. Here are my credentials. What can you tell me about German efforts to make an atomic bomb?*"

Four sets of credentials had been prepared for Donovan's approval, which made him wonder, very unkindly, how much time the Documents Branch—which was charged with preparing counterfeit credentials and identification badges—had wasted on this idiotic idea.

Each set of credentials held a gold badge in one side of a leather folder, and a sealed-in-plastic photo identification card in the other. The photo ID was clearly patterned after the Adjutant General's Office identification cards issued to commissioned officers. There was space for a photo, a thumbprint, and the individual's name, rank, and date of birth.

Besides that, the badges were unlike any other Donovan had ever seen. Donovan had to admit they were both impressive and attractive. In the center was the great seal of the United States. In two curved lines at the top was the legend THE UNITED STATES OF AMERICA, and under that, OFFICE OF STRATEGIC SERVICES.

Under the badge, in a rectangular block, was space for the individual's rank. One of the badges read SPECIAL AGENT; the second, SENIOR AGENT; the third, SUPERVISORY AGENT; and the fourth, AREA COMMANDER.

There were no such ranks in the OSS, and the armed forces rank that an individual might have brought with him into the OSS carried little weight. There were people in charge of this and that, of course, and their assistants and deputies, but authority was given to station chiefs, for example, based on who was the best man for the job, not on his date of rank—if indeed he had a rank.

Donovan's imagination flew again.

Well, hell, we might as well go whole hog.
We can have a badge for Saboteur. And Assassin. And Burglar.
The possibilities are limitless!

He pulled a pad of interoffice memorandum forms to him and picked up his pen. Then he changed his mind.

This was too spectacular of an idiotic idea to be dismissed by one of his "*Not only no but HELL NO!*" memos, with the addendum, "*Destroy these!*"

This dedicated idiocy deserved more. He decided he would think about it after he had dealt with the off-the-wall analysis and then the problem he really shouldn't have to deal with himself but had to.

He put the leather folders back in the accordion folder and turned to the analysis.

The analysis was labeled: "Geo-Political Analysis Division Document #1943.24.04.717. An Analysis of Japanese Infiltration Among the Muslims Throughout the World."

It was a thin document stapled together under a pale yellow cover stamped TOP SECRET at the top and bottom, and carrying the names of the authors who appended PhD to their names. Donovan recognized both names. They were distinguished academics. One had come into the OSS from Yale, the other from the University of Chicago.

Neither of them was a fool—although one of them was truly strange-looking—and Donovan knew he wouldn't be able to dismiss their argument as quickly as he had the badges; he would have to read the entire document.

He was a lawyer, of course, who was capable of not only reading rapidly but also of retaining the important points a document made. Still, it took him ten minutes to read the analysis and sort out its pertinent points.

If the scholars who had prepared the analysis could be believed—and Donovan decided they could be—Japan had been courting the Muslim countries since the 1880s. After the Russo-Japanese War of 1904–1905, Japan intensified its efforts, and as early as 1906 had begun to plant rumors that the emperor was preparing to make Islam Japan's state religion.

In 1909, according to the analysis, the notion was given semiofficial approval when a number of influential Japanese signed "The Muslim Pact," which promised to promote Islam to the Japanese people. Among the Japanese who signed it was Tsuyoshi Inukai, who had later become prime minister. Others who signed it were Ryohei Uchida, who was known to be close to the emperor, and Mitsuru Toyama, who was very active in an odd facet of Japanese politics, the secret societies. On the Muslim side was a well-known and powerful writer,

Abdurrashid Ibrahim, whose writings pushed the idea that the time had come for a worldwide expansion of Islam.

After World War I, the analysis went on, the Japanese began to spread the word in the Muslim world that thousands of Japanese had converted to Islam and that Japan as a whole was ready to convert en masse, because the Mikado himself was coming to see himself as the head of a religion embracing the tenets of Muhammad.

In 1923, the analysis reported, a Japanese named Sakuma, who was reliably reported to have close contacts with the Japanese military, the foreign ministry, and the emperor's closest advisers, went to Shanghai and established "The Society of Light," a Muslim evangelical center with the announced purpose of promoting Islam in China.

More recently, the analysis went on, in the 1930s forward, Japan had been excusing its expansion into Southeastern Asia as "necessary to liberate those countries from Anglo-American tyranny." To Muslims, that might mean from "Christian tyranny," especially when the Japanese were portraying themselves as seriously considering conversion to Islam.

It pointed out that the "cultivate the Muslims" policy was being run by General Sadao Artaki, a former war minister and one of Premier Tojo's closest allies.

The analysis concluded that Japan considered its program a success and very likely would try something similar elsewhere—for example, with a "Catholic Policy" in Latin America. If Muslims could be convinced that the Mikado was about to become a Muslim, why couldn't Latin American Roman Catholics be convinced that the emperor was about to embrace the Pope, and all Japan was trying to do was protect them from the evils of Anglo-American Protestantism?

Phrased in academic jargon, the analysis said that while to Western eyes the Japanese emperor's conversion to Islam was about as likely to happen as the Pope embracing Shintoism, it wasn't how things looked to Western eyes that mattered, but what the people in Asia and South America thought.

The analysis summarized: "Japan has expended on Muslim policy many years of patient labor and has assigned to it some of her ablest political and military leaders. Her cunning and opportunism, her flexible approach and unscrupulous manipulation of the facts have borne fruit in many lands," and then went on to recommend that the OSS immediately begin its own propaganda campaign in Muslim countries exposing "Japan's barefaced duplicity" by documenting what the Japanese were in fact doing, forcing emperor worship on the Muslim populations of territories they had "liberated."

Donovan exhaled audibly. This was the first he'd heard of anything like this—and that was more than a little embarrassing, as he took pride in his knowledge of things like this—and obviously it had to be looked into.

He reached for his pen and the pad of interoffice memoranda forms again, and wrote two. One was to the authors of the analysis: "Thank you. Good job. I'll get back to you. WJD." The second was to the assistant deputy director for Asia, as he knew the deputy director himself was in Asia, trying to reason with General Douglas MacArthur about the potential value of the OSS: "Read this carefully. Look into it. Get back to me soonest. WJD."

Then he turned to the problem that he really shouldn't have to deal with but knew he had to.

It was in the form of an interoffice memorandum: "Bill, I need to talk to you about Frade. I'll be here all morning. AFG."

Donovan recognized the initials as those of the deputy director of the OSS for Western Hemisphere Operations, Colonel Alejandro Federico Graham, USMCR.

And Donovan knew that Frade was Major Cletus Howell Frade, USMCR, an OSS agent presently in Argentina.

Donovan had no idea what Graham wished to talk to him about vis-à-vis Major Frade, but he suspected he wasn't going to like it at all. And he was sure that Colonel Graham wasn't going to like at all what he was planning to tell him vis-à-vis Major Frade. He had planned, until he found Graham's interoffice memo on his desk, to send him one. It would have read much the same: "Alex, I need to talk to you about Frade. I'll be here all morning. WJD."

Donovan leaned forward and depressed the talk switch on his intercom device.

"Helen," he said. "Would you please ask Colonel Graham if he has a minute for me? Bring in coffee, and then no calls—except from the President—until we're through. Okay?"

[THREE]

Colonel A. F. Graham was ushered into Donovan's office. Graham was a short, trim, tanned, barrel-chested, bald-headed forty-eight-year-old with a pencil-line mustache; he wore a superbly tailored double-breasted pin-striped suit that Donovan strongly suspected had come from London's Savile Row. Helen placed a silver coffee service on a low table and left.

"I hope I didn't interfere with your schedule, Bill," Graham said. "But we really have to talk."

"Yes, we do," Donovan said. "I had dinner with the President last night and—"

"How nice for you!" Graham interrupted, mockingly. "And was the First Lady there?"

Colonel Graham was not an admirer of either the President or his wife. It was more or less common knowledge that he had been one of the largest individual contributors to the campaign of his friend Wendell Willkie, who had run against—and been soundly beaten by—Roosevelt in the 1940 presidential campaign.

"No, she wasn't," Donovan said, just a little sharply.

"Well, since we're swapping social tidbits, I had a couple of drinks with Marcus Howell last night."

"How nice for you," Donovan offered sarcastically.

"Yes, indeed. I walked into the bar of the Union League in Philadelphia, and he 'just happened' to be there."

Donovan decided that he would let Graham tell him what Howell—who was chairman of the board of Howell Petroleum; a close friend of Colonel Robert R. McCormick, owner of *The Chicago Tribune*, whose pages often reflected his deep hatred of Franklin Delano Roosevelt; and Major Cletus Howell Frade's grandfather—had said or wanted before he told him what the President had said and wanted.

"And what did you and Mr. Howell talk about?"

"A number of things, but topping the list was that he wants us to bring Cletus Frade home from Argentina."

"Well, now, isn't that an interesting coincidence? Just last night the President wondered if that might not be a good idea." Donovan paused. "He really wants to know who Galahad is, Alex."

Graham met his eye for a moment. "I'm afraid your friend the President is going to be disappointed again. Frade's not going to tell him, and, further, says the situation there precludes his leaving."

He laid Frade's radio message on Donovan's desk.

Donovan read it, then looked at Graham incredulously.

"He has new information regarding Galahad's connections that he'll only give personally to you?" Donovan exploded. "Just who the hell does he think he is?"

"He knows who he is, and that's the problem," Graham said.

"You're not telling me, Alex, that you're even thinking of going down there?"

"I'm on the Pan American Grace clipper out of Miami tomorrow night. I wanted to tell you where I would be, and I wanted to urge you as strongly as I can to do everything within your power to turn off all these people who are trying to find out who Galahad is."

"What I'm tempted to do is order you not to go, and to order that arrogant young man onto the next Panagra Clipper to Miami."

"That would force me to resign, and he wouldn't come. We've been over all this before. Is that what you want?"

It was a full thirty seconds before Donovan replied.

"One time, when we reach that point, I'm going to say, 'Yes, Alex, it is.' "

"But not this time?"

Donovan shook his head.

"What do you think he means about Galahad's connections?"

"I haven't the faintest idea. But I know him well enough now to know he really thinks it's important."

Donovan nodded.

"Okay. Go down and see what he has to say."

"I will."

Graham headed for the door and was halfway there when Donovan realized he hadn't gotten into the second thing Roosevelt had brought up at dinner.

While Donovan held Alex Graham in very high regard, it was also true that their personalities clashed, almost always because Graham was one of the very few people in the world who was not afraid to tell Donovan no and then was uncowed when this inevitably triggered Donovan's temper.

And it just happened again. He told me no, and I became annoyed to the point where not only didn't we have the friendly cup of coffee I set up but, also, I forgot I promised FDR I would have Graham implement his latest friendly suggestion for the OSS.

"Hold it a second, will you, Alex?" Donovan called.

Graham turned.

"There's something else," Donovan said. He waved at the couch and the coffee service. "Have you time for a cup of coffee?"

Graham recognized the olive branch.

"Thank you. I'd love one."

He walked to the couch and sat down. Donovan walked to the coffee table carrying a cigar humidor, offered a cigar to Graham, lit it for him, and then poured the coffee.

"Why does this little bird on my shoulder keep whispering, 'Beware of Irishmen bearing gifts'?" Graham said.

"Because you have a cynical streak in your character," Donovan said.

"True," Graham said.

"FDR had dinner with Hap Arnold night before last," Donovan began. "During which Arnold told him how well aircraft production is going."

General Henry H. Arnold was commanding general, Army Air Forces.

Graham nodded and waited for Donovan to go on.

"Arnold apparently got carried away and said something about almost being at the point where we have more airplanes than we need."

"That's hard to accept," Graham said. "From what I hear, there have been awful losses in Europe."

"It seems Arnold wasn't talking about bombers and fighters," Donovan said. "What has apparently happened, Alex, was that cost-plus contracts were apparently let for all kinds of aircraft, not only fighters and bombers and the larger transports. The aircraft industry rose to the challenge and went on an around-the-clock, no-weekends-off production schedule and has churned out, for example, large numbers of aircraft—the models in question here are Lockheed's Lodestar and Constellation—"

"You mean that *Queen Mary*–size wooden airplane Howard Hughes is building?"

"No. I don't know what they call that wooden airplane, but that's not it. You know what the Lodestar is, of course?"

"Uh-huh. What's the Constellation?"

"Another of Hughes's designs. Great big, four-engine, forty-odd-passenger airplane. It has three tails. It can fly across the Atlantic. Or to Hawaii."

"I've seen pictures."

"Well, neither airplane fits comfortably into the Army Air Force. The Lodestar carries only fourteen people and the door isn't large enough to conveniently drop parachutists. The Douglas DC-3—the C-47—carries twenty-one people and the door is big enough for paratroopers. The Constellation is really a better airplane than the DC-4—it cruises at better than three hundred miles an hour; the DC-4 only goes a little better than two hundred—but the decision was made early on to go with the DC-4 as the standard, and that Lockheed should produce the P-38 fighter instead of more Constellations." He paused and looked at Graham. "You see where I'm going, Alex?"

"No. I don't think this is just polite conversation over coffee, but I don't know where it's leading."

"The President remembered we sent a Lodestar down to Argentina," Donovan said.

"That was a mistake. I suggested that Roosevelt send a Staggerwing Beechcraft down there to replace the one Frade lost—his father's airplane—when he was shot down leading one of our submarines—the *Devil Fish*—to the Reine de la Mer. The President agreed, and told the Air Force to come up with one. They couldn't find one, so they sent the next best thing, a twin-engine, fourteen-passenger airliner, to replace a single-engine six-seater."

"The commander in chief expressed a desire which has the force and effect of law. What were they going to tell him? 'Sorry'?"

"Where's this leading, Bill?" Graham said suspiciously.

"The commander in chief, after being informed by the commanding general of the Army Air Forces that he had more Lockheed Lodestars and Constellations than he really needed, wondered if it wouldn't be a good idea for the OSS to use some of those airplanes to set up its own airline down there, under that stalwart Marine Aviator Cletus Frade."

"You're pulling my leg," Graham said.

"I told the commander in chief that you would implement his suggestion, Colonel Graham."

"No way, Bill. It's a . . . nutty . . . idea."

"After I tell you that FDR really warmed to his idea—he feels that not only would it enhance the image of the arsenal of democracy—"

"Meaning what?"

"That the arsenal of democracy, now in high gear, is so formidable that we can sell the very latest airplanes to friendly—or neutral—foreigners."

Graham grunted.

"And, waving his cigarette holder around, the President smugly suggested that the OSS could probably find some advantage in having its own airline."

Graham sadly shook his head.

"You want to tell him it's a nutty idea, Alex?" Donovan asked.

"If I thought it would do any good, I'd be happy to tell him," Graham said. "But since Roosevelt believes he is divinely inspired—"

"Between us—to go no further than this room—what's wrong with the idea?"

"Off the top of my head, I can think of a number of things wrong with it. For one thing, even if Frade could get permission to set up an airline, which seems unlikely, he's not qualified to run an airline. For God's sake, he really shouldn't even be flying the Lodestar he has."

"Why not?"

"Because he's likely to kill himself doing so. And we need him alive, not spread over some mountain in the Andes."

"I somehow got the idea he's a pretty good pilot," Donovan said. "He's an ace, right? And he has been flying the Lodestar he has?"

"He's a Marine fighter pilot, a young one. He therefore believes he can fly anything. That is known as the arrogance of youth."

"The President is very impressed with him."

"Did the President suggest where the pilots to fly the airplanes of OSS Airways are supposed to come from?"

"Argentina."

"And who's going to train them? Frade?"

"Would you believe me if I told you I tried—hard—to dissuade FDR from this airline idea? And raised the question of pilots to him?"

"And what did he do? Flash that famous smile and say, 'Oh, Bill, that can be worked out'?"

"What he said was that Arnold also told him that the pilot-training program has gone so well that they are getting ready to release the transport pilots commissioned early on to return to the airlines, and that they would be ideal, because of their experience, in setting up an airline."

"You mean transfer them to the OSS?"

"He didn't get into that. But that could be worked out."

Graham snorted.

"Will have to be worked out," Donovan added. "The bottom line, Alex, is that unless you can talk him out of this idea . . ."

"Huh!"

". . . there will be an airline."

Graham shook his head again but said nothing.

"Among the many reasons I like you, Alex," Donovan said, after a moment, "and the primary reason I put up with your—how do I phrase this?— *independent spirit* is that I know if I give you an order, you'll either obey it or tell me, up front, that you won't take the order. You are not capable of accepting an order and then not doing your very best to carry it out."

"I gather this is an order?"

Donovan nodded.

"Keep what you just said in mind, Bill, if I can't make your airline idea . . ."

"The *President's* airline suggestion."

". . . fly."

Donovan smiled, then had another thought.

"Just a second, Alex," he said, and reached for the accordion envelope and handed it to Graham.

"Why don't you stop by the Documents Branch and have these made out for Major Frade and his team before you go?"

Graham examined the credentials, at first curiously and then incredulously. "And whose idiot idea was this?"

"If you mean, Was this another presidential suggestion? No. It came from downstairs."

Graham, shaking his head in disbelief, handed the envelope back to Donovan.

"No, I meant it," Donovan said. "Take the badges down there."

"I'm not following you, Bill."

"What the hell, everybody down there in South America—friend, foe, and ostensibly neutral—knows Frade's in the OSS, so why not? And—I admit this is unlikely—it might just remind him he's in the OSS if you handed him a fancy badge like that."

Graham looked at Donovan for a moment, then said, "Well, I can't see where it would do any harm."

"Have a nice flight, Alex. Keep in touch."

[FOUR]
El Palomar Air Field
Campo de Mayo Military Base
Buenos Aires Province, Argentina
1525 4 July 1943

As the airliner taxied up to the terminal, Colonel A. F. Graham saw—not surprising him at all—that El Coronel Alejandro Bernardo Martín had elected to meet Varig Flight 207.

Martín, wearing a well-cut suit and an overcoat, was standing outside the terminal building with a group of immigration and customs officers. He was a tall, fair-haired, light-skinned thirty-six-year-old who carried the euphemistic title of "Chief, Ethical Standards Office" within the Ejército Argentino's Bureau of Internal Security. In fact, he was the most powerful—and, making him even more dangerous, the most competent—intelligence officer in Argentina.

It had been necessary for Graham to get a visa for travel to Argentina. Said visa had been stamped at the Argentine embassy in Washington inside a diplomatic passport issued with the greatest reluctance by the State Department. The passport identified Graham as a career State Department officer with the personal rank of under secretary. The Department of State, in requesting Graham's visa from the Argentine embassy, had declared he was traveling to Argentina to coordinate security and other matters at the U.S. embassy.

No one was fooled. But both the Argentines and the Americans understood the rules of the game. Graham would have diplomatic status in Argentina, protecting him from arrest. Theoretically, if he was caught with twenty pounds of dynamite in the act of placing it under the Casa Rosada—Argentina's pink equivalent of the White House—all that could happen to him would be to be declared persona non grata and expelled from the country, after which the Argentine ambassador in Washington would "make representations" to the U.S. secretary of State.

As a practical matter, both sides understood that if he were caught trying to blow up Casa Rosada—or in some other outrageous activity—he would be shot, after which the American ambassador in Buenos Aires could "make representations" to the Argentine foreign minister.

There were Argentines in Washington carrying diplomatic passports—most of them running errands for the Germans—with no more right to theirs than Graham had to his. They were under constant surveillance by the FBI, as Graham would be under constant surveillance by the BIS in Argentina.

But as diplomats they were protected against arrest and could not be questioned, which obviated the necessity of coming up with some imaginative excuse to explain one's presence where one was not supposed to be.

Anything less than really outrageous behavior was tolerated by both the United States and Argentina. It was in their mutual interest.

And there was a simple, logical explanation as to why Graham found El Coronel Martín meeting his Brazilian airline flight not surprising. There was no question in Graham's mind that within an hour of his acquiring the visa—no longer than it had taken to encrypt the message—somebody from the Argentine embassy had gone to Western Union, or Mackay Radio, and sent a cable informing the BIS that Graham was coming to Buenos Aires.

What had somewhat surprised Colonel A. F. Graham were the airplanes that had carried him from Natal, Brazil, to Argentina. They were both Lockheed Lodestars.

He'd flown from Miami to Natal—with fuel stops in Trinidad and Belem—in great luxury aboard a Panagra Boeing 314—the same "Dixie Clipper" that had in January flown President Roosevelt to the Casablanca Conference. It was an enormous forty-two-ton flying boat powered by four 1,600-horsepower engines. Aboard was a bar and comfortable bunks, and first-class food had been served by Panagra stewards in crisply starched white jackets.

They'd spent the night in luxurious accommodations in Belem, then flown the next morning on to Natal, an eight-hour flight during which they had averaged a bit over 125 miles per hour. This was as far south as the big seaplanes went. From Natal, they either flew across the South Atlantic to British Gambia on the African Coast or returned to Miami.

The Panagra flights to Natal always carried high-priority supplies and senior officers bound for the large U.S. Army Air Forces base at Brazil's Pôrto Alegre, and thus routinely were met by a USAAF plane from Pôrto Alegre. The last time Graham had gone to Argentina, that aircraft had been a B-24 and everyone had had to sit on the floor.

This time, the airplane had been a Lodestar—one painted olive drab, making it in USAAF parlance a C-60—fitted out to transport seven passengers in the comfort befitting Air Forces senior officers.

That had made Graham wonder how long there had been a plethora of Lodestars before Hap Arnold had confided in Roosevelt the amazing success of the aircraft production system.

And when he'd gone to the civilian side of the airfield at Pôrto Alegre to board a Varig flight to Buenos Aires, he again had been surprised to see that it too was a Lodestar, also apparently brand new, but this time configured as a normal airliner with seats for fourteen passengers.

The stewardess told him that the Brazilian airline had recently acquired a dozen of the airplanes.

This, of course, forced him to think of Roosevelt's "suggestion" that Cletus Frade start an airline in Argentina. He wondered if Roosevelt had other reasons for making the suggestion. In his experience with the President, the reason advanced for one idea or another was most often not the real one.

Graham, admiringly, not pejoratively, thought that Franklin Delano Roosevelt could have given lessons in political maneuvering to Niccolò Machiavelli.

Colonel Martín was standing just inside the immigration and customs booths in the terminal.

"Colonel Martín, what a pleasant surprise!" Graham greeted him cheerfully in Spanish, putting out his hand.

"Have a nice flight, did you, Colonel?"

"Actually, I think you're supposed to call me 'Mr. Secretary,' " Graham said.

"What is that saying of your Corps of Marine infantry, 'Once a Marine, always a Marine'?"

"And that is actually the 'Marine Corps' instead of what you said," Graham replied. "Tell you what: Why don't you call me 'Alejandro'? Or better yet, 'Alex'?"

"I'm afraid that would annoy my German friends—you know how fond they are of their titles and ranks—who might think we were being too friendly, but thank you just the same."

"And we must never forget evenhanded neutrality, right?"

"You understand my problem," Martín said, smiling. "But perhaps, when we are alone, and we are sure no one can hear or is watching, we can call one another by our Christian names."

"I'd like that, but I understand the BIS is always watching and listening."

"So I've heard," Martín said. "Are you going to be with us long, Mr. Secretary?"

"Probably not long at all," Graham said. "Perhaps we could have lunch."

"You'll be staying where?"

"I don't think you're supposed to ask me that," Graham said. "But in the spirit of friendship, I'll tell you: at the Alvear Palace."

"I thought you perhaps might be staying with Major Frade."

"Are you referring to Don Cletus Frade, by any chance?"

Martín, smiling, snapped his fingers and shook his head ruefully.

"I just can't seem to get it straight in my mind that he's no longer an officer of your Corps of Marines, but one of our most respected *estancieros*."

"Perhaps you should write it on the palm of your hand, if you have trouble remembering. And to answer another question you shouldn't be asking: I feel sure that sometime during my visit, I will avail myself of Don Cletus's famous hospitality."

"When you see Don Cletus, please express my regards?"

"I'll be happy to."

"May I offer you a ride into Buenos Aires, Mr. Secretary?"

"I wouldn't want to inconvenience you."

"Not at all. The Alvear is right on my way."

"Then thank you, Colonel."

[FIVE]
Suite 407
Alvear Palace Hotel
Avenida Alvear 1891
Buenos Aires, Argentina
1645 4 July 1943

Graham just had time to go into his suitcase for a change of linen and his toilet kit when there was a knock at his door.

When he opened the door, Cletus Frade was standing there. Behind him was Suboficial Mayor Enrico Rodríguez, Ejército Argentino, Retired. Graham saw that Rodríguez's trench coat, worn over his shoulder, did not entirely conceal the self-loading shotgun he carried against his leg.

Graham waved them into the room.

"I wondered when I was going to see you, Major," Graham said.

"I didn't want to intrude on your conversation with Martín," Frade said.

"You have any idea what that was all about?"

"I think he was sending us both a message that he's watching us."

"Is there a situation here I don't know about?"

"That qualifies as a massive understatement," Frade said.

"What's with the shotgun?"

"Enrico has sworn an oath to God that what happened to my father will not happen to me," Frade said.

Graham met Frade's eyes and saw in them that what he'd said was a statement of fact.

"Unless you really want to stay here, I think you'd be more comfortable at San Pedro y San Pablo," Frade said. "And we have to go there anyway."

"Why do we have to go there anyway?"

"Today is the Fourth of July, and you, Colonel Graham, sir, will be the senior officer present as the local OSS detachment celebrates Independence Day."

Graham met his eyes again and saw that Frade was serious about this, too.

"Won't Martín know?"

"If we leave right now, we can probably get away from here before Martín can get his people in place to surveil you."

Graham closed his suitcase.

"Okay," he said.

———

Frade's enormous Horch was parked in the Alvear Palace's covered, off-the-street driveway, and when Frade, Graham, and Enrico came out of the revolving door, the top-hatted doorman hurried to open the rear door of the car.

Frade, who was carrying Graham's bag, walked quickly to it, threw the bag in the backseat, then closed the door. The car immediately drove off.

Frade took Graham's arm and propelled him out of the drive onto Avenida Alvear. When he saw the confusion on Graham's face, he chuckled and said, "Sorry, mi coronel, it's Ford time."

There was a 1941 wooden-sided Ford station wagon at the curb. Graham saw that Enrico was already in the street and had opened the driver's door.

Frade pointed to the front passenger door, and then as Graham got in, trotted around the rear of the station wagon and got behind the wheel. As soon as Enrico was sure the door was shut, he got in the back, and the station wagon pulled into the flow of traffic.

"What's this all about?" Graham said as they pulled up to, and stayed behind, the Horch.

"The theory is that if they try to bushwhack me, as they bushwacked my father, they'll probably hit the Horch first," Frade said matter-of-factly. "There's two guys with Thompsons in the Horch, and there's another Thompson under your seat. 'Surprise, surprise!'"

"You think that's likely?" Graham said.

Frade looked at him and shook his head in disbelief.

III

[ONE]
Estancia San Pedro y San Pablo
Near Pila, Buenos Aires Province
Republic of Argentina
1925 4 July 1943

Once they were out of the city, the Horch and the Ford station wagon heading south on National Route Two, Graham bluntly had asked: "So, what is it that's so important I had to come down here to get you to share it with me?"

Frade had replied by putting his index finger to his lips, then jerking his thumb toward Enrico, who was sitting in the next row of seats with his shotgun between his knees.

Graham didn't press for an answer.

For two reasons, he thought.

One, if he doesn't want Enrico to hear what he has to say, he probably has a good reason.

Two, pushing him won't work. All that would accomplish would be to make both of us angry.

That portion of the Code for the Governance of the Naval Service requiring immediate and cheerful, willing obedience to orders just doesn't apply in this circumstance.

He knows it. Worse, I know it.

And even worse, he knows that I know it.

Graham had been to the estancia before, but he realized after an hour or so on Route Two, with the glowing needle on the Ford's speedometer seldom dropping below one hundred kph, that he had forgotten how far from Buenos Aires it was.

They turned off Route Two at Lezama and, twenty-odd kilometers later, passed through the village of Pila. The maps of Argentina showed that the macadam road ended at Pila. It didn't, but five hundred meters outside Pila, Estancia San Pedro y San Pablo began. The road here was privately owned, and had been built and was maintained by the proprietors of Estancia San Pedro y

San Pablo and Estancia Santa Catalina. Estancia Santa Catalina was on the other side of Estancia San Pedro y San Pablo.

Graham had known even before he had met Cletus Frade that Estancia Santa Catalina was owned by Señora Claudia de Carzino-Cormano. He knew, too, that Doña Claudia's relationship with El Coronel Jorge Guillermo Frade over a twenty-year period had kept both of them from partaking of the sacrament of communion in the Roman Catholic Church, the canons of which deny the sacrament to those who have shared—in the case of Doña Claudia and El Coronel were sharing continuously and almost notoriously—sexual congress outside the bonds of holy matrimony absent confession and absolution, which carried with it their promise to go forth and sin no more.

Several times Graham had met Doña Claudia—a svelte woman in her mid-fifties with gray-flecked, luxuriant black hair—and had liked her. He wondered if she would be at the estancia. He knew she often was, and this pleased him because he thought of her as a restraining influence—especially with regard to El Coronel Juan Domingo Perón—on Cletus Frade.

Ten kilometers or so down the private road, the headlights of the station wagon illuminated a brick and wrought-iron sign at the side of the road. It read SAN PEDRO Y SAN PABLO. Five hundred meters past the sign, there was a fork in the road. But no signs or arrows indicated where either fork led.

The Horch and the Ford took the left fork. Fifteen kilometers down that road Graham caught a first glimpse of the brightly illuminated, sprawling, white-painted stone main building. It sat with its outbuildings in a three-hectare, manicured garden, all set within a windbreak of a triple row of tall cedars.

As they came closer, he saw, just outside the windbreak, the airfield. There were four airplanes parked there, three Piper Cubs and a Lodestar, the latter painted a glistening red. The paint job was the result of a presidential order.

Franklin Delano Roosevelt had told General Hap Arnold of the U.S. Army Forces that he wanted to send an airplane, a Beechcraft Staggerwing, to an important Argentine to replace one that had been destroyed. The President had not shared with General Arnold how it had been lost, just that it had, and that he wanted the replacement to be as much like the lost plane as possible, including the color. And that it be brand new.

With more important things on his mind, General Arnold had delegated the order to others. Two days later, the USAAF procurement officer at the Beech Aircraft Company in Wichita, Kansas, had reported to his superior that in late 1940, a Staggerwing Beechcraft bright red in color had been sold to a Colonel Frade in Buenos Aires, and this was almost certainly the airplane President Roosevelt had in mind. The procurement officer also reported that no new Staggerwings of any color were available.

To the military mind, this was only a minor problem in executing an order of the commander in chief. The order was immediately amended to provide that an airplane of at least equal quality be obtained, painted Beechcraft red, and sent by the most expeditious means to Colonel Frade. It was soon discovered that Lockheed had delivered a number of Lodestar aircraft to the Air Forces. They were inarguably of at least equal quality, and moreover could be flown down there. A dozen Lodestars had recently been configured as airliners, sold to Varig, the national airline of Brazil, and flown down there by USAAF pilots.

"Colonel," the order had been issued to the procurement officer, "make sure the Lodestar you send to Colonel Frade be painted Beechcraft red, be as nicely configured as the ones we sold to the Brazilians, and get it on its way within forty-eight hours."

Three minutes later, they reached the main house. There were a number of people standing on the verandah.

Somehow, Graham decided, *they knew exactly when we would be here. Which means that he has people—his gauchos—stationed where they can watch the highway.*

One of the men on the verandah was wearing what clearly identified him as a gaucho: a black, wide, flat-brimmed hat; billowing black *bombachas* tucked into calf-high black boots; a wide, red, coin-studded leather belt; a leather vest; and a horn-handled foot-long knife in a silver scabbard at the back of the belt.

Most of the others were armed with Colt .45 ACP semiautomatic pistols carried in leather holsters hanging from web belts.

The gaucho came quickly off the porch, walked up to the Ford wagon, came to attention, and saluted.

"Happy Fourth of July, sir," Chief Radioman Oscar J. Schultz, USN, said. "If the colonel will give me his gear, I'll take care of it."

Graham returned the salute as a Pavlovian reaction, then smiled as it occurred to him that if there was a more blatant violation of the Navy regulation that "naval personnel will not render the hand salute while in civilian attire" he couldn't imagine what it would be.

"Good to see you, Chief," Graham said. "My suitcase is in the Horch."

"I'll handle it for the colonel," Chief Schultz announced, and went to the Horch.

As Graham got out of the Ford, he saw that the other men—two in the uniform of U.S. Army officers, several of the others wearing parts of U.S. Army uniforms, and the rest in the clothing of gauchos—had come to attention. He wondered if someone had actually called "Attention!" or whether popping to attention had been the Pavlovian response on the part of one of the sergeants to the presence of a full-bull colonel, and the others had joined in.

"As you were," Graham ordered, and he walked toward the verandah, smiling and with his hand extended.

There were four sergeants on the roster of what, in a document classified Top Secret in OSS headquarters, was officially known as OSS Western Hemisphere Team 17, code name Team Turtle. A sunken ship is sometimes said to have "turned turtle." The original mission of the team had been to cause the sinking of the *Reine de la Mer,* an ostensibly neutral Spanish merchantman actually engaged in replenishing German submarines in Argentina.

There had been five sergeants until Technical Sergeant David G. Ettinger had been murdered and mutilated in Montevideo. He had been killed with an ice pick in the ear, and his penis had been cut off and inserted into his mouth. Agents of the German SS-SD had correctly decided that the discovery of his mutilated body would make it clear to the German-Jewish communities of Buenos Aires and Montevideo that any contact with a fellow Jewish refugee from Germany now working for the Americans would become known and both would be punished.

Ettinger's assassination had deeply saddened and angered the members of Team Turtle. Especially the team's other Jewish member, Sergeant Sigfried Stein, their explosives expert. Stein, also a refugee from Nazi Germany, said he was not surprised, however, at anything done by the *Gottverdammt* Nazis.

The other two sergeants were Technical Sergeant William Ferris, who was the weapons and parachute expert, and Staff Sergeant Jerry O'Sullivan, who operated the team's highly secret radar.

Standing on the verandah with them were the officers: Captain Maxwell Ashton III and First Lieutenants Anthony J. Pelosi and Madison R. Sawyer III. Ashton and Pelosi, both assistant military attachés at the U.S. embassy, were in uniform, complete to the silver aiguillette of military attachés. Sawyer, whom

Graham was about to tell he had just been promoted to captain, was wearing U.S. Army riding breeches, boots, and a blue polo shirt.

Sergeant Ferris, Captain Ashton, and Lieutenant Sawyer all met the criteria of social prominence that allowed critics of the OSS to complain that the acronym really stood for Oh, So Social. They all came from wealthy, socially prominent families.

Sergeants Stein and O'Sullivan and Lieutenant Pelosi did not. Stein was the only one of them who had a college degree (an E.E., earned at night school at the University of Chicago). Lieutenant Pelosi had barely made it through vocational high school in Chicago. And O'Sullivan had dropped out of high school in his sophomore year.

The latter two had been the beneficiaries of the Army's system of testing all enlisted men for their general intelligence and ability to learn. Scores on the Army General Classification Test determined where one would serve in the Army. Generally speaking, an AGCT score of 100 would send the new soldier to a technical school (the Signal Corps, for example) and an AGCT score of 110 would see the soldier as a ripe candidate for Officer Candidate School.

After basic training, Private O'Sullivan (ACGT 142) was sent to the Signal School at Fort Monmouth for training in the new, still highly secret technology of radio ranging and direction, called "Radar," and Private Pelosi (AGCT 138) went from Fort Dix to Fort Belvoir, from which he emerged just over three months later as a duly commissioned officer and gentleman of the Corps of Engineers.

Now-Sergeant O'Sullivan had volunteered for an unspecified hazardous assignment overseas to get him out of the classrooms at Fort Monmouth, where he had been assigned to teach classes of newly commissioned officers—whose stupidity had astonished him—the basic principles of radio ranging and direction.

Meanwhile, Second Lieutenant Pelosi had volunteered for an unspecified hazardous assignment overseas to get him out of the 82nd Airborne Division, where he had come to understand that engineer second lieutenants spent most of their time digging latrines and fixing roads and looking for land mines, and you had to be at least a captain before they would let you near any real demolition work.

Both applications had been quickly accepted by the OSS, who had put out the call for volunteers, O'Sullivan's because he knew more about radio ranging and direction than the OSS expert who interviewed him, and Pelosi's because several very senior officers of the OSS had done business with the Chicago firm of Pelosi & Sons Demolitions Inc., which enjoyed a fine reputation for being able to take down twenty-story buildings with explosives without shattering windows across the street. One telephone call had confirmed that "Little Tony" was indeed part of the Pelosi clan and had been "taking things down" since he had joined the Boy Scouts.

Pelosi and Ashton were the only two of the Americans who were legally in Argentina. They had diplomatic passports and diplomatic carnets attesting to their status as military attachés.

The others—and the radar set—had been infiltrated into Argentina from the U.S. Army Air Forces base at Pôrto Alegre, Brazil, in a Lodestar flown— after only four hours of instruction—by Cletus Frade, who had never set foot in one before, never mind sat in its left seat.

Frade, who had been born in Argentina, was considered by the Argentine government therefore to be an Argentine, and thus was in the country legally. Some, perhaps most, of his activities in Argentina could be considered treason against the country of his birth, and for some time that had been a genuine concern.

But then, during the coup d'état of 19 April 1943, most doubts vis-à-vis his allegiance to Argentina had been dispelled, at least in the mind of General of Division (Major General) Arturo Rawson, who came out of the coup as president of the Governing Council of the Provisional Government of the Republic of Argentina.

What had happened was that one section of Operation Blue—the plan for the coup d'état—had taken into consideration the possibility that the coup would in fact fail. Blue had been written in large part by El Coronel Jorge Guillermo Frade, Cavalry, Ejército Argentino, Retired, before his assassination, when it was anticipated that he would become president of the Governing Council of the Provisional Government.

In such an event, the leaders of the failed coup would have to have a means to get out of the country—their alternative being the firing squad. And Operation Blue had dealt with that problem: El Coronel Frade was to fly his Staggerwing Beechcraft to the airfield at the Campo de Mayo army base, and use it to transport himself and other senior officers to either Uruguay or Brazil.

By the time the coup began, El Coronel Frade was dead and the Beechcraft on the bottom of Samborombón Bay, having been shot down as Cletus Frade led an American submarine to the *Reine de la Mer.*

Cletus, who had read Operation Blue after he found it in his father's (then his) safe at Estancia San Pedro y San Pablo, decided that since his father had put his fellow officers in danger, Cletus was honor bound to carry out his father's wishes. He flew the Lockheed Lodestar to Campo de Mayo and placed it—and himself—at the disposal of General Rawson.

The coup didn't fail, and the Lodestar wasn't needed.

But toward the end of the coup, as two columns marched toward Argentina's Casa Rosada, General Rawson confided in Cletus Frade that he had lost contact with both columns. He needed to get directions to them, otherwise unnecessary blood would be shed.

That didn't seem to be much of a problem for Cletus Frade, who had been flying Piper Cubs over the prairies of Texas since he was fourteen, and where the standard method of getting messages—and often lunch—to someone on the ground was by dropping them in pillow cases out the window of a Cub. He told Rawson they could do the same thing using one of the Ejército Argentino's Piper Cubs.

Rawson first asked Cletus if he would fly such a mission, and then when Frade—aware he'd put his foot in his mouth again—said he would, Rawson had another thought. He said he would go with him in the Cub, so that he could personally issue the necessary orders.

General Rawson had had very little experience flying in small aircraft, and absolutely none in flying at only two hundred feet above Avenida Libertador in downtown Buenos Aires. He regarded what Cletus Frade thought of as an uneventful short hop to a soccer field and back as a magnificent manifestation of both flying skill and great courage, proving that patriot's blood as great as his late father's coursed through the veins of Don Cletus Frade.

The command structure of the OSS in Argentina as posted on a Top Secret chart in OSS headquarters in Washington differed greatly from the way things actually were in Argentina. That this had not come to the attention of OSS Director Donovan was because all reports from Argentina passed through the hands of Colonel A. F. Graham. As the deputy director of the OSS for Western Hemisphere Operation, Graham filtered anything he suspected would annoy Donovan—sometimes by burning the reports—rather than have Donovan see them.

Most of the reports that complained about how things were going came from Lieutenant Commander Frederico Delojo, USN, who in Buenos Aires was the naval attaché—and, covertly, the OSS station chief—of the Embassy of the United States.

Commander Delojo was a Puerto Rican, a graduate of the U.S. Naval Academy at Annapolis, and had been an intelligence officer from the time he had been a lieutenant junior grade. In theory—on the manning chart at OSS headquarters—Delojo was in command of all OSS personnel and activities in Argentina.

One of the reports that Commander Delojo had sent to the OSS in Washington—and that Graham had burned—reported that then-Captain Cletus Frade, USMCR, had told him that the next time he came anywhere near Estancia San Pedro y San Pablo or tried to establish contact with any of the OSS personnel there he would be shot.

Frade had made a similar threat to Lieutenant Colonel Richard Almond, USAAF, who had gone to Argentina ostensibly to teach Frade how to fly the Lodestar but actually had been sent by Army Intelligence to identify "Galahad," Frade's window into the German embassy, and more.

Colonel Graham wasn't sure that the threats were bona fide, but he suspected Frade meant them. Frade was determined to keep his men and his sources alive.

Captain Maxwell Ashton III was on the manning chart as the commanding officer of Team Turtle, and therefore under the orders of Lieutenant Commander Delojo. However, he actually took his orders from Frade—and Delojo didn't even know where he or any of the others were or what they were doing.

Graham had sent a message to Delojo telling him that not only was he not to consider Captain Ashton and Lieutenant Pelosi subject to his orders, he also was not to inquire into their activities. Delojo's four-page letter of protest about that, sent via the diplomatic pouch to Director Donovan, accordingly had gone up in flames in Graham's wastebasket.

It was Graham's judgment that not only had Frade done a magnificent job so far in Argentina, but if left alone could probably make an even greater contribution to the war effort.

Graham could not think of having a better agent in place, just about equally because Frade seemed to have a natural talent for covert warfare and because of his superb connections. The man leading the junta that had taken over Argentina was personally fond of him. Colonel Juan Domingo Perón, whom Graham believed to be a dangerous man and one destined to assume a greater role in Argentina, had been Frade's father's best friend, and looked on Frade as a beloved nephew.

And all of that didn't get into Frade's connections with people who could tell him the details of the German Operation Phoenix, and the despicable practice within the SS of allowing Jews in concentration camps to be ransomed out, which really had the attention of the President of the United States.

The status quo was not easy for Graham. He had been an infantry company commander—and later, as a major, a regimental intelligence officer—with the Marines in France in the First World War, and there learned to devoutly believe in the principles of leadership and obedience that made the Marine Corps what it was.

He reluctantly had left the Marine Corps after the war, and only because he knew that it would shrink in size to the point where he would be lucky to get a commission as a lieutenant, and that promotions would come as quickly as glaciers melt—if at all.

He had gone into the railroad business and there applied the techniques of leadership he had learned in the Marine Corps. He knew they worked. Before he had gone back on active duty he had been chairman of the board of the nation's second-largest railroad.

And he really disliked the deceit he knew he was practicing with OSS Director Donovan. He genuinely admired and liked Donovan, despite their monumental political differences.

Yet he remained absolutely sure that letting Major Cletus Frade, USMCR, have a freer hand than Graham ever had granted any other subordinate was the correct thing to do.

There were two young women near the men on the verandah—one petite and dark, the other tall, lithe, fair-skinned, and very blond.

When he had finished shaking hands with the men, he turned to them.

"Señora Frade," Graham said in Spanish to the blonde. "I'd really forgotten how lovely you are."

"They call that 'the bloom of pregnancy,' " she replied in English that made her sound as if she would be quite at home in the Royal Enclosure at Ascot. "Unfortunately, it's temporary, and soon I'll be grotesquely swollen and as gray as a dirty sheep."

I'd forgotten that, too. Dorotea Mallín de Frade says exactly what she's thinking.

He smiled and turned to the small, dark young woman. She reminded him very much of his late wife. She looked as Emelia had when he'd met her.

"We've never met," he said, "but I suspect you are Señora Pelosi. My name is Graham."

She smiled shyly, and her reply was so soft he couldn't hear it.

And that, too, reminded him of Emelia.

"Okay, fireworks time," Cletus Frade announced behind him, "after which we can get down to the serious drinking."

Graham turned to look at him.

Frade handed him a bottle of beer.

"No glass," Frade said. "No self-respecting Aggie would drink beer from a glass on the Fourth of July."

"Absolutely not," Graham said, and took the bottle.

They walked back to the airstrip through the formal gardens. Flaming torches lit the path paved with brick. Frade, holding his wife's hand in his left hand and a bottle of Quilmes beer in the right, led the way with Graham at his side. Enrico walked behind them, his shotgun cradled in his arms. The others followed.

As they came out of the garden, just as Graham noticed that chairs and a table loaded with food had been set up, there was a roll of drums. A brass band began to play the song of the U.S. Army Artillery, "The Caissons Go Rolling Along."

Graham saw a twenty-man-strong, ornately-uniformed band lined up next to the Lodestar.

"I'm impressed, Cletus," Graham said, laughing.

"That's the band of the Chapel of Our Lady of the Miracles," Frade replied. "When I found out that most of its members were retired members of the Húsares de Pueyrredón regimental band, I decided to give them a chance."

Graham shook his head and smiled. He knew that Estancia San Pedro y San Pablo was so large and so far from the nearest town and had so many workers that it had its own church, complete with two priests and a cemetery. And he was not surprised that El Coronel Frade had found employment for old soldiers of his regiment. In many ways, the large estancias were feudal fiefdoms, with El Patron—now Cletus Frade—acting as paterfamilias.

By the time they had reached the row of chairs, the band had segued into another march.

"What the hell is that?" Graham asked.

" 'Semper Paratus,' the Coast Guard song," Frade replied. "I'm surprised you didn't know."

"Where the hell did you get the music?"

"I told Pelosi to tell Delojo I needed it. He finally found it somewhere in the embassy's storage. I don't think they used it much; I don't think the box the music came in ever had been opened."

"Did you tell Commander Delojo what you wanted it for?"

Frade took a swig of beer, smiled, then shook his head.

By the time everyone had settled into their seats, the band had made another segue, this time to "The Aggie War Hymn."

Frade and Graham immediately stood. Technical Sergeant Ferris and Lieutenant Sawyer, seeing this, looked at them curiously.

"Atten-hut!" Graham barked. Everyone complied.

"And stay that way!" Frade snarled.

Next came "The Marines' Hymn" and after that the opening bars of "The Star-Spangled Banner." The landing light of the Lodestar came on, illuminating the national colors on a pole, which hadn't been visible before.

Graham put his hand over his heart. Then he saw that Frade was saluting.

You're not supposed to salute in civilian clothing.

Then he saw that all the others were saluting.

Graham felt his eyes water.

Well, goddamn it, why not?

Civilian clothes or not, these are warriors on a field of battle every bit as dangerous as Guadalcanal or the skies over Germany.

Graham moved his right hand, the fingers now stiff and together, from over his heart to his eyebrow.

When the band of the Chapel of Our Lady of the Miracles had concluded their rendition of the National Anthem of the United States of America, they were given a round of hearty applause. Someone—Graham suspected Lieutenant Pelosi—whistled very loudly and shrilly through his teeth.

The Lodestar's landing light went out.

"I didn't have the manpower to present the colors," Frade said. "But that seemed to work pretty well, didn't it?"

When Graham was sure he had control of his voice, he said, "Well done, Major Frade."

"I also couldn't lay my hands on a Marine Corps flag," Frade said. "And God knows I tried. If I could have found one, I'd have put it beside the flag so the Lodestar could have lit it up, too."

"*Semper fi,* Major Frade," Graham said, hoping that Frade hadn't picked up on his throat-tightened voice.

"All right, Pelosi," Frade ordered. "Get your show off the goddamn dime!"

Graham saw Pelosi run across the runway into the darkness. A moment after he disappeared, a skyrocket raced into the night sky and burst into fireballs.

"Where did you get the fireworks?" Graham asked as another skyrocket went off.

"No problem. They use them down here for everything from New Year's Eve to baby christenings."

Graham said what he was thinking: "You'd have made a pretty good company commander, Frade."

"If that's an offer, Colonel, I can be packed in no more than three minutes."

"Just as soon as the Corps gives me the regiment I want and so richly deserve, I'll send for you."

Frade chuckled, and handed Graham a fresh bottle of Quilmes beer.

The celebration at the airstrip lasted another hour. The chapel band played popular music, American and Argentine, and Lieutenant and Mrs. Pelosi danced the tango to the great delight of the others. Graham remembered how embarrassed Emelia had been when he had to explain to her what Mrs. Astor, the Anglo-American socialite, had meant when she described the tango as a "naval engagement without seamen." María Teresa Pelosi reminded him more and more of Emelia Graham.

Graham decided early on that the talk he had to have with Frade could— and should—wait until morning. Not only would it more than likely be confrontational and unpleasant and destroy the good feeling celebrating the Fourth of July on the Argentine pampas had caused, but Frade had never been without a bottle of beer from the moment they had reached the ranch. It would obviously be better to have their meeting bright-eyed and sober in the morning.

[TWO]

As they walked into the house, Frade took Graham's arm.

"Why don't we go into the study?"

"How about in the morning?"

"Now would be better," Frade said.

He started walking down the long, wide corridor toward what had been his father's office, with Enrico trailing after him. After a moment's hesitation, Graham followed them.

When Frade reached the door, he signaled to Enrico to sit in a leather armchair outside the office, then unlocked the door and went in. As Graham followed him inside, he saw that Frade had gone to a table lined with whiskey bottles.

"Close the door, please," Frade said, then announced: "I'm having scotch. What can I fix for you?"

"I'll have a scotch," Graham said. "But we're back to wouldn't it be better to do this in the morning? When you're . . . clearheaded?"

Frade looked at him for a moment until he understood, then chuckled.

"This is my first today, Colonel. There was water in my beer bottle. I didn't want to set the wrong example for the troops."

"Okay. Sorry. That puts us back to my thought that you would have been a good company commander."

Frade didn't reply. He handed Graham a stiff drink, then sat down at what had been his father's desk.

He looked at Graham for a long moment, then shrugged.

"What do you want to hear first?" Frade said.

"Isn't that obvious? What you made me come all the way down here to hear in person."

"I thought maybe you'd ask, 'So how's Galahad these days?' "

"Okay, so how's Galahad these days?"

"Major Freiherr Hans-Peter von Wachtstein is fine, thank you. He did not have to go to Valhalla after spreading himself—as an honorable officer and gentleman—all over the runway at El Palomar."

"What the hell are you talking about?"

Frade did not respond directly. Instead, he said, "And when he told me why he was still among us, it came out that Admiral Wilhelm Canaris is one of the good guys—"

"Oh, come on, Frade!" Graham interrupted, thinking, *My God, where did he get that?* "The head of the Abwehr is a good guy? Somebody's pulling your chain!"

"—which is why I wanted you to come down here," Frade went on, immune to Graham's sarcasm. "I didn't want to send that in a message, for the obvious reasons. You really never know who's reading your radio traffic, or whether somebody in the State Department is reading stuff in the diplomatic pouch before they send it over to the OSS."

Graham looked at him in disbelief.

It was possible that something—anything from a train or airplane crash to a heart attack—would remove William J. Donovan from command of the OSS. That contingency had to be planned for. An immediate successor—someone who knew the most secret of all the secrets—would have to be named.

Two men had been selected.

One was Allen W. Dulles, who was running OSS operations in Europe from Switzerland. Dulles was the archetypical WASP Washington insider. A Princeton graduate, he was the grandson of John W. Foster, who had been secretary of State under President Benjamin Harrison, and the nephew of Robert Lansing, who had been President Woodrow Wilson's secretary of State.

Dulles was very good at what he did, and superbly qualified. As a State Department officer, he had been stationed in Bern, Paris, Istanbul, Vienna, and Berlin.

The other man was Graham.

Graham had been genuinely surprised when Donovan told him that he had been chosen—with President Roosevelt's approval—as one of the two men who were to be prepared to step in immediately as Donovan's successor should that be necessary. Surprised because he was the antithesis of a WASP Washington insider. He was a Roman Catholic Texan of Mexican heritage who had graduated from Texas A&M, and his only connection with politics had been to support—and make substantial financial contributions to—the 1940 presidential campaign of Wendell L. Willkie, whom Roosevelt had soundly beaten.

To be prepared to take over from Donovan, the three met whenever they could find the opportunity. Dulles could rarely get to Washington, so what most often had happened was that Graham would meet with Donovan in Washington, and then Graham would travel to Europe—most often to Portugal, which had air service to Switzerland—and personally tell Dulles what Donovan thought he should know. He had told Dulles of the Manhattan Project, the ultrasecret program to develop an atomic bomb.

And Dulles would tell Graham what secrets he thought Donovan and his possible successor and no one else should know. Two of these secrets involved the identities of anti-Nazi Germans high in the hierarchy of the Thousand-Year Reich with whom Dulles was dealing.

One of these was a man named Fritz Kolbe, who provided Dulles with the identities of German spies around the world and had told him of the German development of a revolutionary German fighter aircraft, the Messerschmitt Me-262, which, powered by a new type of engine—a "jet"—was capable of great speed and posed a real threat to the Army Air Forces' plans to bomb Germany into submission.

And Graham had relayed to Donovan that Dulles was in contact with Vice Admiral Wilhelm Canaris, the chief of the Abwehr, who was dedicated to the overthrow of Adolf Hitler, and there had even been vague talk about a plot to assassinate Hitler.

Canaris's and Kolbe's activities were secrets as tightly held as was that of the atomic bomb.

And, Graham thought, looking at Frade, *if I'm to believe what I'm hearing, Cletus Frade, a very junior and very amateur OSS operative on the pampas of Argentina, has uncovered the Canaris secret.*

That's incredible!

But maybe—even probably—he's simply reporting gossip.

"I find that very hard to believe, Frade," Graham said. "What do you know about Canaris?"

"He's the head of German intelligence."

"And you're telling me he's . . . sympathetic to the Allied cause?"

"That's what I hear. From what you would call an absolutely reliable source."

"And who would that be?" Graham demanded.

"Let me take it step by step," Frade said.

"Okay."

Frade took a sip of his drink, then began: "Himmler knows they've got a traitor in their embassy here. It's pretty obvious. They couldn't get that Operation Phoenix money into Argentina, and lost two of the best guys trying: Colonel Karl-Heinz Grüner, the military attaché who was also the Sicherheitsdienst guy, and Standartenführer Josef Goltz of the SS.

"So Himmler put SS-Brigadeführer Ritter Manfred von Deitzberg, his adjutant, into a Wehrmacht Generalmajor's uniform and sent him down here to find the traitor."

There had been a good many German names and titles in what Frade had said, and Graham realized that Frade had pronounced them correctly and with ease.

"Where'd you get the German?" Graham asked.

"Siggy Stein—Sergeant Stein—asked me if I didn't think I should at least be able to understand some German, so he's been teaching me."

"And doing very well, I must say," Graham said.

"There's not really a hell of a lot to do here on the pampas," Frade said. "There's been plenty of time to try to learn German. I want to get back to that— not much to do—but later. Let me finish."

"Sorry. Go ahead."

"Von Deitzberg, who is smart, tough, and could charm the balls off a brass monkey, decided that maybe the captain of the *Reine de la Mer* knew something that hadn't come out about (a) how come the Argentines knew where they were going to try to land all that money; (b) how much, if at all, the *gottver-dammt Amerikaners* involved in (a) . . ."

Graham smiled at the "goddamned Americans" correctly translated and pronounced in German. Frade smiled back.

". . . and (c) how come von Wachtstein, who was in the boat with Grüner and Goltz, didn't also get his brains blown all over the beach of Samboromón Bay—"

"We got lucky there, didn't we?" Graham interrupted.

"Yeah, we did. I fucked up there big-time; Argentines don't believe the Scripture that says that vengeance is only the Lord's. I should have known that Enrico and Sarjento Gómez would not pass up an opportunity to kill the Germans who ordered my father's murder, tried to murder me, and in the process got Enrico's sister's throat slashed. We got lucky that Enrico knew von Wachtstein had nothing to do with my father's murder and that he's a friend of mine and, when he saw von Wachtstein in the boat, told Gómez."

"I'm as much at fault about what happened on the beach as you are," Graham said. "I didn't come to Argentina for the first time yesterday. I know all about their concepts of vengeance and honor. I should have told Sawyer to watch those two."

"Which would have made him curious why we wanted von Wachtstein kept alive, and we couldn't tell him, could we? And even if we had told him that Enrico and Gómez had more on their minds than covering his ass while he was taking pictures, there was nothing Polo could have said or done to stop them."

" 'Polo'?"

"Sawyer. He's the only one who's not bored out of his skull here," Frade said, smiling. "He spends most of his time on horses, swinging a mallet at a willow-wood ball. He's pretty good; he was a three-goal player before he joined the Army."

"Who does he play with?" Graham asked.

"My father's polo team. Of which, of course, my father was captain. San Pedro y San Pablo. I call them the Pedro y Pablo Hot Shots."

"And how do you explain Sawyer to them?"

"Well, first of all, they live here. El Patron doesn't have to explain anything to them. And Sawyer—and the others—are by no means the first people who have been guests here for extended periods while other people were looking for them. If you're asking, 'Am I putting the team at risk?'—no. The opposite, I would say. Most of the polo players are supervisors of some kind. Which means they run the gauchos who are my perimeter guard. Nobody gets close to this place without my having at least thirty minutes'—more often an hour's—warning."

"How about from the air?"

"We don't get as much warning of somebody flying over," Frade admitted. "But you would be surprised how far the sound of an aircraft engine carries in the pampas. And that's not much of a threat anyway. Martín knows what we're doing here—including that we have the radar—and doesn't seem to care. What he worries about is my guys being loose in Argentina. So I don't let them leave the estancia."

Graham considered that, nodded, and then said, "Well, you don't have to worry about Oberst Grüner and Standartenführer Goltz anymore."

"What makes you think I was worried about them?"

"Weren't you worried they'd have another shot at you?"

"That's a given. If the SS-SD guys in the embassy ever have the chance to kill any of us, and one of Martín's men isn't actually watching them that moment, they'll take it. That's another reason I don't let anybody leave the estancia. Tony Pelosi's safer with his diplomatic passport. We don't try to kill their guys with diplomatic status, and they don't try to kill ours."

"That doesn't apply to what happened to Grüner and Goltz?"

"I think the Germans think they were killed by Argentines, getting revenge for my father. The proof seems to be that no Americans at the embassy have been killed, tit-for-tat. I was sort of hoping they'd get Delojo."

"Your mouth sometimes—often—runs away with you, Frade. You can't really mean that."

"Yeah, I can. I don't trust him. You want to hear the rest of this?"

Graham nodded.

"Where was I?" Frade said.

"Where were you? Himmler was sending his adjutant over here masquerading as a Wehrmacht general—"

"Von Deitzberg," Frade confirmed, "who decided that somebody reliable should talk to the captain of the *Reine de la Mer*. So he went to Canaris and Canaris loaned him his liaison officer to the foreign ministry, a submarine officer slash intelligence officer named Boltitz, Korvettenkapitän Karl Boltitz. Boltitz speaks Portuguese, which was important because the captain of the *Reine de la Mer* didn't speak German.

"So off von Deitzberg and Boltitz go to Portugal and talk to the captain of the *Reine de la Mer*. Boltitz smells a rat about von Wachtstein walking away— actually rowing away, I suppose—from the beach unhurt, but has no proof of anything. Von Deitzberg is very impressed with the way Boltitz has dealt with the Portuguese captain, and with the fact that Boltitz speaks Spanish; he doesn't. So he goes back to Canaris and tells him that he wants to borrow him a little longer, to take him to Argentina with him. Canaris isn't happy with that, but von Deitzberg is Himmler's adjutant, and Canaris decides not to fight.

"So, off to Argentina, where Boltitz noses around—he's clever as hell—and finds out that von Wachtstein tipped us off as to where the *Reine de la Mer* was going to put the money ashore. That he's the traitor, in other words. Now, here's where it gets interesting—"

"Interesting? So far this tale of yours sounds like a screenplay for a cheap spies-and-robbers movie."

"Yeah, I know. Let me finish. Now, Boltitz is an officer and a gentleman. His father is a vice admiral. And he knows that so is von Wachtstein—that *his* father is a generalmajor. Now, when two officers and gentlemen are involved in something like this, there's a set of rules, based on their code of honor.

"So Boltitz goes to von Wachtstein and tells him he knows what's going on, and that he expects von Wachtstein to behave like an officer and a gentleman is supposed to in these kind of situations."

"You're not going to tell me he handed him a pistol with one cartridge and then left him alone?"

"It was a little more complicated than that," Frade replied. "Boltitz went to von Wachtstein and told him that if he had a fatal crash—spread himself all over the runway—at El Palomar when he came back from Uruguay, Boltitz would not turn him in; the family's honor would not be sullied, and his father would not be sent to a concentration camp. And von Wachtstein agreed to do it."

"This is so bizarre I'm beginning to believe it," Graham said.

"Of course, I'm only a *temporary* officer and gentleman by act of Congress for the duration plus six months," Frade said, "but if it had been me . . ."

Graham chuckled.

". . . I'd have said, 'Heil Hitler, Herr Korvettenkapitän!' then killed him and tossed his body into the River Plate."

"What *did* he do?"

"He went to Lutzenberger."

"The ambassador?"

Frade nodded and said, "Manfred Alois Graf von Lutzenberger, ambassador of the German Reich to the Republic of Argentina."

"To confess? What?"

"Lutzenberger is also one of the good guys," Frade said. "He and General von Wachtstein went to college together. He knows that von Wachtstein brought a hell of a lot of money here—and is getting more from Switzerland—for after the war."

"What do you mean for after the war?"

"To send back to Germany, after we win the war, to make sure they don't lose their land."

"This General von Wachtstein thinks Germany's going to lose?"

Frade nodded, and said, "More than that."

"What more than that?"

"You speak German, right?"

"I can read and write it, but when I try to speak it, German-speaking people have a hard time trying not to laugh."

Frade stood up and walked to the bookcases on one wall of the study. He took a firm grip on a shelf and tugged mightily. With a squeak, a section of the bookcase swung outward, revealing a wall-mounted safe. He worked the combination, spun a large stainless-steel wheel, and pulled the door open. From an inside drawer, he took an envelope and handed it to Graham.

"No, you can't have this," he said. "But I think you should read it. When my father read it, it brought tears to his eyes, and when I read it last week, it did the same thing to me."

Graham took the envelope. The lined envelope was fine vellum, and so were the two sheets of paper it held.

Schloss Wachtstein

Pomern

Hansel—

I have just learned that you have reached
Argentina safely, and thus it is time for this
letter.

The greatest violation of the code of chivalry by
which I, and you, and your brothers, and so many of
the von Wachtsteins before us, have tried to live is
of course regicide. I want you to know that before I
decided that honor demands that I contribute what I
can to such a course of action that I considered all
of the ramifications, both spiritual and worldly,
and that I am at peace with my decision.

A soldier's duty is first to his God, and then to
his honor, and then to his country. The Allies in
recent weeks have accused the German state of the
commission of atrocities on such a scale as to defy
description. I must tell you that information has
come to me that has convinced me that the
accusations are not only based on fact, but are
actually worse than alleged.

The officer corps has failed its duty to Germany,
not so much on the field of battle, but in pandering
to the Austrian corporal and his cohorts. In
exchange for privilege and "honors," the officer
corps, myself included, has closed its eyes to the
obscene violations of the Rules of Land Warfare, the
Code of Honor, and indeed most of God's Ten

Commandments that have gone on. I accept my share of the responsibility for this shameful behavior.

We both know the war is lost. When it is finally over, the Allies will, with right, demand a terrible retribution from Germany.

I see it as my duty as a soldier and a German to take whatever action is necessary to hasten the end of the war by the only possible means now available, eliminating the present head of the government. The soldiers who will die now, in battle, or in Russian prisoner of war camps, will be as much victims of the officer corps' failure to act as are the people the Nazis are slaughtering in concentration camps.

I put it to you, Hansel, that your allegiance should be no longer to the Luftwaffe, or the German State, but to Germany, and to the family, and to the people who have lived on our lands for so long.

In this connection, your first duty is to survive the war. Under no circumstances are you to return to Germany for any purpose until the war is over. Find now some place where you can hide safely if you are ordered to return.

Your second duty is to transfer the family funds from Switzerland to Argentina as quickly as possible. You have by now made contact with our friend in Argentina, and he will probably be able to be of help. In any event, make sure the funds are in some safe place. It would be better if they could be wisely invested, but the primary concern is to have them someplace where they will be safe from the Sicherheitsdienst until the war is over.

In the chaos which will occur in Germany when the war is finally over, the only hope our people will have, to keep them in their homes, indeed to keep them from starvation, and the only hope there will be for the future of the von Wachtstein family, and the estates, will be access to the money that I have placed in your care.

I hope, one day, to be able to go with you again to the village for a beer and a sausage. If that is not to be, I have confidence that God in his mercy will allow us one day to be all together again, your mother and your brothers and you and I in a better place.

I have taken great pride in you, Hansel.

Poppa.

Graham read the letter, then looked at Frade.

"Jesus Christ," Graham said softly.

"Yeah."

"And Whatsisname, the ambassador, is 'our friend'?"

"Lutzenberger," Frade furnished.

"How did you come by this letter?"

"From von Wachtstein. He needed help to deal with his money. I owed him."

"What for?"

"He warned me they were going to bushwhack me, remember? That gave him a big IOU on me."

"And are you helping him?"

"My Uncle Humberto is."

Graham looked at him for amplification.

"Humberto Valdez Duarte," Frade explained. "Managing director of the

Anglo-Argentine Bank. He's married to my father's sister. It was their son—my cousin—who got himself killed at Stalingrad spotting artillery, when all he should have been doing was observing."

"If their son was killed with the Germans at Stalingrad, why is he helping?"

"I suppose the real reason is he figured my IOU to von Wachtstein was a family debt of honor."

"And you think he can be trusted?"

Frade nodded. "I think he was forced to face the fact that his son was a fool. But he's not going to do anything to hurt me. Or von Wachtstein." He paused and chuckled, then added: "I'd bet my life on it."

"You realize, I suppose, that not only should you have shown me this letter long before this—"

"I thought about that. And decided not to pass it on. I didn't know what would be done with the information, and I didn't want General von Wachtstein getting hung on a butcher's hook as a traitor because of something I'd done."

"That sort of decision is not yours to make, Major Frade."

"I generally make all my own decisions," Frade said. "Deferring only to people I know are smarter than me."

"Officers senior to you are presumed to be smarter than you."

"That hasn't been my experience."

Graham realized that he was dangerously close to losing his temper, and that would make matters even worse.

"This helping von Wachtstein conceal his money over here, I hope you're aware, could be considered as treating with or giving aid and comfort to the enemy."

"I hope that wasn't a threat."

"It was a simple statement of fact, Frade."

Neither said anything for a moment, then Graham asked, "What happened when von Wachtstein went to the ambassador? Let's get back to that."

"He told him—this is almost a quote—to be careful when he came back from Uruguay; he needed him. Actually, he said, 'Germany needs you.' "

"Why was von Wachtstein flying to Uruguay in the first place?"

"They have a Fieseler Storch. Like a Cadillac version of the Piper Cub. He goes over there all the time, carrying stuff, people, et cetera."

"And then what?"

"Lutzenberger calls Boltitz in and shows him a letter from Canaris, which says Boltitz is to regard any orders from Lutzenberger as if they came personally from him."

"And the orders from Lutzenberger were to lay off von Wachtstein?"

"That, too, of course. But, more importantly, admitting—without actually coming out and saying it—that he's part of the whole resistance to the Nazis, and probably part of—at least a supporter of—the plot to kill Hitler."

"And then von Wachtstein told you what had happened?"

"He flew out here, with Boltitz, in the Storch. They both told me."

"And then you sent me the radio?"

Frade nodded.

"Frade, I can only hope that you appreciate what dangerous ground—what thin ice—you're walking on," Graham said seriously.

"I can only hope that you appreciate your OSS guy down here is in way the hell over his head."

"Is that another shot at Commander Delojo?"

"I was talking about me."

"Commander Delojo is the Argentine OSS station chief," Graham said. "He's my OSS guy down here."

"Then I can only hope you appreciate your OSS guy down here is not only in way over his head, but isn't working exclusively for the OSS."

"What the hell is that supposed to mean?"

"He's an Annapolis ring-knocker, a lifer, who still has dreams of being captain of a battleship. He is not going to do anything that might displease the Navy Department, and, conversely, is going to do anything he thinks will please them—get him his battleship—like sending them anything about what the OSS is doing down here that they might like to know. He scares the hell out of me."

"I don't believe that he's that way."

"If Delojo knew anything about what I've just told you, it would be in the next diplomatic pouch to the Office of Naval Intelligence. And Christ only knows what they would do with it."

God damn it! He's right.

That wasn't considered before—what the hell, the Navy's on the same side in this war—but it should have been. And by me.

Well, as soon as I get back to Washington, I'll get Delojo out of here.

If ONI hears that Admiral Canaris is working against the Nazis, God only knows what they would try to do with their fellow sailor. And what damage that could cause to what Dulles is trying to do.

Or, for that matter, to the OSS.

There's nothing the Navy would like more than to send the chief of Naval Op-

erations to Roosevelt and tell him they've got Canaris in their pocket. And, that being the case, shouldn't the OSS be ordered to back off?

The problem is that there is only one man who can deal with Canaris, and he's not in the Navy. At the first approach the Navy made to Canaris, he'd back off. Not only from the Navy but from Allen Dulles, too.

I can't let Navy Intelligence put its toe in those waters.

"I think you're dead wrong about that, Frade."

"Then I'm sorry. What I was hoping you'd say would be that you would send somebody—Christ, there must be somebody in the OSS—who would know what to do down here."

Nobody with your connections, unfortunately.

And, as a matter of fact, nobody that I can think of who could do a better job, including me.

Okay, Alejandro, truth time. Face the facts.

Your clever idea to send a young Marine officer—with absolutely no experience as an intelligence officer—down here wishfully thinking that maybe he could get his Argentine father to look more fondly on the United States has gotten completely out of hand.

For one thing, that mission is moot—El Coronel Frade is dead.

And it doesn't really matter that young Frade probably can't tilt the Argentine government toward us any more. Not impossible, but improbable. The bottom line here is that that isn't nearly as important as the other things.

Frade is now involved in things far more important. It doesn't matter how he got involved; the fact is that he knows about—is involved with—resistance to the Nazis by senior members of the Oberkommando der Wehrmacht; the German navy; the head of Abwehr; the assassination plot against Hitler; Operation Phoenix; and the ransoming of Jews from concentration camps.

And while he's so painfully right that he's in over his head with all of this, the bottom line there is: So what? He's involved.

"Major Frade, I want you to listen very carefully to what I'm about to say," Graham said seriously.

Frade looked at him quizzically, nodded his head, but said nothing.

"That was an order," Graham said. "To which, as a serving Marine officer, you are expected to reply, 'Aye, aye, sir.' "

Graham saw the look on Frade's face.

Is that contempt? Or amusement?

Probably both: Contemptuous amusement. Or amused contempt.

Frade said, "Aye, aye, sir."

"Is something bothering you, Major?"

" 'Serving Marine officer,' Colonel? So far as I know—with the exception of the Marine guards at the embassy—I'm the only Marine in Argentina. And God knows, I'm not functioning as a Naval Aviator. And as a serving Marine officer, I'm supposed to place myself at the orders of the senior officer of the Navy Department present. That would be Commander Delojo, and I have absolutely no intention of placing myself—or the Army officers, enlisted men, or Chief Schultz, who I *do* command—under Delojo's orders."

"Finished?" Graham asked.

Frade nodded. Then, a long moment later, when he realized Graham was waiting for the expected response, he said, "Yes, sir."

"First, let's straighten out the chain of command," Graham said. "You are a Marine officer seconded to the Office of Strategic Services. As am I. I'm the senior Marine officer in OSS. That makes you subject to my orders. Clear?"

"Yes, sir."

That reply was neither amused nor contemptuous.

I got through to him. At least a little.

A stray thought popped into Graham's head.

The last time I thought of an amused contemptuous look on the face of Major Frade was when I went to the Documents Branch to pick up those absurd credentials Donovan ordered me to bring down here.

I knew that would be his understandable reaction to them.

But can I turn that around?

Christ, it's worth a shot.

And I have to have him under control before I get into what he's going to have to do now that he has stumbled into things he can't control himself.

"You asked me to come down here at a time when I was planning to come anyway," Graham said. That wasn't true, but he saw that he had Frade's attention.

Frade looked at him curiously, but said nothing.

"I'll be back in a minute, Major," Graham said. "While I'm gone, why don't you give some serious thought to the chain of command you'd like to see in place here?"

"Sir?" Frade asked, but Graham was already at the door and didn't reply.

"Very interesting," Frade said after examining the leather folder holding the plastic-sheathed photo identification card and gold OSS badge. "What am I supposed to do with it? Show it to Colonel Martín?"

And there's that sardonic look on his face. And I understand it.

"I can do without the sarcasm, Frade," Graham said icily.

"Sorry," Frade said, not sounding very contrite.

"You noticed, I hope, that in the rank block, you are identified as area commander."

"I saw that. What does it mean?"

"Just what it says," Graham said.

Frade held both hands out, palms upward, signaling he had no idea what Graham was talking about.

"Let me explain," Graham said. "You're not the only officer around with command structure problems . . ."

I'm making this up as I go along.

". . . and this new system is what Director Donovan and I—in consultation with the attorney general—came up with."

"New system?"

"The Rules for the Governance of the Navy—or Army Regulations—just don't provide for situations in the OSS where the best-qualified man to perform a function, or issue orders, is an officer—or often an enlisted man—junior to, and thus subject to the orders of, someone else in his unit."

"That finally occurred to somebody, did it?" Frade asked.

"So we've developed our own OSS command structure, which gives the necessary lawful authority to the individual who should have it, regardless of his rank in his service. At the moment, there are four grades: special agent, senior agent, supervisory agent, and area commander."

Frade pursed his lips thoughtfully.

Not sardonically. Have I got him?

If I don't blow this, I just may have.

"Just about everybody in the field will be a special agent," Graham went on. "Again, without regard to their actual rank in their branch of the service. Those with greater responsibility will hold the higher ranks. I can readily see where a lieutenant—for that matter, a sergeant—will be a senior agent. Frankly, I don't think that many sergeants will be supervisory agents, but if that becomes necessary, it will happen. The important thing about the new system is that it gives lawful authority to those we think should have it."

"Ashton's a good man, but he doesn't know half as much about communications or the radar as Chief Schultz," Frade said. "Or Siggy Stein."

"In that case, if you want to, you could designate Chief Schultz as a senior agent. That would give him the lawful authority over the others he needs."

Frade didn't reply.

He's obviously giving this some thought. Which means he's swallowed it hook, line, and sinker.

"What are you thinking, Frade?"

"That maybe I better apologize for what I was thinking when you handed me this Junior G-Man's badge. This'll work, Colonel."

"My badge reads theater commander. That outranks an area commander."

Where the hell did I get that?

"I was afraid it would," Frade said. "What do I call you, 'theater'? Or 'commander'?"

" 'Sir' will do nicely. This is strictly for internal use. You understand that?"

Frade nodded. "You have these for the other guys?"

"Special agent badges and ID cards for everybody, plus about a dozen blanks—already signed—for the ID cards. When you decide who'll be what, you can fill them out. I also have some senior and one supervisory thingamabobs that go on the badges."

When I took everything away from those morons in Documents, it was to keep them from falling into the wrong hands. I never dreamed they'd be used.

Thank God I didn't have time to destroy them.

"Let me think about it," Frade said.

"Certainly. Now, there's two other things we have to talk about."

"Okay."

"There are three really significant secrets, Frade, that only very few people know about. By very few people, I mean Director Donovan, Allen W. Dulles, and me."

"Who's Dulles?"

"The senior OSS man we have in Switzerland. Like me, a theater director."

Frade nodded.

"One of them is actually two," Graham said. "That's Operation Phoenix and the ransoming of Jews from concentration camps."

Frade nodded again.

"The second is that Dulles is in contact with Admiral Canaris, and that means with the plan to assassinate Hitler."

Frade nodded again. "And the third?"

There was absolutely no reason that Frade should know of the Manhattan Project.

"You don't have the Need to Know," Graham said.

"Fine with me, as long as it's not going to happen here."

"I can assure you it's not going to happen here," Graham said.

"So why is this business about Canaris such an important secret?"

"You make me another drink, and I'll tell you."

". . . So, essentially all I have to do is make sure that nobody talks about Canaris."

"That and keep me posted up to the minute on anything, anything at all, that touches on Canaris," Graham said. "That's even more important, if possible, than keeping me up-to-date minute by minute about anything else you learn—no matter how unimportant it seems to you."

"That's not a problem. There are only two people who know about Boltitz and Canaris—"

"You and who else?" Graham demanded.

"Dorotea."

"Why in hell did you tell your *wife?*"

"She was there when von Wachtstein and Boltitz told me. She knows everything." He paused, then added: "About everything. The radar, Operation Phoenix, what happened on the beach. Everything."

"I don't like that."

Frade didn't reply, which Graham correctly interpreted to mean that Frade didn't much care if he liked it or not.

"And, presumably, you intend to tell her about this conversation?"

"I'd rather have her trusting me to tell her everything than have her suspect I'm keeping something from her and then having her snooping around where she shouldn't be trying to figure out what that is."

And he's probably right about that, too.

"And, of course, Schultz will have to know. He handles the encryption."

"Only him?"

"He taught me how, in case I had to do it sometime, but he does the encryption. And decryption."

"Keep it that way."

Frade nodded.

He didn't say, "Aye, aye, sir."

But there was no sarcastic smile on his face when he nodded. He accepted the order. I'm going to have to be satisfied with that.

The sardonic smile will come back now when I tell him that President Roosevelt wants him to set up an airline.

Graham began: "Now, to the second reason I was coming down here before you sent for me . . ."

He saw that Frade was listening attentively.

"Is this airline supposed to be a cover for what we're doing down here?" Frade asked when Graham had finished.

There's no wiseass smile on his face.

"Obviously, it would be. But I don't think that's the primary purpose the President had in mind."

"Then what's he after?"

"He didn't confide that in me. He doesn't have to. He's the commander in chief. And, actually, I haven't talked to him. He told Donovan, and Donovan told me to do it."

"Maybe he wants to stick it into Juan Trippe and Pan American Grace," Frade said.

"Why would you want to say that?"

"My grandfather hates Roosevelt, but he says he's smarter than hell. What was the name of that Italian family who went around poisoning everybody who got in their way? Machi-something."

"Machiavelli," Graham furnished.

"Right. My grandfather says Roosevelt is *Machiavellian*. Trippe has South America sewn up as far as airlines go—hell, he's got the world sewn up. So give him some competition. Cut him down to size."

"That's pretty far-fetched, Frade."

On the other hand, it may be right on the money.

I have no idea what Roosevelt was thinking when he came up with this airline idea or what it's supposed to accomplish.

Frade chuckled.

"What's funny?" Graham asked.

"I was just thinking: What does Donovan's badge say, 'world commander'?"

"I suppose. Either that or 'friend of the President.' Can this airline be done, Frade?"

Frade nodded.

"I'll have to set up a company, and get some partners. . . ."

"Who, for example?"

"My Uncle Humberto—that is, the Anglo-Argentine Bank. And the proper officials in the ministry of transportation; things work much faster down here if the official with the rubber stamp has a piece of the action. And maybe—maybe hell; absolutely—my Tío Juan."

"El Coronel Juan Domingo Perón?"

"He told me he wants me to think of him as my loving uncle," Frade said, shaking his head in what could have been either disbelief or disgust. "If I can get him on board—and I think I can; he needs the money—that will keep Martín off my back."

He looked at Graham for a moment, then went on: "Not that I'm going to use this airliner for anything of which Martín might disapprove. You understand that, right?"

"You'll use it for any purpose the President or I direct."

"You want to blow my contacts with Canaris, von Wachtstein's father, and the rest of it?"

"Of course not."

"Then it has to be kept as far away from the OSS as I can keep it."

"Understood."

We'll cross that bridge when we get to it.

If there is some OSS need for these airplanes, we'll damn well use them for it.

Frade said: "Varig has got a bunch of Lodestars. Where'd they get them?"

"I have no idea."

But I would not be at all surprised if Roosevelt was involved.

Frade raised an eyebrow, then drained his glass and said, "Lockheed must have some kind of operation in Brazil. Americans, I mean. Engineers, mechanics. And somebody in charge. What about having Lockheed send the guy in charge down here to try to sell Don Cletus Frade their airplanes? No mention of the OSS, of course, or that I'm an American. I'm a rich Argentine who Roosevelt, for his own reasons, wants to be nice to, and already gave me one Lodestar to prove it. And can get Don Cletus export licenses to buy some more now that I want to start an airline?"

"Sounds good, but slow down. All I really know about this is that Donovan—the President—wanted to know if it could be done—"

"You made it sound like an order."

Graham ignored the interruption. He went on: "—and now that you tell me you think it can, I'll get into the details when I get back to Washington."

"When's that going to be?"

"I'd like to leave tomorrow."

"This airline's that important, is it?"

"No. But everything else you've told me is. I want to get back to Washington as quickly as I can."

"Okay."

"And the sooner I get back, the sooner I can get a replacement for Commander Delojo down here."

That didn't produce the reaction Graham expected.

"I'd rather you leave him where he is," Frade said. "Just watch him. And I'll have Ashton and Pelosi watch him. And don't tell him about this agent business with the badges. I'd rather have him there than somebody I don't know. I told Delojo if he snoops around here or my people, I'll kill him. I think he believes me. A new guy might not."

"Your call," Graham said.

These credentials really got to him.

And when you're on a roll . . .

"There's the oath of office to be administered to your officers and men," Graham said. "It's too late—and there's been too much beer—to do that tonight. First thing in the morning?"

"Fine," Frade said.

He also swallowed that hook, line, and sinker.

"I'd like to do it in the field," Graham went on, "rather than here. Would that cause problems?"

"Where they are now is about five kilometers from here. Except Schultz, who never leaves the radar. But he can leave that for an hour or so. What I could do is tell him to meet us at the house, and you and I could go there."

"Fine."

"You up to riding a horse, Theater Commander, sir?"

"Do I have to remind you that I'm a Texan and an Aggie?"

"Okay. Breakfast at seven-thirty, then we'll ride out there."

"Seven-thirty. And now I'm going to go to bed. It's been a long day."

"Yeah," Frade agreed.

Before he took a shower and went to bed, Graham sat at the desk in his room and tried to recall the words of the oath an officer swore when he accepted the commission. He started to write them down. He had a good memory, but he knew when he looked at what he had written that he didn't have it all, and that what he did have was not right.

It doesn't matter. I'll change the wording anyway.

[THREE]
Casa Núrmero Veintidós
Estancia San Pedro y San Pablo
Near Pila, Buenos Aires Province
Republic of Argentina
0925 5 July 1943

There were more than seventy numbered casas scattered around the three hundred forty square miles of Estancia San Pedro y San Pablo. The term *casa*, meaning "house," was somewhat misleading. There was always more than just a house. There were stables and barns and all the other facilities required to operate what were in effect the seventy farming subdivisions of the estancia. And on each casa there was always more than one house; sometimes there were as many as four.

Some of them were permanently occupied by the supervisor—and, of course, his family—of the surrounding area, the people who worked its land. And some of them were used only when there was a good deal of work to be done in the area, and the workers were too far from their houses or the village near the Big House to, so to speak, commute.

House Number 23 was one of the larger houses. It looked—probably by intention—like a small version of the Big House. Built within a stand of trees, against the winds of the pampas, it was surrounded on three sides by four smaller houses. The casa itself had a verandah on three sides. Inside, there was a great room, a dining room, an office, a kitchen, and five bedrooms. It had, as did the two- and three-bedroom smaller houses, a wood-fired *parrilla* and a dome-shaped oven. One building housed a MAN diesel generator, which powered the lights, the water pumps, the freezers, and the refrigerators. El Patron had taken good care of his workers.

It was an ideal place for Team Turtle to make their home. Comfortable and far from prying eyes.

When Frade and Graham rode up to it, the members of Team Turtle were waiting for them, looking much like they had the previous day, except that Graham suspected that when they "went home" from the Big House last night, more than one of them had had a nightcap or three. Or more.

"Gentlemen, if you'll gather around me," Graham said, "I'll explain what's going on."

He delivered that lecture much as he had practiced it in his head on the ride over. And was pleased that everybody was paying attention, and there were no looks of displeasure.

"And under this new system," he concluded, "Major Frade has been made area commander. Chief Schultz has been appointed—because of the nature of his cryptographic duties, primarily, but for other reasons as well—as senior agent. All the rest of you will be special agents."

And nobody seems to object to that either. Or be surprised.

"So now, gentlemen, if you'll form a rank and come to attention, I will administer the oath of office and present you with your credentials. Which you don't get to keep, by the way. Area Commander Frade will keep them for you."

They formed a ragged line.

Graham barked, "Atten-hut!" and they came to attention and the line straightened out. When it had, Graham barked, "Attention to Orders. Headquarters, War Department, Washington, D.C., General Orders No. 150, 25 June 1943. Paragraph 117. First Lieutenant Madison Sawyer, 0567422, Cavalry, is promoted Captain, with date of rank 25 June 1943."

Captain Sawyer's response was not what Graham expected. He smiled broadly. Captain Ashton reached over and shook his hand. The others applauded.

Graham had another fey thought.

What the hell, why not? God knows they deserve it.

And when I get back to Washington, I'll make it legal if I have to intercept General George Catlett Marshall on his morning canter through Rock Creek Park.

"Paragraph 118," Graham bellowed. Everyone looked at him in confusion. "The following enlisted men, Detached Enlisted Man's List, are promoted as follows: Technical Sergeant William Ferris to be Master Sergeant; Staff Sergeant Jerry O'Sullivan to be Technical Sergeant; Sergeant Sigfried Stein to be Staff Sergeant."

Since I thought of it only sixty seconds ago, those promotions came as a surprise. But their faces show how much they're pleased.

So what do I do now for the chief?

"This is unofficial," Graham went on, "but shortly—promotion processes seem to take longer in the Naval Service—I expect there will be a communication from the chief of Naval Operations informing Chief Schultz that he has been commissioned Lieutenant, USN (Reserve) (Limited Duty) with immediate effect, and concurrent call to active duty."

"I'll be a sonofabitch!" Chief Schultz said.

And there will be such a message, if I have to go to the commander in chief to get him to personally order the chief of Naval Operations to send it.

"Raise your right hand and repeat after me: 'I—state your name and rank—' "

There was a jumbled muttering of names and ranks.

" '—do solemnly swear that I will support and defend the Constitution of the United States against all enemies, foreign and domestic; that I will bear true faith and allegiance to the same; and that I will obey the orders of the President of the United States and the orders of the OSS officers appointed over me; that I will well and faithfully discharge the duties of the office upon which I am about to enter; that I will guard with my life until my death, unless sooner relieved of this obligation by competent authority, all classified material entrusted to me, or which I acquire through the execution of my duties; that I take this obligation freely, without any mental reservations or purpose of evasion whatsoever; so help me God.' "

When he was finished, Graham walked down the line and handed everybody their leather folder that held the gold badge and photo identification card.

Everybody looks pleased.

More than pleased. This fraudulent little exercise of mine is for them a solemn occasion.

I should be ashamed of myself, but I'm not, and not only because I thought it was necessary to make the fraud, but because it's made these guys feel important and necessary.

And they damn sure are.

Chief Schultz's Dorotea—a pleasantly plump thirty-five-year-old Argentine who supervised the servants of Casa Número Veintidós and whom he perhaps ungallantly but accurately described as his live-in dictionary—served coffee and croissants that had been baked in the wood-fired outdoor oven. Graham collected letters that he would make sure were mailed in the United States when he got home. Frade collected the credentials and put them into his saddlebag.

Graham shook everybody's hand, then he and Frade got on their horses and rode back across the pampas to the Big House.

At four-thirty in the afternoon, Graham was back at El Palomar, where he boarded the Lockheed Lodestar that was Varig Flight 107 for Pôrto Alegre, Brazil.

IV

[ONE]
**Aboard the Motor Vessel *Ciudad de Cádiz*
48 Degrees 85 Minutes South Latitude
59 Degrees 45 Minutes West Longitude
1200 7 July 1943**

El Capitán José Francisco de Banderano, a tall, slender, hawk-nosed, some-what swarthy forty-five-year-old wearing a blue woolen, brass-button uniform with the four golden stripes of his rank on the sleeves, stood on the flying bridge of his ship with binoculars to his eyes. He was making a careful scan of as much of the South Atlantic Ocean as he could see.

There's nothing out there—not even whitecaps. Just a smooth expanse of ocean.

De Banderano over the years had seen his share of action—had damn near been killed—and knew that an enemy man-o'-war quickly could turn a peace-ful patch of ocean violent. Thus he was on a high alert, acutely aware—certainly in broad terms, if not in detail—that while elsewhere in the world the war raged more dramatically, it just as easily could literally explode here.

Indeed, the three-day-old Battle of Kursk—it would last till 23 August—was pitting about three thousand Soviet tanks against roughly that many Ger-man tanks. It would become the largest tank battle ever, with the Germans and Russians each losing almost all of their tanks.

Meanwhile, on that very day of 7 July, an Allied fleet of 2,760 ships—primarily from Norfolk, Virginia, and Scotland's River Clyde—was converging on a rendezvous point in the Mediterranean Sea near Malta. Three days hence, American troops under Lieutenant General George S. Patton and British troops

under General Sir Bernard Law Montgomery would execute Operation
Husky—the invasion of Sicily.

It would be the first Allied assault on German-occupied Europe.

De Banderano went back on the bridge, set the binoculars in their rack by his
chair, and rubbed his hands. The high seas of the South Atlantic in July were
cold.

"Herr Kapitän!" announced a young man wearing the white jacket of a
steward. He offered a tray on which sat a china mug of steaming coffee.

De Banderano took it.

"Danke," he said.

As he started sipping from the cup, he thought:

*It is highly unlikely that luncheon will be interrupted by a signal from the
U-405. It is entirely possible that we will never hear from the U-405, period. The
rendezvous was supposed to be within a forty-eight-hour window. That ran out
twelve hours ago.*

*My options are (1) head for Buenos Aires now, or (2) go at midnight, which
will mean I give them another twenty-four hours beyond the window, or (3) go at
first light, which will mean I will have stayed on station for thirty or so hours beyond the window.*

*I want this mission to be successful, but I can't keep making slow circles in the
South Atlantic forever.*

I will decide over lunch. If not, then at dinner.

"You may serve luncheon whenever it is convenient," de Banderano
ordered.

"Jawohl, Herr Kapitän," the young blond steward replied, clicked his heels,
and marched off the bridge.

Capitán de Banderano, with some disgust, watched him leave. He was
aware that the steward spoke little Spanish—and that he was neither a steward
nor much less a seaman.

The day before the *Ciudad de Cádiz* had sailed from Cádiz, the steward—
eighteen-year-old Rottenführer Paul Plinzer—was one of fifteen Germans
who had boarded the ship. There was "special cargo" aboard, and it had been
decided that it needed the special protection that only the Schutzstaffel could
provide.

There were three officers, Sturmbannführer (Major) Alfred Kötl and Obersturmführers (Lieutenants) Willi Heitz and Ludwig Schmessinger. They wore their uniforms and lived in officer's country.

And there were twelve enlisted men, under an oberscharführer (sergeant); two unterscharführers (corporals); and nine rottenführers (lance corporals). They wore civilian clothing and were berthed with the crew.

Sturmbannführer Kötl had volunteered Plinzer's services as steward almost as soon as they had left port, saying that the young Dresdener might as well do something to earn his keep.

De Banderano suspected that Plinzer's real function was to report to Kötl what happened on the bridge. He had given freedom of the bridge to Kötl alone, and Kötl obviously could not be there all the time. A steward did not have to explain his presence.

De Banderano did not like Kötl. He thought him to be arrogant and more self-important than he had any right to be. The situation was exacerbated because Kötl did not know what the special cargo was, or what it was for, or where it was going, only that he was to protect it; he understandably suspected that de Banderano knew the answers and was not telling him.

De Banderano in fact knew only where the special cargo was going. His secret orders, sealed until they were at sea, were to rendezvous with the submarine U-405 at sea, about 220 nautical miles due north of the Falkland Islands, which were some 260 nautical miles east of the southern tip of Argentina. There he would replenish the U-405's fuel, food, and torpedoes, hand her captain his sealed orders, and, as the last step, transfer to the U-405 the crates of special cargo with Sturmbannführer Kötl, an officer of Kötl's choice, and five of Kötl's men.

He had not told Kötl about that, and was looking forward to doing so. He doubted the SS officer would be happy to get on a submarine, destination unknown.

Once the transfer had taken place, the *Ciudad de Cádiz* was to proceed to Buenos Aires, where she was to take onboard as much fuel as they would sell him, and as much frozen meat and fresh produce as possible. In Buenos Aires, he would be provided with a chart overlay marking half a dozen rendezvous points in the South Atlantic Ocean. Once he had sailed from Buenos Aires, he would be advised by a radioed coded phrase at which of the rendezvous points and on what day and at what time he was to rendezvous with other submarines.

De Banderano had no idea what was in the securely sealed wooden crates of the special shipment, although he doubted that it was what he had been told.

Oberst Karl-Heinz Grüner, the military attaché of the German embassy in Buenos Aires, had come aboard the *Comerciante del Océano Pacífico* when she was at anchor, supposedly with "engine problems," in Samborombón Bay in Argentine waters in the Río de la Plata estuary.

He had told her master—de Banderano—that what he wanted to do was smuggle ashore the special cargo—which contained radios, civilian clothing, and other matériel—to be used to help the interned officers of the *Graf Spee* escape from Argentina and return to the war.

De Banderano hadn't believed that the crates contained radios and clothing—all readily available in Buenos Aires—but had said nothing. He had believed the story about helping the *Graf Spee* officers escape their internment, and that had sounded like a noble effort to attempt.

Two hours later, it had been moot.

Somebody had tipped the Argentines, and as soon as the crates had been placed on the beach of Samborombón Bay from the longboats of the *Océano Pacífico*—de Banderano had commanded one himself—there had been a sudden deadly mass of rifle fire. Oberst Grüner and Standartenführer Goltz had been killed immediately. Only by the grace of God had the third German officer involved, Luftwaffe Major Peter von Wachtstein, and de Banderano himself escaped death. And only the grace of God had permitted von Wachtstein and de Banderano to get the crates of the special cargo back into the longboats and back aboard the *Océano Pacífico*.

Within hours, an Argentine navy launch had drawn alongside the *Océano Pacífico* and handed de Banderano orders to immediately depart Argentine waters and never return.

A week after the *Comerciante del Océano Pacífico* tied up at Cádiz, while de Banderano had awaited further orders regarding the special cargo still in the hold—but absent the bodies of Oberst Grüner and Standartenführer Goltz, which had been removed for shipment to Germany—he had had a visitor.

The visitor had been wearing civilian clothing but identified himself as Fregattenkapitän Otto von und zu Waching. Further, he said he served as a special assistant to Vizeadmiral Wilhelm Canaris.

De Banderano had been concerned that he was about to have trouble because the smuggling operation had failed. Although there was no way he could have known the Argentines would be waiting for them on the beach, he in fact was the master of the *Océano Pacífico* and therefore responsible for not having complied with his orders to land the special cargo safely.

That was only tangentially what Fregattenkapitän von und zu Waching had come to see him about. The first thing von und zu Waching had done—in the privacy of de Banderano's cabin, with only the first officer and the chief engineer present—was to present all three officers, on behalf of Admiral Canaris and the Kriegsmarine, the award of the Iron Cross, Second Class, for their valorous service aboard the *Comerciante del Océano Pacífico* during an extremely hazardous and important voyage.

Then, from another oblong box covered with artificial blue leather, he took an Iron Cross, First Class, award and presented it to Capitán de Banderano. Von und zu Waching, holding the citation, read: "For personal valor on a secret mission for the German Reich during which Kapitän de Banderano demonstrated the finest characteristics of a naval officer under heavy enemy fire."

Then Fregattenkapitän von und zu Waching asked de Banderano if he and his officers would consider undertaking another such mission to Argentina.

De Banderano had glanced at his men, then said, "I am sure I am speaking for all of my officers when I say we would be honored, Herr Fregattenkapitän. But the Argentines have made it quite clear that if the *Océano Pacífico* should ever again appear in Argentine waters, she will be seized as a smuggler."

"So I understand," Fregattenkapitän von und zu Waching replied. "I suspect that what we'll have to do is get you another ship, won't we?" He smiled at de Banderano, then pointed out the bridge window. "How about that one?"

De Banderano and the others had looked where he was pointing and saw tied up at the adjacent wharf a modern freighter, substantially larger than the *Océano Pacífico*. They had all been confused. Von und zu Waching was not the type of officer to make jokes.

He quickly made it clear that he wasn't making a joke now.

"That's the *Ciudad de Cádiz*, which arrived from Hamburg last night," von und zu Waching said. "If you are willing to take another assignment for us, that will be your ship."

He then went on to explain that the *Ciudad de Cádiz* had been launched in late 1941 at the Blohm und Voss shipyard in Hamburg, and that, until two weeks ago, had been registered as the *Stadt Kassel* of the Hamburg-American Line.

"From the time of her launching," von und zu Waching said, "she's undergone extensive conversions at Blohm und Voss. The original idea had been to convert her into a raider, a fast merchantman with armament concealed on her aft- and foredecks. The theory was that she would not raise the suspicions of an enemy merchantman until it was too late for it to take evasive or any other action. The German battle flag would be suddenly hoisted, the false bulkheads around her two 70mm and four 30mm automatic cannon would drop and while the thirties worked over the enemy ship's radio shack and superstructure, the heavier cannon would blast her hull.

"It was a clever idea," von und zu Waching went on, "but the *Stadt Kassel* never put to sea on such a mission, for many reasons, some of them intertwined. For one thing, the U-boats had done a better job of sinking Allied merchantmen in the North Atlantic than anyone had thought they would.

"There was no sense risking a valuable ship like the *Stadt Kassel*—and getting her through the English Channel would pose a very serious risk—when U-boats could do the job.

"And there had been no reason to send the *Stadt Kassel* to the South Atlantic to intercept Allied merchantmen headed from Argentina, Brazil, and Uruguay to England or the Mediterranean Sea. For one thing, the U-boats again were doing a fine job, in large part because they were being replenished in the River Plate by 'neutral' ships while the Argentines looked the other way."

Von und zu Waching had let them absorb all that, then continued: "That situation deteriorated severely and rapidly, as you well know, gentlemen, when the Americans established their air base at Pôrto Alegre, Brazil, from which they fly their specially rigged B-24 bombers on wide-ranging antisubmarine patrols. That had made it necessary for the U-boats to operate outside the B-24's patrolling range.

"Secondly, the Americans caught on to the replenishment by 'neutral' merchantmen in the River Plate. The Americans sent one of their submarines after one of them, the *Reine de la Mer*, sinking her and the U-boat that was tied up alongside for the replenishment.

"The official version of that sinking was 'an unfortunate explosion,' but the Argentines let us know they would be very unhappy if we attempted to resume replenishment activities anywhere in Argentine waters.

"And your unfortunate experience in Samborombón Bay has made it clear they were perfectly willing—no matter their personal sympathies—to do what was necessary to protect their neutrality.

"For obvious reasons—although we tried it and are continuing the effort— use of U-boats converted to replenishment vessels is an unsatisfactory solution to the problem. By the time the replenishment submarines rendezvous with the hunter U-boats, they have barely enough of their own fuel to take them home, and little—sometimes no—fuel available to transfer.

"And as they have no refrigerator compartments, they cannot bring adequate supplies of frozen food to their sister submariners. And further, transferring heavy machinery—much less torpedoes—from one U-boat to another on the high seas was something that had not been considered when the U-boats had been designed. As you well know, it is difficult to move anything heavy in smooth seas, and just about impossible to transfer torpedoes in anything rougher.

"At this point, Admiral Raeder, Admiral Canaris, and others took another look at the *Stadt Kassel*. With only minor additional modifications—the installation of auxiliary fuel-storage tanks and the addition of winches and pumps, primarily, and ports near the waterline—she readily could be converted to a splendid submarine replenishment vessel. Getting her through the English Channel remained risky, but in present circumstances, that risk seemed justified. The U-boats in the South Atlantic were out of fuel, out of torpedoes, out of food. The conversions were ordered.

"Admiral Canaris then suggested, and Admiral Raeder agreed, that it would be better to reflag the *Stadt Kassel*. Not only could a neutral—say, Spanish—vessel pass through the English Channel immune to British interference, but she could call at Montevideo and Buenos Aires and other ports, and there purchase food and other supplies, obviating the need for her to sail back and forth to Europe.

"The question then became where could we find a competent crew for what was now the *Ciudad de Cádiz*? A crew not only in sympathy with the aims of Germany, but of proven devotion and courage?"

Von und zu Waching had taken a moment to look each man in the eye, then had said, "You have just answered that question for me, gentlemen. I salute you."

And his right arm had shot out in the Nazi salute.

Ten minutes later, Rottenführer Plinzer returned to the bridge to tell Capitán de Banderano that luncheon was served.

He nodded his understanding, took one last look at the empty South Atlantic, then left the bridge for the wardroom.

The wardroom was large enough for a dining table used for nothing else. It had not been that way on the *Océano Pacífico*. Her one wardroom table had to be used for everything that required a flat surface.

When Capitán de Banderano walked into the wardroom, all those officers who were not standing rose quickly to their feet. They were all neatly uniformed, and there were far more of them than were normally found on a freighter of this size.

"Please be seated, gentlemen," Capitán de Banderano said as he slid into his chair at the head of the table.

The officers sat down. Unless there was an emergency requiring their services, they would remain seated until Capitán de Banderano left the table or he formally excused them.

The wardroom customs of the *Ciudad de Cádiz* were very much the customs of ships of the line of the Royal Spanish Navy. This was not only because Capitán de Banderano was a graduate of the Spanish Naval Academy—as three generations before him had been—and because before the Civil War he had been a lieutenant commander in the Royal Spanish Navy and master of the frigate *Almirante de Posco*. It also was because the *Ciudad de Cádiz* was, in Capitán de Banderano's judgment, not an ordinary freighter but a de facto man-of-war, and had to be run accordingly.

Before the Civil War, de Banderano had every reason to believe that he would rise in rank to capitán—his father had—or possibly even to almirante—as had his grandfather. But the godless Communists and their friends had destroyed that ambition, as well as most of Spain itself.

Early in the Civil War, de Banderano had been detached from the *Almirante de Posco* to serve on the staff of El Generalissimo Francisco Franco shortly after that great man saw it as his Christian duty to take over the reins of government from the king and expel the godless Communists from Spain in order to restore Spain to her former greatness.

As the Civil War dragged on and on, de Banderano's duties had less and less to do with the navy; but they had taken him to all fronts and given him the opportunity to see what the Communists had in mind for Spain. And he had seen that they *were* godless, the anti-Christ. With his own eyes, he had witnessed the murdered priests and the raped nuns and the results of mass executions.

And he had seen, too, that the Germans and the Italians—both fully aware of the threat communism posed to the very survival of Christian civilization—had come to the aid of a fellow Christian nation that once again had infidel hordes raging at her gates.

It was de Banderano's professional opinion as an officer that without the help of German weapons provided to General Franco's army, without the aerial support of the German Condor Legion, without the sixty thousand troops the Italians had sent, the war probably would have been lost.

The English and the Americans had remained "neutral" in the conflict. But that in practice had meant they were helping the enemy. The Americans had even sent soldiers, formed into the Abraham Lincoln Brigade, to aid the Communists.

The behavior of the English and the Americans had baffled de Banderano. The usual explanation of it was that they were not Roman Catholic, and that their "churches" had been infiltrated and corrupted by Communists; but he thought that was too simple an answer. A large number of the Germans who came to help Spain were Protestant. He also thought the other answer was too simple: that the Jews controlled both England and America.

Too many good Spanish Jews had fought as valiantly as anyone on the side of El Caudillo—Franco—for anyone to believe that all Jews were allied with the anti-Christ.

By the time General Francisco Franco had finally, after three bloody years, brought the godless Communists to their knees, Spain was destitute—and not only because the Communists had stolen almost the entire gold stocks of the kingdom; literally tons of gold taken to Russia.

There was hardly enough money to operate, much less construct, men-of-war. The once-proud Spanish navy was on its knees again, thanks to the Communists. By then Capitán José Francisco de Banderano had understood there would be no command of a man-of-war for him in the Royal Spanish Navy post–Civil War.

Yet both his ability and his faithful service had not gone unnoticed. He was rewarded with a command in the Spanish merchant navy.

Before he was approached by the German naval attaché and offered command of the *Comerciante del Océano Pacífico*, he had seen with his own eyes and heard with his own ears American navy ships roaming the North Atlantic.

The Americans were searching for German submarines, the latter of which had under international law every right to sink vessels bound for England laden with war matériel. When the American ships found a U-boat they reported their positions by radio, in the clear. In the clear meant that radios aboard English men-of-war were given the positions of German submarines—near the supposedly "neutral" American men-of-war.

The notion of violating the rules of warfare by violating anyone's neutrality would have deeply offended him before the Civil War. Now it seemed only right. The actions of the English during the Civil War were blatantly antagonistic to neutrality. And, later, the actions of the Americans after the beginning of the current war, but before they themselves joined the hostilities, were equally contrary to neutrality.

Whatever their reasons for opposing Hitler, for refusing to accept that the war Hitler was waging against the Communists was their own war, the fact was that England and America were fighting Germany, and that was sufficient cause for Capitán José Francisco de Banderano to do whatever he could to oppose them.

Capitán de Banderano hadn't hesitated a moment before accepting the German offer to take command of the *Comerciante del Océano Pacífico,* and he had been honored by their offer for him to take command of the *Ciudad de Cádiz.*

[TWO]
Aboard U-boat 405
48 Degrees 85 Minutes South Latitude
59 Degrees 45 Minutes West Longitude
1250 7 July 1943

Kapitänleutnant Wilhelm von Dattenberg, twenty-six years of age, was a large but gaunt Swabian—since leaving the submarine pens at St. Nazaire four months earlier, he had lost forty of his normal 190 pounds. Von Dattenberg took his eyes from the now no-longer-resilient rubber pads of the periscope and saw that both his chief of the boat and his number one had their eyes on him.

He issued two orders by making two gestures, first signaling by pointing to the deck . . .

"Down periscope!" the chief of the boat bellowed.

. . . then, accompanied by a smile, jerking his thumb upward.

"Prepare to surface!" the chief of the boat bellowed.

"Signals lampman, stand by to go to the conning tower," Kapitänleutnant von Dattenberg ordered.

"With the Herr Kapitänleutnant's permission?" the chief of the boat asked softly.

He wants to operate the signal lamp himself?

Well, why not?

Von Dattenberg nodded.

"That's either the *Ciudad de Cádiz,* Erich," von Dattenberg said to his executive officer, Oberleutnant zur See Erich Müllenburg, "or His Brittanic Majesty's cruiser *Ajax* very cleverly camouflaged."

Müllenburg nodded and smiled, but said nothing.

He didn't trust himself to speak. He was one of the very few aboard who knew their fuel supply was down to only ten hours of cruising. Alternate plans had already been made, in case the *Ciudad de Cádiz* was not at the rendezvous point. They would make for the Falklands. When close, or the fuel ran out, whichever came first, the boat would be scuttled and the crew would try to make it to the remote islands in one dinghy, what rafts they could jury-rig, and the four fifteen-man rubber boats.

"Send 'Sorry to be late,' " von Dattenberg ordered.

The chief of the boat put the lamp to his shoulder and flashed the message.

There was an immediate reply from the *Ciudad de Cádiz.*

The chief—unnecessarily, as von Dattenberg could read Morse code—waited until the message had finished, then reported: "The reply, sir, is, 'Better late than never.' "

"Send. 'Request permission to lay alongside.' "

Sixty seconds later, the chief reported, " 'Permission granted,' sir."

"Put the boat alongside, Oberleutnant Müllenburg," von Dattenberg ordered. "Carefully. We don't want to ram her."

As the U-405 inched carefully up to the *Ciudad de Cádiz,* a huge water-tight door near the waterline swung outward from her hull. A cushion—a web of old truck tires—was put over the side, and a series of neatly uniformed seamen tossed lines to crewmen of U-405 standing on the submarine's deck.

As the lines were made tight, von Dattenberg saw neatly uniformed officers lined up behind a man with the four gold stripes of a captain on his sleeves. And then he saw that all the uniforms were not naval. Three of them were black.

The SS! What the hell is that all about?

Two gangways—one a simple ribbed plank, the other with rope railings—were put out from the *Ciudad de Cádiz.* The gangways were nearly level with the deck of U-405, with a slight upward incline.

If there was any fuel in my tanks, there would be a slight downward incline.

"You have the conn, Erich," von Dattenberg said. "The chief and I are going aboard that absolutely beautiful ship."

"Jawohl, Herr Kapitän."

Von Dattenberg and the chief of the boat climbed down from the conning tower and made their way to the gangplank with the rope railings.

The U-boat commander suddenly remembered his appearance. His beard was not neatly trimmed. He wore a sweater that was dirty and full of holes, a pair of equally dirty and worn trousers, a uniform tunic that was missing buttons, grease-soaked, oily tennis shoes, and an equally filthy brimmed cap.

He marched up the gangplank, not touching the railing, and stopped just inside the *Ciudad de Cádiz*. There he saluted.

"Kapitänleutnant von Dattenberg, commanding U-boat 405," he announced. "Request permission to come aboard."

He saw that everyone was saluting as he had, by touching the brims of their uniform caps. Everyone but the SS officers—they gave the Nazi straight-armed salute.

"Permission granted," Capitán José Francisco de Banderano said, then walked to the end of the gangplank and offered his hand. "Welcome aboard, Kapitän. I am Capitán de Banderano, master of the *Ciudad de Cádiz*."

Von Dattenberg clicked his heels.

"Perhaps you would care to join me in my cabin, Kapitän, while my engineering officer shows your man our refueling facilities?"

"You are very kind, sir."

"Make yourself comfortable, Kapitän," de Banderano said when they were in his cabin. "Perhaps taking a chair at the table might be best. I somehow suspect that you will be gracious enough to accept my offer of a little something to eat."

"With all respect, Capitán," von Dattenberg replied not unpleasantly, "I'll hold off on eating until my crew has had a little something."

"I've taken the liberty of ordering my stewards to send sandwiches aboard to give a little something to eat to half of your men, while the other half come aboard and go to the galley for a little something. Does that meet with your approval, Kapitän?"

"You are indeed very kind, sir."

"How does ham and eggs sound for a little something for you, Kapitän?"

"Like manna from heaven, Capitán."

De Banderano picked up his telephone and dialed a number.

"Ham and eggs to my cabin immediately," he ordered. Then he went to a cabinet and came back with a bottle of Johnnie Walker scotch.

"I regret that when the *Ciudad de Cádiz* was turned over to me by the Kriegsmarine they somehow failed to ensure that she had even one bottle of schnapps in her supplies. Can you force yourself to drink this decadent English whiskey? I brought this from my previous command."

"Under the circumstances, I think I can force myself," von Dattenberg said.

De Banderano poured three fingers of scotch in each of two glasses and handed one to von Dattenberg.

"We found each other," de Banderano said. "I wasn't sure it was going to happen."

Von Dattenberg nodded solemnly. "I was down to between six and maybe nine hours of fuel," he said.

Their eyes met for a moment, then de Banderano touched his glass to von Dattenberg's. They took healthy swallows of their drinks.

Von Dattenberg exhaled audibly, then took another healthy sip, draining his glass.

De Banderano poured more for him and asked, "At the risk of being indelicate, Kapitän, would you mind a suggestion about your uniform?"

"A decent burial at sea?" von Dattenberg said. "What do you suggest I do with it?"

"We have clothing stocks aboard. If you will give me your measurements, by the time you have a shower, the ship's tailor will have a proper uniform for you."

"For my crew, too?"

De Banderano nodded, then said: "I think they, too, would prefer to wait until they've had a little something to eat."

"At the risk of being indelicate, Capitán, my underwear is as dirty as my outerwear."

De Banderano nodded.

"Once you give me your sizes," he said, "by the time you come out of there, there will be fresh underwear."

He pointed at a door that von Dattenberg correctly suspected led to the Master's Bath. Then he handed von Dattenberg a pencil and a notebook so that he could write down his sizes.

Ten minutes later, Capitán de Banderano was not in his cabin when von Dattenberg came out of the shower wrapped in a towel. But there was clean white underwear on the table. And an array of plates under chrome domes.

He had not shaved, and he wasn't sure if that was because he thought it would be impolite to use de Banderano's razor or because he had come to like the beard.

He took the underwear back into the Master's Bath and put it on, then went to the table. Reminding himself that if he ate like a pig he was probably going to throw up, he sat down and started carefully lifting the domes.

He ate everything the domes had concealed, and was wondering when his stomach would rebel when there was a knock at the door.

"Come."

A steward, young and blond and in a white jacket, came into the room carrying a uniform on a hanger.

He gave a Nazi salute and barked, "Heil Hitler!"

Von Dattenberg didn't return the salute, but asked, "You're German?"

"Rottenführer Plinzer, Herr Kapitän," the boy barked.

Von Dattenberg took the uniform.

"That will be all, Plinzer. Thank you."

"Jawohl, Herr Kapitän," Plinzer said, threw out his arm, barked, "Heil Hitler!" again, then stood there, obviously waiting for von Dattenberg to return the salute.

He almost didn't.

Fuck the Nazis and their salute!

What'll this kid do, report me to one of the SS officers?

And, anyway, what the hell could they do to me on a submarine-replenishment vessel off the Falkland Islands?

For that matter, what the hell is the SS doing on a submarine-replenishment vessel off the Falkland Islands?

In the end, he returned the salute by raising his arm from the elbow.

That arrogant kid would've reported me for not saluting.

But he's not going to complain that my salute wasn't as crisp or enthusiastic as he thought it should've been.

Capitán de Banderano came back to his cabin moments after von Dattenberg had put on the new uniform, still smelling of camphor mothballs.

He smiled and raised his hands in a gesture that said, *Well, what a change!*

Von Dattenberg smiled back.

"When the fuel's running low, the first thing that gets shut down is the seawater distiller," von Dattenberg said.

De Banderano nodded his understanding.

"Is there anything else I can get you?"

"I don't suppose you have a well-breasted blonde—or two—who just loves sailors?"

De Banderano chuckled as he shook his head.

"Thank you very much for all you've given me so far, Capitán."

"My privilege, Kapitän," de Banderano said. He looked at the young U-boat captain for a moment—he had liked him from the moment he saw him in the conning tower of the U-405—and decided to go ahead with what he had just about decided to do somewhat later.

"I have your orders, Kapitän," de Banderano said. "I'm familiar with them. Would you like to have them now, or wait until Sturmbannführer Kötl, to whom the orders also apply, can join us?"

Without hesitation, von Dattenberg replied, "I'd prefer to have them now, if you don't mind."

De Banderano went to a wall safe, took three large gray manila envelopes from it, and handed one of them to von Dattenberg.

"Sir, the seal is broken," von Dattenberg said.

"My orders gave me the authority to open yours," de Banderano said.

M O S T   S E C R E T

Oberste Hauptsitze der Kriegsmarine

Berlin

2 June 1943

Kapitänleutnant Wilhelm von Dattenberg

Commanding U-boat 405

   (One): You have been entrusted with a mission of great importance to the Reich. You will be informed of the details thereof as considered necessary. The details of this mission will be shared with as few people as possible, consistent with executing the mission.

(Two): For the purposes of this mission, inasmuch as Kapitän Jose Francisco de Banderano, master of the motor vessel Ciudad de Cádiz, is acting at the direct orders of the undersigned, and despite his civilian status, he will be considered the senior officer of the German Reich present.

(Three): You will receive from Kapitän de Banderano a special cargo which you will in absolute secrecy see safely ashore at a location in Argentina to be later identified to you. Attached are chart overlays and signal cryptographic matériel to be used in this connection.

(Four): Sturmbannführer Kötl will board the U-405 together with a small detachment of SS to protect the cargo until it is safely ashore. If the discharge operation is successful, the SS will remain ashore. If the mission encounters difficulty, the priorities are (1) to return the special cargo to the U-405 and (2) return the SS to the U-405.

(Five): Sturmbannführer Kötl's responsibility and authority is limited to the protection of the special cargo. The decisions to attempt to land the special cargo, the methods of doing so, and, should it be necessary, to break off the attempt are entirely your responsibility.

(Six): The packaging of the special cargo is not to be opened under any circumstances.

(Seven): From the time the special cargo is placed aboard U-405, you will not engage any enemy warships or merchant vessels under any circumstances until the special cargo is safely ashore. Similarly,

if the landing attempt is unsuccessful, and the
special cargo is taken back aboard the U-405, you
will undertake no hostile action of any kind until
the special cargo is placed back aboard the Ciudad
de Cádiz or other disposition of same is made.

Doenitz
Karl Doenitz
Grand Admiral

Concur:

Himmler
Heinrich Himmler

J. v. Ribbentrop
Reichsprotektor Joachim von Ribbentrop
Foreign Minister

Canaris
Wilhelm Canaris
Rear Admiral

MOST SECRET

Kapitänleutnant von Dattenberg looked at Capitán de Banderano.

"What is this 'special cargo'?" von Dattenberg said.

"Six wooden crates, each a meter long, three quarters of a meter wide, and three quarters of a meter deep."

"And in them . . . ?"

"When we tried this the first time, I was told they contain radios and civilian clothing and other items intended to facilitate the escape of the officers from the *Graf Spee* from their internment."

"When you tried this the first time?"

De Banderano nodded.

"Obviously without success," von Dattenberg said. "What happened?"

"The Argentines were waiting for us. Oberst Grüner, the military attaché in Buenos Aires, and Standartenführer Goltz were killed."

"But you managed to save the special cargo, obviously?"

"God spared Major von Wachtstein and me; we were able to get the crates off the beach."

"Who did you say? Von Wachtstein?"

"A distinguished Luftwaffe officer. He received the Knight's Cross of the Iron Cross from the Führer personally."

Von Dattenberg smiled. "He was not always that respectable, Capitán."

"You know him?"

"We were almost sent down from university together. I mean, he was sent down, and I was lucky. He went into the Luftwaffe and became a corporal pilot. He flew in Spain with the Condor Legion. I'd heard, after he got the Knight's Cross, that he'd been commissioned, but I didn't know he'd been promoted major. One of the world's good people, Capitán. And he's involved in this, whatever it is?"

De Banderano was pleased to hear that von Dattenberg and von Wachtstein knew each other, that they were friends. He thought they were both fine young officers.

"I think his role was much like yours, Capitán, to assist in getting the special shipment ashore. Not more than that."

"Radios and clothing to help the *Graf Spee* officers escape sounds fishy," von Dattenberg said, making it a question.

"That's what I was told; I didn't ask questions."

"An SS-sturmbannführer to guard some radios and clothing?" von Dattenberg pursued.

De Banderano shrugged.

"If I may offer a suggestion, Kapitän. It might not be wise to express your questions to Sturmbannführer Kötl."

"I am young, Capitán, and inexperienced, but not stupid."

"Shall I ask the sturmbannführer to join us?"

———

Sturmbannführer Alfred Kötl looked up after having read his orders. "This is highly unusual," he objected, "subjecting an SS officer to the orders of a foreign citizen."

"Perhaps that is why Reichsprotektor Himmler personally signed the concurrence of the SS to the Grand Admiral's orders," von Dattenberg offered.

"If you wish clarification of the orders, or confirmation, whatever, we can radio Berlin and get that in perhaps ten or twelve hours," de Banderano said.

"When will the replenishment of your submarine be finished, von Dattenberg?" Kötl asked bluntly. "Certainly that won't take an additional ten or twelve hours."

"There will be time to send a message, Kötl, if that's what you want to do," de Banderano said. "It is my decision that the crew of the U-405 should not undertake this mission until they have had twenty-four hours to recuperate from the ordeal of their voyage so far. Several hot meals and a night in a real bunk should do wonders for them."

"I didn't mean to suggest, Herr Kapitän, that I was questioning your orders. I merely was stating that they were highly unusual."

"In other words, you don't want me to radio Berlin?"

"No, thank you. That won't be necessary."

"When you have selected the men you'll be taking with us, Herr Sturmbannführer," von Dattenberg said, "please instruct them that they may bring aboard one extra uniform, two changes of linen, one spare pair of shoes, their toilet kit, and such personal items as they may be able to hold in their armpit."

"I don't believe I can get even my smallest suitcase under my armpit," Kötl said, smiling at his wit.

"And no suitcases, Herr Sturmbannführer. Space is at a premium aboard submarines."

[THREE]
Third Floor Lounge
Hipódromo de San Isidro
Buenos Aires Province, Argentina
1255 7 July 1943

Humberto Valdez Duarte, a tall, slender, superbly tailored man of forty-seven, with a hawk nose and, plastered to his skull, a thick growth of black hair, walked into the lounge and looked around until he saw Cletus Frade, then walked quickly toward him.

The Hipódromo de San Isidro—the racetrack—provided seats in six stands for a hundred thousand spectators. Today, there was perhaps half that number of racing aficionados seated in them.

The Third Floor Lounge was reserved for members, and thus sat atop the members stand. Its plate-glass windows offered a clear view of the finish line and of the entire 2.8-kilometer racing oval.

Frade, wearing a necktie and tweed sports coat and slacks, was sitting alone at a table near the windows. He was puffing on a large black cigar and his hand rested on a long-stemmed wineglass.

As Duarte approached the table, he fondly called out, "Cletus!"

Frade smiled at the voice, stood up and put out his hand—then retracted it. He suddenly remembered he was in Argentina, where male relatives and good friends exchange kisses, not shake hands.

Frade thought of Humberto Duarte as both a good friend and a relative. Duarte was married to his father's sister and had proved to be a good friend.

They embraced. Duarte detected that Cletus was uncomfortable with the physical greeting but not offended.

"How's my Tía Beatrice?" Frade dutifully asked.

Beatrice Frade de Duarte had, as Frade somewhat unkindly thought of it, gone around the bend on learning that her only child had gotten himself killed at Stalingrad. She was under the direct attention of a psychiatrist—almost around the clock—and in a tranquilized fog. Seeing Frade, who was the same age as her late son and alive, usually made her condition worse.

Duarte's face contorted, and he held up both hands in a helpless gesture.

Before Frade could say anything, Duarte asked, "Have any trouble finding it?"

He sat down, and raised his arm to catch the attention of a waiter.

"Finding it?" Frade said. "No. Enrico knew where it was. Getting in posed a couple of problems."

Duarte frowned. "How so?"

"When I went to the gate to this place, a guard asked if he could help me, so I said, 'How do I get to the Third Floor Lounge?' He put his nose in the air and asked why I wished to go to the Third Floor Lounge. I didn't like his attitude, so I told him I wanted to get a couple of drinks and maybe pick up some girls. Then he put his nose up even higher and told me that was quite impossible, the Third Floor Lounge was for members only. I asked him if he had a list of members, and if so to have a look at it, as I thought I might be a member. And gave him my name. So he stiffly told me to wait, please, and disappeared. Then he showed up with two other guys—they were wearing dinner jackets and looked like a headwaiter and his assistant. The older of them asked me if I was really Don Cletus Frade of Estancia San Pedro y San Pablo. I said, 'That's me.' They were considering this when Enrico, having parked the car, showed up—"

"Cletus, you didn't try to bring Enrico up here!" Duarte said, chuckling.

"Yeah, I did," Frade said, and discreetly pointed to a table at the side of the room. Enrico Rodríguez was sitting there with what looked like an untouched glass of beer. A raincoat covered a long, thin object that could have been a shotgun. "Actually, if the headwaiter hadn't recognized Enrico, I'd still be downstairs arguing with him."

"But they did let you in," Duarte said, shaking his head.

"Only after I was so kind as to put this on," Frade said, lifting a necktie.

"You came here without a necktie?" Duarte said, chuckling again.

"I almost came in khaki pants and a polo shirt, but Dorotea wouldn't let me out of the house that way."

"Cletus, you are impossible. A delight, but impossible."

Two men in dinner jackets were now hovering near the table.

"Don Humberto," the older of the two said. "It is so nice to see you, sir."

"Manuel, I don't think you know my nephew, do you? Cletus, this is Señor Estano, the general manager."

"I don't believe I have had that privilege," Estano said. "I regret, Don Cletus, the difficulty earlier. I can assure you it will not happen again."

"And I assure you, señor, that I shall never appear at the door again without a necktie," Frade said, putting out his hand. "I'm sorry about that."

"They should have known," Estano said, nodding at one of the oil paintings on the wall. "The physical resemblance is undeniable."

"Yes, isn't it?" Duarte said, then added, "I'll have some of whatever Don Cletus is drinking."

"What else would he—or you—drink but a pinot noir from Bodegas de Mendoza?"

"Indeed, what else?" Duarte said.

"This is a '39," Estano said.

He snatched a glass and then a wine bottle from the waiter.

"We still have several cases here, and there's more on Calle Florida, of course."

He poured wine into the glass and Duarte sipped it appreciatively.

"Very nice," he said.

"I, from time to time, have a small sip myself," Estano said. "Would you like menus now, or perhaps wait a few minutes?"

"Give us a few minutes, please," Duarte said as Estano added wine to both their glasses.

After Estano had left, Cletus said, "Okay. You want to explain all that to me?"

"All what?"

"Why was he so sure we would drink this? I told the waiter to bring me a nice, not-too-sweet red."

"You own Bodegas de Mendoza," Duarte said. "Which is well known—perhaps even famous—for the quality of its pinot noir. And '39 was a particularly good year."

"I thought I owned a vineyard called Bodegas Frade."

"You do. You own both. Actually, you own four vineyards."

"Well, that explains that, doesn't it? And why are there cases of it on Calle Florida?"

"Because that's where the Jockey Club is."

"Oh, yeah. My father took me there. Fantastic place."

"You haven't been back?"

Frade shook his head.

"Your father must have arranged for your membership right after you came down here."

"I suppose. I know he did that at the Círculo Militar."

"We could have had lunch there," Duarte said. "Either the main club, or the Círculo Militar."

It was a question Frade elected not to answer. "And what was that business about the 'undeniable physical resemblance'?"

"Six men are credited with founding the Jockey Club, in 1876, in a restaurant called Foyot de Paris. Your great-grandfather, second portrait from the left, was one of them."

"Oh, boy!"

"And now may I ask you a question?"

"Sure."

"Why the sudden interest in the Hipódromo de San Isidro?"

"That was Dorotea's idea. I asked her where we could have lunch so that (a) I could be pretty sure the guy at the next table was not working for El Colonel Martín, and (b) I would not run into my Tío Juan. She first said at the Jockey Club, then changed her mind and said here would be even better."

"I knew it was too much to hope that you'd developed a sudden interest in thoroughbred racing. Well, Dorotea was right. I don't think Martín could get past the guard downstairs."

"And my Tío Juan?"

Duarte shook his head.

"This and the Jockey Club are beyond his pocketbook, Cletus. Well beyond."

"Then I'm not liable to run into him here?"

"No, you're not. But if you want my advice—which I'm sure you don't—maybe you should invite him here for lunch sometime."

"I can't stand the sonofabitch. You know that."

"El Coronel Perón can be very useful to you, Cletus."

"So everybody keeps telling me. Actually, that's the reason I asked you to meet me here. I wanted to ask you how useful he would be to me if I wanted to start an airline."

" 'Start an airline'?" Duarte parroted, almost startled by the announcement.

Frade nodded.

"You mean here?"

Frade nodded again.

"Argentina has an airline."

"Not a very good one," Frade said. "The few airplanes Aeropostal has are small and old, and they only fly to a couple of places, none of them out of the country." He paused. "Not like Varig, for example."

"Cletus, you will forgive my asking, but has this anything to do with what El Coronel Martín and some others—completely without justification, of course—think you are doing?"

Frade ignored the question.

"Varig, the national airline of Brazil, is flying Lockheed Lodestars—just like mine—all over South America. As an Argentine, I feel a little embarrassed that Argentina isn't. Doesn't this embarrass you?"

Duarte rolled his eyes.

"Cletus, you may or may not know this, but Brazil is an ally of the United States in their war with Germany, and the Americans—"

"Humberto, you may or may not know this, but I seem to remember that America is also at war with the Japanese—actually, I have some painful memories of their airplanes—and with Italy, too, although from what I hear, the Italians don't seem to have their heart in it. How many hundred thousand of them surrendered in Africa?"

Duarte, smiling, shook his head and went on: ". . . and the Americans are therefore willing to sell to Brazil certain aircraft they are not willing to sell to Argentina."

"Well, if the Americans think that the Argentines think the Germans and the Japanese are going to win the war, doesn't that make sense?"

"Argentina is neutral in this war, Cletus, and you know it."

"So people keep telling me. But let's not go down that street. If what you say is true, why doesn't Aeroposta buy some airplanes from Germany? Could it be that Germany doesn't have any airplanes to sell?"

"Are you suggesting that the Americans would be willing to sell airplanes to Argentina?"

"Just for the sake of argument, let's say I have reason to believe this Argentine could buy, say, a dozen—maybe more than a dozen—Lockheed Lodestars."

"You didn't answer me before when I asked if this has anything to do with what El Coronel Martín—and others—suspect you are doing for the OSS."

Ignoring the reference again, Frade went on: "Just think what that would mean, Humberto, if you went out to El Palomar to catch a plane to Pôrto Alegre and instead of getting a Brazilian airplane, you could get on one with the flag of Argentina painted proudly on the vertical stabilizer? Wouldn't that make your heart beat proudly?"

Duarte shook his head but didn't reply.

"Or you wanted to fly to Mendoza, where I know you do business, and there at El Palomar was a shiny new Lodestar with—what? 'Argentine Air Lines' has a nice ring to it—painted on the sides of the fuselage to fly you there in comfort and safety, instead of one of Aeropostal's junkers?"

"Now that I know you're serious about this, may I suggest we have our lunch and afterward continue this conversation while I show you around the hipódromo?"

"That's probably a very good idea. I may be paranoid, of course, but I feel curious eyes burning holes in the back of my head.'"

"You're not paranoid," Duarte said. "Some of those looking at you curiously were wondering who you were, at first sitting here all by yourself with no member having you as his guest. The others, having asked Señor Estano and been told, are naturally curious to see what El Coronel Frade's long-lost American son looks like."

"How do they know I'm an American? You just told me I look like my great-grandfather."

"Cletus, you are slumped in your chair with your legs stretched out in front of you, something that's not often seen in here, and on your feet are boots of a type never seen here and certainly not in the Jockey Club."

"If I had known everybody was going to be so curious about me, I'd be working on a chaw of Red Man."

" 'Red Man'?"

"Chewing tobacco. That'd give them something to talk about when I spit." He mimed the act.

"Oh, God, Cletus! For a moment I thought you were serious."

"What makes you think I'm not?"

Duarte shook his head and waved his hand over his head to summon a waiter.

Frade pointed to a family crest engraved in a two-foot square of pink marble set in the wall beside what was the entrance to a long, vine-covered stable.

"This mine, too?"

Duarte nodded and smiled.

"Your grandfather used to say he made a lot of money breeding thoroughbreds for the family while his brother—your Granduncle Guillermo—lost even more betting on them."

"Not only money," Clete said. "My father told me he bet on a slow horse and lost the guesthouse across from the downtown racetrack."

"Your grandfather bought it back, and your granduncle was banished to Mendoza. When your grandfather died, your father and Beatrice stopped racing altogether. Your father said there was enough of a gamble in just breeding and dealing in horses. You're still pretty heavily invested in that. I was hoping you were going to become involved yourself. You know horses."

When my grandfather died, Frade thought, *his property, under the Napoleonic Code of Inheritance, was equally divided between his two children.*

My father then bought out his sister's share; that money became her dowry for when she married Humberto.

And now, when Beatrice and Humberto die, since Cousin Jorge went for a ride he shouldn't have taken in a Storch at Stalingrad and there being no closer blood relative, everything will come to me.

Jesus Christ, what a screwed-up law!

Even my father thought so.

When he explained it to me, he used as an example a family with two children, a son and a daughter. The son takes off for Paris and spends his life chasing women, boozing it up, never even sending a postcard. The daughter spends her life caring for their parents, and can't even get married.

Yet, when the parents die, the Napoleonic Code splits everything fifty-fifty.

"Instead of doing what El Colonel Martín suspects I'm doing, you mean?" Frade asked.

Duarte nodded.

"Let's go find ourselves a clean stall in here and talk about that," Frade said.

"I really believe, Humberto, that El Colonel Martín and I have reached an accommodation," Frade said, his arms crossed and leaning with his back against the wooden wall of an empty stall.

"How so?"

"This is my opinion, okay? Backed up by what's happened, or hasn't happened."

"Understood."

"I was sent down here—Martín has figured this out—to stop the Germans from replenishing their submarines from quote neutral unquote ships in the Río de la Plata. I've done that. The *Reine de la Mer* was sunk by an American submarine. Martín—and everybody else, including General Ramírez—knows that, and that I had something to do with it.

"Sinking the *Reine de la Mer* proved that we know what they were doing, know the identity of the ships that are violating Argentine neutrality, and are prepared to send submarines—or whatever else it takes—into the Río de la Plata to stop it. Argentineans, no matter how much they dislike Americans or love Der Führer, do not want naval battles in the Río de la Plata. Somebody high up in the government has told the Germans to do their submarine replenishment somewhere else. And that's what they're doing. They send supply U-boats from Europe and they rendezvous on the high seas."

He waited a moment, and after Duarte nodded his understanding, went on: "I know—but they don't know I know—that my aircraft mechanic, his name is Carlos Olivo, works for Martín. So Martín knows that every time our radar picks up something interesting, a ship we don't know about, I get in the Lodestar and fly out over the muddy waters of the Río de la Plata and have a look at it. If it's suspicious, Martín gets an 'anonymous' call. Martín knows where it comes from. I keep my people on the estancia, and Martín doesn't come onto the estancia looking for them or the radar, or ask where I've been in the Lodestar."

"You seem pretty sure of all this," Duarte said.

"I am. Now, while I have no idea why President Roosevelt wants an airline down here—"

"Roosevelt? *That's* where this idea comes from?"

Frade nodded. "There's all sorts of possibilities, one being that he wants to stick it to Juan Trippe of Panagra, but I just don't know. Anyway, it has nothing to do with what I'm doing for the OSS. I'll see to that.

"Martín, being Martín, will suspect otherwise. I would, in his shoes. So what I have to do is convince him that I'm as pure as the driven snow. To that end, the pilots of this airline will be Argentine. The whole operation, except for maintenance supervisors and some American airline pilots who will come down here to train the pilots and maintenance people and set it up, will be Argentine. And the cherry on the cake will be that my Tío Juan will be one of the investors and play an active role. I don't know if he'll be suspicious or not."

"You can count on it that he will, Cletus."

"Then good. Let him snoop wherever he wants to. There will be nothing for him to find, because there will be nothing."

"You said you want Perón to be one of the investors."

"Right."

"Before we get to who the others might be, where is Perón going to get the money to invest? He doesn't have anything but his army pay."

"The Anglo-Argentine Bank is going to loan it to him. When I talk to the sonofabitch, I'm going to tell him that I'm absolutely confident that the Anglo-Argentine Bank would be delighted to loan an important man, such as himself, whatever he needed for this business venture."

"The board won't like that," Duarte said. "Where's the collateral?"

"You've just been telling me how wise I would be to be nice to the son-ofabitch, that he's destined to become really important. Tell the board the same thing."

"If you're going to be in business with him, it might be a good idea for you to stop referring to him as 'the sonofabitch.' "

"Yes or no? If necessary, I'll guarantee his loan, but I'd rather he thought I had nothing to do with it. And that Martín learned that, too."

Duarte didn't reply directly. "And the other investors?"

"Why do I think you're not slobbering at the mouth to get a piece of my get-rich-quick scheme?"

"Because I'm a banker, and I recognize a risky venture when I see one. Who else, Cletus?"

"My father-in-law, for one. Señora Carzino-Cormano, for another, and possibly even—I don't know if she has any money—Señora Alicia Carzino-Cormano de von Wachtstein."

"Alicia? Because of her husband?"

"How could I possibly be doing something anti-German with my airline if the wife of Major Freiherr Hans-Peter von Wachtstein is a major investor? I suspect the Germans would tell him to get as close to it as he could."

"But not with the money we hope the German embassy doesn't know about?"

Frade shook his head.

"Not with that money, no," he said. "I don't care who the investors will be so long as I hold sixty percent. I need fifty-one percent for control, and the other nine because I don't want something unexpected to happen that will cut my piece below fifty-one percent."

Duarte looked at him for a long moment.

"Cletus, you are very much like your father," he said. "Remembering your father showing up in the Third Floor Lounge drunk as an owl and in full gaucho regalia—which happened more than once—I was not surprised to see you there, in cowboy boots and tie-less. But I confess I am surprised a little to see that you also have his business acumen. You've given this airline idea a good deal of thought, haven't you?"

Frade nodded, then said, "Does that mean you're not dismissing the idea out of hand as lunatic?"

"Actually, it seems like a pretty good idea. I'll have to ask some questions, and give it some thought, of course."

"Of course. Thank you, Humberto."

[FOUR]
The Office of the Reichsführer-SS
Berlin, Germany
2255 7 July 1943

"You wished to see me, Herr Reichsprotektor?" Obersturmbannführer Karl Cranz asked as he entered the office of Heinrich Himmler.

Cranz was a good-looking, blond, fair-skinned man in his early thirties.

"I wished to see you an hour and a half ago," Himmler said.

"I regret that Sturmscharführer Neidler had trouble finding me in the air raid shelter, Herr Reichsprotektor."

Sturmscharführer (Sergeant Major) Neidler was Himmler's de facto private secretary. He rarely left Himmler's side. That he had been sent to find Cranz had told Cranz there was absolutely no question that Himmler wanted to see him.

"You were not at home?"

"I took my wife to the opera, Herr Reichsprotektor. Neidler knew where I was."

Himmler waved him into a chair.

"While you were at the opera, Cranz, Admiral Canaris came to see me. He would have liked to have had a word with you, but as you said, Sturmscharführer Neidler apparently had difficulty locating you, and the admiral could not wait."

"Whenever you are through with me, Herr Reichsprotektor, I will go to see the admiral and offer my most sincere apologies."

Himmler did not respond to that.

"Canaris had two things on his mind, Cranz. First was that there had been a radio message from the *Ciudad de Cádiz*. Two words: 'Smooth seas.'"

"Well, that's good news, Herr Reichsprotektor."

"Meaning the special cargo is already aboard U-405."

"Yes, sir."

"The second thing Canaris wanted to tell me was that he had a talk a few days ago with Parteileiter Bormann. Bormann told him that a couple of things had been decided. First, that Gradny-Sawz would be the man charged with enlisting Oberst Perón in the plans we have for him, and second, on the recommendation of Brigadeführer von Deitzberg, that Korvettenkapitän Boltitz will become the naval attaché of our embassy in Buenos Aires, whose additional duties will be threefold: supervising the execution of Operation Phoenix, keeping an eye on Gradny-Sawz, and finding the traitor—or possibly the spy—in the embassy."

Himmler looked at Cranz as if expecting a reply, and when none was forthcoming, said, "Comments, Cranz?"

"Sir, the Herr Reichsprotektor did not tell me he had made those decisions."

"I didn't tell you that I had because I hadn't. Parteileiter Bormann apparently has taken it upon himself to make them for me and Admiral Canaris. And in the case of Boltitz, acting on the recommendation of Brigadeführer von Deitzberg, who was presumably speaking for me."

Himmler stared at Cranz for a full thirty seconds to give him time to consider what he had just said.

"Admiral Canaris further told me that he had told Bormann that while he considers Boltitz a fine officer, he does not consider him qualified for those sort of intelligence and security duties. Off the top of my head, Cranz, thinking aloud, so to speak, what I replied to that was, 'I'd really rather have someone like Obersturmbannführer Cranz in that role.' "

Cranz didn't reply.

"The problem now, of course, Cranz, is that Bormann has made his decisions known. The only way to have them reversed would be for Canaris and me to go directly to the Führer. For obvious reasons—the Führer's time is fully occupied, for one thing, and Canaris and I believe that our Führer would be reluctant in any case to overturn any decision of Parteileiter Bormann—we don't want to do that."

"I think I understand the problem, Herr Reichsleiter."

"I hope so, Cranz," Himmler said. "But there is, if I might coin a phrase, a silver lining to the black cloud. If Bormann feels he may make unilateral decisions, it would seem that Admiral Canaris and I have the same right."

"Yes, sir?"

"For example, despite that Wehrmacht Generalmajor's uniform he is wearing while offering suggestions and recommendations on my behalf to Bormann, Brigadeführer von Deitzberg is a member of the Schutzstaffel, and consequently subject to my orders. I can, for example, order him back to Berlin without having to consult with anyone."

"Is that your plan, sir?"

"It is my *decision*, Cranz. There's a difference. Admiral Canaris went on to say that he thinks Boltitz would make a fine naval attaché and probably would be very useful in the other areas I mentioned had he someone skilled in those areas to advise him. Which brings us back to what popped into my head earlier—'I'd really rather have someone like Obersturmbannführer Cranz in that role.'"

"I'm not sure I follow you, Herr Reichsprotektor."

"I have every hope, Cranz, that when you permit me to finish, everything will be clear to you."

"I beg your pardon, Herr Reichsprotektor."

"Foreign Minister von Ribbentrop was good enough to come here when Canaris called him," Himmler went on. "Canaris told him that inasmuch as Gradny-Sawz had not been entirely cleared of suspicion of involvement, he and I were both a little uncomfortable with Bormann's decision to put him in charge of Operation Perón and having him continue his role in Operation Phoenix without having someone more skilled than Korvettenkapitän Boltitz watching him. And Canaris told the foreign minister that we were understandably loath to bother the Führer with the problem.

"Von Ribbentrop asked if we had any ideas, whereupon I said that the ideal solution would be to have someone in the foreign service with the necessary skills—someone already privy to Operation Perón and Operation Phoenix—who could advise Boltitz and keep an eye on everybody. I asked the foreign minister if he could think of such a person he could send. He said that without making that person privy to both operations, he could not. Whereupon Canaris asked me, 'What about your man Cranz, Himmler?'

"I replied that you would be ideal for that duty, were you a member of the Foreign Service. To which von Ribbentrop responded that he could see no reason why you could not be seconded to the foreign ministry—the precedent having been set with the seconding of von Deitzberg to the Wehrmacht—and sent to Buenos Aires as, say, the commercial attaché."

He paused and smiled. "Congratulations on your new duties, Foreign Service Officer Grade Fifteen Cranz."

"Sir, when is this going to happen?"

"Your credentials and diplomatic passport will be delivered to you just before you board the Lufthansa Condor flight at Tempelhof at seven tomorrow morning."

"So quickly."

"Does that pose a problem, Cranz?"

"No, sir. But I did have a thought—"

"Which is?"

"I think fewer questions would be raised about my assignment to the embassy if I were accompanied by my family."

"Being accompanied is obviously out of the question," Himmler said simply. "You will be on the plane tomorrow. But I can see the merit of your suggestion, so perhaps your family could join you there later."

"Yes, sir."

"Insofar as 'fewer questions' is concerned, Admiral Canaris said that fewer questions would be raised by Boltitz being named naval attaché if he had the appropriate rank. He brought this to the attention of Grand Admiral Doenitz, who agreed. So you will be taking with you Korvettenkapitän Boltitz's promotion orders to fregattenkapitän dated several months ago, and which somehow became lost in the bureaucracy. When his appointment as naval attaché is announced to the diplomatic community, it will be as Fregattenkapitän Boltitz. A month or six weeks from now, he will be promoted kapitän zur see."

Cranz nodded.

"May I ask my role vis-à-vis Kapitän zur See Boltitz, Herr Reichsprotektor?"

"May I be the first to offer my congratulations on your promotion, Herr Standartenführer Cranz?" Himmler said, smiling. "Since your promotion will predate Boltitz's promotion to kapitän zur see, when that comes through, you will be the senior officer in the embassy."

"Thank you very much, sir."

"Under the circumstances, your promotion will not be made known to Brigadeführer von Deitzberg until he's back here. You will carry to him a letter ordering his return to his duties in Berlin. Since you have no idea why I am recalling him, those orders will be as much of a surprise to you as they are to him."

"I understand, Herr Reichsprotektor."

"That raises the question of Sturmbannführer Raschner," Himmler said. "Would you prefer that he return to Berlin with von Deitzberg, or would he be useful to you?"

Cranz considered that for a moment.

"I think he would be very useful to me there, Herr Reichsprotektor."

"All right, he's yours. But don't tell him until von Deitzberg is on his way back here."

"Yes, sir."

V

[ONE]
Tempelhof Airfield
Berlin, Germany
0725 8 July 1943

Lufthansa Kapitän Dieter von und zu Aschenburg, a tall, blue-eyed, blond-haired, fair-skinned Prussian, sat in the pilot seat of the Focke-Wulf 200B "Condor," impatiently tapping the balls of his fingers together.

He had hoped to get off the ground before seven o'clock, and here it was nearly half past, and the only information he could get from the goddamn tower was that permission for him to take off "would be coming momentarily." They had been telling him that for half an hour.

Lufthansa Flight 1007 was about to begin a journey of some 8,500 miles to Buenos Aires, Argentina. The flight would be made in four legs, and it was arguable which of them was the most dangerous. None of them was anything approaching safe.

The sleek and slender aircraft, powered by four 870-horsepower BMW engines, looked much like the smaller, dual-engine American DC-3, especially in the nose and cockpit area. It would fly—*presuming the goddamn tower ever gives me permission for takeoff*—first across Germany and German-occupied France, then over neutral Spain, and on to Lisbon in neutral Portugal.

That was the shortest leg—1,435 miles—well within the Condor's maximum range of 2,200 miles. The danger here was from American and British aircraft over Germany and occupied France. Most of the real danger came from Allied fighters rigged as photo-reconnaissance aircraft. They were fitted with extra fuel tanks, and often most of their machine guns were removed. They were charged with photographing the previous night's bomber target to see how much damage had been done and which targets needed to be bombed again.

Von und zu Aschenburg knew that not all of the photo-recon aircraft had had their machine guns removed, leaving the fighters with two .50-caliber weapons perfectly capable of shooting down an unarmed Condor if they crossed paths with one—and fast enough to chase it if that was necessary. It was perfectly legal under the rules of warfare for the Allies to shoot down a transport aircraft that had red swastikas, outlined in white, painted on the sides of the fuselage and vertical stabilizer.

Presuming the Condor made it safely to neutral Portugal, the next leg of the flight would be 1,800 miles—safely within the Condor's range—from Lisbon to Dakar, in the French colony of Senegal on the west coast of Africa.

The danger between Lisbon and Dakar was again Allied aircraft, both long-range bombers on antisubmarine patrol and fighters operating from Moroccan airfields now in American hands, all of whom would regard the Condor as fair game.

Presuming the Condor was not shot down en route to Dakar, the airplane would be inspected and otherwise prepared for the next leg of the trip, 2,500 miles across the North Atlantic Ocean to Cayenne in French Guiana in the northeast of the South American continent.

The work would be done by "technicians" of the German Armistice Commission stationed in Dakar to ensure French neutrality after the Armistice of 1940.

The problem on the Dakar–Cayenne leg was the distance. It was 300 miles, more or less, greater than the Condor could safely fly with its standard load of twenty-six passengers, two stewards, and a ton of cargo. The solution to covering that additional distance, then, was to carry no more than thirteen passengers, plus a steward, and just about no cargo whatsoever. The weight thus saved could be used to carry additional fuel.

Presuming that headwinds or other atmospheric conditions did not cause the Condor to run out of fuel before it reached Cayenne, it would again be inspected and made ready for the final leg of the flight by "technicians" of the German Armistice Commission assigned to French Guiana.

The final leg to Buenos Aires was not only the longest—2,700 miles, 500 farther than the published maximum range of the Condor—but also involved danger from Allied aircraft again. Brazil was at war with Germany, and American B-24 bombers, modified for use as long-range antisubmarine aircraft, here patrolled the Atlantic Ocean all the way to Buenos Aires. Most of their machine-gun positions had been removed, but there were still machine guns in the forward and aft turrets, more than enough to shoot down a Condor should they happen upon one.

But the greatest danger on the final leg was the distance. If there were headwinds and they ran out of fuel, the only option would be to ditch at sea near the shore of Brazil and try to make it ashore in rubber boats. Landing in Brazil would see the Condor fall into Allied hands, and it had been made quite clear to Kapitän Dieter von und zu Aschenburg that doing so would be tantamount to treason.

But what was most galling about the Buenos Aires flights, von und zu Aschenburg had often thought, was that there was no reason even to make them—other than for their propaganda value.

Doktor Paul Joseph Goebbels—that clubfooted minister of propaganda for the Third Reich—can boast: "Germany's great airline Lufthansa flies a regularly scheduled transatlantic service, while the Allies cannot—therefore Germany and National Socialism are superior!"

Von und zu Aschenburg also thought, very privately if not a bit bitterly, that Goebbels was entirely capable of insisting the flights be kept up because when one of them—inevitably—got shot down or, for that matter, just disappeared, he would be sure of headlines all around the world: *Allies Shoot Down Unarmed German Civilian Airliner Carrying Neutral Diplomats and Medical Personnel.*

On today's flight there were three French diplomats to satisfy the "neutral diplomats" portion of that claim, as well as two German doctors and seven nurses en route to Buenos Aires's German Hospital. There was no shortage of work for German medical personnel in Germany which was being bombed daily. And there was no shortage of competent medical personnel in Argentina. Yet still came the doctors and nurses.

Propaganda was very valuable to the Thousand-Year Reich.

Kapitän Dieter von und zu Aschenburg knew that the Condor manifest also listed a German diplomat. But that luminary had not boarded, which was almost certainly the reason the tower's permission for von und zu Aschenburg to start his engines and take off now had been delayed "momentarily" for more than a half hour.

"Herr Oberst," the co-pilot said, bringing von und zu Aschenburg back from his thoughts.

He had been addressed as "Herr Oberst" because—airline pilot uniform or not—he was a Luftwaffe colonel. All of Lufthansa was in fact in the Luftwaffe, but that was not for public consumption. Both "First Officer" Karl Nabler and "Flight Engineer" Wilhelm Hover were actually Luftwaffe hauptmanns who had been assigned to the Condor flights after "distinguished service" as Junkers Ju-52 pilots on the Eastern Front.

Somewhat cynically, von und zu Aschenburg thought that their "distinguished service" meant they had somehow miraculously avoided getting shot down. The tri-motor, corrugated-skin Ju-52, derisively known as "Auntie Ju," was easy prey for Russian fighters.

Von und zu Aschenburg wondered why he liked Willi and loathed Nabler. For all he knew, Willi might be an even more zealous National Socialist than Nabler. He had never discussed the war, or politics, with either of them.

As an intelligent man, a warrior who had seen his share and more of combat, von und zu Aschenburg was not anxious to give his life for the German Reich. But if that was going to happen as he did his duty, he preferred that he die as a soldier, in uniform. He had not volunteered to fly back and forth over the Atlantic; he had been told he had been honored by being selected for that duty. There was no question in his mind that one day he wouldn't make it.

It was one of the many reasons he loathed the Nazis.

He often thought, *If the swine could read my mind, I would be hanging from a butcher's hook.*

First Officer Nabler was pointing to the tarmac. An open Mercedes, a big one, was coming out from the curved terminal building, obviously headed for them.

Two things immediately caught von und zu Aschenburg's attention. First, that the license plate of the car incorporated the lightning flashes of the Schutzstaffel. And second, that it held a family. There was one child in front with the driver—and the driver was in an SS uniform—and two more children in back with two adults, almost certainly the parents.

Von und zu Aschenburg thought it was entirely possible that he was about to get into an argument with the man.

Those SS bastards are so impressed with themselves they really believe they can rescind the laws of physics. Or, at the very least, cause the deplaning of lesser persons so that the wife and kiddies can go flying.

There's simply no way I'm going to take off with the wife and three kids.

"I will see that our distinguished passenger is seated," von und zu Aschenburg said, and unfastened his seat belt.

"Jawohl, Herr Oberst."

Von und zu Aschenburg went quickly through the passenger cabin and down the steps.

The man in the Mercedes was already out of the car, and the driver was taking a suitcase from the trunk.

"Captain," the man said with an ingratiating smile. "My deepest apologies. I know how important it is for you to leave on schedule. Believe me, this couldn't be helped."

"It's not a problem, sir," von und zu Aschenburg said.

He then surprised himself by taking the suitcase from the SS driver.

"If you'll come with me, sir, we'll get you settled."

Herr Karl Cranz of the Foreign Service kissed Frau Cranz and their three children good-bye, shook hands with the SS-sturmscharführer, then followed von und zu Aschenburg up the steps and into the Condor.

[TWO]
Office of the Managing Director
Banco de Inglaterra y Argentina
Bartolomé Mitre 300
Buenos Aires, Argentina
1205 10 July 1943

"Come in, Cletus," Humberto Duarte said as he opened one of the pair of heavy wooden doors to his office.

Frade and Duarte embraced in the Argentine fashion, then they walked into the office, trailed by Enrico Rodríguez.

"Very nice," Clete said, looking around the luxuriously furnished office. "I guess foreclosing on widows and orphans pays you bankers pretty good, huh? No offense."

"None taken. And would you be offended—either of you—if I said you are splendidly turned out? Good morning, Enrico."

Enrico nodded.

"Blame my wife," Frade said. "She's responsible."

Duarte's eyebrows rose in question as he waved Frade into a chair in front of his enormous, ornately carved desk. Enrico took a chair near the door and rested on the floor the butt of the shotgun that he concealed in his top coat.

"Our suits were my father's," Clete said. "In what is now my bedroom, he had a closet full of them. Right after Dorotea and I married, I showed them to her and said we really ought to give them to somebody who could use them.

Most looked like he'd never worn them. She said she knew just the people who could really use them, so I told her to have at it. Two days later, an Englishman showed up, a tailor—"

"An Englishman or an Anglo-Argentine?"

"I'd guess an Anglo-Argentine. He talks like my father-in-law . . . or you. His name is Halsey."

"I know him well," Duarte said. "And let me guess, he stood you on a stool and took out his tape measure and a piece of chalk?"

Clete smiled and nodded. "And now Enrico and I look like advertisements in *Esquire*. All he had to do was take them in a little for me, and let them out a little for Enrico."

"Has Claudia seen you wearing one?" Duarte asked.

Clete shook his head.

"Well, be sure to wear one when she invites you to dinner, which will probably be the day after tomorrow. She'll be pleased."

"Why, twice? Why will she be pleased, and why is she going to invite me to dinner?"

"She will be pleased because whenever she could drag your father into Halsey's place of business, she ordered suits for him. Most of which he hung in his closet and he never wore. And Claudia is going to have you to dinner because of what I want to talk to you about now. After which, we'll walk over to the Jockey Club and have lunch."

"I just had one of my better ideas," Clete said. "Why don't we walk over to the Jockey Club now and talk about whatever you want to talk about while we eat? Enrico and I were up at dawn moving bulls. I'm starved. I was starved *before* Dorotea came after us and told me you were going to buy us lunch here, and I had to get dressed and in the airplane *right now.*"

"You flew in?"

"It's the only way to travel. I thought I told you that. It took us longer to drive here from El Palomar than it did to fly in from Estancia San Pedro y San Pablo in the Piper Cub."

"Well, I'm sorry to tell you you're going to have to live with your starvation a little longer. The rules of the Jockey Club forbid talking business in the dining room."

"Why?"

"That's just the way it is, Cletus."

"If my grandfather and his pals couldn't talk business in the dining room of the Petroleum Club in Dallas, hardly a hole would've been drilled."

"This is Buenos Aires, Cletus. Try to keep that in mind."

"Okay. But before we get into what you're going to try to sell me, which we can't talk about over lunch, since this is Buenos Aires, what about my airlines idea? Have you given that any solemn thought?"

Duarte, smiling, shook his head.

"What's funny?"

"You'll never guess who else has been thinking about an airline for Argentina," Duarte said.

"I give up."

"President Ramírez."

"And what the hell does that mean? I can't start one because this is Argentina and the president doesn't like competition?"

"Just about the opposite," Duarte said. "Your Tío Juan Domingo came to see me yesterday. He told me that Ramírez had called him in, said that it was embarrassing for Argentina not to have an airline with modern transport aircraft like Varig. And since he didn't think the Americans would sell airplanes to Argentina, what about the Germans? And since Perón had such close ties with the Germans, why didn't Perón look into it?"

"*And?*" Frade said, not believing his ears.

"And he did. And Ambassador Lutzenberger told him that just as soon as there was final victory, Germany would be delighted to help Argentina with the most modern aircraft in the world, probably even the Condor. But at the moment, there had been small reverses on the battlefields, and he didn't think any aircraft would be available right now."

Frade shook his head in disgust. "Ramírez actually believed that the Germans would sell him airplanes? I thought he was smarter than that."

"Your Tío Juan Domingo was both surprised and disappointed," Duarte said. "He admitted as much when he came to me and asked if the Banco de Inglaterra y Argentina could induce the British to sell us some transport aircraft."

"Jesus Christ!"

"So with Juan Domingo sitting right there"—he gestured at Frade—"where you are, I called the British ambassador and asked him if he thought the English were in a position to sell some transport planes to Argentina. He said he didn't think so, but to ask him again after the war."

"All of which leaves me where?" Clete said.

"I then told him that you had come to me, said you thought you could get your hands on some Lockheed passenger airships, and then you asked if I thought you could get permission to start an airline, and that I told you that I thought getting permission would be just about impossible."

"Why did you tell him that?"

"Because in addition to being a good banker, I'm a good lawyer, and all good lawyers are devious. I'm surprised you don't know that."

"And what was his reaction to that?"

"He asked—he's actually very clever, Cletus, something you should keep in mind—if your grandfather was involved, to which I replied, I didn't know, but I thought it was likely, because of his relationship with Howard Hughes. To which Colonel Perón replied, 'I thought it was probably something like that.' Does Mr. Howell know Mr. Hughes, Cletus?"

"Very well, as a matter of fact. Hughes's father was in the oil business. He invented a tool that goes on the end of the string."

"Explain that, please."

"When you put down a hole—that is, drill an oil well—there's a string of pipes screwed together—'the string'—that goes into the ground. At the end of the string, there's a cutting tool."

He held his hands, fingers extended, about eight inches apart, indicating the size of the ball-shaped tool, then went on, "Some really tough steel cutters— they look like meshing gears—chew up the dirt and rock, which gets washed out of the way. Hughes's father came up with a hell of an improvement of the tool and, more important, was smart enough to bury it with patents. He started the Hughes Tool Company, and the Hughes Tool Company made him a *very* rich man. And Howard inherited the whole thing. That's where he got the money to go into the movie business and to buy Lockheed."

" 'Howard'? You know him, Cletus?"

Frade nodded.

"Even better," Humberto said.

"What's that got to do with anything?"

"The first thing suspicious people—like Colonel Martín and Colonel Perón—would think when they heard that you—whom they suspect of having ties with the OSS—could get your hands on airplanes in the middle of the war was that you were getting them from the OSS."

"You just finished saying Tío Juan Domingo has figured out I'm getting them from my grandfather's pal, Howard Hughes."

"I told him that the reason I told you getting permission would be impossible was because of the suspicions people like Colonel Martín would have that it was somehow connected with the OSS. To which, after thinking this over for perhaps two seconds, he replied, 'There are ways to put such suspicions to rest.' "

"And did he tell you what they would be?"

"Having someone like himself on the board of directors, and making sure all the pilots, from the chief pilot downward, are Argentines. He even mentioned a Major Delgano for that position."

"Well, Delgano does know how to fly a Lodestar," Clete said.

"How do you know that?"

"I taught him."

"Isn't that the fellow who was your father's pilot?"

Frade nodded.

"Maybe Tío Juan is smarter than I'm giving him credit for being," he said.

"I would say that's a given," Duarte said.

"All the time that Capitán Delgano quote retired unquote was my father's pilot he actually was working for Martín—the BIS. It was only when Martín decided that the coup was going to work, and enlisted in that noble enterprise, that that came out."

"What do you mean?"

"When my father wrote Operation Blue, he made plans to avoid the firing squad in case they couldn't pull it off. Delgano was to take his Beechcraft Staggerwing to Campo de Mayo and have it ready to fly my father, Rawson, and Ramírez to Paraguay. By the time they were ready to start Operation Blue, my father had been assassinated, and the Staggerwing was on the bottom of Samborombón Bay.

"Delgano came to me three days before they were to go, told me that he had been working for Martín all along, and that Martín wanted to use the Lodestar to get people out of the country. So I spent two days teaching him how to fly it, and then decided if my father had wanted to get rid of Castillo and his government so badly, I was obliged to put my two cents in. So I flew the Lodestar to Campo de Mayo."

"I never heard any of this before."

"My role in the coup became something like a state secret. Nobody, maybe especially me, wanted it to come out."

"You sound as if you did more than fly the Lodestar to Campo de Mayo."

"I flew General Rawson around in one of their Piper Cubs when the two rebel columns were headed for the Casa Rosada. They had lost their communication and were about to start shooting at each other."

"And you kept that from happening?"

Clete nodded.

"Ramírez knows this?"

Clete nodded.

"Wouldn't that tend to make him think you're a patriotic Argentine, instead of an American OSS agent?"

"Well, maybe if Delgano hadn't been in Santo Tomé when I flew the Lodestar in from Brazil, with an OSS team on it."

"He saw them?"

"He saw them, and he knows that I flew them to Estancia San Pedro y San Pablo. And since the day after the coup Delgano was back in uniform—a newly promoted major working for BIS—I have to assume Colonel Martín has got a pretty good idea what everybody looks like."

"Are you saying you don't want this man looking over your shoulder in your airline?"

"Not at all. Let him look. I'm not going to be doing anything, now, that I don't want him to see or Martín or anyone else to know about."

"And later?"

"We'll see about later. Why does Perón want to be on the board of directors? To keep an eye on me?"

"That, too, probably, but there would be an honorarium."

"A generous one?"

"Since you are going to be the majority stockholder, that would be up to you. I would recommend a generous one."

"And he does what to earn it?"

"He gets permission for you to have the airline."

"In other words, I'm bribing him."

"We lawyers don't use terms like this here, Cletus. We recognize things for being the way they are."

"Okay. What's the next step?"

"We form the S.A.—Sociedad Anónima, literally translated, 'Anonymous Society,' like an American corporation—and everybody signs it, and then you come up with, say, two million two hundred thousand dollars."

"What did you say? Two million two hundred thousand? Why do I think you just made that figure up?"

"The aircraft are in the neighborhood of a hundred twenty-three thousand dollars U.S. each," Humberto said. "And you're going to need at least a dozen to get started, and fourteen would be better. . . ."

Is he making that up, too? Where did he get all that?

"Fourteen of them comes to about one and three-quarter million. Doubling that—to provide for spares, salaries, operating capital, et cetera, in our preliminary planning—comes to a little less than three and a half million. Sixty percent of that, to ensure your control, comes to the two-million-two figure I mentioned."

"Why fourteen airplanes?"

"Aeropostal has a dozen," Duarte said.

"Where's the other forty percent coming from?"

"Claudia and I will take twelve-point-five each, and the bank the remaining fifteen percent. As I said, my board of directors feels it's a sound investment."

"When did they decide that?"

"I should have said, 'The board will feel that it's a sound investment after I have a chance to tell them about it.' "

"And when is this all going to take place?"

"Claudia's going to give a small, sort of family-only dinner tomorrow night, if Colonel Perón can find the time. If not, the next night. We can sign everything at the dinner."

"I don't know how long it'll take me to come up with that kind of money."

"The bank regards you as a good credit risk."

"You're amazing, Humberto."

"How kind of you to say so. Shall we walk over to the Jockey Club?'

[THREE]
El Palomar Airfield
Buenos Aires, Argentina
1605 12 July 1943

"El Palomar, Lufthansa Six Zero Two," came over the speakers in the El Palomar tower.

The call was faint, and in German. The latter posed no problems—just about all the tower operators spoke German—but the faintness of the call did.

The operators hurriedly put on headsets. One of them went to the radio rack to see if he could better tune in the caller. Another leaned over a shelf and spoke—in German—into a microphone.

"Lufthansa Six Zero Two, this is El Palomar."

There was no answer, so the operator tried again, and again got no answer. There was another call to the tower.

"El Palomar, Lufthansa Six Zero Two. El Palomar, Lufthansa Six Zero Two."

Everybody knew what was happening; it had happened several times before. The Siemens radio transmitters aboard the Lufthansa airplane had greater range than did the radios in the tower. It wasn't supposed to be that way, but that's the way it was.

It produced mixed feelings in both of them, embarrassment that their tower had terribly mediocre communications equipment, and vicarious pride as Germano-Argentines in the really superb German equipment aboard the Lufthansa aircraft.

One of the operators picked up a telephone and dialed a number from memory.

It was answered, in Spanish, on the third ring.

"Embassy of the German Reich."

"Let me speak to the duty officer, please," the tower operator said in Spanish.

An interior phone rang three times before it was answered in Spanish.

"Consular section. Consul Schneider speaking."

The tower operator switched to German.

"Herr Untersturmführer, here is Kurt Schumer at El Palomar."

Untersturmführer Johan Schneider also switched to German.

"How can I help you, Herr Schumer?"

"We just had a radio call from Lufthansa Six Zero Two, Herr Untersturmführer."

"And?"

"We can hear him, Herr Untersturmführer, but he cannot hear us, which suggests he is some distance away."

"We have had no word of an incoming Condor," Schneider said.

Schumer didn't reply.

"Which, of course," Schneider went on, "does not mean that a Condor is not on its way here. Thank you, Herr Schumer. I shall take the necessary steps."

"My pleasure, Herr Untersturmführer."

"Heil Hitler!" Schneider barked, and broke the connection.

There was, of course, a protocol spelled out in great detail in the embassy of the German Reich for a situation like this. At the moment, it wasn't working very well.

Untersturmführer Schneider, who was listed on the embassy's manning chart as an assistant consul, was a member of the Sicherheitsdienst (the Secu-

rity Service, known by its acronym, SD) of the Sicherheitspolizei (the Security
Police, known by its acronym, SIPO), which in turn was part of the Reichssicherheitshauptamt (the Reich Security Central Office, known by its acronym,
RHSA) of the Allgemeine-SS. The SS itself was divided into two parts, the other
being the Waffen-SS, which was military in nature.

Untersturmführer Schneider was very much aware that he was the senior
SS officer presently assigned to the embassy of the Reich in Buenos Aires. This
was pretty heady stuff for an untersturmführer, which was the SS rank corre-
sponding to second lieutenant.

In theory, he was answerable only to the ambassador, Manfred Alois
Graf von Lutzenberger, but on the day Schneider had reported for duty, von
Lutzenberger had told him that the military attaché, Oberst Karl-Heinz Grüner,
was the reichssicherheitshauptamt's man in Buenos Aires. He also told him
that Reichsführer-SS Heinrich Himmler himself, to facilitate Grüner's carrying
out of those duties, had commissioned Grüner an honorary oberführer-SS.
Consequently, Schneider was to consider himself under Grüner's orders.

Oberst/Oberführer Grüner had immediately named Untersturmführer
Schneider Officer-in-Charge of Security Documents, which meant that he
would have responsibility for the reception, care, and transmission of all documents containing secrets of the embassy.

In carrying out his duties, Grüner told Schneider, he would wear civilian
clothing, refer to himself as a consular officer, and not make use of his SS
rank, as he himself never made reference to his SS rank. It was better, Grüner
had told him, that it not become public knowledge that the SS was in the
embassy.

Furthermore, Grüner had told him, he would serve as his deputy in matters of counterintelligence, which duties he could better carry out if no one was
aware he was an officer of the Sicherheitsdienst. He was to make immediate and
secret reports to Grüner—and only Grüner—of any activity that he found
suspicious.

There were ancillary duties as well, among them responsibility for the diplomatic pouches. He was to meet every incoming Lufthansa flight and take from
its steward the incoming diplomatic pouch, which he would take to the embassy and hand over to Grüner personally. Similarly, he would get the Berlin-
bound diplomatic pouch from Grüner and personally hand it to the Condor
steward just before the Condor headed home.

The protocol had become unworkable when Oberst/Oberführer Grüner
had given his life for the Fatherland at Samborombón Bay. Untersturmführer

Schneider remained subordinate to the military attaché, but the military attaché—the *acting* military attaché until another could be sent from Berlin—was Major Freiherr Hans-Peter von Wachtstein of the Luftwaffe, who, as far as Schneider knew, had no SS connection whatsoever.

More than that, Schneider on several occasions had been ordered to surveille von Wachtstein by following him around Buenos Aires and by tapping his telephones in the embassy and at his apartment. This at least suggested that either Oberst Grüner or Ambassador von Lutzenberger—or both—were suspicious of him. Schneider himself thought there was something very strange in von Wachtstein's having come through the gunfire at Samborombón Bay unscathed when Oberführer Grüner and SS-Standartenführer Josef Goltz both had been shot to death.

But orders are orders and remain in effect until changed by competent authority—which in this case would be Ambassador von Lutzenberger, who had not even mentioned the protocol, much less any change in his duties, to Schneider since Grüner had been killed. Schneider had no choice but to follow protocol, which required him on being notified of the imminent arrival of a Lufthansa flight to notify the military attaché who, protocol dictated, "would provide further instructions as necessary."

He found Major von Wachtstein in his—rather than Oberst Grüner's—office. He was in civilian clothing, smoking a long thin cigar, and reading an American magazine, *Life.* The first time Schneider had seen von Wachtstein reading enemy reading material—a copy of the London *Times*—he had reported him to Grüner, who had told him that von Wachtstein was doing so because he was ordered to do so, to see if there was anything in *The Times* which would be of interest to the Abwehr.

When von Wachtstein finally looked up from the magazine and saw Schneider, Schneider threw out his arm in the Nazi salute and barked, "Heil Hitler!"

Von Wachtstein returned the salute, not very crisply.

"What is it, Schneider?"

"Herr Major, I have just learned of the soon arrival of a Condor at El Palomar."

"What's a 'soon arrival'? *When* is a 'soon arrival'? In the next ten minutes? Tomorrow? Friday?"

"Herr Major, I believe the aircraft is about to land at El Palomar."

"I was not aware we were expecting a flight. Were you?"

"I was not, Herr Major."

"You will go downstairs and wake up Günther Loche and tell him to bring a car around, Herr Schneider, while I go by the ambassador's office to tell him that you and I are on our way to El Palomar."

Günther Loche, a muscular twenty-two-year-old with a blond crew cut who von Wachtstein regarded as more zealous a Nazi than the Führer himself, was a civilian employee of the embassy. He had been born in Argentina to German parents who had immigrated to Argentina after the First World War. He had been Oberst Grüner's driver, and until a replacement for Grüner was assigned, he was von Wachtstein's driver.

"You will be going with me, Herr Major?" Schneider said.

Oberst Grüner had rarely done that.

"No. The way that works, Untersturmführer Schneider, is that inasmuch as I am a major and the acting military attaché, *you* will be going with *me*."

"*Jawohl, Herr Major,*" Schneider said, then threw out his arm again and barked, "Heil Hitler!"

Schneider suspected—he had no idea why—that von Wachtstein didn't like him. But he was not offended by von Wachtstein's curt—even rude—sarcasm. For one thing, an officer who had received the Knight's Cross of the Iron Cross for extraordinary valor in aerial combat was entitled to be a bit arrogant.

And for another, I was wrong; I should have been more precise than "soon arrival."

And I had no right to question his orders.

After the first call, Lufthansa Six Zero Two had attempted to contact the El Palomar tower once a minute for the next eleven minutes. Finally, the El Palomar tower operators had gotten through: "Lufthansa Six Zero Two, this is El Palomar."

The response had been immediate.

"El Palomar, Lufthansa Six Zero Two has entered Argentine airspace at the mouth of the River Plate. Altitude three thousand five hundred meters, indicated airspeed three eight zero kilometers. Estimate El Palomar in four zero minutes. Request approach and landing permission."

"Lufthansa Six Zero Two, El Palomar understands you are approximately one four zero kilometers east of this field at thirty-five hundred meters, estimating El Palomar in forty minutes."

"That is correct, El Palomar."

"Permission to approach El Palomar is granted. Begin descent to two thousand meters at this time. Contact again when ten minutes out."

"Six Zero Two understands descend to two thousand meters and contact when ten minutes out."

"Lufthansa Six Zero Two, that is correct."

"El Palomar, Lufthansa Six Zero Two."

"Go ahead, Six Zero Two."

"Six Zero Two is at two thousand meters, indicating three zero zero kilometers. Estimate El Palomar in ten minutes."

"El Palomar clears Lufthansa Six Zero Two as number one to land on runway Two Six. Winds are negligible. Report when you have El Palomar in sight."

Eleven minutes later, Lufthansa Six Zero Two was on the ground.

When von und zu Aschenburg shut down the Condor's engines, he noted in his log that he had fuel remaining for another hour and perhaps ten minutes of flight. That was unnerving, but he had landed here before with less than a half hour's remaining fuel.

When he looked out the window he saw that the reception committee from the German embassy included—in addition to that SS asshole Schneider, who always met Condor flights—an old friend, Major Hans-Peter Baron von Wachtstein.

Almost a decade earlier, an eighteen-year-old Hauptgefreiter (Sergeant) Wachtstein had flown a Messerschmitt Bf 109B on Oberleutnant von und zu Aschenburg's wing in the Condor Legion in Spain, and later a Hauptfeldwebel (Flight Sergeant) Wachtstein had flown a Messerschmitt Bf 109E on Major von und zu Aschenburg's wing in the war in France, the Battle of Britain, and over Berlin.

Oberstleutnant von und zu Aschenburg had presented a newly promoted Oberleutnant Baron von Wachtstein to their Führer on the occasion of von Wachtstein's award of the Knight's Cross of the Iron Cross for extraordinary valor in aerial combat over Berlin while flying a Focke-Wulf 190 as one of von und zu Aschenburg's squadron commanders.

So long as he had been an enlisted man, von Wachtstein had not used the aristocratic "von" and his noble rank, so as not to embarrass his father. This was the new Germany, of course, but there was still enough of the old Germany left that Generalleutnant Graf Karl-Friedrich von Wachtstein had been more than a little uncomfortable to have a son serving in the ranks.

It was another of the reasons that Oberst von und zu Aschenburg liked von Wachtstein.

He had several thoughts when he saw von Wachtstein.

Well, Hansel's out of the insanity in Germany, at least for right now. With a little luck, he can fly that Storch around the pampas until the war is over.

Good for him. He did his duty. Enough is enough.

And thank God he's here. I can give him his father's letter right here at the airport without the SS asshole being the wiser.

Otherwise, I'd have had to carry it around until I could get it to him, and that might have been—hell, would have been—dangerous.

Von und zu Aschenburg turned to First Officer Nabler.

"If you will deal with the paperwork, Nabler, I will deal with our distinguished passenger."

"Jawohl, Herr Oberst," Nabler replied crisply.

If there was room, he'd have clicked his heels and given me the Nazi salute.

As von und zu Aschenburg walked past the flight engineer's station, Flight Engineer Hover met his eyes and said, "I make it an hour and five minutes of remaining fuel, Herr Oberst."

"What shall we do, Willi, burn it off going back to Montevideo?"

Von und zu Aschenburg pushed open the door from the cockpit and entered the passenger compartment. There were twenty-five seats, eight rows of three—a single seat on the left of the aisle and two on the right—plus a single seat next to the door to the toilet in the rear, but there were only thirteen passengers plus the steward.

Von und zu Aschenburg had seated Cranz in one of what he thought of as the best seats on the Condor, then told the steward that nobody was to be seated with him.

The best seats were just behind the trailing edge of the wing, so there was a good view downward from their windows; they were near the center of gravity of the aircraft, so there was less movement; and they were only a few steps from the toilet, which was located at the rear of the passenger compartment.

There were three of these best seats, one on the left side of the aisle and two on the right. Herr Cranz was sitting in the window seat on the right. He smiled charmingly at von und zu Aschenburg.

"Dare I hope our flight is really over, Kapitän?"

Von und zu Aschenburg smiled back.

"There are representatives from the embassy waiting for you, Herr Cranz, so whenever you're ready—"

"I saw Baron von Wachtstein. Who's the young one?"

He knows von Wachtstein? I wonder how.

"That's Untersturmführer Schneider," von und zu Aschenburg said. "He comes to take charge of the diplomatic pouch. Today, pouches, four of them." He paused. *Let's get it out in the open; see what happens.* "You know my old comrade von Wachtstein, do you, Herr Cranz?"

Cranz smiled charmingly again.

"Your old comrade, Kapitän?"

Why do I think—hell, know—*that you know all about Hansel and me, and are simply playing dumb?*

"Hansel and I flew Me-109Bs with the Condor Legion," von und zu Aschenburg said.

" 'Hansel'?" Cranz parroted, still smiling. "Is *Hansel* in keeping with the dignity that comes to an officer decorated with the Knight's Cross of the Iron Cross?"

"Only if one has known the holder of the Knight's Cross since he was an eighteen-year-old hauptgefreiter who had to shave only every third day, Herr Cranz."

"You're right, you're right," Cranz said. "That would have a certain bearing, wouldn't it?"

He smiled once again, then got out of his seat and followed von und zu Aschenburg to the door.

The instant von und zu Aschenburg stepped onto the shallow flight of roll-up steps, Untersturmführer Schneider threw out his arm in the Nazi salute and barked, "Heil Hitler!"

Major Hans-Peter Baron von Wachtstein was so surprised to see Cranz standing in the door behind him that he almost didn't salute at all.

Oh, shit! What's that bastard doing here?

The first time von Wachtstein had seen the affable, charming SS officer was in Lisbon in early May.

As soon as word of what happened at Samborombón Bay had reached Berlin, an investigation personally directed by Reichsführer-SS Heinrich Himmler had begun. Himmler's adjutant, Brigadeführer Manfred von Deitzberg—wearing the uniform of a Wehrmacht generalmajor—and Sturmbannführer

Erich Raschner, von Deitzberg's deputy, had been on the next Condor flight to Buenos Aires.

Within twenty-four hours of their arrival, von Deitzberg had ordered First Secretary Anton Gradny-Sawz, Sturmbannführer Werner von Tresmarck, the senior SS officer in Uruguay, and von Wachtstein to be on the returning Condor flight, "to assist in the investigation."

They had all understood that they were the primary suspects for being the traitor responsible for the disaster. Proof of that had come when their Condor flight had been met in Lisbon by Cranz and a navy officer, Korvettenkapitän Karl Boltitz, who immediately began the interrogation. The interrogation had been no less thorough—or frightening—because it had been conducted with smiles . . . a conversation between loyal officers of the German Reich simply trying to deduce what had happened.

Cranz and Boltitz had shown up a week later in Augsburg. Cranz was in charge of the elaborate funerals of Oberst Grüner and Standartenführer Goltz. By then, von Wachtstein had decided that while the SS officer was far more charming than the naval officer, he was also the most dangerous.

When von Wachtstein had been ordered back to Argentina, he thought he had seen the last of Cranz. And now here Cranz was in Argentina, where he was liable to find out not only that von Wachtstein was the man responsible for letting the enemy know what had been about to happen at Samborombón Bay but that Boltitz and Ambassador von Lutzenberger were also actively engaged in treason against the Führer and his Thousand-Year Reich.

Cranz was traveling on a diplomatic passport, so there were virtually no immigration or customs formalities.

Cranz smiled at the Argentine official who returned his passport, saluted, then, smiling even more broadly, walked up to Schneider and von Wachtstein.

Schneider gave another stiff-armed Nazi salute. Cranz ignored it and put out his hand to von Wachtstein.

"I am flattered that you could tear yourself away from your bride to meet me, Peter," he said.

"Well, for one thing, Herr Obersturmbannführer, I didn't know you were coming," von Wachtstein said.

Schneider assumed an even more rigid posture, as befitting a junior SS officer in the presence of a senior one.

"Yes, that's true, isn't it?" Cranz said. "And, Peter, I have been seconded to the foreign ministry. It would be best if you forgot my SS rank for the time being."

"Yes, sir," von Wachtstein said, then turned to von und zu Aschenburg. "It is always a pleasure to see you, Herr Oberst."

"You are only saying that, Hansel, because I am no longer your commanding officer."

"The Herr Oberst is absolutely correct," von Wachtstein said.

Cranz laughed delightedly.

"But I must tell you both," von Wachtstein said, "that I met you because I have the duty. If I did not, Schneider here would have been your welcoming committee. But all that aside, welcome to Argentina."

Von und zu Aschenburg thought: *Well, why am I surprised that the charming Herr Cranz is actually Obersturmbannführer Cranz? He showed up at Tempelhof in an SS Mercedes.*

But why isn't Hansel awed by the Herr Obersturmbannführer?

Is that stupidity, or on purpose?

"What's this about a bride, Hansel?" he asked.

"You hadn't heard about that?" Cranz put in.

Von und zu Aschenburg shook his head.

"One of Argentina's great beauties found our man irresistible," Cranz went on, pleased with himself. "Or was it the other way around, Peter?"

"Modesty obviously precludes my answering that question," von Wachtstein said, then: "Herr Cranz, may I present Untersturmführer Schneider?"

Schneider clicked his heels and rendered yet another crisply perfect Nazi straight-arm salute. Cranz returned it casually.

"I understand you're responsible for the diplomatic pouch—*pouches*—Schneider?"

"I have that privilege, Herr Obersturmbannführer."

"Didn't you hear what I just said to Major von Wachtstein?" Cranz snapped. "Do not use my rank again!"

There was a moment's silence, enough to give von Wachtstein time to think, *That little sonofabitch is so scared of Cranz he can't talk!*

Cranz went on, unpleasantly: "Then why don't you get them? I want to get to the embassy as quickly as possible."

"Jawohl, meine Herr," Schneider said, and saluted again. He hurried onto the Condor.

"What did you mean before, Peter, when you said you 'had the duty'?" Cranz asked.

"The embassy protocol stipulates that the military attaché is next in line when the first secretary is not able to perform his duties," von Wachtstein explained. "Gradny-Sawz is in Montevideo. I'm the acting military attaché."

"What's Gradny-Sawz doing in Montevideo?" Cranz asked.

"I have no idea."

"And if Ambassador von Lutzenberger ordered him back here, right now, how long would that take?"

Von Wachtstein looked at his watch and then at the sky.

"If I left right now, as long as it would take to fly back and forth to Montevideo," he said. "That presumes the telephone lines are in, and that First Secretary Gradny-Sawz would be at the airport there when I arrived."

"You have an aircraft immediately available?"

Von Wachtstein pointed to the hangar where the Storch was parked.

"This solution is possible?" Cranz asked.

"Possible, but not likely," von Wachtstein said.

"Why not? The telephone lines might be out?"

"That, too. But what I was thinking is that the duties of the first secretary probably will keep him from getting to the airport in Carrasco in time for us to take off and make the return flight in daylight. And he does not like to fly at night."

"But Ambassador Lutzenberger will have ordered him to return," Cranz challenged.

"So what I think would likely happen," von Wachtstein said, "after he couldn't make it to the airport in time for me to fly him back here today, would be that he would say, 'Now that it's impossible to fly, the obvious thing to do is take the boat. That will get me to Buenos Aires earlier than I could flying with you in the morning.' Actually, he's not enthusiastic about flying in the Storch at all."

"You're not suggesting that First Secretary Gradny-Sawz is afraid of flying?" Cranz said.

"Perish the thought," von Wachtstein said, his smile making it perfectly clear that that was exactly what he was suggesting. "If you have to see him right now, I could fly you over there."

Cranz did not reply directly. Instead, he said, almost as if he were thinking aloud, "I have to see everybody, but not necessarily tonight. Generalmajor von Deitzberg is here?"

"No, sir. The Generalmajor and Sturmbannführer Raschner went with Gradny-Sawz to Montevideo."

"Do you know why?"

"No, sir."

"Peter, if the ambassador should send for them, how would they return?"

"By the boat."

"Tell me about that."

"There is an eleven P.M. boat from Montevideo to Buenos Aires. It's usually an eight- or nine-hour ride. There're cabins on the boat, and a bar and a nice restaurant."

"I can see where First Secretary Gradny-Sawz would prefer that to flying in that little airplane," Cranz said, then added, "And Boltitz? Where is he?"

"Also in Montevideo. If Ambassador Lutzenberger hadn't told me how much he needs me to help run the embassy, I would think that no one likes me."

Cranz laughed. He put his arm around von Wachtstein's shoulder.

"I like you, Hansel," he said. "And Oberst von und zu Aschenburg likes you. Isn't that so, Herr Oberst?"

"Can I have some time to think about that?" von und zu Aschenburg said.

Cranz laughed again.

"I can see why you're friends," he said. "Well, then, let's go to the embassy. I can report to Ambassador Lutzenberger and see what he thinks is the best way to get everyone together."

Cranz looked impatiently at the door of the Condor.

"What's taking him so long?"

[FOUR]
The Embassy of the German Reich
Avenue Córdoba
Buenos Aires, Argentina
1735 12 July 1943

"Where did you meet Herr Cranz, Hansel?" Dieter von und zu Aschenburg asked after von Wachtstein had led him into his office and waved him into a chair.

"Charming man, isn't he?" von Wachtstein said, pointing to the light fixture on the ceiling and then at the telephones on his desk.

Von und zu Aschenburg nodded his understanding.

"I met him when I was in Germany," von Wachtstein said.

"You mean recently?" von und zu Aschenburg asked. He looked around the room, then motioned for von Wachtstein to come close.

"In May," von Wachtstein said.

"I didn't know you'd been in Germany, Peter."

"Oh, yes."

Von und zu Aschenburg handed him a thick, airmail-weight envelope and mouthed the words *Your father.*

Peter took the envelope and mouthed, *Thank you, Dieter.*

"Doing what?" von und zu Aschenburg asked, as von Wachtstein walked across the room and sat behind his desk.

"Apropos of absolutely nothing, have you heard that there is a new Messerschmitt with a new kind of engine?"

"When I'm not an airline pilot, I'm a Luftwaffe officer. General Galland was kind enough to show me what he's doing in Augsburg. Unfortunately, I was unable to convince my superiors that I could make a greater contribution to the final victory with a squadron of Me-262s than I am flying a transport back and forth here."

"I know exactly how you feel," von Wachtstein said. "I was in Augsburg and had just passed my check ride in the Me-262 when I was sent back here."

Von und zu Aschenburg looked at him, asking with his eyes if that was the truth, rather than having been said for the benefit of the hidden microphones. Von Wachtstein nodded.

"That's unusual. Why? What are you doing here that's so important?" He stopped himself, then went on. "I should not have asked that."

"What's more than a little embarrassing, Dieter, is the reason I was sent back."

"Which you cannot tell me for reasons of security?" It was more a statement for the recorder than a question.

"Which I don't want to go any further than this room."

Von und zu Aschenburg nodded his understanding.

"I was about to become a father."

"So they got you out of Germany to keep you from an unsuitable marriage? One that would embarrass the Luftwaffe?"

"I was, *I am*, about to be a father *here*," von Wachtstein said.

"I don't understand."

"When the lady who is now my wife learned that she was in the family way, she went to her priest, a Jesuit named Welner. He went to Colonel Juan Domingo Perón—"

"Who's he?"

"One of the more important colonels. And the least important colonels in Argentina, I've learned, are at least as important as one of our Generalmajors. Tío Juan Domingo, as my wife calls Colonel Perón, is 'special assistant' to General Ramírez, the president. I'd say that he's the second or third most powerful man in Argentina."

"And?"

"Anyway, Alicia went to her Jesuit, the Jesuit went to Perón, and Perón went to Lutzenberger. Then Lutzenberger sent a cable to Berlin, and it was decided at the highest levels that I could make a greater contribution to the final victory by coming back here and doing the right thing as a Luftwaffe officer and gentleman—marrying the lady, in other words—than I could shooting down B-17s flying an Me-262."

"Somehow, Hansel, I'm getting the idea they didn't have to march you to the altar at the point of a bayonet."

"I love her, Dieter. I really love her."

"Then what's the problem?"

"I should be flying Me-262s, and I know it, but I'm glad I'm here."

"You can have a clear conscience, Major," von und zu Aschenburg said. "You are an officer doing what you were ordered to do."

"So I have been telling myself. Sometimes I almost believe it."

There was a knock at the door, and before von Wachtstein could open his mouth, it opened and Cranz came in.

I wonder if the sonofabitch was hoping to catch us at something—anything?

Well, when he listens to the wire recording of what Dieter and I said to each other, he won't hear anything he shouldn't.

"Ambassador Lutzenberger," Cranz announced, "has decided the best way to handle things will be for everybody in Uruguay to come here on the overnight boat. Which means that leaves my evening free. I hope that you and the Baroness von Wachtstein are free to have dinner with me. I'd really like to meet her. And I'm sure Kapitän von und zu Aschenburg would."

Von Wachtstein nodded, but said, "Unfortunately, my wife—who is known here as Señora Carzino-Cormano de von Wachtstein, but who I suspect would love having you call her 'Baroness'—is at her mother's estancia. And as I have the duty—"

"And going there would be out of the question?" Cranz interrupted.

"I have the duty until Gradny-Sawz returns, unfortunately."

"Ambassador Lutzenberger says there's no reason Schneider can't fill in for you tonight," Cranz said. "'Señora Carzino-Cormano de von Wachtstein'? That's a mouthful, isn't it?"

"Think how bad it would be if she'd married Dieter here," von Wachtstein said. " 'Señora Carzino-Cormano de von *und zu* Aschenburg.' Now, *that's* a mouthful."

"It's a good thing you're buying dinner, Hansel, or you'd pay for that," von und zu Aschenburg said.

Cranz smiled at both of them.

"Or would that be a real imposition, Peter?" Cranz finally asked. "Having von und zu Aschenburg and myself at your mother-in-law's home?"

"I'm sure it would be no problem," von Wachtstein said. "Actually, unless you really want to go to a hotel, we could spend the night out there. There's plenty of room."

"If you're sure it would be no imposition . . ."

"Let me call them and let them know we're coming," von Wachtstein said, and reached for the telephone.

[FIVE]
Estancia Santa Catalina
Near Pila, Buenos Aires Province
2215 12 July 1943

That afternoon, when Don Cletus Frade, El Patrón of Estancia San Pedro y San Pablo, on hearing that El Coronel Juan Domingo Perón had found time in his busy schedule to accept the kind invitation of Doña Claudia de Carzino-Cormano of Estancia Santa Catalina to a small, "just family" dinner, Frade had taken several steps to make sure things went smoothly.

For one thing, he told his wife, Señora Dorotea Mallín de Frade, to make sure Señorita Isabela Carzino-Cormano, the elder daughter of Doña Claudia de Carzino-Cormano, was aware that not only were they coming to the dinner for Tío Juan Domingo but that he probably was going to bring at least one American officer with him.

"El Bitcho," as Clete thought of Isabela, not only disliked him intensely on a personal basis but was more anti-American than Mussolini. With just a little bit of luck, he hoped, El Bitcho would suddenly remember a previous engagement which, sadly, would preclude her presence at the "just family" dinner with Tío Juan Domingo.

Dorotea had done what her husband asked, but it hadn't worked.

When they had driven over to Estancia Santa Catalina in time for the cocktail tour, El Bitcho was there in the sitting room, dressed in black, and again playing the tragic role of widow-in-everything-but-name of the late Capitán Jorge Alejandro Duarte, who had fallen nobly on the field of battle at Stalingrad.

Clete knew that his uncle, Humberto Duarte, while deeply mourning the loss of his only son, did not hold Clete's father—who had arranged for Jorge to be an aerial "observer" with Von Paulus's Sixth Army in Russia—much less Clete responsible for what had happened.

But Isabela sure as hell made it clear that she did. Jorge had been killed by the godless Russian Communists, who were allied with the Americans. Cletus Frade was an American. It was as simple as that.

When Clete and Dorotea had walked into the sitting room of the big house at Estancia Santa Catalina, Isabela, sniffling into a lace handkerchief, had walked out in an air of high drama.

Custom required that Clete embrace and kiss everybody. Kissing Doña Claudia and Alicia von Wachtstein posed no problems. Kissing his Uncle Humberto was, as usual, a little awkward. Kissing his Aunt Beatrice made him both uncomfortable and a little ashamed of himself. That she was playing with far less than a full deck wasn't her fault, obviously, but the cold fact was that kissing her made him feel uncomfortable.

But not as uncomfortable as kissing Tío Juan Domingo had made him feel. Notwithstanding the fact that he had been his father's best friend and the best man at his parents' wedding, he couldn't stand the sonofabitch.

To help get himself through the greeting ritual that experience had taught him was inevitable, Clete had told himself that he was behaving like a child. He certainly could not afford to act as such, and reminded himself that Perón had done nothing to him and had, in fact, done things *for* him, and the last thing he should do now, when he needed Perón's influence to get the airline off the ground, was piss off the bastard.

There were two people in the sitting room he was not expected to kiss and didn't. One of them was Gonzalo Delgano, a short, muscular man of about forty, and the other a bespectacled, slim, fair-skinned man of about the same age whose name was Kurt Welner. Both of them were wearing well-cut suits and striped neckties.

"How are you?" Frade said, offering Delgano his hand. "More important, what do I call you? 'Señor'? Or 'Major'?"

"I could ask just about the same thing of you," Delgano replied. "But how about 'Gonzalo,' Don Cletus?"

"How about dropping the 'Don'?"

"Agreed. Good to see you again, Cletus."

Frade next offered his hand to Welner, who, when he had seen Clete kissing Perón, had smiled approvingly, causing Clete to give him the finger behind Perón's back. Smiling broadly, Father Kurt Welner, S.J.—who only rarely wore the clerical collar associated with his profession—had countered the gesture by making the motions of a priest benignly blessing a beloved member of his flock.

Welner had been Clete's father's friend and confessor; Clete wasn't sure which had been the more important role. Welner was also the confessor for the Duartes and the Carzino-Cormanos. He wasn't sure what Welner's relationship with Perón was, although Perón treated him with great respect.

"What's the latest from Rome?" Clete asked.

" 'Love thy neighbor as thyself,' " Welner replied unctuously.

They both laughed. Claudia looked dismayed.

"Why don't we go in the library and get our business out of the way?" Humberto Duarte suggested.

All the men—including Father Welner, which Clete thought was a little unusual—plus Doña Claudia de Carzino-Cormano went into the library, where a long table was just about covered with blue folders.

Everyone sat down but Duarte, who stood at the head of the table.

"Aside from a name for this enterprise," he said, "I think everything is ready for signatures. And since Cletus is going to be the majority stockholder, I suggest that he has the right to name it. Once he does, I think you should all read the documents carefully, and if you find nothing wrong with them, sign them."

Everyone looked at Frade.

"I first thought of calling it 'Trans-Andean Airways,' " Frade said. "You know, over the Andes to Santiago. But then I found out there are mountains between here and there that are higher than seven thousand meters. And 'Through and Around the Andes Airways' doesn't have the same appeal, does it?"

There was polite laughter. Frade considered Major Delgano's smile as genuine, and thought, *The only thing I have against him is that he's an intelligence officer, and God knows I'm in no position to hold that against anybody.*

"How about 'South American Airways'?" Frade went on. "It is going to be international."

"I think that's fine," Claudia said.

"I don't think el señor Trippe's going to like it," Colonel Perón said, "but I do."

Why am I surprised that he knows Juan Trippe owns Pan American Airways?

Because you're not listening to Humberto, Clete, who keeps warning you Tío Juan is a lot smarter than you give him credit for being.

"We're not a Sociedad Anónima until everything has been signed," Duarte said, "so a vote isn't necessary. When everyone has signed, it will be for the establishment of South American Airways, S.A. Agreed?"

No one said anything, but no one raised any objection.

Ten minutes later, all parties involved having signed the necessary documents, South American Airways, S.A., was in business.

"And now, Father Welner," Duarte said, "would you ask God's blessing on this enterprise?"

Welner stood up, and everyone bowed their heads.

"Dear Lord, we ask . . ."

Clete didn't pay much attention to the prayer. He was thinking that the Roman Catholic Church—or at least the Society of Jesus of the Roman Catholic Church—now knew as much about South American Airways, S.A., as any of the investors or officers.

When they all filed back into the sitting room, champagne and hors d'oeuvres were waiting for them.

And moments later—as Clete thought she probably would—Isabela made a dramatic reentrance and resumed giving her quite credible portrayal of a young woman courageously bearing up as well as she could under the tragic circumstances.

She had just been "talked into" having a glass of champagne by Father Kurt when Clete learned that the other steps he had taken to ensure they would have Perón's undivided attention while discussing and ultimately signing the documents for the airlines idea had also gone awry.

The telephone wires to Estancia Santa Catalina from the junction box of the government-owned and -operated telephone service in Pila crossed Estancia San Pedro y San Pablo. It had not been hard at all for Chief Schultz to go to several of the repeater stations—there were nine in all—and provide means for both eavesdropping on all calls on both estancias and a means for the lines "to go out."

The latter was more sophisticated than simply breaking the connection. Schultz and Sergeant O'Sullivan had rigged a "random noise generator" to the circuitry. Clete had no idea what it was, but he had seen how it worked. When switched on, it produced on the telephone line what sounded like static—what most would describe as "a bad connection"—and effectively prohibited conversation.

More important, it fooled the technicians of the government telephone service into believing that "there was trouble on the line or in one of the repeater stations" rather than a severed line caused by a fallen pole, a failed transformer, a shorted insulator, et cetera.

Clete had ordered that there was to be "trouble on the line" to Estancia Santa Catalina from the moment El Coronel Perón (or more likely his chauffeur or bodyguard) hung up after reporting to the Edificio Libertador that Perón had arrived safely at Estancia Santa Catalina. The line was to remain out until they heard from Don Cletus—or one of the switchboards—to turn off the trouble/random-noise generator.

The system worked perfectly. As soon as Colonel Perón's bodyguard had notified the Edificio Libertador that the Secretary of Work & Social Welfare had arrived safely at Estancia Santa Catalina, and hung up, Chief Schultz had turned on the random-noise generator.

The unplanned result of this was that when Major Hans-Peter von Wachtstein attempted to call his wife from the German embassy to ask her to tell her mother that he was coming for dinner—with two guests—the operator reported that there was trouble on the line and suggested he try to place the call later.

Two hours later, when a black Mercedes touring car bearing diplomatic license plates came racing down the road from Pila and entered upon Estancia San Pedro y San Pablo, the gaucho on duty there quickly got on the telephone, shut off the random-noise generator, and told the switchboard operator to quickly connect him with either El Jefe or Don Cletus.

He got El Jefe first. El Jefe shut down the random-noise generator and caused the telephone to ring in the sitting room of the big house on Estancia Santa Catalina. There the telephone was passed to Don Cletus.

"Heads up, boss," Chief Schultz reported. "There's a Mercedes with diplomatic tags and four people in it headed your way. The gaucho at the gate says that it looks like Doña Alicia's German is in the front seat."

Clete put the telephone handset back in the cradle. He saw that just about everybody was looking at him.

"Señora Carzino-Cormano de von Wachtstein," Frade said, "it would appear that your wandering husband is about to join this festive occasion. He and three other people."

"Three other people?" Alicia asked.

Clete shrugged, and when his wife looked at him questioningly, he shrugged again.

"Hans-Peter is coming?" El Coronel Perón said. "Wonderful!"

[SIX]

"Turn the lights off and stop right here," Major Hans-Peter Freiherr von Wachtstein ordered sharply.

Günther Loche braked the Mercedes so heavily that it skidded before coming to a stop. Both Obersturmbannführer Cranz and Oberst von und zu Aschenburg slid off the rear seat.

"What is it?" Cranz demanded.

"It would seem we have guests I didn't know about," von Wachtstein said.

Cranz looked out the windshield at the line of cars drawn up in the drive of the big house. There was a shiny new black Rolls-Royce, a black 1940 Packard 280 convertible coupe, an olive-drab Mercedes, a red-and-black Horch touring car, and a 1942 Buick Roadmaster.

"That Horch is really the last thing I would have expected to see out here in the middle of nowhere," Commercial Attaché Cranz said.

"It belongs to Cletus Frade, Karl," Peter von Wachtstein said. "It was his father's. His father was riding in it when he was murdered."

"You mean Frade is here?" Cranz asked.

"Either he or his wife. I would suspect both. Shall we turn around?"

"What is he doing here?"

"I would suspect having dinner. His wife and my wife are very close," von Wachtstein said. "They grew up together. And my wife knew I had the duty and wouldn't be here to make things awkward."

"And who else would you say is here?"

"The open Packard is Father Welner's. He's the family's Jesuit. The Rolls belongs to the parents of Hauptmann Duarte, who died at Stalingrad. They're

Frade's aunt and uncle. The army Mercedes is almost certainly Colonel Perón's. And the Buick is my mother-in-law's."

"And her relation to Frade?"

"Very close. She looks on him as a son."

When Cranz didn't reply for a long moment, von Wachtstein asked again, "Shall we turn around? If we go in there, it's going to be more than a little awkward."

"You don't get along with Frade?"

"For some reason," von Wachtstein said more than a little sarcastically, "he thinks we Germans were responsible for the murder of his father."

Again, Cranz didn't reply for a long moment. Then he said, "Peter, we are in a neutral country. We are gentlemen, and I think we may presume that Frade will do nothing to embarrass a woman who thinks of him as her son. I had hoped to get to know Colonel Perón while I was here, and at least get a look at Señor Frade. Fortune may well be smiling on us. Loche, put the lights back on and drive up to the entrance."

"May I ask who these people are?" von und zu Aschenburg said.

"Colonel Juan Domingo Perón is a very important Argentine army officer," Cranz began, "known to be sympathetic to National Socialism, and a man who a number of people believe will become even more important in Argentina. Frade is the son of the late Oberst Frade, who, until he was assassinated by parties unknown, many thought would be the next president of Argentina. His son, like you and Peter, is a fighter pilot of some distinction. You'll have a lot in common. But be careful, please, Oberst von und zu Aschenburg. He is also the head of the American OSS in Argentina, and a very dangerous man."

"I'm not good at this sort of thing, Cranz," von und zu Aschenburg said. "Why don't I just wait in the car?"

"I understand your feelings, Herr Oberst. Let me go off at a tangent. May I have your permission, Herr Oberst, to address you by your Christian name? And that you call me 'Karl'? And that, especially, both of you remember not to use my rank?"

"In other words, you think I should go in there with you?"

"I would be very grateful, Dieter, if you would."

Von Wachtstein kissed his wife and then his mother-in-law on their cheeks.

"Mama," he said to Claudia Carzino-Cormano, "I had no idea you were having guests. I tried to call, but the lines were out again. . . ."

"This is your home," she said in Spanish, and put out her hand to von und zu Aschenburg. "Welcome to our home. I'm Claudia Carzino-Cormano."

Von und zu Aschenburg took her hand, clicked his heels, bowed, and kissed her hand.

"Please pardon the intrusion, la señora," he said in Spanish. "Hansel and I are old friends, and I really wanted to meet his bride. My name is Dieter von und zu Aschenburg."

" 'Hansel'? As in Hansel and Gretel?"

"In German, it means 'Little Hans,' señora," he replied. "I have known him that long."

"You'll forgive me, señor, I don't recognize your uniform."

"I have the honor to be a pilot for Lufthansa, señora. We just arrived, and I haven't had time to change out of my uniform."

"So you're not a soldier?"

"An airline pilot, señora."

Cletus Frade thought: *In a pig's ass you're not a soldier; Lufthansa is entirely owned by the Luftwaffe.*

And who's the other guy? He obviously doesn't speak Spanish. His smile is more than a little strained.

"And how should I call you?"

Try "Oberst," Claudia.

They don't let second lieutenants fly the Condor.

"I would be honored, señora, if you bring yourself to call me Dieter."

"And you will please call me Claudia," she said, and turned to Cranz. "Welcome to our home, señor. And you are?"

"I regret, madam, I do not speak Spanish," Cranz said in German.

"He says he's sorry he doesn't speak Spanish, Claudia," Frade offered helpfully in English.

"That's not a problem, Cletus," she said in German. "Because I do speak a little German."

"My name is Karl Cranz, *gnädige Frau*," Cranz said. "I'm newly assigned to the German embassy here. As the commercial attaché. Please forgive our intrusion."

Frade glanced at Major Delgano and saw in his eyes that he didn't believe that "commercial attaché" announcement, either.

Doña Claudia said, "And your mother is Austrian or you have spent some time there. *Gnädige Frau* is pure Viennese."

"Guilty, *gnädige Frau*. My mother is a Viennese. You know Vienna?"

"I once spent a wonderful month there while visiting a friend who was in school in Germany. Let me introduce the others. . . ."

When they went in to dinner, Clete saw that Claudia had not only given some thought as to who would sit where but had also somehow arranged for name cards—even for the unexpected guests—to be placed on the table in silver holders so that everybody would know where to sit.

She sat at one end of the long table. As the guest of honor, Perón was seated at her right. Peter von Wachtstein was seated at the other end, apparently signifying his new role as the man of the house, separated from his mother-in-law by two candelabra and an enormous bowl of flowers.

Cranz was seated across from Perón, and von und zu Aschenburg was seated next to von Wachtstein, with Father Welner next to him, and Isabela next to him. Clete was near the middle of the table, beside Alicia von Wachtstein and across the table from his Aunt Beatrice and Uncle Humberto. Dorotea was next to Humberto, and Delgano sat beside her.

Clete was impressed with Claudia's seating arrangements. They were designed, he decided, to provide an ambiance where polite conversation would be encouraged, and the opposite—verbal battles between, for example, himself and Isabela—be made difficult.

The only interesting thing Clete noticed during the course of dinner was that Cranz was really charming both Claudia and Perón and that both seemed to like it.

There's something about that sonofabitch that bothers me.

After dinner, the gentlemen retired to the library for brandy and cigars. Over the fireplace hung a huge oil portrait of a tall, heavyset man in the full dress uniform of the Colonel Commanding the Húsares de Pueyrredón Cavalry Regiment.

"Would it be indiscreet of me to guess that's the late Señor Carzino-Cormano?" Cranz asked. "And what is that marvelous uniform?"

"That's my father, Señor Cranz," Clete said in German. "The late Oberst Jorge Guillermo Frade."

"A fine-looking man," Cranz said.

"What's that phrase? 'Tragically cut down in the prime of his life'?"

"In one of those interesting coincidences, Captain von und zu Aschen-burg," Colonel Juan D. Perón said hurriedly and in Spanish, changing the direction of the conversation, "we were talking, just before you arrived, about airlines."

"Really?"

"We just started one," Perón said. "South American Airways."

This was translated by von und zu Aschenburg for Cranz.

Cranz replied, "How interesting!"

Von und zu Aschenburg smiled, then made the translation of that for Cranz into Spanish: "Herr Cranz said he's a bit surprised that aircraft would be available to start an airline."

Clete smiled warmly at Cranz.

"Actually, that's why I'm going to start an airline," Frade said. "I found out that we—that's my American half talking; I'm half American, half Argentine—that is to say, we North Americans have a bunch of brand-new Lockheed Lodestars that nobody wants and that South American Airways can buy cheap."

That translation was made. Cranz smiled but did not reply.

"Forgive me for saying this, Señor Frade," von und zu Aschenburg said, "but I would be just a little wary of airplanes that can be had cheaply because nobody wants them. Are you a pilot?"

"I've flown a little," Clete said.

"What kind of airplanes?"

"Mostly Piper Cubs, planes like that—"

"Cletus, I just can't let that pass," Perón interrupted. He turned to von und zu Aschenburg. "The truth, Captain von und zu Aschenburg, is that before he was medically discharged from the American Corps of Marines, Cletus distinguished himself as a fighter pilot in the war in the Pacific. His late father"—he waved his arm dramatically at the oil portrait of the late Colonel Frade—"my best friend, may he rest in peace, was very, very proud of him."

"You weren't flying Piper Cubs in the Pacific, were you, Señor Frade?" von und zu Aschenburg asked.

"Actually, yeah. Sometimes I did. We used them like you use your Storch, for artillery spotting, things like that. Other times, I flew Grumman F4F Wildcats."

"He was an ace," Perón proclaimed. "And, in a situation the details of which I'm not at liberty to discuss, he recently applied his extraordinary flying skills and demonstrated his courage here in Argentina, the land of his birth. His father would be, as I am, very proud to say that he has earned the respect and admiration of many senior officials, including our president."

As von und zu Aschenburg translated this for Cranz, Cranz looked between Frade and von Wachtstein.

Frade thought: *I'm sure I'm right. The airline pilot is a good guy, and the diplomat a bad one. A bad one and a dangerous one. Why do I know that?*

And thank you, Tío Juan Domingo, for that passionate little speech.

While I am tempted to blush, the bottom line is that you have told these guys, and one or the other of them—probably both—is going to pass it on to somebody in the German embassy that Don Cletus Frade has many friends in high places, and that should be taken into consideration the next time somebody suggests killing him would solve a lot of problems.

Cranz spoke to von und zu Aschenburg, who then translated: "Mr. Cranz . . . Karl . . . remains curious about the availability of transport aircraft for a civilian enterprise in . . . in the present conditions."

"The present conditions" meaning the war, right?

Oh, I'll love answering this one.

"From what I've been told," Frade said, "what aircraft are available are those the Air Forces or our airlines don't need. I don't think there's any DC-3s or -4s available, is what I mean. What is available are some Lockheed Lodestars nobody really has any need for. And our airlines don't need them either. They're pretty much settled on the DC-3. But the Lockheed's fine for our purposes."

Cranz said something else in German. Frade understood him to ask "How soon?" but waited before replying until von und zu Aschenburg had paraphrased what Cranz had said in Spanish. The delay was ostensibly for the benefit of the others, though it also allowed Frade to fully consider an appropriate answer.

Frade looked at Cranz and said: "Right away, as a matter of fact. El Señor Delgano and I will start looking for facilities in Mendoza and Uruguay in the next couple of days."

"You already have the airplanes?" von und zu Aschenburg asked.

"No. But I have a Lodestar, which I will rent to Through and Around— excuse me, *South American Airways*—to get us started."

Then he stood up.

"I have to be going," he said. "It's been a pleasure meeting you, Captain, and Mr. Creez, was it?"

"*Cranz*," Cranz said carefully.

Frade shook hands with Father Welner and Delgano, then kissed Claudia, Perón, and Duarte, and then nodded at the Germans as he walked out of the library.

He stopped in the corridor outside the library.

"You have to understand, Herr Cranz," he overheard Juan Domingo Perón say in German, "that he lost his father to a very cruel and unwise decision by one of your SS officers."

"I had no idea," Cranz said, mustering a tone that he hoped sounded like genuine surprise.

"I think the best way to deal with that subject," Doña Alicia said, "which is painful to all of us, is not to discuss it."

VI

[ONE]
Office of the Director
Office of Strategic Services
National Institutes of Health Building
Washington, D.C.
0930 29 June 1943

"Why is it, Alex," OSS Director William J. Donovan said, looking up from his desk to meet Colonel Alejandro Graham's eyes, "that I suspect I'm not going to like that cat-who-has-just-swallowed-the-canary smile on your face?"

"Bill, you know that I always love to bring you proof that one of your orders has been carried out with alacrity."

"Try telling that to your man Frade."

"As a matter of fact, I have just heard from Major Frade."

"And you're smiling. So what's the bad news?"

Graham extended a message fresh from the radio room. Donovan snatched it from his hand and scanned it. His eyes widened and his eyebrows rose as he read it more thoroughly:

PRIORITY

TOP SECRET LINDBERGH
DUPLICATION FORBIDDEN

FROM TEX

MSG NO 205 0405 GREENWICH 13 JULY 1943

TO AGGIE

REFERENCE AIRLINE

HUMBERTO DUARTE, HEREAFTER TÍO HANK, MANAGING
DIRECTOR, BANCO DE INGLATERRA Y ARGENTINA, HEREAFTER
BANK, ADVISED ABSOLUTELY IMPOSSIBLE TO OBTAIN
PERMISSION TO FORM AND OPERATE AIRLINE WITHOUT
PARTICIPATION OF SENIOR ARGENTINE OFFICER, ENTIRELY
ARGENTINE FLIGHT CREWS, AND APPOINTMENT OF BUREAU OF
INTERNAL SECURITY OFFICER, HEREAFTER BIS, AS CHIEF
PILOT TO ENSURE AIRLINE DOES NOT CARRY OUT OSS
ACTIVITIES.

SOUTH AMERICAN AIRWAYS, S.A., HEREAFTER SAA, FORMED
LAST NIGHT WITH INITIAL CAPITALIZATION OF
$3,432,000. TEX SIXTY PERCENT MAJORITY STOCKHOLDER
AND MANAGING DIRECTOR WITH INVESTMENT OF $2,200,000
OBTAINED FROM BANK WITH LOAN AGAINST LOCAL
PROPERTIES.

BANK HOLDS FIFTEEN PERCENT OF REMAINDER. SEÑORA
CLAUDIA CARZINO-CORMANO, HEREAFTER TÍA CLAUDIA, AND
TÍO HANK 12.5 PERCENT EACH. THEY WILL SIT ON BOARD
OF DIRECTORS WITH COLONEL JUAN DOMINGO PERÓN,
HEREAFTER TÍO JUAN. MAJOR GONZALO DELGANO, BIS,

QUOTE RETIRED END QUOTE, HEREAFTER HAWK, HAS BEEN
NAMED CHIEF PILOT.

PLEASE ARRANGE FOR FOURTEEN PARROTS PLUS SIXTY-DAY
SUPPLY OF SPARES TO BE SENT TO BIRDCAGE FOR PICKUP
BY TEX AND HAWK. ONE PARROT NEEDED IMMEDIATELY,
OTHERS AT SEVEN- TO FOURTEEN-DAY INTERVALS.

ALSO URGENTLY NEED SIX REPEAT SIX 500-WATT COLLINS
MODEL 295 TRANSCEIVERS AND ADEQUATE REPEAT ADEQUATE
SPARES FOR SAME.

ADVISE HOW YOU INTEND TO PAY FOR ALL THIS.

FISHING NONPRODUCTIVE

ACKNOWLEDGE

TEX

"You believe this?" Donovan asked.

"I have no reason not to."

Donovan shook his head unbelievingly.

"What does he mean by that 'fishing nonproductive' remark?"

"Presumably, that he has found no replenishment ships in the River Plate."

"Okay. I presume 'parrots' means airplanes—"

"Lockheed Lodestars," Graham confirmed.

"Does he have enough money to buy *fourteen* of them?"

"They go for about a hundred and twenty-five thousand dollars. Fourteen would be one and three quarters million."

"I know who Perón is, but who are these other people?"

"Aunt Claudia was Frade's father's . . . how do I put this? . . . great and good friend."

"You mean 'mistress'?"

" 'Mistress' means to me some young tootsie being supported by a sugar daddy. Señora Carzino-Cormano is just about as well off as Frade was. As our Frade now is. I'm guessing that she's an investor and on the board, because if she is, there won't be some other Argentine. Same thing for Uncle Hank, whose wife is the late Colonel Frade's sister. Or, equally possible, both of them saw it as an interesting investment. The bank's in for fifteen percent."

"Presuming we send him the airplanes—"

"I think we are morally obliged to send him the airplanes. We told him the President wanted an airline, and he's set up one."

Donovan ignored the interruption, and went on: "—what good is this airline going to do the OSS? With an Argentine intelligence officer as the chief pilot? With all pilots Argentine?"

"I don't know. Do you think in his Machiavellian way Roosevelt had another purpose besides helping the OSS when he ordered the OSS to set up an airline?"

"Like what?"

"Like sticking it in Juan Trippe."

"If he did, he'd never admit it."

"There's one way to tell," Graham said. "First you tell him the good news, that there's going to be an airline down there. Then you tell him the bad news, that the OSS can't use it for anything, because there are Argentines deeply involved in it just to keep that from happening. Then you compare his reactions. If he's not really unhappy about the bad news . . ."

"Why don't you tell him? I'm going to the White House for cocktails at five, and I'm sure the President would be delighted if you came. Then you could judge his reactions for yourself."

"If I did that, he likely would be able to ask who Galahad is again, and God only knows where that would lead."

"That thought ran through my mind, frankly. Why don't I meet you in the lobby at, say, quarter to five? That way, we can be sure that nothing will happen to keep you from going."

"I really don't want to go over there, Bill."

"Yeah, I know. But Allen Dulles is going to be there."

Graham didn't reply. But he certainly was curious as to why Dulles, the OSS station chief in Switzerland, was in the States.

Donovan went on: "I think Dulles is the real reason the President wants to know who Galahad is. And I think the President would like you to tell him why you won't tell him."

"I presume my invitation to this is in fact an order?" Graham asked coldly.

Donovan nodded. He met Graham's eyes for a long moment, then said, "Yes, Colonel, it is. And in the meantime, why don't you start working on getting a Lodestar on its way to Pôrto Alegre?"

"To where?"

"Our air base at Pôrto Alegre, Brazil—the 'birdcage.' "

"You remembered the code name!" Graham said in mock awe.

"I forget very little, Colonel Graham. It might behoove you to keep that in mind. For example, I'm not about to forget quarter to five in the lobby."

"What about the radios he wants?"

"I guess I'm not perfect after all. I forgot that."

"I can't believe that."

"Call the Army Security Agency, tell them you need the radios and some expert who'll know how to set them up. We'll send him and the radios down there on the first Lodestar."

"And what do I respond to Frade?"

"Why don't you wait until you have his reaction to the news that you're sending the first of fourteen Lockheed Lodestars that will be of little or no use to the OSS in Argentina?"

"And what about the financing of this enterprise?"

"You can ask the President that, too. I would guess that since he would have to repay Frade that two point two million from his unvouchered funds, he would be pleased if Frade used his own money. As you point out, he's got lots of it."

"That's not fair, Bill."

"We're in the OSS, Alex. The word 'fair' is not in our lexicon."

[TWO]
Embassy of the German Reich
Avenida Córdoba
Buenos Aires, Argentina
0855 13 July 1943

Manfred von Deitzberg, a tall, slim, blond forty-two-year-old wearing a brand-new gray double-breasted pin-striped suit, marched through the door of the office of Ambassador Manfred Alois Graf von Lutzenberger. Von Deitzberg thrust out his arm. "Heil Hitler!"

Von Lutzenberger returned the salute, none too crisply, then said, "If you please, gentlemen, give the Herr Generalmajor and me a moment alone."

First Secretary Anton von Gradny-Sawz—a tall, almost handsome, somewhat overweight forty-five-year-old with a full head of luxuriant reddish-brown hair—SS-Sturmbannführer Erich Raschner—a short, squat man of the same age—and Korvettenkapitän Karl Boltitz, the latter two also wearing obviously new suits of clothing, and all of whom had obviously intended to enter von Lutzenberger's office, stopped so suddenly that they bumped into each other.

"And close the door, please," von Lutzenberger said, then waited until it was before he said, "And how was the voyage, von Deitzberg?"

Von Deitzberg, unsmiling, ignored the question. "I presume there was an important reason why you summoned me here?"

"I was complying with my orders," von Lutzenberger said, and handed him a sheet of paper.

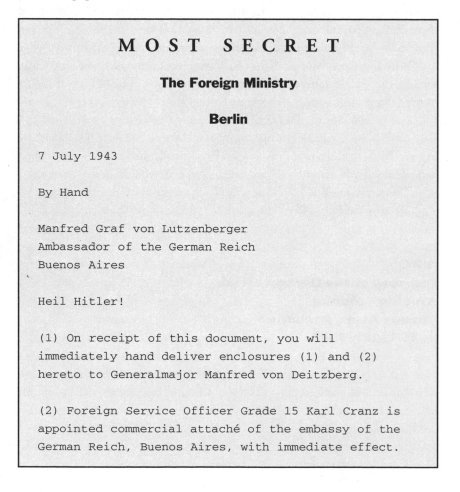

MOST SECRET

The Foreign Ministry

Berlin

```
7 July 1943


By Hand


Manfred Graf von Lutzenberger
Ambassador of the German Reich
Buenos Aires


Heil Hitler!


(1) On receipt of this document, you will
immediately hand deliver enclosures (1) and (2)
hereto to Generalmajor Manfred von Deitzberg.


(2) Foreign Service Officer Grade 15 Karl Cranz is
appointed commercial attaché of the embassy of the
German Reich, Buenos Aires, with immediate effect.
```

Vice Foreign Service Officer Grade 15 Wilhelm
Frogger will return to Berlin to assume new duties
in the foreign ministry as soon as the turnover can
be effected.

(3) Kapitän zur See Karl Boltitz is appointed naval
attaché to the embassy of the German Reich, Buenos
Aires, with immediate effect. In this position,
Kapitän zur See Boltitz will be the senior military
officer of the embassy.

(4) Major Hans-Peter Baron von Wachtstein is
appointed attaché for air to the embassy of the
German Reich, Buenos Aires, with immediate effect.

Concur:

Himmler

Heinrich Himmler

J. v. Ribbentrop

Reichsprotektor Joachim von Ribbentrop
Foreign Minister

Canaris

Wilhelm Canaris
Rearadmiral

MOST SECRET

"By hand, Herr Ambassador?" von Deitzberg asked.

"That was hand-delivered to me by Herr Cranz. Yesterday afternoon."

"And where is he?"

"He and the pilot of the Condor, a Captain von und zu Aschenburg, accepted von Wachtstein's invitation to have dinner with von Wachtstein's family at their farm. Cranz called the duty officer later to say they would be spending the night there, and coming here at nine this morning."

"It's nine now."

"Then they should be here. Sometimes there is traffic."

"May I have the enclosures mentioned, please?"

"Certainly," von Lutzenberger said, opened his desk drawer, and handed von Deitzberg a bluish-gray note-sized envelope and a large thick manila envelope.

Von Deitzberg opened the small envelope first. It contained a sheet of Reichsprotektor Heinrich Himmler's personal notepaper.

Der Reichsprotektor

```
7 July 1943

Brigadeführer von Deitzberg,

You are immediately needed here.

If necessary, you are authorized to delay the return
flight of the Condor by as much as twenty-four hours
until the turnover to Cranz, who will assume all
your responsibilities in Argentina, is accomplished.

Heil Hitler!

Himmler
```

The large manila envelope was so securely bound that von Deitzberg couldn't open it until von Lutzenberger's secretary, Fräulein Ingebord Hässell, a middle-aged spinster who wore her graying hair drawn tightly against her skull, was summoned and finally produced a huge pair of shears.

It contained a letter and several packets of charts and data.

M O S T   S E C R E T

Reichssicherheitshauptamt

Berlin

7 July 1943

SS-Brigadeführer Manfred von Deitzberg

By Hand

(One): You will immediately make these orders known to Ambassador von Lutzenberger and SS Obersturmbannführer Cranz for the necessary actions on their part.

(Two): There has been confirmation that the special cargo has been transferred from the motor vessel Ciudad de Cádiz to U-405, Kapitänleutnant Wilhelm von Dattenberg commanding. Sturmbannführer Kötl and a small SS detachment are accompanying the special cargo.

(Three): Enclosed are chart overlays and signal cryptographic matériel to be used in seeing that the special cargo is safely put ashore in absolute secrecy at a location in Argentina to be determined by Cranz and von Lutzenberger in consultation with von Dattenberg.

(Four): If the landing operation is successful, the SS detachment will remain ashore to ensure the security of the special cargo and to perform other missions as determined by Cranz. If the landing encounters difficulty, the priorities are to (A) return the special cargo to the U-405 and (B) return the SS personnel to the U-405.

(Five): Sturmbannführer Kötl's responsibility and authority is limited to the protection of the special cargo. The decisions to attempt to land the special cargo, the methods of doing so, and, should it be necessary, to break off the attempt are entirely the responsibility of Kapitänleutnant von Dattenberg. The location of the offloading is to be determined by consultation between Cranz and von Dattenberg.

(Six): There are additional SS personnel aboard the Ciudad de Cádiz who, following the successful unloading of the special cargo, may be brought into Argentina to further ensure the security of the special cargo and to perform such other duties as Cranz may prescribe. Ambassador von Lutzenberger is charged with acquiring the necessary documentation for all SS personnel whose presence in Argentina must obviously not come to the attention of the Argentine authorities.

(Seven): As the senior officer of the German Reich in Argentina, Ambassador Lutzenberger will continue to exercise that authority, including over U-405 while U-405 is involved in this mission. It is understood, however, that inasmuch as von Lutzenberger cannot be expected to have the

expertise of Cranz and von Dattenberg, he will seek
their counsel.

Himmler

Heinrich Himmler
Reichsprotektor

Concur:

J. v. Ribbentrop

Joachim von Ribbentrop

Doenitz

Karl Doenitz Foreign Minister
Grand Admiral

Canaris

Wilhelm Canaris
Rearadmiral

MOST SECRET

"Are you familiar with the contents of this, Your Excellency?" von Deitzberg asked.

Von Lutzenberger shook his head. Von Deitzberg handed him the order. Von Lutzenberger read it carefully and handed it back.

"It would seem the next step is to make Obersturmbannführer Cranz aware of these orders," he said.

"Would you do me the courtesy, Your Excellency, of giving Cranz and me a few minutes alone?"

"Herr Generalmajor, there is an unfortunate implication in your request that there is something you wish to discuss with Cranz that you don't wish the ambassador of the German Reich to hear," von Lutzenberger said.

"It was my intention, Your Excellency, to ask Cranz, man-to-man, if he has anything he can tell me why the reichsprotektor is recalling me to Berlin on such short notice. I have no objection to your hearing that question, or the reply."

Von Lutzenberger depressed a lever on his intercom device.

"Fräulein Hässell, will you ask Herr Cranz to come in, please?"

Von Deitzberg thought: *The sonofabitch knows there's no way he can keep me from talking to Cranz privately later. He's doing this just to put me in my place. I guess he didn't like being ordered to "seek the counsel" of Cranz.*

Fräulein Hässell opened the door for Cranz a moment later. He marched into the office, threw out his arm, and barked, "Heil Hitler!"

"It would appear, Cranz," von Deitzberg said, "that I am urgently needed in Berlin. Do you have any idea why?"

"No, sir, I don't."

"And it would also appear that in addition to your new diplomatic duties, you are to assume all of my responsibilities here vis-à-vis both the Reichssicherheitshauptamt and Operation Phoenix."

"Jawohl, Herr Brigadeführer."

"You are learning this for the first time, are you, Cranz?"

"Yes, sir. All the reichsprotektor told me was that I was to come here, bearing certain documents for the ambassador, and be prepared to stay for an indefinite period of time."

"Well, I think you had better have a look at our orders, Cranz. And then I will entertain your suggestions as to how the turnover may be accomplished in the least possible time."

"Jawohl, Herr Brigadeführer."

Von Deitzberg handed him the orders from Himmler.

[THREE]
Office of the Commercial Attaché
Embassy of the German Reich
Avenida Córdoba
Buenos Aires, Argentina
1105 13 July 1943

The commercial attaché, Foreign Service Officer Grade 15 Wilhelm Frogger, turned out to be just what Obersturmbannführer Karl Cranz expected him to be.

He had, of course, read Frogger's dossiers—both of the foreign ministry and the Sicherheitspolizei—in Berlin immediately after the unfortunate business on the beach of Samborombón Bay. He also—just before going out to Estancia Santa Catalina with von Wachtstein and von und zu Aschenburg the night before—had ordered Untersturmführer Schneider to get from the safe the dossier on Frogger that Oberst Grüner had been keeping on him in Argentina.

All of these showed Frogger to be a fairly ordinary career civil servant, perhaps a little less intelligent than most. Cranz somewhat cynically decided that Frogger's rise to Grade 15 had more to do with his having joined the Nazi party early on. And even more cynically, he had decided that Frogger had joined the party more because he was from Munich, where the Führer had first begun to achieve success, rather than because he had seen National Socialism as the wave of the future.

Frogger and his wife had three sons, all of whom had become Wehrmacht officers. Two had died in the service of the Fatherland, one early in the war in Belgium and the second in the early days of Operation Barbarossa, the invasion of Russia. The third had been captured while serving with Rommel's Afrikakorps.

As Frogger had worked his way up the foreign service ladder, he had been stationed at half a dozen embassies, none of them as important as Buenos Aires, and until Buenos Aires, always as the Assistant or Deputy This Or That, never the principal, even when he had been in Leopoldville, in the Belgian Congo. There he had been a deputy counsel, which, Cranz had decided, probably meant he had spent most of his time dealing with the maintenance of the German World War I military cemeteries in what had been, before the Versailles Conference, Germany's African Colonies. He had been assigned to Argentina— probably to get him out of the way while important things were being done— in April of 1940.

There had been no objection by anyone when Frogger and his wife had been placed in the unofficial Not Likely To Be Traitors column with Fräulein Ingebord Hässell.

When Cranz went into Frogger's office, he immediately decided that Frogger was precisely what he had thought after he'd read his dossiers.

Physically, he was a plump little man who wore what was left of his hair combed over his bald dome. He also had a neatly trimmed square mustache under a somewhat bulbous nose. Cranz wondered if that was because Frogger thought it made him look masculine or sophisticated, or whether he had grown it in emulation of Adolf Hitler.

They exchanged Nazi salutes.

"His Excellency has told you I am to assume your duties, Herr Frogger?"

"Yes, he has, Herr Cranz."

"There is more to that than appears," Cranz said. "With the caveat that this is a State Secret and therefore be shared with no one, I hereby inform you that to carry out a mission that is none of your concern it has been decided at the highest levels that an officer of the SS be assigned secretly to the embassy here, and that he assume your duties as the means to carry out his mission in secrecy. I am SS-Obersturmbannführer Cranz."

"It is an honor to meet you, sir. How should I address you?"

"As Herr Cranz, please."

"How may I be of assistance, Herr Cranz?"

"I confess I have absolutely no knowledge of your duties. Why don't you tell me what they are?"

Frogger thought the question over for a long moment before replying, "The basic role of a commercial attaché, Herr Cranz, is to foster commerce between the Reich and what we call the 'host country.' In normal circumstances, I would be doing whatever I could to encourage the Argentines to purchase, for example, Siemens radios and phonographs, Leica cameras, Mercedes-Benz trucks and autos, et cetera, and at the same time facilitating the purchase by German businesses of what Germany needs, mostly foodstuffs, wool, and leather, at the lowest possible prices."

He looked at Cranz for an indication that Cranz understood him.

Cranz nodded.

Frogger went on: "In the present circumstances—"

"You mean the war?"

"Yes."

"Go on."

"I was thinking just the other day, Herr Cranz, that what I have become in the present circumstances is a 'purchase facilitator.' "

"Which means?"

"In the present circumstances, Germany has very little to offer for sale to Argentina. Our industry is devoted entirely, as I'm sure you are aware, to production to bring us to the final victory as soon as possible. At the same time, Germany's need for foodstuffs, wool, and leather is so great that, if we were able, we would take their entire production."

"Why aren't we able?"

"The Americans, primarily, and, to a lesser degree, the English."

"I don't think I fully understand."

"It is a rather complicated problem, Herr Cranz."

Cranz made an impatient gesture.

"First of all, it is a question of shipping, Herr Cranz. Our Kriegsmarine is unfortunately not able to protect our shipping. Which means we have to ship in neutral bottoms. Spanish, French, and Portuguese, primarily. Sometimes Swedish. And recently, we have had to make sure that merchandise owned by Germany is not aboard a, say, French ship."

"Why?"

"Because the Americans announced they were going to stop and inspect neutral vessels on the high seas to make sure they were not carrying contraband, by which they meant anything owned by Germans."

"And they're doing that?"

"The threat was enough to make the Swedes and the French, et cetera, refuse to take aboard German-owned merchandise. It has been necessary for us to arrange for Spanish or Portuguese, et cetera, firms to purchase, for example, frozen beef, which is then shipped to Spain or Portugal on neutral bottoms. Once ashore in Spain, it can then legally be sold to Germany and sent by rail.

"So one of the things I do, Herr Cranz, is guarantee the sight drafts of, say, the Spanish Beef Importing Company of Madrid—"

"What's a 'sight draft'?"

"Something like a check. Payable 'on sight.' The Argentine beef producers want their money before they will allow their beef to be loaded aboard ship. So I see to that. Berlin advises me how much the Spanish Beef Importing Company—which we control, of course—is allowed to bid for the beef, and then I—the Hamburg-Argentine Bank—guarantees their sight draft for payment."

"Berlin advises you? What's that all about?"

"Because the Americans also bid for the beef, driving the price as high as they can to inconvenience us. It's sort of a game we play."

"A *game*? What sort of a game?"

"At the weekly sale, the American beef packers here, Swift and Armour, enter a bid for so many tons of beef. So does the Spanish Beef Importing Company. Say the Americans enter a bid of fifty dollars per hundredweight. We—the Spaniards—counter with a bid of fifty-five dollars. They raise their bid to sixty dollars, we raise ours to sixty-five, et cetera."

"The bidding is in American dollars?" Cranz asked incredulously.

Frogger nodded.

"Where do we get American dollars?"

"In Switzerland, primarily. Some in Sweden. Even some in France. We have to pay a premium for them, of course."

"Of course," Cranz said bitterly.

"As I was saying, the bidding goes back and forth until one side stops. Recently, frozen beef has been closing at about one hundred five dollars a hundredweight."

"Why does one side stop bidding?"

"We stop when it reaches the maximum Berlin has stated."

"And the Americans?"

"Whenever they want us to have the beef at an outrageous price. They don't really want the beef."

"Then why do they bid on it?"

"To either keep us from getting it or to make us pay very dearly for it."

"And they never take the beef? Win the auction?"

"Oh, yes, Herr Cranz. They take it frequently. Whenever we don't top their bid."

"And if they don't want it, what do they do with it?"

"They—that is to say, Swift and Armour—corn it and tin it."

"And what exactly does that mean?"

"The meat is treated with brine and then tinned. I'm sure you've seen the tins, Herr Cranz." He gestured with his hands. "One end of the tins is larger than the other."

"I've seen them," Cranz said. "Let me see if I have this straight. If the Americans win the auction of frozen beef sides, they thaw the sides and then convert the entire side—steaks, roasts, everything—into tinned corned beef?"

"Precisely, Herr Cranz."

"Doesn't that make the tinned beef prohibitively expensive?"

"What I believe happens, Herr Cranz, is that the Americans—there is a man at the American embassy, a man named Delojo, who is actually a lieutenant commander in the American Navy and who is the American OSS chief in Argentina—"

"The OSS gets involved in these beef auctions?"

"And in the auctions for leather and wool, everything we want and they don't want us to have. What he does in the case of the beef is compensate Swift and Armour for the difference between what the beef is worth and what they have paid for it. In other words, if the frozen sides are worth—"

"I get the picture," Cranz interrupted. "And what do they do with all this tinned beef?"

"They ship it to the United States in neutral bottoms, some Argentine, and then transship the majority of it to England in their convoys."

"How do you know all this?"

"From my experience, of course. I know about the American OSS man from the late Oberst Grüner. He kept a pretty close eye on the OSS, as you can imagine."

"And the same sort of thing, you say, goes on with wool and leather?"

"And all foodstuffs," Frogger said. "The details of the transactions are somewhat different, you will understand, but you will see that you will be kept rather busy."

Cranz looked at his watch.

"Why don't we see about lunch?" he asked. "We can continue this conversation while we eat. Is there somewhere close?"

"The ABC is near. At Lavalle 545."

"And what is the ABC?"

"Probably the best German restaurant in Buenos Aires, Herr Cranz."

"Sounds fine," Cranz said. "Why don't we go there?"

And the first thing I'm going to do when we get back is have Ambassador von Lutzenberger cable the foreign ministry and have the orders sending you home canceled.

I have a job of great importance to do here, and I can't do it if I have to spend all my time in an auction bidding war against the goddamn OSS over tinned corned beef!

[FOUR]
Office of Ethical Standards, Bureau of Internal Security
Ministry of Defense
Edificio Libertador, Avenida Paseo Colón
Capital Federal, Buenos Aires, Argentina
1220 13 July 1943

Major Gonzalo Delgano, Argentina Air Service, Retired, stood outside the office door of Colonel Alejandro Bernardo Martín, chief of the Office of Ethical Standards, and waited patiently until Martín sensed he was there and looked up at him.

Martín smiled and waved Delgano into his office.

"And how is the soon-to-be chief pilot of South American Airways doing this morning? Have you got time for lunch?"

"Not only do I have time, I need sustenance badly," Delgano said. "I spent the morning marching around what is to be the airfield of South American Airways."

"Really? And where is that?"

"In Morón, about seven kilometers from El Palomar."

"You're serious, aren't you?"

"Absolutely. No sooner had I hung up talking to you this morning than Frade was on the phone. He said he would meet me in half an hour at El Palomar, and wanted my opinion of what he called 'the base.' I thought he was going to show me some maps—"

"But?" Martín interrupted, smiling.

"When I got to El Palomar, one of his bodyguards—not Enrico Rodríguez . . . the other one?"

"Sargento Rodolfo Gómez, Retired?"

Delgano nodded. " . . . Gómez was there, with a Ford station wagon. And a few minutes later, Frade landed in a Piper Cub."

"And where was Sergeant Major, Retired, Rodríguez? In the Piper Cub?"

Delgano nodded again. "With his shotgun. Which I had the feeling he wanted to use on me. Anyway, Rodríguez got out of the airplane and I got in, and off we took. Five minutes later, we landed on what I later learned was the feeding field for Frade's slaughterhouse. You know, where they hold the beef if too many show up at once?"

"I know the place."

"There must have been five hundred heads on the field, being rounded up and loaded on trucks by his gauchos—I later learned it was for movement to another slaughterhouse he owns out by Pilar—plus a small army of surveyors, plus half a dozen pieces of engineering equipment—bulldozers, scrapers, that sort of thing—waiting for the surveyors to finish putting flags in the ground so they could get to work."

"He's building an airfield out there? Did he tell you why?"

"He did," Delgano said, smiling. "He said he thought at first he'd build 'the base' on Estancia San Pedro y San Pablo but had decided against it . . ." He stopped, shook his head, chuckled, then went on. ". . . because he wanted to spare you having to drive all the way out to the estancia all the time to make sure he wasn't doing anything he shouldn't be."

"He actually said that?" Martín asked, smiling.

Delgano nodded.

"And that he didn't want to rent hangars and shops—or build them—at El Palomar because he thought they'd want too much rent. And he had been thinking of closing the Morón slaughterhouse anyway."

"What we have here, Gonzalo, is another incident of Don Cletus telling us the truth but making us wonder what he's not telling us."

"Yes, sir, I think that's the case."

"But he's right. We can keep an eye on South American Airways easier in Morón than we could at Estancia San Pedro y San Pablo. I'm presuming it is suitable for an airfield?"

"Ideal, actually. He can put in two runways without much leveling, and there's a railroad siding. Where cattle have arrived until now, railway wagons of stone from Mendoza will soon start arriving to pave the runways. He's got everything pretty well figured out."

"That's what worries me," Martín said. "Can he finish his airfield by the time he gets airplanes?"

"Probably not," Delgano said. "He said we ought to be hearing when the first Lodestar will be at Pôrto Alegre in the next couple of days."

"You have to admire his self-confidence. He doesn't have permission from the interior ministry to start his airline, and he's already building an airfield for it, and buying airplanes."

"Fourteen of them," Delgano said. "Which poses the problem of getting the right kind of pilots for them."

Martín didn't respond directly.

"On the other hand, I can't imagine the interior ministry dragging its feet, much less looking unfavorably upon a request for the necessary licenses presented to them by Colonel Perón."

"That does seem unlikely, doesn't it?" Delgano said dryly. "What are we going to do about pilots?"

"How many pilots are required for fourteen aircraft?"

"Don Cletus, when he told me my first job was to recruit pilots, said we'd best plan for four per aircraft at a minimum. That's fifty-six. Call it sixty, at least."

"We can't get that many from the air service," Martín thought aloud.

"And that's probably as many pilots as Aeropostal has."

"They have seventy-one," Martín said. "Seven of whom are quote inactive end quote air service officers."

"If we have half a dozen air service officers to watch the others and keep their eyes open, generally—"

"Can we find that many willing to quote resign end quote?" Martín asked. It was obvious he didn't expect an answer. "Let me think about that, Gonzalo."

"Yes, sir. And while we're just a little off the subject of airlines, Clete—"

" 'Clete'?" Martín parroted.

"I realize it's not very professional of me, Colonel, but the cold fact is I like him. He's a nice chap, funny. And you have to admire the way he jumps in and gets things done."

"I agree with everything you say, Gonzalo. But Frade—despite his not-at-all-convincing denials—is a serving officer of the American Corps of Marines in the OSS. What he's trying to do is not necessarily—indeed, rarely—in the best interests of Argentina."

"Who's going to win the war? Don't answer that if it puts you on a spot."

"It doesn't matter who I think will win it. There are a lot of people here, including President Ramírez and Colonel Perón—perhaps most importantly, Colonel Perón—who think German efficiency and the invincible Wehrmacht will come out on top."

"The Wehrmacht was run out of Africa, and just a couple of days ago, the Allies invaded Sicily. And it's Berlin that is being bombed just about daily, not Washington."

"It would not behoove either of us as Argentine officers to publicly disagree with our president's—or, again, perhaps more importantly, Colonel Perón's—assessment of the world situation. For one thing, we might well be wrong. The late Colonel Frade also thought the Germans were going to be invincible."

"For which he got himself shot."

Martín met Delgano's eyes for a long moment.

"Before we got into this potentially dangerous conversation, Gonzalo, you started to say something? 'A little off the subject of airlines'?"

"Oh, yeah. I told you that von Wachtstein brought two friends with him to dinner at Estancia Santa Catalina? The Lufthansa pilot and the new commercial attaché for the German embassy?"

"What about them?"

"Frade managed to make me understand that he didn't think the commercial attaché was what he said he was, and that I should make you aware of this."

"How so?"

"The implication was he wasn't either a friend of von Wachtstein's or a diplomat."

"He has a diplomatic passport," Martín replied. "And there has been no word from our embassy in Berlin suggesting he's not bona fide."

"Do you think it's possible there are people in our embassy who might close their eyes—"

"What about the Lufthansa pilot?" Martín asked, shutting off the question.

"Well, he's what he says he is. He and von Wachtstein flew together all over Europe and Russia. And we know he flies the Condor."

"Why are you smiling, Gonzalo?"

"Señorita Isabela Carzino-Cormano was quite taken with him," Delgano said. "And vice versa. As we speak, they're having lunch in the Alvear. She's going to show him around Buenos Aires."

"That amuses you?"

"The possibility Estancia Santa Catalina might ultimately come into the hands of a couple of Luftwaffe pilots does."

"You think that's likely?"

"Ten minutes after she met him, she was miraculously transformed from grieving widow, sort of, into . . ." His eyebrows went up.

"Into what?"

"She did everything but back into him, wagging her tail," Delgano said. "Doña Claudia saw it. She didn't know what to think."

Martín shook his head and smiled.

"Tell you what, Gonzalo. Nose around Aeropostal and see who you think would be useful to us and South American Airways—in that order. I'll look into the new commercial attaché."

[FIVE]
Office of the Military Attaché
Embassy of the German Reich
Avenida Córdoba
Buenos Aires, Argentina
1405 13 July 1943

Sturmbannführer Erich Raschner, a thoughtful look on his face, handed Himmler's handwritten order, the directive from the foreign ministry, and von Deitzberg's personal orders from the reichssicherheitshauptamt, back to von Deitzberg but said nothing.

"And your opinion of all this, Erich?" von Deitzberg asked.

"There's no telling—there's not much to go on."

"Off the top of your head? I won't hold you responsible."

"It's odd that I'm not being ordered back to Berlin with you."

Von Deitzberg nodded his agreement. "And what would be your guess about that?"

"The reichsprotektor wants me here," Raschner said, matter-of-factly, with no suggestion that he was being flip.

"And why would he want you here?"

"To keep an eye on things," Raschner replied. "We still haven't found the traitor, and . . ." He let his voice trail off.

"And?" von Deitzberg said.

"Have you shown me everything?"

Von Deitzberg nodded.

"Have you learned anything more about the reichsprotektor in that connection?"

"As far as I know, he knows nothing about it," von Deitzberg said.

"You don't think maybe the reason you're being recalled so suddenly is because he's found out?"

Von Deitzberg stared at him coldly.

"I thought of that," he said, finally. "But if that were the case, don't you think he'd have recalled both of us and not sent Cranz here?"

In August 1941, in the Reich Chancellery, Hitler had personally promoted Brigadeführer Reinhardt Heydrich, Himmler's adjutant, to gruppenführer. And

Hitler made von Deitzberg—newly appointed as first deputy adjutant—an obersturmbannführer.

After a good deal of champagne at the promotion party at the Hotel Adlon, von Deitzberg confided to Heydrich that, although the promotion was satisfying for a number of reasons, it was most satisfying because he needed the money.

Two days later, Heydrich handed him an envelope containing a great deal of cash.

"Consider this a confidential allowance," Heydrich said. "Spend it as you need to. It doesn't have to be accounted for. It comes from a confidential special fund."

With his new position as first deputy adjutant to Reichsführer-SS Himmler came other perquisites, including that of a deputy. Heydrich sent him—"for your approval; if you don't get along, I'll send you somebody else"—Obersturmführer Erich Raschner, whom Heydrich identified as intelligent and trustworthy. And who "having never served in either the Waffen-SS or the Wehrmacht," Heydrich went on, "had been taught to respect those of his superiors who had."

Raschner turned out to be a short, squat, phlegmatic Hessian, three years older than von Deitzberg. He had come into the SS as a policeman, but a policeman with an unusual background. He had originally been commissioned into the Allgemeine-SS, which dealt mainly with internal security and racial matters, rather than the Waffen-SS. Later, he had been transferred to the Sicherheitspolizei.

Von Deitzburg had sensed that, for some reason, it was important to Heydrich that he and Raschner get along.

When, several weeks later, Heydrich asked von Deitzberg for his opinion of Raschner, von Deitzberg gave him the answer he thought he wanted: They got along personally, and Raschner would bring to the job knowledge of police and internal security matters that von Deitzberg admitted he did not have.

"Good," Heydrich said with a smile. "He likes you, too. We'll make it permanent. And tonight we'll celebrate. Come by the house at, say, half past seven."

At a little after half past seven, they opened a very nice bottle of Courvoisier cognac, toasted the new relationship, and then Heydrich matter-of-factly explained its nature.

"One of the things I admire in you, Manfred," Heydrich said, "is that you can get things done administratively."

"Thank you."

"And Erich, on the other hand, can get done whatever needs to be done without any record being kept. Do you follow me?"

"I'm not sure."

"The confidential special fund is what I'm leading up to," Heydrich said. "I'm sure that aroused your curiosity, Manfred?"

"Yes, it did."

"What no longer appears on Erich's service record is that he served with the Totenkopfverbände," Heydrich said.

The Death's-Head Skull Battalions were charged with the administration of concentration camps.

"I didn't know that."

"You told me a while ago you were having a little trouble keeping your financial head above water. A lot of us have that problem. We work hard, right? We should play hard, right? And to do that, you need the wherewithal, right?"

"Yes, sir," von Deitzberg said smiling.

"Has the real purpose of the concentration camps ever occurred to you, Manfred?"

"You're talking about the Final Solution?"

"In a sense. The Führer correctly believes that the Jews are a cancer on Germany, and that we have to remove that cancer. You understand that, of course?"

"Of course."

"The important thing is to take them out of the German society. In some instances, we can make them contribute to Germany with their labor. You remember what it says over the gate at Dachau?"

" 'Arbeit macht frei'?"

"Yes. But if the parasites can't work, and can't be forced to make some repayment for all they have stolen from Germany over the years, then something else has to be done with them. Right?"

"I understand."

"Elimination is one option," Heydrich said. "But if you think about it, realize that the basic objective is to get these parasites out of Germany. Elimination is not the only option."

"I don't think I quite understand," von Deitzberg confessed.

"Put very simply, there are Jews outside of Germany who are willing to pay generously to have their relatives and friends removed from the concentration camps," Heydrich said.

"Really?"

"When it first came to my attention, I was tempted to dismiss this possibility out of hand," Heydrich said. "But then I gave it some thought. For one thing, it accomplishes the Führer's primary purpose—removing these parasitic vermin from the Fatherland. It does National Socialism no harm if vermin that cost us good money to feed and house leave Germany and never return and then cost others money to feed."

"I can see your point."

"And if, at the same time, it takes money from Jews outside Germany and transfers it to Germany, there is also an element of justice. They are not getting away free after sucking our blood all these years."

"I understand."

"In other words, if we can further the Führer's intention to get Jews out of Germany, and at the same time bring Jewish money into Germany, and at the same time make a little money for ourselves, what's wrong with that?"

"Nothing that I can see."

"This has to be done in absolute secrecy, of course. A number of people would not understand; and an even larger number would feel they have a right to share in the confidential special fund. You can understand that."

"Yes, of course."

"Raschner will get into the details with you," Heydrich went on. "But essentially, you will do what I've been doing myself. Inmates are routinely transferred from one concentration camp to another. And, routinely, while the inmates are en route, members of the Totenkopfverbände remove two, three, or four of them from the transport. For purposes of further interrogation and the like. Having been told the inmates have been removed by the Totenkopfverbände, the receiving camp has no further interest in them. The inmates who have been removed from the transport are then provided with Spanish passports and taken by Gestapo escorts to the Spanish border. Once in Spain, they make their way to Cádiz or some other port and board neutral ships. A month later, they're in Uruguay."

"Uruguay?" von Deitzberg blurted in surprise. It had taken him a moment to place Uruguay; and even then, all he could come up with was that it was close to Argentina, somewhere in the south of the South American continent.

"Some stay there," Heydrich said matter-of-factly, "but many go on to Argentina."

"I see," von Deitzberg said.

"Documents issued by my office are of course never questioned," Heydrich went on, "and Raschner will tell you what documents are necessary. You will also administer dispersals from the confidential special fund. Raschner will tell you how much, to whom, and when."

"I understand."

"We have one immediate problem," Heydrich said. "And then we'll have another little sip of this splendid brandy and go see what we can find for dinner."

"An immediate problem?"

"We need one more man here in Berlin," Heydrich said. "Someone who will understand the situation and who can be trusted. I want you to recruit him yourself. Can you think of anyone?"

That had posed no problem for von Deitzberg.

"Josef Goltz," he said immediately. "Obersturmbannführer Goltz."

Heydrich made a *Give me more* sign with his hands.

"He's the SS-SD liaison officer to the Office of the Party Chancellery."

Heydrich laughed. "Great minds run in similar channels. That's the answer I got when I asked Raschner for ideas. Why don't the two of you talk to him together?"

In addition to his other duties, Gruppenführer Heydrich had been named Protector of Czechoslovakia. On 31 May 1942, he was fatally wounded when Czech agents of the British threw a bomb into his car in Prague.

Before leaving Berlin to personally supervise the retribution to be visited upon the Czechs for Heydrich's murder, Himmler called von Deitzberg into his office to tell him how much he would have to rely on him until a suitable replacement for the martyred Heydrich could be found.

Meanwhile, von Deitzberg was faced with a serious problem. With Heydrich's death, he had become the senior officer involved with the confidential fund and the source of its money. But von Deitzberg had never learned from Heydrich how much Himmler knew about it.

He quickly and carefully checked the records of dispersal of money; he found no record that Himmler had ever received money from it.

It was of course possible that the enormous disbursements to Heydrich had included money that Heydrich had quietly slipped to Himmler; that way there would be no record of Himmler's involvement.

Three months later, however, after Himmler had asked neither for money nor about the status of the confidential fund, von Deitzberg was forced to conclude that Himmler not only knew nothing about it but that Heydrich had gone to great lengths to conceal it from the reichsprotektor.

It was entirely possible, therefore, that Himmler would be furious if he learned now about the confidential fund.

The reichsprotektor had a puritanical streak, and he might consider that Heydrich had actually been stealing from the Reich, and that von Deitzberg had been involved in the theft up to his neck.

When von Deitzberg brought up the subject to Raschner, Raschner advised that as far as he himself knew, Himmler either didn't know about the fund—or didn't want to know about it. Thus, an approach to him now might see everyone connected with it stood before a wall and shot.

They had no choice, Raschner concluded, except to go on as they had— but of course taking even greater care to make sure the ransoming operation remained secret.

Obersturmbannführer Josef Goltz had died at Samborombón Bay with Oberst Karl-Heinz Grüner. That meant only four people, all SS officers, were left who knew the details of the confidential special fund: Von Deitzberg, Raschner, Cranz, and their man in Uruguay, Sturmbannführer Werner von Tresmarck.

And von Tresmarck wasn't really in the same league as von Deitzberg, Raschner, and Cranz. He wasn't really a *senior* SS officer, for one thing. And for another: his sexual orientation.

Von Tresmarck had come to von Deitzberg's attention when a Sicherheitspolizei report of his relationship with a young SS officer had come to his desk for action.

At the time, von Deitzberg had needed someone reliable in Uruguay. Reasoning that someone whose choices were doing precisely what he was told to do—and keeping his mouth shut about it—or swapping his SS uniform and the privileges that went with it for the gray striped uniform of a Sachsenhausen concentration camp inmate—with a pink triangle on the breast—would be just the man he needed.

And von Dattenberg had spelled it out to von Tresmarck in just about those terms.

If von Tresmarck would marry someone suitable immediately, his Sicherheitspolizei dossier would remain in von Deitzberg's safe while he went to Uruguay and did what he was told to do.

He even defined someone suitable for him.

"One of the ladies who spends a good deal of time around the bar in the Adlon Hotel is a Frau Kolbermann. Inge Kolbermann. She is the widow of the late Obersturmbannführer Kolbermann, who fell for the Fatherland in Russia and left her in pretty dire straits financially. And there are other reasons she will probably accept a proposal of marriage. You had better hope she accepts yours."

She indeed had accepted von Tresmarck's proposal, as von Deitzberg thought she would. He knew a good deal about Frau Kolbermann, both professionally and personally. She was no stranger to his bed. If she was in Uruguay, she posed far less of a threat to embarrass him.

And so far, both of them had performed adequately.

Almost visibly thinking, Raschner hadn't replied for a long moment.

"I don't believe in good luck," he said finally. "But sometimes things happen randomly that others might consider good luck."

"Meaning?"

"The pie, with Goltz gone, can now be sliced into three parts, not four."

"Yes, that's true. I hadn't thought about that."

"The weak links in the chain are von Tresmarck in Uruguay and those I think of as the worker bees in Germany, those who—"

"I take your point."

"You will be there. You can arrange things so the worker bees about whom you have any suspicions, or who know too much, can be sent to work in other hives or otherwise disposed of. And von Tresmarck can continue accepting contributions to the confidential fund as he has been doing, with Cranz keeping a close eye on him. And me keeping a close eye on both of them."

"And Cranz," von Deitzberg said, "as commercial attaché, will be able to make the right kind of investments."

"With me watching him," Raschner said.

"And me watching you," von Deitzberg said smiling. "Keep in mind always, Erich, that you work for me, not Cranz."

"Of course," Raschner said. "Are you going to tell him that?"

"Of course. As a matter of fact, I'll tell him right now. Go get him, would you, please? He's with Frogger."

[SIX]
Army Security Agency Facility
Vint Hill Farms Station
Near Warrenton, Fauquier County, Virginia
1940 13 July 1943

As the black 1942 Buick Roadmaster approached the small frame guard shack, floodlights came on and a large military policeman—one of three on duty—came out of the shack. He held up his right hand in an unmistakable *Stop right there!* gesture.

When the car had stopped, he walked to the driver's window.

"You didn't see the sign, 'Do Not Pass—Restricted Military Area'?"

"We're expected, Sergeant," Colonel A. J. Graham said from the backseat of the Buick.

The MP sergeant shined his flashlight in the backseat and saw a well-dressed civilian.

"My name is Graham, Sergeant."

"*Colonel* Graham?" the MP asked dubiously.

"That's right."

The flashlight went off.

"Lieutenant!" the MP sergeant called.

Graham saw a barrel-chested young Signal Corps officer push himself off the hood of a jeep where he had been sitting. He marched purposefully toward the Buick.

"Is there a problem?" the lieutenant asked in a booming voice.

"Sir, there's a civilian in the backseat of the Buick, says he's Colonel Graham."

" 'Civilian'?" the lieutenant parroted, making it clear he thought that what he had been told was highly unlikely.

He marched to the Buick and boomed, "Colonel Graham?"

"That's right."

"We expected a Marine colonel," the lieutenant boomed.

"And that's what you got," Graham said, and held out his identity card.

The lieutenant examined the card, and then Graham, very carefully.

Then he handed the card back, came to attention, saluted, and boomed, "Good evening, sir. Sir, I am Lieutenant McClung, the officer of the day. If the

colonel will have his driver follow me, I will take you to the colonel, who is waiting for you, sir."

"Thank you," Graham said.

"The colonel will understand that when I said we expected a Marine colonel,
we expected one in uniform, sir."

"That was reasonable," Graham said. "Thank you, Lieutenant."

"To what do I owe this unexpected pleasure, Colonel?" Colonel Raymond J.
Scott, Signal Corps, commanding Vint Hill Farms Station, asked as he shook
Graham's hand.

"I didn't mean to make waves, Colonel," Graham said. "But I had to come
out here as soon as I could, and I'd never been here before, so I asked our
commo officer, Colonel Lemes, to set it up."

"Well, what he did was call the Office of the Chief Signal Officer, and his
deputy called here and said you—Colonel Graham of the Marines *and* the
OSS—was on his way out here and to give him—you—whatever you wanted.
So I sent Iron Lung to the gate—"

" 'Iron Lung'?" Graham chuckled. "I can't imagine why you call him that."

"He does give new meaning to the phrase 'voice of command,' doesn't he?
Actually, he's a fine young officer."

"That was the impression I formed," Graham said. "He'd have made a fine
drill instructor at Parris Island."

"Actually, before he came here, he was a tactical officer at Signal Corps
OCS at Fort Monmouth."

"What was that, the round peg in the round hole?"

Scott laughed.

"So how can we help the OSS?" Scott said, waving Graham into a chair.

"I've got a team in the field that needs better radios than they have to communicate with Washington."

"Where are they?"

"South America. They've asked for six Collins Model 295 Transceivers."

"Well, they know what to ask for, but . . ."

"There's a problem?"

"How skilled is your commo sergeant?"

"He's a long-service Navy chief radioman. About as smart as they come. As
a matter of fact, he's about to be commissioned."

"Then no problem. They're great radios, but they need people who know what they're doing when they go down. And, as matter of fact, to set them up. When do you want them?"

"Would tomorrow morning be too soon?"

"You're serious?"

"Within the next couple of days."

"How are you going to ship them?"

"By air. In an airplane that's also going down there."

"Can you give me forty-eight hours?"

"That would work fine."

"Happy to be able to oblige," Colonel Scott said. "Where do you want them?"

"We're in the National Institutes of Health complex on—"

"I know where it is. I'll have Iron Lung personally check them out and deliver them himself."

"I'm really grateful, Colonel. Thank you."

"Anything else the Army Security Agency can do for the OSS?"

"No. That's about it," Graham said. Then he changed his mind. "This is a wild hair . . ."

"ASA deals with wild hairs all the time."

"Cryptography."

"You came to the right place. What's the problem?"

"When we augmented the team down there, we sent an Army M-94 cylindrical cipher device with them, thinking it would be an improvement over the hand encryption they're using. El Jefe refuses to use it. He says it's too easy to break."

"El Jefe? The Chief?"

Graham, smiling, nodded.

"Well, he's right. Who's liable to intercept?"

"The Germans, most likely. Others."

"Apropos of nothing whatever, Colonel, does the term *Enigma* mean anything to you?"

"Yes, it does."

"I thought it might. Well, the bad news is we don't have anything nearly as good. The M-94 is pretty primitive. We have another one called the SIGABA, which is almost as good, as safe as the one whose name is classified."

"We have those at several places," Graham said. "But when I asked Colonel Lemes, he said that not only are they awfully expensive—"

"Is that a problem for you?" Scott interrupted.

Graham shook his head and went on. "—but that they are large, heavy, delicate—apparently they've never successfully dropped one by parachute—difficult to operate, and a mechanical nightmare."

"Unfortunately, he's right. About the only place they work reliably, outside of fixed bases, is aboard ship."

"How common is that? I mean, would they have one aboard a destroyer?"

"What destroyer? Some do, some don't."

"The USS *Alfred Thomas*, DD-107," Graham said.

"You want me to find out?"

"Could you?"

"Sir," Lieutenant McClung boomed from the door. "I have—more precisely Lieutenant Fischer has—the information the colonel requested vis-à-vis the SIGABA aboard a Navy vessel."

"Is he out there with you?"

"Yes, sir," McClung boomed.

"Bring him in."

The two young officers marched into Colonel Scott's office.

Second Lieutenant Leonard Fischer, Signal Corps, was nowhere as large as First Lieutenant McClung.

"What did you find out, Len?" Scott asked.

"Sir, there is one aboard the *Alfred Thomas*. My source in the Navy says he doesn't know if it's operable, and probably is not, because the chief radioman who knew how to operate it and repair it was taken ill and removed from the ship somewhere in South America—Argentina or Uruguay, he wasn't sure."

Colonel Scott and Colonel Graham looked at each other, but neither responded directly.

"Lieutenant, let me ask you a question," Graham said. "What would you say the chances are that a SIGABA could be shipped about five thousand miles on one airplane—I mean, it would be loaded aboard the airplane in Washington and off-loaded at its destination, not go through depots, et cetera—without suffering irreparable damage?"

"It would need a lot of work, sir," Lieutenant Fischer said, after thinking about it. "Five thousand miles in an airplane is a lot of vibration, and there would be, I'd guess, half a dozen landings and takeoffs to make it that far. But *irreparable*? No, sir. Presuming the parts were available, and we know pretty well which parts will fail, and there was someone who knew what he was doing to make the repairs, it could be made operable."

"Thank you," Graham said, and looked at Scott.

"That'll be all for right now, but stay close," Scott said.

"Yes, sir," McClung boomed, drowning out whatever Fischer replied.

Scott looked at Graham after the two had left.

"Did I ever tell you, Colonel, that in addition to everything else we do here, some of us read minds?"

"Read mine," Graham said.

"How long will Lieutenant Fischer be on temporary duty with you?"

"It's important, Colonel, or I wouldn't ask," Graham said. "Can I have him for thirty days?"

VII

[ONE]
Office of the Commercial Attaché
Embassy of the German Reich
Avenida Córdoba
Buenos Aires, Argentina
0915 14 July 1943

Commercial Attaché Karl Cranz had come to work in a very pleasant frame of mind. There was only one problem to deal with that he could see, and it wasn't at all a major one. There was no question in his mind that the foreign ministry would, as a result of his cable yesterday, cancel Commercial Attaché Wilhelm Frogger's orders to return to Berlin. That caused the small problem of having two commercial attachés in the embassy.

Cranz had decided that could easily be solved by changing his own title to deputy commercial attaché. It didn't matter, really, what official title one carried, so long as everyone understood who had the authority.

Reminding Frogger that he was, in fact, Obersturmbannführer Cranz and in Argentina on an important and highly secret mission would keep Frogger in his place, leaving Frogger free to continue his auction bidding war with the Americans over the tinned corned beef.

What was amusing in all this was that he really wasn't Obersturmbannführer

Cranz at all, but actually Standartenführer Cranz, although he had to keep that under his hat until von Deitzberg was on the Condor on his way home.

When he was free to let everyone know his real rank, that would put a number of potential problems in order. As Standartenführer Cranz he would be both the senior service officer in the embassy and the senior SS officer in this part of South America.

That would make him senior to the just-promoted Fregattenkapitän Boltitz, the new naval attaché. Not that he anticipated any trouble with Karl Boltitz or his new number two, Military Attaché for Air Major Peter von Wachtstein. He had just about decided that whoever the traitor in the embassy was, it wasn't von Wachtstein. If indeed there was a traitor. It seemed more and more likely that what had happened at Samborombón Bay was entirely an Argentine reaction to the elimination of Oberst Frade.

He would also put Raschner straight about why he had not been recalled to Berlin. Raschner obviously thought he still would be working for von Deitzberg, and in that capacity keeping an eye on Commercial Attaché Cranz. Immediately after advising Raschner of his actual rank, Cranz would make it clear to him that the reason Raschner remained in Buenos Aires was that Standartenführer Cranz had asked Himmler for his services and, accordingly, Raschner no longer worked for von Deitzberg.

Raschner—he was not a fool—would immediately recognize on which side of his bread was the butter and was probably going to be very useful.

And just as soon as von Deitzberg left for Berlin, Cranz would have von Wachtstein fly him to Montevideo, where he would assert his authority over both Councilor Konrad Forster and Sturmbannführer Werner von Tresmarck in the embassy there.

Councilor Forster was actually Hauptsturmführer Forster of the Sicherheitsdienst. His primary function in the embassy—known only to Ambassador Schulker—was counterintelligence. Cranz would firmly tell Forster that Forster was now under his orders, and that Cranz was to be immediately furnished with any information he developed.

Forster was not privy to anything concerned with the confidential special fund, and Cranz had no intention of telling him.

But if von Tresmarck did something stupid—something that might call attention to anything, which included the fund—Cranz told Forster that he wanted to hear about it right away.

Von Tresmarck would also be told that he now was directly responsible to

Cranz, and bluntly reminded that he had one foot on the slippery slope to a pink triangle on a gray Sachsenhausen inmate's uniform.

Cranz saw no potential problems with any of this, and was delighted with what he saw as his future here in Buenos Aires. Neither was he worried that anything would happen in Germany to see him recalled. That couldn't be done without the acquiescence of everyone involved with Operation Phoenix—and that group included Martin Bormann. Karl Cranz was much closer to Hitler's right-hand man than anyone thought, and Bormann wanted Cranz in Buenos Aires. Bormann knew more about the confidential special fund than anyone thought, because Cranz had gone to him and told him.

Bormann's reactions had not been what Cranz had expected. The Reichsleiter had not gone to Himmler with the information that von Deitzberg was conducting what Himmler probably would have considered a treasonous fraud against the Third Reich. Nor had he asked to be included in the distribution of the fund's munificence.

"What I want you to do about that, Karl," he'd said, using Cranz's Christian name for the first time, "is play along with them. Sometimes, something sordid like that can be transformed into something useful. And don't worry. If it comes out, I'll tell the Führer you were acting on my orders."

Cranz had asked Bormann what to do about taking money from the special confidential fund, saying that it would look suspicious if he didn't. Bormann had said, somewhat cryptically, "Don't do anything that would cause suspicion," and Cranz had decided that that was permission to keep taking the money.

The money was one of the reasons Cranz also was pleased about what life in Buenos Aires promised to be, especially after Ilse and the children joined him. Frogger had told him that there was a generous Foreign Service allowance for renting an apartment, adding that he didn't use all of his and pocketed the difference, which was permitted.

Cranz had immediately decided to do the opposite, to augment the rental allowance with money from the special confidential fund. When Ilse and the children joined him, they'd find a very nice apartment—perhaps even a chalet in one of the suburbs—waiting for them.

He'd also used some special confidential funds the night before. He'd sort of tricked Boltitz into taking him to his tailor by asking him what he planned to do about new uniforms to go with his new rank. When Boltitz had replied that he'd have to go—and soon—to von Wachtstein's tailor to have the extra golden stripe added to the sleeve, Cranz had said, "I'll go with you, Karl. I need some suits, and I might as well take advantage of not having to worry about a clothing ration."

He'd ordered half a dozen suits, shirts, and neckties. Not that it mattered, but they were really inexpensive. And when they walked back onto the street, he'd seen a lingerie store with what looked like silk stockings in the window.

Silk stockings were hard to come by in Berlin, even in the special stores for senior officers. The opposite was apparently true in Buenos Aires. The store had shelf upon shelf of them, and at quite reasonable prices.

He bought a dozen pair of the best quality the store offered. He would get Captain von und zu Aschenburg, the Condor pilot, to take them to Ilse. He would put a note in the box, suggesting that Ilse give a pair or two of them to her friend Gerda. She would probably do so anyway, but it was best to make sure. Gerda, the daughter of Walter Buch, chairman of the party's court for the determination of NSDAP legal matters and internal discipline, was married to Martin Bormann.

Von und zu Aschenburg, too, was going to be useful. Once he got in the habit of taking small packages from South America to Berlin, those packages in the future could contain Swiss francs, English pounds, and American dollars for von Deitzberg.

One of the problems with the special confidential fund was that the payments made to gain the freedom of the Jews in the concentration camps were transacted in Uruguay. That required converting the funds to currency usable in Germany. Reichsmarks were hard to come by in Argentina and Uruguay without going through either the Buenos Aires branches of the Deutsche Bank or the Dresdnerbank—which of course being German kept detailed records, which of course was not a good thing. Thus, von Tresmarck had to send the cash in the diplomatic pouch, and that raised the risk of Hauptsturmführer Forster—who was both zealous and until now under no one's authority—finding out what von Tresmarck's little packages contained.

Cranz had arrived in what arguably was his office at five minutes to nine. His good feeling lasted until he glanced at his watch and saw that it now was quarter past nine.

One would have thought that Frogger would have come in a bit early, not a bit late.

He said and did nothing even then, instead glancing through the *Argen-*

tinisches Tageblatt, the German-language newspaper. Somebody—he couldn't remember who—had told him that the Argentines, who regarded the *Tageblatt* as a "guest newspaper," would not permit it to publish much of anything at all except announcements of church meetings, births, weddings, deaths, and the like unless the items first had been published in an Argentine newspaper—and then only if the translation was approved by the Argentine government and the paper ran both the German translation and the original story in Spanish, either side by side or one after the other.

Reading it now, Cranz thought that were it not for the notices of the deaths of Argo-Germans in Africa and Russia, and pleas to contribute to *Winterhilfe*— which asked Germans abroad to aid Germans impoverished by the war—one would never know a war was on.

He quickly tired of reading news of the Buenos Aires German community's church suppers and such.

He looked at his watch again.

Nine twenty-five.

Where the hell is he?

He couldn't remember the name of Frogger's secretary, so he couldn't call for her. Instead, he got up from Frogger's desk and walked to the outer office.

"Señora," he asked politely, "you don't happen to know where El Señor Frogger is, do you?"

She smiled, then said she was sorry, she had no idea.

"What time does he usually come to work?"

"He's usually here, señor, when I come in."

"And when do you usually come in, señora?"

"El Señor Frogger likes to have me at my desk at eight, señor."

"He didn't send a message that he would be late?"

"No, señor."

"Would you please try to get him, or La Señora Frogger, on the telephone for me, please?"

Three minutes later, she reported that there was no answer at El Señor Frogger's home number or at the Café Flora, where he and La Señora Frogger sometimes went for breakfast.

Cranz smiled and thanked her, gave the situation a moment's thought, then went looking for First Secretary Anton von Gradny-Sawz.

Cranz had already formed several opinions about Gradny-Sawz, none of them very flattering. He had decided Gradny-Sawz was shrewd but not very bright; that it had been a mistake by Bormann to name him to try to enlist Colonel Perón—that Cranz probably would have to take that task onto himself—and that while Gradny-Sawz probably was not the traitor, neither was he trustworthy.

But Gradny-Sawz was first secretary of the embassy, and thus Frogger's immediate superior, and Cranz didn't want to go to the ambassador about something petty like Frogger not showing up for work on time.

When Cranz got to Gradny-Sawz's office, von Deitzberg was in there with Gradny-Sawz and looked at Cranz with annoyance.

"Will this wait, Cranz?" von Deitzberg snapped.

"Frogger hasn't come in, and I was going to ask the first secretary if he perhaps knew anything about it."

"Did you call him at home?" von Deitzberg asked.

"There's no answer," Cranz said.

"Let me check with Fräulein Hässell," Gradny-Sawz said, and dialed a number.

Fräulein Hässell had no idea why Herr Frogger had not come to work.

Nor did Ambassador von Lutzenberger, who suggested it might be a good idea to send Untersturmführer Schneider around to their apartment to make sure that nothing was wrong.

"You go with him, Cranz," von Deitzberg ordered, "and take Raschner with you."

The Frogger apartment was on the fourth floor of a turn-of-the-century apartment building on Calle Talcahuano. A park separated it from the Colón Opera House.

When there was no answer to the in-house telephone, the concierge said the Froggers must have gone out before he came on duty at nine, then gave the men a good deal of trouble when they said they wanted to have a look in the apartment.

Cranz was perhaps disloyally amused at Raschner's coldly angry reaction to that.

He's going to have to remember that this is not Germany and that a Gestapo badge is absolutely meaningless here.

Cranz's charm, diplomatic passport, and a small cash gift overcame the concierge's reluctance to let them into the apartment. The concierge was visibly relieved when Schneider produced a key.

The Froggers were not in the apartment. The beds were made, and there was no sign that they had had their breakfast there. There was nothing suspicious about that. They were Germans. When Germans got out of bed, they made the bed. When they had breakfast, they cleaned the table and the plates and silver and the kitchen.

Yet there also was not any lingering smell from someone having cooked a breakfast meal.

"Herr Obersturmbannführer," Raschner called softly from a table in the sitting room.

Cranz walked to him.

"What looks like a photo frame has recently been removed from here," Raschner said, pointing to barely discernible disturbances in a very light coating of dust.

Cranz raised his eyebrows in question.

"I noticed the absence of photographs of the sons," Raschner said. "There are no photos anywhere. Then it seemed to me that there were photo frames missing from the arrangement on the mantel"—he gestured with his finger toward the mantelpiece—"and then I found this."

Cranz nodded.

"May I proceed, Herr Obersturmbannführer?"

"Proceed to what, Sturmbannführer?"

"While I see if I can find a photo album anywhere, I will send Schneider to the garage to see if their auto is there."

"You're suggesting what, Sturmbannführer?"

"Let me see if we can find the car and a photo album before I suggest anything, Herr Obersturmbannführer."

"Please call me 'Herr Cranz,' Sturmbannführer."

"May I proceed, Herr Cranz?"

"Go ahead."

[TWO]
Estancia San Pedro y San Pablo
Near Pila
Buenos Aires Province, Argentina
1030 14 July 1943

Don Cletus Frade sat at a small glass-top table on a small verandah outside the master bedroom of the big house waiting for his wife to join him. He was reclined in his chair, his feet resting on the other chair, and holding a brown manual in his hands.

The manual, published by the Aeronautics Division, Ministry of the Interior, Republic of Argentina, was titled "A Practice Examination for Those Intending to Take the Qualifying Examination Leading to the Award of the Rating of Commercial Aviation Pilot."

The manual had come to him from Major Gonzalo Delgano, Argentina Army Air Service, "Retired," now the chief pilot of South American Airways. He had pointed out, reasonably, that inasmuch as the "understanding" was that all SAA pilots be Argentine nationals, it might be better if Don Cletus got an Argentine pilot license as an Argentine citizen.

It would be, Delgano had said at the time, a mere formality. Then he had come back and reported that the examining officer was being a "bit difficult" and Don Cletus would have to go to El Palomar and take the examination. It would probably be a matter of simply showing up—Delgano would meet him there—and signing a few papers.

Reasoning that while Delgano was probably right, this still was Argentina, and that it was better to be safe than sorry.

Clete had called Tío Juan Domingo and explained the problem.

Colonel Perón said that it was nonsense, not to worry about it, that he would have a word with whoever it was in charge of such things. Then he had called back and said "there were formalities," and that he would need to go to El Palomar and sign a few papers. And he would meet him there to make sure things went smoothly.

The "practice examination" seemed to have been written for people who really didn't have much practical aviation experience. Among other gems, offered as True or False, it asked would-be aviators "Should seat belts be worn at all times?" and "Should flights over bodies of water be undertaken only in good weather?"

Doña Dorotea Mallín de Frade came onto the verandah in her negligee and a robe, both pale blue. Don Cletus's heart jumped.

That has to be the best-looking woman in the world.

For the first time in my life, I understand why people go bananas when they see the Virgin Mary with the Baby Jesus in her arms.

My God, I'm the luckiest man in the world to have that beautiful, wonderful, loving woman carrying our child!

"Get your goddamn feet off my chair, Cletus!" Doña Dorotea greeted him. "I've told you a hundred times!"

He took his feet off her chair and put the manual on the floor.

Antonio LaVallé, the butler, trailed by one of the maids, appeared.

"Would Doña Dorotea prefer her eggs soft-boiled or scrambled?"

"The thought of either makes me nauseous," Doña Dorotea said.

"You have to eat, precious," Clete said.

"Yes, I know. I'm eating for two. What is that wonderful American phrase? 'Up yours,' Cletus."

"Give her the eggs scrambled, with toast and orange juice, please," Cletus said.

Doña Dorotea had managed to get everything down without nausea and was mopping at her plate with a piece of toast when Antonio came back onto the verandah.

"Don Cletus," he announced, "four people, one a woman, in an American auto with diplomatic license tags have just come onto the estancia."

Clete nodded his thanks and wondered aloud, "I wonder who the hell that is? A woman?"

Dorotea shrugged.

"In twenty minutes, you will know."

"In twenty minutes, I have to take off for El Palomar."

"In a Cub, darling, right?"

"In a Cub, my love."

After a second glass of after-dinner Argentine brandy the previous evening, Clete had confided to Dorotea that he was thinking of flying the Lodestar to El Palomar for his pilot's test.

"I mean, how could they question my ability to fly a transport if I flew there in the Lodestar?"

"They would question your sanity for flying it alone," she said. "And if you ever fly it alone again, you will thereafter sleep in it alone. You are about to be a father. Perhaps, as you say, you should write that down."

Not quite twenty minutes later, Clete and Dorotea had a second cup of coffee on the verandah as they waited for the mysterious American car with diplomatic license tags to appear.

It turned out to be a 1941 Chevrolet sedan. Captain Max Ashton was driving, and beside him in the front seat was a plump, balding, forty-nine-year-old who looked like a friendly shopkeeper. Clete knew who he was, and his curiosity was now in high gear.

Milton Leibermann was accredited to the Republic of Argentina as one of the five legal attachés of the United States embassy. It was technically a secret that he was also the special agent in charge of the Federal Bureau of Investigation's Argentine operations, and that all "legal attachés" were FBI agents.

In what Colonel Graham had described to Clete as yet another wonderfully Machiavellian move of President Franklin D. Roosevelt, the President had assured FBI Director J. Edgar Hoover that the FBI was responsible for all intelligence and counterintelligence activities in the Western Hemisphere. The President had also told OSS Director William J. Donovan that Central and South America were of course included in the OSS's worldwide responsibilities.

The result of this was that there were two U.S. intelligence agencies operating throughout Central and South America who regarded themselves as being in competition with each other and therefore had as little to do with each other as possible. And in Argentina—where Major Cletus Frade, chief of OSS Western Hemisphere Team 17, code name Team Turtle, did not trust the OSS Station Chief, Argentina, Lieutenant Commander Frederico Delojo, USN, as far as he could throw him—that meant there were three American intelligence agencies whose members did not talk to each other.

The exception to this was the relationship between Major Frade and Mr. Leibermann. There was a strong feeling of mutual admiration. Leibermann was a first-generation American who had learned his German and Yiddish from his parents and his Spanish from the Spanish-Harlem section of Manhattan.

He had developed contacts with the German and German-Jewish communities in Buenos Aires and elsewhere. Frade—with the caveat that Leibermann not pass it on to his FBI superiors—had told Leibermann about the operation the SS had ransoming concentration camp inmates. Leibermann had agreed to keep the secret, because he personally believed the OSS was better equipped to deal with the problem than was the FBI. The FBI's expertise lay in solving crimes and ransoming operations of an entirely different nature.

Leibermann was the only person not in Team Turtle who knew that "Galahad," Frade's man in the German embassy, was Major Hans-Peter Baron von Wachtstein. He had kept this secret, too, although, as the SAC in Buenos Aires, he had been tasked "as the highest priority" to find out who Galahad was.

Leibermann and Frade had agreed early on that the less they were seen together the better it would be for both. They maintained contact through Ashton and Pelosi, and the latter took care to see that their contacts took place not only inside the embassy but out of sight of Commander Delojo as well. It was not in either Frade's or Leibermann's interests that Delojo know of their association.

The last time Leibermann had been at Estancia San Pedro y San Pablo was for the wedding of Clete and Dorotea. Frade was genuinely surprised to see Leibermann now, and concerned. Agents of the BIS knew who Leibermann was and kept him under pretty tight surveillance.

The mystery grew even more when instead of pulling into the parking area in front of the big house, Ashton stopped just long enough for Leibermann to get quickly out of the car, then drove away.

Leibermann trotted up the stairs and across the verandah—passing Clete and Dorotea—and went into the house.

Enrico picked up his shotgun and looked down the drive as if he expected someone to be chasing the Chevrolet.

"I think he's headed for the hangar, Enrico," Clete said. "Go down there and see if you can be useful." Then, when he saw the look of reluctance on the old soldier's face, he added: "Go! We'll be all right. There's a Thompson in the vestibule."

When Clete and Dorotea went into the house, they found Leibermann in the vestibule.

"Where's the resident BIS agent?" Leibermann asked.

"Delgano's waiting for me at Campo de Mayo," Clete said. "Where today, after dutifully cramming for it all last night, I take my pilot's exam."

"What he meant to say, Milton," Doña Dorotea said, "was: 'Good morning, Milton. How are you? Nice to see you. You're looking well. Can we offer you a cup of coffee? Or some breakfast?' "

"What I meant to say is: 'What's the hell's going on, Milt?' "

"At half past eight this morning, the commercial attaché of the German embassy appeared at my apartment door with his wife and surrendered," Liebermann said. "They're in the car with Ashton."

"What do you mean, *surrendered*?" Clete asked.

"They've been recalled to Germany, and he doesn't want to go. So he wants me to get them to Brazil, where he can get them interned."

"He tell you why?" Clete asked, but before Leibermann could reply, he asked another question: "What's their relationship to you?"

"Well, I've been trying to recruit them, but until this morning, when they showed up at my place, I had no idea that I'd even caught their attention."

"Recruit them for what?"

Leibermann's face showed he thought that was a really stupid question.

"Can you do that? Get them to Brazil?" Clete asked.

"Not without permission,'" Leibermann said. "Which means I would have to ask the ambassador, who would ask your friend Commander Delojo . . ."

"Another stupid question: Why can't they get themselves interned here?"

"Because neutral Argentina is not granting political asylum to Germans. Or, for that matter, to Americans. Brazil is at war . . ."

"Okay. Back to my first question: Why doesn't he want to go back to Germany? What did he tell you?"

"Nothing that I believe," Leibermann said. "But what I think is very likely is that he's afraid he's going to be identified as Galahad."

"But he's not."

"I know that, and you know that, and probably so does Generalmajor von Deitzberg, who was sent here to find the traitor and he's not going to fail. Or at least that's what Frogger is worried about."

"That's his name?"

Leibermann nodded. "Wilhelm Frogger."

"So what's wrong with letting Delojo have him?"

"Delojo's going to ask why he came to me, and I have solemnly promised him I would let him know in advance before I tried to recruit anybody, so there would be 'no duplication of effort.' "

"And Delojo," Dorotea said, "would certainly ask him who he thought the traitor really was, and this man would probably give him a list of names, including the right one."

Leibermann looked at her and nodded.

"I wonder what this guy knows about Operation Phoenix and the ransoming operation," Clete wondered aloud.

"I don't know. He probably knows something he doesn't know he knows. Presuming he doesn't know all about both operations," Leibermann said.

There was the sound of a car pulling up outside.

"Now what the hell?" Clete said.

It was Enrico and Max Ashton.

"I told you to make yourself useful at the hangar," Clete said less than kindly.

"Rodolfo is at the hangar, Don Cletus," Enrico said.

Cletus was about to bark at Enrico, then just in time remembered, *Never give a subordinate an ass-chewing in the presence of others*, and turned back to Leibermann.

"Well, what we're really saying is that we should hide these people someplace until we make up our minds what to do with them," he said.

"And pick their brains about what they might not know they know," Leibermann quickly agreed.

"Which is why you brought them here, right?" Clete said. "Why the hell didn't you come right out and say so?"

"I didn't want to suggest something that could endanger your operation. But once it was your idea . . ."

"Well, we can hide them here, I guess."

"This is the first place Colonel Martín would look for them," Dorotea said. "If he doesn't think you kidnapped them, the Germans will make that suggestion."

Leibermann didn't say anything, but it was clear on his face that he agreed with Dorotea.

"Don Cletus?" Enrico said.

"What?" Clete asked, somewhat impatiently.

"Is it important that we hide these people where El Coronel Martín and his clowns cannot find them? Or the Germans?"

"Yes, it is."

"We could hide these people in Casa Chica, Don Cletus."

"What's Casa Chica?" Frade said. "One of the casas on the estancia? Didn't you hear what Doña Dorotea just said? This is the first place Martín's going to look. And, God damn it, the people who work for him are not clowns; they're good."

"This is somewhat delicate, Don Cletus."

"*Delicate?* What the hell are you talking about?!"

"Casa Chica is a very small estancia near Tandil in the hills between La Pampas and Mar del Plata," Enrico explained. "No more than maybe two hundred hectares."

"Whose estancia is it?"

"It is yours, Don Cletus."

"How come I never heard of it?"

"It was one of your father's most closely kept secrets, Don Cletus," Enrico said.

"You mean during the . . . before the coup? Because of that?"

"No, Don Cletus," Enrico said uncomfortably. "Señor . . . it was where he and Doña Claudia would go when they wished to be alone."

Leibermann smiled. Frade glared at him.

"There is an airstrip and a nice little house. Very romantic, Don Cletus. There is a very nice view of the hills. There is a waterfall, not a very big one, but a very nice one. And—"

"And nobody knows about this place?" Clete shut him off.

"No, señor. Only myself and Rodolfo. When El Coronel and Doña Claudia went there, he took with them only Rodolfo or me, and Mariana María Delores, may she be resting in peace."

Frade's mind flashed the image of Enrico's sister, Señora Mariana María Dolores Rodríguez de Pellano, her throat slashed during the failed attempt to assassinate Frade.

When Clete didn't reply, Enrico went on: "There are just a few servants there, Don Cletus. All of them my family. They know how to keep their mouths shut."

"That sounds ideal, Clete," Leibermann said.

"Can we get these people there without anyone seeing them?"

"In the back of a truck," Enrico said.

"Honey, I really have to go," Clete said. "If I'm late getting to Campo de Mayo, the first thing they'll think is that I'm involved in this."

Dorotea nodded.

"Call Casa Número Veintidós. Tell Chief Schultz to send Sergeant Stein here with a truck and a couple of Thompsons. Tell Stein to dress like a gaucho. And then, Enrico, truck these people out to this place in Tandil. Don't let them be seen, and don't let them near a telephone."

"I will go with you, Don Cletus," Enrico said softly.

Clete ignored him.

"I have no intention of riding in the back of a truck," Dorotea said. "I'm pregnant, in case you haven't noticed. Factor that into your planning, Napoleon."

"What are you talking about?" Clete asked. "You're not going to this place, wherever it is. Jesus Christ!"

"Permission to speak, Don Cletus?" Enrico asked.

When Frade looked at him, he saw Enrico was standing at attention.

Restraining a smile, Clete barked, "Stand at ease, permission granted," and then glowered at Ashton, who was smiling.

"Señor, if I am not with you at Campo de Mayo, questions would be asked . . ."

Jesus, he's right about that!

". . . but if Rodolfo were to drive Doña Dorotea in the Horch and the truck following them was carrying furniture, and provisions. . . ."

"Good idea, Clete," Leibermann said. "Nothing suspicious about that. What do they call that? 'Hiding in plain sight'?"

Clete considered that a moment, then agreed. "Yeah, it is. You sure you're up to this, baby?"

"Of course I am. All I do is ride over there—I've never been to the estancia, but I've been to Tandil; I'd guess it's about two hours from here—unload the provisions and the furniture, and ride back. As long as Rodolfo and Seigfried don't hang out a sign, no one will suspect that we're hiding a couple of Nazis in what is now *my* little love nest in the hills."

Clete was surprised at her use of the term *Nazi* and then wondered why. He quickly decided that was because the word called up images of Nazis in steel helmets or SS uniforms in B movies, not the dumpy looking guy and his matching wife he had seen in the back of the Chevrolet.

He turned to Leibermann.

"And you and Max head back to Buenos Aires and hope nobody saw you come out here."

[THREE]
Office of the Ambassador
Embassy of the German Reich
Avenida Córdoba
Buenos Aires, Argentina
1140 14 July 1943

"I suggest for the moment," Ambassador von Lutzenberger said, "that we accept Sturmbannführer Raschner's premise that Herr Frogger has chosen to desert his post—"

"What other reason for his disappearance could there possibly be?" von Deitzberg interrupted almost indignantly.

Von Lutzenberger ignored him and went on: "—which then poses the question of why."

"He did not wish to go home, obviously," Gradny-Sawz said.

"If so, wouldn't that raise the question why?" von Lutzenberger said.

"Isn't that equally obvious?" von Deitzberg said sarcastically. "He's the traitor we've been looking for."

Cranz had several thoughts, one after the other:

Nonsense.

Frogger not only had no reason to be a traitor but was psychologically incapable of being one.

Does von Deitzberg actually believe what he's saying?

Of course not.

Von Deitzberg was sent here to find the traitor, and failed.

But he can now say that he suspected Frogger all along, and was getting close to having enough proof when Frogger somehow found out—or simply sensed it—and deserted.

That makes him look a lot better than having failed to find the traitor.

And if there is a traitor, knowing that Frogger has been "exposed" might just make him relax enough so that he'll make a mistake. If that happens, von Deitzberg will get credit for catching both.

My God, he's good!

"Cranz," von Deitzberg asked, "wouldn't you agree?"

"I'm only wondering, Herr Generalmajor, how it is that Frogger managed to escape the attention of Herr Gradny-Sawz, Oberst Grüner, and Untersturmführer Schneider."

"Or mine," von Lutzenberger said. "I'm as culpable as they are."

And so you are, Your Excellency, Cranz thought.

You are nobly accepting responsibility for something over which you had no control, and could not be expected to, with a senior Sicherheitsdienst officer—now conveniently dead—in charge of that sort of thing.

The proof of that came immediately.

"Your Excellency," von Deitzberg said smoothly, "I admire your position, but I respectfully suggest that if Oberst Grüner—an expert in these matters—could not detect this traitor, you really couldn't be expected to."

Now he's "Your Excellency"?

And you "respectfully suggest," von Deitzberg?

You're now friends, are you?

"I am the ambassador of the German Reich, Herr Generalmajor, and responsible for everything that happens—or doesn't happen—on my watch," von Lutzenberger said. "But, readily acknowledging your expertise in these areas, may I ask what you suggest we do now?"

And if you go along with that, von Deitzberg, won't that dump the responsibility for whatever happens next in your lap? I know you're too smart not to see that.

So the question becomes, How are you going to react? As a professional, and agree with von Lutzenberger that the responsibility is in fact his? Or will your ego take over?

Von Deitzberg took a moment to reply. When he finally did, Cranz thought his ego had overridden his common sense.

"Let's consider other possibilities before we decide on a course of action," von Deitzberg said. "And, please, feel free to interrupt me at any time."

"Jawohl, Herr Generalmajor," Cranz said.

"The first question, it would seem to me," von Deitzberg began, "is, Where is this swine? Did he just put his wife on a train and go somewhere? Or—and we know he had to plan for this—are the English or the Americans perhaps involved?"

"Frogger was of course under routine security surveillance," von Lutzenberger said. "And Gradny-Sawz and I read all of the reports that Schneider and others submitted to Grüner. There was nothing that ever suggested any contact with the Americans or the English. Isn't that so, Gradny-Sawz?"

"I never saw anything, Your Excellency."

"His social life, such as it was," von Lutzenberger went on, "was limited to participation in activities of the German community. The Froggers were Protestant and regularly attended church services at the German community church—"

"Where, so far as we know, the man on his knees next to them," Cranz interrupted, "might well have been from MI-5, right? Or the OSS?"

"More likely MI-5, Karl," von Deitzberg said. "I don't think the Americans are that smart."

Cranz chuckled his agreement.

I'm now "Karl," am I, Herr SS-Brigadeführer von Deitzberg?

Well, since we are now friends and dealing with a common problem, I will not argue with your assessment of the ability of the OSS by saying the Americans were smart enough to find and sink the Reine de la Mer.

"Frogger," von Deitzberg went on, "was obviously far more clever than even

Oberst Grüner thought. I don't think, therefore, that we stand much chance at all of locating them by ourselves. It would be my recommendation, Your Excellency, that we report they are missing to the Argentine authorities."

"And what will we tell the Argentine authorities?" Cranz asked.

The ambassador said, "What we know for sure: that they are missing. And we are naturally concerned for their safety."

"Mentioning nothing about their possibly having deserted?" Gradny-Sawz asked.

It earned him a withering glare from von Deitzberg.

"We don't *know* that they have deserted, do we?" von Deitzberg said. "For all we *know*, Gradny-Sawz, they may have been stolen by gypsies or taken bodily into heaven."

"Gradny-Sawz will call the foreign ministry," von Lutzenberger said as he pushed his telephone to him. "And I suggest, Herr Generalmajor, that we get Boltitz and von Wachtstein in here and explain the situation."

"Go get them," von Deitzberg ordered, gesturing to Cranz. Then he had a second thought. "But before we do that . . . Is there any way Herr Frogger and his wife could just disappear? Do we know anyone who could arrange that?"

"I don't," von Lutzenberger said. "Oberst Grüner dealt with things like that."

"Not too well, apparently," von Deitzberg said. "Well, if the situation presents itself, that would be a satisfactory solution to this problem. Keep your eyes and ears open, Raschner. Take whatever action seems appropriate."

"Jawohl, Herr Brigadeführer."

Von Deitzberg looked at him as if he was about to remind him that he was to be addressed as "Herr Generalmajor" but then changed his mind.

[FOUR]
Diplomatic Liaison Section
Foreign Ministry of the Republic of Argentina
Plaza San Martín
Buenos Aires, Argentina
1205 14 July 1943

The first call El Señor Alfredo Mashewitz, the chief of Diplomatic Services, made after assuring First Secretary Anton Gradny-Sawz of the German embassy that he would "get right on this" was to the chief, Office of Ethical Standards,

Bureau of Internal Security, Ministry of Defense, in the Edificio Libertador on Avenida Paseo Colón.

The call was taken by Warrant Officer Frederico Attiria, who said that El Coronel Martín was not available—that he was with the president of the Republic, General Arturo Rawson, who was attending some sort of luncheon function at the Campo de Mayo military base. Attiria said that he would get word to him as quickly as possible.

Señor Mashewitz next called Comisario Santiago Nervo, chief of the Special Investigations Division of the Policía Federal, and got him on the phone. He told him what had happened.

Nervo said he would send an official of appropriate rank to the German embassy immediately, and asked if Mashewitz had notified the office of the president of the Republic, as he was sure they would want to hear about this.

Mashewitz said that he would telephone the office of the president of the Republic immediately, but that he had reason to believe the president himself was attending a luncheon function at Campo de Mayo.

"Well, then, I suppose I had better be getting out there myself, hadn't I?" Nervo replied, then added, "And I think it would be a good idea if you called BIS and let them know about this. I presume you have the number?"

Mashewitz, deciding that it would only complicate matters if he said that his first call had been to BIS, simply replied that he had the number.

When he hung up, he did not call the office of the president, but instead went to lunch. The foreign minister, who would of course have to be told as soon as possible, was taking his lunch at the Jockey Club, where of course talk of business was verboten, and the foreign minister did not take kindly—to put it mildly—to being disturbed during his meal. The news would wait until the foreign minister returned from lunch. In the meantime, he would have a lamb shank and a glass or two of merlot at a restaurant just around the corner from the ministry.

[FIVE]
El Palomar Airfield
Campo de Mayo Military Base
Buenos Aires Province, Argentina
1245 14 July 1943

Don Cletus Frade saw El Coronel Juan Domingo Perón waiting for him as he taxied the Piper Cub up to what on an American base would be called Base Operations.

Perón, in uniform, was sitting somewhat regally in the back of his official car, a glistening olive-drab Mercedes touring sedan, which, despite the chill of the wintry July day had the top down. Major Gonzalo Delgano, Army Air Service, "Retired," was in civilian clothing and seated in the front beside the soldier driver. Delgano looked uncomfortable.

Perón appeared displeased when he saw Sergeant Major Rodríguez, Retired, get out of the backseat, then take out his Remington Model 11 self-loading shotgun. Rodríguez rested the shotgun against the landing gear and began to tie down the Cub and put its wheel chocks in place.

Oh, hell, Frade thought. *I don't know what's going on. But the last thing I want to do is make a full day of this, with a long lunch at the club and where everybody will be making their manners to Perón—which is obviously what he has in mind.*

What I have to do is get the hell out of here—fly to Tandil, wherever the hell that is, make sure that Dorotea made it all right, then make sure the Germans are firmly locked up where they won't be seen, then get back to the estancia while there's still enough light to fly.

Which means: I will need a chart to find Tandil.

And gas. I can't make it with the fuel aboard—the J-3 Cub holds only twelve gallons of fuel, giving it a range of about 190 miles. And it's farther than that from El Palomar to Tandil.

He turned his back to the Mercedes.

"Enrico, we have to go to Tandil. Get a twenty-liter can of gas and a map, and put them in the plane. And make sure the tank on the Cub is full."

Enrico nodded.

"Aren't you glad you brought me along, Don Cletus?"

"Yes, I am," Frade said, and squeezed his shoulder. Then he walked toward the Mercedes.

Perón descended somewhat regally from the Mercedes.

Don Cletus wondered: *What's the protocol? Does one kiss a colonel in a class "A" uniform on a military base?*

When in doubt, kiss.

"I was becoming worried that you would be late, Cletus," Perón said after they had kissed.

"Punctuality is my only virtue, Tío Juan," Clete said as he offered his hand to Delgano. "You said one o'clock, and I'm ten minutes early."

"You had best get in back with us, Delgano," Perón ordered, "and let the sergeant major sit with the driver."

"Enrico's going to fuel the airplane," Clete said.

Perón looked relieved. But even though Enrico was not going, Delgano got in the backseat. The three of them were all large men, and it was a tight fit.

"Well, where do I take the exam?" Clete asked. "Last night I felt like a schoolboy studying up for it."

Perón smiled at him but did not reply.

Five minutes later, the Mercedes pulled up in front of the Officers' Casino. Cars of all sizes lined the driveway.

"Tío Juan, it looks like half the Ejército Argentino is having lunch. Why don't I take the examination now? And we can come back when there aren't so many people?"

Perón didn't reply. He got out of the car.

Shit!

They walked through the ornate doors and into the marble-floored lobby.

Major Cletus Frade, USMCR, looked up at an enormous crystal chandelier and thought: *Boy, this is really one hell of an O club. I'd forgotten how fancy it is.*

Probably because the last time I was here, there was a good chance I'd be stood against a wall.

The O club at Fighter One was a couple of picnic tables under a canvas flap.

On great occasions, there was a can or two of beer. Warm beer.

A major wearing a uniform draped with gold aiguillettes marched up to them.

"This way, mi coronel," he said.

He walked to a double door and pulled the right side open.

Perón motioned for Clete to precede him.

Just as soon as he was through the door, the major with the aiguillettes barked, "Mr. President, gentlemen, our guests!"

There was the sound of shuffling feet as the room full of officers came to their feet, and then the sound of applause.

I don't know what's going on with Tío Juan Domingo, but I am going to find a chair at the rear of the room.

Perón firmly grasped Clete's arm and marched him along the side of the dining room, then behind the head table.

General Arturo Rawson, president of the Republic of Argentina, was standing there in uniform. He wore a broad smile and had his arms ready to embrace somebody.

"My great friend Cletus!" Rawson exclaimed, then wrapped him in a bear hug and kissed him on both cheeks.

What the hell is going on here?

Clete's hand was then enthusiastically shaken by a dozen officers, none of whom he recognized, as a beaming Perón watched.

Everybody sat down but General Rawson.

"Gentlemen," Rawson began, "in this very room—well, not exactly, in *that* little room . . ."

He pointed to the bar, and there was dutiful laughter.

". . . my dear friend, the late Coronel Jorge Guillermo Frade, whom God has seen fit to remove from our midst, talked many times to me of two things. One was the role he saw for light aircraft in the army. Frankly, I didn't agree with him. But I never argued with him, because a wise man never argued with Coronel Jorge Guillermo Frade. And he spoke with great pride of his son, Cletus, who was born here but raised by his mother's family in the United States, after the tragic death of his mother when he was an infant.

"His son, Cletus, was an officer of the American Corps of Marines, a pilot. Jorge was not surprised. The blood of Juan Martín de Pueyrredón ran through his veins. Jorge told me with great and justifiable pride that Cletus had shot down seven of the enemy's planes and been twice decorated with the Distinguished Flying Cross for his valor.

"And then Cletus was released from active duty for a physical problem, and came here to the land of his birth to be with his father. Then God in his wisdom took our beloved Jorge from us, just as he was about to lead us in the action we found it necessary to take in order to restore our beloved Argentina to democracy.

"Technically, that was none of Cletus Frade's business. He was an American. But he knew that his father had been the principal author of Operation Blue. And when that action began, the blood of Pueyrredón, the blood of Jorge Guillermo Frade, coursing through his veins overcame consideration of legal technicalities. He saw his duty.

"Cletus Frade flew his father's airplane here to Campo de Mayo and placed it and himself at the service of the Ejército Argentino. If our action had failed, there is no question in my mind that he would have been standing beside me as we faced a firing squad.

"As our columns advanced on the Casa Rosada, I saw them. I saw them from a light airplane being flown with extraordinary skill by Cletus Frade. There was no longer any question in my mind about what El Coronel Frade believed about the role of light aircraft in the army.

"From the moment Cletus landed us back here on that historical day I wondered how I could recognize Cletus's service to Argentina. He was not an officer in the Ejército Argentino, so I could neither promote him nor decorate him. Indeed, if I had decorated him, it would have gotten him in trouble with the U.S. government.

"And then, several days ago, El Coronel Juan Domingo Perón came to me and we talked about Juan Domingo's godson, Don Cletus Frade. He told me that Cletus has actually become an Argentine. He has married an Argentine, and God is about to bless that union with a child. He has assumed control of his father's business ventures. And El Coronel Perón told me that he is going to apply his aviation skills here in Argentina. South American Airways will soon take to the skies under our flag.

"And El Coronel Perón said, 'What's a little funny, Mr. President, is that Cletus will have to go through all the licensing examinations to get a pilot's license, just as if he never flew before.'

"And at that moment, gentlemen, I knew how I could in some small way express my gratitude—indeed, that of the nation—to Don Cletus Frade for his valiant service to the republic.

"Gentlemen, as president of the Republic of Argentina, it is my pleasure to announce that Don Cletus Frade has been certified by the Aeronautics Division, Ministry of the Interior, Republic of Argentina, as a commercial aviation pilot. And more than that, his certificate will bear the signature of the president of the republic as the approving officer."

He gestured to the aiguillette-draped major, then to Cletus to join him. The major now held a gold-framed document in his hands. As Rawson took it from him and handed it to Frade, the officers in the room stood and applauded.

General Rawson pumped Frade's hand, then embraced and kissed him. Then Colonel Perón pumped Frade's hand and kissed him.

"Thank you, Tío Juan," Frade said.

Perón embraced him again.

Over his shoulder, Frade saw Colonel Alejandro Martín, chief of the Ethical Standards Office of the Bureau of Internal Security, looking at him and smiling.

Frade thought the smile was one of amusement, as if he and Frade shared a secret.

Colonel Martín showed up at the airfield as Frade was loading Enrico, the shotgun, the framed commercial aviation pilot certificate, and the twenty-liter can of aviation gas into the close confines of the rear seat of the cub.

Martín saluted Perón, shook hands with Delgano, and offered his hand to Frade.

"Congratulations on your certification, Don Cletus," he said.

"Thank you."

"May I ask a layman's question?"

"Certainly."

"Why are you taking gasoline with you?"

"To make sure that I have enough gasoline to get back to Estancia San Pedro y San Pablo."

Martín's face was questioning.

"But if you flew here from Estancia San Pedro y San Pablo . . ."

You clever sonofabitch, you!

"Why do I need more gas to fly back than I did to get here?"

Martín nodded.

"It's known as 'winds aloft,'" Frade said. "If the wind is blowing on your tail, 'a tailwind,' you add the speed of the wind to the speed of the airplane to get your speed over the ground. However, if it is blowing against your nose, a 'headwind,' then you subtract the speed of the wind from the speed of the aircraft over the ground. I had a tailwind coming here, which meant that I had more than enough fuel. But I expect a headwind on the way back."

"And what if you had had a headwind on your way here?"

"Then I would have had to turn back, come by car, and miss getting my license."

"So, if you have to refuel on your way home, you will land on the pampas?"

"If I have to refuel, I will land on a road on the pampas, if I can find one. If not, then I would have to take a chance landing on the grassland."

"Fascinating!"

"You must come fly with me sometime, Colonel."

"I would like that, Don Cletus," Martín said. "Actually, I came here for a quiet word with Colonel Perón. Normally, I would ask for a moment of the colonel's time in private, but after that sterling tribute to your Argentine patriotism by General Rawson, I can see no reason I shouldn't share this with you as well."

"Share what, Martín?" Perón asked, more than a little impatiently.

"It would seem, sir, that the commercial attaché of the German embassy has disappeared."

"What do you mean, 'disappeared'?" Perón asked.

"They can't find him or his wife," Martín said, looking directly at Frade.

"What do you think happened to them?" Frade asked.

"I haven't the faintest idea right now, Don Cletus, but I think we'll find out something soon."

"If I happen to run into them," Frade said, "you'll be the first to know."

"This is not a joke, Cletus," Perón said sternly. "This is serious business. I need to find a telephone to call Generalmajor von Deitzberg and assure him the Argentine government will do everything in its power to get to the bottom of this."

[SIX]
Near Olavarría
Buenos Aires Province, Argentina
1540 14 July 1943

The navigation chart being used by newly licensed commercial aviation pilot Don Cletus Frade did not have, so far as he could see, the location of any airfield marked on it. It had been published by the Automobile Club of Argentina for the use of touring motorists.

It had proved perfectly adequate, however, to get him where he was now, at an indicated altitude of fifteen hundred feet and about that far to the right of National Route Three.

The only man-made break in the sea of grass that was the pampas was Route Three, and he had seen very few cars and trucks on that narrow two-lane highway.

Clete put the Cub in a gentle climbing bank to the right, taking him farther away from Route Three. When he no longer could see the highway, he saw that the altimeter showed he was at thirty-five hundred feet. He straightened out and looked slowly at the pampas from horizon to horizon. There was absolutely nothing down there but cattle, clumps of trees, and grass.

He put the nose down and dropped to five hundred feet.

Then, as he looked over his shoulder and indicated with a pointing finger that they were going down, Enrico smiled wanly and made the sign of the cross.

Clete retarded the throttle until he felt the little airplane show the first signs of a stall.

Then he dropped the nose further, flared, and put the Cub on the ground. There was no sense making a flyover to see if he could see any obstacles in the grass; the grass was high enough to conceal a rock or tree stump or something else that would cause him to dump the plane.

He had dumped Cubs a half-dozen times while landing on the Texas prairie, twice flipping over, but without hurting himself. He thought that was the worst that could happen here—he'd dump the Cub and have to take a long hike over the pampas to Route Three, then wait for somebody to pick them up.

He knew that he had to see what was going on with the German couple from the embassy as soon as he could, although he wasn't sure why. It probably would have been smarter to go back to the Big House at the estancia, then drive over to Tandil. But he had given in to his gut feeling that it was important to get there as soon as possible, and that meant flying there from Campo de Mayo, knowing that he'd have to make a fuel stop in the middle of nowhere, and risk dumping the Cub.

Ten minutes after having transferred the gas in the can to the tank, he was airborne again.

And ten minutes after that, as a line of hills almost suddenly rose from the flat pampas, Enrico touched his shoulder and pointed at one of the higher hills. Clete turned toward the hill and in a few minutes saw that there was a house—and some small outbuildings—near the top of one of the hills.

Enrico touched his shoulder again and pointed.

Clete nodded, acknowledging that he had seen the landing strip. He was surprised a moment later to see a windsock to one side of the short strip.

He put the nose down and into the wind, looked at Enrico, and saw that Enrico was again invoking the mercy of the Deity.

As he landed, he got a pretty good look at the house—the strip had been carved out of the hill below the house. It was more of a cottage than a house, with a red-tile roof and a large plate-glass window in the front. There was even a small swimming pool.

A hilltop lovenest, he thought, and smiled at the thought of his father, with Claudia in the backseat, flying a Cub—maybe this one—into here with a weekend of whoopee on their minds.

He hadn't seen the Horch or a truck, which meant that Dorotea was already on her way back to Estancia San Pedro y San Pablo, if not already there.

He turned the Cub around at the end of the runway and shut it down. From the house, two gauchos came trotting down a wide stairway; the steps appeared to be railroad ties.

One was Sargento Rodolfo Gómez, Argentine Cavalry, Retired. The other was Staff Sergeant Siegfried Stein, Signal Corps, U.S. Army. Gómez cradled a Mauser hunting rifle in his arms. Clete thought it was most likely the rifle—once his father's—that Gómez had used to take out Oberst Grüner and Standartenführer Goltz at Samborombón Bay. Stein had a Thompson submachine gun hanging from his shoulder, and the butt of a Model 1911-A1 Colt could be seen sticking out of his wide gaucho belt.

When Clete had climbed out of the Cub, Stein saluted not very crisply. Gómez looked at him, then saluted.

Clete casually returned the salutes. To show he appreciated the incongruity of the situation, he smiled and, as a colonel might do on the parade ground, barked, "Stand at ease, men!"

Stein grinned. "I'm a little surprised you could find this place."

"I had an ACA road map," Frade said. "How's our guests?"

"Several answers to that," Stein said. "Physically fine. They're in the living room."

"And the other answer?"

"She's a real Nazi bitch, Major."

"*She* is?"

"I have the feeling that if she could find some Gestapo guy, it would take her about ten seconds to denounce her husband."

"Then why did she come?"

"Women change their minds, and, oh boy, has this one changed hers."

"She say anything?"

"Only that she—meaning him, too—will deal only with an 'officer of suitable rank.' "

"And she pegged you as a sergeant?"

"She pegged me as a Jew—maybe something about my accent—and she can't believe a Jew would be an officer." He smiled. "I heard her tell him to tell the 'Jüdisch Gefreiter' that she was hungry."

"Well, let's go see her. I'll tell her that you're actually a Jüdisch Oberst."

"I don't think that would work. I think you're even going to have a hard time getting her to believe you're a major."

Frade didn't reply directly; he had had another thought.

"Did you bring any gas with you?"

Stein nodded. "Four jerry cans from the hangar. I hope it's avgas."

"If you got it from the hangar, it is," Frade said. "Enrico, gas it up. I want to get out of here while it's still light."

Frade looked at Stein, who waved him up the steps to the house.

Commercial Attaché and Frau Frogger were sitting side by side on a couch in the living room. The couch faced a large plate-glass window offering a view of the valley and the next range of hills.

Frade could imagine his father and Claudia sitting there—maybe Claudia had had her head in his father's lap as he smoked a cigar and they shared a glass of wine watching the sunset.

He felt a wave of anger at the two Germans sitting on his father's and Claudia's couch.

This is not the time to do something stupid!

Frogger, after a moment, stood. His wife clutched her briefcase-sized purse against her stomach and looked at Frade coldly.

"All right, Herr Frogger," Frade said in German. "What have you got to offer me?"

"Who are you, please?" Frau Frogger demanded.

Frade ignored her.

"Well?" he pursued.

"I don't really know what you mean," Frogger said.

"We insist on dealing with an officer of appropriate rank," Frau Frogger said.

"You are in no position to insist on anything," Frade said. "Major, did you find anything interesting in their luggage?"

Staff Sergeant Stein accepted his promotion without question. He popped to attention and said, "No, sir. I thought I would wait until you got here, Colonel."

"Where is it?"

"I put the bags in the housekeeper's room, sir."

Frade switched to Spanish and turned to Gómez. "Take the man to get their luggage," he ordered.

"Sí, mi coronel," Gómez said, and gestured with the muzzle of the Mauser for Frogger to start moving.

"Let's have a look at what she's got in that purse," Frade said in English, as much to see from her reaction whether or not she spoke English. He saw that she both spoke English and was very unhappy with the notion of having him see what her purse contained.

You're a regular Sherlock Holmes, Frade!

"Please empty the contents of your purse on the table," he said in German, pointing.

"Nothing but personal items," she said.

"Empty the purse on the table," Frade said coldly.

"We have diplomatic immunity," she protested. "This is an outrage."

For a moment, Frade thought of ordering Stein to take her purse, but one look at Stein's face showed that the last thing he wanted to do was snatch a purse from someone—Nazi bitch or not—who looked like a grandmother.

Frade took four quick steps to Frau Frogger and snatched the purse from her hands. He found the zipper, opened it, turned the purse upside down, and started to shake the contents onto the floor.

When he glanced at her, he saw pure hate in her eyes.

Frade looked at the pile of miscellany from a woman's purse and saw a silver-framed photograph. He bent over and picked it up.

It was of three nice-looking young men, all wearing Wehrmacht uniforms. It was fairly obvious these were the Frogger children. The oldest of them was wearing a large floppy beret, and from some recess of his mind he recalled that German armed forces wore berets. He had no idea what ranks they held—as a matter of fact, he wasn't even positive that they were all officers.

For an intelligence officer, Frade, you have enormous voids in your professional knowledge.

"Please give that back to me," Frau Frogger said, not at all belligerently.

He looked at her, resisted the temptation to hand her the photograph, and instead carried it out of the room, knowing he was going only where Rodolfo Gómez had led the man.

The door led to the kitchen. Frogger, carrying two large leather suitcases, was walking across it. Frade motioned for him to stop. He held the photo out to him.

"These are?"

"My childr—our sons."

"And they are where?"

"Two have been killed in the war. The third is in the United States."

"In the United States?"

"Wilhelm, this one"—he pointed at the man wearing the oversized floppy beret—"was captured while serving with the Afrikakorps."

"His name is Wilhelm Frogger?"

Frogger nodded. "Oberstleutnant Wilhelm Frogger."

"He is young to be a lieutenant colonel," Frade said.

"If you will excuse me, Herr Oberst, you look young to hold your rank."

Well, he swallowed that colonel bullshit. Or he's pretending he did.

Okay, where do I go from here?

Jesus, I wish I had had more time to talk to Milton!

Milton said they deserted because they didn't want to go back to Germany.

Okay. Let's go with that.

"Mr. Leibermann tells me that you want to be interned in Brazil."

"That is correct."

"I'm the only person who can get you into Brazil, and right now I can see no reason why I should do that."

Frogger's eyes widened, but he didn't reply.

"Actually, Leibermann made a mistake in bringing you to me."

"We have surrendered," Frogger said.

"What you have done is desert your post at the embassy and put yourselves into the hands of a man whose father was assassinated on the orders of the German embassy."

"But we have *surrendered*," Frogger repeated. "We wish to be granted political asylum in Brazil."

"Then you should have gone to the Brazilians. You didn't."

"I am prepared to cooperate," Frogger said.

"Meaning what?"

"I have information which would be of value to you."

"Information about Operation Phoenix, for example?"

"Excuse me?"

"Operation Phoenix."

"I don't know the term. I'm sorry."

"Then you are either stupid or a liar, probably both. Stupid, certainly, for thinking you could come and expect help to desert your post, with nothing to offer us."

"I have information . . ."

"But not about Operation Phoenix?"

"I know nothing about any Operation Phoenix."

"You are lucky you brought your wife with you," Frade said. "Otherwise, you would already be in an unmarked grave on the pampas. I don't like to kill women unless I have to."

"Then simply return us to Buenos Aires."

"My God, you *are* stupid, aren't you? You've already seen too much to be allowed to remain alive."

He gestured with his hands, indicating Frogger should carry the suitcases into the living room. Gómez went next, then Frade followed them in.

"Open them and dump them on the floor," Frade then ordered coldly.

"Those are our personal possessions!" Frau Frogger complained indignantly.

"Dump them on the floor," Frade repeated.

When that had been done, he spotted the photo album, went to it, and picked it up. He flipped through it, then tossed it atop the pile of clothing and personal items.

In Spanish, he ordered Gómez to put "these swine" into the house-keeper's room.

"If they look like they're even trying to get away, shoot them," Frade ordered, "put them in a hole in the pampas, pour gasoline on them, then set them afire and leave them for the buzzards."

"I have information—"

"Shut your mouth, you slimy bastard!"

Staff Sergeant Stein met Frade's eyes but said nothing.

"You ever watch cop movies, Siggie?" Frade asked when Gómez had led the Froggers away.

Stein nodded. "Sometimes."

"Then you're familiar with good cop/bad cop?"

Stein nodded.

"I have just been the bad cop," Frade said. "I don't know how convincing I was, but that's what I was trying. I threatened to kill and burn them—"

"I don't think they have buzzards down here, Major."

"I don't know if they do or not. But I don't think that they know either."

Stein smiled at him.

"You're about to become the good cop, *Major* Stein. The way you do that is to confirm their suspicions that Colonel Frade is an unmitigated sonofabitch who hates Nazis because they killed his father—that's not far from the truth, incidentally, but I have people like that sonofabitch Cranz in mind, the SS, not a miserable little shit like this guy. Anyway, being the good guy, tell them you may—just may—be able to talk me out of killing them if they have something to offer . . ."

"Like what?"

"He says he never heard of Operation Phoenix, and I don't know if he's lying or not. But work on that. Start—unless *he* starts on Operation Phoenix, or the ransoming operation, which I think is unlikely—by getting him to give us the manning chart of the embassy. We can have von Wachtstein check that, see if he's lying."

"Major, I've never done anything like this in my life."

"Welcome to the club, Sergeant Stein. Neither have I."

Stein shrugged.

"When will you be back?"

"In a couple of days. I want to talk to Leibermann. It's going to be tough. Martín showed up as I was about to take off from Campo de Mayo. He suspects we're involved in this. BIS agents are going to be all over everybody."

Stein nodded, then shrugged, but didn't reply directly.

"You better get going, Major. You're about to lose daylight."

Frade thought aloud: "Jesus, I wish I could get von Wachtstein out here. He'd know how to deal with them."

"But then they would know he's Galahad."

"What makes you think he hasn't already figured that out?"

"Or her," Stein said. "Can you get him out here?"

"I don't know. I'll work on it. But in the meantime . . ."

"Yes, sir."

[SEVEN]
Estancia San Pedro y San Pablo
Near Pila
Buenos Aires Province, Argentina
1905 14 July 1943

When Clete dropped the nose of the Piper Cub on his final approach to the landing strip, he saw that the Horch and Dorotea's Buick were parked side by side at the end of the runway. A dozen other vehicles were parked on either side of the strip, positioned so their headlights would illuminate the strip.

The "emergency lighting system" wasn't needed yet, but in another fifteen minutes it would have been.

Dorotea set that up.

Jesus Christ, what a great woman!

And then he saw her, standing up in the front seat of the Horch, waving a welcome to him.

You sonofabitch, how did you wind up with a woman like that?

Because God takes care of fools and drunks, and you qualify on both counts?

The Horch and the Buick came up as he and Enrico were tying down the Piper Cub. Chief Schultz was driving the Buick.

"We was about to send out a search party," he said, then added, "And we just got word that Delgano just came onto the estancia."

"Then you better get the hell out of here," Frade said.

Schultz nodded but held out a piece of paper.

"You better read this and see if you want to answer right away," he said, handing him a message typed on an all-caps typewriter that had once been in the communications room of the *USS Alfred Thomas,* DD-107. "It took me forever to decrypt the goddamn thing, but I was glad I did."

Clete didn't know what that meant. Schultz offered no explanation beyond a smile.

URGENT

TOP SECRET LINDBERGH
DUPLICATION FORBIDDEN

FROM AGGIE

TO TEX

ARRANGE TRANSFER SOONEST OF TWO MILLION DOLLARS
($2,000,000.00) ACCOUNT LOCKHEED AIRCRAFT COMPANY
FIRST NATIONAL BANK OF BURBANK, BURBANK CALIFORNIA,
AS INITIAL PAYMENT FOR FOURTEEN (14) LOCKHEED MODEL
18B AIRCRAFT AND APPROPRIATE SPARES.

FIRST TWO (2) AIRCRAFT WILL DEPART US FOR BIRDCAGE
WITHIN 48 HOURS.

ETA BIRDCAGE DEPARTURE TIME PLUS SEVENTY-TWO (72)
HOURS. LOCKHEED AIRCRAFT WILL NOT REPEAT NOT
AUTHORIZE RELEASE OF REMAINING TWELVE (12) AIRCRAFT
UNTIL AFOREMENTIONED PAYMENT IS RECEIVED.

ESSENTIAL YOU BE PRESENT BIRDCAGE TO RECEIVE
AIRCRAFT AS SIX (6) COLLINS MODEL 295 TRANSCEIVERS
PLUS APPROPRIATE SPARES WILL BE ABOARD FIRST
DEPARTING AIRCRAFT IN CARE OF MR. LEONARD FISCHER OF
COLLINS RADIO CORPORATION WHO WILL ASSIST IN SETTING
UP SUBJECT RADIOS.

ADDITIONALLY, IN RESPONSE TO REQUEST OF LT SCHULTZ,
MR. FISCHER IS BRINGING WITH HIM, TOGETHER WITH
APPROPRIATE SPARES, AN ELECTRICAL TYPEWRITER OF THE
TYPE LT SCHULTZ OPERATED ABOARD USS ALFRED THOMAS
AND WILL ASSIST IN SETTING IT UP.

ADVISE YOUR ETA BIRDCAGE

AGGIE

Frade looked at Schultz and said, "Why are you smiling, Jefe? Because we're getting six radios? Or because you're now apparently a goddamned officer and gentleman, *Lieutenant?*"

"That, too, Major, sir, but the only electrical typewriter on the *Alfred Thomas* was a SIGABA."

"And you're going to tell me what a Sigaba, whatever, is, right?"

"Last word in encryption/decryption machines. Not only is the encrypted stuff absolutely unbreakable, but it's as fast as a horny sailor heading for a . . . uh . . . Sorry, Doña Dorotea."

"Heading for a Christian Science Reading Room, right?" Dorotea said.

"I was thinking of an ice-cream parlor," Schultz said.

"Who's this guy they're sending with it?" Frade asked.

"I'd bet he's either a sergeant or a smart young lieutenant from the ASA. The SIGABA needs an expert to set it up and fix it." He paused. "And also to guard it while it's being moved. That's a piece of really secret machinery."

"What's the ASA?"

"Army Security Agency. They handle this sort of thing for all the services."

"Message Aggie that I'll have the Banco de Inglaterra y Argentina wire the money first thing in the morning, and that I'll be at Birdcage within seventy-two hours."

"Aye, aye, sir."

"And now get out of here, before Delgano sees you."

"What are you going to do about Delgano while you're gone?" Dorotea asked. "If they think we have the Nazis, he'll be all over the place."

"I'm taking him to Brazil with me," Clete said. "The minute he shows up here, the managing director of South American Airways is going to tell Chief Pilot Delgano to get us seats on the first Varig flight."

VIII

[ONE]
Aboard Varig Flight 525
Above Durazno, Uruguay
1505 17 July 1943

"Yes, I would. Thank you very much," Cletus Frade said in response to the stewardess's question if he would like another glass of merlot.

"And me, too, if you please," Gonzalo Delgano said, flashing his most dazzling smile at her.

And then he watched her walk forward in the cabin.

"I forgot about that," Frade said. "But you really are going to enjoy that, aren't you, Señor Jefe de Pilotos?"

"Forgot about what?"

"You get to pick the stewardesses."

"Excuse me?"

"You ever see an American football game, Gonzo?"

"In the newsreels," Delgano said, confused.

"All those enormous young men, rushing at each other, knocking each other down, getting their teeth knocked out, breaking their arms and legs?"

Delgano nodded.

"Ever wonder why they do it?"

"It is sort of brutal, isn't it?"

"In the newsreels you saw, did they show the cheerleaders?"

"Excuse me?"

"The pretty young girls in short skirts bouncing around?" He raised his arms above his head in a punching motion. " 'Go Aggies! Go Aggies!' They're called 'cheerleaders.' "

"Yes, now that you mention it. Very interesting."

"That's why they do it," Clete said seriously.

"That's why who does what?"

"The young men are so willing to have their arms broken and their teeth knocked out. The winning team gets their pick of the cheerleaders. If you score more than twelve points, you get two."

Delgano looked at him in shock, then realized his chain had been pulled.

"Holy Mother of God, Cletus, for a moment I actually believed you."

"Same thing with chief pilots," Frade said. "If he doesn't dump more than one airplane in six months, or forget to put the wheels down for the same period of time, he gets his pick of the stewardesses."

Delgano shook his head in disbelief.

"If I didn't know better, I would think you're a lunatic."

The stewardess returned with their wine.

"My friend here tells me you can't get to be a Varig stewardess unless you are forty years old or the mother of three or more children," Frade said to her. "I told my friend that couldn't possibly be true. Is it?"

"Do I look like I'm forty? Or have children?"

"That's what I told him," Frade said, nodding agreeably. "As I said, I didn't believe it."

"You will have to excuse him, señorita," Delgano said, his face flushed with embarrassment. "He's a *norteamericano,* and they're all crazy."

Frade pulled his Argentine passport from his suit jacket and held it out to the stewardess.

"Two glasses of wine and he gets like that. I wouldn't give him any more, if I were you."

The stewardess smiled brightly at Frade, gave Delgano a dirty look, and retreated down the aisle.

Delgano shook his head again.

"I'm glad I did that," Clete said.

"You mean, made an ass of yourself?"

"A chief pilot is not permitted to lose his temper. You might want to write that down. No, what I meant was take my passport out."

"I'm afraid to ask why."

"Because it reminded me I'm an Argentine citizen."

"You remembered! But what does that mean?"

"When we get to Pôrto Alegre, I think it would be best if you dealt with the local officials."

"Now I'm really afraid to ask why."

"Well, the last time I was here—when I picked up my Lodestar—I left under something less than ideal conditions."

"Meaning what?"

"I now understand that the tower was ordering me to return immediately. But I don't speak Portuguese, so I didn't understand him, and kept going."

"Holy Mother of Christ!"

"Well, actually, I did understand him, but I really didn't want to go back and have to explain who the people I had aboard were, and why we hadn't gone through immigration."

"Ashton and the others and the radar," Delgano said, shaking his head.

El Capitán Gonzalo Delgano of the Bureau of Internal Security had been waiting at the landing strip of the Second Cavalry Regiment in Santo Tomé when Cletus Frade had landed the Lodestar after flying it there from Pôrto Alegre.

There had been an unofficial arrangement with senior officers involved with Operation Blue for Clete to use the Santo Tomé airstrip to get the Lodestar into Argentina against Brazilian wishes. They wanted it available to Generals Ramírez and Rawson—and other senior officers—so they could flee the country if the coup d'état failed.

Clete had seen this as an opportunity to get Team Turtle—and more important, the radar—off the American air base in Pôrto Alegre and into Argentina surreptitiously and without running the risk of having the radar grabbed by either Brazilian or Argentine authorities.

It would have worked had not the decision to put Operation Blue into action been made. This meant that the Operation Blue officers needed the airplane at Campo de Mayo as soon as possible, and Delgano had been sent to Santo Tomé to make sure they got it.

The discovery that the Lodestar carried a heavily armed OSS team and a radar set complicated things more than a little. Clete announced that if Delgano and the BIS arrested Team Turtle they could get someone else to fly the Lodestar—knowing they had no one qualified to do so.

In the end, in the opinion of then-Lieutenant Colonel Martín of BIS, who by then had allied himself with Generals Ramírez and Rawson, having the plane available overrode all other considerations. Team Turtle and its radar had gone to Estancia San Pedro y San Pablo, and Clete had flown the Lodestar to Campo de Mayo.

The coup d'état was successful. Martín and Delgano were promoted for their contributions, and neither of them seemed to recall that there were half a dozen American OSS agents operating a radar station and doing only God knew what else on Estancia San Pedro y San Pablo.

"Yeah," Clete said. "Ashton and the others and the radar."

"I didn't know this before," Delgano said.

"Yeah, I know. For all I know, the Brazilians have stopped looking for an American name C. Frade. And I am now an Argentinean businessman with the same name, a passport to prove it, and intend to cross all the *t*'s and dot all the *i*'s when we go through immigration at Pôrto Alegre. Having said that, I still think it would be best if you dealt with the Brazilian authorities."

Delgano considered that and nodded.

"You're an amazing man, Cletus. Nothing you do surprises me anymore. I wouldn't be surprised if you had Frogger and his wife in your luggage."

"Who?" Clete asked, smiled, and raised his glass of merlot to Delgano.

[TWO]
Canoas Air Base
Pôrto Alegre, Brazil
1935 17 July 1943

As Frade got out of the taxi, he saw that there were four military policemen in the guard shack at the brightly lit entrance to the base, two Brazilian and two American.

As he walked up to the shack, one of the Brazilian MPs stepped out of the booth and none too courteously inquired, "Señor?"

Well, I guess with this haircut, I look like a Latin American.

Is that good or bad?

His hairstyle had been among the other things that changed with marriage. Dorotea had announced that the trim—a crew cut he'd worn since his first haircut at the U.S. Navy Flight Training Facility at Pensacola, Florida—made him look like a criminal. His current cut hung over his collar and partially concealed his ears. He thought it made him look like a pimp, but he found that a newlywed, one giddy with love, will make all sorts of sacrifices to retain the affection of his bride.

He saw one of the American MPs glance at him, then dismiss him as unimportant.

"I would like to see Colonel Wallace. My name is Frade," he said in Spanish.

Colonel J. B. Wallace, U.S. Army Air Forces, commanded the 2035th Training Wing—and the American portion of the Canoas Air Base—and Clete was reasonably sure that Colonel Wallace would be less than overjoyed to see him. But he had to establish contact with someone who knew who he was, and Wallace was the only name he knew or had been given.

And he couldn't expect any immediate help from Colonel Graham. There had been no reply to the half-dozen messages Frade had just sent to Graham— one about the money being on its way to Lockheed's account in California; another a report of progress on the registry of the Lodestars; then one asking that Graham arrange for him to get sent the airframe numbers of the planes that by then were en route to Brazil; two follow-up messages, then the final one saying that he would be aboard Varig Flight 525.

"Who, señor?"

"El Coronel Wallace. *Norteamericano,*" Clete said.

He knew there was enough similarity between Portuguese and Spanish that the MP understood him.

"There is no such person, señor," the MP said.

Oh, shit. Now what?

He tried again. "El Coronel Wallace?"

The Brazilian MP shrugged.

"Then any American officer."

"Tomás," one of the American MPs asked in really bad Portuguese, "what did the señor say his name was?"

The Brazilian MP obviously didn't understand.

"El Coronel Wallace," he said, and shrugged to show he had no idea what the señor wanted.

"Hey, pal, you speak any English?"

Clete nodded, and said, "Frade."

"Oh, shit," the MP said. "Major Frade, U.S. Marine Corps?"

Clete nodded. "But I'd rather people didn't know that."

"You got some ID, sir?"

I have a very fancy gold badge identifying me as an OSS area commander. Even has a photo ID.

But I left it in my safe, as I am here masquerading as an Argentine.

Besides, I don't think I'm supposed to show it to anyone anyway.

But next time, I'll bring it. It would have solved this problem.

Clete shook his head.

"Just a minute, please, sir," the MP said, and went into the guard shack.

In about sixty seconds, the MP came back out of the shack and repeated, "Just a minute, please, sir."

Three minutes after that, the headlights of a 1942 Ford sedan appeared as it raced up to the guard shack. Frade saw that it had a covered plate on the front bumper, and a chrome pole on the right fender, covered with an oilcloth sleeve. He had just put everything together and concluded that this was the personal auto of a general officer when the proof came: Out jumped a young Air Forces captain wearing wings, a fur felt cap with a crushed crown, and the aiguillette of an aide-de-camp.

He looked at Frade, almost visibly decided the man in the rather elegant suit whose hair now covered the collar and most of his ears could not possibly be a major of Marines, looked at the MP, then back at Frade after the MP pointed to him.

"Major Frade?"

Clete nodded.

"You have some identification, sir?"

Clete shook his head.

It clearly was not the answer the captain hoped for.

"Sir, I'm General Wallace's aide . . ."

"He got promoted, did he?"

"Sir, if you'll come with me, please?"

He held open the Ford's rear door.

Three minutes later, the Ford pulled into the driveway of a pleasant-looking Mediterranean-style cottage with a red tile roof. A neat little sign on the neatly trimmed lawn read: BRIG. GEN. J. B. WALLACE, U.S. ARMY AIR FORCES.

"If you'll come with me, Major?" the aide asked, and led him into the house, then to a closed interior door, on which he knocked.

"Come in, please," a male voice, somewhat nasal, called.

"Right in there, sir," the aide said, opened the door, then closed it after Frade had passed through.

Frade expected General Wallace. He got instead a white-haired civilian of about fifty who had a somewhat baggy suit, a bow tie, and a mustache that would have been Hitlerian had it not been almost white. He looked very much like the Reverend Richard Cobbs Lacey, headmaster of Saint Mark's of Texas, an Episcopal preparatory school in Dallas at which a fourteen-year-old Clete had had a brief—five months—and ultimately disastrous association.

"Ah," the man said. "Major Frade. I have just helped myself to some of the general's whiskey. May I offer you one?"

It's almost eight p.m. Why not?

"Thank you," Frade said.

But who the hell is this guy?

The man walked to a table on which were bottles of whiskey, glasses, bottles of soda, and a silver ice bowl.

"What's your preference, Major?"

"Is that Jack Daniel's?"

"Indeed. And how do you take it?"

"Straight, with a couple of ice cubes."

The man made the drink, then handed it to Clete and put out his hand.

"Allen Welsh Dulles," he said.

"Cletus Frade."

The man's grip was firm.

"Yes, I know," the man said. "How was your flight?"

"Very nice, thank you. Who are you?"

"I told you. My name is Allen Welsh Dulles."

"That's your name"—*your three-part name, just like Richard Cobbs Lacey, and it's for some reason vaguely familiar*—"not who you are."

Dulles smiled.

"We have mutual friends."

"We do?"

"Your grandfather, for one."

Clete's eyebrows rose.

"That's not precise," Dulles said. He raised his glass. "Cheers!"

Clete tapped the glass and took a sip.

Taking this drink is probably not very smart.

This guy wants something from me, and I've already decided he's smarter than I am.

What the hell is going on?

"Actually, my brother—John Foster Dulles—is an attorney in New York City. Among his firm's clients are Cletus Marcus Howell and Howell Petroleum."

"Is that so?"

"I've never had the privilege of meeting Mr. Howell—which I am led to believe is often an interesting experience—but nevertheless I relay, through my brother, your grandfather's best wishes."

Okay. Now I know what's going on.

This guy wants to know who Galahad is.

As a friend of the Old Man, he thinks he's got an in with me.

Fuck you, you three-name sonofabitch!

"And as does, of course, Alejandro Graham," Dulles added.

Jesus!

"I had dinner with Alex several nights ago in Washington," Dulles went on. "We have been friends for a long time."

Frade didn't reply.

"Major Hans-Peter Baron von Wachtstein," Dulles said.

"Excuse me?"

"Is Galahad," Dulles said.

That's nothing but a guess.

"Who?"

Dulles smiled at him.

"Major Hans-Peter Baron von Wachtstein is Galahad," Dulles said. "Which is something the FBI, the Office of Naval Intelligence, the Army's Chief of Intelligence, and of course SS-Brigadeführer Ritter Manfred von Deitzberg—and others—would dearly like to know."

Jesus, he knows about von Deitzberg?

"I have no idea what you're talking about," Frade said.

Dulles smiled at him, then took a sip of his drink.

"Well, they won't hear it from me," Dulles said.

"Hear what from you?"

"The identity of Galahad."

"We're back to the fact that I have no idea what you're talking about."

Dulles smiled at him.

"Let me tell you about my dinner with Alex Graham," Dulles said. "Your drink all right? Need a little top-off?"

"My drink is fine, thank you."

"It was in the Hotel Washington," Dulles said. "You know it?"

Frade shook his head.

"Right around the corner from the White House," Dulles said, "which is convenient when the President, as he did a couple of nights ago, wants to have a private dinner away from the White House."

"The President?" Frade blurted.

"The Secret Service just rolls his wheelchair into a laundry van, drives it around the corner to the service entrance of the Washington, then rolls him through the kitchen in the basement to the service elevator, and on up to an apartment they keep for him there."

"He can't walk?" Frade blurted.

Dulles shook his head. "Not much farther than that door"—he pointed—"and that's pretty exhausting for him."

"I didn't know that."

"Not many people do," Dulles said. "Anyway, it was a small dinner. Just the President, Graham, Donovan, Putzi Hanfstaengl, and me."

"Am I supposed to know who Putzi Haf . . . whatever you said . . . is?"

"I'd be surprised if you did. Putzi Hanfstaengl—Ernst is his name; we just call him 'Putzi'—is a German. He was at Columbia with Roosevelt and Donovan. Got pretty close to Hitler. He was smart enough to get out just in time—before they were going to see he had a fatal accident. As an enemy alien in the U.S., he's under arrest, of course. The Army has posted guards on him in his quote cell end quote at the Washington, which just happens to be down the corridor from the President's apartment. Staff Sergeant Ernst Hanfstaengl—same name as his father, you might note—is in charge of that guard detail. So far Putzi hasn't tried to escape."

"This all sounds . . . fantastic!"

"And I have barely begun, Major Frade. You sure you wouldn't like me to refresh your drink?"

"I think that would be a very bad idea, Mr. Dulles."

"Please call me 'Allen.' And if I may, I'd like to call you 'Cletus.' "

"I could no more call you Allen, sir, than I could call Colonel Graham by his first name."

"Give it a shot. It may not be as difficult as you might think. But may I call you 'Cletus'?"

"Yes, sir."

"Thank you. Well, the reason Putzi was there was because we were talking about the war against Germany—"

"Who the *hell* are you?" Frade blurted.

"I do, in Bern, Switzerland, what you are doing in Buenos Aires. I keep an eye on the Germans and try to make trouble for them. I'm the OSS station chief in Switzerland."

That's it! Graham told me about a Dulles!
So this could all be true, of course.
But it could also be some sort of trap.
Have I admitted Galahad is von Wachtstein?
Cletus, ol' pal, you're way in over your depth here.
"The regional commander?"

"Excuse me?"

"You're the OSS regional commander?"

"I suppose you could phrase it that way. But I concentrate on the German and Italian high commands. The sabotage and espionage, that sort of thing, is run by David Bruce out of London."

I've got a badge. All my people have badges.
How come you don't?
What have I got to lose by asking?
"I don't suppose you have your credentials handy, do you, Mr. Dulles?"

"Excuse me?"

"Your credentials. Your badge."

"Now I don't know what you're talking about."

"Then how do I know you're who you say you are?"

"I suppose you'll just have to take my word for it. May I continue?"

Frade raised both hands in a *Have at it* gesture.

"Your name came up," Dulles went on. "We talked of other things, of course, but your name came up."

Frade didn't reply.

"The President said that Alex had a loose cannon running around in Argentina, who—believe it or not—refused to share the name of his mole in the German embassy in Buenos Aires with his commander in chief."

Frade continued to keep his mouth shut.

"I told the President (a) that I knew who Galahad was, and (b) I wasn't going to tell him or Donovan either. Which predictably set off Wild Bill's Irish temper. Then I told them why. I told them Galahad's identity was too important a secret—right up there with the Manhattan Project, in my judgment—"

"The what?"

"The Manhattan Project. I'll get to that in a minute. Far too important a secret to be shared with everyone in the intelligence community, and that if I didn't identify Galahad for them, they could truthfully tell the Chief of Naval Operations, the Chief of Staff, and J. Edgar Hoover that they didn't know."

"You say you know it's von Wachtstein. How do you know that?"

"Because I am privy to a secret known to no more than eight or nine Americans, one of whom, Cletus, is you."

"What secret is that?"

"General von Wachtstein intends to assassinate Adolf Hitler," Dulles said. "We are in communication. One of his co-conspirators is a chap, a lieutenant colonel, named Claus von Stauffenberg, *Count* von Stauffenberg, who is a close friend of young von Wachtstein."

Jesus! He's got to be who he says he is!

Otherwise, he couldn't know any of this.

Frade, carefully choosing his words, said, "Peter told me he'd gone to see von Stauffenberg in Munich. But until just now, I thought this 'regicide' that his father was talking about was just wishful thinking."

"It is not."

"And they're calling this operation the Manhattan Project?"

Dulles laughed.

"No, it is not. The Manhattan Project involves the development of a bomb of enormous power, incredible power. It involves nuclear energy and an element known as uranium. One of my jobs in Berne is to see how far along the Germans are with their development of what is now called an 'atomic bomb.' And to do whatever I can to throw a monkey wrench in their works. Whoever creates this bomb first is going to win the war. It's as simple as that."

"My God!"

"Indeed," Dulles said. "And one of your tasks when you get back to Argentina, almost as your first priority, is to report immediately anything you hear about uranium or a superbomb or heavy water—"

"Heavy water?"

"I don't understand much of this, but apparently when an extra atom, or several extra atoms, are added to water it becomes deuterium oxide—or 'heavy water'—and this heavy water is somehow necessary to create a nuclear explosion. The Germans had a facility to make heavy water in Denmark. The British trained some Danes as commandos and sent them in to destroy the facility or render it inoperative. I'm not privy to the details, but their mission was successful and so set back the Germans somewhat."

"This is all new to me."

"It's all new to all of us," Dulles said. "Anyway, David Bruce told me that he's just parachuted an OSS team into Denmark—run by a fellow Princetonian, Lieutenant Bill Colby, a chap about your age, Cletus—ostensibly to do commando-type things with the Norwegian resistance, but actually to see what the Germans are doing with their now partially destroyed heavy-water plant. So keep your eyes and ears open vis-à-vis anything nuclear but—importantly—without anybody noticing."

Frade nodded.

"Now, the Germans— presuming they don't develop their nuclear bomb before we do; and the indications are they will not—have lost the war. This is apparent to their senior officers, to everybody but Hitler. Most importantly, it is apparent to Admiral Canaris, chief of Abwehr intelligence. Which is why he's been talking to me. That's another secret to which you are privy, along with no more than perhaps a dozen others. Am I going too fast for you?"

"Yes, sir. You are. My head is spinning."

"Well, then, let me finish, and when I have, I'll try to clarify what you may not fully understand. All right?"

"Yes, sir."

"The question then becomes, when will they lose the war? The sooner the better, obviously. But there are some problems. For one thing, they are somewhat ahead of us in the development of jet fighter aircraft. Our XP-59A didn't get into the air until the first of October 1942—"

"We have a jet fighter?" Clete blurted in surprise.

Dulles nodded. "—and is nowhere near operational. The German Messerschmitt Me-262, on the other hand, is near operational status."

"Peter flew one," Frade said, "in Augsburg. He said it went six hundred miles an hour and has thirty-millimeter cannons."

"Your friend Peter has flown this aircraft?"

Frade picked up on something in Dulles's voice.

"He's my friend. He saved my life, okay?"

"You didn't make any sort of a report of this test flight?"

Frade shook his head.

He said, "I just presumed we knew about it. Had spies. . . ."

His voice trailed off as he realized how lame that sounded.

Dulles's eyes narrowed.

"Well, we don't," he said coldly. "If you can fit it into your busy schedule when you get back to Argentina, you might consider talking some more to your friend Peter about the Me-262. I'm sure the Army Air Forces would dearly love to hear what someone who has actually flown the Me-262 thinks about it."

Frade did not reply.

"If the Germans can build enough of them quickly enough, they can inflict bomber losses on the Air Forces and the RAF to the point where the bombing will have to be called off. That would permit them to continue the war for an extended period. Under that circumstance, your delicate feelings about asking your friend about the Me-262 aren't really important, are they?"

"Is that what you were thinking?" Frade asked.

"Isn't that what you were thinking?"

"I was thinking it was stupid of me not to have thought the AAF would want to hear about the Me-262," Frade said. "And then that it really didn't matter, because I don't think he knows much beyond its performance, armament, and how hard or easy it is to fly. He didn't get that much time in it, and he's a pilot, not an engineer."

Dulles considered that a long moment, then said, "You're probably right. And anyway, we've gone off at a tangent.

"To backtrack: Putzi said that probably every senior Nazi knows the war is lost. Hitler is psychologically unable to face that, and the senior officers around him are not going to suggest it. But Bormann—who is probably the most powerful man after Hitler—does, or we wouldn't have Operation Phoenix.

"The ransoming operation is probably simply a personally profitable sideline for senior officers of the SS, headed by von Deitzberg. Himmler—as always—is a mystery. I don't have a clue as to whether he's involved with the ransoming operation or not, or whether von Deitzberg is running it under his nose. The upper ranks of the SS, according to Canaris, are riddled with criminal types.

"The question of what to do about both came up at dinner, and was decided by the President, based on a number of factors. Starting with the ransoming operation, Roosevelt said the question was saving lives, however that could be done. Exposing the operation would serve only to ensure that all the Jews in the camps were exterminated.

"Similarly, exposing Operation Phoenix—which seems so incredible on its face that the Nazis could not only deny it but ridicule the accusation—would accomplish very little."

"You're saying you're just going to let them continue?"

"I'm saying you are. With an important caveat. We want to know everything about it. We want the money traced from the moment it arrives in Argentina. We want to know what was bought with it, and from whom. The names of the Argentine—and Paraguayan and Uruguayan—officials who have been paid off. Everything.

"The thinking is that if we went to General Ramírez or General Rawson now with what we have, or what you might dig up, they would tell us to mind our own business. The Argentines are not convinced the Germans have lost the war.

"When Germany surrenders— How much do you know about the Casablanca Conference?"

"What I read in the newspapers, and that wasn't much."

"I was there," Dulles said. "It started out almost as a propaganda stunt. Stalin didn't want to come—which was the reason Churchill wanted it, so that he and Roosevelt could gang up on Stalin—and Chiang Kai-shek wasn't invited.

"There was not much need for a conference between Churchill and Roosevelt; they were and are pretty much agreed on everything, which actually means just about everything Churchill wants.

"But there they were: Roosevelt—who is actually quite ill—looking chipper as he became the first President ever to leave the country during wartime, with his good friend Churchill.

"Three things were decided at Casablanca. Churchill lost two of the decisions."

"Excuse me?"

"Churchill wants to invade Europe through its 'soft underbelly,' meaning the Mediterranean coast of France. George Marshall wants to invade across the Channel. Roosevelt backed Marshall, so that's where it will happen. Secondly, Charles de Gaulle will not meet an accident—"

"Who?"

"Colonel Charles de Gaulle. Great long drink of water? Who has appointed himself leader of the Free French?"

"Okay, I know who you mean. Accident?"

"Churchill thinks—and he's probably right—that he's going to be more trouble than he's worth. But the President made it clear he would be very unhappy indeed if de Gaulle had any kind of an accident.

"And the third thing decided—the only decision made public—was that we are going to demand the unconditional surrender of Germany, Italy, and Japan. I personally thought that was a bad idea, as there is a chance that if General von Wachtstein and von Stauffenberg succeed in removing Hitler, an armistice could quickly be agreed upon. But that question was decided in Churchill's favor.

"That's bad, because it will extend the war, especially insofar as the Japanese are concerned. The Italians, if there weren't so many German troops in Italy, would surrender tomorrow morning. The Germans will hang on as long as possible, but ultimately, they will surrender unconditionally.

"And what *that* means, under international law, is that the moment the Germans sign the surrender document, everything the German government owns falls under the control of the victors. Things like embassy buildings, other real estate, bank accounts. Are you following me, Cletus?"

"I hope so."

"The moment the Germans surrender, our ambassador will call upon the Argentine foreign minister, present him with a detailed list of all German property in Argentina—which you will have prepared, to include bank account numbers, descriptions of real estate, et cetera—and inform him that we're taking possession of it.

"The Argentine government may not like it, but it's a well-established principle of international law, and it really would be unwise of them to defy that law. I rather doubt they will. Nations, like people, tend to try to curry favor with whoever has just won a fight."

"Jesus Christ!"

"That your only comment?"

"What I'm thinking is that I'm in way over my head. Why don't they send somebody to Argentina who has experience and knows what he's doing?"

"Ask yourself that," Dulles said.

"Because he wouldn't have my contacts."

"And because he would be more carefully watched than you are."

"They're watching me pretty carefully right now, as a matter of fact."

"What have you done to cause that?"

"They suspect I had something to do with the disappearance of the commercial attaché of the German embassy and his wife. On the way up here, Delgano, who is ostensibly my chief pilot but who is—and he knows I know—a BIS agent, said he wouldn't be surprised if I had them in my suitcase."

"I don't quite understand. You had something to do—"

"They showed up at Milton Leibermann's door and said they wanted to 'surrender'—"

"And Leibermann is?"

"The FBI guy in Buenos Aires."

"The FBI chap in Berne seems to think I am invisible," Dulles said.

"Leibermann is a good guy. We work well together. Anyway, he brought them out to the estancia, and we're hiding them until somebody tells me what to do with them."

"On your estancia?"

"On another one I'd never heard of ten days ago. They're safe."

"And Leibermann has reported this to the ambassador? And/or the FBI?" Frade shook his head.

"Why did they . . . 'surrender'?"

"They wanted Leibermann to get them to Brazil so they could be interned. Leibermann thinks, and I agree, that they were afraid to go back to Germany because von Deitzberg or Cranz—Frogger's replacement, actually an SS-obersturmbannführer—have not been able to identify von Wachtstein as the spy and are going to hang it on Frogger."

"This man's name is Frogger?"

"Wilhelm Frogger. His son and namesake—he had three sons; two got themselves killed—is an oberstleutnant who got himself captured with the Afrikakorps. He's now in a POW camp in the States."

"They've probably got him in Camp Clinton," Dulles said, almost to himself.

"Excuse me?"

"This chap in the Afrikakorps?"

"Yeah. I think so. Do tank officers wear big black berets?"

Dulles nodded.

"Then he was—is—a tank officer," Frade said. "What's Camp Clinton?"

"A POW camp in Mississippi. We sent a lot of Afrikakorps officers there—including, significantly, General von Arnim. It's where we plan to hold all German general officers and the more important staff officers."

Frade's face showed he had no idea who General von Arnim was.

"Hans von Arnim," Dulles explained. "He took over the Afrikakorps from Erwin Rommel. He surrendered what was left of it when Tunisia fell. In early May." He paused and chuckled. "Starchy chap. About so tall"—he held his hand out to indicate a short height—"with a Hitlerian mustache and a large—forgive me—Semitic nose."

"You know him?" Frade asked in surprise.

"I went to Tunisia to see him. I'm afraid I got nowhere with him."

Dulles paused thoughtfully again, then asked, "You didn't report this to Colonel Graham?"

"I sent him half a dozen messages and never got a reply. So I guessed he was out of Washington, and I didn't want somebody else reading about Frogger if Graham wasn't there."

"What are you doing with these people now?"

"One of my sergeants—Stein, good guy, smart, Jewish, got out of Germany just before they would have packed him off to Sachsenhausen or someplace—

is trying to convince them that the only way he can keep me from shooting and burying them in an unmarked grave on the pampas is for them to come up with something I can use. Starting, for example, with a manning chart of their embassy. If he lies about that, von Wachtstein will be able to tell."

"And if he's not lying, then what?"

"Then I will see what else I can get out of him."

"I'm sure you can see how valuable this man could be in providing the information about German assets I mentioned."

No, Stupid here didn't even think about that.

"Mr. Dulles, I have to tell you that that never entered my mind."

Dulles looked at him a moment and smiled.

"As you said, your head's been spinning. I'm sure that the potentially vast importance to us of this man Frogger would have occurred to you sooner or later."

Frade shook his head.

"And if he is?" Dulles went on. "Lying to you, I mean. Then what?"

"I don't know. I don't want to kill them, but they know too much—about Leibermann, Stein, me, et cetera—to turn them loose."

"Don't kill them just yet, please, Clete. Let me give this some thought."

Frade looked at Dulles and saw that he was smiling.

"Did I say something that amused you, Mr. Dulles?"

"A minute ago you said something that amuses me now."

"What was that?"

"Something to the effect that you're in over your head and why don't they send someone to Argentina who knows what he's doing."

"That's funny?"

"Alex Graham said, vis-à-vis you, something to the effect that the first impression you give is of a dangerously irresponsible individual who should not be trusted out of your sight. And then, depending on how much experience one has with really good covert intelligence officers, quickly or slowly comes the realization that one's in the company of a rare person who seems to be born for this sort of thing."

My face feels flushed.

Am I blushing?

Jesus H. Christ!

"That sounds almost like a compliment," Frade said after a moment.

"I'm sure it was intended as one," Dulles said.

"Does that mean you're going to tell me what this airline business is all about?"

"Alex and I talked about that, and Colonel Donovan told me he'd asked the President. No one knows anything except that Franklin Delano Roosevelt thinks it's a good idea, and that he was pleased to learn of your remarkable progress in getting one going."

"Jesus!"

"Your glass is nearly empty, Cletus."

"I don't know if another's a good idea."

"We're through for today. We'll talk again in the morning. You can get a really nice American breakfast at the officers' club here. Half past eight, shall we say?"

"I've got Delgano with me."

"Oh, bring him. Tell him I'm an assistant consular officer trying to straighten out your problems with Brazilian immigration."

He saw that Frade was looking at him curiously, as if trying to guess if he was kidding or not.

"That story will explain where you have been now, and where you will be after we have our breakfast."

"That being the case, sir, I think I will have another little taste."

[THREE]
Plaza Pôrto Alegre Hotel
Pôrto Alegre, Brazil
0830 18 July 1943

The Plymouth staff car that had come to the Canoas Air Base entrance the day before was sitting at the curb when Frade and Delgano came through the revolving door of the hotel.

An AAF sergeant was at the wheel today, and General Wallace's aide-de-camp was leaning against the rear door.

The aide straightened when he saw Frade and Delgano, opened the door, then as they approached greeted them in really bad Spanish: "Good morning, Señor Frade. General Wallace hopes that you will take breakfast with him and Mr. Stevens."

Frade picked up on both "Señor" and the poor Spanish, then wondered who the hell Mr. Stevens was.

"That's very gracious of the general," he replied in Spanish.

There were two men sitting with Brigadier General J. B. Wallace, U.S. Army Air Forces, at a table in a small room off the main dining room of the Canoas Air Base Officers' Open Mess. Cletus Frade saw that one of the men was Allen W. Dulles and the other a smallish, stocky young man with a crew cut.

If I were a betting man, and I am, I'd bet he's a second john, not long out of Officer Candidate School.

Wallace stood up, put out his hand, and asked as if he had never seen Frade before in his life, "Señor Frade?"

Frade nodded.

"I'm General Wallace, the base commander. And these gentlemen are Mr. Stevens, of the War Production Board, and Mr. Fischer, of the Collins Radio Corporation."

Dulles was "Stevens" and the second lieutenant in civvies was Fischer.

They shook hands, and Frade introduced Delgano.

General Wallace waved them into seats, and two waiters appeared. One handed them menus while the other put a folding partition across the opening to the room to screen it off from the main mess.

Frade examined the menu.

I have no idea what this role-playing is all about, or who is supposed to be fooling who, but I am not going to be a good little boy and play an Argentine businessman who has only coffee and a roll for his breakfast.

Not when faced with an American menu like this.

I'll play the part halfway; I'll order all I want—but in Spanish.

When the Portuguese waiter looked to him for his order, Frade said in Spanish, "I'll have grapefruit juice, please, a large glass of milk, a double stack of the buckwheat pancakes, a couple of fried eggs over easy, and a double order of the bacon on the side."

The waiters' eyes, and those of Delgano, widened.

"Mr. Stevens" smiled and asked, "Are pancakes common in Argentina, Señor Frade?"

Frade shook his head. "And, I am shamed to admit, we don't have very good bacon, either."

"I'll have the same," Dulles said to the waiter in Portuguese. "But just a regular order of pancakes and bacon, please."

"What are pancakes?" Delgano asked.

"Bring him what Mr. Stevens is having," Frade ordered in Spanish.

"My orders, Señor Frade," General Wallace said when the table had been cleared of everything but coffee, "are to fully cooperate with the War Production Board in the movement of the Lodestar aircraft through Canoas Air Corps Base to Argentina. When we transfer title to you here, they will have been inspected by my maintenance people. They will be in tip-top shape, or as close thereto as we are able to get them."

"That's very kind of you, General."

"Mr. Stevens didn't seem to know if you or Señor Delgano will require any instruction in the operation of the Lodestar," Wallace said. "The pilots who flew it here are available if you do."

"Captain Delgano, who is chief pilot of South American Airways, has been checked out in the Lodestar," Frade said with a straight face, "but I am one of those who believe there is no such thing as too much training. So we gratefully accept your kind offer, General."

"Then why don't I see if I can round up the pilots and have them come here to set that up?"

"And while you're doing that, perhaps Mr. Stevens can let me know what has to be done about the documentation?"

"Good idea," General Wallace said. "So if you will excuse me, gentlemen?"

Two middle-aged men, both wearing four-stripe epaulets identifying them as airline captains, appeared several minutes later.

"Good morning, gentlemen," one of them said in Spanish. "I'm Captain McMurray of Lockheed. I understand someone needs a little time in the Lodestar?"

Delgano's relief that Spanish was being spoken was evident.

Introductions were made and they left, taking Delgano with them.

Dulles waited until the folding partition screen had been replaced, then asked, "Is he a good pilot, Clete?"

"He's a very good pilot, with far more multiengine time than I have. He's also a better—"

He stopped, realizing he was about to say something that he shouldn't: "intelligence officer."

This earned him a small smile from Dulles.

"Let me make the proper introductions," Dulles then said. "Major Frade, this is Lieutenant Fischer of the U.S. Army Signal Corps."

"Sir," Fischer said.

"How are you, Lieutenant?" Frade said.

"I think I should begin this by telling you Fischer has been cleared for Top-Secret Lindbergh," Dulles said.

"He knows who Galahad is?" Frade blurted.

"Not yet," Dulles said, "but if you think about it, he's going to figure that out even if you and I don't tell him. One of the problems no one talks about in this area is those people who encrypt and decrypt messages get to read them."

Frade nodded.

"Colonel Graham found Lieutenant Fischer at Vint Hill Farms Station," Dulles went on, and when he saw on Frade's face that he had no idea what that was, he explained. "That's the Army Security Agency base near Washington. The ASA does signal intelligence—intercepts, that sort of thing—and communications counterintelligence. And cryptography. That's where Fischer primarily comes in; he's an expert."

Frade nodded.

"The original idea," Dulles went on, "when Colonel Graham decided you needed better cryptographic equipment than you have was to get you something better from the ASA. They offered a SIGABA, and then the services of someone—Fischer here—to accompany the device to Argentina. The equipment is quite delicate, I understand."

"So my commo man tells me," Frade said.

"But then the situation changed a bit when Graham realized first that the President is determined to learn who Galahad is, on one hand, and, on the other, is quite concerned that the ransoming operation does not become known to people who shouldn't know about it."

"He knows about that, too?"

"Only in the most general of terms," Dulles said. "But that brings us back to those who handle encrypted material get to read it. So when Colonel Graham and I discussed this, we decided that we had to bring Fischer on board, so to speak."

"Can you explain that?"

"Once Fischer gets both the SIGABA device and the Collins transceivers up and running, he will return to Vint Hill Farms Station. All your communications vis-à-vis the ransoming operation, Galahad, and that regicide business we were talking about yesterday will, with their own code, be routed through Fischer at Vint Hill, and passed only to Colonel Graham and myself."

"Not to General Donovan?"

"Colonel Graham and I will decide what General Donovan is to get in these areas."

Frade pointed at Fischer. "For Christ's sake, he's a second lieutenant." He paused and looked at Fischer. "Right?"

"Yes, sir," Fischer said. "I'm eligible for promotion in sixty days."

"And you don't think Donovan is going to send some colonel out to Vint—whateverthehell—"

"Vint Hill Farms Station," Dulles furnished.

"—to stand *Second Lieutenant* Fischer at attention and tell him Donovan gets a copy of everything?"

"Both Colonel Graham and I have told General Donovan that if something like that happens, he and I will personally deliver our resignations to the President."

"And," Frade challenged, "you don't think General Donovan could think of a way around that? 'And not only will you give me a copy of everything, Second Lieutenant Fischer, but I order you not to tell anyone—including but especially Graham, Dulles, and Frade—that you're going to do it.' "

"Actually, that potential problem occurred to Fischer," Dulles replied. "And he came up with a rather clever simple means to let us know if that has happened."

Frade looked at Fischer and made a *Come on, let's hear it* gesture.

"Yes, sir. Sir—"

"Whoa," Frade interrupted. "No 'sir.' No 'major.' From right now."

"Yes, si— What do I call you?"

"Clete. And you?"

"Len. Leonard."

"Okay, *Len:* How are you going to keep Donovan from standing you tall?"

"There's no way I can do that, but if it happens, when I open the net in the morning . . ."

"Explain that, please."

"There will be a regular contact every day at a time to be determined. First, the contact is established. Then there is a brief gibberish message, encoded, to test the SIGABA and its signal operating code. You know, something like 'Mary had a little lamb'; 'There is nothing to fear but fear itself'; 'Lucky Strike Green has gone to war'; 'Play it again, Sam' . . ."

"Okay, I get the picture."

"If I have been compromised, I send yesterday's gibberish as the test encryption."

Frade thought it over and said what he had been thinking.

"That'd work. But how do we know you'd do it?"

"Two reasons. One, I'm a Jew, and I think the President is right. If this ransoming operation gets out, no more Jews will be able to get out of German concentration camps. . . ."

"You told him about that?" Frade challenged Dulles.

Dulles nodded. "He would have come to know anyway."

Frade raised his eyebrows, then looked at Fischer.

"And reason two?"

"Colonel Graham made certain threats about what would happen to me if I betrayed the trust he was placing in me. I believe him, and I'm a devout coward."

Frade said nothing for a long moment.

"What are you thinking, Cletus?" Dulles asked, finally.

"I was thinking that Len and I already have something in common," Frade said. "I think we both wish we had never heard of any of this. Or of the fucking OSS."

Dulles's face showed no expression.

After a long moment, Dulles said, "There is one other thing."

He stopped and leaned to the side of his chair. After a moment, Frade understood he was reaching for something. Something he probably had in a briefcase.

Dulles came up with a leather case containing a camera and slid it across the table to Frade.

"What's this?"

"It's a thirty-five-millimeter camera," he said. "Specifically, a Leica I-C."

"German?" Clete asked as he opened the case.

"German," Dulles confirmed.

"It looks brand new."

"It is. I bought it—actually, I bought three; all they had—in a camera store in Zurich a week or so ago."

"What am I supposed to do with it?"

"When you're in Argentina, I want you to take Len to see Herr and Frau

Frogger," Dulles said. "While he is with them, I want you to take a picture of Len with them. I want one of the Froggers to be holding that day's *La Nación* newspaper."

What the hell is this all about?

"Am I allowed to ask what this is all about?"

"Take at least a half-dozen shots, then change film and take another half-dozen. When you've done that, have the film developed. You have someplace where that can be done discreetly, I suppose?"

"I'm sure I can find one."

"Then give one set of the negatives to Len, who will bring them to the United States when he returns. The other set is to be given to Commander Delojo at the embassy with instructions to send them in the diplomatic pouch, eyes-only Colonel Graham."

"If I gave a roll of film to that sonofabitch, there would be prints at the Office of Naval Intelligence before Graham got the negatives. Didn't Graham tell you about him?"

"Colonel Graham said that you weren't especially fond of Delojo."

"Delojo doesn't know I have the Froggers. And I don't want him to know. If Graham wants the ONI to have copies of these pictures—and learn I have the Froggers—I guess I can't stop him. But I'm not giving Delojo any pictures. And what the hell are they for, anyway?"

"I have a feeling that the Froggers may be of some genuine use to us in several areas. I haven't given it a good deal of thought so far, beyond thinking it would be very interesting if someone called on Oberstleutnant Frogger at Camp Clinton and showed him the photograph of his parents."

"You're sure he's there?"

Dulles nodded.

"I sent a message last night, after we met. I got the confirmation just before we came here. He's fully recovered from his wounds, and is regarded as a Class III, which I found interesting."

"What's a Class III?"

"I have no idea. I presume Colonel Graham thought I knew. I don't. I sent a message asking for an explanation, but there's been no answer, and now there's no time for one."

"Why not?"

"Because my plane leaves in about an hour, and I want to go to the base store—what do they call it?"

"The PX?" Fischer furnished.

"Close, but not correct. The Air Forces calls their stores something else. In any event, I need toothbrushes and toothpaste and hair tonic." He stood up and put out his hand. "So, gentlemen. It's been a pleasure meeting both of you. And we'll be in touch, of course."

And when they had shaken hands, Dulles walked out of the room.

[FOUR]
El Palomar Airfield
Campo de Mayo Military Base
Buenos Aires Province, Argentina
1115 19 July 1943

"El Palomar, South American Airways Zero Zero One," South American Airways Chief Pilot Gonzalo Delgano said into his microphone.

His co-pilot, Señor Cletus Frade, restrained a smile.

I am learning. If I hadn't let him sit in the left seat for this, he never would have forgiven me.

"South American Zero Zero One, Palomar."

"Palomar, South American Zero Zero One is at two thousand meters, twenty-five kilometers from your station, indicating three hundred forty kph."

"Zero Zero One, Palomar. What is your airspeed?"

"Palomar, I repeat. Indicated airspeed is three four zero kilometers per hour. I repeat, three four zero kilometers per hour. Request approach and landing instructions."

If you said "three four zero" one more time, Gonzalo, you would have popped the buttons on your shirt.

"Gear is down and locked, Captain," co-pilot Frade reported. "You have twenty-degrees of flap. We are indicating one hundred twenty-five kph."

"That was a very fine landing, Captain," the co-pilot said. "If I may be permitted to say so. What we call a greaser."

"Actually, for an aircraft of this size, it's not at all that hard to fly, is it, Cletus?"

"It's not an easy one to fly, Gonzalo," Frade said seriously.

Captain Delgano beamed.

I have made a friend for life.

But how that will, of course, affect our professional relationship in the other profession we practice—but don't talk about—remains to be seen.

Frade's good feeling disappeared sixty seconds later when he looked out the cockpit window and saw the welcoming party waiting for them. It included— in addition to Suboficial Mayor Enrico Rodríguez, Retired, the Horch, and a Ford ton-and-a-half stake-bodied truck with ESTANCIA SAN PEDRO Y SAN PABLO painted on the doors—two Argentine officers, El Coronel Juan D. Perón and El Teniente Coronel Alejandro Martín.

How the hell did they know we were coming?

And what the hell do they want?

They knew we were coming, Stupid, because your new friend for life called the Argentine embassy in Rio de Janeiro—

Or maybe there's an Argentine consulate in Pôrto Alegre—

Or maybe Martín has one of his guys in Pôrto Alegre and my pal for life Gonzalo just happened to run into him in the lobby of the hotel.

—and told him, them—somebody—when we were leaving and when we expected to arrive.

And what our welcoming party wants—or at least Martín wants—is to see what interesting things I'm smuggling into Argentina.

And then, to cover his ass—or perhaps he wanted a witness when he caught me smuggling something into Argentina—Martín called Perón, and Tío Juan called the estancia and told Enrico.

The radios I can explain.

But how do I explain the SIGABA device?

Frade waved cheerfully out the window to Perón and Martín as Delgano taxied the Lodestar up to the hangar South American Airways had rented until the hangars—and the runways—being built in Morón were completed.

Frade was first out the door.

"Where's the brass band?" he called as he walked to Perón and Martín. "You two are all we get? No crescendo of trumpets, no roll of drums?"

The intended humor failed. Both Martín and Perón looked confused.

He kissed Tío Juan, then—*what the hell!*—Martín.

"A pleasant flight, Cletus?" Perón asked.

Delgano answered for him.

"Two hours and sixteen minutes from Pôrto Alegre, mi coronel," he proclaimed. "At an average speed of three hundred forty!"

"That fast? You were trying to set a record?"

"No, actually, we didn't try to do anything but get here safely," Frade said.

"It is a beautiful machine," Perón said.

"Would you like to see the inside, mi coronel?" Delgano said.

"I would, thank you," Martín said.

Len Fischer came down the stairs.

"This is Mr. Fischer, of the Collins Radio Corporation," Frade said. "He's here to set up our base station radios."

Perón smiled politely. Martín didn't seem to be surprised to see him.

"We might as well unload them, Fischer," Frade said. "They'll have to pass through customs."

Two customs officers were standing not far away.

That was your cue, Tío Juan, to say, "Oh, that won't be necessary."

"I'd like to see those myself," Martín said.

Okay. A communications radio is a radio. Radios look like radios. And I made sure I told Delgano we were bringing in two radios.

But the SIGABA? How the hell am I going to be able to explain that?

"Can we get some help?" Frade asked.

Tío Juan snapped his fingers, and the older of the customs officers quickly walked to him.

"Be so good as to help this gentleman remove some cargo," Perón said.

Two minutes later, six large wooden crates and a smaller one sat on the tarmac.

The crates had latches. Opening the first of the large ones was simple and quick.

"And there's five more," Fischer said, pointing at the others.

"What's that?" Martín inquired politely, pointing at the smaller crate.

"What is that, Mr. Fischer?" Frade asked in English.

"That's the tape repeater, Mr. Frade," Fischer replied in English.

Frade made the translation.

"What does it do?" El Teniente Coronel Martín asked in Spanish.

"The colonel would like to know what it does," Frade said.

"I'll show you," Fischer said. "You'll have to translate."

"Okay," Frade said, and switched to Spanish. "He's going to show you, and I will translate."

"Muy amable," El Teniente Coronel Martín replied.

"It works with the communications transceivers, in the larger crates," Fischer said, "in the radio-direction-finder function."

Frade made the translation as Fischer took from the crate what looked very much like a typewriter mounted to a metal box.

"The crew of the aircraft, when they are some distance from the field," Fischer explained, "listen for a Morse code signal being transmitted by the transceiver."

Frade made the translation.

"They can then head for the source of that signal," Fischer went on. "Radio propagation is sometimes directional."

Frade translated.

"But of course they have to be listening to the right signal, which means it has to be identified," Fischer went on. "That means sending a message. Now, supposing the airfield here is looking for South American Airways Zero Zero One"—he gestured—"this aircraft."

Frade translated.

"In that case, the message would be 'South American Airways Zero Zero One.' "

Frade translated.

I now have Tío Juan's and Martín's fascinated attention.

Where is Fischer getting this bullshit?

"Which would normally be transmitted, over and over, by a radio operator sitting at a desk and tapping his key."

Frade translated.

Fischer said, "Dit dit dit dot dit dot dot dit dit."

Tío Juan and Martín signaled that that required no translation by nodding their understanding.

"He would do this, over and over, for an hour. Or even longer," Fischer said.

Frade translated.

"But with the Model SIGABA here," Fischer said, patting the device much as if it were a beloved family puppy, "all we have to do is type the message once."

He mimed typing.

Frade translated.

"And the SIGABA produces a perforated tape, like this."

He held up a three-foot-long strip of brown paper tape and handed it to Frade.

Frade translated as they examined it. He saw that it was perforated along its length with small holes. Over each grouping of holes was a letter. In this case, it spelled out PLAY IT AGAIN SAM.

He handed the tape to Martín, who examined it. Tío Juan moved in for a closer look, took the tape from Martín, then looked at Fischer for a further explanation.

"Then all we have to do is feed the tape back into a Model 7.2 transceiver," Fischer went on, "and throw a switch, and the Model 7.2 will broadcast the message on the tape over and over, perfectly, until it is turned off."

Frade translated.

"Very clever," Martín said.

"Brilliant!" Tío Juan said enthusiastically.

"When we have it set up, I'll be happy to demonstrate it," Fischer said.

Frade translated.

"I'd like to see that," Tío Juan said.

"Well, as soon as we get it set up, Tío Juan, at Estancia San Pedro y San Pablo, I'll arrange a demonstration for you and El Coronel Martín."

"Please," Perón said.

"Captain Delgano," Frade said, "would you be good enough to show these gentlemen around Zero Zero One?"

"It would be my honor, Don Cletus."

"Jesus, Fischer," Frade said when the others were inside the Lodestar, "where did all that tape repeater yarn come from?"

"I spent most of the trip down here wondering what I was going to do if somebody asked me what the SIGABA was. I didn't want to have to pull the D-ring."

"What D-ring?"

"The one that sets off the thermite grenades. There's two of them in the crate, in boxes labeled 'Perforatable Tape.'"

IX

[ONE]
Estancia San Pedro y San Pablo
Near Pila
Buenos Aires Province, Argentina
1730 19 July 1943

Second Lieutenant Leonard Fischer, Signal Corps, U.S. Army, looked with interest as a native Argentine cowboy—called a *gaucho,* he had learned from a magazine photo essay—pushed himself off the tailgate of a Ford Model A pickup and walked toward the Horch that had carried them from the airfield to what Major Frade had described as "my farm."

The gaucho looks just like the ones in the pictures in National Geographic: *He's got the wide leather belt decorated with silver, the big knife slipped in the belt at the back, the billowing breeches tucked into leather boots—everything.*

But what's a gaucho doing here? This place looks more like the campus of a boarding school for rich kids than a farm.

And take a look at that! Jesus, that's a good-looking dame!

I thought all these people would look like Chiquita Banana—dark skin, black hair, a whatchamacallit tied over their heads—not a long-haired blonde in a blouse and a horse riding skirt.

The blonde kissed Major Frade in a manner that was both respectable and interesting, then put her hand out to Fischer.

"Welcome to Estancia San Pedro y San Pablo," she said. "I'm Dorotea Frade."

"Thank you. My name is Fischer."

Frade said, "Second Lieutenant Leonard Fischer, Signal Corps, this is my communications officer, Lieutenant Oscar Schultz, USN. And that is the last time we will use our ranks."

Both Fischer and Schultz had personal thoughts before they shook hands.

Fischer wondered, *Frade's not talking about the gaucho—is he?*

Schultz thought, *This kid is supposed to be expert on the Collins Model 7.2 transceivers and the SIGABA?*

"How do you do, sir?" Fischer said politely.

"And kill the 'sir' business, too," Frade added.

"What do you say, Fischer?" Schultz said.

"What do I call you?"

"We call him El Jefe," Dorotea said. "It means 'the chief.' "

Fischer nodded his agreement.

"Well, come in the house and we'll have tea," Dorotea said.

"Can I pass on that, Dorotea?" Schultz said. "I want to look at what they brought. I figured we'd do that in the hangar?"

"So would Carlos like to have a look at what we brought," Frade said, then explained Carlos to Fischer. "He's my mechanic, hired at the strong recommendation of Delgano, which means he works for El Coronel Martín."

"Carlos went into town yesterday," Schultz said. "I thought he'd be back today, but he's not here. I checked on that when I heard you'd come onto the estancia."

"So would I like to see what you brought home," Dorotea said. "So tea will be served in the hangar. There also will be beer, Mr. Fischer, a very nice merlot, and bourbon, as that's what my husband drinks. But we have about anything else you might want."

"Beer will be fine, ma'am," Fischer said. "Ma'am, do you have a vacuum cleaner?"

"Yes, of course."

"Could I borrow it, please? One with a hose would be just what I need."

"One vacuum cleaner with a hose coming up," Dorotea said.

"What's with the vacuum cleaner?" Schultz asked.

"I packed the transceivers and the . . . electric typewriter . . . with popcorn," Fischer said.

"You did what?"

"I used popcorn as a cushioning material," Fischer explained.

"I'll be goddamned!" Schultz blurted.

"Quite probably," Dorotea said, "if you keep taking His name in vain."

"Well, I'll be a sonofabitch," Chief Schultz said in awe, then winced. "Sorry again, Dorotea."

They were in the hangar, looking into the innards of the SIGABA device, the cover of which had been carefully removed. There was not much to see, other than an odd wire rising from a sea of popcorn kernels.

"You did that to the Model Seven-Twos, too?" Schultz asked.

"Yeah. It really works."

"You've moved one of these before?" Schultz asked doubtfully.

"I've moved a bunch of them," Fischer said.

Fischer turned to Enrico Rodríguez, who was somewhat awkwardly, if not comically, holding his shotgun in one hand and an upright vacuum cleaner by its handle in his other. Fischer took the vacuum from him and found a power outlet.

There was a thin, foot-long hollow wand attached to the vacuum cleaner hose. Fischer pulled it off, then turned on the vacuum and carefully lowered the now-large, open end of the hose into the SIGABA.

There was a rattling in the hose as the machine sucked up the popcorn. It didn't take long to get most of it out, and then Fischer put the wand back on the hose and used that to suck out what was left from among the vacuum tubes and rat nests of wiring in the cavity.

"I'll be a sonofabitch," Schultz said again. This time he didn't apologize.

"Now let's see what happens when we plug it in," Fischer said.

Dorotea handed him a power cord.

"One-ten or two-twenty?" Fischer asked.

"Two hundred twenty volts," Schultz answered for her.

Fischer threw the voltage-selector switch on the side of the SIGABA device, then made the connection.

"You better stand back, Chief. Sometimes there's a flash fire," Fischer said seriously.

Schultz looked at him in disbelief but took a step back.

Fischer pushed the main power switch.

There was a hum, but no fire.

Fischer smiled at Schultz, who, smiling, shook his head.

A row of dials slowly came to life.

Both Fischer and Schultz examined them carefully.

"Jesus, better than I thought," Fischer said thoughtfully.

"You don't have any juice on the DC feed to the secondary oscillator," Schultz said.

"Oh, hell!" Fischer said, then added, "But no problem. I'll just say the magic words!"

"The what?"

"Mumbo jumbo, fish boom bah," Fischer intoned, and with his index finger tapped the dial that showed no indication of power. The indicator needle leapt to life and indicated twelve volts DC.

"If that didn't work, I would have kicked it. That usually works," Fischer said. "But sometimes I have to use a hammer."

"You're a real wiseass, aren't you?" Schultz said, smiling.

Fischer shrugged. "I'm a Signal Corps second lieutenant. It goes without saying."

"It's working?" Frade asked.

"If I hadn't watched it myself, I wouldn't believe it," Schultz said. "Okay, Fischer. Fair's fair. If that popcorn is your idea, you're one clever sonofabitch."

"Call me 'Len,' " Fischer said.

Frade said, "Talk about clever: You should have heard the line of bull he fed Martín and Tío Juan about this thing. Which they swallowed whole. Tell the chief, Fischer."

Fischer related the story.

"And they believed that?" Schultz then said.

"Swallowed it hook, line, and sinker," Frade confirmed.

"Well, then, they must not know a hell of a lot about the way RDF works."

"What do you mean?" Frade asked.

"There's no long message like that—*'South American Airways Zero Zero One'*—what he said. What the field RDF transmitter sends is a couple of letters. Like P-A-L for Palomar. That's all. You don't know that?"

"I do," Frade replied. "But so what? Martín and Perón don't."

Then he had a thought that chilled him, almost making him sick to his stomach.

Oh, shit!

Delgano was there when Fischer was handing that bullshit story to Perón and Martín!

He's a pilot. He knows about RDF call signs as well as I do! Every time he goes into Palomar, he homes in on PAL.

He looked at Fischer.

Fischer looked embarrassed.

"I know about radios," he said. "I don't know much about airplanes."

"Obviously," Frade said, somewhat sharply. And was immediately sorry.

This is my fault, not his.

So why didn't Delgano say anything?

Was he waiting until we were gone, and was going to tell Martín then?

That doesn't make any sense.

If he was going to tell Martín, he would have told him when he was showing him and Perón around the airplane.

And if he had told Martín, Martín wouldn't have been so obliging about us loading the SIGABA and the Collins transceivers on the truck and bringing them out here.

At the very least, Martín would have "suggested" we leave everything in the hangar at Palomar.

"Something you ate, darling?" Dorotea asked. "You look as if you're about to be sick."

"We didn't fool Delgano with that story," Clete said. "He's a pilot."

"Oh, shit!" Schultz said.

After a moment, Dorotea asked very softly, "You think he told Martín?"

"I think if he had, the SIGABA device now would be in Martín's office, being examined by his technicians, and I would be explaining to Tío Juan why I was smuggling a cryptographic device into Argentina. Or I'd be in a cell."

"Delgano's a good guy, Clete," Schultz said. "I know you don't like him, but . . ."

"But what? The sonofabitch spied on my father for years."

"That was his job," Schultz argued. "His *duty*. That don't mean he didn't like your father. Or that he liked spying on him."

"Meaning?"

"And he's not stupid."

"No, he's not. But what does that mean?"

"I don't think he liked what the Krauts did to your father. Either personally, or as an Argentine officer. And then you proved you're not exactly Argentina's Public Enemy Number One by taking this"—he pointed to the nose of the Lodestar, which was just inside the hangar—"to Campo de Mayo and flying General Whatsisname . . ."

"Rawson," Dorotea furnished.

". . . around in their Piper Cub—"

"I know where you're going, Chief," Clete interrupted. "But I don't share your optimism. I have a somewhat darker view."

"Such as?" Dorotea asked.

"Arresting me—or even Fischer here—as a spy is something that's not going to happen without General Rawson's permission. They're not going to just say, 'Gotcha. Up against the wall!' "

"If you think you're being clever and funny, you're not," Dorotea said.

"I'm obviously not clever, sweetheart, and this is not at all funny. So I think we have to consider the very real possibility that, any minute now, Rawson having given his permission, reluctantly or otherwise, the gauchos will report that a small convoy of Ejército Argentino vehicles have come onto the estancia . . ."

Dorotea inhaled audibly and put her hand to her mouth.

". . . to arrest me. And, of course, Fischer. And to grab the SIGABA."

"You don't know that," Schultz said.

"No. But I always look for the dark lining of the dark cloud," Clete said. "The question then becomes what do we do with Fischer."

"We take him out in the boonies," Schultz said.

"No," Frade said. "We fire up the Lodestar and take him to Uruguay. He heads for the Brazilian border, then home. I wait there until I hear from some-body here . . . you, sweetheart . . . what the Ejército Argentino did when they learned we were gone."

"Or if they came here at all," Dorotea said.

Clete nodded. "And based on that information, I decide what to do next."

"Or if they came here at all," Dorotea repeated.

Clete looked at her.

She added, "You're assuming a lot has happened and will happen that may not have happened or will not happen at all."

"Honey, I just can't cross my fingers and hope for the best," Clete said. "Okay. Get the tractor, Chief, and we'll drag the Lodestar out of here."

"I'm going with you," Dorotea said.

"No, you're not. If you did that, you would be an accomplice. Right now, you're just a wife who had no idea what her crazy American husband was up to. They're not going to bother you. And we'll get you to Uruguay or Brazil or wherever later."

"I'm going with you," she insisted.

"No," he said flatly.

"What about the pictures Mr. Dulles wants of me and the Nazis?" Fischer asked.

"Oh, Jesus!" Frade said.

"What pictures?" Dorotea asked. "What Nazis? Who's Mr. Dulles?"

"I had the feeling he thought that was pretty important," Fischer said.

"Yeah, so did I, God damn it," Clete said.

"Are you going to tell me what's going on, please?" Dorotea asked.

He looked at her, then suddenly turned and walked toward the hangar door.

"What are you doing?" she called after him. "Where are you going?"

When Clete left the hangar, Dorotea started after him.

Chief Schultz caught her arm. She looked at him in surprise.

"Sometimes, when you have to make a decision, it's better if you're alone," Schultz said. "And he has to make the decisions here by himself."

She continued looking at Schultz for a long moment, then nodded her understanding.

She turned to Fischer.

"The Nazis you were asking about? Did you mean the Froggers?"

"That's the name—I think—he used. Mr. Dulles—"

"And who is Mr. Dulles?"

"I don't really know. I mean, he's OSS. I know that. But he's more than that. He's somebody important."

"How do you know that?" Schultz asked.

"Well, when we landed at Pôrto Alegre, he was there with the commanding general, an Air Forces brigadier named Wallace. They met the plane, I mean. And Mr. Dulles shakes my hand and says, 'What brings you to Pôrto Alegre, Lieutenant?' and I say, 'I'm looking for a man named Frade,' and the general says, 'That makes two of us.'

"The way he said it made it pretty clear that he wasn't going to hang a Hawaiian lei around this Major Frade's neck. So Mr. Dulles says, 'You think you know Major Frade, do you, General?'

"And General Wallace says—I don't remember exactly, but something like— 'Yes, I do. The last time he was here he took off without permission, defied my orders to return to the field, and got me in all sorts of difficulties with the Brazilian authorities. I've really been hoping to see that young man again, and soon.'

"And then Mr. Dulles says, very soft, 'I'm afraid you're mistaken, General. You have never seen Señor Frade before.'

"And the general says, 'Oh, yes, I have. And I look forward to taking that young man down a peg or two.'

"And Mr. Dulles says, 'General, I'm afraid you're not listening. I just told you that you never before saw the Señor Frade who's coming here to pick up the Lodestar aircraft. You won't recognize him today or at any other time he might be back here. Is that clear, or is it going to be necessary for me to call General Arnold and have him tell you that personally?' "

"Who's General Arnold?" Dorotea asked.

" 'Hap' Arnold, commanding general of the Army Air Forces," Schultz furnished. "The *whole* goddamn AAF."

"Yeah," Fischer went on. "So this General Wallace looks like he's going to sh . . . *explode*. But then he says, 'Yes, sir. I mean, no, sir. It will not be necessary for you to call General Arnold.'

"And Mr. Dulles says, 'Thank you.'

"And then—later, not when the general was there—he told Major Frade that I had been given a Lindbergh clearance, and that I was going to find out who Galahad is . . ."

"Jesus!" Schultz said.

". . . because I'll be handling all the traffic from here when I get back to Vint Hill Farms."

"That makes sense," Schultz said. "We can't have everybody at Vint Hill doing the decryption."

"What about the Froggers?" Dorotea asked. "Did he know about them, too?"

"I guess Major Frade told him, because just before he left, he gave him a German camera—something with an *L*—"

"Leica?" Dorotea offered.

Fischer nodded. "And told him to take pictures of me with these people. Holding a copy of that day's newspaper."

"To do what with?" Schultz asked.

Fischer shrugged. "All I know is that I'm going to take the film with me when I go to the States. Mr. Dulles wanted to send a second copy through some Navy officer in our embassy—Delojo?—but Major Frade said he didn't trust him—"

"What *Major* Frade said earlier," Frade's voice suddenly announced, startling everyone, "*Lieutenant* Fischer—and it was an order, Fischer—was to stop using ranks."

Everyone turned to see Frade coming back inside the hangar.

"Sorry," Fischer said as he noticed the pronounced change in Frade's body language.

"I'm going to tell it like it is, Fischer," Frade said with some force. "If my stupidity blows this operation—for allowing you to run with that line to Martín and Perón while not recognizing Delgano, a pilot, knew it was bullshit—there's going to be real problems. And that's the great understatement of the day. If— probably when—we get caught, I don't think much will happen to me. I'll be kicked out of country, but they're not going to shoot me."

He glanced at the others. "You, however, you're something else. And so are the rest of the people on the estancia. I don't think they'll shoot everyone. But you will be tried as spies, sentenced to death, and thrown in a cell. Unless we can do something to get you out, and I don't think we can—'we' meaning me and the U.S. government—you'll be in that cell for the duration of the war and—what is it they say?—'plus six months.' "

"Yes, sir," Fischer said meekly.

"And that means, of course, that we won't have the radar to make sure the Germans haven't brought another submarine-replenishment vessel into Samborombón Bay . . ."

"Shit," Schultz said.

". . . And that while you're all in some cell—before and after your court-martial—the Germans will probably try to have you killed."

"They can do that?" Fischer blurted.

Frade exhaled audibly. "Yeah, Fischer, they can do that. My Uncle Juan Domingo is not the only Argentine officer who thinks Hitler's a good guy and that the Germans and Japs and Italians—The Axis—are going to win the war."

"Oh, boy!" Fischer said.

"And to answer your specific question: The organized crime down here is very much like ours in the States. When the Germans wanted my father dead—and, for that matter, me whacked—they didn't try to do it themselves. They hired professional killers from whatever they call the Mafia down here. They took out my father but didn't get me. That was dumb luck; somebody told me they were coming, and I was waiting for them. They're not nice people. They found my housekeeper, a really nice lady, in the kitchen and slit her throat, just because she was there—"

"Jesus!"

"Yeah, Jesus. Now pay attention, Fischer: I can get you out of the country, into Uruguay, right now. And have you in Brazil tomorrow."

"Yes, sir."

"The Froggers are at Casa Chica, a small farm I own near Tandil, in the hills between La Pampas and Mar del Plata—"

"I don't know where any of those places are," Fischer interrupted.

"Let me finish, Fischer," Frade said coldly.

"Yes, sir."

"It's about a two-hour drive from here," Frade went on.

"Yes, sir."

"And every twenty miles or so, I expect there will be a checkpoint. Either army or police."

"Yes . . . I understand."

"I think those pictures are more important than I understand—"

Fischer, nodding, interrupted: "Mr. Dulles made that pretty clear without coming right out and saying so, or saying why."

After a long silence, Frade said, "I am not going to order you to go out there, Fischer."

Fischer met his eyes for a moment, then shrugged. "When do I go? Right now?"

"If we're going to go, yeah, right now. You're willing to take the chance?"

Fischer nodded again.

Frade raised his eyebrows. "The first thing I learned when I went into the Marine Corps was never to volunteer for anything."

"Yeah, well, what the hell, I've never seen a real Nazi," Fischer said.

"Taking into consideration that that goddamned Carlos may have sneaked back onto the estancia—"

"I don't think so, Clete," Schultz said. "Those gauchos of yours know if a damn rabbit comes on the place."

Frade ignored the comment. "—and is watching us through binoculars to see what we're doing before they come to arrest me. So, what we now are going to do is get in the Horch. Fischer gets in the backseat and lies on the floor until we're a couple of miles from here. And we go to Casa Chica."

"A couple problems with that, sweetheart," Dorotea said.

Clete turned quickly to look at her.

"You don't know how to get there," she explained reasonably. "The only time you've been there, you flew the Piper Cub. And . . . when I am sitting with you in the front seat, and if Carlos is watching us, he will decide that you and I have gone off for a romantic interlude. If I'm not with you, *that* would be suspicious. Most *Marines* would not think of leaving their bride the same night they came home."

Clete saw out of the corner of his eye that Schultz and Fischer were trying very hard not to smile.

Clete nodded. "Okay, okay, sweetheart, you can go."

"Oh, you're just so *good* to me!"

He shook his head—but he was smiling.

"Chief," Frade then said, "take the SIGABA device out to the radar site. Make sure it and the radio and the code machine and everything else is rigged with thermite grenades."

"And the Collins radios?"

"Leave them here. If Carlos is watching, taking them out of the hangar would be suspicious."

Schultz nodded.

"If they come after me," Frade went on, "torch everything, then go hide on the estancia."

"I know just the place. *Places,*" Schultz said. "We'll just lay low until we see what happens. Not that I think anything will."

Frade raised his eyebrows, not convinced. He said, "When we get to Casa Chica, we'll take the pictures of the Froggers—we'll need a copy of *La Nación . . .*"

"There's one in the sitting," Dorotea said.

". . . And then we'll spend the night. We'll leave there at seven, seven-thirty in the morning. Which should put us back here, or onto the estancia, at about half past nine. Have a gaucho meet us somewhere if everything's okay. If there's no gaucho . . . then we'll play it by ear."

[TWO]
Estancia Casa Chica
Near Tandil
Buenos Aires Province, Argentina
2015 19 July 1943

Dorotea had to tell Clete where to turn off the macadam-paved highway onto Estancia Casa Chica. There was no sign visible from the highway, but one hundred meters down a road paved with small, smooth riverbed stones, the powerful headlights of the Horch lit up two short pillars formed from fieldstone. A sturdy rusty chain was suspended between them, and hanging from the center of the chain was a small sign that read: CASA CHICA.

"Oh, damn!" Dorotea Frade said. "I don't have a key."

"Great!" Clete said.

Enrico Rodríguez got nimbly from the car the moment it stopped, found in the shadows the padlock fastening the chain to the left pillar, tugged at it a moment, then matter-of-factly pulled from his shoulder holster his .45-caliber pistol—an Argentine copy of a Colt Model 1911 semiautomatic—took aim, and fired.

Clete noticed that Enrico had not first worked the action, which meant he had been carrying the pistol with a round in the chamber.

The first shot dented the massive brass padlock, but it still securely held the chain. Enrico fired again, then again. The lock then dropped off the chain and the chain dropped to the road.

"Did he have to do that?" Dorotea asked, seemingly taking the abuse of the lock somewhat personally.

"Well, since unnamed persons didn't have the key . . ."

Enrico came back to the Horch, stopping to stand in the beam of the head-lights. Clete could see that the hammer still was back and locked. Enrico re-placed the magazine in the pistol with a fresh one, then put the pistol back in the shoulder holster.

That means he's back to eight available shots, Clete thought, *seven in the magazine and the one he left in the throat.*

Now what the hell is he doing?

What Enrico was doing was recharging the magazine he'd taken from the pistol. When he'd finished, he slipped it into the left front pocket of his pants and got nimbly back into the car.

He didn't say one word, Clete thought, smiling as he put the Horch in gear.

Three hundred meters down the road, just past a curve, a two-wheeled horse cart was blocking the road.

Clete slammed on the brakes, pushed Dorotea down onto the floor, and got out, grabbing a Remington Model 11 12-bore self-loading shotgun from under the seat as he did so.

"It's all right, Don Cletus!" a familiar voice quickly called from the dark-ness. "It's Sargento Gómez here."

A moment later, Sargento Rodolfo Gómez, Argentine Cavalry, Retired, stepped into the light of the headlights. He had a 7mm Mauser carbine cradled in his arms like a hunter.

And, a moment after that, Staff Sergeant Sigfried Stein, Signal Corps, U.S. Army, came running down the road carrying a Thompson .45-caliber subma-chine gun. Before he reached them, two gauchos on horseback, both carrying shotguns, came onto the road.

"I heard shots," Stein said, but made it more a question.

"Enrico had to shoot the padlock off the chain," Frade said.

"I forgot the key," Dorotea said. "For which sin, I was just shoved onto the floor."

"Don Cletus was protecting you, Doña Dorotea," Enrico said.

"I've been trying to convince myself of that," Dorotea said without con-viction.

"Sorry, baby," Clete said, then turned. "Sergeant Stein, say hello to Lieutenant Fischer."

The two shook hands.

Frade looked at Fischer and said, "Around here, we use ranks to dazzle our guests. Siggy is Major Stein and I am El Coronel." He turned to Stein. "Speaking of our guests?"

"José," Stein said, and pointed to one of the gauchos, "his wife is with Frau Frogger. Frau Frogger's not talking to Herr Frogger."

"Why not?"

"Because he came to me and told me that if we didn't watch her close, she was going to try to get back to Buenos Aires."

"Oh, Jesus," Frade said. "Fischer, you are now another major." He paused. "Oh, hell! Fischer, how's your German?"

"Not bad."

"Okay, we don't introduce you. When Siggy and I talk to you, it will be as Mister Fischer. Got it?"

"Jawohl, Herr Oberst," Fischer said.

"Get in, Siggy. We'll go see the lioness in her cage."

"I can just ride on the running board," Stein said.

"Get in," Frade ordered. "If you fell off and broke your leg, we'd really be screwed."

Commercial Attaché Wilhelm Frogger got quickly to his feet when Frade walked into the sitting room. Frogger had been in an armchair—*my father's armchair, you sonofabitch!*—reading a book.

Frogger was wearing a suit and necktie. His face was cleanly shaved and his mustache trimmed.

A gaucho with a flowing mustache and holding a shotgun in his lap was sitting in a wooden chair tipped against the wall near the door.

He neither said anything nor got out of the chair, but nodded at Frade and the others.

Frade glared at Frogger but didn't speak to him.

"The woman?" Frade said to the gaucho.

"In her room."

"Go get her, please."

The gaucho nodded and left the room.

Fischer walked to Frogger and gestured for him to hand over the book.

Frade examined it, shrugged, then handed it back.

"Goethe, *Römishe Elegien,*"Wilhelm Frogger announced in German, then translated to English. *"Roman Elegy.* Love poems."

"I know," Frade replied in English. "My father spoke German."

Then an unpleasant thought occurred to him: *Is that bastard holding a book from which my father used to read to Claudia?*

Frau Frogger appeared a moment later, trailed by a short, squat female.

That has to be José's wife, Frade thought, then remembered hearing that among the gauchos the sacrament of marriage was often ignored. *Whatever her marital status, she's formidable.*

"Have Frau Frogger comb her hair and otherwise have her make herself presentable," Frade ordered the squat female in Spanish. "We are going to take her photograph."

"I refuse," Frau Frogger said.

"If necessary, tie her to a chair," Frade ordered.

Frade motioned for Stein and Fischer to follow him. "Come with me, please, gentlemen," he said, then quickly added, "And lady."

"Thank you ever so much," Dorotea replied icily.

Frade led them through the kitchen to a galley at the rear of the house. And then he went back in the kitchen, coming out a moment later with a bottle of wine and a handful of long-stemmed glasses.

"What, Clete?" Stein asked as Frade worked the corkscrew.

"Two things," Frade said. "First, I'm sure my lovely bride would like to have witnesses while I grovel in apology for shoving her down on the floor of the Horch—"

"And for almost forgetting your lovely bride in there just now," Dorotea said.

"I am groveling, my love."

"Good."

"And I wanted Stein to tell Fischer—who glared in outrage at me when I told José's wife to tie Grandma to a chair—who's the real Nazi in there."

"Unequivocally, she is, Mr. Fischer," Stein said. "She thinks Hitler was sent by God to save the world from the likes of you and me." He saw the look on Fischer's face and added: "I shit you not, Lieutenant. Grandma not only is a real Nazi—but a three-star bitch to boot. Sorry, Dorotea."

Dorotea made an *It's not important* gesture.

"Call me Len," Fischer said idly, then went on. "Well, neither one of them is what I expected. He looks like a librarian, and she looks like . . . well, 'grandma' fits. Not at all what I expected."

"That's probably because you expected them to look like the evil men in the black uniforms in Hollywood Nazi movies," Stein said.

"Probably," Fischer admitted, chuckling.

"Most of the Nazis you see in movies are Jews, Len, I hope you know."

"Are they really?" Fischer asked, smiling.

"So my father tells me," Stein went on. "He tells me that when he goes on the Sabbath to Temple Israel on Hollywood Boulevard, he sees so many familiar Nazi faces that if it wasn't for the yarmulkes he'd think he was in the Reichstag."

"You're teasing, right?" Dorotea asked.

"No, I'm not," Stein said.

"Let's talk about the Nazi librarian," Frade said. "Did you get anything out of him, Siggy?"

"I don't know how good it is, but I got a lot out of him," Stein said. "That's one of the reasons Grandma is pissed at him. But I don't know if that's an act, too."

"What did you get?"

"All sorts of lists and organizational charts about the German embassy. You know, boxes and arrows, saying who's responsible for what, and who takes orders from whom. Phone numbers. Addresses. Things like that. Shall I get it?"

"What would I do with it now? We'll have to have von Wachtstein look at it"—he saw the look on Stein's face, stopped, then went on—"to see if he's telling us the truth."

Then he stopped again, and formed his thoughts before going on.

"Fischer, you now know who we have in the German embassy. If the wrong people learn that name, he—and a lot of other good people— are going to die as painfully as the Krauts can kill them."

"How do you know you can trust . . . Who did you say, von Wachtstein?"

"Major Hans-Peter Baron von Wachtstein, of the Luftwaffe," Frade said. "Onetime fighter pilot. Awarded the Knight's Cross of the Iron Cross by Hitler himself."

"And you trust him?"

Frade nodded solemnly. "He saved my life. And there's more, but I just decided you don't need to know more."

"You mind telling me why?"

"There's a very strong possibility that the wrong people will be asking you questions. And you obviously can't tell them something you don't know."

"Do I get an explanation of that?" Stein asked.

Frade looked at Stein a moment.

"Yeah, sure," he said. "If this operation of ours blows up the way I think it might—probably will—you, Siggy, are going to be the Lone Ranger out here."

"Blows up?" Stein said.

"Just before we came out here, I told Chief—sorry—*Lieutenant* Schultz to rig thermite grenades on the radar, the radios, and the new code machine Fischer brought down here with him. His orders are that the moment he hears the Argentines have come onto the estancia to arrest me, he's to torch everything and try to find some place on the estancia for everybody to hide until something can be done to get everybody out of Argentina, probably to Uruguay."

"Jesus!"

"You're stuck here with the Froggers."

"You're sure this is going to happen?" Stein said.

"I'm not, and neither is Schultz," Dorotea said.

Frade glanced at her, then looked back to Stein.

"I'll tell you what I told my wife and Schultz: I can't afford to be an optimist."

Stein shrugged in understanding.

"So I'll take it from the top, Siggy. You can decide for yourself whether I'm right."

Stein nodded.

Frade began: "When we—Delgano and I—went to Pôrto Alegre to pick up the Lodestar, the radios, the SIGABA, and Fischer, there was a man waiting for me . . ."

"So you came here to take Grandma's picture," Stein said after Frade was finished. "Because you think it's important to this Mr. Dulles?"

It was more of a statement than a question.

Frade nodded. "And because I thought I might be able to salvage at least the pictures of her for him from the smoldering ruins of our operation."

"You don't know that, Cletus!" Dorotea said, and when he looked to her, she repeated, " 'The smoldering ruins.' "

"Baby, you don't know how much I hope you're right and I'm wrong, but I can't go with crossed fingers and wishful thinking."

"For the sake of argument, Clete," Stein said, "say you're right. What do I do with the Froggers if I hear they've arrested you?"

"They know too much, Siggy," Frade said.

"I was afraid of that," Stein said. He shrugged. "What the hell."

"You can have Enrico do it, or Gómez, if it comes to that," Clete said.

"If it comes to that, I'll do it," Stein said. He looked at Fischer. "What are a couple of nice Jewish boys like us doing here, doing things like this?"

Fischer raised his eyebrows in an expression that said *Hell if I know.*

Frade went on: "We'll spend the night here, and leave for the estancia at first light. Gauchos will meet us as soon as we come onto the estancia. If—and I don't think this is likely to happen—they say the cops or whatever haven't come yet, then I'll fire up the Lodestar and fly Fischer to Uruguay. That will at least get him and one roll of the film out of here."

"And if you're right," Dorotea said, "and the police or whatever are looking for you, then what?"

"Then you will drive to the house—taking one of the rolls of film with you; which you will somehow manage to get to the embassy—and tell the cops you have no idea where your crazy husband is. Enrico will go with you. Fischer and I will get on horses and ride off into the sunset and hope we can hide until I figure out how to get him and me and everybody else out of the country."

"I've never been on a horse," Fischer said.

"Then that should be interesting," Frade said.

"Well, let's go take the goddamn pictures," Stein said.

"New problem," Frade said. "It's dark. You can't take pictures in the dark, can you? Maybe we'll have to wait until tomorrow morning."

"That depends on the camera," Stein said.

Dorothy took the camera from her purse and handed it to him.

"My God," Stein said. "A Leica I-C. Looks brand-new."

"Is it a good camera?" Frade said. "More to the point, can we take pictures with it tonight?"

"Is it a good camera? Yeah. About as good as they come. You have film?"

Dorotea handed him four film cassettes, which he examined quickly.

"Jesus, this is hard to come by, too. ASA 200. *Very* fast. No problem with this. We just take the shades off the lamp."

"You know about photography, Siggy?"

"My father's in the camera business—motion and still—in Los Angeles."

They watched as he loaded film into the camera with a practiced skill.

"Okay, let's go," Stein said when he'd finished.

———

Frau Frogger was sitting stiffly in a wooden chair, her hands folded in her lap.

Fischer and Stein were rearranging the light fixtures in the room to Stein's satisfaction.

"Just her, or the librarian, too?" Stein asked when they finished with the lighting.

"How many pictures can you take?"

"These are thirty-six-exposure rolls; there's two of them."

"Priority one is her with Fischer and *La Nación,*" Frade said. "When you're sure you have her, then we can take more with him. And what the hell, with me, too."

"I protest," Frau Frogger said in Spanish, then repeated it in German.

"One more word out of you, señora," Dorotea said coldly, "and we will take photographs of you without clothing."

Frau Frogger snorted.

Dorotea slapped her face very hard.

"Hey!" Clete protested without thinking.

"You tell me that I can, Cletus, and when we finish taking her picture, I'll take her out onto the pampas myself."

Frade's first reaction, of course, was surprise that Dorotea had slapped the woman. That was really out of character for Dorotea.

His second reaction was husbandly pride.

God, what a wife! She understands we have to keep this woman afraid, and is doing whatever is necessary to do it.

His third reaction, somewhat slow in coming, was far less pleasant.

Jesus Christ! That was no act. She slapped that woman with hate!

Confirmation of this came from the looks on the faces of Fischer and Stein and Enrico. Stein and Fischer had seen what Frade had seen—and were shocked and repelled. Enrico's face showed approval.

Did she mean what she said about taking them out herself and killing them?
Of course not.
You're pissing in the wind, Cletus.
The no-longer Virgin Princess, the angel walking the earth carrying your child, meant every word of what she said!

Confirmation of this came from the terrified faces of the Froggers.

Jesus H. Christ!

Then another thought he had heard somewhere—and had promptly dismissed as probably bullshit—now popped into his mind: *The female of the species is always the more deadly.*

I will be goddamned!

Well, you're a Marine officer. You know the tactic to be applied here. When you've broken through the enemy's defenses, don't stop, continue the attack!

"Fischer, stand her up, hand Grandma *La Nación*, and smile for the birdie."

Don Cletus Frade did not discuss with Doña Dorotea Mallín de Frade what had happened, not even after he had had more than his fair share of several bottles of merlot.

The reason was simple. He didn't know what to say.

And he had thoughts later, after they had retired and shared conjugal relations, that he knew he didn't dare share with his wife.

From their very first coupling, Dorotea—and she then really had been the Virgin Princess—had always been an enthusiastic partner.

But tonight was different!

Not a complaint, certainly, but tonight she really wanted to mate, and her response was nothing like any previous responses.

She literally couldn't get enough.

And it had nothing to do with her being pregnant.

[THREE]
Estancia Casa Chica
Near Tandil
Buenos Aires Province, Argentina
0650 20 July 1943

"Since my husband devoutly believes that enormous breakfasts are a hallowed American custom," Doña Dorotea announced brightly at breakfast, "I have done my best to be a good wife. There is grapefruit juice and milk, toast, coffee, and ham steaks. And as I understand that those of your religious persuasion aren't allowed to eat pork, I had the cook grill some steak to go with the eggs. I hope that will be satisfactory."

"Anything's fine, Dorotea," Stein said.

"I thought the least I could do,"Lla Señora Frade said, trying to smile brightly, "was feed the condemned men a last hearty meal."

Clete said, "Baby, nobody's going to die—"

"At least not today, probably," she interrupted.

"—but I admit there is a good chance we'll be playing cops and robbers later this morning."

Stein suddenly laughed. "Oh, I wish I could be there to see Fischer getting on his first horse and riding off on the pampas. 'Hi, ho, Silver, away!' " He paused, and then went on "That probably should be, 'Oi veh, Silverman, away!' "

"Sergeants are not allowed to mock commissioned officers and gentlemen such as myself, Sergeant Stein," Fischer said good-naturedly. "Perhaps you should keep that in mind."

"You know, when they sent the Lone Ranger movie down here, they had to change Tonto's name," Stein said.

Frade said, "You're a fountain of Hollywood information, aren't you, Siggy?"

"I shit you not, Major," Stein said. " 'Tonto' means 'stupid' in Spanish."

"That's right, it does," Dorotea said, and giggled. " 'The Masked Rider of the Plains, and his faithful Indian companion, Stupid.' "

Everyone started laughing.

Jesus, Frade thought, *the laughter is coming close to being hysterical.*

I'd probably put them over the edge if I mentioned the name of where we've built the airfield for South American Airways—Morón."

Then Frade wondered if he was the only one thinking that nervousness—hell, not only that but fear and terror, too—was causing the hilarity.

As they were getting in the Horch, Sargento Rodolfo Gómez walked up to Frade.

"May I have a moment, Don Cletus?"

Frade followed him out of earshot of the people in and around the car.

"What's on your mind, Rodolfo?"

"So you will not worry about Sargento Stein, Don Cletus . . ."

"Worry about him? Why?"

"Enrico says he does not think Sargento Stein has it in him to kill the Nazi bitch."

"I think Enrico is wrong, Rodolfo. And I don't want either of the Germans killed unless it is necessary."

"I understand, Don Cletus. But if I see that Sargento Stein thinks he has to do it, I will do it for him. My conscience will not bother me later. Enrico is like my brother. His sister, may she be resting in peace with all the angels, was like my sister. You understand, Don Cletus?"

"I understand, Rodolfo, and I thank you."

"Que Dios lo acompañe, Don Cletus."

[FOUR]
Estancia San Pedro y San Pablo
Near Pila
Buenos Aires Province, Argentina
0915 20 July 1943

They had gone a little over a mile onto Estancia San Pedro y San Pablo when a gaucho, where the road passed close to a thick grove of ancient eucalyptus trees, moved his horse onto the road.

Frade braked the Horch with a sinking feeling. There was no immediate danger, but he felt sure the gaucho had been sent to tell him that at the big house were agents of the Bureau of Internal Security—or the Policía Federal— and that he was about to have to start running.

If not running for his life, then running away from spending a long time in a miserable prison cell.

The gaucho politely nodded when Frade had stopped, but didn't say anything.

Frade looked into the grove, expecting to see saddled horses. What he saw in addition to three saddled horses and three horse-borne gauchos and the Model A Ford pickup that Lieutenant Oscar Schultz, USN, used for his transportation over the pampas was Schultz himself, wearing his gaucho outfit and walking toward the road.

Clete turned off the ignition. If he was going to go riding off into the pampas, Dorotea would drive the car to the big house.

Dorotea reached for his hand and held it.

"Well, I'll tell you what's happened," Schultz said, quite unnecessarily.

"Thanks," Clete replied sarcastically, and was immediately sorry, even though the sarcasm had sailed over Schultz's head.

"Delgano is at the big house," Schultz said. "He's been there since half past seven. He's alone, and nobody else has come onto the estancia."

"He's alone?"

Schultz nodded.

"They told him you and Dorotea were off somewhere on the estancia."

"He didn't think that was odd?"

"Your butler—what's his name?"

"Antonio," Clete furnished.

"Lavallé," Dorotea furnished.

Antonio Lavallé had been El Coronel Jorge Guillermo Frade's butler, at both the "money sewer" mansion on Avenida Coronel Díaz in Buenos Aires and the big house at Estancia San Pedro y San Pablo, for longer than Clete and Dorotea were old.

"Yeah," Schultz continued, "he managed, without coming right out and saying it, to tell him that you and Dorotea went off to find a little romantic privacy, if you take my meaning."

"And?" Clete said.

"He asked when you would be back, and Antonio said, 'Probably before lunch.' Delgano said that he really had to see you, and that he would just wait."

"And?"

"Antonio gave him coffee and rolls, and according to the last word I got, Delgano's sitting on your verandah waiting for you to come home."

"When was your last word?"

"Just before we heard you'd come onto the estancia. Maybe ten minutes ago."

Frade, obviously in thought, didn't reply.

"Come on, my darling," Dorotea said. "Give us your worst-case scenario; you're very good at that."

"Okay. I will. He's going to tell me that the Bureau of Internal Security would prefer that we handle the unfortunate situation in a civilized manner."

"Meaning what?"

"Meaning he would rather that I just get in his car with him and go to Buenos Aires, thereby avoiding a shoot-out with my army of gauchos."

"That's absurd," Dorotea said.

Clete didn't think she really thought it was absurd.

"Possible, but I don't think so," Schultz said.

"Why not?" Frade challenged.

"I just don't think so," Schultz said. "I think if that was the case, he'd have at least brought one guy with him." He paused, then explained: "In case you changed your mind on the way to Buenos Aires."

"So what's he doing here? Just paying a social call?" Frade asked.

"I think you have to find out," Schultz said. "You open to a suggestion?"

"Wide open."

"I take Fischer with me. Can you handle a Thompson, Fischer?"

"No," Fischer said simply. "The only weapons I've ever fired was in Basic Officers' School—the .45 and the M1 Garand."

"Okay, I'll give you my .45," Schultz said, and took his pistol from his waistband. "Watch it; it's locked and cocked."

Fischer looked at him in confusion.

"All you have to do is take the safety off," Schultz said. "Push this down." He demonstrated. "There's a round in the chamber, ready to fire."

"Okay," Fischer said without much enthusiasm as Schultz locked the weapon and handed it to him.

"Now that he's got a loaded pistol, what's he going to do with it?" Frade asked.

"He's coming with me in the truck. To the house. Give us a ten-minute head start, then drive slow. See what Delgano's up to. If he gives you the 'come with me' business, you make a signal—scratch your ear, something like that—and we come out of the garden and tie him up. Then you take off."

"That's your suggestion?" Dorotea asked, her tone on the edge of sarcasm.

"You got a better one, Dorotea?" Schultz asked.

"You come out of the bushes," Frade added thoughtfully, "tie Delgano up, and then you go out to the house, torch the radar, bring everybody to the hangar, and I fly everybody to Uruguay."

"That'd work," Schultz said.

"Everybody presumably includes me?" Dorotea asked.

"Of course," Frade said. "Jesus! Did you think I'd leave you here?"

She didn't respond directly.

"And the Froggers?" she asked softly.

Enrico said, "I will send a gaucho to Casa Chica and have Rodolfo take them out on the pampas. For the time being, Sargento Stein can stay there."

Frade looked doubtful.

"We don't have time to go back and get them," Dorotea said. "And if we did manage to get them to Uruguay, what would we do with them there?"

Clete felt a chill.

She's right. But I'm supposed to make that decision, and she's supposed to be horrified.

"When we get to Uruguay, I'll contact the OSS guy in the embassy there," he said, speaking slowly. "Maybe he can think of some way to get them to Uruguay, and what to do with them there. They're important to Dulles, and I don't want to kill them unless I have to."

Did I mean that? Or am I just unable to order their assassination?

"That's risky, Cletus," Dorotea said.

"Maybe. But the last time I looked, I'm in charge. Enrico, you will stay on the estancia. I'll get word to you one way or the other."

"I will go with you," Enrico said.

"No one will be trying to kill me in Uruguay. And once this is over, one way or the other, you can come to Uruguay with Sargento Stein."

"Don Cletus . . ."

"I'm not going to argue with you, Enrico. You will do what I say."

After a long moment, Enrico said, *"Sí, señor."*

"Okay, let's do it," Frade said. "I'll give you fifteen minutes. If, when you get to the big house, something smells, send somebody to warn us."

Enrico nodded.

"Don't shoot yourself in the foot with that .45, Fischer," Frade said.

Captain Gonzalo Delgano, chief pilot of South American Airways, who was sitting in a wicker chair on the verandah of the big house and resting his feet on a wicker stool, got up when he saw the Horch with Don Cletus Frade at the wheel and Doña Dorotea Frade beside him roll majestically up the driveway.

Clete saw that Delgano was wearing a well-cut double-breasted suit.

Implying that he's really not Major Delgano of the Argentina Army Air Service, Retired.

Except that he's not—and never has been—retired from the army and, more important, has never severed his connection with the Ethical Standards Office of the Bureau of Internal Security.

And that, charming or not, he is one dangerous sonofabitch.

Dorotea waved cheerfully at him as Clete stopped the car.

Delgano came down the shallow flight of stairs from the verandah.

"Gonzalo! What a pleasant surprise!" Dorotea said.

"I'm sorry to intrude, Doña Dorotea," Delgano said. "But something important has come up."

"Oh, really?"

"What's up, Gonzo?" Frade asked as they embraced and kissed.

"I had hoped to see Mr. Fischer," Delgano said.

"He's not here?" Dorotea asked.

Delgano shook his head.

"Well, he's probably taking a ride," she said. "He's quite a horseman."

"Why do you want to see Fischer?" Clete asked.

Antonio Lavallé appeared. He was wearing a crisp white jacket.

"May I get you something, Doña Dorotea? Don Cletus?"

"I'd like some coffee, please," Dorotea said. "Darling?"

"That'd be fine," Clete said.

"I was hoping Mr. Fischer would demonstrate his machine for me," Delgano said. "The one that cuts the paper tapes so that air base transmitters can endlessly repeat the station identifier."

"Why would you want him to do that?" Clete asked.

"Well, El Coronel Jorge G. Frade Airfield needs one," Delgano said.

"Excuse me?" Dorotea asked.

"A tape that will permit the transmitter to endlessly send 'JGF, JGF, JGF, JGF,' " Delgano said, meeting Clete's eyes. "So that pilots can find the field."

"You've lost me, Gonzo," Frade said.

"After you left El Palomar yesterday, Cletus, El Coronel Perón and I drove over to the airfield. It's amazing how much work has been done. One hangar is almost up and a good deal of work has been done on the terminal building. One runway is just about complete—not paved, but ready for the pavement, with whatever they call what goes under the concrete."

"Well, I'm glad to hear that."

"And El Coronel Perón said, 'Delgano, this place needs a name. What would you suggest?' "

"And I said, 'Mi coronel, only one name comes to me.' And he said, 'I wonder if we are thinking the same thing? I was about to suggest Aeropuerto Coronel Jorge G. Frade.' And I said, 'I think that would be entirely appropriate, mi coronel,' and he said, 'I will have a word with the president.' "

Clete said nothing.

"I was very fond of your father, Cletus," Delgano said. "And I hope it will not embarrass you if I tell you how much the two of you are alike, and how much I value your friendship."

"Thank you," Clete said.

"And I thought it would be very nice when you and I return from Pôrto Alegre with the next Lodestar in a few days or a week, if we could home in on JGF, JGF, JGF. And think of your father."

"That would be very nice, Gonzo," Clete said, his voice breaking.

He heard himself.

Shit, I can't even talk!

The next thing he knew, he was embracing Delgano.

He found his voice ninety seconds later when Antonio appeared with a coffee service.

"Is there champagne in the refrigerator, Antonio? If so, get us a couple of bottles! We have something to celebrate!"

Dorotea went to Delgano and kissed him, then went to her husband and took his hand.

[FIVE]
Estancia Santa Catalina
Near Pila
Buenos Aires Province, Argentina
2015 20 July 1943

Cletus Frade's first reaction when he saw the black Mercedes drop-top sedan with a *cuerpo diplomático* license plate parked in front of the great house of the estancia was to think, *Thank God, he's here.*

Frade was carrying the information outlining the workings and personnel of the German embassy that Stein had obtained from Frogger. If Major Freiherr Hans-Peter von Wachtstein had not been at his wife's mother's home, Frade would have had to have given the papers to La Señora Alicia Carzino-Cormano de von Wachtstein to pass to her husband.

Clete didn't want to do that.

Alicia was not Dorotea. And that was something Clete had known long before Dorotea had manifested that cold ruthlessness at Casa Chica that he hadn't suspected she was capable of. The less Alicia was involved in the business between Clete and Peter, the better. For a number of reasons, not limited to her inability to handle—it bordered on sheer terror—what her husband was doing.

And that presumed Alicia would be here. If she wasn't, that would have meant he would have had to give the material to Alicia's mother, and have her pass it to Alicia to pass it to Peter. And he would have had to tell Claudia what it was, and how he had come by it. He didn't want to do that either. Claudia Carzino-Cormano was tough, but there was no reason to bring her into a potentially dangerous situation unless it was absolutely necessary.

Clete had another unpleasant thought. The Mercedes was the car assigned to the military attaché of the German embassy. It had been Peter's to use—after Oberst Grüner, the military attaché, had been killed at Samborombón Bay—

as the *acting* military attaché. But that had changed with the arrival of Korvettenkapitän Karl Boltitz, who had been named the military attaché.

Is Boltitz here with Peter?

As if reading his mind, Dorotea said, "That's the official car. That means Boltitz is probably here, too."

"Yeah," he said, and looked at her.

Jesus Christ, she even thinks like I do!

When they walked up on the verandah, they could see Korvettenkapitän Boltitz through the sitting-room window. He was in an armchair. La Señorita Isabela Carzino-Cormano was sitting on a footstool next to him, hanging on his every word.

Looks like El Bitcho has become just another goddamn Nazi, Clete thought. *She's as bad as Frau Frogger.*

Alicia saw them through the same window and seemed less than overjoyed at their arrival. Although she and Dorotea had been close friends since childhood, and although she knew that if it hadn't been for Clete going to El Coronel Perón, who had gone to some of his high-ranking Nazi friends to request a favor, right now Peter von Wachtstein would be in Germany flying the Me-262 jet fighter instead of here safe—relatively—in Argentina.

Alicia got off the couch and was standing behind the Carzino-Cormano butler when he opened the door.

"Peter is here," she greeted them. "And Karl Boltitz."

That it was a warning showed in her eyes.

"How nice," Dorotea replied cheerfully. "Are you going to ask us in?"

"Of course," Alicia said, then raised her voice. "Mama, Dorotea and Cletus are here."

She led them into the sitting room.

Von Wachtstein and Boltitz stood.

"Oh, how nice," Claudia Carzino-Cormano said, smiling bravely. "You're just in time for dinner."

"Then our timing is perfect," Cletus said, went to her, really kissed her cheek, and thought: *I'm glad you don't know there's two other Nazis at Casa Chica, one of them sitting on your couch reading from my father's copy of Goethe's love poems.*

He turned to the men.

"And how is the diplomatic corps tonight?"

"Señor Frade," Boltitz said. "How nice to see you. And you, señora."

"Hello, Frade," Peter said. "How are you? Dorotea?"

"Can I get you something to drink?" Claudia asked.

"I thought you'd never ask," Clete said. "If that's merlot that Major von Wachtstein is drinking, I'd love some of that."

He sensed Isabela's eyes and looked at her. Her eyes were as hateful as he expected.

"What a joy it is to see you, Isabela," Clete said. "And you seem so happy. Been pulling the wings off flies again, have you?"

"Cletus!" Dorotea and Claudia said, almost in unison.

"Karl," Claudia then said, "you'll have to forgive him. He's always teasing Isabela."

"I am not!" Cletus said.

"Changing the subject," Peter said. "There's a rumor going around that your first airplane has arrived."

"Not a rumor at all," Clete said. "It's at El Palomar. After a two-hour-and-sixteen-minute flight from Pôrto Alegre."

"That's fast."

"Fast and smooth," Clete said. "American aviation genius at work."

That earned him, as he expected it would, another dirty look from Isabela.

"Not as fast as the Condor, certainly," Isabela said.

"I don't know," Clete said innocently. "How fast is the Condor, Isabela?"

Her expression showed that she did not have a clue. She looked at Peter.

"It'll do a little better than three hundred kph," Peter furnished. "It cruises at around two fifty-five."

"The Lodestar tops out at a little better than three forty-five," Clete said.

"But it won't cross an ocean, will it?" Isabela challenged.

Gotcha, El Bitcho!

"Isabela," Clete explained politely, "the Lodestar, first, never was designed for long flights. And, second, it's obsolete. That's why they've sold them to South American Airways. We—the Americans—don't need them anymore."

"Then you Americans *don't* have an airplane like the Condor that will cross oceans?" she pursued.

"I didn't say that, Isabela," Clete went on, trying not to sound condescending. "Right now, the Americans every day fly the Douglas DC-4 across both the Pacific and the Atlantic. And there's a new Lockheed—"

"There is?" Peter asked.

Clete turned to him. "The Lockheed pilots who delivered the Lodestar to Pôrto Alegre told me their new one—they call it the 'Constellation'—has just been certified. At cruise altitude, seventy-five hundred meters, it cruises at five hundred seventy kph. For eighty-seven hundred kilometers. With a full load. Thirty passengers."

"Very impressive," Peter said, meaning it.

"I'll believe it when I see it land at El Palomar," Isabela said.

"That's probably never going to happen, Isabela," Clete said, paused, and when he saw she was about to snap back at him, added, "When the first Constellation lands here, it'll belong to South American Airways, and will of course land at Aeropuerto Coronel Jorge G. Frade."

"The two of you stop it!" Claudia said. After a moment, she asked, "What did you just say, Cletus?"

"About where the Constellation will land when it comes here, you mean?"

"You know very well that's what I mean. What are you talking about?"

"The chief pilot of South American Airways—you remember him, Claudia, Major Delgano?"

She nodded. "And?"

"He came to see us this morning to tell me that he and my Tío Juan"—he paused and looked at Boltitz—"El Coronel Juan Domingo Perón is not really my uncle, korvettenkapitän, but he likes me to call him that. Anyway, Tío Juan and Major Delgano thought it would be nice if we named our new airport after my father, and wanted to know what I thought of the idea."

"Damn you, Cletus!" Claudia said, having trouble with her voice. "You are just like him! Same awful sense of humor!"

"Oh, I don't think they were fooling, Claudia. Tío Juan told Delgano he was going to have a word with the president. I wouldn't be surprised if somebody's already painting a temporary sign."

"If la señora is so pleased," the butler announced from the door to the dining room, "dinner can now be served."

"As our hostess," Clete said while the coffee was served, "already is offended by my bad manners—"

"And with damned good cause," Claudia interrupted, "thank you very much, Cletus."

Clete nodded once, then went on: "—I would not dare anger her further by filling the room with cigar smoke. I am therefore going to take my coffee onto the verandah for a smoke. If anyone would care to join me . . . you, perhaps, Isabela?"

She snorted.

"All are welcome," Clete went on. "I have cigars but regrettably no cigarettes."

"I'd like a smoke," Boltitz said. "With your permission, la señora?"

"Go," Claudia said.

The three men went not only onto the verandah but off it and into the garden, where they could not be overheard. There, Frade extended his cigar case.

"I don't use them, thank you," Boltitz said.

"Put one in your mouth anyway," Frade said. "In case El Bitcho is watching us out the window, as I suspect she is. Or will be."

Boltitz nodded and took a cigar.

Von Wachtstein took a cigar, lit it, and puffed appreciatively.

"Nice," he said.

"They make them in Tampa, Florida," Frade said between puffs on his. Then he added, "Peter, turn your back to the house. I'm going to give you an envelope, and I don't want Isabela to see me doing it."

The transfer took perhaps thirty seconds.

"What's in the envelope?" von Wachtstein said.

"Information about your embassy. I need to know how accurate it is."

"Where did you get it?" Boltitz asked.

Frade didn't reply.

"So you have the Froggers, Cletus?" von Wachtstein asked, but it was more of a statement.

"The who?"

"You would be surprised to learn that the former commercial attaché of the embassy, Herr Wilhelm Frogger, and Frau Frogger have gone missing?" Boltitz asked.

"You don't say?" Frade said.

"On Estancia San Pedro y San Pablo?" von Wachtstein asked.

Frade shook his head.

"Someplace where they will be hard to find, I hope?" Boltitz asked.

Frade looked at him but did not reply.

"Major Frade, if I'm not mistaken, SS-Brigadeführer von Deitzberg has ordered the present commercial attaché, the former Obersturmbannführer Karl Cranz, to eliminate them when and where found."

"Why would von Deitzberg want to do that?"

"Because he could then tell Himmler that Frogger was the traitor in the embassy and that he had been eliminated."

"But that's not true."

"And if von Deitzberg later found the real traitor, he could then tell Himmler that there were two traitors and he had found both. And I would guess that
he would hope the currently unrevealed traitor, or traitors, would relax a bit after
learning Frogger had been identified, and that would help him catch them."

"You're pretty good at this, aren't you, Boltitz?" Frade said. His tone of
voice showed that he meant the compliment.

"Admiral Canaris once told me that any intelligence officer who thinks he's
pretty good is sadly mistaken," Boltitz said.

"He's obviously a wise man," Frade said. "Well, if I happen to bump into
your man Frogger, I'll mention that his friends are looking for him."

"I suspect he knows that," Boltitz said. "What he really should worry about
is that Frau Frogger thinks they are really friends."

"You know that, too, do you?" Frade said.

"What do you want done with what you gave Peter?"

"Just let me know if it's accurate. If it is, call my house in Buenos Aires and
leave word that my new suit is ready."

"And if it's not?"

"Leave word that I have to come in for another fitting," Frade said.

Boltitz nodded.

"We should probably rejoin the ladies," von Wachtstein said. "Before El
Bitcho comes out to wag her tail at Karl."

X

On 10 July 1943, Allied troops invaded the island of Sicily. General Bernard
Montgomery's Eighth British Army landed at five places on the southeastern tip of
the island. Lieutenant General George S. Patton's United States Seventh Army went
ashore on three beaches to the west of the British.

There was little opposition, and Patton's troops quickly took Gela, Licata, and
Vittoria before nightfall. The British took Syracuse on the day of the landing, Palz-
zolo the next day, Augusta the day after that, and Vizzini on 14 July. On the same
day, the Americans took Niscemi and the Biscani airfield.

Patton moved to the west and his II Corps, under Lieutenant General Omar

N. Bradley, struck out to the north. British forces were being held up by German forces under Field Marshal Albrecht Kesselring.

On 22 July 1943, the U.S. Seventh Army's Third Infantry Division, under Major General Lucian Truscott, took Palermo, and in so doing cut off fifty thousand Italian troops from their intended path of retreat. Patton then started to move on to Messina, intending, he announced, to get there before General Montgomery.

[ONE]
Aeropuerto Coronel Jorge G. Frade
Morón, Buenos Aires Province, Argentina
0915 22 July 1943

Clete Frade pointed out to the left to show Len Fischer that they were almost at the airfield. Fischer, his arms wrapped around his small suitcase, nodded and smiled somewhat wanly.

Frade had learned only that morning—just before they boarded the Piper Cub—that Fischer had about as much experience with light aircraft as he had with horses—none—and it was a toss-up which of the two made him more uncomfortable.

Frade now made gestures with his hand to show—if not warn—Fischer what he intended to do with the aircraft, which was make at least one low pass over the field to make sure that it would be safe to land.

Not on the runways. These were cluttered with heavy machinery, tractors, graders, dump trucks, and cement mixers. Instead, Frade planned to land—presuming he found nothing parked or dumped there—on the grass of what had only recently been a cattle-feeding lot.

He made two passes to ensure his intended "runway" was clear, then turned to signal Fischer that he was about to set down the airplane.

From the look on Fischer's face, it was obvious that, until this moment, Fischer had never considered the possibility that they would not be landing on a wide and smoothly paved runway.

His concern—terror—was evident.

Frade felt sorry for him, but they had to land. Otherwise, none of the items on what Clete thought of as "the list" were going to be addressed.

And there were a number of critical items on the list, ones that Frade had been unable to neatly categorize as Priority One, Priority Two, and so on, because they were all interrelated with one another.

For example, they had to make sure they got electrical power run to the control tower, then make sure the Collins transceiver there worked, then use the Collins to call Delgano aboard SAA Zero Zero One.

Also high on the list: getting Second Lieutenant Len Fischer safely out of Argentina.

There had of course been the temptation to get Fischer out of the country immediately, but there were problems with that. One of them was that it would be suspicious if he left before the Collins transceivers were set up and operating at the field at Estancia San Pedro y San Pablo and at what was now Aeropuerto Coronel Jorge G. Frade.

Setting up the radios was what Fischer was supposed to be doing in Argentina. If he seemed to be fleeing, Martín would certainly wonder why—*If someone warned him, who?*—and that finger would point at Delgano.

Delgano was a card Frade was unwilling to play, because he simply didn't know how far Delgano was willing to go to close his eyes to things Martín would (a) certainly want to know and (b) expect to hear from Delgano.

Delgano hadn't told Martín what the SIGABA device was. But there was no guarantee he would do the same sort of thing ever again.

And, for that matter, it was possible—not likely, but possible—that Delgano had told Martín about the SIGABA device, and the two of them were in the clever process of lulling Señor Frade into thinking he had no problems.

What Clete had decided to do was keep Fischer around until the Collins radios were functioning—but only at the estancia and here, in the control tower of what he in aviator shorthand had already begun to think of as "Jorge Frade."

The problem with that was there was no electrical power at the terminal building. In fact, the terminal building itself was nowhere near finished, and when it was electrical power would be about the last thing installed. And no power in the terminal meant no power in the tower.

Frade thought—indeed had been told—that he had solved the no-power problem by calling the electrical contractor and applying a West Texas business tactic: Clete had offered him a bonus if there was power to the unfinished control tower by quitting time—six p.m.—yesterday.

It was the same technique he had earlier used to get all the contractors working almost feverishly. And he'd done it over the objections of the SAA board of directors—"Cletus, things are just not done that way in Argentina" was the way Humberto Valdez Duarte, financial director of South American Airways, had put it.

As they were about to let the contracts, Frade had insisted that the contracts include bonus and penalty clauses. And so, there were generous bonuses provided for completion of the various aspects of the construction ahead of schedule, and increasingly heavy penalties if the work was not completed when it was promised.

Frade landed the Cub without incident—neither from the aircraft nor from his squeamish passenger—and taxied to the terminal building behind one of the three hangars under construction. This one was almost done. Workmen were hanging the sliding doors. More important, there was a gasoline-powered generator at the base of the still-unfinished control tower, with a cable snaking up the tower and through an opening that would eventually hold a window.

"Greed triumphs, Len," Frade said after he had shut down the engine.

"What?"

"Never mind." He pointed to the tower. "Let's climb up there and see if the Collins will work."

Thirty minutes later, with a pleased smile, Second Lieutenant Leonard Fischer, Signal Corps, USA, handed Major Cletus Frade, USMCR, a headset.

"Your cans, sir," Fischer said.

Frade put them on and heard a distinct metallic sound: *dit dah dah dah, dah dat dit, dit dit dah dit.*

He smiled.

There was a pause, then his smile broadened as *dit dah dah dah, dah dat dit, dit dit dah dit* came again.

And, after another pause, the Morse code for JGF sounded again. And again. And again.

"If you weren't so ugly, Lieutenant, I think I'd kiss you."

Fischer smiled, handed Frade a microphone, and threw a switch.

"That's ready, too?" Frade asked, surprised.

Fischer nodded.

Frade pressed the TALK button on the microphone.

"South American Airways Zero Zero One," he said in Spanish, "this is Jorge Frade."

There was no reply. Over the next few minutes, Frade made the call again, and again, and again. Still, no reply. He shook his head and shrugged, and started to take the earphones from his head.

"Jorge Frade, this is South American Zero Zero One. Go ahead."

Frade recognized Delgano's voice.

"Zero One. What is your position?"

"Jorge Frade, Zero One is fifteen kilometers north of El Palomar at two thousand meters, indicating three hundred kph."

"Zero One, Jorge Frade, report reception of our RDF signal."

"Frade, Stand by."

There was a minute's silence as Delgano tuned his radio direction finder.

"Frade, Zero One. Receiving RDF signal loud and clear."

"Zero One, using RDF signal as navigation device, proceed to Frade, descending to one thousand meters, report when field is in sight."

"Zero One understands proceed Frade using RDF, descend to one thousand meters, report when in sight of field."

"Zero One, Frade. That is correct."

"Frade, Zero One has field in sight."

"South American Airways Zero Zero One, you are cleared to make a low-level east-west pass over Jorge Frade at an altitude of your choice."

Frade expected Delgano to make the pass at a minimum of fifteen hundred feet above ground level. Thirty seconds later, South American Zero Zero One flashed along the east-west runway of Aeropuerto Coronel Jorge G. Frade at no more than five hundred feet AGL—her engines roaring, the throttles apparently against their stops.

Fischer watched in amazement as startled ground workers on and near the runway raced for cover.

Frade watched the aircraft roar past, then dramatically pull up and bank.

As her tail disappeared into the distance, he thought, *Goddamn, that's one pretty airplane!*

It was a moment before Frade trusted his voice. Then he said, "South American Zero Zero One, proceed to El Palomar and terminate your flight."

[TWO]
Aeropuerto de El Palomar
Buenos Aires Province, Argentina
1030 22 July 1943

South American Airways Chief Pilot Gonzalo Delgano was standing beside SAA's Lodestar, tail number Zero Zero One, when Frade taxied up to it in the Piper Cub. Five other pilots of South American Airways also stood there. They were all in uniform, a powder blue tunic with four gold stripes on the sleeves, and darker blue trousers.

Frade wondered how Delgano had come up with the uniforms so quickly. He recognized several of the faces but couldn't come up with a single name.

Delgano marched up to the Piper Cub as Frade and Fischer got out.

Then he spread his arms wide.

"Cletus," he said emotionally. "El Coronel would be so proud!"

Then he wrapped his arms around Frade, wetly kissed both of his cheeks, and hugged him tightly.

Fischer looked uncomfortable.

Then one by one the other pilots marched up to Frade and solemnly shook his hand.

"And we are so grateful to you, Señor Fischer," Delgano said, turning to him, "for your skill and hard work."

He embraced Fischer and kissed him with almost as much emotional enthusiasm as he had shown with Frade. Fischer smiled bravely. Then the pilots advanced on Fischer and shook his hand.

"I'm happy to have been able to be of service, Captain," Fischer said.

"El Señor Fischer will be going with us on the Varig flight, Gonzalo," Frade said. "It is time for him to go home."

"I have been thinking about that, Cletus," Delgano said. "Perhaps it will not be necessary to subject our friend El Señor Fischer to the rigors—perhaps even the danger—of flying with our competition."

Frade immediately thought, *Oh, shit!*

Getting Fischer safely out of Argentina—with the two rolls of high-speed 35mm film that when processed would show Fischer, looking uncomfortable, standing beside a scowling Frau Frogger holding a copy of *La Nación*—had become Priority One on the list.

Frade had considered, and decided against, having the film developed and copies made. If El Coronel Martín of the Bureau of Internal Security suspected—which was entirely likely—that not only was Fischer more than the technical representative of the Collins Radio Company of Cedar Rapids, Iowa, but further suspected—which also was entirely likely—that Cletus Frade had something to do with the missing Froggers, he might suggest that the customs officials pay special attention to Fischer's luggage before he was allowed to board the Varig flight to Rio de Janeiro, Brazil.

If the film were developed, there would be the proof that not only was Fischer more than a radio technician but—there he was, standing beside Frau Frogger—a kidnapper of a German diplomat and his wife.

Fischer—surprising Frade—said he was willing to take the risk.

After Frade accepted that, he said, "Then what you're going to do, Len, if it looks as if you're going to be searched, is ruin the film by pulling it out of the cassettes."

"Those pictures are important to Mr. Dulles. You know that, Clete."

Frade had then ordered, "What you're going to do, Lieutenant Fischer, if it looks as if you're going to be searched, is pull the film out of the cassettes. Say, 'Yes, sir.' "

Getting Fischer on the Varig flight to Rio had depended on getting the Collins transceiver at Morón's not-yet-completed Aeropuerto Jorge G. Frade up and running, so they could contact South American Airways Chief Pilot Gonzalo Delgano in SAA's Lodestar, call sign Zero Zero One, and thus prove that his technical duties had been completed and he could leave Argentina.

When they had left Jorge Frade just now, Clete had decided that that much had been accomplished, and all that remained to be done was to get Fischer on the Varig flight to Brazil with himself and Delgano.

And now Delgano doesn't want to subject Fischer to the "rigors and danger" of flying on Varig?

What the hell?

Get him to install the radios, then arrest him?

"I think we should not say unkind things about our competition, Gonzalo," Frade said. "No matter how tempting that may be."

"What I was thinking, Don Cletus, is that we should fly to Canoas in Zero

One, taking these gentlemen with us"—he nodded at the pilots—"which would give them more time at the controls. You could serve as the instructor pilot on the way back here in Zero Zero Two."

Thank you very much, Chief Pilot.

It didn't take you long to forget who taught you to fly a Lodestar, did it?

"Otherwise," Frade said, "Zero One would just be sitting here until you and I got back and no one would get any cockpit time. Right?"

Delgano nodded.

"Can we do that?" Delgano said. "I mean will they let us land there? I had the feeling that the American general doesn't like you very much."

"We'll just have to find out," Clete said. "I think that's a hell of a good idea."

"I thought you would agree," Delgano said, smiling, and pointed to a fuel truck that had just rolled up beside Zero Zero One, one he'd clearly arranged for before bouncing his idea off Frade.

"Gonzo, I'd like to make sure nothing happens to the Collins while we're gone. We turned it off, but . . ."

"I think the control tower should be manned around the clock starting right now," Delgano said. *"We* know the runways are not yet usable, but a Varig pilot just might hear our RDF signal and think that they are. I will have operators there within the hour."

Thirty minutes later, they took off for Canoas. Frade rode in the back, the first time he had ever been in a Lodestar passenger seat.

Once Frade felt the aircraft break ground and heard the hydraulic whine as its landing gear retracted, he heaved a mental sigh of relief. He had succeeded in getting Len Fischer—and equally important, perhaps even more important, the two cassettes of 35mm film—out of Argentina. In about two hours and thirty minutes, the Lodestar—and the film—would touch down at the U.S. Army Air Forces field at Canoas.

That left only one problem—that of protecting the Froggers—on what hours before had become The List of Things That Might—Probably Would—Go Wrong.

That remained a serious problem—Boltitz had told him that von Deitzberg had ordered their assassination when and where found—but that too looked as if it might go away.

When he had gone to Enrico to discuss that question with him, the old sergeant major told him he had already dispatched a dozen workers of Estancia San Pedro y San Pablo—all retirees of the Húsares de Pueyrredón Cavalry Regiment—to Casa Chica.

"They will know what to do, Don Cletus," Enrico had said confidently.

Frade had asked for an explanation.

"If the same kind of people who tried to kill you and who killed El Coronel and my sister—may they be resting in peace with all the angels—come to Casa Chica, they will be left on the pampas for the birds to eat."

"And if it is the army or the police?"

"Then the Nazis will be taken onto the pampas. I know how to deal with this, Don Cletus."

"I don't want the Froggers killed unless it's absolutely necessary—"

"So you have said, Don Cletus."

"And when I have Fischer out of Argentina, we will have to find some other place to keep them."

"There are places, Don Cletus. I will think on it."

Frade now thought: *I could very well be pissing in the wind, but this just might work out okay.*

He took a cigar from a leather case and bit off a piece of its closed end.

"You don't happen to have another of those, do you?" Len Fischer asked from his seat across the aisle.

Frade offered him the case and said, "I didn't know you smoked cigars."

"This will be my first ever," Fischer said. "But I feel like celebrating, and a cigar . . ."

[THREE]
Canoas Air Base
Pôrto Alegre, Brazil
1305 22 July 1943

Captain Gonzalo Delgano, who was in the co-pilot seat of the Lodestar, consulted his chart, the needle of the radio direction finder, and looked out the side window of the cockpit. Then he looked over his shoulder at the managing director of South American Airways standing behind him, pointed at the chart, the ground, and then the RDF indicator.

Frade nodded his understanding of what he had been shown, then said, "I think it would be better if I worked the radio."

Smiling at Captain Francisco Sánchez, who was in the pilot seat, Frade said, "Can I get in there, please, Captain?"

"Yes, of course, señor," Sánchez said, then unfastened his harness, stood up, and squeezed past Frade.

"It might be best, Captain," Frade said, his tone very serious, "if you went in the back and strapped yourself in. Captain Delgano will be landing the aircraft, and more often than not that is both a frightening and bumpy experience."

"Mother of God!" Delgano said in disbelief, shaking his head.

Captain Sánchez tried but failed to restrain a smile.

Frade fastened his harness, then keyed the microphone.

"Canoas, this is South American Airways Zero Zero One," he said in English, "thirty miles south of your station at five thousand feet, indicating one eight zero knots. Request approach and landing."

The reply did not come immediately. When it did, it was an American voice.

"Aircraft calling Canoas, be advised that Canoas is a Brazilian air base closed to civilian traffic."

Frade looked at Delgano, said, "I thought that might happen," then pressed the mike button.

"Canoas, South American Airways Zero Zero One has aboard aircrews to pick up a Lodestar that you have on your field. If you have any questions, please contact General Wallace. Tell him the pilot in command is Señor Frade."

"South American Zero Zero One, Canoas. Stand by."

"South American Zero Zero One, Canoas."

"Zero One."

"Zero One, state your type of aircraft and position."

"We're a Lodestar a couple of miles south, passing through two thousand feet, indicating one five zero knots. I have the field in sight."

"Canoas has you in sight, Zero One. Canoas clears Zero Zero One for a straight-in approach to Runway Three-Five. Be advised that a Follow-Me will meet you at the end of your landing roll."

"Understand straight in to Three-Five. Thank you."

[FOUR]
Office of the Commanding General
U.S. Army Air Forces Establishment
Canoas Air Base
Pôrto Alegre, Brazil
1400 22 July 1943

"Yes, sir," a portly, middle-aged USAAF master sergeant wearing aircrew wings said to his intercom box, then looked somewhat disapprovingly at Frade. "The general will see you now, Señor Frade."

"Thank you," Frade said, and, motioning Fischer to come with him, walked through the door to the office of Brigadier General J. B. Wallace, U.S. Army Air Forces.

Wallace was sitting behind a highly polished desk. It held a leather-bound green blotter, a telephone, a pen holder, a sign reading *Brig Gen Wallace,* and nothing else.

"Thank you for seeing me, General," Frade said politely.

Wallace nodded but did not reply.

"General, I'm going to need some assistance," Frade said.

"Is that so?" General Wallace asked in his somewhat nasal tone.

"Yes, sir. The first thing—"

"Forgive me, *Señor* Frade," Wallace interrupted, "but what gives you the authority to demand anything of me?"

Frade took a leather folder from his trousers pocket and laid it on the general's desk. It was his set of the credentials that Colonel Graham had issued to everyone on Team Turtle on 5 July. His identified him as the OSS regional commander.

"Those credentials do, sir. And you are advised that those credentials are classified Top Secret, and you are not permitted to disclose to any of your subordinates that I have shown them to you."

The general picked up the folder and began to examine it.

"And my *superiors?*" he challenged, sarcastically. "Am I *permitted* to disclose to them that you have shown me whatever this is?"

"You may inform your superiors, in the grade of major general or above, that I presented them to you, but not the circumstances under which I have done so. Any questions you or they may have about the credentials or me should be directed to the Office of Strategic Services in Washington."

General Wallace tried to stare Frade down. He failed.

The general examined the credentials again, this time very carefully. Finally, he raised his eyes to Frade.

"Frankly, I've never seen anything like this before."

"Very few people have, sir."

"What is it you want me to do, Mr. Frade?"

I thought those credentials would dazzle you, you pompous sonofabitch!

"I want you to fly Mr. Fischer to Rio de Janeiro as soon as possible so that he can catch the next Pan American Airways flight to the United States."

"That shouldn't be a problem," General Wallace said.

"I want him escorted, very discreetly, of course, by armed officers—one of whom should be at least a major—who will stay with him until they see the Pan American plane take off."

"That can be arranged. And what else?"

"I need to send a small package by officer courier to Washington," Frade said. "I thought perhaps one of your pilots flying up there—a major or more senior officer?"

"Again, that should be no problem to arrange. Am I permitted to ask what's in the package?"

Frade did not answer immediately. Instead he gestured to Fischer.

"Let me have one of those cassettes, Len."

When Fischer had handed him one, Frade held it up for General Wallace to see.

"This is also classified Top Secret," he said.

"I understand," General Wallace said seriously.

"I will need three large manila envelopes—better make it four, right, Mr. Fischer? You're the expert here."

"Four would be better," Fischer agreed.

"And a grease pencil and Scotch tape. The wider the better."

"Sergeant!" General Wallace raised his voice.

The portly master sergeant appeared at the door.

"Mr. Frade will require four large manila envelopes, Sergeant, some Scotch tape, and what else was there, Mr. Frade?"

"A grease pencil, black, please, Sergeant," Frade said. "And if you have some of the two-inch-wide Scotch tape?"

"Yes, sir," the master sergeant said. "Right away."

Frade used the grease pencil to write *Unexposed Film Top Secret Eyes Only DDWHO* in large letters on both sides of one of the manila envelopes, put the film cassette he'd shown Wallace in it, and wrapped it tightly with the Scotch tape.

Then he repeated that operation twice, creating a thick roll of envelopes and tape. He put the roll into the fourth envelope, then on that outer envelope wrote *BY OFFICER COURIER TOP SECRET EYES ONLY DDWHO OR GENERAL DONOVAN.* He sealed the envelope, then signed *C. FRADE, AREA COMMANDER* on the flap, and covered his signature with more Scotch tape.

"Do you think that'll do it, Mr. Fischer?"

"I think that should do it," Fischer said. "General, you don't happen to have a courier's briefcase we could use, do you?"

"I don't know what a courier's briefcase is," General Wallace said.

"They have sort of a stainless-steel wire and handcuff arrangement," Fischer said, "so the briefcase can be attached to the courier."

Where the hell did Len get that?

"Perhaps we could improvise something," General Wallace said.

"That would be helpful," Fischer said. "Thank you."

"May I ask what DDWHO means?" General Wallace asked.

"Deputy Director, Western Hemisphere Operations," Frade said. "The courier doesn't need to know that. All he has to do is take the briefcase to the National Institutes of Health Building, ask for the duty officer, and give it to him."

"I understand," General Wallace said. "May I make a suggestion?"

"Certainly."

"We have an aircraft—a B-24—leaving within an hour or two for the United States. Perhaps Mr. Fischer could travel on that?"

Why not? That would save Len the trip to Rio de Janeiro.

But it's a long goddamn ride in the bomb bay of a B-24 from here to the States.

"Ordinarily, General," Frade said, "that would be a splendid idea. But there are reasons why Mr. Fischer should travel on Pan American Grace"—*for example, sitting in a softly upholstered seat while a steward in a white jacket serves him chilled champagne and a five-course meal*—"that make that ill-advised. Perhaps the B-24 pilot—presuming he's a field-grade officer—could serve as the officer courier, but my priority now is to get Mr. Fischer to Rio de Janeiro just as soon as possible."

"I understand," General Wallace said, and raised his voice again: "Sergeant!"

The master sergeant appeared in the door a moment later.

"Sir?"

"Call Base Ops and have a C-45 readied for an immediate flight to Rio. Priority One."

"Yes, sir."

"Thank you," Frade said.

Besides, if Len went on the B-24, that would put both film cassettes on the same plane, and that would not be a good idea.

"Is there anything else I can do for you, Mr. Frade?"

"I can't think of a thing, General."

"If you'll be with us tonight, perhaps we could have dinner."

"That's very kind of you, General, but just as soon as I see Mr. Fischer's plane lift off, I'm going wheels-up myself back to Buenos Aires."

"Sergeant!"

"Sir?"

"Have my car brought around to take these gentlemen to the field."

As they walked across the tarmac to a USAAF Beechcraft C-45 Expeditor, Fischer smiled at Frade and said, accurately mimicking General Wallace's somewhat nasal speech, " 'Is there anything else I can do for you, Mr. Frade? Dinner, perhaps?' "

Frade chuckled.

"You really put that stuffy sonofabitch in your pocket," Fischer said.

It wasn't me, Frade thought.

It was that OSS badge that put Wallace in my pocket.

"I'm a Marine officer, Lieutenant," Frade replied with a mock-serious tone. "Perhaps you should keep that in mind." Then he smiled and, when Fischer smiled back, put out his hand.

"Thanks, Len. You've done a wonderful job."

"I'm a Signal Corps second lieutenant," Fischer said, mimicking Frade's tone. "Perhaps the major might want to keep that in mind."

Clete laughed, then, surprising the both of them, they embraced in the Argentine manner—except neither kissed the other.

"I'll see you around, Clete. And we'll be in touch."

"Yeah, we will."

Frade punched Fischer in the arm, then watched as Fischer ducked through the small door of the small twin-engine aircraft.

Frade didn't move as the Expeditor taxied to the end of the runway, ran up its engines, and took off. It wasn't that he was that interested in watching the airplane take off. He was considering the fact that, once again, he was about to be a prick.

Fischer was under the impression that he was going back to the safety of Vint Hill Farms Station.

Tough luck, Len, ole buddy. I need you.

If not here right now, then kept on the shelf to be taken down and expended as needed.

[FIVE]
Estancia San Pedro y San Pablo
Near Pila
Buenos Aires Province, Argentina
1810 22 July 1943

It was admittedly a little dark when Frade lined up the Piper Cub to land on the estancia runway, but not as dark as Doña Dorotea Mallín de Frade apparently thought it was. There were half a dozen vehicles lined up on the sides of the runway, their headlights illuminating the runway boundaries.

I could have made it in here no problem, but it's really nice to know that Dorotea is really trying to take care of me.

As he taxied up to the hangar, he saw that Schultz's Model A pickup was part of the improvised landing light system, and that Enrico was at the wheel of the Buick convertible and that Dorotea was at the wheel of the Horch.

"Thanks, baby," he said as he embraced his wife.

"First, did Len get away all right?" she asked.

"At this moment, he is in the Copacabana Palace Hotel in Rio sipping champagne and ogling the near-naked ladies on the beach."

"I'm serious," she said, not amused. "What about the film?"

"So am I. I should have added, he has an armed guard, courtesy of the U.S. Army Air Forces, who will stay with him until he—and the film—takes off in the Pan American clipper. And second?"

"Why did you have to fly down here in the dark?"

"Well, for one thing—not that I'm not grateful for the landing lights—it wasn't dark."

"You were taking an unnecessary chance. The station wagon's at the house; you should have driven."

"I had two things in mind. In addition to knowing when there wouldn't be enough light to land here."

"Which were?"

"My stomach told me to go home to get something to eat. I didn't get to eat any lunch. And I needed to see that ugly gaucho." He turned. "How goes it, El Jefe?"

Schultz, who of course was wearing his gaucho costume, smiled at him.

"If you weren't such a bloody ass," Dorotea said, "the proper response would have been, 'I couldn't wait to be with my beloved wife.' "

Clete smiled. "That, too, of course."

Enrico walked up.

"Everything okay at Casa Chica, Enrico?"

"It is under control, Don Cletus."

"Then it's time for my supper," Clete said. "A *bife de chorizo*, I think, with a glass—perhaps a bottle—of merlot. And during supper, Jefe, I will dictate a message to Graham which I want you to get out an hour ago."

"That won't be necessary," Dorotea said.

"Excuse me?"

"After consulting with Oscar and Enrico, I've made some changes in our operation."

Now what?

"Made some changes in our operation"?

"Oh, really? Such as?"

"It will save time if I show you," she said, "rather than trying to explain."

When they got to the big house, Dorotea led everybody to what had been El Coronel Frade's study. Schultz walked quickly ahead of them and unlocked the heavy door.

Where the hell did Schultz get a key? Enrico's got one, but I never gave Schultz one.

Which means Dorotea did.

What the hell is going on?

The answer to that became apparent the moment the lights were switched on in the study. Something had changed. It still was lined with books and framed photos, but the furniture had been rearranged and a sturdy table added. The new table sat close to one wall. On it was a Collins transceiver and the SIGABA encryption device.

Jesus H. Christ! What's that doing in here?

"Is someone going to tell me what's going on here? Maybe you, Jefe?"

"Well, Dorotea and Enrico and I talked things over," Schultz said. "And decided that putting the equipment in here made more sense than having it out in the boonies."

"For one thing, darling," Dorotea said, "it's rather obviously both a nuisance and time-consuming for the team to have to run back and forth to Casa Veintidós every time you get a message, or want to send one."

He nodded and waited for her to go on.

Schultz picked up their reasoning. "Enrico said your father thought the study—when he was setting up the revolution—was the safest place on the estancia to do things in the dark. . . ."

"Otherwise, Don Cletus," Enrico chimed in, "El Coronel, may he be resting in peace in heaven with all the angels, would have gone onto the monte himself. He worked here."

"And what if El Coronel Martín decides to raid the place?" Frade challenged.

"I rigged thermite grenades," Schultz said. "We'd have more time to torch this stuff here than if it was in Casa Veintidós. I showed Enrico and Dorotea how to do that. There wasn't time to teach anyone else, and anyway, Enrico's still making up his mind about who else he wants to know about this."

"You know how to set off the thermite grenades?" Frade asked his wife.

She nodded. "And I also know how to operate the SIGABA."

"You know how that thing works?"

She nodded again. "Would you like me to demonstrate?"

"May I ask why I wasn't asked whether I thought this was a good idea?"

"Well, for one thing, it's obviously the thing to do," Dorotea said. "And this was the time to do it. Carlos isn't here—"

"Where is he?"

"He told me that Delgano wanted him at El Palomar to assist in teaching mechanics what he knows about the Lodestar," she said.

What the hell is that all about?

Interest in South American Airways?

Or to get him out of here?

For what reason?

Dorotea went on, "We of course don't know, darling, when Carlos will show up here again. But since he *wasn't* here, he wasn't able to see Oscar and Enrico moving the equipment into the house and setting up the antennae. And of course you and Delgano were flying back and forth to Brazil, so Delgano doesn't know. For those reasons, darling, Oscar, Enrico, and I decided that this was the moment to do it. Did we do wrong?"

Frade exhaled audibly.

"No. The only thing you've done is embarrass me for not thinking of this myself."

Dorotea, Enrico, and Oscar looked very pleased with themselves.

"Is it up and running?" Frade said.

"We got the first message right after you took off this morning," Schultz said. He took a folded sheet of paper from his pocket and handed it to Frade.

```
URGENT
VIA ASA SPECIAL


TOP SECRET LINDBERGH
DUPLICATION FORBIDDEN


FROM AGGIE


TO TEX


GREAT INTEREST HERE IN FUNCTIONING OF YOUR NEW LEICA


IMMEDIATELY ADVISE WHEN AND HOW YOU PLAN TO SEND
FAMILY PHOTOS AND REPORT OF HOW FAMILY IS DOING


THIS IS MORE IMPORTANT THAN YOUR VACATIONING IN RIO
AND SHOULD BE ACCOMPLISHED FIRST


ACKNOWLEDGE RECEIPT


AGGIE
```

"You've seen this, baby?" Frade asked.

"Of course," Dorotea said.

"Well, Graham is obviously talking about the Froggers," Frade said. "But why in this cutesy code language if that thing is any good?"

He indicated the SIGABA device.

"He's got his reasons, I guess," Schultz said. "You want to answer it now? Or wait until you get something to eat?"

"With as much naval service as you have, Lieutenant Schultz, I am shocked that you don't know that nothing gets between a Marine and his chow." He paused, then asked, "Is there anything else you three have done that I should know about before I chow down?"

" 'Chow down'? Good God!" Dorotea said. "I'm married to a savage! But to answer your question, my darling, the only thing that's happened was that your tailor left a message at the house in Buenos Aires that your suit is ready, and you may pick it up at your convenience."

"Well, that's good news!" Clete said happily.

"Since I know your idea of formal dress is hosing the mud off your cowboy boots," Dorotea said, "your enthusiasm for a new suit piques my curiosity. Tell me all, darling."

He told her.

Dinner for Frade was the New York strip steak he had thought of earlier, plus two fried eggs, home-fried potatoes, and a tomato and cucumber salad, which additions he thought of as he watched one of the maids open a bottle of merlot.

By the time it was over, not only had a second bottle of merlot been emptied by Clete, Enrico, and Oscar, but Frade was just about prepared to answer Graham's radio message. Dorotea had first written it down, then gone to the study, typed it out, shown it to him for his approval, then returned to retype it with his corrections, and then finally to show him the final version.

After dinner, he went with her and El Jefe to the study, and watched how the operation worked.

First, she typed the message on the SIGABA keyboard, which produced a very long strip of perforated paper on which the now-encrypted message had been punched.

"Oscar will have to contact Vint Hill, darling," Dorotea said. "He hasn't yet had time to teach me how to do that."

"Won't you have to learn Morse code first?"

"Of course, but that shouldn't take long."

He didn't argue.

It didn't take the former chief radioman long to establish contact with Vint Hill. Frade heard Schultz twice key in *dit dit dit, dah dit dit dit,* which he recognized as being SB, for "Stand By."

Schultz waved graciously at Dorotea, who then took the perforated tape, fed it into the Collins, and with a delicate finger pushed a button.

The Collins began to swallow the tape, far faster than Clete expected. Finally, it had gone through the machine and come out another opening.

"Another beauty of this setup is that it transmits so fast," Schultz said. "You can resend—in other words, send twice—in less time than it would take me to key this in by hand. Less time for anybody to triangulate us, even if they happened on the frequency we're using."

"Very impressive," Clete said, meaning it.

He gestured to Dorotea, who fed the tape into the Collins again.

When it started to come out of the Collins, Schultz moved a small metal wastebasket under the transceiver to catch it.

"And now all we have to do is burn the tape," he said. "And of course Dorotea's notes and the drafts, and we're done."

"Not in here, Oscar," Dorotea commanded. "Burning that paper will smell up the whole house."

They carried the wastebasket onto the verandah.

Schultz took out a Zippo lighter, lit a piece of paper, and dropped it, flaming, into the wastebasket.

Clete saw something in the dark that shouldn't be there—the flare of a match in the garden—touched Enrico's arm, and pointed.

Enrico worked the action of his shotgun.

Then there was another flare of light in the garden, this time long enough for Frade to see that it was a match that a gaucho on horseback was using to light a cigar. And to see that the gaucho held a 7mm Mauser carbine across his saddle.

"There are always two watching the house, Don Cletus," Enrico said matter-of-factly.

Frade replied softly so that only Enrico could hear.

"What are you talking about?" Dorotea demanded.

"I just told Enrico that I'm so pleased with all you learned that tonight you can stay; he won't have to take you back to the village."

"You bah-stud!" she said loudly.

Schultz laughed.

"And you, too!" Dorotea said.

[SIX]
Office of the Director
Office of Strategic Services
National Institutes of Health Building
Washington, D.C.
0845 23 July 1943

"If you have a moment, Bill?" the deputy director for Western Hemisphere operations of the Office of Strategic Services inquired of the director of the OSS from the latter's office door.

"I always have time for you, Alejandro," William J. Donovan said, waving him in. "But only if you're the bearer of good tidings."

"We have a response from Frade," Graham said, gesturing with the folded sheet of paper in his hand.

"From our loose cannon? Why am I afraid what you bear in your hands is not good tidings? Let me see it."

"Shit," Graham said.

"Alejandro!" Donovan said in mock horror. "I'm shocked."

"Well, I was so pleased with it, and anxious to tell you, that I forgot to leave it in my office."

Donovan gestured for him to hand it over.

"There are things in here I'm not going to like?" Donovan said.

"Almost certainly."

Graham gave it to him, then walked to a couch, stretched out his legs, and waited while Donovan read the message.

```
URGENT
VIA ASA SPECIAL


TOP SECRET LINDBERGH
DUPLICATION FORBIDDEN
```

FROM TEX

TO AGGIE

1—YOUR MESSAGE RE: LEICA ACKNOWLEDGED

2—INASMUCH AS LIEUTENANT FISCHER (HEREAFTER FLAGS)
HAS DEPARTED AND I CAN'T ASK HIM HOW GOOD THE NEW
TOY YOU SENT IS, I WILL USE THE SAME CUTE VERBAL
CODE WITHIN AN ENCRYPTED MESSAGE THAT YOU DID.
PLEASE ADVISE IF I HAVE TO DO THIS IN THE FUTURE.

3—FLAGS LEFT BIRDCAGE APPROXIMATELY 1400 TODAY TO
CATCH THE NEXT BUS HOME FROM YOU KNOW WHERE. HE HAS
WITH HIM UNEXPOSED ROLL OF FILM SHOWING FROGGERS
(HEREAFTER TOURISTS) HOLDING COPY OF DAY-OLD LOCAL
NEWSPAPER. HERR TOURIST (HEREAFTER GOOD KRAUT) GAVE
US SOME DATA ABOUT LOCAL DIPLOMATIC ORGANIZATION
THAT GALAHAD HAS CONFIRMED AS ACCURATE. FRAU TOURIST
(HEREAFTER OLD BITCH) REGRETS GOOD KRAUT'S ACTIONS
AND WOULD RETURN HOME IN A MINUTE IF GIVEN THE
CHANCE.

4—TOURISTS ARE IN THE BEST, MOST REMOTE AND MOST
SECURE LOCATION I CAN PROVIDE.

5—A SECOND ROLL OF UNDEVELOPED FILM, ESSENTIALLY THE
SAME PICTURES, ADDRESSED TO YOU OR YOUR BOSS, EN
ROUTE VIA USAAF OFFICER COURIER, WHO IS PILOTING A
BIRDCAGE BIRD UP NORTH.

6—BRIGADIER CHICKEN AT BIRDCAGE, AT FIRST VERY
DIFFICULT, BECAME PICTURE OF COOPERATION AFTER I
SHOWED HIM MY CREDENTIALS. NOT ONLY DID HE PROVIDE A
SPECIAL BIRDCAGE BIRD TO TAKE FLAGS TO THE BUS STOP
BUT PROVIDED ARMED GUARD TO MAKE SURE FLAGS GOT

SAFELY ON THE BUS. HE EVEN OFFERED TO BUY ME DINNER
BEFORE I FLEW HOME.

7—I CONFESS THE FIRST TIME I SAW THOSE CREDENTIALS,
I THOUGHT, NO SURPRISE, THAT SOMEBODY UP THERE
WASN'T PLAYING WITH A FULL DECK. I APOLOGIZE
ABJECTLY. GIVE THE SOB BOTH EARS AND THE TAIL.

8—WITH REGARD TO FLAGS: NOT ONLY IS HE ONE HELL OF A
TECHNICIAN, BUT A HELL OF A FINE OFFICER. IT LOOKED
FOR ABOUT TWENTY-FOUR HOURS AS IF WE WERE ALL ABOUT
TO BE STOOD AGAINST A WALL. I OFFERED TO GET HIM OUT
OF THE LINE OF FIRE. FLAGS SAID HE WOULD TAKE HIS
CHANCES AS HE FELT THE PICTURES THE CAMERA GUY
WANTED WERE MORE IMPORTANT THAN MAYBE WE UNDERSTOOD.
CAN YOU GET HIM A MEDAL?

9—MORE IMPORTANT, CAN YOU GET HIM TO QUOTE VOLUNTEER
END QUOTE FOR THE BOY SCOUTS THE WAY YOU DID ME? FOR
ONE THING, HE ALREADY KNOWS WHERE MOST OF OUR
SKELETONS ARE BURIED, AND WILL LEARN ABOUT THE REST
WHEN HE'S WORKING THE OTHER END OF THE TELEPHONE. IF
THAT'S NOT POSSIBLE, I VERY STRONGLY RECOMMEND THAT
YOU GET HIM A BADGE AS SOON AS POSSIBLE. THERE'S
BOUND TO BE A GENERAL OR COLONEL CHICKEN AT HIS
PLACE OF WORK WHO WILL BE TOO CURIOUS ABOUT WHAT
HE'S DOING FOR THE BOY SCOUTS, AND A BADGE WILL
CERTAINLY HAVE THE SAME BENEFICIAL EFFECT ON HIM
THAT IT DID ON GENERAL CHICKEN AT BIRDCAGE.

10—FOR YOUR GENERAL INFORMATION, THERE WAS A STORY
IN LA NACIÓN THAT SAID SOUTH AMERICAN AIRWAYS WILL
SHORTLY RECEIVE ITS SECOND LODESTAR AIRCRAFT, WITH
MORE COMING SOON, AND THAT OPERATIONS WILL SOON
BEGIN FROM SOUTH AMERICA'S NEWEST AIRFIELD, WHICH,
AT THE SUGGESTION OF COLONEL JUAN D. PERON, HAS BEEN

NAMED AEROPUERTO CORONEL JORGE G. FRADE. THE STORY
WENT ON TO SAY THAT INITIAL OPERATIONS WILL BE TO
MONTEVIDEO, URUGUAY, AND POSADAS, WITH OTHER
DESTINATIONS TO BE ADDED AS AIRCRAFT AND PILOTS FOR
THEM BECOME AVAILABLE.

11—I WILL BE OUT OF TOUCH FOR THE NEXT THIRTY-SIX
HOURS AS I WILL BE VISITING GOOD KRAUT TO SEE WHAT
ELSE HE CAN TELL ME, AND TO KEEP OLD BITCH FROM
GOING HOME. IN THIS CONNECTION, GALAHAD INFORMS THAT
A CONTRACT HAS BEEN PUT OUT ON BOTH BY VON
DEITZBERG, WHEN AND WHERE FOUND.

TEX

"I don't think, Colonel Graham, I have ever seen a document quite like this," Donovan said.

"That's why I regret forgetting to forget it in my office," Graham said. "I thought you might react that way."

"It's not an intelligence report, or at least like any other report from the field that I have ever seen."

"Think of it as good news, Bill."

"I'll need a little translation of what Major Frade calls 'the cute verbal code within an encrypted message.' "

"I'll do my best. It might be easier if I wrote you a memo."

"Let's do it now, please, Alejandro. Why does he call this ASA officer 'Flags,' for example, do you think?"

"I think it makes reference to the Signal Corps insignia—you know, the crossed semaphore flags?"

Donovan nodded.

" 'Tourists' I think I understand. But 'Good Kraut' and 'Old Bitch'?"

"I think he means Frogger is cooperating and Frau Frogger is not."

"That's the first time I have even seen 'old bitch' in an official communication," Donovan said, and dropped his eyes to the sheet of paper again. " 'Brigadier Chicken'? "

"As in 'chickenshit.' Implying the general was reluctant to understand that our operations don't always follow established protocol or regulations."

"And I see that I was right when I told you take those badges down there." Graham shook his head in mock disgust.

"That's the lawyer coming out in you again, Bill. Twisting the facts to support your position. You wanted to impress on Frade that he was in the OSS with a badge saying so. That's all. You didn't any more think that he would wag them in some Air Forces general's face than I did."

Donovan smiled, then went on, " 'Give the SOB both ears and the tail'? "

"I think that Frade is suggesting that the SOB who got him the credentials—which would be you, of course—be given, as is a very good matador in a bullfight, both ears and the tail."

Donovan shook his head.

"What about this Lieutenant Flags? Can we recruit him?"

"Only, Bill, at the risk of greatly annoying the Army Security Agency. Let me think about that."

"Well, obviously we can't give him a medal."

"You could write him—or I will write and you can sign—a very nice letter to the ASA extolling his many virtues."

"And the badge Frade says we should give him?"

"That makes sense. I want to talk to Fischer just as soon as I can."

"When will that be?"

"There's a B-26 waiting for him to get off the Clipper in Miami. Six, seven hours after that."

"The film?"

"I don't know which will get here first, the one Fischer has with him, or the one the pilot-courier is bringing."

"And we won't know, will we, until we get the film developed, if there's anything useful on either roll?"

"There you go again, Counselor, looking for the black cloud. Look on the bright side."

"Which is?"

"The next-to-last paragraph," Graham said. "Your friend Franklin's got the competition to Juan Trippe's Pan American that he wanted."

"You think that's it, Alejandro? That Roosevelt wants to stick it to Trippe with that Argentine airline?"

"That's all I can think of."

"I want to see that film the moment it's developed," Donovan said. "You think we should send Allen Dulles a message telling him it's on the way? He's really—"

"It may be all blank. Why don't we wait and see?"

Donovan considered that a moment, then said, "You're right. That makes— what?—twice this year, doesn't it?"

"Three times. My secretary said you really are a bastard, and I agreed with her."

Donovan laughed out loud and waved the message.

"Can I have this?"

"You're the boss."

"I'm going to put it in the safe under 'Documents of Historical Interest' and let some historian try to figure it out fifty, sixty years from now."

Graham laughed, pushed himself off the couch, and extended his hand to Donovan with the first and index fingers crossed.

"What's that for?" Donovan asked.

"Crossed fingers. Let's hope those pictures are usable."

They shook hands; then Graham walked out of Donovan's office.

XI

[ONE]
Office of the Commercial Attaché
Embassy of the German Reich
Avenida Córdoba
Buenos Aires, Argentina
0910 23 July 1943

"You wished to see me, Herr Cranz?" Fregattenkapitän Karl Boltitz asked at the door of SS-Standartenführer Karl Cranz's office.

Cranz, who was wearing one of his new suits in the guise of commercial attaché, gestured for Boltitz to come in.

"I asked to see you *and* von Wachtstein," Cranz said, his tone making it a question.

"I believe he went quite early to El Palomar airfield, Herr Cranz. I had the impression you wanted him to fly to Uruguay." His tone, too, made it a question.

"Is that what he told you?" Cranz asked, indicating that Boltitz should come around his desk to look at something he had laid out on it.

"What he said, Herr Standart . . . Sorry, sir."

Cranz made a *it doesn't matter* gesture, then smiled and said, "Actually, Karl, today I feel more like a standartenführer than a bidder for frozen cubed beef."

"I doubt the Standartenführer ever feels like a natural bidder for frozen cubed beef," Boltitz said.

"I can hear one day my nephew asking, 'And what was your most painful experience in the war, Oncle Karl?' And I can hear me replying, 'Standing in a freezing warehouse on the docks in Buenos Aires, leibling, trying to buy frozen cubed beef.' "

Boltitz chuckled dutifully.

"Did von Wachtstein tell you I wanted to go to Uruguay in the Storch?" Cranz asked.

"Yes, sir, I did," Major Freiherr Hans-Peter von Wachtstein said from the office door. "If I had known you wanted to see me, sir, I would have tried—"

"No matter, von Wachtstein," Cranz interrupted him. "You're here. Is the Storch flyable?"

"Yes, sir. And if we leave in the next hour, we can arrive in Montevideo in time for a nice lunch at the casino in Carrasco."

"We're not going to Uruguay," Cranz said.

"I had the impression, sir—"

"Impressions are often wrong, von Wachtstein."

"Yes, sir, I suppose that's true."

"I tried, and apparently succeeded, von Wachtstein, to give you the erroneous impression that I wanted you to fly me to Uruguay."

Von Wachtstein stood silently and thought, *What the hell is this bastard up to?*

"Doesn't that make you curious?" Cranz went on.

"Yes, sir, it does."

"But not enough to ask me why I would do that?"

"No, sir. I assume you had your reasons."

"Are you a naturally curious man, von Wachtstein?"

"I think I am, sir."

"But you never asked me about something I feel sure arouses your curiosity," Cranz said. "Do you take my meaning?"

"No, sir. I'm lost."

"You were curious about the special shipment, weren't you?" Cranz asked, smiling.

Peter felt the base of his neck tighten.

"Yes, sir, I admit that I was. Am."

"Two weeks ago, I told you the special cargo had been loaded aboard U-boat 405. Weren't you curious, von Wachtstein, about what was going to happen next?"

"Yes, sir, I was."

"But you never asked me about that, did you?"

"No, sir. I thought you would tell me when you thought I should know."

"Did you perhaps ask the fregattenkapitän?"

Von Wachtstein looked at Boltitz, then back to Cranz. "Yes, sir, I did."

"And what did he tell you?"

"Essentially that I would learn about it when you decided I should know, sir."

"Is that all you asked the fregattenkapitän?"

That's a loaded question.

And I don't like the smile on his face.

But this is not the time to hesitate in replying.

"The truth, sir, is that I asked Karl—"

" 'Karl'? Not the 'fregattenkapitän'?"

Von Wachtstein exchanged a glance with Boltitz and decided Boltitz also had no idea where Cranz was going with his line of questioning.

"No disrespect was intended, sir," von Wachtstein said to Cranz. "I had the privilege of the fregattenkapitän's friendship before he became a fregattenkapitän."

"So you did. So what did you ask your friend the fregattenkapitän?"

"Sir, I asked him if he knew and wouldn't tell me, or whether he didn't know anything himself."

"And the fregattenkapitän's response?"

"The fregattenkapitän told me that was none of my business, sir, and that I should have known better than to have asked him something like that."

Cranz smiled broadly and laughed.

"And indeed that's what Karl should have told you, Hans," he said. "But you are forgiven. And Karl didn't know any more than you did. What he was doing was what most officers—including this one—do: give their subordinates the erroneous impression they know more than they actually do."

Boltitz chuckled dutifully.

"It is not kind to make fun of a simple fighter pilot," von Wachtstein said.
Cranz and Boltitz both laughed.

"Speaking of flying," Cranz said, and motioned for von Wachtstein to come
around the desk.

Von Wachtstein did. There was a map of the Argentine coast laid out on
it. He saw that the map had come from the Ejército Argentino's Topographic
Service.

Cranz took a pencil from a jar on his desk and pointed at the map, to a point
on the Atlantic Ocean von Wachtstein estimated to be about two hundred
kilometers south of Samborombón Bay.

*If that isn't where they intend to bring that special cargo ashore, I can't imag-
ine what it is.*

"If I told you I wanted you to fly me there, von Wachtstein, what would be
your reply?" Cranz asked softly.

" 'Yes, sir, with qualifications.' "

"Meaning?"

"If you wanted to land there, sir, I would need somewhere I could put
down the Storch."

"And?"

"If you wanted to come back, I would need fuel. I can make it there with
a comfortable margin of safety, but to get back . . ."

"A smooth field would suffice, am I correct?"

"Yes, sir."

"And two hundred liters of aviation-grade gasoline? Would that be enough?"

"Yes, sir. More than enough."

"And how long would it take us to get there?"

"I would guess," von Wachtstein said, and made a compass with his fingers,
and then put them on the map scale, "that that's about five hundred kilometers from El Palomar . . ."

"Four hundred eighty-three, to be precise," Cranz corrected him, just a little smugly.

"Then a few minutes more than three hours, Herr Cranz."

"It's now twenty-two past nine," Cranz said. "If we left here now, and it takes
us an hour to get to El Palomar and to take off, that's ten-thirty. Plus three
hours. That means we could be at Necochea at one-thirty. Correct?"

Von Wachtstein made a rocking gesture with his hand that meant *more
or less.*

"How much is . . . ?" Cranz mimicked von Wachtstein's gesture.

"No more than thirty minutes, perhaps even less, either way, sir. Depending on weather, winds, et cetera."

"Then that, as I said, would put us down there at a little after one, wouldn't it?" Cranz said, and without waiting for a reply turned to Boltitz: "A car will pick you up at half past nine at the door, Boltitz. An American Packard. It will take you and Sturmbannführer Raschner to meet us at Necochea."

"Yes, sir," Boltitz said, then added, "An American Packard?"

"A dark blue one," Cranz said.

There was a moment's silence.

"Neither of you has any questions?" Cranz said.

"None that I dare ask," von Wachtstein confessed.

"Correct, von Wachtstein," Cranz said, smiling, then grew serious: "What we're about to do is important business both to the Reich and to ourselves. If we succeed, we can take pride in having successfully performed our mission. If we fail, I would have to report our failure to Reichsprotektor Himmler, something I really would be loath to do. I came here to Argentina determined not to fail. Do you understand me, gentlemen?"

Both said, "Yes, sir."

"My decision not to make either of you privy to the details of the landing of the special cargo was based on several factors, including the fact that we suspect—but do not know—that Herr Frogger was the traitor in our midst. In your case, von Wachtstein, there are those who felt your escaping from the debacle at Samborombón Bay without a scratch was a little suspicious. I did not share in this suspicion, of course, but it was there. Now, since I have not taken even Fregattenkapitän Boltitz into my confidence, he could not possibly have taken you into his. If there is trouble today, I will know—and can inform the reichsprotektor—that neither of you could possibly be the traitor.

"If it goes well—and Sturmbannführer Raschner and I have worked very hard to ensure that it will—it will tend to give some credibility to my belief that Frogger is, was, our traitor. Unfortunately, I'm afraid that it will not wipe completely from his mind what suspicions the reichsprotektor has about you, von Wachtstein."

"Excuse me?" von Wachtstein said.

"You could hardly have informed your friend Major Frade—or anyone else—of the planned landing of the special shipment, could you, since you didn't know, still don't know, what those plans are, could you? That's not quite the same thing as saying you would not have, had you been aware of them. And you won't, now, have that opportunity."

Von Wachtstein didn't reply.

"You're not going to stand there with a look of indignation on your face, are you, Hans? Pretending you didn't know you were—indeed, still are—under suspicion?"

"I knew I was, Herr Standartenführer," von Wachtstein said coldly. "At first. But in my naïveté, I thought I had been cleared by both you and Boltitz."

"Neither Boltitz nor I think you're our traitor, Hans. But there are those—Raschner among them, I'm afraid, as well as the people in Berlin—who still wonder about you. We live in that kind of world, I'm sorry to say."

Von Wachtstein didn't reply.

"If there are no further questions, gentlemen, I suggest we be on our way," Cranz said. He looked at von Wachtstein. "No questions, Hans?"

"No questions, sir."

"You called me Herr Standartenführer a moment ago."

"I apologize, sir."

"You were a little upset," Cranz said. "Understandably."

"It won't happen again, sir."

"Actually, I'm glad it happened. When we get to Necochea, and while we're there, I think that if you and Boltitz addressed me by my rank, it would have a salutary effect on the people who will be there. God knows, it's hard to work up a lot of respect for a commercial attaché in his new suit."

Cranz stood, then took a 9mm Luger P-08 pistol from his drawer, ejected the magazine, then after ensuring it was full put it back in, worked the action to chamber a cartridge, clicked on the safety, and finally slipped the weapon inside his waist band.

Von Wachtstein had several thoughts:

Ready to do battle for the Thousand-Year Reich, are you, Standartenführer?

Why am I not surprised he's got a P-08?

Most of these SS bastards never have heard a shot fired in anger; for them a Luger's like those stupid daggers they wear on their dress uniform—a symbol, rather than a tool.

The first thing that Dieter von und zu Aschenburg did when I showed up with a Luger in Spain was take it away from me and give me a .380 Walther PPK.

"A Luger's for looks, Hansel, my boy. If you're going to shoot somebody, you'll need something that doesn't jam after the first shot. Or before the first shot."

As he and Cranz walked across the sidewalk to get into the embassy Mercedes, he had three more thoughts:

I still have the PPK; it's in the bedside table in my apartment.

Cranz didn't say anything about me taking a gun.

My God! Was there some sort of threat in him making sure I saw he had the P-08 ready to fire?

[TWO]
El Palomar Airfield
Campo de Mayo Military Base
Buenos Aires Province, Argentina
1035 23 July 1943

"Tell me something about the radio in the Storch, von Wachtstein," Cranz said as they walked up to the aircraft.

"What would you like to know, Herr Standartenführer?"

"How do they work? What do they do?"

"Well, this one has the latest equipment. There's a transmitter-receiver—"

"Which does what?"

"Permits me to communicate with the control tower here, to get permission to taxi, to take off and land, to check the weather, things like that."

"Can you communicate with anyone else?"

"If there were other German aircraft here, and within range, I could talk to them."

"Not to an Argentine aircraft?"

"We use different frequencies, Herr Standartenführer. Theoretically, yes; actually, no."

"Anything else?"

"It has an RDF receiver, Herr Standartenführer. That round antenna on top?" He pointed to it and, when Cranz nodded, went on: "It rotates. There's a control in the cockpit, and a dial. First you tune in the frequency of the airfield. You hear a Morse code signal. Here, that's PAL: Dit dah dah dit. Dit dah. Dit dah dit—"

"I know Morse code, von Wachtstein."

"Yes, sir. I should have known that. No offense intended, sir."

"None taken. And?"

"When I hear that repeated, I rotate the antenna. Signal strength is shown on a dial. When the dial shows the strongest signal strength, it does so on a compass. That shows me the direction of the field."

"Very interesting."

"It's effective, sir."

"Just as soon as we get into the air, von Wachtstein, I want you to turn off the transmitter-receiver."

"Jawohl, Herr Standartenführer."

Jesus Christ! He thinks I'm going to get on the radio and tell somebody where we're going!

"Does that answer your question, Herr Standartenführer?"

"Yes, it does, thank you. I have one more."

"Yes, sir?"

"Will our route take us over your wife's farm? Let me rephrase: Is it necessary that we fly over your wife's farm, or that of your friend Frade?"

"I had planned to fly down National Route Three, Herr Standartenführer. It goes all the way to Necochea. My mother-in-law's estancia touches Route Three."

I don't think he's angling for an invitation to call on Doña Claudia.

"Can you avoid doing so?"

"Certainly, Herr Standartenführer."

"Do so," Cranz ordered curtly.

"Jawohl, Herr Standartenführer!"

Does he really think I'll try something to tell somebody what's going on?

He's too smart for that.

Then is he trying to scare me?

If so, why?

What the hell is going on here?

Jesus Christ!

My vivid imagination has just gone into high gear:

When we get to the beach at Necochea, he's going to use that Luger on me.

"As you suspected all along, Herr Reichsprotektor, von Wachtstein was our traitor. As soon as he learned where the special cargo was to be brought ashore, he attempted to tell our enemies again. I would have preferred that he could have been brought for trial before a People's Court—traitors don't deserve an Officer's Court of Honor—but with the safety of the special cargo at risk, I decided it was necessary to eliminate him then and there. And did so. Heil Hitler!"

Von Wachtstein began his preflight walk-around inspection of the Storch.

You're paranoid, Hansel! Absolutely out of your fucking mind!

Maybe not.

Or I am paranoid—which really wouldn't surprise me—but that doesn't mean that Herr Standartenführer Cranz isn't prepared to kill me to make himself look good with Himmler . . . and incidentally get rid of someone who really might be a traitor.

Which of course I am.

As he worked the rudder back and forth with his hand, he glanced at Cranz, who was watching him with some interest.

Well, one thing is for sure. He's not going to shoot me while we're in the Storch. He doesn't know how to fly, and the Herr Standartenführer is very good at protecting his ass.

If I live through this, I will have to remember to get my PPK out of the damn drawer and start carrying it with me.

Why didn't I think of that before? I know these people are murderers.

Clete goes around armed to the teeth, as if he's on the way to that gunfight in the Wild West. What was it called—"The Easy Corral"?

No. The O.K. Corral. That's it. The O.K. Corral.

What the hell is a corral?

Just when the elapsed-time clock mounted at the top of the Storch's windscreen showed that they had departed El Palomar two hours and fifty-five minutes earlier, Major von Wachtstein felt something push at his shoulder. He turned and saw that Standartenführer Cranz was holding a celluloid-covered map out to him.

He took it and saw that it was another Argentine Army Topographic Service map, this one of a smaller scale. It was centered on Necochea and showed little else. Arrows indicated that some place called General Alvarado was to the north, near the Atlantic Ocean, and a place called Energia was to the south, what looked like a kilometer or two inland from the ocean.

The reason it doesn't show much more than a couple of dirt roads is that there probably isn't anything else down there.

What the hell. You don't want anybody around when you're trying to smuggle things ashore.

A long oblong had been drawn with a grease pencil on the celluloid covering the map. It was labeled *Landeplatz 1,200 M.* It was located, von Wachtstein estimated, about three hundred meters from the ocean, at right angles to it.

He looked over his shoulder at Cranz, and gestured to him that he should put on his headset.

Cranz nodded, and thirty seconds later, "Hello, hello, hello. Can you hear me?" came over von Wachtstein's earphones.

"I hear you clearly, Herr Standartenführer."

"Can you locate the airfield?"

"I will have to fly much lower, Herr Standartenführer."

"Then do so," Cranz ordered impatiently.

Reasoning that an SS-standartenführer was certainly a courageous man—at least in his own mind—von Wachtstein dropped the nose of the Storch almost straight down, and allowed the airspeed indicator to get very, very close to the red line before pulling out at about three hundred feet.

The wind whistled interestingly—it sounded like a woman screaming in pain—as it whipped around the gear and fuselage of the Storch at close-to-tearing-the-wings-off speed.

Five minutes later, after dropping even lower—so low that he had to go around, rather than over, various clumps of trees on the pampas—he thought he saw what had to be the so-called airfield. In the middle of nowhere, there were four Ford ton-and-a-half trucks parked in a line about three hundred meters from the South Atlantic.

Two men stepped in front of the line of trucks and began to wave their arms.

"I believe that's it, Herr Standartenführer," von Wachtstein said, pointing. "To our left."

"Are you going to have enough runway to land?"

I can land this thing, if I have to, in about two hundred meters at forty kph.

"I believe I can manage, Herr Standartenführer. I presume that someone has walked the landing area to make sure there are no obstructions."

There was a perceptible hesitation before Cranz, without much conviction in his voice, said, "I'm sure that's been done, von Wachtstein."

Von Wachtstein flew the length of the makeshift runway, could see nothing on it, and noted nothing that suggested strong crosswinds.

"It would have been helpful, Herr Standartenführer, if someone had thought to erect a windsock," he said, then stood the Storch on its wingtip, leveled out, and landed.

[THREE]
Near Necochea
Buenos Aires Province, Argentina
1415 23 July 1943

When von Wachtstein taxied the Storch up to the trucks, he saw that the straight-arm Nazi salute was being rendered by perhaps a dozen men, all but one of whom were wearing the dark blue coveralls of Argentine workmen. The lone man not in coveralls wore a suit.

You are not only paranoid, Hansel, but certifiably insane.

A couple of hours ago, you were scared shitless that Cranz was going to execute you out of hand. Now you're having a hard time keeping a straight face at the gray pallor of your passenger.

He shut down the engine.

"Well, we're down, Herr Standartenführer."

"I see that we are," Cranz snapped. "Why was this flight so rough?"

"I regret that, Herr Standartenführer, but landing on a dirt strip with the winds coming off the ocean is not like landing at El Palomar. But not to worry, sir. The Storch is a splendid airplane."

The man wearing the suit walked up to the airplane and again gave the Nazi salute as soon as Cranz had climbed out.

Von Wachtstein busied himself taking tie-down ropes from the Storch and, when he had them in hand, said, "I wonder if anyone has a hammer for the tie-down stakes, Herr Standartenführer?"

"Erich," Cranz was saying to the man in the suit, "this is my pilot, Major Freiherr von Wachtstein, who received the Knight's Cross of the Iron Cross from the hands of Der Führer himself."

Now he's going to dazzle this guy, whoever he is, with my *Knight's Cross?*

The man threw another Nazi salute and said, "A great honor, Herr Major. I am—"

Cranz silenced him midsentence with an imperiously raised hand.

"I think it better, *Herr Schmidt,* that the fewer facts von Wachtstein knows about you, the better. No telling who's liable to be asking him questions. Am I right, von Wachtstein?"

"The Herr Standartenführer is quite correct. How do you do, *Herr Schmidt?*"

They shook hands.

"Now, what is this about tie-downs, whatever you said?" Cranz asked.

"The Storch has to be tied down, sir. I have the ropes and the stakes, but I need something to drive the stakes."

"If I may, Herr Standartenführer?" Herr Schmidt said.

Cranz nodded.

Schmidt turned toward the workers at the trucks and bellowed, "Two men and a hammer. Two hammers. Here. Immediately!"

There was sudden frenzied activity at the trucks to comply with the order.

Which, von Wachtstein decided, was indeed an order.

"Herr Schmidt" gave it like an officer.

And those guys are responding to it like soldiers.

He talks funny. I can generally tell where somebody's from in Germany by their accent; I can't with this guy.

So, what does that mean?

That he's not a German? Somebody like Günther Loche, maybe? A German who came here from Germany.

What do they call them? Argo-Germans.

The Loche family are better Nazis than Hitler.

And those soldiers understood his German, making them more Argo-Germans?

Argo-German Nazis in the Argentine Army?

What the hell is going on here?

Two of the men in blue coveralls, each carrying a heavy iron hammer, trotted over to them.

"Major von Wachtstein will tell you what he needs done," Herr Schmidt said.

"Jawohl, Herr Oberst," the older of the two said, then saluted von Wachtstein.

Von Wachtstein crisply returned the Nazi salutes.

"What I need you to do, Stabsfeldwebel, is have your man drive these stakes so that I can make sure my airplane doesn't get blown away."

He pointed to the ground where he wanted the stakes driven.

"Jawohl, Herr Major," the man said. He turned to the man with him and said, "You heard the Herr Major."

And then he turned back to von Wachtstein. "Actually, it's Oberfeldwebel, Herr Major."

So, not sergeant major, but master sergeant.

Close enough. A sergeant.

Oh, you are clever, Hansel!

"How did you know he was a soldier, von Wachtstein?" Cranz asked.

And stupid, too.

"Well, before I was commissioned, Herr Standartenführer, I was an unterfeldwebel. Willi Grüner and I both were unterfeldwebels, commissioned the same day. One feldwebel can always recognize another, right, Oberfeldwebel?"

The master sergeant smiled happily.

"I would say that's so, Herr Major."

"Willi Grüner?" Herr Schmidt said. "By chance, the son of our Oberst Grüner? I know he had a son in the Luftwaffe."

"Yes," von Wachtstein said simply. "The sad duty of telling him the circumstances of his father's death fell to me in Berlin not long ago."

Von Wachtstein exchanged a glance with Cranz.

So is this where the standartenführer decides that I really am a loyal officer?

Or that I am not, in which case Cranz takes out his Luger and shoots me?

No, probably not here. He'd have to drive back to Buenos Aires.

Maybe a little later—maybe when we're back in Buenos Aires—when he can come up with a credible story. Maybe that he caught me trying to tell the enemy about this operation.

"Oberst Grüner died for the Fatherland, for National Socialism," Schmidt said. "I am proud that he was my friend."

"I regret that, while I did know him, I cannot claim to have been his friend," Cranz said. "But back to duty. Major von Wachtstein said that if there had been a windsock, our landing would have been safer."

"You will have to understand, Herr Major, that I am an officer of mountain troops and know very little about aircraft."

"A windsock indicates to the pilot how the wind is blowing," von Wachtstein explained.

"I suspect that this will not be the last time we will meet on a windy beach," Cranz said. "Have a windsock the next time."

"*Jawohl, Herr Standartenführer.* I assure you that omission will not happen again," Schmidt said.

"See that it doesn't," Cranz said. He then smiled and asked, "I hope you did give some thought to our lunch?"

Schmidt pointed to an area behind the trucks, where von Wachtstein saw a tent fly had been erected over a folding wooden table.

"It is not much, Herr Standartenführer, but it will stave off starvation."

It turned out to be sort of an Argo-German picnic lunch, served from insulated containers whose markings made it clear they belonged to the Argentine army. They were painted a dark olive drab, showed signs of frequent and hard use, and had serial numbers stenciled on them in white.

They contained empanadas, knockwurst and sauerkraut, leberwurst, butter and condiments, kaiser rolls, and loaves of rye bread of a kind von Wachtstein hadn't seen since leaving Germany. It was all served on a white tablecloth by a young man in blue workman's coveralls.

Von Wachtstein refused both beer and wine, saying he had to fly.

When lunch was over and the table cleared, another map was produced.

"Be so good as to explain to Major von Wachtstein his role in the operation," Cranz ordered.

"*Jawohl, Herr Standartenführer,*" Schmidt said. He used a pencil to point at the map. "The U-405 is here, Herr Major, just outside Argentine waters. In other words, twenty-one kilometers; twenty to comply with maritime law, plus one kilometer as a safety factor. Our last communication with it—"

"The Kriegsmarine would say 'her,' " Cranz corrected.

"*Jawohl, Herr Standartenführer,*" Schmidt replied, then went on: "The last communication with *her* was early this morning. There be will no other radio communication with *her* unless there is an emergency of some sort. Now that we have the airplane, that won't be necessary. U-405 currently is submerged. At sixteen-thirty, she will come to the surface, where she will hope to see you, Herr Major, in your Storch. That will—"

"Presumably, von Wachtstein," Cranz interrupted, "you will be able to find U-405, now that you know where she is?"

"If she's where the Herr Oberst indicated, I can, Herr Standartenführer."

"Why did you refer to Herr Schmidt as 'Herr Oberst,' von Wachtstein? And don't tell me that it's because all obersts recognize one another."

Because my old friend the oberfeldwebel addressed him as such, you arrogant prick.

"It was a slip of the tongue, Herr Standartenführer. I can't imagine that Herr Schmidt would be an Argentine coronel."

"Of course not," Cranz said.

They all smiled at each other.

Schmidt continued: "Seeing the Storch will be the signal for the U-405 that everything is going according to plan. She will acknowledge seeing you by some means. Will you be low enough to see someone waving a flag?"

"I can fly low enough to see someone smiling at me, *Herr Schmidt,*" von Wachtstein said, and they all smiled at each other again.

"The U-405 will then submerge," Schmidt resumed, "and head toward the beach, to this, the fifty-fathom line. At ten knots, she should be there in under an hour—"

"By which time," Cranz interrupted again, "Sturmbannführer Raschner and Fregattenkapitän Boltitz will be here."

What the hell is Raschner doing with Boltitz?

I know he said they were driving here in an American Packard, but why?

"Yes, sir?"

"At seventeen forty-five," Cranz explained, "U-405 will rise to periscope depth and look for a signal which Fregattenkapitän Boltitz will transmit with a signal lamp. On receipt of that signal, she will surface and come closer to the beach. . . ."

Cranz gestured somewhat imperiously at Schmidt to pick up the story.

"This is the ten-fathom line," Schmidt said, pointing to the map with the pencil. "It is, as you can see, about five hundred meters from the beach."

"Yes, sir," von Wachtstein said.

"During this period, we will have communication with the U-405 with the signal lamp," Schmidt went on. "When she is in position, she will launch rubber boats to bring the special cargo ashore. As soon as it is ashore, the U-405 will move to the fifty-fathom line, submerge, and return to the high seas."

"And while all this is going on, von Wachtstein," Cranz said, "you will be flying overhead the shoreline to make sure that Herr Schmidt's plans to make sure no one happens to come up the beach have been as good as he assures me they will be. And as soon as you see the rubber boats heading for the beach, you will land in case something has come up that will require your aviation skills."

"Yes, sir."

"Do you have any questions, von Wachtstein?"

"No, sir. But I think I had best see about refueling the Storch."

"Can Schmidt's men handle that?"

"I'd rather do it myself, sir."

"Speaking of Schmidt, is there any reason Schmidt could not go with you when you go to signal the U-405?"

Afraid you might get your feet wet, Herr Standartenführer?

"No, sir."

"I think his splendid work setting this up has earned him that privilege," Cranz said.

"Yes, sir. So do I."

[FOUR]
38 Degrees 26 Minutes South Latitude
58 Degrees 59 Minutes West Longitude
Off Necochea, Buenos Aires Province, Argentina
1625 23 July 1943

Herr Erich Schmidt had become visibly nervous when he could no longer look over his shoulder and see the landmass that was Argentina, but not nearly as nervous as Standartenführer Karl Cranz had looked when von Wachtstein had descended rapidly on their way to Necochea.

Von Wachtstein almost regretted telling him, "No, sir. There are no life preservers on the aircraft. When the standartenführer told me we were not going to fly over the River Plate, I removed them."

And Cranz saw me take them out.

Which is more than likely—likely, hell!—OBVIOUSLY the reason he rewarded Schmidt with the privilege of going out to meet the U-405.

Right after takeoff, von Wachtstein had done the navigation in his head.

Course: Due east. Altitude: 1,000 meters should do it. Length of flight: Winds off the ocean at probably 20 kilometers, indicated airspeed of 150, so that's 150 minus the 20-kph headwind, or 130. And 130 into 21 kilometers is—what?—hell, call it a fifth of an hour.

Twelve minutes into the flight by the elapsed-time clock mounted above the windscreen, he started to examine the surface of the ocean.

No whitecaps, just rolling seas.

Wait, there's a whitecap . . . no, that's not a whitecap.

The rushing wave he'd spotted grew larger and whiter, then turned into a pole racing across the sea.

A sub periscope.

Goddamn! There she is, Lindbergh!

You get the Luftwaffe Prize For Dumb Luck Dead-Reckoning Navigation.

"There she is, sir," von Wachtstein said, banking the Storch to give Schmidt a better look.

The periscope was now visibly atop a submarine's conning tower. Then a deck-mounted cannon broke through the waves. People appeared in the conning tower. One of them pointed at the Storch. Another ran aft of the conning tower to a sort of iron-pipe railed platform.

Von Wachtstein saw a flag appear as the U-405 came completely to the surface.

Not the swastika flag.

That's the Kriegsmarine battle ensign—what Langsdorff arranged to fall on when he shot himself.

He picked up a little altitude, then made a steep descending turn and flew back to the submarine. He lowered flaps, flying as slowly as he could and as close to the waves as he dared.

I'll be a sonofabitch . . . that's an SS uniform on the guy giving that stupid fucking Nazi salute.

There were several Kriegsmarine officers on the aft platform and in the smaller area atop the conning tower. He could tell because they were wearing officer's brimmed caps and sweaters. The SS asshole was wearing a white shirt and tie.

The officers waved—broad, wide-spread arms—but not one saluted.

When von Wachtstein was past the submarine, he dumped the flaps and shoved the throttle to full emergency power. The Storch quickly gained speed and altitude . . . *Like a goosed stork,* he thought with a grin, imagining Schmidt's pucker factor reflex to the maneuver.

As soon as he could, he turned and dropped back to the surface of the sea.

Now the Kriegsmarine battle flag was gone, as were all the men but one— an officer, on the conning tower, who waved a final time, then disappeared into the boat as the U-405 began to submerge.

Thirty seconds later, the submarine was gone.

Von Wachtstein turned the nose of the Storch due west.

After crossing the coastline, he flew low and slow enough over the trucks so that he could signal with an upraised thumb that they'd made the rendezvous with U-405. Then he flew for several kilometers over the beach and finally flew several kilometers inland.

There were three dirt roads leading from a paved road to where the trucks sat on the rise overlooking the beach. Each road had been blocked by a truck and soldiers. These men were in uniform, not in the blue workman coveralls that all the others wore beside the beach.

When he returned to the landing strip, as he was landing, he saw two things he hadn't seen on his flyovers. One was a large four-door sedan, which had to be the American Packard in which Sturmbannführer Erich Raschner and Fregattenkapitän Karl Boltitz had driven from Buenos Aires. The other was that there were now two machine guns and their crews—in uniform, not blue coveralls—in position so they could cover the beach.

He recognized the model of the machine guns.

I didn't know the Argentines had Maschinengewehr 34s; I thought they were still using World War I Maxims.

And why are some of these mountain troops in uniform, and the rest in blue coveralls?

Okay. Civilians in coveralls with Maschinengewehr 34s would really make people, like the local authorities, curious.

This way Herr/Oberst Schmidt can get away with saying he's running some sort of repel-the-invaders field exercise.

But, that being the case, why the coveralls on the others?

Then he saw where he was relative to the ground, made the necessary corrections to his flight path, and softly set down the Storch.

[FIVE]
Near Necochea
Buenos Aires Province, Argentina
1705 23 July 1943

"I thought I made it clear that your role in this was to fly along the beach," Standartenführer Cranz said when von Wachtstein walked up to him.

"Sir, I landed for several reasons, among them being that I thought the Herr Standartenführer would want confirmation from Herr Schmidt that we made rendezvous—"

"Quite right."

"—and that we saw nothing out of the ordinary. And I thought Herr Schmidt wanted to be here—"

"Very well."

"—and I wanted to top off my tanks, and I thought you might have further orders for me, Herr Standartenführer."

"Only those that I gave you earlier: to maintain an alert observation and to return to the field the moment you see the rubber boats leave the submarine."

"Jawohl, Herr Standartenführer. Sir, am I permitted to make a suggestion?"

Cranz made an impatient gesture for him to go on.

"Sir, if you flew with me, you would be much better able to see what's going on than you can from here."

Cranz considered that for a full fifteen seconds—which seemed longer—in the process looking at Schmidt and almost visibly deciding that he had survived the flight without permanent damage, then said, "Good thinking, von Wachtstein. What was it you said, 'top off' your tanks?"

"Yes, sir."

"Well, then, do that immediately. We're running out of time."

There're possibly three reasons you agreed to go along with me:

One, you may be worrying that if I'm up there by myself, I'll get on the radio and tell somebody what's happening;

And/or, two, if something does go wrong, we'll be already in the air and can just go back to Buenos Aires, leaving you out of the mess, and leaving Raschner and Boltitz to sort things out;

And/or, three, you'll now be able to tell Himmler that you personally risked your life by flying over the actual landing of the special cargo.

At seventeen forty-five, von Wachtstein, flying five hundred meters offshore and two hundred meters off the surface of the sea, saw what he thought was the periscope of U-405 slicing through the water. He looked at the beach and saw the flashes of light Boltitz was sending with his signal lamp.

A minute or so later, U-405 surfaced, then slowly turned toward the beach.

Von Wachtstein saw that the battle ensign was again flying from the platform aft of the bridge.

Men began to appear on the deck forward of the conning tower, struggling to get something up and out from inside the submarine.

And then rubber boats took shape, apparently inflated with some sort of air tank. First one, then a second, then a third.

At the sub's stern, there was the bubbling of water as the propellers were reversed. And then she stopped. Seamen put the rubber boats over the side.

Five men in black Schutzstaffel uniforms appeared on the deck. Two of them made their way carefully down the hull of the submarine, using a rope. Then a wooden crate appeared on the deck.

That's the special cargo. God only knows how much money is in that box!

With great effort, the crate was very carefully lowered into the rubber boat.

When it was in place, two men—both officers, one navy and one SS—followed it into the boat. The navy officer went to the stern of the rubber boat and jerked the starter rope of a small outboard motor. When the motor started, the boat turned away from the submarine and headed for the shore.

Von Wachtstein looked over his shoulder and saw that Cranz had a Zeiss 35mm camera to his eye.

Good God!

"I took these myself, Herr Reichsprotektor, while I was risking my life by flying overhead."

"When would you like me to land, Herr Standartenführer?"

"I'll let you know. I want to take some photos for the reichsprotektor. I'm sure he would like to see them."

"Would you like me to fly a little lower, Herr Standartenführer?"

"No!" Cranz snapped, then recovered, and added evenly, "This height is perfect for my purposes."

A minute later, the Storch encountered some turbulence, which caused the Zeiss to bump against Cranz's face.

He suddenly ordered von Wachtstein, "Okay, return to the shore and land. I will get some shots of the actual landing of the boats."

There was some more turbulence during the landing, causing the Storch to bounce twice back into the air.

"Sorry about that, Herr Standartenführer," von Wachtstein said once he'd stopped the Storch and shut down the engine. "The winds coming off the sea . . ."

Cranz wordlessly got out of the plane and trotted toward the beach.

I think I'm supposed to stay here.

But, on the other hand, I wasn't ordered to.

And if I go to the beach, "Perhaps I can be of some help to the Herr Standartenführer?"

By the time von Wachtstein got there, two rubber boats had unloaded their crates and were already making their way back to the submarine for others. A dozen men in blue coveralls were with some difficulty carrying the heavy wooden crates across the loose sand of the beach and toward the trucks.

Standartenführer Karl Cranz, Fregattenkapitän Karl Boltitz, Sturmbannführer Erich Raschner, and "Mr. Schmidt"—all in civilian clothing—were standing with a navy officer, an SS-sturmbannführer, and two SS enlisted men. They were in somewhat wet uniforms. The SS men all stood at rigid attention.

Either Cranz or Raschner is giving them hell about something.

The third rubber boat approached the beach.

"You and your men get that crate out of that boat," Cranz ordered coldly. "And I don't give a damn how wet you get! And that includes you, Sturmbann-führer!"

The SS officer gave the Nazi salute, then shouted at his men, who ran into the surf to meet the rubber boat. The SS officer splashed in after them.

I suspect the Herr Standartenführer has just taught the Herr Sturmbannführer that it is not beneath an SS officer's dignity to get one's uniform wet in the performance of his duty.

Von Wachtstein saw that the navy officer—who was in a somewhat informal uniform, with a battered brimmed cap, a sweater, and shapeless navy blue trousers—was smiling at the sight of the SS splashing around in the surf.

In that moment, as von Wachtstein—to his great surprise—recognized the navy officer, Kapitänleutnant Wilhelm von Dattenberg spotted him.

"Hansel!" he cried happily. "You sonofabitch! I couldn't believe it was you in that ugly little airplane! "

"Willi! You ugly bastard!" von Wachtstein cried back, then ran across the sand to him.

They embraced, pounding each other's back.

"I gather you gentlemen are acquainted?" Cranz said.

Neither von Dattenberg nor von Wachtstein paid any attention to him.

"They were at school together, Herr Standartenführer," Boltitz offered. "I learned they knew each other only just now."

"Herr Kapitänleutnant," Cranz said. "If I may have a moment of your time?"

Von Dattenberg looked at him but didn't speak.

"Is there any reason the rubber boats cannot stay here?" Cranz went on.

"How would I get back aboard my boat?" von Dattenberg asked jokingly. "That's a long way to swim."

"You are talking to a SS-standartenführer!" Sturmbannführer Raschner snapped.

"I'm sure the kapitänleutnant meant no offense," Cranz said, putting oil on the troubled seas.

"I meant none," von Dattenberg said to Cranz, then nodded toward Raschner, "but I take offense at *his* tone of voice."

"Easy, Willi," Boltitz said.

"You will have to understand, Herr Kapitänleutnant," Cranz said, "that

Sturmbannführer Raschner really has no idea of the stress you and your men have been under. I believe you owe the kapitänleutnant an apology, Raschner."

Von Wachtstein thought, *What the hell is Cranz up to?*

Does he want the boats that much?

He doesn't want to have a fracas in front of Schmidt?

Or for it to get back to Himmler that there was a fracas on the beach because his flunky didn't like the way the U-boat commander talked to him?

"If I in any way offended you, Herr Kapitänleutnant, I apologize," Raschner said.

Von Dattenberg nodded his acceptance.

"There are more boats on the *Ciudad de Cádiz,*" von Dattenberg said, turning to Cranz. "Could you make do with two?"

The Ciudad de Cádiz*?*

Oh, the new supply ship.

"I've been making do with none," Cranz said charmingly. "If you could spare me two, Herr Kapitänleutnant, I really would be grateful."

Von Dattenberg raised his voice.

"Everybody into one boat, we're leaving two here!"

A seaman replied, *"Ja, Kapitän."*

"And you'd better show someone how to deflate them," von Dattenberg said.

The sailor replied by taking a wicked-looking knife from his boot and waving it menacingly.

"No, you idiot," von Dattenberg said, laughing. "Open the valves."

"I can do that, Willi," Boltitz said. "I think it would be a good idea for you to put to sea."

Von Dattenberg popped to attention. *"Jawohl, Herr Fregattenkapitän.* By your leave, sir?"

"Resume your conn, Kapitänleutnant."

"Jawohl, Herr Fregattenkapitän."

Von Dattenberg then saluted, clicked his heels, and took a step backward. He turned to von Wachtstein.

"Hansel, if you remember to take a bath every day and stop trying to screw every female over the age of thirteen, maybe they'll give you a real airplane again."

"Go fuck yourself, Willi," von Wachtstein said smiling, and wrapped his arms around him again.

Von Dattenberg looked at Cranz and Schmidt, nodded his head, said, "Herr

Schmidt, Herr Standartenführer," then trotted to where his sailors were about to launch the rubber boat back into the sea.

"Smooth seas!" Cranz called a moment later.

"I'll help you deflate the rafts," von Wachtstein said to Boltitz.

There was a flicker of surprise in Boltitz's eyes, but he said nothing.

They went to the rafts. Boltitz got in and began unlashing the cover of the exhaust valve.

Von Wachtstein leaned in, as if to see what he was doing.

"Karl, if you've got a pistol, give it to me," he said softly. "And don't let anyone see."

Boltitz looked at him long enough to see that he was serious, then said, "Get in here and give me a hand, please."

Von Wachtstein climbed into the rubber boat.

Below the gunwale, out of the view of others, Boltitz handed him a Luger P-08. Von Wachtstein stuffed it in the below-knee pocket of his flight suit, then shoved a scarf into the pocket so the outline of the pistol wouldn't be seen.

"Why?" Boltitz asked.

"I think Cranz is going to kill me as soon as we're back at El Palomar."

"Why?" Boltitz asked softly.

"My skin crawled a while back," von Wachtstein said. "I'm not sure whether he's intentionally trying to make me afraid, or whether he's really going to get rid of me on the general principle of covering his ass and making himself look good. So, better safe than sorry."

"And what are you going to do?"

"If he killed me, he would have to explain that he found out about me. That would get my father hung on a meat hook."

"So would your killing him."

Von Wachtstein nodded.

"The choice, Karl, is either two dead von Wachtsteins—which would mean the end of the bloodline—or one von Wachtstein left alive and one SS sonofabitch dead. And more of them dead later."

"Hans, don't do anything impetuously," Boltitz said, then, really surprising von Wachtstein, added: "I will pray for you." He raised his voice. "Now just stand on it to force the air out, von Wachtstein. Don't jump; that will puncture the fabric."

Cranz walked up a moment later.

"Is there a reason Schmidt's men can't stand on there?" he asked. "We should be getting back to El Palomar, von Wachtstein."

"Jawohl, Herr Standartenführer."

"That sounded good, von Wachtstein, but from this moment, I again am Commercial Attaché Cranz."

Von Wachtstein nodded.

"We'll see you back in Buenos Aires, Boltitz. Make it in the morning. I think we have all done enough for the day."

[SIX]

It was a three-hundred-meter walk up an incline from the shoreline to where the Storch was parked beside the trucks. Cranz walked behind von Wachtstein, and all the way von Wachtstein was very much aware of how the Luger P-08 in the low pocket was banging against his leg.

Not because it was uncomfortable—that too, of course—but because he didn't see how Cranz could not notice it.

As they approached the trucks, the first of them moved off, and by the time they got to the Storch, only two were left.

"Good!" Cranz said, and a moment later von Wachtstein took his meaning. One of the soldiers in blue coveralls was standing ten feet away from the Storch. Beside the soldier were two twenty-liter gasoline cans.

Herr Standartenführer wants to make sure we don't run out of benzene on the way to Buenos Aires.

As von Wachtstein topped off the tanks, he was afraid the swinging bulge on his right leg would attract Cranz's attention. It didn't. Cranz was watching one of the last two trucks drive off.

The last, its doors open, was just about empty. This truck apparently would carry the rubber boats and what men remained. The others had carried off the half-dozen wooden crates and the rest of the soldiers, both those uniformed and those wearing the blue coveralls.

"Can you hurry that up a bit?" Cranz called to von Wachtstein.

"I just finished, Herr Sta . . . Cranz. We're ready to go anytime you are."

By the time they'd gotten into the Storch and taxied to the end of the landing strip, the last of the trucks was moving off. Aside from some tire and foot marks, there was nothing on the beach that would tell anyone what had happened here.

By the time the runway lights of El Palomar appeared, von Wachtstein was not nearly so afraid of being shot once Cranz was safely on the ground as he had been.

Cranz had spent almost the entire flight wallowing in the success of the operation, first thinking about it, then sharing his thoughts with von Wachtstein, as if seeking his confirmation:

"All things considered, von Wachtstein, I'd say that Oberst Schmidt did a fine job. Just about as good as a German officer could have done. Wouldn't you say?"

"I thought he did a splendid job, sir. And his men were obviously well-trained and well-disciplined."

"I don't think it would be rash to think, now, that the U-405 is safe from detection, do you?"

"I think once she reached the fifty-fathom line and submerged, sir, that she was as safe as she'll ever be."

"Zeiss makes a fine camera. I think those photographs will come out well, don't you?"

"Zeiss is a fine camera, sir, and there was plenty of light."

"The vibration—is that what you call it, 'the vibration'?—of the airplane won't make them, what, out of focus?"

"I think the speed of the exposure will keep that from happening, sir."

"I'm sure the reichsprotektor—and others, of course, as well—will be interested in the photos."

"You know what they say, sir. A picture is worth a thousand words."

"I was wondering why Sturmbannführer Raschner and Kapitänleutnant von Dattenberg took such a dislike to each other."

"Are you asking for my opinion, sir?"

"Please."

"I would say that Raschner didn't like von Dattenberg's somewhat casual uniform. . . ."

"You can hardly imagine the kapitänleutnant walking into the Kriegsmarine building dressed like that, can you?"

"No, sir. And Raschner probably thought that von Dattenberg didn't treat you with the proper respect. And on von Dattenberg's part, he is a captain, and they are kings in their castle."

"I didn't think von Dattenberg was being disrespectful, did you?"

"No, sir. I did not."

An embassy Mercedes was waiting for them—or at least for Cranz—at El Palomar. Untersturmführer Johan Schneider was driving it, and had dozed off behind the wheel while waiting for his passenger to arrive.

This was not the behavior expected of a very junior SS officer when dealing with a very senior one—even one in a happy, self-congratulatory frame of mind—as Cranz made clear the moment he saw Schneider with his mouth open and his eyes closed.

Cranz got in the backseat finally, and the Mercedes drove off.

There was just time for von Wachtstein to conclude that he wasn't going to be shot tonight when the car braked, then backed up to him.

The rear door opened.

"You'll have to excuse me, von Wachtstein. I'm a little distracted."

"That's perfectly understandable, sir."

"Get in. Where are you headed?"

"To my apartment, sir."

"The baroness is there?"

Take the chance. All he can say is no.

"No, sir. She's at the estancia. Sir, may I ask a favor?"

There was a just-perceptible pause before Cranz said, "Certainly."

"While I will make every effort to report for duty on time tomorrow, may I ask your indulgence if I were to be as much as an hour, or an hour and a half, late?"

"You want to go to the estancia, right?"

"Yes, sir. If that would be possible."

"Schneider!" Cranz ordered. "After you drop me at my apartment, you will take the Herr Major to his estancia."

"Jawohl, Herr Cranz."

"And try to stay awake, Schneider," Cranz said. He turned to von Wachtstein. "That's what's known as killing two—no, three—birds with one stone. I am simultaneously being a kind superior, rewarding a subordinate for a good day's work, and punishing another subordinate for falling asleep on duty."

"Thank you very much, sir."

[SEVEN]
Estancia San Pedro y San Pablo
Near Pila
Buenos Aires Province, Argentina
0020 24 July 1943

Von Wachtstein saw the glow of what had to be the headlights of Cletus Frade's Horch—what other car could possibly be racing down the private macadam road connecting Estancia Santo Catalina and Estancia San Pedro y San Pablo at this time of night?—long before he saw the headlights themselves.

He pulled his mother-in-law's Buick to the side of the road and threw the switch so the headlights went off and the parking lights came on.

When the approaching headlights were two or three hundred meters distant—close enough to blind von Wachtstein—they suddenly turned to dying glows, then went completely out.

What the hell!

It took perhaps twenty seconds for his eyes to regain their acuity, and then he could see very little except the patch of gravel shoulder illuminated by his parking lights.

After a moment, he got out of the Buick. He stood on the road, looking down it into the dark.

"You are alone, señor?" a familiar voice said behind him.

Von Wachtstein turned and saw Enrico, his self-loading shotgun pointing at the ground.

"You really thought I was going to ambush him, Enrico?"

"We are perhaps a kilometer from where El Coronel and I were ambushed, Señor Wachtstein," Enrico said, then added pointedly, "Either by Germans or by pigs working for the Germans."

He walked in front of the Buick and signaled into the darkness that it was all right to come closer.

The enormous Horch headlights came back on and the car approached. When it was perhaps fifty meters distant, von Wachtstein could see that Doña Dorotea Mallín de Frade was driving, and that her husband was riding on the running board next to her, a Thompson submachine gun slung from his shoulder.

When the Horch had stopped parallel to the Buick, Frade jumped to the ground.

"We're going to have to stop meeting this way, Hansel," Frade greeted him. "People will talk."

Von Wachtstein didn't reply for a moment, then he said, "At about eighteen hundred tonight, six wooden crates—each a meter long, three quarters of a meter wide, and three-quarters of a meter deep—were brought ashore from the U-405, loaded onto Argentine army trucks, then taken I have no idea where."

"My God!" Dorotea said.

"What was in the crates?" Frade asked softly.

"Almost certainly money. Probably gold and jewels, too. It's the special shipment, Clete."

"Where was this?" Dorotea asked.

"On a deserted beach near Necochea."

"Necochea's a small town on the coast," Dorotea explained to her husband, "about ninety kilometers south of Mar del Plata."

"How do you know they were Argentine army trucks?" Frade asked.

"Well, they were under command of a colonel of mountain troops, and some of them were wearing uniforms."

"That's some five hours ago," Frade said. "Too late to do anything about the goddamned submarine."

"I really hope so," von Wachtstein said.

"Excuse me?" Dorotea said.

"Kapitänleutnant Wilhelm von Dattenberg, her commander, is an old friend of mine. We went to school together."

XII

[ONE]
Office of the Director
Office of Strategic Services
National Institutes of Health Building
Washington, D.C.
0845 24 July 1943

"What brings you to work so early, Alex?" OSS Director Donovan said to Deputy Director for Western Hemisphere Operations Graham. "I didn't think you Latinos got out of bed before ten."

"With all possible respect, Mr. Director, sir," Graham said as he made a rude upward gesture with his middle finger, "I beg to inform you that I have been hard at work since about five, in order that you would find something on your desk to do when you came to work, almost certainly hungover from a late-evening—perhaps an into-early-morning—soiree with our commander in chief, his charming wife, and your dear pal J. Edgar Hoover."

"You heard about that, did you?"

"I hear about everything," Graham said. "I thought you knew that."

Donovan shook his head and asked, "You want some coffee?"

"Since I was not at all sure you would be so charmingly hospitable, I told her to bring me a cup."

Donovan smiled and chuckled and then pointed to the thick stack of eight-by-ten-inch photographs on his desk.

"I presume you have seen these?"

Graham nodded. "I watched as most of them appeared miraculously on paper in that tray of whatever chemical it is in the photo lab."

"And the lieutenant—'Flags,' nice-looking young man—where is he?"

"I sent him out to Vint Hill Farms in my car. I told him to stay loose, and my driver to stay there until he hears otherwise. Flags—Fischer—was pretty beat."

"What about him?"

Donovan's secretary came in with a simple coffee service of two china mugs and a thermos bottle on a plastic tray, set it down, then filled the mugs.

Graham waited until she had left the office and closed the door behind her before answering: "I said he was pretty beat. I should have said 'in shock.' Forty-eight hours ago, he thought he was going to be either thrown in a cell or shot, then all of a sudden he's back in Washington."

"He came here?"

"I met the B-26 that brought him up from Miami. I wasn't kidding when I said I've been up and at it since five."

"Well, the pictures came out," Donovan said. "Would I be far off if I guessed that the other young man—the handsome chap in a racetrack tout's plaid jacket with the foulard at his neck and in desperate need of a barber—is Major Cletus Frade, USMCR?"

"You never saw *Don Cletus* before?"

Donovan shook his head.

"I think I'll have that shot blown up and use it as a dartboard," the OSS director said. "Can you guess what the President—and, for that matter, Eleanor—and of course J. Edgar wanted to talk about last night?"

"What you solemnly promised Allen Dulles and me you wouldn't talk about?"

"J. Edgar is humiliated that he hasn't been able to make good on his promise to FDR that he would find out who Galahad is. I think that's why the subject came up. Roosevelt wanted to suggest to J. Edgar that J. Edgar's not as sublimely efficient in all intelligence matters as J. Edgar thinks he is."

"You did tell the President how far along his airline is?"

Donovan sipped at his coffee, then said, "And he seemed pleased."

"And by any chance did the subject of the Germans trying to buy sanctuary in Argentina come up?"

"Yeah, it did. The President asked J. Edgar what he knew about it, to which J. Edgar replied that he's working on it, and would have something on it for him soon."

"Which means he's still in the dark," Graham thought aloud.

Donovan nodded his agreement.

"About Operation Phoenix or our involvement in it?" Graham asked.

"I think J. Edgar has heard the term, but I suspect that's all he knows. I know he knows there's the program concerning the ransoming of concentration camp inmates, because I was there when Roosevelt told him he wanted to know what the FBI found out about it, and ordered him to take no action without his specific approval. I don't think he knows how deeply we're involved, or whether we're involved at all."

"Then you would say—Roosevelt would have told you—if he'd changed his mind about just letting the Phoenix program go ahead, and we'll deal with it after the war?"

"I think Roosevelt is less interested in Operation Phoenix than he is in not interfering with the ransoming operation. As despicable as that is, it keeps some Jews alive."

Graham nodded.

"Which is not to say that FDR is not interested in Operation Phoenix," Donovan said.

"Then why don't you read this," Graham said, handing him several sheets of paper, "and tell me what you think we should do about it?"

```
URGENT
VIA ASA SPECIAL


TOP SECRET LINDBERGH
DUPLICATION FORBIDDEN


FROM TEX


TO AGGIE


1—AT APPROX 1700 LOCAL YESTERDAY GALAHAD AND POPEYE
WITNESSED THE UNLOADING OF SIX (6) HEAVY WOODEN
CRATES AND HALF A DOZEN (6) SS GUARDS FROM U-405
NEAR NECOCHEA APPROX SIXTY (60) MILES SOUTH OF MAR
DEL PLATA. IT WAS ALMOST CERTAINLY THE QUOTE SPECIAL
SHIPMENT END QUOTE THE GERMANS PREVIOUSLY FAILED TO
GET ASHORE AT SAMBOROMBÓN BAY.


2—THE OPERATION WAS CONDUCTED BY STANDARTENFÜHRER
KARL CRANZ (HEREAFTER LIMBURGER), WHO OSTENSIBLY IS
GOOD KRAUT'S REPLACEMENT AT EMBASSY, AND LITTLE-Z.
```

BIG-Z HAS BEEN RECALLED AND HAS DEPARTED FOR BERLIN, LEAVING LIMBURGER AS SENIOR OSS OFFICER. GALAHAD AND POPEYE WERE NOT INFORMED OF OPERATION UNTIL IT WAS UNDER WAY AND THERE WOULD BE NO CHANCE FOR EITHER OF THEM TO TELL SOMEBODY ABOUT IT.

3—GALAHAD REPORTS THE FORCE ON THE BEACH WAS ARGENTINE ARMY MOUNTAIN TROOPS UNDER COMMAND OF A GERMAN-SPEAKING COLONEL. SOME SOLDIERS WERE IN WORKMAN COSTUMES, OTHERS IN UNIFORM. COLONEL WORE CIVVIES AND USED PHONY NAME. CRATES AND SS GUARDS WERE LOADED ONTO ARGENTINE ARMY TRUCKS THEN DRIVEN OFF TO UNKNOWN DESTINATION OR DESTINATIONS. PROBABLY, AS THEY WERE MOUNTAIN TROOPS, TO THE CHILEAN BORDER AREA IN THE ANDES MOUNTAINS.

4—GALAHAD REPORTS THAT U-405 CAPTAIN WAS KÄPITANLEUTNANT WILHELM VON DATTENBERG (HEREAFTER GUPPY) WHOM GALAHAD KNEW IN COLLEGE AND WITH WHOM POPEYE HAD SAILED IN OTHER U-BOAT. GALAHAD FURTHER REPORTED THAT GUPPY LET SLIP THAT U-405 HAD TAKEN SPECIAL CARGO ABOARD FROM SPANISH-FLAGGED CIUDAD DE CADIZ OFF FALKLAND ISLANDS APPROX TWO (2) WEEKS EARLIER. VESSEL APPARENTLY HAS BEEN CONVERTED TO REPLENISHMENT VESSEL WITH FUEL TANKS, REEFERS, CLOTHING STORES, TORPEDOES, AND SO ON.

5—GALAHAD REPORTS THE OPERATION WAS VERY SKILLFULLY PLANNED AND EXECUTED AND THAT FROM REMARKS OF LIMBURGER, GUPPY, AND OTHERS THIS WAS NOT A ONE-TIME OPERATION.

6—MY CHANCES OF FINDING THE CRATES ARE PRACTICALLY NONEXISTENT, BUT I WILL WORK ON IT. LET ME KNOW WHAT YOU WANT ME TO DO IN CASE I GET LUCKY.

7—ALSO PLEASE ADVISE IF THE CAMERA WORKED AND WHAT I
AM SUPPOSED TO DO WITH THE TOURISTS.

8—PLEASE ADVISE WHEN FLAGS WILL ANSWER THE PHONE.

TEX

Donovan looked up from the papers and said, "Well, just to be sure we know what and whom we're talking about, who's Popeye?"

"Oh, no, Bill," Graham said while wagging his right index finger for effect. "Allen Dulles and I know who he is. But so that you can look FDR straight in the eye and truthfully say you don't know who he is, we're not going to tell you."

Donovan exhaled audibly, but didn't respond directly.

"And Big-Z is von Deitzberg, right?"

"Himmler's adjutant," Graham confirmed. "SS, but he was sent to Argentina in a major general's uniform."

Donovan nodded.

"Presumably to run the smuggling operation," Graham added, "in addition to Phoenix."

"And now he's been recalled to Berlin? Any idea why?"

Graham shook his head.

"And his replacement, Limburger?" Donovan asked.

"Another member of the SS inner circle."

"Who kept both Popeye and Galahad in the dark about when and where, et cetera?"

"That's what it says."

"And the Argentine army was involved?"

"Same answer."

"How come Galahad gave Frade his friend the U-boat skipper's name?"

"Why not? What could Frade do with it?"

"And there's a new replenishment ship?"

"So it would appear."

"Can we do anything about it, now that we know the name?"

Graham shrugged, then said, "I haven't made up my mind yet whether we should. And I don't know if we can. We can't board her on the high seas. I don't understand that decision, but the President made that very clear."

Donovan looked at Graham for a long moment.

"Okay, Alex, what do you want to do?"

"Let me throw something else into the equation. Lieutenant Colonel Frogger, who's now in that VIP POW camp—Camp Clinton, in Mississippi—has been classified as a Class Three."

"Am I supposed to know what that means?"

"I had to ask. Class One is a professional officer and dedicated National Socialist. Class Two is a Nazi who holds commission; it includes all members of SS and most other officers. Class Three is a professional officer not known to be a Nazi, or to be sympathetic to the idea. Apolitical."

"And is there a Class Four?"

"An officer who professes to see the errors of his ways and is ready to do what he can to help us rid the world of those terrible Nazis."

"You don't seem to approve of the Class Fours."

"I generally don't trust people who find it easy to change sides."

"How do you feel about Putzi Hanfstaengl?"

"Putzi didn't become anti-Nazi until Adolf Hitler decided to eliminate him, now did he?"

"The President trusts him."

"FDR also trusts Henry Wallace, and I know J. Edgar has told the President that he knows Wallace is at the very least a Communist sympathizer."

"How do you know that?"

"What? That Henry Wallace is somewhat to the left of Joe Stalin, or that J. Edgar told Roosevelt that he is?"

"Either, both."

"Hoover told me. In the strictest confidence, of course."

"Not to leave this room, of course, but J. Edgar told me the same thing, in the strictest confidence, of course. And I confided—in the strictest confidence, of course—in J. Edgar that I had told Roosevelt precisely that when he picked Henry Wallace for his Vice President."

They shook their heads and smiled at one another.

"We seem to have digressed," Donovan said. "So what does this Afrikakorps lieutenant colonel's classification as a Three suggest to you that you should do?"

"You're sitting down; I can tell you," Graham said, and paused. "I'm going to bring Frade up here to see if he can enlist Colonel Frogger in our noble cause."

"Which noble cause would that be?"

"Giving his father some backbone. A conservative estimate of what's in those special shipment crates is a hundred million dollars. I suspect it's more than that. I don't want to lose track of it. And more will be coming. The key to keeping track of it is Frogger's knowledge of who the German embassy has in its pocket."

"Backbone?"

"His wife is the real Nazi in the family."

"This woman?" Donovan asked incredulously, pointing to a photo of Frau Frogger standing beside Len Fischer.

Graham nodded. "And she's been working on him to go back. I don't know whether she thinks all will be forgiven, or whether she'll denounce her husband."

"Frade's not going to let her go, is he?"

"Absolutely not. And Frogger's too smart, too scared, to think all would be forgiven."

"Then what's the problem?"

"He's a bureaucrat. He's going to take the middle ground. Tell us just enough to keep us hoping for more, but not everything he knows. We need his full cooperation; he has to be really turned. And the way to do that is through the son."

"And what makes you think the son will go along with this? You said he's been classified as apolitical."

"I don't know if he will or not. But I think we have to try."

"Alex, I don't think this is a good idea."

"That makes it two to one, Bill. You lose."

"Meaning what?"

"Allen thinks it's worth a shot."

"You talked to Dulles about this?"

Graham nodded. "I called him as soon as I saw the picture of Frau Frogger and what looks like her grandson."

"You mean Fischer?"

Graham nodded again. "Allen's original thought was that I would take Fischer and the pictures of Frogger's mother and father to Camp Clinton and between us we could turn this guy—"

"Presuming you *could* turn him," Donovan interrupted, his tone on the edge of sarcasm, "what would you do with him, take him to Argentina?"

If Graham heard the sarcasm, he ignored it along with the question.

"—but when I saw the picture of the two of them, Frau Frogger and Fischer, I realized that a nice-looking young Jewish second lieutenant like Fischer was not going to have much of an impact on an Afrikakorps lieutenant colonel. So I called Allen."

"You talked about this on the telephone?" Donovan asked, both incredulously and on the edge of anger.

Graham saw this, and his lips tightened.

"Yeah. And Allen and I also chatted about the plot to assassinate Hitler, the Manhattan Project, Operation Phoenix—"

"All right, all right," Donovan said. "Sorry."

"—and other subjects of high interest," Graham finished. "Then Allen asked me what I thought of having Frade deal with Colonel Frogger."

"He asked you that?"

"Yes, he did. He also said that if I hadn't called, he would have called me. Great minds, you may have heard, run in similar paths."

"I'm getting the feeling, Alex, that you're not in here asking my opinion of this idea of yours and Allen's, much less for permission to carry it out."

"That's because you're perceptive, Bill. Probably a result of your legal training."

"But I am permitted to ask a question or two?"

"Certainly."

"How are you going to get Frade to come here? I've always had the impression that he might ignore an order to come home. And how is he going to explain his absence to his Argentine friends?"

"Allen and I have a plan."

"Which is?"

"If I told you, you would be in a position to say, 'I told you so,' should it not turn out as well as we hope it will."

[TWO]
Office of the Managing Director
Banco de Inglaterra y Argentina
Bartolomé Mitre 300
Buenos Aires, Argentina
1650 30 July 1943

"Well, that was quick, Cletus," Humberto Valdez Duarte said as he waved Frade into his office. "We didn't expect to see you so soon."

Frade came into the office trailed by Captain Gonzalo Delgano. Frade wore aviator sunglasses, a battered long-brimmed aviator's cap, khaki trousers, an open-collared polo shirt, a fur-collared leather jacket bearing a leather patch with the golden wings of a Naval Aviator and the legend C.H. FRADE 1LT USMCR, and a battered pair of Western boots. Delgano was in his crisp SAA pilot's uniform.

They crossed the office to Duarte's desk and shook his hand.

"The message we got," Frade said, "was that you wanted to see us as soon as possible. So here we are."

"The message was addressed to you, Señor Frade," a voice said behind them. "Captain Delgano will not be required."

Frade was surprised. He hadn't seen anyone but Duarte when he and Delgano came into the office. Then he realized that the voice had come from the adjacent conference room. He walked to its doorway and looked inside.

South American Airways corporate counsel Ernesto Dowling—a tall, ascetic-looking, superbly tailored fifty-odd-year-old—was sitting near the head of a long conference table. Next to him was Father Kurt Welner, S.J., and beside the superbly tailored cleric was Doña Claudia de Carzino-Cormano, who wore a simple black dress adorned with what looked like a two-meter-long string of flawless white pearls. El Coronel Juan Domingo Perón, in uniform, was sitting at the far end of the conference table.

"Not to worry, children," Frade called to them cheerfully. "The Marines have landed and the situation is well in hand."

That earned him a very faint smile from Father Welner. No one else smiled, and Dowling looked at him with disapproval.

Either they have never heard that before, or they don't know what it means.
Or they're all constipated.

"If I'd known there was going to be a meeting of the board, I'd have worn a necktie," Frade then added.

He went to Claudia and kissed her, meaning it; next kissed Perón, not meaning it; and shook Welner's hand, telling him that the Lord's distinguished representative was again surrounded by sinners and thus had his work cut out for him.

Then Frade offered his hand to Dowling.

Fortunately, I don't know the sonofabitch well enough to have to kiss him.

And what an arrogant sonofabitch!

Delgano is SAA's chief pilot, not some flunky who can be dismissed with: "Captain Delgano will not be required."

"Captain Delgano!" Frade called. "The party's in here. We've apparently missed the champagne, but no doubt the dancing girls are on the way!"

Claudia shook her head. Everyone else seemed uncomfortable or reproachful.

I think I have just failed inspection.

Well, I'm not running for office.

Delgano came into the office.

"Sit here beside Colonel Perón and me," Frade ordered. "With a little luck, we won't have to talk to the civilians."

Perón smiled at that.

Duarte came into the room and took the seat at the head of the conference table.

"Can I get either of you coffee or anything?"

"No, thanks," Frade said. "What I'm hoping is that whatever this is won't take long, and Delgano and I can go to the Círculo Militar for a couple of well-deserved jolts of their best whiskey. We'll take you along with us, Tío Juan, if you'll pay."

Perón laughed, which earned him disapproving looks from everybody but Father Welner.

" 'Well deserved,' Cletus?" the Jesuit asked.

"Delgano and I spent the day flying."

"When I spoke with Dorotea, she said you were in Uruguay," the priest said.

Frade nodded. "Back and forth thereto. Three times. Each."

"In this weather? I could hardly see to drive in the fog."

"Lesser men could not. Captain Delgano and myself can and did. Taking with us a total of eight SAA pilots who woke up this morning holding the erroneous belief that one cannot fly across the River Plate unless there are no clouds and the sun is shining. We converted them, though, didn't we, Gonzo?"

"Yes," Delgano replied with a grin, "we did."

"And of course you and your superiors benefited," Frade said seriously.

"And how is that, Cletus?" the Jesuit asked suspiciously.

"To a man, once we were out of sight of land, they put their hands together"—Frade placed his palms together in an attitude of prayer—"and solemnly vowed to God that if He would let them land safely, they would sin no more forever."

The priest and Perón laughed out loud. Claudia and Humberto smiled.

"You've been flying back and forth to Uruguay, over the Río de la Plata, all day?" Dowling said.

Frade heard both surprise and disapproval in Dowling's voice.

Fuck you, he thought, but said, "Yes, we have. Flying's the only way to travel, Ernesto. You really should try it sometime."

"You were almost certainly uninsured," Dowling said. "I shudder to think what would have happened had you crashed, or gone lost."

That sonofabitch is not talking about people getting killed.

What he's shuddering about is money.

"Excuse me?" Frade said.

"Forgive me, Ernesto," Duarte said politely. "But what I read in that was that SAA cannot fly passengers."

"Perhaps I misread it," Dowling said, and took a pink manila folder from his briefcase and began to paw through it.

"If SAA cannot start flying paying passengers," Frade said, "and soon, we may have just a little trouble meeting the payroll."

There were no smiles, much less laughter. And nobody replied.

Frade glanced around the room. "May I ask what the hell is going on here?"

"There has been a very disturbing development, Cletus," Perón said. "Which I lay at the feet of the English."

"The *English?*"

"If this wasn't such a serious problem, Cletus, I'd be amused," Duarte said. "This will probably be a crushing blow to your ego, but Seguro Comercial, S.A., has notified us that you are not legally qualified to be flying passengers—that no South American Airways pilot is."

Frade smiled, then said jokingly, "Tío Juan, tell the nice man that I have a commercial pilot's certificate signed by the president of the Republic of Argentina himself."

Perón, who did not look amused, did not reply.

Dowling began to read from a sheet of paper he had taken from the pink manila folder.

That looks like a Mackay Radiogram.

" 'Until you are able to provide us the appropriate documentation certifying that the pilots of South American Airways, S.A., have satisfactorily completed examinations leading to the ATR Rating in Lockheed Type 18 aircraft . . .' "

Dowling stopped and looked at Frade.

" 'Lockheed Type 18 aircraft' would be the Lodestar," Dowling said, almost seeming to enjoy himself. "Correct?"

"Correct," Frade said.

Oh, shit!

Dowling's eyes fell to the paper, and he went on: " '. . . such examinations having been taken at either the manufacturer's plant or at a facility approved by the U.S. Federal Aviation Administration, the undersigned must regretfully decline to insure any South American Airways flights of Lockheed Type 18 aircraft while such aircraft are carrying passengers.' " Dowling stopped again, then added, "It's signed 'Geoffrey Galworth-Moore for Lloyd's of London.' "

"Correct me if I'm wrong, please, Ernesto," Duarte said, "but what I heard just now is that we can't get insurance to fly passengers."

Dowling considered that for a long moment.

"Yes," he said. "It does imply that they will be willing to insure us if we don't carry passengers."

"My God!" Claudia exploded. "Why should we have an airline that can't fly passengers?"

"Well, I've heard air freight is the wave of the future," Frade said flippantly. "We could move polo ponies around, I suppose. And certainly chickens."

Dowling looked as if he couldn't believe what he heard. Duarte shook his head. Perón frowned. Claudia glared at him.

"That's the sort of really stupid remark your father would make when he thought he was being clever!" she said.

Now Perón smiled.

Dowling's attitude and behavior had had Frade boiling under the skin, and now something in Claudia's attitude made him really angry. It pushed him over the edge, although he didn't realize this until he had finished replying.

With an edge to his tone, Frade blurted: "I find it just a little difficult to behave as the managing director of this airline should behave because I have no idea what's going on. You're right, Claudia. That was a flip remark, and thus stupid. It won't happen again." He looked at Humberto Duarte. "I presume the meeting has been called to order?"

Duarte raised an eyebrow. "Actually, no, Cletus. I didn't think it was necessary."

"Well, it is, and get your secretary in here to take the minutes."

"Is that supposed to be clever, Cletus?" Claudia challenged sarcastically.

"I really hope so, señora. But not clever in the sense that you have been using the term." He turned back to Duarte. "You going to get her in here or not, Humberto?"

Duarte picked up a telephone and politely asked his secretary to come right in and bring her notebook with her.

As she came through the door, Frade stood.

"Please sit here, señora," he said. "You'll be able to hear better."

She sat down.

"I'd like to sit there, Humberto," Frade said, pointing at the chair at the head of the table—which happened to be where Duarte was seated. "All right?"

Duarte's face showed he didn't at all think that it was all right, but he gave up the chair.

"Why don't you sit by Claudia?" Frade said, then sat down at the head of the table.

"Are you ready, señora?" Frade asked Duarte's secretary.

She nodded, her pencil poised over her stenographer's notebook.

There was a large glass water pitcher sitting upside down on the table. Clete pulled from his right boot a hunting knife with a five-inch blade and gave the thick glass pitcher a healthy whack.

The sound was startling.

Frade then formally announced: "This special meeting of the board of directors and of the stockholders of South American Airways, S.A., is hereby convened in the Banco de Inglaterra y Argentina building, Bartolomé Mitre 300, Buenos Aires, Argentina, at seventeen hundred hours and eight minutes on 30 July 1943 by Cletus Howell Frade, managing director."

He looked around the room.

"Also present are board members Señora de Carzino-Cormano, Señor Humberto Duarte, and Coronel J. D. Perón. Also present are Father Welner, SAA Chief Pilot Captain Gonzalo Delgano, and Señor Ernesto Dowling. There being a quorum present, I move the waiving of the minutes of the last meeting."

They were all looking at him in bewilderment that bordered on shock.

"Am I going to hear a second of the motion on the floor, or will it be necessary for me to put the question to the stockholders?"

Duarte raised his hand and softly said, "Second."

Frade nodded once. "The vote is called. All those opposed signify their opposition by raising their hands." He silently counted a three-second pause, then went on: "The chair, seeing no opposition, announces the motion carries. There being no old business requiring action at this time, the chair calls for new business. Señor Dowling, would you be so kind as to brief the board in detail on any insurance problems SAA is experiencing or may experience in the future?"

Dowling looked as if he was going to stand but then changed his mind.

"May I ask a question, Don Cletus?" Dowling said.

Frade didn't say anything but gestured somewhat impatiently for Dowling to ask what he wanted to ask.

"What did you mean a moment ago when you asked if it was going to be necessary for you to put the question of your motion to the stockholders?"

"Frankly, Señor Dowling, the question surprises me a little. As an attorney, as SAA's corporate attorney, I would have thought you would understand, even if some of the others present might be a little fuzzy on the precise details, how things are supposed to be run around here."

Frade kept eye contact with him as he let that sink in a moment, then went on: "So, for your edification, as well as theirs, the way things work around here is pretty much the way they work in the United States. I took the time to read the Argentine law on the subject."

He glanced around the table and saw that he now had everyone's rapt attention.

"The board of directors of a company like ours, as well as the managing director, are elected by the stockholders. The directors make recommendations to the managing director, and, presuming he agrees with them, he carries out what the board wants done.

"If the managing director doesn't like the recommendations of the board and doesn't think they should be carried out, he can appeal to the stockholders at the present or a future meeting of the stockholders. The stockholders can then by a simple majority of votes cast—one vote for each share of stock the stockholder owns—sustain either the managing director or the board of directors.

"I think everyone heard me convene both this meeting of the board and this meeting of the stockholders.

"Now, when I didn't immediately hear a second to my motion—the chair's motion—to waive the reading of the minutes of the previous meeting, I had two choices: either sit here and waste time while the secretary found the minutes and then read them, or take my motion to the stockholders.

"It didn't get to that. There was a second to my motion, and the board in its wisdom voted to waive reading of the minutes. If there had been no second, or after there was a second the board had voted down the motion, then the managing director would have appealed to the stockholders.

"And I'm sure the stockholders would have voted to support the managing director for the simple reason that stockholder Cletus Howell Frade holds sixty percent of the stock of this corporation."

Frade paused as he stared at Ernesto Dowling.

"Does that answer your question, Señor Dowling? And if there are no questions regarding my explanation of how things work around here, I'll presume that now everyone understands where I fit in."

There was a long silence before Perón broke it.

"You seem to be suggesting, Cletus," he said just a little uneasily, "that you can do just about anything you want to do with the company, whether or not the rest of us agree."

"Yes, sir," he said, meeting El Coronel Juan Domingo Perón's eyes. "That's pretty much the way it is."

Frade recalled a leather-skinned and leather-lunged Old Breed gunnery sergeant from shortly after he'd joined the Corps. The gunny had told Frade and the thirty other young men about to become Marine officers: *When you gotta tell somebody something they won't like, look 'em in the goddamn eye! They damn sure won't like you or what you're going to make them do any better, but they'll know you're not afraid to fuck with 'em!*

Frade had found it sage advice in his service as a Marine Corps officer and in the OSS, and had put it into practice now.

Perón shifted his gaze to Humberto Duarte, who looked both surprised and uneasy.

"Is Cletus correct, Humberto?"

"I'm afraid he is, Juan Domingo," Duarte said.

Frade slowly looked around the table. Father Welner appeared both curious and amused. Claudia Carzino-Cormano could have been angry or sad, or both. When he looked at Captain Delgano, Delgano was shaking his head in either surprise—even shock—or amusement. Ernesto Dowling looked quietly

furious. And when he returned his gaze to Perón, he saw that Perón was looking at him very thoughtfully.

"As a practical matter, of course," Frade went on, "I am delighted to defer
to the greater expertise of every member of the board. But I thought it important that all of you understand where I stand."

There was no response.

"Cletus, I'm impressed," Father Welner said. "Where did you get that mas-
tery of procedure?"

Frade saw that Perón was waiting with interest for his answer.

"From my grandfather. I watched him conduct meetings of Howell Petroleum. He's the majority stockholder." He paused. Then, without thinking first,
added: "He once told his board that they should keep in mind they were window dressing, nothing more."

Humberto Duarte and Ernesto Dowling looked almost as shocked as Claudia Carzino-Cormano.

Father Welner smiled. "He actually said that to his board, Cletus?"

"I believe it, Father," Perón said. "I know Señor Howell. He is a . . . *formidable . . . man.*"

"So Jorge led me to believe," the priest said dryly.

Frade looked at him and thought, *You're a slippery sonofabitch, Welner.*

*From that answer neither Dowling nor Delgano would suspect that my father
and my grandfather loathed and detested each other.*

And that you damn well know it.

"But I was just thinking," Perón went on, "that there's blood in here, too."

Now what the hell are you talking about?

"Excuse me?" Claudia said.

"Not only of his grandfather," Perón explained, "but of his father. Look at
him standing there, Claudia, his eyes blazing, his chin thrust forward, his hands
on his hips, just daring someone—*anyone*—to challenge his authority. That
doesn't remind you of Jorge?"

She looked and, after a moment, she nodded.

"Yes, it does," she said. "I often told Jorge he was the most arrogant man
I'd ever known."

"It is arrogance, my dear Claudia, born of confidence," Perón said. "And I,
for one, applaud it."

Claudia glared at him, whereupon Perón put action to his words: He began
to applaud. Duarte and Dowling looked at him incredulously.

Then Father Welner, smiling, clapped his hands, and, a moment later, Delgano followed. Then without much enthusiasm Duarte and Dowling joined in, and finally Claudia, with no enthusiasm at all.

I will be goddamned! Frade thought, then cut short the applause by gesturing toward Dowling and announcing, "To the business at hand. If you please, señor?"

"Well, you heard me read the radiogram we got—actually Seguro Comercial got—last night from Lloyd's of London—"

"It should be read into the minutes," Frade interrupted, "but before you do that, tell me this: Did Seguro Comercial send a letter when they sent you that cable? If so, that should be read into the record, too."

"What actually happened, Señor Frade, is that the radiogram was delivered to me when it arrived at Seguro Comercial last night."

"That sounds a little odd," Frade said. "Why would they do that?"

"I also represent Seguro Comercial, Señor Frade. I thought you knew that."

"No, I didn't," Frade snapped. "How can you represent the both of us? It seems to me you have to be either our lawyer or theirs."

"Is there some reason I cannot be both?"

"Yeah, there is. Whose side are you going to be on if we take them to court?"

" 'Take them to court'?"

"Correct me if I'm wrong," Frade said, "but we went to them for insurance. And they sold us insurance. We wrote them a very large check. Deal done. Right?"

"That was before they heard from Lloyd's of London, of course," Dowling said. "That obviously changes things."

"Not for me. Not for SAA. Seguro Comercial sold us insurance; therefore, we're insured. If Seguro Comercial can't reinsure, that's their problem, not ours. If they try to get out of our deal, so far as I'm concerned, it's breach of contract, and we'll take them to court."

"Let me try to explain this to you, Señor Frade," Dowling said, tight-lipped. "We purchased ninety days' coverage, with the understanding that the price would be renegotiated before the ninety days were up and the contract extended—"

"I wondered about that," Frade interrupted.

"Excuse me?"

"I saw the contract. It was for fourteen aircraft. We have four, and when the ninety-day period is up, we *may* have eight or ten. But not fourteen. So why are we paying to insure either four or six airplanes we don't have? I sent Señor Duarte a note asking that question."

Dowling did not reply.

Frade turned to Duarte. "Humberto, did you raise the question with Señor Dowling?"

Duarte nodded, and looked at Dowling. "I sent you a memorandum asking about that, Ernesto."

Frade said, "So what did Seguro Comercial say when you asked them, Señor Dowling?"

"I was planning to bring up the matter at renegotiation time," Dowling said, more than a little lamely.

"Señor Dowling," Frade went on, "did you not recognize that there was a flaw in the contract you negotiated between your two employers?"

"I take offense at that, Señor Frade."

"About ninety seconds ago, Señor Dowling, I was going to offer you the choice between working for SAA or Seguro Comercial. But not now."

"Cletus!" Claudia said warningly.

"What exactly does that mean?" Dowling asked.

"It means that thirty seconds ago, I decided that I don't want you working for SAA. Your employment is terminated as of now."

"You can't do that, Cletus!" Claudia said furiously.

"Yes, I can. And I just did." Frade looked at Dowling. "Good evening, señor."

Dowling stuffed the Mackay Radiogram back in his briefcase and looked at Duarte.

"Cletus . . ." Duarte said.

"Good evening, Señor Dowling," Frade repeated.

Dowling, white-lipped and with his dignity visibly injured, walked out of the conference room.

When there was the sound of the outer door closing, Duarte said, "Cletus, that was a serious mistake. Ernesto and I have been friends for years. We were at school togeth—"

"The matter is closed," Frade interrupted icily.

"You're out of control, Cletus!" Claudia said. "You simply can't do things like that."

"Will you take my word, Claudia, that I can, or are we going to have to go to the stockholders?"

"You went too far, much too far," Duarte said. "Things just aren't done that way in Argentina."

"And that's what's wrong with Argentina," El Coronel Juan Domingo Perón said.

Frade looked at him.

What the hell is this?

"Excuse me?" Claudia asked.

"I said that's wrong with Argentina," Perón said. "We do business with people we knew at school, and wink-wink when the rules are bent or broken. What we need here is what Cletus just demonstrated: an ability to see things as they are, even when that's uncomfortable, and then to make the necessary corrections without regard to personal feelings."

"I don't know what to say, frankly, Juan Domingo," Duarte said.

"Then say nothing, Humberto," Perón said, coldly angry. "Or perhaps, 'Thank you, Cletus.' "

"Thank him for insulting a man who not only is a close personal friend but one of the most respected members of the bar?"

Perón looked at Duarte a long moment with an expression that Frade thought could have bordered on contempt, then said: "If he's one of the most respected members of the bar, I shudder for the legal system of Argentina. Good God, Humberto. Didn't you hear what was said? Ostensibly as our attorney he said nothing when Seguro Comercial, *whose attorney he also is,* took our money to insure aircraft that we don't even have. Did you hear that or not?"

"I heard it, Juan Domingo, and obviously that was wrong. But there are other ways to deal with it than the way—"

"And didn't you just hear me say that the way to deal with such problems is to see them clearly—admit to them—then deal with them as brutally as necessary, paying no attention to our personal feelings?"

Duarte nodded slowly. "I heard you, Juan."

Jesus Christ, Frade thought, *where did all that come from?*

And that wasn't Tío Juan taking care of me.

He was as mad at Dowling as I was.

Frade's eyes turned to Father Welner, who was looking at him with a strange expression.

Perón said, "May I suggest, señor managing director, that we now turn our attention to the insurance problem?"

"Ernesto took the Lloyd's of London radiogram with him," Claudia said.

"Well, why not?" Frade said. "It wasn't addressed to us anyway. But we know what it said."

Perón said, "The goddamn English are behind that, Cletus. I'm sure of it."

Frade looked as if in thought, then said, "Before we turn to the problem, there's one thing I would like to do."

"I'm almost afraid to ask what that is," Claudia said.

Frade formally announced: "The chair moves the election of Captain Delgano to the board of directors."

"Splendid idea," Perón said.

"I'll take that as a second," Frade said. "Are there any other comments?"

No one said anything.

"Are there any objections?"

The handle of the knife caused the water pitcher to resonate shrilly.

"Hearing none, the motion carries," Frade said. "Welcome to the board, Gonzalo."

"I don't remember being asked if I wanted to be, as your grandfather would put it, window dressing," Delgano said.

"You didn't have to," Frade said. "I read minds."

Frade looked at Duarte. "Okay, Humberto, tell us what you think is really going on, presuming you agree with me that it has nothing to do with the qualifications of our pilots?"

"If I may, Cletus," Perón said. "As I said, the British are behind this."

"Explain that to me, please."

"Before the war, the British controlled the Argentine railroads. They were already talking back then about either taking over Aeropostal or starting their own airline. That had to be delayed by the war, but there is no question that that is still their intention. From their viewpoint—I am not among those who think the British will win this war—they see two obstacles to doing that. Varig and Pan American Grace—"

"Not Aeropostal?" Duarte interrupted.

"A moment ago," Perón said, "I said something about seeing things the way they are, not as we wish they were. As an Argentine, I am ashamed of Aeropostal. We can do better, Humberto. And you know it."

Duarte shrugged. "No argument."

"As I was saying, Cletus," Perón went on, "the English simply do not understand that England no longer rules the waves. In their ignorance, their *ar-*

rogance, they believe that as soon as the war is over—which they believe they will win—they can come back here and take control of our commercial aviation just as they did with our railroads.

"There's not much they can do about Varig and Pan American, and they're not worried about Aeropostal. But South American Airways? Better to nip that little flower in the bud—when it is easy to do so. Just step on it. How? By telling Lloyd's of London to find some excuse not to insure us."

Frade looked at Welner, who was nodding his agreement.

"You agree with that, Humberto?" Frade then asked.

"That's probably part of it, but—"

" 'Probably part of it'?" Perón parroted indignantly.

"Let him finish," Frade said curtly.

This earned him a look of both surprise and indignation from Perón, but after a moment Perón gestured regally for Duarte to continue.

"Cletus," Duarte said carefully, "I was a little surprised to learn that you have been flying back and forth to Montevideo. That is, that the Uruguayan authorities permitted you to do so."

"Why wouldn't they?"

"I heard some talk at the Jockey Club that Varig is more than a little upset that South American Airways has started up and, worse, started up with aircraft they had been led to believe they were going to get."

Frade raised an eyebrow. "I thought you weren't supposed to talk business at the Jockey Club."

"That doesn't apply to the steam bath," Humberto replied absently, then went on: "And I would really be surprised if Varig hasn't casually mentioned in passing to the Uruguayan authorities that Lloyd's of London has canceled SAA's insurance because our pilots are not qualified."

"That would seem to buttress my argument," Perón said. "Not refute it."

"I wasn't disagreeing with you, Juan Domingo, merely suggesting that there's more here than Winston Churchill having a word with some school chum at Lloyd's Coffee House. For example, I wouldn't think Señor Juan Trippe of Pan American Airways was thrilled to learn he will have competition from another Argentine airline. And I don't think he would be above trying to do something to inconvenience us."

Duarte and Perón quietly looked at each other a long moment.

Frade thought: *This problem can be solved overnight by messaging Graham that FDR's airline is about to be shot down by an English insurance company or by Juan Trippe—or by both.*

But if the problem suddenly went away, how could that be explained?

That would cause the OSS's head to pop out of the gopher hole.

Okay. So we get insurance from the same place Eastern Airlines and Transcontinental and Western Airways get theirs.

And where is that? I don't have the foggiest fucking idea.

Has to be America—so the solution is we get American insurance.

And how to do that?

There's nothing wrong with our airplanes. They're brand-new Lockheeds.

We're back to the pilots. Nobody is going to write insurance on us if they think our pilots are a bunch of wild Latinos who learned to fly last week.

And that brings us right back to getting ATRs for our pilots.

"Gonzo," Frade said, "how much time do our pilots have?"

Perón and Duarte looked at him in curiosity.

"That would depend on the pilot, Don Cletus," Delgano said.

"How many have a thousand hours of multiengine time?"

"Maybe a dozen, possibly a few more than that."

"And how many of that dozen speak English?"

"Most of them have enough English to fly."

" 'Enough English to fly'?" Perón parroted.

"Mi coronel, English is the language of air traffic control in Uruguay and, in large matter, Brazil and Chile, as well. We've all flown there."

"Why is the language of air traffic control English?" Perón challenged, as if this offended him personally.

"I don't really know, mi coronel," Delgano replied as if this outrage was his fault.

"The solution to this little problem of ours," Frade said, "is to get American insurance, and the way to do that is to get our pilots an American ATR rating."

Now everyone, including Claudia, was looking at him as if he had lost his mind.

"Anyone got a better idea?" Frade asked.

"How are you going to get our pilots this rating?" Delgano asked. "Where?"

"At the Lockheed plant in Burbank."

"Where?" Perón said.

"California. Burbank is in California."

"You're serious, aren't you?" Duarte asked.

"Yes, I am."

"May I play the devil's advocate?"

"Go ahead."

"To do that, you of course would have to get our pilots to Burbank, California."

Frade nodded and motioned impatiently with his hand *Get to the point.*

"To get them to California," Duarte went on, "they would need two things. First, a visa. And if the English—and, for that matter, Mr. Trippe—have the influence to get Lloyd's of London not to insure us, isn't it possible they have the influence to suggest to the U.S. government that giving visas to a dozen Argentine pilots is a bad idea—"

"I take your point, Humberto," Frade interrupted, and thought, *I didn't think about that; you're probably right.*

"—inasmuch as the time and effort to train them could be better spent, for example, training their Brazilian allies," Duarte went on to sink his point home.

And Graham could fix that, too, except that would see the OSS's ugly head again popping out of the gopher hole.

Frade said, "What's the other thing you think we would need to get our pilots to Burbank?"

"A means of getting them there," Duarte said. "Do you think Mr. Trippe might suggest to the American Embassy in Rio de Janeiro—which issues the priorities necessary to get on any Pan American flight to the States—that there are more Americans or Brazilians deserving of a priority than some Argentines?"

Frade didn't immediately reply because he couldn't think of anything to say.

And again Duarte drove home his point: "And there is no other way but Trippe's Pan American Airways to travel by air to the U.S., which means we're talking of at least three weeks' travel time by ship, and that's presuming you could get the necessary visas . . ."

"Is that all that the devil's advocate can think of?" Frade said.

"Isn't that enough? I don't like it, Cletus, but I'm following Juan Domingo's idea that we should see things the way they are, rather than as we wish they were."

Frade nodded. "True, but"—*Where did this come from?*—"there are two flaws in the devil's argument."

"Never underestimate the devil, Cletus," Father Welner said.

Jesus, is he serious?

"Are there really?" Duarte said.

"First of all," Frade went on, "Pan American is not the only way to fly to the States. The Lodestars were all flown down here; there's no reason one couldn't be flown back."

"Could you do that?" Perón asked.

"It is possible, mi coronel," Delgano said.

Frade added, "And it would also solve the visa problem. Aircrews don't need visas."

"They don't?" Perón asked dubiously.

Delgano shrugged. "We don't need them to fly to Chile, Brazil . . . anywhere. I can only presume the same is true of the United States."

"It is," Frade said with certainty.

I have no idea if that's true or not.

The first question that comes to mind is whether I can call twelve guys sitting in the back "aircrew" just because they're pilots.

But I have to run with this until I can get a message to Graham.

"When can you leave, Cletus?" Perón asked.

"At first light the day after tomorrow. It will take us that long to prepare. Right, Gonzo?"

Delgano nodded.

"Well, there you have it, Humberto," Perón said.

"Excuse me, Juan Domingo?"

"An hour ago, I saw no solution to this problem," Perón said. "And now, thanks to Cletus, we have one."

Frade studied Perón.

Does he believe that?

Then Frade announced: "There being no other new business, is there a motion to adjourn?"

"So moved," Claudia Carzino-Cormano said.

"Second?"

"Second," Duarte said.

"Are there any objections? Hearing none, the motion carries, and this meeting is adjourned."

He rapped the water pitcher with his knife again.

[THREE]
Estancia San Pedro y San Pablo
Near Pila
Buenos Aires Province, Argentina
2030 30 July 1943

Enrico had insisted on driving, so on the long ride to the estancia, Clete had the opportunity to think about what had happened, what was probably going to go wrong, and what difficulties he was likely to—or certainly would— encounter.

Heading the latter category was the reaction of Doña Dorotea Mallín de Frade on her learning (a) that her husband very shortly was going to fly to the United States, (b) that he didn't know how long he would be gone, and (c) that, no, she couldn't go along with him.

His lady greeted him at the door. He kissed her.

"You're just in time for dinner, darling. Why do I suspect that's either pure coincidence, or that you've done something really awful, and this is your way of making amends?"

"A lot's happened, baby. I've got to message Graham, and I'd rather do that before we eat."

"And are you going to tell me what's happened?"

"How about I write the message, you run it through the SIGABA, and then I answer the questions you're certain to have?"

She nodded.

"I did a random network check about an hour ago," she said as they went inside and closed the door. "The Collins is up."

"And you know how to operate it. That's more than I know how to do."

"That's because I'm smarter than you are, darling."

She waved him down the corridor toward the study.

Twenty minutes later, Clete watched as Dorotea thoughtfully and methodically tore into six-inch lengths the long tape that had run though the SIGABA device.

"What are you thinking, baby?" he finally asked.

"That there has to be a better way to get rid of the tape than tearing it into

pieces," she said matter-of-factly, "then taking it onto the verandah and burning it. But so far—"

"That's all?"

She met his eyes.

"That, and that you can take the portrait of your mother with you to give
to your grandfather."

"Excuse me?"

"The one in the upstairs corridor in your Uncle Guillermo's house on Libertador."

"*Grand*uncle Guillermo," he corrected her automatically. "I have no idea
what you're talking about."

"There is a portrait," she explained patiently, then spread her arms wide to
illustrate the size, "a large oil portrait of your mother. It's hanging in the upstairs corridor in your *Grand*uncle Guillermo's house. You grandfather wanted
it. I gave it to him. There was no way he could take it with him. I tried to ship
it, but that proved impossible. The war, don't you know? You can fly it with you
to the United States. Do you understand now?"

"That's all you've got to say about my going to the States?"

"What is there to say? You obviously have to go, for the reasons you gave
in your message to Colonel Graham. And, as obviously, I can't go with you for
a number of reasons, including of course our Nazi houseguests."

[FOUR]
4730 Avenida del Libertador
Buenos Aires, Argentina
2030 31 July 1943

"In the best of worlds," Dorotea said as the Horch rolled up to the massive iron
gates of the house across the street from the hipódromo, "we would be living
here, and your beloved Tío Juan would be living somewhere, *anywhere*, else."

"That thought has run through my mind," Clete said.

"I am really offended at what he does in what I think of as our first bedroom," Dorotea said. "And I suspect he suspects that."

"Why?"

"When I called to tell him we would be coming over to get the painting, he said that he was so sorry he would not be here to receive us; that he had a dinner engagement."

"Maybe he just had a dinner engagement."

"Ha!"

The gates were opened and the Horch drove into the basement garage. There in the garage was a 1940 Ford station wagon and a 1938 Ford coupe, but Perón's official Mercedes was nowhere in sight.

"Good!" Dorotea said. "He's not here. Now I won't have to smile and pretend to be charmed."

"You're sure it's here? The portrait?"

"I called and checked on that, too. I also told the housekeeper to find a well-worn comforter or two and some twine to pack it."

"And while you and Enrico are doing that, I think I might have a glass of my nice wine. Presuming he left me some."

"Would you be shocked to hear, my darling, that I was just now trying to think of some reasonably tactful way to keep you from offering your expert advice as to how I might better pack the portrait?"

"You want a glass?"

"I'll wait, I think, until we're in the house we have to live in because Guess Who is living here. But thank you just the same."

"Cletus! I think you'd better come up here!"

"Yes, my love."

He was sitting, his legs stretched out before him, on one of the eight high-backed chairs that lined the walls of the foyer. He pushed himself out of the chair, drained his glass of merlot, set the empty glass on a side table, then trotted up the wide stairs to the second floor.

When he got there, he saw a large flat object leaning against the wall. It was cushioned with what had to be at least two well-worn comforters held in place by what looked like three hundred feet of sturdy twine.

Dorotea and Enrico were nowhere in sight.

Uh-oh! She's in the bedroom!

Two significant things had happened to Clete in the master bedroom of the mansion.

The first involved two Argentine assassins-for-hire who had tried to elimi-

nate Cletus Howell Frade on behalf of the German government while he slept
in his granduncle's bed. They had failed—and died for their efforts—but not
before killing the housekeeper, who happened to be Enrico's sister.

And shortly thereafter, in the same bed, the former Señorita Dorotea Mallín had not only lost her right to the title of the Virgin Princess but had become
with child.

It was this last that made Clete worry about what she was up to in the
bedroom—now Tío Juan's bedroom. Clete would not have been surprised to
find her doing something really outrageous.

*Or, more likely, she has already done something outrageous—and now I have
to make it right.*

At first, Clete didn't fully comprehend what he was looking at.

Dorothea was standing at the head of bed and Enrico at the foot. She was
holding the Leica I-C 35mm camera in one hand.

Dorotea said, "Maybe you better do this, darling, and I'll hold the map flat."

"What map?" Clete said.

"This one," she said unnecessarily. "I found it in that thing." She pointed
to a meter-long leather tube that he recognized as an Ejército Argentino map
case. "It's off the coast south of Mar del Plata. There are marks and notes on it
around Necochea. I'll bet when Peter sees the photo I'm making, he'll say it's
where the submarine landed. Isn't that interesting that Tío Juan would have a
map of that area?"

"Why the hell did you go in his map case?"

"You don't want to know."

"Yes, I do."

She looked at him unapologetically, then said, "I thought maybe it would
contain something naughty." She paused. "But this is better, isn't it?"

"It is if he doesn't walk in on us taking a picture of it."

"Well, then take the damned camera and make the picture!"

The rolled map would not go back in the case. There was something else inside that stopped it.

"Baby, when you took out the map, was it by itself or rolled with something else?"

"There was another map, of South America, rolled around it."

Clete, not without effort, got the map of South America out of the map case
and unrolled it on the bed.

"Now give me that one, sweetheart," he said, motioning for the first one that they'd photographed. He casually glanced at the second map. "Wait a minute. What the hell is this?"

He looked more closely, and saw clearly that it was a map of the South American continent. But something about it did not look right.

The map bore a label stating that it had come from the Map and Topographic Office of the Supreme Command of the Wehrmacht in Berlin. It was labeled VERY SECRET and carried the title *Sud-Amerika Nach der Anschluss.*

"Oh, shit!"

That translates as "South America, After the Annexation"!

He scanned the map and noticed that Uruguay and Paraguay no longer existed as sovereign countries; they now were part of Argentina, much as Austria had become part of Germany *Nach der Anschluss.* The map also showed Peru and Bolivia divided more or less equally between Argentina and Brazil.

"What is it?" Dorotea said.

"It's why Tío Juan hopes the Germans will win the war. Put a fresh roll of film in the camera, honey. I want to take pictures of this to Washington, too."

XIII

[ONE]
Office of the Director
Office of Strategic Services
National Institutes of Health Building
Washington, D.C.
1425 1 August 1943

"Waiting to see me, Alex?" the director of the Office of Strategic Services inquired of the OSS deputy director for Western Hemisphere operations, who was sitting in an upholstered chair in Donovan's outer office, holding a copy of *The Saturday Evening Post.*

"Oh, you are a clever fellow, aren't you? You take one look at someone and you can tell just what they're up to."

"I asked him if he wanted to go in, General Donovan," Donovan's secretary said, just a touch self-righteously.

Donovan signaled for Graham to go into his office, then turned to his secretary. "Bring me and the Latin Bob Hope here some coffee, will you, please, Margaret?"

"I've never been called that before," Graham said.

"And I'm sorry I did," Donovan said. "I hope Hope doesn't hear about it. I really like him."

Graham waited until Donovan took his seat behind his desk, then handed him a manila folder stamped TOP SECRET in red.

"I hope this is good news," Donovan said.

"As far as I'm concerned, it is," Graham said, and sat in one of the two leather armchairs facing Donovan's desk.

Donovan opened the folder and read the message.

```
URGENT


TOP SECRET LINDBERGH
DUPLICATION FORBIDDEN
2100 LOCAL 30 JULY 1943


FROM TEX


TO AGGIE


SEGURO COMERCIAL IS ABOUT TO INFORM SOUTH AMERICAN
AIRWAYS THAT SINCE LLOYD'S OF LONDON HAS REFUSED TO
REINSURE SAA THEY ARE FORCED TO CANCEL OUR
INSURANCE.

LLOYD'S REASON FOR REFUSING TO REINSURE IS THAT OUR
PILOTS DO NOT HOLD US AIR TRANSPORT RATINGS.
STRONGLY SUSPECT THAT LLOYD'S GOT THEIR INFORMATION
ABOUT OUR PILOTS FROM CERTAIN INDIVIDUALS AT VARIG
WHO THINK THAT SAA'S LODESTARS SHOULD HAVE GONE TO
THEM, AND WHO NOW ARE TRYING TO CUT OFF COMPETITION.
```

IT IS EQUALLY PROBABLE THAT PAN AMERICAN, EITHER
INDEPENDENTLY OR WORKING WITH THOSE AT VARIG, HAS
ALSO MENTIONED OUR NON-ATR-RATED PILOTS TO LLOYD'S
BECAUSE THEY DON'T WANT ANY COMPETITION EITHER.

TIO JUAN THINKS THAT THE BRITISH ARE INVOLVED IN THE
CANCELLATION, EITHER ALONE OR IN CONJUCTION WITH
VARIG AND/OR TRIPPE, BECAUSE THEY PLAN TO RUN
ARGENTINA'S AVIATION AFTER THE WAR THE WAY THEY RUN
THE ARGENTINE RAILROADS AND WANT TO NIP COMPETITION
IN THE BUD.

WHILE IT SEEMS PRETTY CLEAR TO ME THAT OUR FRIEND IN
SWITZERLAND PROBABLY COULD FIX THINGS WITH LLOYD'S,
AND THE MAN WHOSE AIRLINE IDEA THIS WAS CERTAINLY
COULD DO SO, HAVE THEM BUTT OUT REPEAT HAVE THEM
BUTT OUT UNTIL I HAVE A CHANCE TO TRY TO FIX THIS
MYSELF.

FORCING LLOYD'S TO REVERSE ITSELF WOULD NOT ONLY
ANNOY THEM, WORD ALSO WOULD GET OUT ABOUT IT AND
THEN QUESTIONS ASKED ABOUT WHO IT IS THAT'S LEANING
ON THEM. NO DOUBT VARIG AND PAN AMERICAN WOULD BE
ANNOYED AND PROBABLY WOULD START ASKING THE SAME
QUESTION. THAT WOULD CERTAINLY SCREW UP THINGS FOR
ME AND SAA BOTH IMMEDIATELY AND IN THE FUTURE.

UNLESS I AM GIVEN SOME GOOD REASON NOT TO DO SO, I
INTEND TO FLY FOURTEEN (14) SAA PILOTS TO BURBANK AS
SOON AS POSSIBLE, PROBABLY WITHIN THIRTY-SIX (36)
HOURS, AND GET THE PILOTS THEIR ATRS. AS I DOUBT
THIS WILL SATISFY LLOYD'S OR SEGURO COMERCIAL FOR
REASONS STATED ABOVE, I WILL HAVE TO GET SOME U.S.
INSURANCE COMPANY TO INSURE SAA. ANY IDEAS?

TEX

"Two questions," Donovan said when he had finished reading. "Why do you think this is good news? FDR will have a fit when he hears about it."

"You said two questions?"

"This is dated two days ago. You just got it?"

"I got it two days ago. I was waiting for the second message I just gave you"—he gestured toward the manila folder—"the one you chose to ignore."

"I didn't see the second message," Donovan said as he went back into the manila folder, found the message, took it out, and began to read it:

```
URGENT


TOP SECRET LINDBERGH
DUPLICATION FORBIDDEN
1000 LOCAL 1 AUGUST 1943


FROM COWGIRL


TO AGGIE


TEX AND FRIENDS LEFT FOR BURBANK 0645 TODAY


TEX BRINGING WITH HIM PHOTOS OF TWO VERY INTERESTING
MAPS OF THIS AREA


EL JEFE AND I HOLDING THE FORT AND CARING FOR
TOURISTS


COWGIRL
```

Donovan looked up from the sheet. " 'Cowgirl'?"

"The feminine of 'cowboy.' Taking a wild guess, Señora Dorotea Mallín de Frade."

"She knows too much, period."

"They're newlyweds; he tells her everything. And beneath her really extraordinary beauty there is a highly intelligent and very, very tough young woman."

Donovan looked past Graham a long moment as he considered that. "Okay.

I'll take your word for it. Now, tell me why you think this is good news. The maps?"

"I have no idea what they are."

"Then what, Alex?"

"You think Juan Trippe is capable of going to Lloyd's?"

Donovan thought about that for perhaps two seconds, then nodded. "Yeah, Juan's capable of that. Especially if he heard, and I'm sure he has, that the airline in Argentina is Roosevelt's idea."

"You think he's heard?"

Donovan nodded again. "He's heard that an Argentine airline is starting up. Hell, that was in the newspapers down there. And then he wondered where they were getting their airplanes. And then he wondered how neutral Argentina was getting Lodestars that allies—for example, Canada and Mexico—would love to have. Who would have the authority to order that besides FDR? Sure, he knows."

"What about Varig going to Lloyd's?"

"Same story. They wanted the Lodestars. Argentina got them. 'Let's knock off the competition before it gets off the ground.' " He paused. "I heard the pun. Unintentional. It just came out that way."

"And the Brits? Do you think somebody there, wanting to make sure nobody else starts an airline in Argentina before they get around to it, went to Lloyd's?"

"Why not? All of the above."

"What about Allen Dulles? Do you think he might have gone to Lloyd's?"

"Why would Allen want to do . . . ? Alex!"

Graham nodded, then explained: "As part of the Air Transport Rating examination, there is a cross-country flight. Frade will be one of the first pilots to take the check-ride. His flight will take him to Jackson, Mississippi, which is a half-hour's car ride from Camp Clinton."

"You've got the whole damn thing set up."

"I did the setup. But it was Allen's idea. He really wants to turn Colonel Frogger—"

"All this to track the Operation Phoenix money in Argentina?" Donovan interrupted.

"I suspect there probably is more, but Allen didn't say anything."

"And you didn't ask him?"

"Allen does things one step at a time. If Frade can turn Frogger, and there is more, I suspect Allen will tell me."

"Why not now?"

Graham shrugged. "Of the three of us, who would you say really knows what he's doing?"

Donovan could have taken offense, but he didn't. Instead, he said, "Point taken." After a moment's silence, he asked, "When does this happen?"

"Sometime in the next thirty-six to forty-eight hours they'll have to land in Mexico to get permission to enter the United States. Probably Nogales, maybe Sonora."

"You don't know?"

Graham shook his head.

"Allen's idea. Frade believes everything he sent in that message. If he doesn't know anything, he can't let anything slip. Anyway, the Air Force's North American Air Defense Command, which issues the clearance to enter U.S. airspace—and normally would issue it to an airliner of a neutral country in maybe an hour—has been told to wait five hours. That'll do several things. It will almost certainly give the pilots with him—at least one of whom is an Argentine intelligence officer taking notes—a chance to witness Frade showing genuine frustration and maybe even losing his temper."

Graham took a sip of his coffee, then added, "And it will give me a little time to get out to Burbank."

He drank again from the cup, then said, "The permission will finally come, and they'll fly to the Lockheed plant in Burbank, where they will not be expected, and will be met by indignant and curious immigration officers and by curious Lockheed officials who more than likely will be annoyed. Frade and his group won't be arrested, but they will be escorted to their hotel by an immigration officer and told not to leave it until everything is cleared up.

"Sooner or later, somebody at Lockheed is going to call the War Production Board and ask what to do with the SAA pilots who have just dropped in on them unexpected and uninvited—"

"How do you know they'll do that?" Donovan interrupted.

"Because, if they don't, Howard Hughes will tell them to do so."

"Howard Hughes is in on this?"

Graham nodded. "But only him."

"How much did you have to tell him?"

"Only that I needed a favor. He knows Frade, you know."

"You told me that."

"Anyway, when somebody at Lockheed calls the War Production Board, there will be a couple of hours' delay and then someone will tell Lockheed to do whatever South American Airways wants done."

"And how do you know that will happen?"

"Julius Krug, the chief of the War Production Board, knows that the air-line is Roosevelt's idea."

"There's a long list of things that could go wrong in that scenario, Alex."

"O ye of little faith!"

"But even if nothing goes wrong, what if Frade can't turn the Afrikakorps colonel—?"

"*Lieutenant* Colonel Wilhelm Frogger," Graham furnished. "If Frade and Fischer—and of course me—can't turn him, then because he will have heard too much to be allowed to go back in the POW cage, I'll have to decide what to do with him."

"I don't like the sound of that. He's entitled to the protection of the Geneva Convention."

"If that gets to be a real problem—which means if *he* does—we'll talk again about his having an accident. But right now I'm thinking of sending him to the Aleutian Islands, where he can sit out the war with our homegrown Communists."

"You're serious?"

"There would be a certain poetic justice in that, don't you think? A devout Nazi being guarded by American Communists?"

"Before you do that, Alex, I'll want to talk about it again."

Graham shrugged, then drained his coffee cup.

[TWO]
Lockheed Air Terminal
Burbank, California
1805 4 August 1943

Clete had moved into the Lodestar's pilot's seat as they had approached the U.S.–Mexican border. He decided that it would be better to have an American voice—and one familiar with American procedures—dealing with the en route controllers and the Lockheed Terminal tower than a Spanish-tinged one who didn't really know what he was doing.

And as there were military air bases all over Southern California, he had also thought it possible, even likely, that they would be intercepted by Air Force or Navy—or even Marine—fighters because someone hadn't got the word about an Argentine airliner having been cleared to enter the country. He knew how to talk to another American fighter pilot; none of the others did.

But no fighter had appeared off his wing, and when he called the Lockheed Terminal tower for approach and landing instructions, the air traffic personnel matter-of-factly gave them to him.

When Frade turned the Lodestar on final and felt he could finally relax, a warning message came from a remote corner of his brain:

Not yet, stupid.

You've come too far to get sloppy at the last minute and dump the airplane on landing.

If Lindbergh—probably then as tired as I am now—had dumped the Spirit of Saint Louis *while trying to land at LeBourget, he wouldn't have been remembered as "Lucky Lindy, America's Hero."*

No, he'd now be remembered—or forgotten—as just one more crazy man who had tried and failed to complete a flight across the Atlantic.

I'd bet dollars to doughnuts that when Lindbergh was on final to LeBourget, he told himself, "Careful, Charley, don't fuck it up now!"

Ninety seconds later, Frade greased the Lodestar in. For a moment he was elated, but then he had the further presence of mind to tell himself: *And not yet either, stupid. You won't be finished until they put the wheel chocks in place. You really don't want to run over the Follow-Me truck before you're parked.*

Three minutes later, when the ground handler signaled that he should cut his engines, and he had done so without anything falling off or blowing up, he smiled at Delgano.

"Gonzo, we have apparently cheated death again."

Delgano smiled back and shook his head, then started to unfasten his shoulder harness.

Clete decided, with an audible sigh, that now he *really* could relax.

Then he looked out the side cockpit window and saw that ground handlers were not the only people who had met the Lodestar. There were assorted uniformed police, Border Patrol officers, two Military Policemen, and several other men in business suits waiting to greet the visitors from Argentina.

[THREE]
The Chateau Marmont
8221 Sunset Boulevard
Hollywood, California
1950 4 August 1943

The convoy of three mostly identical 1942 Chevrolet Carryalls—truck-based vehicles that could be described as station wagons on steroids; one white, two black, and all bearing U.S. government license plates and with the legend FOR OFFICIAL USE ONLY painted on their doors—was stopped in the eastbound lane of Sunset. The Carryalls waited until there was a break in the flow of traffic, then turned left and rolled up a steep side street, then immediately into a drive- way and stopped.

The passenger door of the lead truck, the white one, opened. A stocky man in a light brown military-type uniform, complete to Sam Browne belt and a hol- stered Colt .45 ACP revolver, got out. The epaulets on his uniform carried the twin silver bars of a captain. The patch on his shoulder was stitched: UNITED STATES OF AMERICA BORDER PATROL.

"Okay, gentlemen," the Border Patrol captain said as he folded down the back of the front seat, "here we are."

Cletus H. Frade got out first. He was unshaven and he otherwise showed the effects of having spent most of the previous ninety-six hours flying across the South American continent, over Central America, and finally from Sonora to Burbank.

Frade looked around the dark and cool brick parking area. "And where is here? *What* is here?"

"This is where you'll be staying until we get your status cleared up," the cap- tain said.

"That sounds like we're under arrest," Clete challenged.

"You're being detained," the captain said. "I told you that at the field. There's a difference."

"What is it?"

Delgano and two other pilots climbed out of the back of the Carryall.

"If you leave the hotel grounds," the Border Patrol captain explained, "you'll be *arrested* and taken to the Los Angeles County Jail. It's not nearly as com- fortable as the Chateau Marmont."

"*Chateau Marmont*"? Frade thought.

Christ, this is a high-dollar Hollywood starlet hotel.

And either it's my ears still ringing from the flight, or he mispronounced its name.

He said it like it was that yellow-bellied groundhog, the marmot.

But it's built like a French manor, and pronounced, Chateau Mah-MO.

What in hell are we doing here?

Frade said, "What exactly has to be cleared up?"

"I told you that, too, Mr. Frade. For these gentlemen, why they have no visas."

"And I told you, they're aircrew, they don't need visas."

"And you were told, Mr. Frade," the Border Patrol captain went on, his voice suggesting he was about to lose his patience, "that for our purposes, aircrew are people actually involved in flying the airplane. Being able to fly the airplane doesn't count." He paused. "And in your case, Mr. Frade, you have to clear up why you don't have a draft card, or a certificate of discharge from the Armed Forces, and why your passport doesn't show when you left the United States. For all we know, you could have sneaked out of the U.S., probably via Mexico, and gone to Argentina to dodge the draft."

"Wait a damn minute . . ." Frade began, then stopped himself.

I'm screwed. . . .

I didn't get my American passport stamped because I went down there on my Argentine passport.

But I can't tell you that because that would open the dual-citizenship can of worms.

And I don't have a draft card or a discharge because I am a serving officer of the U.S. Marine Corps.

But I can't tell you that, either, because Delgano and the other SAA pilots would hear me. And even if I did say it, you'd probably never look past this long-haired Argentine haircut that my wife so loves—and the last damn thing a Marine would have.

And then there's my OSS area commander's badge. I can't show you it because (a) you probably wouldn't know what the hell it was and (b) I don't want Delgano or anyone else to see it.

So, all things considered, Clete ol' boy, what you should do is just keep your mouth shut until you can get on a telephone and call Colonel Graham.

If you weren't so goddamned tired, you would have thought of that before you got into an argument with this guy.

The Border Patrol captain looked at Frade, waiting for him to go on.

"Do whatever it is you were about to do," Frade said.

"May I have your attention, please, gentlemen?" the Border Patrol captain said, raising his voice. "If you'll gather around me, please?"

He waited until they had done so, then said: "This is the Chateau Marmont Hotel, where for the next day or two you'll be housed as the guests of the Lockheed Aircraft Company. You are not permitted to leave the hotel grounds, and you are not permitted to use the telephone or send a telegram or a letter. You will not be permitted visitors. If you violate any of these simple rules, you will lose your status as 'detainees' and be arrested, handcuffed, and taken to the Los Angeles County Jail for illegal crossing of the United States border.

"My advice, gentlemen, is to enjoy Lockheed's hospitality until your status can be cleared up. If you've done nothing wrong, you have nothing to worry about. Welcome to Los Angeles and the United States."

He waved them toward a wide, shallow, curving flight of stairs that apparently led to the hotel's interior.

[FOUR]

The room to which Frade was taken was more like a small apartment—*a real apartment*, he thought, *not a hotel apartment.* It had a comfortable bedroom, a complete kitchen with a full-size refrigerator and gas stove, a dining table that could easily seat six, and a large, well-furnished living room—which made him wonder what the Chateau Marmont was really all about.

The refrigerator held a half-dozen bottles of beer, and he grabbed one by the neck, opened it, and took a healthy swallow. Then he sat at the table.

He realized that he was really exhausted and that that had caused him to almost lose his temper. Twice. Once, about being "detained," and, the second time, when the customs officer had made the crack about him possibly being a draft dodger.

Well, I didn't, thank God.

And I got everybody here from Buenos Aires.

So, after I finish this beer, I'll grab a shower, then get in the rack, and when I wake up, I'll be full of piss and vinegar and able to decide rationally what to do next.

I'm not really in trouble. And my ace-in-the-hole is Graham. I'd call him now if I wasn't convinced the Border Patrol hadn't cut off the phones.

As he finished his beer, he glanced at the telephone beside the table and, just to be sure, put the phone to his ear. It was dead.

He gave the finger in the direction of the front door, the Border Patrol captain being somewhere the other side of it, and then went into the bedroom, found his toilet kit, and went into the bath and took a long shower and then shaved.

He decided that a second bottle of beer was in order, and wrapped a towel around his waist and went into the kitchen and opened the refrigerator. There were three bottles of beer in it.

I'd have sworn there were a half-dozen the first time I was in here.

He took one of the remaining bottles and looked for the opener.

Where did I put the goddamn bottle opener?

He went to the stove to open the bottle using the edge of the stove. When he sort of squatted to see that he would open the bottle and not break its neck, the towel around his waist fell to the ground.

He rather loudly uttered a lengthy vulgar and obscene curse in the Spanish language, then with the heel of his hand knocked the cap neatly off the bottle.

He had just put the bottle to his lips when a familiar voice said, "Unless you knew better, you'd never guess that that sewer-mouthed, naked man in dire need of a haircut was a Marine officer, would you, Howard?"

"Oh, I could," another male voice said. "You can always tell a Naval Aviator by the tiny dick and huge wristwatch."

Frade snatched the towel from the floor, wrapped it around himself again, and went into the living room. There the mystery of the missing beer bottles was explained, as was the missing bottle opener.

Colonel A. F. Graham, USMCR, was seated in an armchair and holding one of the bottles. Howard Hughes, sitting in a matching armchair across the coffee table from Graham, held another bottle. The opener was on the table between them.

Hughes wore scuffed brown half-Wellington boots, stiffly starched khakis, a crisp white-collared shirt, and an aviator's leather jacket. Even slumped in the armchair, it was clear that he was a commanding and confident figure: a tall— if somewhat sinewy—ruggedly handsome man with slicked-back black hair and deeply intelligent eyes.

"How goes it, Clete?" Hughes said casually in a clearly obvious but not thick Texas accent. "Long time no see."

"Hello, Howard," Frade said, then looked at Graham. "Good evening, sir."

"I'll be goddamned," Hughes said. "He's so surprised he's almost polite."

"I didn't expect to see you here, Howard."

"With Alex, you mean?" Hughes asked.

Clete nodded. "Or him, either."

"I'm the reason you're here with him," Hughes said.

"What?"

"Alex was out here about—what, Alex? A year ago?"

"Fourteen, fifteen months," Graham furnished.

"Doing what?" Frade asked.

"That's none of your goddamn business, Clete," Hughes said with a smile. "Particularly since that Border Patrol guy thinks you're a draft dodger."

"You heard that?"

"Alex and I were playing house detective in the lobby," Hughes said, and mimed holding up a newspaper to hide his face. "Anyway, Alex was here a little over a year ago, and I told him I had just thought of something, and asked him if he remembered Cletus Marcus Howell from the trial. . . ."

"I'm afraid to ask, but what trial?"

"Right after my father died, my goddamn relatives were stealing me blind. I was a minor; they had themselves appointed my guardians, and they headed right for the Hughes Tool cash box. Your grandfather saw it, didn't like it one bit, and neither did A. F. here. So I borrowed from your grandfather the money I needed for lawyers and we went to court. Your grandfather and A. F. told the judge what an all-around solid citizen I was, wise beyond my years, and got me liberated—"

"*Emancipated,*" Graham corrected him. "Declared an adult."

"Right. Anyway, I saw your picture in the L.A. *Times.* You'd just made ace on Guadalcanal. It made me think, so I told Alex about your Argentine father, and since Alex was in the spy business—"

"You know about that?" Clete blurted.

"Yeah, I know about that. What did you think Alex was doing out here, chasing movie starlets?"

"As a matter of fact . . ." Clete said.

"*Watch it,* Major," Graham said, but he was smiling.

"Are you going to tell me what's going on?" Clete asked.

"You look kind of beat, Clete," Graham said. "You sure you want to do this now?"

"I am beat. But as beat as I am, I know I'd never get any sleep not knowing . . ."

"Okay. Your call." Graham took a sip of his beer, clearly composing his thoughts, then went on: "Roosevelt has decided—and, for once, I agree with him—that the best way to deal with Operation Phoenix is not to try to stop it but, instead, to keep an eye on it and grab the money, et cetera, once the war is over."

Clete had just enough time to be surprised that Howard Hughes was privy to Operation Phoenix when Hughes confirmed it:

"Otherwise," Hughes said, "they'd just find some other way to get the money in. Nobody ever accused Bormann, Göring, Goebbels, and Company—or, for that matter, Franklin Roosevelt—of being stupid. Many other pejoratives apply, but not 'stupid.' "

Graham chuckled and went on: "And Allen Dulles thinks you—and the Froggers—are the key to doing that. He thinks the key to getting the Froggers to help, really help with Phoenix and more, is to go to Mississippi and turn their Afrikakorps son. More important, Allen thinks you're our best hope to turn him."

"I don't have any idea how I would do that," Clete said.

"So far," Hughes offered, "you've turned one Kraut with the Knight's Cross of the Iron Cross and another Kraut who works for Canaris. . . ."

"You told him that?" Clete blurted angrily.

Graham didn't reply.

Hughes added: "You're obviously pretty good at turning Krauts. So why should turning the one in Mississippi be so difficult?"

Frade looked at Graham, who went on: "So the problem was to get you to the States without raising any more suspicions in Colonel Martín's fertile mind. And Allen said the way to do that was not to tell you anything was going on until you got here. He was betting that you would understand the only way to get around the problem of your pilots not having ATRs was to get them rated, and since the only place you could do that was here, you'd figure out some way to get them—and you—here without making anybody suspicious. And he was right. Again."

"Allen Dulles was behind Lloyd's canceling our insurance?" Clete asked incredulously.

Graham nodded.

"I'll be damned!" Clete said admiringly.

"I don't think I want to play poker with Dulles," Hughes said.

"What are the maps Dorotea was talking about?" Graham said. "And, incidentally, I sent her your love and told her that you arrived safely. A radiogram to South American Airways. She'll get it, right?"

"I have trouble picturing you as a happily married man," Hughes said.

"That's because you haven't seen her," Clete said to Hughes, then looked at Graham. "Yeah, she'll get it. Thanks."

"The maps?" Graham pursued.

"God, I forgot about them. We went to my Granduncle Guillermo's house to pick up a picture of my mother that my grandfather wants. Perón is staying there. He wasn't there when we were, but Dorotea saw an Argentine army map case and took the maps from it. One shows the coastline south of Mar del Plata where U-405 . . ." He looked at Hughes. "You know about that, too, Howard?"

"I know everything," Hughes said.

"Of course," Clete said, then picked up where he'd left off: ". . . where U-405 landed the special shipment, which means that Perón knew all about it."

"That surprised you?" Graham asked.

"Yeah, a little. Even after I've had time to think about it."

"Dorotea said 'maps,' plural."

"The other one was from the Oberkommando of the Wehrmacht. It shows South America 'after the annexation.' Paraguay and Uruguay are shown as provinces of Argentina."

"Zimmerman," Graham said thoughtfully. "That's interesting."

"What?" Clete asked.

"Stranger things have happened," Graham said, as if to himself. Then he asked, "Where's the film?"

"In my toilet kit."

Graham said, "You have some place where it can be developed right now, Howard?"

Hughes rose gracefully from his armchair, walked to a closet, unlocked it, reached inside, came out with a telephone, and, putting the phone to his ear, leaned on the doorjamb.

"We need a little room service," he announced into the telephone, then put it back, closed the door, and locked it.

He saw the look on Frade's face.

"We couldn't take the chance that one of your pals would catch you trying to get Alex on the phone," Hughes explained. "And Alex was worried what kind of a hooker you'd get if you tried that."

Frade gave him the finger.

A moment later, there was a knock at the door and someone called, "Room service."

Hughes opened the door to a stocky man wearing a white cotton waiter's jacket, and motioned him into the room.

The man looked expressionless but carefully at Frade.

"Get your film, Clete," Hughes ordered.

"Is this guy room service or not?" Clete asked.

"You're hungry?" Graham asked.

Frade nodded.

"Tell them to start serving dinner," Hughes ordered the man. "Bring three here. And then take a film cassette the gentleman in the towel is about to give you out to the studio. Have it souped. I want prints large enough to read. And I want them yesterday. Bring the film back with you. Got it?"

"Yes, Mr. Hughes," the man said, and turned and looked at Frade again.

Clete went to the bathroom, took the film cassette from his toilet kit, and started to return but changed his mind. He got dressed first, then went back to the living room. The "waiter" still stood where he had been standing.

Clete handed him the film cassette.

"And when you bring my dinner . . ." he began, then looked at Hughes. "Do I have any choices?"

"The usual jailhouse fare," Hughes said.

Frade turned back to the waiter. "Bring a bottle of Jack Daniel's and a good bottle of merlot or pinot noir."

The man looked at Hughes for direction.

"That," Hughes added, "and a bottle of gin and some ice and a martini mixer, or shaker, or whatever they call it. Serve wine with the others' meals, but no hard stuff. I don't want anybody finding the liquid courage to start a jailbreak."

"Yes, Mr. Hughes."

"You heard me say I want those prints yesterday?"

"Yes, Mr. Hughes."

The man turned and left the room.

"What did you say before?" Clete asked Graham. " 'Zimmerman'?"

Graham shook his head in exaggerated disappointment. "You were apparently asleep during Modern American History 101 at our alma mater. You really don't know?"

"No, I really don't know."

"Neither do I, Alex," Hughes said. "And I very nearly finished high school. What the hell are you talking about?"

"In 1917, the British had a cryptographic operation they called 'Room 40.' Big secret, because they had broken the Imperial German diplomatic code—"

Hughes interrupted: "Like the Navy has broken the Imperial Jap Navy Code?"

"You didn't hear that, Clete," Graham said furiously. "My God, Howard!"

"Well, you said we were going to tell him about Lindbergh and Yamamoto; he'd have heard that then," Hughes said unrepentant.

Frade looked from Hughes to Graham and back again.

Lindbergh? Lucky Lindy?

And who? Yamamoto, the Jap admiral?

Graham shook his head and went on: "And one day in January 1917, Room 40 broke a message that Zimmerman, the German foreign minister, had sent to Count von Bernstorff, the German ambassador in Washington, with orders to forward it to the German ambassador in Mexico, a man named von Eckhardt."

"What was in the message?" Frade asked.

"Two things. That Germany was going to resume unrestricted submarine warfare as of the first of the month. And that Eckhardt was to tell the president of Mexico that if Mexico declared war on the United States, after the war—which Germany would win, of course—Mexico could have Texas, New Mexico, and Arizona."

"You're pulling my leg," Hughes said.

"No, I'm not. You really never heard this before?"

"No, I haven't. You, Clete?"

"This is all news to me."

Graham shook his head in disbelief, then went on: "So the Brits, after thinking about it for a month, decided to tell us, even though they knew this would mean the Germans would know they had been reading their mail."

"And what happened?" Clete said.

"Then President Wilson sat on the telegram for a week, before finally releasing it to the press on March first. The American people were furious, and a lot of them seemed more annoyed with Mexico, who hadn't said a word to us about the telegram, than with the Germans. Anyway, a month after that we declared war on Germany."

"I'll be a sonofabitch," Hughes said indignantly. "Those goddamn Mexicans!"

Graham laughed. "See what I mean? 'All's fair in love and war,' Howard. Write that down."

"You think they're trying to pull the same thing again, with Argentina?" Hughes asked.

"On the way up here," Clete said, "I wondered if Tío Juan had really been careless, or whether he wanted me to find those maps."

"Tío Juan? This Argentine colonel?" Hughes asked, and when Clete nodded, added, "Why would he do that?"

"It's a long way up here from down there," Clete said. "I thought of a lot of possibilities."

There was a knock at the door and a new voice called, "Room service."

This time there were two "waiters" who entered the room. They could have passed as brothers of the first "waiter." They were pushing a food cart and a smaller cart holding an assortment of bottles, an ice bucket, an array of glasses, and a martini shaker.

Clete lifted one of the chrome domes over a plate and saw that it covered a hot turkey sandwich, which explained the very quick service.

"Everybody gets the same thing?" he asked.

Hughes nodded.

"That should be interesting," Clete said. "They don't have turkeys in Argentina. . . . Or cranberry sauce."

"I didn't think about that," Graham said.

"Not a problem. If they're as hungry as I am, it won't make any difference."

And then Clete's brain went off on a tangent:

Maybe I could raise turkeys on Estancia San Pedro y San Pablo.

They're probably no harder to raise than chickens.

Build some pens.

Hell, let 'em run loose.

They hunt wild turkey in Alabama.

That might be fun.

Hell, why not get some pheasants, too?

What about foxes? Do we have foxes down there, some other predator that would eat my turkeys and pheasants?

What the hell am I doing?

Am I that tired, that my brain goes off the track?

Or is it shutting down?

"Are you going to eat that, Clete?" Howard Hughes inquired. "Or just stand there holding that chrome thing and looking at it?"

"I think I just fell asleep standing up."

"You want to just forget talking, Clete?" Graham asked.

"Let's see what a healthy jolt of Jack Daniel's does for me," Clete said, and reached for the bottle and a glass, then poured three fingers of whiskey.

Hughes jerked his thumb at the waiters, signaling them to leave. Both said, "Yes, Mr. Hughes."

When they had left the room Clete said, making it a question: "You seem to be pretty well known around here, Howard."

Hughes shrugged but didn't reply.

"You were saying Colonel Perón wanted you to see those maps?" Graham said.

"I think that's possible," Clete said.

"Why would he want to do that?"

"All kinds of possibilities," Clete said. "The bottom line to all my thinking on the way up is that my Tío Juan is a lot smarter than I've been giving him credit for being."

Graham grunted. "I tried to make that point to you."

Frade raised his glass in a gesture of a toast, took a long sip of the drink, and when he'd swallowed and exhaled, went on: "Too smart—knowing Dorotea and I were going to the house—to leave something incriminating just lying around where I was likely to find it. And I thought that he's smart enough to have put a hair or something in the lid of the map case that would tell him it had been opened."

"You're right, Alex," Hughes said. "Our little Cletus has developed a real feel for the spy business, hasn't he?"

"Fuck you, Howard," Clete said sharply, raising his glass in Hughes's direction in another mock toast, and taking another drink.

Hughes looked at him coldly.

"What did you say?" he asked incredulously after a moment.

"You're out of line, Howard," Graham said. "Clete, when I told him what I think of you, what Allen Dulles thinks of you, it was complimentary. The phrase 'Little Cletus' never came up."

Unrepentant, Hughes blurted: "I've known him since he was in short pants, for God's sake!"

"That was a long fucking time ago, Howard," Clete said. "I'm a big boy now. The next time you say something like that to me, I'll knock your goddamn teeth down your throat."

Hughes assumed a boxing position. "Just a precaution, Major Frade, sir, in case you don't take this as a compliment."

"What?"

Hughes moved his fists and his feet around like a boxer.

Clete fought off the temptation to smile.

Hughes went on: "Boy, he's really the old man's grandson, ain't he, Colonel Graham, sir?"

"Oh, shit," Clete said, and laughed.

"I would take that as both a compliment and an apology, Clete," Graham said.

"Still, I think I'd rather whip his ass," Clete said, but he was smiling.

Graham, also smiling, asked, "Can we now get back to the spy business?"

"I'd *much* rather whip Howard's ass," Clete said.

"Be that as it may, Major Frade," Graham said, "you were about to tell us why you think Perón wanted you to see what he had in his map case."

Frade sipped at his glass, shrugged, then said, "There's a lot of possibilities, but as absurd as this may sound, I think he might be trying to turn me."

"That's interesting," Graham said. "Why would he want to do that?"

"He's got all of his ducks in a row but me," Clete said. "He's the *éminence grise* behind the president now, and—"

"When I knew him he didn't know what that meant," Hughes said.

"God damn it, Howard!" Graham snapped. "Enough. And I mean it."

Hughes threw up both hands in apology and surrender.

Clete looked at Hughes, shook his head, and went on, "—there's no question in my mind that he wants to be president, and probably will be."

"How much of a Nazi do you think he really is?" Hughes asked.

"I think he really believes that fascism, National Socialism, whatever, would bring some really needed efficiency to Argentina, but I don't think he thinks the Germans are going to win the war any more than I do."

"Really?" Graham asked softly.

"And I think the Germans have cut him in for a piece of the action in Operation Phoenix. I don't know if he's involved in the concentration camp inmate-ransoming operation or not. Or even if he knows about it."

"Serious question, Clete," Hughes said. "If you're in his way, why doesn't he take you out?"

"He's my godfather. They take that seriously down there. That's one reason. The second reason, probably, is that my father was very popular there, and if I were to get whacked, a lot of questions would be asked about who did it and why. Everybody knows the Germans had my father killed and had a shot at killing me. They'd be suspect. But if I had to bet, I'd bet on the godfather busi-ness. I think the sonofabitch really likes me."

"But you don't like him, right?" Hughes said. " 'The sonofabitch.' Why?"

"For one thing, he's a dirty old man."

"How so?"

"He likes young girls."

"So does Errol Flynn," Hughes said. "He almost went to jail last year for diddling a couple of fifteen-year-olds. He's still a good guy. What does it say in the Good Book? 'Judge not, lest ye be judged'?"

"Tío Juan likes them younger. Like thirteen."

"*That's* a dirty old man," Hughes agreed.

"Is that really it, Clete?" Graham asked. "You disapprove of his morals?"

"That's part of it, certainly. I just don't like him."

"Your father did. And I'm sure he knew of the colonel's proclivities."

"Yeah, he knew. Enrico told me. Maybe it's because he likes me. That makes me uncomfortable. I met the sonofabitch for the first time when I first went down there, and he treats me like the beloved nephew."

"Or maybe the son he never had?" Graham pursued.

Clete considered that a moment, then said, "Well, maybe. Can we get off this subject? Tell me about Lindbergh and Yamamoto."

"Roosevelt hates Lindbergh," Hughes said. "Which may be—probably is—why he wants you to start an airline."

"I don't understand that at all," Clete said.

"You want to tell him, Alex?"

"You tell him," Graham said.

"Okay," Hughes said. "Lindbergh was big in the America First business. They didn't think we should get involved in a European war or, for that mat-ter, with the Japs."

"So was my grandfather an America Firster," Clete said. "And so was Sen-ator Taft. And Colonel McCormick, and a lot of other people. So what?"

"But Roosevelt couldn't get Senator Taft. Or your grandfather. Or Colonel McCormick. Or, for that matter, me. But Lindbergh left himself wide open when he went to Germany. Göring gave him a medal, and Lindbergh said the Germans had the best air force in the world."

"You're saying Roosevelt thinks Lindbergh is a Nazi?" Clete asked incredu-lously.

"No, I don't think that," Graham said. "What I think is that Roosevelt likes to get revenge on people he thinks have crossed him. And he can take it out on

Lindbergh. America First went out of business when the Japanese bombed Pearl Harbor."

"On December eighth," Hughes said, "Charley Lindbergh—'Lucky Lindy,' America's hero, whose wife's father is a senator and who's a colonel in the Army Reserve—volunteered for active duty. Never got the call. Roosevelt had told Hap Arnold that he was not to put Lindbergh back in uniform, period."

"Easy, Howard," Graham cautioned.

"Jesus Christ!" Clete exclaimed.

"Colonel McCormick was going to put this story on the front page of all his newspapers," Hughes said. "Lindbergh asked him not to. He said it was personal between him and Roosevelt, and it wouldn't help us win the war. He said he could make himself useful out of uniform."

"How?"

"He went to work for Lockheed," Hughes said.

"What's your connection with Lockheed?" Clete said. "You own it?"

"I own TWA—which, by the way, I renamed from Trans-Continental and Western to Trans-World Airlines, to annoy Juan Trippe—and there's a law that if you own an airline you can't own an aircraft factory, so I don't own Lockheed."

"What's the point of that?" Clete asked. "I never heard that before."

"There are some critics of our commander in chief," Hughes said, "who feel Roosevelt had that law passed to punish Juan Trippe, who had the bad judgment to hire Lindbergh after Lindbergh gave his professional opinion that the Luftwaffe was the best air force in the world. I mean, what the hell, compared to Roosevelt, what did somebody like Lindbergh know about the Luftwaffe?"

"I didn't know Lindbergh worked for Trippe," Clete said.

"In addition to being a hell of a nice guy, Charley is a hell of a pilot and a hell of an aeronautical engineer," Hughes said. "He not only laid out most of Pan American's routes in South America for Trippe, but worked with Sikorsky to increase the range of the flying boats. You didn't know that?"

"I heard he'd been in South America," Clete said. "I didn't know what he was doing."

"Anyway, Trippe's smart enough—particularly after Charley pointed it out to him—to understand that flying boats are not the wave of the future. So he wanted to take over Don Douglas's Douglas Aircraft. Roosevelt heard about that and had the law passed. Trippe had the choice between owning Pan American and getting a monopoly on transoceanic flight or buying Douglas. He chose Pan American, and having got the message, fired Charley. Politely, of course, but fired him."

"Jesus Christ!"

"I gave him a job at Lockheed—"

"I thought you don't own Lockheed," Clete interrupted.

Hughes ignored the interruption. "—where he went to work on increasing the range of the P-38. There are some people who suggest that I had something to do with the design of the P-38."

"I heard you had a lot to do with the design of the Jap Zero," Clete said. "I remembered that when I got shot down by one of them."

Hughes ignored that, too, and went on: "Charley went to the Pacific, to Guadalcanal, as a Lockheed technical representative—"

"Lindbergh was on Guadalcanal?"

"Meanwhile, the Navy in Pearl Harbor, having broken the Jap Imperial Navy Code, was reading their mail. They knew—"

"Be careful here, Howard," Graham said.

Hughes nodded his understanding. "They knew that Yamamoto made regular visits to Bougainville in a Betty—you know about Bettys, don't you, ace? Two of your seven kills were of that not-at-all-bad Jap bomber—in what he thought was complete safety because Bougainville was out of range of our fighters."

Graham made a *Slow it down* gesture, and Hughes nodded.

"Well, I just happened to overhear a rumor that the range of the P-38 was greater than anyone thought it was because of the efforts of a certain Lockheed tech rep on Guadalcanal. And I just happened to mention this to a mutual friend of ours, also a Texan, when he was out here chasing starlets.

"And, lo and behold, the next thing we hear is that on the eighteenth of April, Admiral Isoroku Yamamoto, commander of the Combined Fleet of the Imperial Japanese Navy, was shot down—and killed—by Army Air Force P-38s operating out of Henderson Field on Guadalcanal."

Hughes paused and looked at Graham.

"Did I say anything I wasn't supposed to, Alex?"

"Not yet."

"A couple of weeks after that," Hughes went on, "I was in Washington and ran into an old pal of mine—"

"Whose name you are not at liberty to divulge," Graham interrupted.

Hughes nodded. "—who has a lot of stars on his shoulders and I know personally admires Charley. And I asked him if he knew what Charley had done on Guadalcanal, and he said he didn't want to talk about that, so I asked him what did he think would happen if I went to Colonel McCormick and told him what I knew.

"He said that after Yamamoto had been shot down, he'd tried to bring up the subject of Charley to—"

"Watch it, Howard," Graham said.

"—to a man who lives in a big white house on Pennsylvania Avenue—"

"Oh, God, Howard!" Graham said, shaking his head.

"—and was, so to speak, shot down in flames. This *unnamed man* told him—and this is where it gets interesting—that he was going to tell him what he had told Juan Trippe no more than an hour before: 'It would be ill-advised to ever raise Lindbergh's name to me again.'

" 'Me,' of course, meaning—"

"He knows who you mean, Howard," Graham said with a sigh.

"So, cleverly assembling the facts, Alex and I concluded that Juan Trippe went to this unnamed man and told him, considering what Charley had done to knock the head Jap admiral out of the war, that it was time to forgive him. An hour later, Ha . . . *my friend* went there and offered the same argument. This man is not known to appreciate being shown where he has made an error in judgment.

"And the next day, or maybe the day after, he told Wild Bill Donovan to set up an airline in South America, no reason given," Hughes concluded.

"Does General Donovan know about this?" Clete asked.

"General Donovan is very good at figuring things out," Graham said.

"But he hasn't said anything to you, right?" Hughes asked Graham.

"He probably knows that Juan annoyed FDR and is being punished with South American Airways," Graham said, "but I don't know if he knows Hap— oh, hell, the cow's out of the barn—if he knows Hap Arnold also went to Roosevelt. And he hasn't told me because I would be liable to tell Howard—Wild Bill refers to Howard as my Loose Cannon Number One—"

"Guess who's A. F.'s Loose Cannon Number Two, Clete," Hughes interrupted, laughing.

Graham finished: "—who would be capable of going—even likely to go— to Colonel McCormick and telling him (a) what Lindbergh did vis-à-vis Yamamoto and (b) what FDR did in grateful appreciation."

"What I'd like to do is go whisper in Alphonso's ear," Hughes said.

"God damn it, don't even joke about something like that," Graham said furiously.

" 'Alphonso'?" Clete asked.

"The A in Senator Robert A. Taft's name stands for Alphonso," Hughes said. "That's a secret right up there with Leslie Groves's superbomb."

Graham looked at Hughes almost in horror, then his eyes darted to Clete.

Clete said, "I don't know who—what did you say, 'Leslie Groves'?—I don't know who she is, but I know about the superbomb."

"Who *she* is?" Hughes said, laughing. "Clete, the *guy* who runs the Manhattan Project is a barrel-chested gray-haired major general named Leslie Groves."

"Allen Dulles told you about the Manhattan Project?" Graham asked.

Clete nodded.

"He somehow neglected to mention that to me," Graham said.

"Maybe he thinks you're a loose cannon," Hughes said.

Graham flashed him an angry look.

"He also told me about some German ex-Nazi in the Hotel Washington," Clete said. "Tell me about him."

"He did tell you how secret the Manahattan Project is, I hope," Graham said.

Clete nodded, then said, "Tell me about the German in the Hotel Washington."

Graham said, "You're thinking he might be useful in turning Colonel Frogger?"

"I don't know. It looks to me as if I need all the help I can get. What about him?"

"I'm somewhat embarrassed that I never thought about this at all," Graham said. "What did Allen Dulles tell you about Hanfstaengl?"

"That he was an early supporter of National Socialism," Clete said, "and became a pal of Hitler, a member of the inner circle. Then he got on the wrong side of Martin Bormann or Goebbels or Göring or Himmler—or all four—who didn't want him close to Hitler. Somebody warned him that one of the above—or maybe Hitler himself—was going to have him whacked, and he got out of Germany just before that was going to happen, and came here and looked up his college chum, FDR, who installed him in the Hotel Washington, where he tells Roosevelt what Hitler and friends are probably thinking."

Graham nodded and said, "That's the story."

"You sound like you don't believe it," Hughes said.

"I have trouble believing people who change sides," Graham said.

"If Clete thinks he'd be useful, and he probably would be," Hughes said, "we could pick up ol' Putzi in Washington and take him with us to Mississippi. Or take the Kraut with the funny name to Washington to see Putzi."

"Ol' Putzi would probably be useful"?

Howard knows about this guy?

Not only knows about him, but sounds as if he knows him.

"We could pick up ol' Putzi and take him with us to Mississippi"?

"Who is 'we' and 'us'?" Clete asked. "As in '*we* could pick up ol' Putzi and take him with *us* to Mississippi'?"

Graham started to reply, then stopped.

"I don't have the Need to Know, right?" Clete said.

"What's going to happen now, Major Frade," Graham said, "is that you're going to bed before you fall asleep standing up again. You will be awakened at eight, and informed that the Immigration Service people will pick you up in the driveway at nine and return you to Burbank."

"And what's going to happen when we return to Burbank?"

"That's what I'll decide before you return to Burbank," Graham said.

"Why can't you tell him now?" Hughes protested.

"Tell *either one* of you now?" Graham asked, and then answered his own question. "Because I just realized that both of my loose cannons would probably approve of what I'm thinking, and when that happens I want to really be careful."

He stood.

"Good evening, Major Frade," he said. "Try to get a good night's sleep. Whatever ultimately happens tomorrow, I suspect it will be a busy, busy day." He turned to Hughes. "Let's go, Howard. And if you're even thinking about sending somebody to keep Clete company, don't."

He walked to the door. Hughes pushed himself out of his chair and walked after him.

XIV

[ONE]
Grand Reception Room
Embassy of France
Cerrito 1399, Buenos Aires, Argentina
2205 4 August 1943

German Ambassador Manfred Alois Graf von Lutzenberger, attired in the splendiferous gold- and silver-encrusted diplomatic uniform prescribed for ambassadors of the Third Reich, stood with First Secretary Anton von Gradny-Sawz, whose uniform was only slightly less laden with gold thread embroidery. They were holding champagne stems and making polite conversation with Mexico's ambassador to the Republic of Argentina, José Enrico Tarmero.

Despite von Lutzenberger's smile, he was having unkind thoughts about many things, starting with Ambassador Tarmero's uniform, which outshone his own.

Then there had been Tarmero's inquiry.

The Mexican ambassador had asked the German ambassador if he could offer—in confidence, of course—his opinion of the ultimate effect on the war of King Victor Emmanuel having dismissed Benito Mussolini and then appointed Marshal Badoglio to replace him.

Von Lutzenberger had thought: *The simple answer to your question, you stupid man, should be self-evident.*

The King understands the war is lost and wants to salvage whatever he can, then dodge, as well as he can, the wrath of the Allies.

I would not be at all surprised to learn that as we stand here dressed like characters in a Hungarian comic opera—in this grand reception room in the embassy of what pretends to be a neutral sovereign state but is in fact Axis-leaning—officers of the American OSS are meeting with Badoglio—probably in Rome, maybe in the Vatican—discussing with him the capitulation of Italy.

And with that in mind, Mister Ambassador, I dare to suggest that your question is something less than diplomatic.

But what von Lutzenberger had told the ambassador was that, in his opinion, once it became evident that Italy could not function without Il Duce, particularly when it came to throwing the British and the Americans off Sicily, Mussolini would be restored to power.

Von Lutzenberger also had unkind thoughts about the minister extraordinary and plenipotentiary of the United States of America to the Republic of Argentina, who, while standing across the room under the magnificent chandeliers and before a portrait of Napoleon, had had the gall to raise his champagne stem and smile.

But, von Lutzenberger told himself, the American ambassador was nodding and smiling at Tarmero—not at von Lutzenberger.

One does not nod at the ambassador of a nation with which your nation is at war.

Von Lutzenberger glanced again at the American ambassador.

In a pig's ass he's smiling at Tarmero!

The sonofabitch is smirking at me!

And his gottverdammt *smirk is asking, "Heard about Sicily, Mr. Ambassador of the Third Reich? Or about Il Duce getting the boot? Getting the message, are you?"*

And what's particularly galling is that he has every right not only to smirk but also to mock me and just about every other ambassador in the room by his dress. He is in white tie and tails, rather than any sort of diplomatic uniform. And there is nothing whatever—no silken sash nor ornate decorations, not even miniature medals of any kind—on his jacket or sleeves or anywhere else to suggest his rank or even his nationality.

He looks as if he could be a gigolo or a headwaiter.

But what he is—and everybody knows it, including this moron of an ambassador from Mexico—is the representative of the most powerful nation on earth, which inevitably will be the ultimate victor of the second world war to end all wars.

Von Lutzenberger drained his glass and put it on a table.

And if I have any more of this splendid champagne—which, aside from pâté de foie gras, is about the only thing the French do well—I am almost certain to make an ass of myself.

I have to think of some way to get out of here without violating any diplomatic protocol.

Now, how the devil am I going to do that?

Not quite thirty seconds later, the problem was solved.

Assistant Consul Johan Schneider—wearing civilian clothing, of course—

was being led to him by a young man who was almost certainly one of his French peers—that is to say, a junior officer on the French ambassador's staff.

I wonder if he suspects that Schneider is an SS-untersturmführer?

Schneider announced: "I regret the necessity, Excellency . . ."

Von Lutzenberger tried but failed to shut him off with a gesture.

". . . of this interruption," Schneider plunged ahead, "but there has been an important communication from—"

"I understand, Herr Schneider," von Lutzenberger cut him off abruptly, thinking, *It certainly is not Ambassador Tarmero's business to know from whom I have an important message, and possibly none of Gradny-Sawz's.* "And where is this communication?"

"—from Berlin," Schneider plunged on, and then patted his chest.

Von Lutzenberger gestured impatiently for Schneider to hand over the message.

Schneider took a gray manila envelope from his jacket pocket and handed it to von Lutzenberger, who then looked at Tarmero and Gradny-Sawz.

"Will you be so kind, gentlemen, as to excuse me for having to answer the call of duty?"

He didn't wait for a response. He gestured for Schneider to follow him and went to the men's room. He had been in the French embassy often enough to know where it was, and also that it would reek of perfume to mask the odors from the plumbing, which apparently had been installed about the time of the Franco-Prussian War and not repaired since.

It was not occupied.

Thank God. Now I won't have to go in one of the indoor pissoirs.

"Don't let anyone else in," von Lutzenberger ordered.

"Jawohl, Excellency," Schneider said, and stood beside the door, prepared to defend the men's room with his life.

Once von Lutzenberger was inside, despite what he had originally decided not to do, he went into one of the stalls, which did indeed smell like a pissoir on the Champs-Élysées, and latched it closed before he tore open the gray manila envelope.

It contained a white letter-sized envelope stamped MOST SECRET and closed with an official stamp, not unlike a postage stamp, across which, following the protocol, Schneider had written his name.

Von Lutzenberger tore it open, took out several sheets of paper, and began to read them.

CLASSIFICATION: MOST URGENT
CONFIDENTIALITY: MOST SECRET
DATE: 4 AUGUST 1943

FROM: PARTEILEITER MARTIN BORMANN
     NATIONAL SOCIALIST GERMAN WORKERS PARTY
     BERLIN

TO: IMMEDIATE AND PERSONAL ATTENTION OF THE REICH
AMBASSADOR TO ARGENTINA, BUENOS AIRES

HEIL HITLER!

WITH REGARD TO THE MATTER OF COMMERCIAL ATTACHÉ
WILHELM FROGGER AND FRAU GERTRUDE FROGGER IT HAS
BEEN DECIDED BY THE PARTEILEITER, ADMIRAL CANARIS,
AND SS-BRIGADEFÜHRER VON DEITZBERG ON BEHALF OF
REICHSFÜHRER-SS HIMMLER THAT THE PRESS OF DUTIES
UPON OUR FÜHRER ADOLF HITLER IS SUCH THAT THIS
MATTER SHOULD NOT BE BROUGHT TO HIS ATTENTION
AT THIS TIME SO THAT OUR FÜHRER CAN DEVOTE HIS
FULL ATTENTION TO BRINGING GERMANY TO FINAL
VICTORY.

CONFIDENTIAL AND UNOFFICIAL CONFERENCES BETWEEN
CANARIS, VON DEITZBERG, AND THE UNDERSIGNED HAVE
REVEALED ASPECTS OF OUR OPERATIONS IN ARGENTINA
BEARING UPON OPERATION PHOENIX AND OTHER MATTERS
THAT WERE NOT KNOWN, IN THE INTERESTS OF SECURITY,
TO OFFICIALS OF THE GERMAN EMBASSY OR TO ALL OF THE
SIGNATORIES HERETO. SPECIFICALLY:

THE UNDERSIGNED HAS FOR SOME TIME EMPLOYED FRAU
GERTRUDE FROGGER AS HIS CONFIDENTIAL AGENT TO REPORT
DIRECTLY TO THE UNDERSIGNED HER OBSERVATIONS OF THE

ARGENTINE/GERMANS, HER HUSBAND, AND OTHERS INVOLVED
OR PLANNED TO BE INVOLVED IN OPERATION PHOENIX. THIS
MISSION WAS NOT TO BE REVEALED TO ANYONE, INCLUDING
HER HUSBAND, BUT WITH REGARD TO THE LATTER, WE MUST
PRESUME THAT SECURITY HAS BEEN BREACHED BECAUSE OF
THE MARITAL RELATIONSHIP.

ADMIRAL CANARIS HAS FOR SOME TIME EMPLOYED WILHELM
FROGGER AS HIS CONFIDENTIAL AGENT, CHARGING HIM WITH
REPORTING ON GERMAN AND NON-GERMAN PERSONNEL WORKING
IN THE EMBASSIES IN BUENOS AIRES, MONTEVIDEO, AND
SANTIAGO, CHILE. FROGGER WAS SPECIFICALLY CHARGED BY
CANARIS WITH DETERMINING WHICH OF THE AFOREMENTIONED
INDIVIDUALS HAD BANK ACCOUNTS AND, IF SO, WHERE AND
WHAT ACTIVITY THERE HAS BEEN THEREIN, AND IF ANY
SUCH PERSONNEL HAD ACQUIRED PROPERTY IN ARGENTINA
AND URUGUAY OR ELSEWHERE AND, IF SO, THE SOURCE OF
THE FUNDS INVOLVED.

WHILE HE WAS IN ARGENTINA, VON DEITZBERG, ACTING ON
THE AUTHORITY OF BOTH REICHSFÜHRER-SS HIMMLER AND
FOREIGN MINISTER VON RIBBENTROP, WAS, TOGETHER WITH
VON GRADNY-SAWZ, IN SUCCESSFUL CONTACT WITH COLONEL
PERÓN. PERÓN WAS OFFERED SUBSTANTIAL FINANCIAL
REWARDS FOR HIS ASSISTANCE TO OPERATION PHOENIX,
GERMAN SUPPORT FOR HIS AMBITIONS TO BECOME PRESIDENT
OF ARGENTINA, AND IMPLIED GERMAN SUPPORT FOR THE
INTEGRATION OF URUGUAY, PARAGUAY, AND OTHER
TERRITORIES INTO ARGENTINA FOLLOWING OUR FINAL
VICTORY.

WHILE IT IS POSSIBLE THAT THE FROGGERS HAVE BEEN
ABDUCTED — EITHER BY BRITISH AGENTS, AS ADMIRAL
CANARIS THINKS IS MOST LIKELY, OR BY THE AMERICANS,
SPECIFICALLY FRADE — IT MUST BE CONSIDERED THAT

FROGGER OR HIS WIFE, OR BOTH, DESERTED THEIR POST
EITHER TRAITOROUSLY IN THE BELIEF THE WAR WILL BE
LOST, OR THAT THEY DESERTED THEIR POSTS FOR
FINANCIAL CONSIDERATIONS. CANARIS STATES THE BRITISH
HAVE PRACTICED THE LATTER SUCCESSFULLY IN A NUMBER
OF SITUATIONS.

WHATEVER THE CIRCUMSTANCES, IT IS AGREED BETWEEN US
THAT THE FROGGERS ARE IN POSSESSION OF KNOWLEDGE
(PERHAPS UNWITTINGLY) OF INFORMATION THAT COULD
CAUSE SERIOUS DAMAGE TO OPERATION PHOENIX
SPECIFICALLY AND BE EMBARRASSING TO THE GERMAN REICH
SHOULD IT BECOME PUBLIC.

THEREFORE, CANARIS AND THE UNDERSIGNED ARE AGREED
THAT VON DIETZBERG WAS BOTH CORRECT AND ACTING
WITHIN HIS AUTHORITY WHEN HE ORDERED THE ELIMINATION
OF BOTH INDIVIDUALS WHEN AND WHERE FOUND. IDEALLY,
THERE WOULD BE AN OPPORTUNITY TO INTERROGATE BOTH TO
DETERMINE HOW MUCH INFORMATION HAS BEEN PASSED TO
THE ENEMY BEFORE THEY ARE EXECUTED, BUT THIS IS A
SECONDARY CONSIDERATION.

THE QUESTION THEN BECOMES HOW TO LOCATE THEM. WE ARE
IN AGREEMENT THAT OUR BEST CHANCE TO DO THIS IS
THROUGH COLONEL PERÓN. ONCE IT IS POINTED OUT TO HIM
THAT THE DISCLOSURE OF HIS CONNECTION WITH OPERATION
PHOENIX — SPECIFICALLY INCLUDING BUT NOT LIMITED TO
PROVIDING ARGENTINE ARMY PROTECTION OF THE LANDING
OF THE SPECIAL CARGO — WOULD ALMOST CERTAINLY
PRECLUDE HIS EVER BECOMING PRESIDENT OF ARGENTINA,
IT IS FELT HE WOULD LEND HIS CONSIDERABLE INFLUENCE,
BOTH MILITARY AND ON THE GOVERNMENT GENERALLY, TO
THE RESOLUTION OF THIS PROBLEM.

AS AN IMMEDIATE SOLUTION OF THE PROBLEM IS OBVIOUSLY
NECESSARY, THIS MESSAGE SHOULD BE IMMEDIATELY
BROUGHT TO THE ATTENTION OF VON GRADNY-SAWZ,
STANDARTENFÜHRER CRANZ, STURMBANNFÜHRER RASCHNER,
AND KAPITÄN ZUR SEE BOLTITZ ONLY REPEAT ONLY.

AS AMBASSADOR, VON LUTZENBERGER WILL BE IN OVERALL
COMMAND, BUT IT IS BELIEVED AND EXPECTED THAT VON
LUTZENBERGER WILL DEFER IN MOST CASES TO THE
PROFESSIONAL JUDGMENT OF CRANZ BECAUSE OF HIS
GREATER EXPERIENCE IN THESE AREAS.

EFFECTIVE IMMEDIATELY, BOLTITZ WILL TRANSMIT A DAILY
REPORT TO ADMIRAL CANARIS OF PROGRESS BEING MADE.

THIS MESSAGE WILL BE ACKNOWLEDGED IMMEDIATELY ON
RECEIPT.

HEIL HITLER!

MARTIN BORMANN
PARTEILEITER

CONCUR
WILHELM CANARIS
VIZEADMIRAL

MANFRED VON DEITZBERG
SS-BRIGADEFÜHRER

Von Lutzenberger, shaking his head, folded the sheets of paper and put them back into the letter-sized envelope. This he absently tried to put into his suit jacket. But he wasn't wearing a suit jacket; he was in his uniform, and it had no pockets. He ultimately learned that there were hip pockets on the uniform trousers, though none deep enough to take the white envelope without it first being folded.

This he did. He thought he would give the manila envelope to Schneider to take back to the embassy and destroy. Then he decided he would leave it in the pissoir, on the floor, where the French would find it and wonder what it might have contained.

He wordlessly left the men's room and found Schneider still at his post.

"Go in there, Schneider," he said, nodding at the Grand Reception Room, "and tell Herr von Gradny-Sawz that he is to immediately pick up Herr Cranz and Herr Raschner and bring them to the embassy on a matter of some importance."

"*Jawohl,* Excellency."

"Tell Herr von Gradny-Sawz that I am going to pick up Kapitän Boltitz on my way."

"*Jawohl,* Excellency."

Von Lutzenberger scanned the room and thought: *I hope it won't take me too long to find the French ambassador to express my gratitude for his splendid hospitality and my regrets that duty calls. I really want Boltitz to see this message before we meet with the others. Maybe—very possibly—he will see something in it that I have missed.*

[TWO]
The Chateau Marmont
8221 Sunset Boulevard
Hollywood, California
0905 5 August 1943

When the managing director of South American Airways—wearing a tweed jacket, khaki slacks, a white polo shirt, and well-worn Western boots—walked off the elevator into the lobby of the hotel, he found eleven SAA captains and one U.S. Border Patrol captain already there.

The Immigration Service captain was in uniform. So were the SAA pilots, each nattily attired in a woolen powder-blue tunic with the four gold stripes of a captain on the sleeves, darker blue trousers, a crisp white shirt, and a leather brimmed cap with a huge crown. On their breasts were what Clete thought of as outsized golden wings, in the center of which, superimposed on the Argentine sunburst, were the letters SAA.

Chief Pilot Delgano, as was probably to be expected, had five golden stripes on his tunic sleeves and the band around his brimmed cap was of gold cloth.

To a man, they looked at him askance.

I think I just failed inspection, Frade thought.

What did they expect, that I would be wearing a SAA uniform?

And what the hell are they doing in those ridiculous uniforms, anyway?

I don't think it's coincidental. Somebody told them to wear them.

Let's find out who and why. . . .

He said, "I see that everyone is properly—I should say 'splendidly'—turned out. Your idea, Captain Delgano?"

"I thought it would be appropriate, Señor Frade," Delgano replied seriously.

"And so it is," Frade said.

"I'm so glad you could find time for us in your busy schedule, Mr. Frade," the Immigration Service captain said somewhat sarcastically.

"Well, I always try to be properly turned out myself, and that takes time." He smiled triumphantly, then said, "So, what happens now?"

"That will be explained to you later. Shall we get in the Carryalls?"

"We are completely in your hands, Captain," Frade said.

[THREE]
Lockheed Air Terminal
Burbank, California
0935 5 August 1943

They were taken to an unimpressive two-story masonry building that was just inside the fence and perhaps three hundred yards from the gate. It was not the same building to which they had been taken the night before.

As they were getting out of the Carryalls, a Border Patrol officer with major's insignia on his epaulets came out of the building and signaled to the captain that he wanted a word with him out of hearing of the others.

"Wait here, please, gentlemen," the Border Patrol captain ordered more than a little arrogantly.

At the last moment, Frade resisted the temptation to pop to attention, salute, and bellow, "Aye, aye, sir!" Instead, he gave the captain a thumbs-up signal, which he was pleased to find seemed to annoy the captain.

Clete took a closer look at the building.

A legend had been cast into the concrete over the door:

LOUGHEAD AIRCRAFT
MANUFACTURING COMPANY

"Loughead"?

Can't they spell?

How do you pronounce that? "Lewg-head"? "Log-head"?

Maybe that was the original name and Howard changed it. He said he changed Trans-continental and Western Airways to Trans-World Airlines.

There came the sound of multiple powerful aircraft engines on takeoff power. Everyone quickly looked for the source—and then found it. There was a runway running parallel to the building and the fence.

Coming down the runway was a brand-new P-38 glistening in the early-morning California sun. By the time the twin-engine, twin-tail Lightning reached them, it was airborne, its landing gear nearly retracted. The pilot apparently had pulled back on the stick the moment he had gotten a green gear-up-and-locked light, because the nose of the fighter lifted as he made a steep climbing turn to the right.

Clete heard himself grunt.

That's what the hell I should be doing, flying something like that.

I'm a fighter pilot, not a damn fly-gently-so-as-to-not-disturb-the-passengers aerial bus driver.

As the Lightning rapidly grew smaller as it climbed, there came the sound again of powerful engines at takeoff power, and another P-38 roared down the runway. This one also had its gear retracted by the time it reached them and had begun a steep climbing turn in the direction of the first fighter. Sixty seconds after that second Lightning passed them, there again came the sounds of engines on takeoff power, and a third P-38 took off.

Clete watched the third plane until it vanished from sight, then looked at the SAA captains. He saw from their faces there was no question that they were awed.

Well, why not? The hottest planes in the Argentine air force are the Curtiss P-36 Hawks. They were obsolete even before we sold them to Argentina before the war.

"Those were the P-38 Lightning, were they not, Cletus?" Delgano asked.

"Yes, they were."

"Is that what you flew when you were in the Corps of Marines?"

"No, I flew a single-engine Grumman Wildcat, the F4F."

"Like the Lightning?"

Clete shook his head. "No. Single engine. Designed to be flown off aircraft carriers. Nice airplane."

The Border Patrol major walked up to them.

"I was just telling Captain McNeil that everything seems to be in order now," the major announced.

"Oh?" Frade said.

He saw the captain, who did not seem happy and was carefully avoiding looking at them, walk to the white Carryall and get in.

"Well, I'm sure it's the same in your country," the major explained. "From time to time, things don't go as they're supposed to. But it's all cleared up now."

Why do I think Colonel Graham had something to do with that?

"What we're waiting for now," the major went on, "is for Immigration Service officers to come here and issue the necessary visas. Then you'll be free to get on with your business. I understand that people from the War Production Board and Lockheed are already waiting for you at Lockheed."

Ten minutes later, the immigration officers appeared. It took just under half an hour for them to issue visas. When the SAA captains and Clete came out of the Loughead Aircraft Manufacturing Company building, a bus with LOCKHEED AIRCRAFT lettered on its sides was waiting for them.

The bus carried them to the far side of the airfield, past long, double lines of parked aircraft. There were more P-38s than Clete could count, at least two dozen PV-1 Venturas, which looked something like an armed version of the Lodestar, then another two dozen or more Lodestars. Six of the latter aircraft were painted in the South American Airways color scheme.

On seeing their aircraft, there was a sudden wave of pride felt among all the SAA pilots, including Clete—which suddenly was greatly diminished when they saw the four aircraft sitting near the end of the tarmac.

These four airplanes had their own row; they were too large to park one behind another like the others.

"Clete, is that the Constitution you told us about?" Delgano asked.

"Constellation," he corrected without thinking.

I boasted about that airplane without ever having seen one.

Jesus Christ, she's beautiful!

"Three tails?" one of the SAA pilots asked.

"Vertical stabilizers," Clete again corrected without thinking. "The only way

they could get enough vertical-stabilizer control surface and get the tail into a hangar was to have three vertical stabilizers instead of one great big one."

"That's an incredible airplane!" another of the pilots said.

Yeah, it is.

Makes that Kraut Condor look like . . . a Lodestar.

"Maybe we can get a closer look at one while we're here," Clete said.

Howard ought to be able to arrange that.

Send these guys back to Argentina dazzled with American aviation genius.

"Gentlemen," a gray-haired man in a well-fitting suit said. "Welcome to the United States and to Lockheed Aircraft. I regret the confusion when you first arrived, but all the problems have, I think, been solved. Including . . . Which of you is Mr. Frade?"

Clete raised his hand.

"Including insurance," the man went on, "which I understand has posed something of a problem for you. United States Fidelity and Guaranty—just before we walked in here just now—telephoned to say that they'll be happy to insure South American Airways' flight operations, and that a temporary policy has been issued covering your activities here, with the final policy to follow shortly, covering everything."

"That's excellent news," Frade replied.

The man nodded. "Presuming, of course, we can get your pilots their ATRs. Importantly, you will be insured while operating your Lodestar aircraft here so that your pilots not only can use them for training and qualification but also can fly them to Argentina once they're rated.

"So let's turn to that. The Federal Aviation Administration has informed me that—for the purposes of meeting the flight-time prerequisites, et cetera, for the Air Transport Rating—they will recognize your records as maintained by the government of Argentina. Which means they will require your flight records to be here, which means that you're going to have to get them authenticated by the U.S. consulate in Argentina and then get them up here from Buenos Aires, then authenticated by the Argentine consulate in San Francisco. Is that going to pose a problem, Mr. Frade?"

"No. I'll send a radiogram down there, and have the records flown to Rio de Janeiro and put on the Panagra flight to Miami."

"I'll leave that in your hands, Mr. Frade, as you will have more time on your hands than these gentlemen. I have been led to believe that you have been an Army pilot?"

"A Naval Aviator," Frade corrected him firmly. "I was a Marine."

"My mistake. No offense intended. The FAA will be able to get your flight records from the Navy, and you won't have to go through the basic training and examinations that these gentlemen will."

Clete nodded his understanding.

"In your case, purely as a formality, you'll have to take a cross-country check ride to make you current in multiengine aircraft."

"Fine," Frade said.

"And with that in mind—aware as we are how anxious everyone is to get through this as soon as possible—we've arranged for you to make that flight immediately."

"Immediately?"

"There's a Follow-Me truck outside which will take you to what we call the Used Car Lot—"

"Excuse me?"

"That's what we call the parking tarmac," the man said. "As you know, Mr. Howard Hughes—you know who I mean, of course?"

"I know who he is," Frade said.

"Mr. Hughes has both a certain influence around here and what some think is a fey sense of humor. Our engineering facility is known as the Skunk Works."

Frade chuckled and nodded.

The pilots of South American Airways, to a man, frowned as people are prone to do when not understanding what has been said.

"When you return," the man went on, "which should not take more than a couple of days, these gentlemen will be well on their way to their ATRs."

"Good," Frade said. "Now, what about the Follow-Me?"

The man motioned for the door.

"Right outside. As I said, it'll take you to the Used Car Lot, where an aircraft and your instructor pilot are waiting. Is that all right with you?"

Frade nodded agreeably. "It's fine with me. Thank you."

The Follow-Me—a 1941 Chevrolet pickup truck painted in a black-and-white checkerboard pattern and bearing large checkerboard flags flying from the front bumper and the rear of the bed—drove Frade to the end of the Used Car Lot.

"Here we are," the driver said.

Clete saw the SAA Lodestars, got out of the truck—which then immediately drove away—and walked toward the Lodestars. There was no sign of activity, no ground auxiliary power equipment, no fire extinguishers, no instructor pilot, nothing.

Somewhat annoyed—*that sonofabitch just dropped me at the wrong place*—Clete put his hands on his hips and looked around.

There was a Constellation sitting alone. The three others were a hundred yards farther away.

The lone Connie bore military markings, and around it *was* activity. There were a fire truck and crew, a pickup-mounted auxiliary power unit humming smoothly, and half a dozen ground handlers, one of whom had wands in his hands. There was also a pickup truck with a ladder leading to the aircraft's rear door.

It took Frade almost ten seconds to decide that he would really piss off people if he went up that ladder and had himself a good long look at the insides of that big, beautiful sonofabitch, thus delaying its imminent takeoff, and that unless he trotted over there, it would take off before he could do so.

He was surprised that no one stopped him when he went quickly up the ladder and ducked through the doorway and entered the fuselage.

He was even more surprised when a large man in a white jacket immediately stepped to the doorway, signaled for the stair truck to back away from the door, and began to close the door.

Then the large man gestured for Frade to walk toward the cockpit.

The guy who this guy expected to get aboard is really going to be pissed when he gets here and sees the Connie taxiing away.

"Good morning, Major Frade," a familiar voice said. "I'm so glad you finally could join us."

Frade looked at him but didn't reply.

"Why don't you go in there," Colonel A. J. Graham said, pointing toward the cockpit, "and make your manners to the pilot?"

Well, I guess that check-ride to make me current in multiengines story was bullshit for the benefit of the SAA pilots.

We're on our way to Mississippi.

Clete walked to the front of the passenger compartment and went through the door.

To his left, an Air Force master sergeant sat at the radio console. A Collins Model 7.2 transceiver had been bolted on rubber mounts to the floor. To his right, closer to the pilots' seats, a man in civilian clothes—obviously the flight engineer—sat before an impressive array of dials and switches and levers.

Clete took the last eight steps and found himself standing between the pilot's and co-pilot's seats, the latter empty.

The pilot turned to look at him.

"Why, hello there, Little Cletus," Howard Hughes said.

Clete gave him the finger.

"If you sit down there, Little Cletus," Hughes went on, ignoring the vulgar gesture and pointing to the co-pilot's seat, "and fasten the straps and put your earphones on, Uncle Howard will let you play with his new toy."

Clete sat down.

The instant he had the earphones in place, Hughes's voice came over them.

"See if you can wind it up, Ken."

"Yes, Mr. Hughes," the engineer replied, then began working his control panel. "Starting Number Three . . ."

There was the whine of the starters and then the sound of an engine—somewhat reluctantly—coming to life. The aircraft trembled with the vibration of a 2,200-horsepower Wright R-3350-34 engine running a little rough.

"Starting Number Two."

The second engine started more easily.

"I show Two and Three running and moving into the green," Hughes's voice said.

"Confirmed, Mr. Hughes."

"Disconnect auxiliary power."

"Yes, Mr. Hughes."

"I see auxiliary power disconnected," Hughes said after a moment, "and Two and Three in the green."

"Confirmed, Mr. Hughes."

"Lockheed," Hughes announced. "Three Four Three at the Used Car Lot. Request taxi and takeoff."

Howard Hughes turned to Clete Frade.

"Pay attention, Little Cletus," Hughes's voice came over the earphones, "and try to learn something."

Three minutes later:

"What the nice man just said, Little Cletus, is that we're cleared for takeoff. Now, the way we do that is you put your hand on those levers and push them to where it says 'Takeoff Power.' Then you steer down the runway. The controls will come to life at about forty knots. It will just about take itself off at about ninety. When I call 'one hundred,' ease back on the yoke."

"Yes, sir," Clete said, and put his hand on the throttle quadrant.

[FOUR]
Jackson Army Air Base
Jackson, Mississippi
1745 5 August 1943

"Do you think you can put it down there, Clete?" Howard Hughes asked.

They were flying over a small airfield at an altitude of two thousand feet as slow as Clete dared to fly the Constellation. He had his hand on the throttles, ready to firewall them the moment he suspected they were close to a stall.

Howard's now serious; otherwise he'd have said "Little Cletus."

When in doubt, tell the truth.

"I don't know, Howard. It would be helpful if I knew how long that run-way is, and what the Constellation needs."

"I like you so much better when you are cautious and modest," Hughes said.

Clete flashed him a dirty look.

"Let me put it this way," Hughes said. "I could get us in there . . ."

"You want to land it, go ahead. I have a total of five hours thirty in this air-plane, one takeoff, zero landings. I really don't know how to fly it."

"At the risk of repeating myself," Hughes said, "I like you so much better when you are cautious and modest. What I was going to say is: *I* would come in low and slow, full flaps, lots of power. *I* would try to touch down as close to the threshold as *I* could, and *I* would chop the power the moment before *I* heard the chirp. *I* would then judiciously apply the brakes, so as not to burn them out, and then, when *I* was halfway down the runway, *I* would decide whether *I* had enough runway and brakes left or should firewall the throttles."

Clete didn't reply.

Hughes then said, "It occurs to me that if *you* were to steer and work the brakes, and *I* worked the throttles and flaps, this would be educational for you. Do you want to have a whack at trying that?"

He wouldn't make the offer unless he thought I could handle it.

"What about me shooting a touch-and-go—*a couple* of touch-and-goes—first?"

"I was about to make that very suggestion," Hughes said. He picked up the microphone: "Jackson, this is Army Three Four Three. As you may have noticed, we've been flying around your field. The reason for this is there is a student pilot at the controls who has been gathering his courage to shoot a couple of touch-and-goes. He has found the courage, but considering his youth, lack of experience, and all-around flying ineptness, you might want to wake up the fire truck drivers and have an ambulance on standby."

The controller was laughing as he replied, "Three Four Three, you are cleared for multiple touch-and-goes. You are number one to land."

Twenty minutes later, Cletus Frade, having approached the runway threshold as low and slow as seemed appropriate based on the experience of two previous aborted landings, touched down very close to the threshold, quickly retarded the throttles, and, a moment later, gingerly applied the brakes. Long before he reached the halfway point of the runway, he decided he had more than enough of it left to stop before burning out the brakes.

"We're down, Howard. We seem to have cheated death again."

Hughes chuckled. "For a moment, I wasn't too sure about that. Not bad, Little Cletus. There may be hope for you yet."

"This is a great airplane," Clete said.

"We think so. Just remember when you go to turn it around that it's a great *big* airplane."

The proof of that came ten minutes later, when they tried to get off the Constellation. The airfield—which was apparently used as an auxiliary field for Air Force pilot training; Clete saw on the tarmac maybe a dozen North American AT-6 Texan two-seat advanced trainers, four Beech C-45 Expeditors used for twin-engine pilot training and for navigator training, and maybe a dozen Vultee BT-13 basic trainers—was not equipped with any sort of stairs or even maintenance scaffolding for an aircraft as high off the ground as the Constellation.

The problem was finally solved—as what looked like all the pilots and student pilots of the AT-6s, the C-45s, and the BT-13s gathered to watch—by leaning against the Constellation's fuselage a very tall stepladder otherwise used to change the lights in the hangar ceilings.

By the time that was done, there were two staff cars and two lieutenant colonels on the tarmac.

"Let me deal with this," Colonel Graham said, and carefully got on the ladder and climbed down it.

Three minutes later, he climbed back up.

"I'm going out to Camp Clinton to have a look at Colonel Frogger," Graham announced to Howard and Clete. "I may or may not be back tonight. The base commander here will take care of the enlisted people. There's a transient BOQ here, and an officers' club. Do I have to remind you two to behave yourselves?"

[FIVE]
Officers' Club
Jackson Army Air Base
Jackson, Mississippi
1745 5 August 1943

The officers' club was almost the opposite of elegant. It occupied the lower floor of a simple wooden two-story building. Twelve Transient Bachelor Officers' Quarters—cubicles of plywood furnished with two beds, two tables, and two chairs—were upstairs and had a common latrine.

There were two virtually identical buildings on either side of the officers' club, all four devoted to housing transient officers—almost always instructor pilots and their students—who for one reason or another had to spend the night at the auxiliary field.

There were two parts to the club, The Mess and The Lounge. The mess was a cafeteria serving Army-style food. Two tables, each seating four, had white tablecloths and bore signs lettered FIELD GRADE OFFICERS, which meant majors and up.

They had waiter service. Everybody else walked the cafeteria line while holding a Masonite tray on which they loaded food selected from steam trays, then carried their tray to one of the thirty four-place tables covered with oilcloth.

When Hughes and Frade walked into the officers' mess, Major Frade, who was a field-grade officer in another life, took one look at the field-grade officers' tables and motioned for Hughes to get into the cafeteria line.

There was a small problem after they had selected their dinner and tried paying for it. Hughes attempted to pay the cashier—an Air Forces sergeant—with a crisp hundred-dollar bill, one of a sheaf of hundred-dollar bills he had in his shirt pocket.

"I can't cash something like that, for Christ's sake!" the sergeant said.

Cletus Frade, likewise, had nothing smaller than hundred-dollar bills in his wallet. He also had some Argentine, Brazilian, and Mexican currencies, but the Air Forces sergeant quickly rejected these as well, asking, "For Christ's sake, does this look like a fucking bank?"

Five minutes later, the cashier returned from The Lounge and counted out and handed to Howard Hughes his change. It came in the form of bills, nothing larger than a five, and several rolls of nickels, dimes, and quarters—a total of $99.30, the cost of each of their meals being thirty-five cents.

By then, there were perhaps twenty officers, almost all of them pilots and lieutenants, backed up behind them in the line, each holding their Masonite tray of dinner.

The food was surprisingly good.

Afterward, they went into The Lounge. It was somewhat dimly lit. There was a bar with a dozen stools and twelve or fifteen four-man tables, these covered with festive bright red oilcloths. The bar stools were all occupied, as were all but two tables at the far end of the room.

Clete and Howard headed for these. They sat at one of them and almost immediately were able to deduce that the tables had not been occupied because they were right in front of an enormous wall-mounted fan that sucked the outside Mississippi midsummer's humid air into the building and forced it through The Lounge in the hope that it would cool.

Five minutes after that, Clete concluded there was no waiter service.

"I think we have to go to the bar," he announced.

"Go see if they'll sell us a bottle, Cletus. We can take it to our room."

"I don't have any money they'll take."

"And after all I've done for you today!"

Hughes walked to the bar, patiently awaited his turn, and returned to the table holding two glasses, each holding what looked like a single ice cube.

"They won't sell us a bottle, and you can't take glasses out of the room," he reported.

"What is this?" Clete said after sipping his drink.

"Rye whiskey."

"No bourbon?"

"Stupid question, Little Cletus."

"Mud in your eye, Howard!"

"Fuck you, Little Cletus!"

They tapped glasses.

Five minutes later, three Air Force officers—two captains and a lieutenant, all wearing wings—approached the table.

"Oh, shit . . ." Hughes and Frade muttered almost simultaneously.

"Good evening, gentlemen," the captain said.

"Good evening," Frade and Hughes replied almost simultaneously.

"Could you spare a moment for the Army Air Force?" the shorter of the two captains said.

"Certainly," Hughes said.

They're half in the bag, Frade thought. *And belligerent.*

How do I handle this?

Show them my Marine major's identification?

Or my OSS badge?

Either one will raise more questions with these guys than it will answer.

"You came in with that big airplane, am I right?" the short captain went on.

"Yes, we did," Hughes said.

"I never saw one of those before. What is it?"

"It's a Lockheed C-69. They call it the Constellation," Hughes said.

"You were flying it, were you?"

"Yes. He and I were flying it," Hughes said, indicating Frade with a nod of his head.

"Had a little trouble, did you? That's why you set down here?"

"We erred on the side of caution," Frade said.

"You 'erred on the side of caution'? You mean, you were just being careful?"

"Yes, that's right," Frade said.

"Where'd you come from? In other words, where are you based?"

"At the Lockheed plant in Burbank," Hughes replied.

"And where are you headed? Where *were* you headed, before you *erred on the side of caution* and landed here?"

"I'm afraid that's classified," Frade said.

The short captain's chest seemed to puff out. "What did you say?"

"I said, I'm afraid that's classified," Frade repeated.

"You're a civilian, right?"

"That's right."

"But you do recognize this uniform? You understand I'm a captain in the Army Air Force?"

"Of course," Frade said.

"So here you sit, a goddamn civilian in an Army Air Force officers' club on an Army Air Force field, into which you flew an Air Force airplane—"

"Excuse me, Captain," a voice said somewhat sharply.

Frade turned and in the dim lighting saw an Army MP officer, a major, in full regalia, MP brassard, and a white leather Sam Browne belt with a .45 ACP pistol in a white holster.

What the hell is this all about? Clete thought, then took a closer look at the military police officer. *Jesus, am I losing my mind?*

"All I was doing, Major," the Army Air Force captain said, suddenly not so cocksure, "was asking this civilian—"

"You didn't get the word that no one was to attempt to speak to these gentlemen? To communicate in any way with them?" Second Lieutenant Leonard Fischer, Signal Corps, demanded rather nastily.

"Huh?"

"The response I expect from you, Captain, is 'Yes, sir' or 'No, sir.' Now, which is it?"

"No, sir. I didn't hear anything about anything like that."

"Well, now you have," Fischer said.

"Yes, sir."

"I suggest that on your way to your quarters, you spread the word."

"Yes, sir."

The two captains and the lieutenant made a beeline for the door.

Fischer turned to Hughes and Frade.

"Now, what are you two doing in here? You were told to be as inconspicuous as possible."

"We were going to have a drink in our room, *Major*," Clete said. "But they wouldn't sell us a bottle or let us take glasses from the bar."

"Well, if you insist on drinking, you'll have to do it in your quarters," Fischer said. "Go to them now. I will bring you something to drink. You understand I'll have to tell the colonel about this."

Five minutes later, the MP major, carrying a bottle of rye whiskey, glasses, and a small tin bucket full of ice, walked into BOQ Room 7, which was being shared by Frade and Hughes.

"A little warm in here, isn't it?" the MP said.

"Howard, say hello to Second Lieutenant Len Fischer of the Signal Corps," Frade said.

Hughes did not appear to be surprised to learn Fischer was neither a major nor an MP. The two wordlessly shook hands.

"Actually, it's first lieutenant," Fischer said. "As of two days ago."

Hughes relieved Fischer of the bottle of whiskey and the glasses and began to pour.

"You are going to tell us where you got the MP uniform? And the major's leaf?" Frade asked.

"At Fort Myer," Fischer said. "Early this morning. Two guys from the OSS showed up at Vint Hill Farms with a letter of instructions and the photographs we took of the Froggers at Casa Chica—"

"Where?" Hughes interrupted.

"Casa Chica," Frade explained, "a small estancia where we've stashed the Froggers." He turned to Fischer and asked, "What instructions?"

"The letter said I was to go to Camp Clinton, as an MP major, give the photographs to Colonel Frogger, say nothing, answer no questions, and wait for him there."

"You've seen Frogger?" Clete asked.

Fischer nodded. Hughes handed him a drink.

"What's he like?"

"More like his father than his mother. Smaller than I expected him to be. Anyway, they took me to the MP battalion at Fort Myer, got me suited up like this, and then took me to Bolling Air Force Base, loaded me on a B-26—that was an experience—and flew me down here.

"A light colonel from Camp Clinton met me, and took me out there, and put me together with Frogger. They had him in a room in a small wooden building. He had a duffel bag with him."

"And?" Clete asked.

"I did what Colonel Graham's letter said to do. I walked in and saluted, and said, in German, 'Colonel Frogger, I have been instructed to give you these photographs,' and gave them to him. They shook him up, obviously, and he asked what was going on. I told him he would be informed in good time, saluted him again, and left. And waited for Colonel Graham to show up."

"You think he recognized you in the pictures?" Clete said. "You were in civvies."

Fischer shrugged, then took a close look at Hughes.

"You're Howard Hughes," he said.

"Yeah, I know," Hughes said.

"The pilot, the movie guy," Fischer went on.

"Right again, Len," Frade said. "You have just won the cement bicycle for celebrity spotting. Give him your autograph, Howard."

Hughes gave Frade the finger.

"What are you doing here?" Fischer asked.

"The same thing you are, pal," Hughes said. "Waiting for Graham to tell me what to do."

"Welcome to the OSS, Len," Frade said.

"You're in the OSS?" Fischer asked Hughes.

"Sometimes it feels that way, but, technically, no."

"And I am?" Fischer asked.

"I don't know if you are, technically," Frade said. "But if I had to bet, I'd say you are."

"I'm out of Vint Hill Farms? Out of the ASA?"

"I think when this is over," Frade said, "Graham will send you back there. You're very useful there. Unless something unexpected comes up, of course, and something unexpected will probably come up."

"So what happens now?" Fischer asked.

Now Frade shrugged.

"I know not what course others may take," Hughes intoned solemnly, "but as for me, give me rye whiskey when bourbon and scotch are not available."

He reached for the bottle.

Colonel A. F. Graham came into BOQ Room 7 ninety minutes later, just as Howard Hughes was shaking the last drops of the rye whiskey into his glass.

"You're out of luck, Alex, the booze is all gone," Hughes said.

"You two are going to have to fly tomorrow," Graham said. "And you're drinking?"

"Only this one bottle," Hughes said. "And it was nowhere near full when Len here brought it to us."

Graham didn't reply. He turned to Frade.

"I really wish you had a uniform. And a haircut. But there wasn't time, so we'll have to go with what we have."

"Go where? And what do we have?" Frade asked.

"Don't push me, Clete," Graham said. "I'm not in a very good mood."

"You couldn't turn the Kraut?" Hughes asked.

Graham shook his head. "I'm still working on shaking him up. And I haven't done well at that. He knows all about the Geneva Convention and enough about the United States to know we scrupulously follow them."

"A real Nazi, huh?" Frade said. "A chip off the ol' block—his mother's block?"

"No. He's more like his father. Go by the book. The book says don't cooperate with the enemy, and that's it, so far as he's concerned."

"What did he have to say about us having his parents?"

"I refused to discuss that. And when I asked him how familiar he was with Putzi Hanfstaengl, he said he'd never heard of him. Where he is now is in a room, alone, guarded by a couple of MPs. I told him he is not going back into the camp as a prisoner. I wouldn't discuss that, either. I'm going to let him stew there overnight, and let you have a go at him in the morning. You, or you and Fischer. Your call."

"I want Len there."

"Okay. Now, why don't we all go to bed?"

XV

[ONE]
Senior German Officer Prisoner of War Detention
Facility
Camp Clinton, Mississippi
0915 6 August 1943

It had been a thirty-minute drive in a 1941 Chevrolet Army staff car from Jackson Army Air Base to the POW camp, down a narrow macadam road that cut through the loblolly pine trees of rural central Mississippi.

When they got close to the base—signs on what had been a farmer's fence read KEEP OUT! U.S. GOVERNMENT PROPERTY—Frade started looking for the barbed-wire fences and observation towers of a POW camp. There were none.

Their driver turned off of the macadam onto a rutted red clay road, and two hundred yards down that saw a guard shack in the center of the road manned by a pair of armed MPs in uniform. A curved sign erected over the shack read PRISONER OF WAR CAMP. Below that, in smaller letters, it said CLINTON, MIS-SISSIPPI, and below that was a square sign reading, VISITING PROHIBITED.

Frade noted that now there was a single coil of concertina marking the perimeter.

"Not much barbed wire," he observed aloud as the staff car pulled to a stop at the guard shack.

"Yeah," Fischer said. "Why is that?"

"Where are they going to go if they escape?" Graham replied. "This is the middle of nowhere. The wire's more of a psychological barrier; it serves as a re-minder of where they are."

One of the guards in the shack came out, looked into the car, and then sort of came to attention and saluted. Graham was in uniform, as was Fischer, who was riding in the front seat.

Frade was annoyed: *If a Marine saluted a full bull colonel that sloppily, he'd find himself suddenly practicing the rendering of the hand salute for the next two weekends.*

"We're expected," Graham said as he returned the salute.

"Yes, sir," the guard said, and walked to a counterbalanced striped barrier pole and raised it. Then he gestured somewhat impatiently for the staff car to pass.

Five hundred yards from the gate was a copse of trees and beyond that another fence. It was a standard chain-link fence that looked as if it belonged in some-one's backyard and might, Clete thought, pose a problem for a six-year-old to climb over.

Inside the fence line were small groups of German officers, perhaps two dozen men in all, apparently out for a morning stroll.

"The little one with the big nose," Graham offered, "is General Hans-Jürgen von Arnim, who has the dubious distinction of having surrendered the Afrikakorps."

Frade found General von Arnim—who wore a khaki uniform and had his hands folded on his back—marching purposefully over the sparse grass, trailed by four other officers.

Graham went on: "He's not looking at us, of course, but I'm sure he's wondering what's going on. By now, he knows we've taken Frogger from the general population."

"He's not the only one wondering what's going on," Clete said. "Are you going to tell me what I'm supposed to do? Or am I supposed to wing it?"

"Actually, Major Frade, I've given the question of how you should handle this a good deal of thought. If I knew what you should do, I'd tell you. But I don't know. I could tell you to wing it, but that's a little too casual. So I think that you should use your best judgment. I'll back whatever you decide to do."

Clete didn't reply.

"The expected response, Major, was, 'Aye, aye, sir.' "

"Aye, aye, sir."

There was another copse of trees on the other side of the field, where the Germans were having their morning constitutional, and then the camp itself. It looked like any other hurriedly-built-to-last-five-years temporary military installation, like Jackson Army Air Base.

There were no hangars, of course, but there were many more "colonel's quarters" than Frade expected to see. These were small, one-story frame buildings intended for the use of senior officers. They held two bedrooms, a living room, a dining room, a kitchen, and a bath.

The staff car pulled up before one of them, and the driver got out to open Graham's door.

Graham looked at Frade. "Do you want us to come in with you?"

It was a moment before Clete had time to consider the question.

"You go in first," he finally said. "Then Len goes in—I want this guy to recognize him from the photos—then I'll come in. Neither one of you say anything to him. If I give you a signal, leave us alone."

Graham's face tightened. He had just been given an order, not a suggestion. Marine majors do not give orders to Marine colonels.

He decided this was not the time to raise the subject.

After a moment, he nodded and said, "Okay."

[TWO]

Inside the larger bedroom of Building T-402, Oberstleutnant Wilhelm Frogger heard the crunch of tires on the pebbles on the driveway. He stood up and went to the window and looked out through the steel mesh.

Frogger was dressed, like General von Arnim, in the tan desert uniform of the Afrikakorps. It was nearly new. The Americans had captured matériel as well as prisoners, shipped it to the United States, and now were issuing it to their prisoners.

The room was furnished with a standard U.S. Army steel cot, a simple wooden table, and a folding metal chair. A door led to a basic bath with a sink, a water closet, and a shower. On the table were an ashtray fashioned from a can of Planters peanuts, a stainless-steel water pitcher, a china mug, and a Masonite tray holding the remnants of the breakfast—scrambled eggs, bacon, toast, milk, and apple jelly—he had been served at half past seven.

There also was a cardboard box; today was Ration Day, and his ration had been delivered with his breakfast.

The cardboard box held a box of kitchen matches; a carton of Wings cigarettes; an unopened can of Planters Peanuts; a tube of Colgate toothpaste; two Hershey chocolate bars; two bars of soap; a pad of lined paper; a Prisoner's Mail form, which, when filled in, would serve as his weekly letter home; and two pencils.

Frogger had taken nothing from the box but a package of cigarettes. When they had brought him to Camp Clinton, he had been ordered to bring all his personal property, and the U.S. Army duffel bag on the floor held all the things he had needed except cigarettes. The carton-a-week ration always ran out a day or two before Ration Day, no matter how hard he tried to make it last the whole week.

Next to the ration carton was the manila envelope filled to capacity with eight-by-ten-inch photographs of his family that the military police major had given him yesterday.

Frogger saw through the window that the same military police officer was getting out of the front seat of the staff car. And, a moment later, the man who had come to see him early last evening got out of the backseat.

Now he's in uniform.

But it's not a U.S. Army uniform.

What do they call their naval infantry—Marines?

Ja . . . the man is wearing the uniform of a colonel of the Corps of Marines.

And then another got out of the car. A civilian with long hair.

He's the other man in the photographs of my parents.

That confirms it. The military police major is the other man in the photographs.

I have no idea who they are, or what they want from me, but I am going to have to be very careful.

Frogger looked at the table. He had taken several photographs from the envelope to look at them again, and had not returned them. He turned from the window, walked quickly to the table, put the photographs back in the envelope, then arranged it neatly beside the ration box.

He took a pack of Wings cigarettes from his shirt pocket, removed one cigarette and lit it with a kitchen match, then sat down in the metal folding chair to wait for whatever was going to happen next.

Oberstleutnant Wilhelm Frogger stood up and came to attention as military courtesy dictated when Colonel A. F. Graham, USMC, walked into the room followed by the military police major. A moment later, Frade entered the room.

"*Guten Morgen, Herr Oberstleutnant,*" Frade said.

"*Guten Morgen.*"

"My name is Frade."

"Oberstleutnant Frogger, Wilhelm, Identity Number 19-700045."

Frade gestured with his hand for Graham and Fischer to leave.

"And please close the door," Frade said.

Graham and Fischer left the room and the door clicked shut.

Frogger picked up on that.

This man is younger than the Corps of Marines Oberst.

But apparently he is in charge.

Frade looked Frogger square in the eye.

"Do you speak English, Colonel? My German is not that good."

"Lieutenant Colonel Wilhelm Frogger, Identity Number 19-700045."

"The way you said that, Colonel, suggests you think you are about to be interrogated."

"I believe that under the Geneva Convention," Frogger said in vaguely British-accented English, "by which both our nations are bound, giving my name, rank, and identity number is all that can be required of me."

"I'm not going to question you because you have no information I need. The Afrikakorps no longer exists. You may sit if you like."

Frogger decided that standing at attention served no useful purpose, sat down, and picked up his cigarette from the Planters peanuts ashtray.

Frade took a cigar from a leather case, bit off one end, took a kitchen match from the box and struck it on the tabletop, then carefully lit the cigar.

"You've heard, no doubt, that we have taken Sicily," Frade said after exhaling a large cloud of cigar smoke, "and that Mussolini has been removed from office and replaced by Marshal Badoglio. If I were a betting man, and I am, I'd bet that negotiations for Italy's surrender are under way as we speak."

Frogger did not reply.

Frade puffed his cigar, then added, "But you probably have not heard about this. It just came in."

He handed a sheet of teletype paper to Frogger:

```
OFFICE OF WAR INFORMATION
WASHINGTON
2305 5 AUGUST 1943


UNCLASSIFIED


DISTRIBUTION LIST A—GENERAL


GERMAN PROPAGANDA MINISTER JOSEF GOEBBELS IN A 2130
(BERLIN TIME) 5 AUGUST 1943 NATIONWIDE BROADCAST
RECOMMENDED THE IMMEDIATE EVACUATION OF ALL NON-
ESSENTIAL PERSONNEL FROM BERLIN.


THIS IS THE FIRST ADMISSION THAT BERLIN WILL SHORTLY
BE UNDER HEAVY AERIAL BOMBARDMENT ATTACK WHICH THE
GERMANS BELIEVE NEITHER ANTI-AIRCRAFT NOR THE
LUFTWAFFE WILL BE ABLE TO SUCCESSFULLY RESIST.


A FULL TRANSCRIPT OF THE GOEBBELS BROADCAST HAS BEEN
TRANSMITTED TO DISTRIBUTION LIST A—HEADS OF AGENCIES
AND WILL BE MADE AVAILABLE TO INTERESTED PARTIES BY
CONTACTING OWI ATTENTION: OFFICIAL GERMAN BROADCASTS
SECTION.


END


UNCLASSIFIED
```

After Frogger read the teletype, he wordlessly laid it on the table, then puffed at his cigarette.

Frade said: "That doesn't have much personal impact on you, does it? You have no family remaining in Berlin—in Germany, for that matter. Your brothers are dead, and we have your parents."

Frogger didn't respond in any way.

"As a professional soldier, of course, it might suggest to you—if you haven't already come to this conclusion—that you've lost the war."

Frogger met Frade's eyes but didn't reply.

"I said a moment ago that this is not an interrogation. Quite the opposite. I'm going to tell you about myself and about your parents. I'm free to do this, because as of now you are not going to be in a position to pass what I tell you to anyone who could pass it on. Have you ever heard of the Aleutian Islands?"

Frogger frowned as he considered the question.

"North Pacific Ocean?" he said.

Frade nodded. "Sort of a tail coming off Alaska."

Frogger nodded.

"You're a field-grade officer," Frade said. "A staff officer, so it will probably come as no surprise to you that we have people in uniform we don't completely trust. Communists, in particular—especially people who fought in Spain with the Abraham Lincoln Brigade—but others as well. We think that some are Germans who still consider Adolf Hitler and the Nazi party the hope of the world, just as some Italians feel the same way about Mussolini. I'm sure you understand what I mean."

Frogger remained silent.

"I suppose in Germany that these sort of threats to the common good would be shot out of hand, if they were not lucky enough to be put in a concentration camp."

Frade let that sink in, then went on: "We, however, don't shoot people out of hand, and with the exception of what we did to Japanese-Americans right after we got in the war, we don't put them in concentration camps. That was something that shouldn't have happened, and most Americans are ashamed that it did.

"Still, we have a saying that just because you're paranoid doesn't mean that little green men from Mars aren't after you with evil intent."

A smile flickered briefly across Frogger's lips.

"So we had the problem of what to do with people we have concerns about. Does Sergeant A, or Major B, feel his allegiance is to the Kremlin or the Pentagon? Since we have no proof, we can't just shoot them, but on the other hand, we can't just let them run free, which might pose a threat to national security.

"So what we do with them is send them to defend the Aleutian Islands, which I suppose could fairly be described as a concentration camp. No barbed wire or guard towers—much like Camp Clinton. Those sort of things are not needed. The only way to get to the Aleutian Islands is by ship or airplane. All we have to do is make sure that when a ship or airplane leaves the Aleutians no one's on it who's not supposed to be on it. Getting the picture?"

Frogger nodded curtly as he lit another cigarette.

"If we can't come to some sort of agreement here, Colonel Frogger, you will be flown to the Aleutians and kept there until the war is over, when we will decide what to do with you."

"That would bring us back to the Geneva Convention, wouldn't it?" Frogger said, unmoved. "What you have described to me would be in violation of the convention."

"Probably, it is. It also almost certainly violates our own constitution. But in wartime, winning is what counts, not the fine points of law. During our own Civil War, Abraham Lincoln suspended the right of habeas corpus."

He took a puff of his cigar, exhaled a gray-blue cloud, then went on:

"Now, let me tell you who I am. I'm an American. An intelligence officer. I'm half-Argentine. My father was not only a colonel in the Ejército Argentino, but active in politics. He was a graduate of your Kriegsschule, and until I finally opened his eyes what scum are running Germany he was really hoping the Axis would win this war.

"What I'm doing in Argentina is—"

"Apparently kidnapping German diplomats and their wives," Frogger blurted.

"—going to be hard for you to believe. You're just going to have to take my word for it."

Frogger's eyes showed how likely that was going to be.

Frade continued: "With the possible exception of Hitler himself, and perhaps a handful of his intimates, a number of senior German officials—Martin Bormann, for one—realize that the war is lost. They have a contingency plan for this. It's called Operation Phoenix. What they are trying to do is purchase sanctuary in South America, primarily in Argentina but in Uruguay, Paraguay, and Brazil as well, to which the senior Nazis will escape and hide until such time as they can rise, Phoenix-like, from the ashes."

"You don't really expect me to believe that."

"I told you that you were going to have to take my word for it. And it gets even more sordid and unbelievable. A number of senior SS officers close to Himmler, although we don't think he's personally involved, saw a chance to make lots of money and took it.

"Jews in concentration camps can buy their way out. They are taken to the Spanish border, then given passports and passage on neutral ships to Argentina and Uruguay. The ransom money goes into the pockets of the SS officers involved."

Frogger shook his head in disbelief.

Frade went on: "When it came to the attention of the SS in Buenos Aires that I was investigating both Operation Phoenix and the ransoming operation, they decided to have me assassinated. An officer in the German embassy, a decent man, decided his officer's honor would not permit him to stand silent while this happened. He warned me. When the people—local gangsters—came to assassinate me, I was ready for them and eliminated them. But not before they had slit the throat of my housekeeper."

"You will forgive me, sir, for saying this sounds like the plot of a bad movie."

"It does indeed. Is there a saying in German, 'Truth is stranger than fiction'?"

Frogger snorted.

"The next thing the Germans decided was that the assassination of my father would serve two purposes. One, it would remove him from power, which was important, because following a planned coup he was to become president of Argentina, and having an Argentine president who was no longer pro-Nazi was unacceptable. And two, it would also, they believed, send a message to the Argentine officer corps that Germany would not hesitate to eliminate any officer who got in their way.

"That assassination was successful. My father was shot to death—two twelve-gauge, double-ought-buckshot loads to the head—and his driver, his former sergeant major, was severely wounded."

They now locked eyes.

"The assassination of my father did not cow the Argentine officer corps. Almost to a man they were offended and angry. More important, they did everything but cheer when the German military attaché and the senior SS officer in the German embassy were shot to death while trying to unload from a U-boat crates of currency, gold, and other valuables intended to finance Operation Phoenix."

"You shot them?" Frogger blurted.

"No. They were shot by my father's former sergeant major—whose sister, by the way, was my housekeeper the assassins murdered—and another old sergeant who had served with my father."

"Forgive me, but I get back to the bad movie plot," Frogger said.

Frade studied Frogger and decided he hadn't said that with much conviction.

"A decision was made at the highest level of our government—hell, by President Roosevelt himself—that as sordid as the ransoming of Jews is—and I was prepared to stop it—it should be allowed to continue because at least some Jews were being saved from the gas chambers."

Frade didn't like the look in Frogger's eyes.

"If you think the stories of the gas chambers are fantasy, I'm probably wasting my time with you. But I suggest you hear me out, as we're getting to your parents."

They locked eyes again.

"Go on, please," Frogger said finally.

"My orders now are to let both operations, Phoenix and the ransoming, continue. I am to find out as much as I can about how the Operation Phoenix funds are being spent. And there's a great many of them. A U-boat successfully landed the crates they had previously failed to, and I'm sure more are on the way. We will deal with the situation after the German surrender."

Frogger looked at him intently but said nothing.

"And then God, so to speak, dumped your parents in my lap."

"What, exactly, does that mean?"

"By now, the Germans understood there was a traitor, or traitors, in the embassy. And of course there are. But no one in the embassy has been able to identify the traitors, and the pressure from Berlin to find them is enormous.

"Your father, who is not one of the traitors, was ordered back to Germany. He thought that once he was in Germany—he knows how these people think, how they operate—he and your mother would be thoroughly interrogated and then shot. Or hung from a butcher's hook."

"But you just said he isn't a traitor."

"He's not. But these people needed to find a traitor, and your father was available. I think—but do not know—that your father also knows many details of Operation Phoenix and maybe of the ransoming operation as well. That would be enough for these people to kill him. And your mother."

Frogger said nothing.

"So your father, knowing the alternative was the meat hook, took off."

"And they went to you?"

"Not directly. To someone else who brought them to me."

"And you're holding them."

"I have no choice. They have seen too much for me to let them go. But that's moot, Colonel. The SS will kill them where and when found."

"How do you know that?"

"You'll have to take my word for that, too."

Frogger thought about that a moment, then said, "What exactly is it that you want from me?"

"I want you to come to Argentina and convince your father that his—and your mother's—only hope to stay alive is to cooperate fully with me in tracking the Operation Phoenix and ransoming money."

"I thought you have spies—traitors—in the embassy. They can't provide that information?"

Frade shook his head.

"If they could, I wouldn't be wasting time here talking to you."

Frogger considered that a moment, then carefully extinguished his cigarette and stood.

"Very imaginative," he said.

"Excuse me?"

Frogger popped to attention.

"Oberstleutnant Frogger, Wilhelm, Identity Number 19-700045."

"Sit down, Frogger. I'm not through with you."

"Oberstleutnant Frogger, Wilhelm, Identity Number 19-700045."

"I'm not going to tell you again," Frade said softly.

"Oberstleutnant Frogger, Wilhelm, Identity Number 19-700045."

"You're back in the plot for a bad movie, are you?"

"Oberstleutnant Frogger, Wilhelm, Identity Number 19-700045."

"Then this is the place in that movie where the interrogator loses his temper and starts punching you? Or puts burning matches under your fingernails?"

"Oberstleutnant Frogger, Wilhelm, Identity Number 19-700045."

"The place where the hero decides that his parents and he himself must die painfully and bravely for the good of the Thousand-Year Reich, the Fatherland, and of course the Führer?"

"Oberstleutnant Frogger, Wilhelm, Identity Number 19-700045."

"And then the Berlin Philharmonic starts playing 'Deutschland, Deutschland über Alles'?"

Frogger glowered at him.

As if leading the Berlin Philharmonic with both hands, Frade began to loudly sing: " 'Deutschland, Deutschland über alles, über alles in der Welt . . .' " He stopped, then added in German, "Nice melody. But no, Willi, that's not going to happen."

Frade walked to the door and opened it.

"Major, will you please come in and handcuff Colonel Frogger? Put him in the car." As Fischer entered, Frade pointed at the table. "And have someone bring all that stuff. He's going to need it in the Aleutians."

"Yes, sir," Fischer said.

Frogger stiffened.

As Fischer approched, Frogger announced, "Under the Geneva Convention, I am entitled to an audience with the camp commander."

Frade walked out of the room.

[THREE]

"Well, I'm not surprised that you gave up," Colonel A. F. Graham said to Major Cletus Frade as they stood out of the sun in the cool shade of a magnificent magnolia tree and watched Fischer load Frogger in the backseat of the staff car. "That sonofabitch is tougher than he looks. But I wonder if maybe you quit a little too soon."

"Colonel, I haven't quit. I'm just starting."

"What do you have in mind?"

"The Kraut who Roosevelt has stashed in the Hotel Washington."

"You want to take him to Washington to see Hanfstaengl?"

Frade nodded. "By way of Fort Bragg."

"What's at Fort Bragg?"

"I heard it's even bigger than Camp Pendleton, and there should be a lot of planes on the air base because of the paratroopers."

"You're trying to impress Frogger?"

Frade nodded again.

"I don't think that will work, and I don't think taking him to see Putzi Hanfstaengl in Washington is a good idea."

"Oh, Jesus Christ!" Frade said in exasperation.

"By now, you should know that the way this works is I make the decisions and you make them happen."

"Colonel, what you said was, 'Use your best judgment. I'll back whatever you decide to do.' This is my best judgment. If you don't want to do it, Colonel, sir, that's your call."

"I don't like your tone of voice, Major," Graham said coldly.

Frade's face showed that he didn't much care whether Colonel Graham liked the tone of his voice or not.

After a long moment, Graham said, "You showed him that Office of War Information radioteletype about warning people to get out of Berlin?" When Frade nodded, Graham added, "If you really want to impress him, we could quote refuel end quote at Newark."

"What's going on at Newark?"

"It's the jump-off point for B-17s, B-24s, and whatever else can make it across the Atlantic. The last time I was there, it was a sea of bombers."

Frade nodded his understanding.

"And on the way," Graham said, warming to his own idea, "we could fly over Manhattan—which has not been bombed—and then over the shipyards in New Jersey and around Baltimore . . . and finally Washington, the White House, and all those buildings untouched by the war."

He saw the look on Frade's face.

"Okay, Clete, I'm going to give you the benefit of the doubt. Allen Dulles thinks turning the Froggers is important."

Frade did not reply.

"This isn't the first time that I've given you the benefit of my very serious doubts, is it?"

"I don't think I'd better answer that."

"Don't let it go to your head," Graham said.

Frade didn't respond.

"There are several problems with taking him to see Putzi at the Hotel Washington," Graham went on. "For one thing, Frogger says he never heard of him—"

"He's heard of him," Frade said flatly.

Graham grinned. "Odd, we've found something we agree on. I'll have to give Putzi a heads-up we're coming, and why."

"Just tell him we want him to convince Willi that Putzi was a pal of Adolf and his cronies, and—"

"I know what to tell him," Graham cut him off. "What I'm thinking is that taking a German officer, in Afrikakorps uniform, into the Hotel Washington may raise some eyebrows."

"If anybody asks, tell them he's a character in one of Howard's movies."

Graham shook his head.

"And speaking of Howard," Frade said, "are those guys in the white jackets on the Constellation his or yours? They're the same ones who were in the Chateau Marmont, right?"

"You mean Howard's Saints? I wondered how long it was going to take you to get around to asking about them."

" 'Howard's Saints'?"

"They're Mormons. Members of the Church of Jesus Christ of Latter-Day Saints. They don't drink, they don't smoke, they don't even drink coffee. They protect Howard from all sorts of threats—some real, some imagined. He pays them very well."

"Do they carry guns? Can they help Fischer guard Frogger?"

Graham nodded.

"Can we get Howard on the phone while Fischer and Frogger are on their way to the airport? Give him a heads-up?"

Graham nodded and said, "You're not going with them?"

"Let him worry what you and I are up to," Frade said. "And then be dazzled by the airplane while he's waiting for us."

Graham considered that, then nodded. "Okay."

Frade walked to the staff car. Frogger was in the backseat, his hands handcuffed behind him. Fischer was standing by the door.

"Get Colonel Frogger out of the hot sun, Major," Frade ordered. "Put him on the plane. Cuff him to one of the seats halfway down the fuselage. If he tries to escape, shoot him in the foot; try very hard not to kill him. What I don't need right now is a noble martyr to the Nazi cause."

"Yes, sir," Fischer said.

[FOUR]
Bolling Air Force Base
Washington, D.C.
1730 6 August 1943

Clete didn't know, of course, whether Oberstleutnant Frogger was impressed with his tour of the Eastern Seaboard from Connecticut to Washington, D.C.—with a side trip to North Carolina to Pope Air Force Base and Fort Bragg—but as Frade lined up the Constellation with the runway at Bolling, he didn't see how Frogger could not be. He had been dazzled himself.

After the flyover of Bragg and Pope—and they had been lucky there; an enormous fleet of C-47s was in the process of disgorging a regiment of paratroopers as they flew over—they had flown to north of New York City, where Hughes had called Air Traffic Control and reported they were having pressurization problems, and requested an approach to the field at Newark at no higher than five thousand feet.

That allowed them to fly at that altitude over Manhattan Island. The Hudson River was full of ships, and they got a look at the bustling shipyards in New Jersey. Taking on fuel at Newark gave them forty minutes on the ground, which in turn gave them—and, more important, Frogger—that long of a time to see row after row of glistening new B-17 and B-24 heavy bombers preparing to fly to Europe.

Hughes again called Air Traffic Control, reported they were still having pressurization problems, and requested—and received—permission to fly to Bolling at five thousand feet.

Their routing took them over Delaware, then Baltimore, and finally Washington. It was a sunny day and all the buildings of the capital were on clear display, every one untouched by any sign of bombing.

They were third in the pattern to land at Bolling, after a B-26 light bomber and a four-engine Douglas C-54 transport. Frade then greased in the Constellation. He really thought it was a combination of a nice day, a low, slow approach, and a lot of beginner's luck, but was nonetheless pleased when he heard Howard Hughes say over the intercom, "Not bad, Little Cletus."

The tower directed them to the tarmac before a remote hangar on the opposite side of the field from Base Operations. The hangar was under heavy guard—submachine-gun armed MPs on foot and others in a three-quarter-ton weapons carrier and a jeep. Frade was curious about that and even more curious to see that a dozen or more men were in the hangar polishing the aluminum skin of a C-54.

Hughes answered his question before Frade could put it into words.

"The Sacred Cow," he said.

"The what?"

"The Sacred Cow," Hughes explained, "is the President's personal aircraft. He really should have one of these; they're faster, have a longer range, and are more comfortable. But Lockheed makes these, Charley Lindbergh works for Lockheed, and our commander in chief is cutting off his nose to spite his face because he's got a hard-on for Charley."

"You're serious?"

"Don't tell anyone, Little Cletus, but our noble commander in chief can be a vindictive sonofabitch. Ask your grandfather."

Ground handlers pushed steps against the Constellation's rear and behind the cockpit doors. A closed van backed up to the steps rising to the door behind the cockpit. On its sides was a sign: CAPITOL CATERING. A 1940 Packard limousine pulled up to the stairs leading to the passenger compartment. A chauffeur got out and the rear door opened.

Frade walked down the aisle to Frogger, who was handcuffed to one of the seats. A fold-down shelf on the rear of the seat ahead of him held a coffee cup and an ashtray.

Frade squatted in the aisle.

"Welcome to Washington, Herr Oberstleutnant."

Frogger did not reply.

"One of two things is going to happen now," Frade said. "I'm going to have the major remove your handcuffs. Then you have your choice of walking forward and going down the stairs and into the van. Or you can be difficult about this, and the handcuffs will be put back on your wrists and you will be led— or carried, if you choose to be difficult—down the wider stairs at the passenger compartment door and put into the van."

"Where am I being taken?"

"To see Herr Hanfstaengl. He's a former close friend of your Führer."

"This entire situation, sir, is a violation of my rights under the Geneva Convention! I demand to see a representative of the International Red Cross!"

Frade stood and looked at Fischer.

"Have them cuff Herr Oberstleutnant's hands behind his back and put him in the van."

Frade stood in the passenger door and watched as two of Howard's Saints marched Frogger down the stairs and to the rear door of the CAPITOL CATERING van. Fischer followed them. The van's door closed and it drove off.

Frade stepped back and motioned for Colonel Graham to precede him down the stairs. They both got into the limousine and it drove off.

As they left the air base, Frade said, "I don't suppose there's a radio in that van, is there? And one in here?"

"There is," Graham said. "That is, there *are*. But if you're thinking of telling them to drive the extra couple blocks to show Frogger the White House, I already have."

The Packard stopped in front of the Hotel Washington. Graham got out with Frade on his heels, went through the revolving door, and walked purposefully to the bank of elevators. They got on one, and the operator, a burly black man with gray hair, closed the door.

"Good evening, Steve," Graham said politely. "By now they should be waiting for us in the subbasement."

"Excuse me, Colonel," the operator said as he studied Frade and his long locks. "Who's this gentleman?"

"This is Major Frade," Graham said.

"My heads-up said you, an MP major, two of Mr. Hughes's men, and a quote end quote special visitor."

"And that while we're in there nobody else is to be admitted?"

"Yes, sir."

"The MP officer will be in the basement with the special visitor," Graham explained. "I'll vouch for this officer."

"Yes, sir," the elevator operator said, and reached for the elevator control. As he did so, Frade saw that the fabric of the operator's black jacket was tightly stretched over what was almost certainly a 1911-A1 Colt .45 in the small of his back.

"Why do I suspect you're one of us?" Frade asked him, smiling.

"No, sir. I'm Secret Service. We protect the President, the Vice President, their families, and select supposed ex-Nazis."

The elevator stopped and the Secret Service man slid open the door.

Frogger was standing there with one of Hughes's men on each side. Fischer stood to one side.

"Good evening, gentlemen," the Secret Service man said. "I guess you're waiting for the elevator to the Washington Berghof?"

Graham laughed.

"Get on, please, Oberstleutnant Frogger," Graham ordered.

Frogger looked reluctant, almost as if he was going to refuse.

"Get on," Graham repeated.

Frogger didn't move.

"Colonel, you better get on," the Secret Service man said in perfect German. "If I have to come out there and throw you on, you're not going to like it at all."

Frogger came into the elevator and the others crowded in after him.

The Secret Service man took a telephone from its hanger and said into it: "Six on the way up. Clear the corridor."

The elevator began to rise. When the car stopped and its door was opened, there was a small sign announcing SEVENTH FLOOR.

There also were two men in civilian clothing waiting for them. From the respect with which they greeted Colonel Graham—and from their haircuts—Frade guessed they were soldiers, maybe even Marines.

"This way please, Colonel, gentlemen."

They were led to a door at the end of the corridor. One of the men gestured at Howard's Saints, signaling them that the corridor was as far as they were going to be allowed to go, and then opened the door and gestured for Graham, Frade, Fisher, and Frogger to go in. When they had done so, the door was closed after them.

Frade saw they were in a comfortably furnished corner sitting room. Its windows opened on both Pennsylvania Avenue and Fifteenth Street. The White House, a block or so to the west, was clearly visible over the roof of the Treasury Department building.

An interior door opened and a tall man with somewhat sunken eyes and a prominent chin walked in. He was wearing a white shirt, no tie, and the cuffs were rolled up.

"Hello, Alex," he said in Boston—or at least Harvard—accented English.

"How are you, Putzi?" Graham said as they shook hands.

Hanfstaengl looked at Frogger and said in German, "Colonel, I'm Ernst Hanfstaengl. And you can let your breath out. You are not about to be hung on a meat hook."

Frogger glared at him but said nothing.

Hanfstaengl turned to Graham.

"I don't need to know who these gentlemen are, Alex, but it probably would be quite helpful if I knew what it is they—or you—want from the colonel."

"Putzi, I'm afraid that's classified," Graham said.

"Mr. Hanfstaengl," Frade said, "what I would like for you to do is tell the colonel what scum are running Germany."

Hanfstaengl looked at Frade, then raised his eyebrows.

"Well, that wouldn't be hard—I know most of them—but what makes you think he'd believe me? Someone in my position would not be likely to say that Adolf Hitler and the National Socialist Democratic Workers Party are the hope of Western civilization, now would he?"

"Give it a shot, please," Frade said on the cusp of unpleasantness.

Hanfstaengl looked at Graham for guidance.

Graham said, "Tell the colonel, for example, where Hitler got the money to buy the *Volkische Beobachter.*"

"The people's what?" Frade asked.

" 'The People's Observer,' literally translated," Hanfstaengl said. "The Nazi party newspaper. Hitler got it from me. I gave him the money."

"And why did you do that?" Graham asked softly.

"At the time, I believed Hitler was the hope of Germany and possibly the only thing standing between Germany, Europe, Western civilization, and the Communist hordes."

"What made you change your mind?" Frade asked.

"Even if you don't know it yet, the United States is the only hope the world has to stem the Communist hordes."

"You haven't changed your mind about Hitler?" Frade challenged.

"My position on that is a pox on both their houses," Hanfstaengl said. "Goebbels and Himmler tried to have me murdered, as I suspect you know."

"But I thought you were a good Nazi," Frade said.

"Presumably you know what Lord Acton had to say about power. 'Power corrupts, and absolute power corrupts absolutely.' What happened in Germany is unequivocal proof of that."

"Then you would say that Hitler and the people around him are corrupt?" Graham asked.

"Well, if the bastard hadn't murdered his niece, with whom he was having an incestuous relationship, I would say that Hitler is probably less personally corrupt than those around him. He's paranoid, of course. And an egomaniac. Those around him are corrupt beyond description."

He paused and looked at Frogger.

"You are a professional soldier, Herr Oberstleutnant?"

Frogger nodded.

"Then certainly you must be aware that your peers hold the 'Austrian corporal' in deep contempt?"

Frogger didn't reply.

"Let me put it to you this way, Herr Oberstleutnant: Germany has lost the war. The sooner it's over, the fewer soldiers—and civilians—will be killed or mutilated for life. Have you heard that Goebbels has gone on Radio Berlin and advised people to leave? So the sooner Germany surrenders, the better for Germany."

Hanfstaengl looked at Frogger for a response and got none. He shrugged as if he expected that reaction.

Then he coldly added: "Herr Oberstleutnant, if whatever Colonel Graham here is asking you to do will hasten the end of the war, then it is your duty to do so."

"What they are asking me to do has nothing to do with ending the war, Herr Hanfstaengl," Frogger said.

"Perhaps you can't see how whatever he's asking you to do has to do with hastening the end of the war, but I know Colonel Graham well enough to know that unless he thought it was about ending the war, or something nearly that important, he wouldn't have brought you here to me."

Frogger did not respond.

Without breaking eye contact with Frogger, Hanfstaengl said, "May I ask him a question, Alex?"

"Discreetly, Putzi."

"Herr Oberstleutnant, does the term *heavy water*—"

"Stop right there, Putzi!" Graham said sharply.

"—mean anything to you? Because if it does, and you're not giving Graham what he wants—"

"*Shut up,* Putzi!" Graham ordered loudly and furiously.

Graham looked at Frade. "Get Frogger the hell out of here. I knew this was a bad idea. . . ."

Hanfstaengl threw both hands up in a gesture of surrender.

"Herr Hanfstaengl, I have no idea what you're talking about," Frogger said without conviction as Frade reached for him.

"Putzi, you sonofabitch!" Graham said bitterly.

The door from the corridor suddenly opened.

A burly man stepped inside. He held a Smith & Wesson revolver in his hand, the arm extended parallel to his leg. He looked quickly around the room.

"You can put that away, Dennis," Franklin Delano Roosevelt said as he rolled his wheelchair through the doorway. "I know both of them well enough to know it's mostly bark without much bite."

No one in the room spoke for a moment.

"Mr. President," Graham said finally. "Your friend has just been talking about heavy water." His voice was tense with anger.

"I heard you would be here, Alex," the President said, ignoring the outburst entirely. He paused to take a cigarette from a gold case and fit it into an eight-inch-long silver holder. Dennis, the man who had entered the room holding a revolver at his side, quickly produced a cigarette lighter.

Roosevelt took a puff and exhaled thoughtfully.

"As I was saying, Alex, I heard you were paying Putzi a visit, but I didn't hear anything about these gentlemen."

He waved the cigarette holder like a pointer at Frade, Fogger, and Fischer, who had all, without thinking about it, come to attention. Then the cigarette holder pointed at Frogger.

"May I ask who you are, sir?"

Frogger grew even more stiffly erect. He bowed and clicked his heels.

"Oberstleutnant Frogger, Wilhelm, Excellency!" he barked.

"In whose presence Hanfstaengl has been—" Graham began, only to be shut off by Roosevelt's extended palm.

Roosevelt's cigarette holder was now aimed at Frade.

"Before anyone tells me, let me guess. You're Cletus Frade."

"Yes, I am, Mr. President."

"I'm pleased that you finally have found time to come to Washington," Roosevelt said. He turned to Frogger. "Mr. Frade is an interesting man, Colonel. At one time, he was a distinguished fighter pilot. Now he's an intelligence officer who knows the names of the German officers who are planning to—how do I put this?—*permanently and irrevocably* remove Chancellor Hitler from office. Information he refuses to share with me, as difficult to believe as that may be."

He paused and looked at Frade for a long moment.

FDR then went on: "And I have no idea, Colonel, why he's brought you here to see my old friend Hanfstaengl. I'm not at all sure he'd tell me if I asked. But I do know that he would not have done so unless he thought it was rather important."

He took another pull at his cigarette, then looked at Frogger as he slowly exhaled the smoke through his nostrils.

"The reason, Mr. Frogger, that I don't insist that Frade share everything he knows with me is that he enjoys my absolute confidence. You might wish to keep that in mind in your dealings with him."

The President kept his eyes locked with Frogger's for a long moment, then swiveled the wheelchair to face Hanfstaengl.

"This would seem to be a poor time for a visit, Putzi, wouldn't it? I'll come back another time." He paused, then said, "Good evening, gentlemen," and swiveled his wheelchair around so that he faced the door.

The Secret Service agent was just able to get to the door and open it as Roosevelt rolled up to it. And then the President was through it and gone.

A long moment later, Frade said without thinking, "Jesus H. Christ!"

"Is it true, Mr. Frade?" Frogger asked. "That you know the names of those officers who plan to . . . remove . . . der Führer?"

"If it were true, why the hell should I tell you?"

"If it was not true, you would have said it was, to elicit my support," Frogger said.

Frade just looked at him.

"Mr. Frade," Frogger said after a moment, "does the name Oberstleutnant Claus Graf von Stauffenberg mean anything to you?"

Frade didn't reply.

"Perhaps you're not as good an intelligence officer as your President Roosevelt seems to think you are, Mr. Frade. The look in your eyes answered my question."

They locked eyes.

"As the imminent and inevitable collapse of the Afrikakorps became apparent," Frogger said, "von Stauffenberg was trying to arrange my transfer to Germany. I'm rather surprised my name has not come to your attention." He paused, then went on: "Under the changed circumstances, Mr. Frade, I will of course do whatever it is you want me to do."

"For the moment, Colonel Frogger, I'll go along with you," Graham said.

"It will take a day or two for me to verify your connection with von Stauffenberg. If you're lying, I'll have you shot."

"I understood that, Colonel, when I gave you von Stauffenberg's name."

"Fischer, take him back to Bolling. Put him on the Constellation. If he tries to escape, if he tries anything, kill him," Graham ordered.

[FIVE]
Bolling Air Force Base
Washington, D.C.
2205 6 August 1943

The Constellation was not only plugged into a ground-power generator but was also connected with something Frade had never seen—a flexible pipe connected to a truck-mounted air-conditioning unit. Graham had told him that it had been specially made to cool the President's Sacred Cow while the aircraft waited for him on a typical torrid Washington summer day.

Frade was sitting—drinking coffee with Howard Hughes—near the rear door, through which the eighteen-inch-diameter flexible hose was delivering a steady blast of icy air. Frogger was seated about in the middle of the passenger compartment. He was no longer handcuffed. Fischer was sitting across the aisle from him, and two of Howard's Saints were sitting on the aisle just forward of Frade. Frogger wasn't going anywhere.

There were MPs armed with Thompson submachine guns at the foot of the stairs, and just inside the door were two men in suits who Frade supposed were either Secret Service agents or from the OSS.

One of them stepped around the air-conditioning hose and onto the stairs, then a moment later came to where Frade and Hughes were sitting.

"Colonel Graham would like to see you, gentlemen," he said.

They went down the stairway and got into the backseat of the Packard limousine.

"I haven't heard from Allen Dulles," Graham began the moment Hughes had pulled the door closed after them. "No telling where he is, or when I'll hear from him. But I think Frogger's telling the truth, so I think we should get this show on the road."

"Vegas?" Hughes said.

Graham nodded.

"Las Vegas?" Frade asked.

Graham nodded again.

"I think it might be helpful if I knew what's going on," Frade said more than a little sarcastically.

"Ignoring your tone of voice, I will tell you," Graham said. "By now the word is out that we took Frogger to see Hanfstaengl."

"The word's out to who?" Frade said. "And, for Christ's sake, by who?"

"You might want to write this down, Major," Graham said. "There is no such thing as hole-proof counterintelligence. I'm going on the assumption that among the Hotel Washington's staff are some people who are generously compensated for reporting to the Spanish embassy, the Mexican embassy, the Argentine embassy—yeah, Clete, the Argentine embassy—and even the British embassy about who goes to see Putzi Hanfstaengl and even more generously compensated if they can provide photographs of the visitors. So we have to get Frogger out of town as quickly as possible."

"To Las Vegas?"

"Las Vegas is in the middle of nowhere," Graham explained. "The Las Vegas Army Airfield was established there because it offers a lot of room in which aerial gunners can be trained. What most people don't know is that across a ridge line or two is another air base, no name, where we conduct tests of various things we don't want anybody to know about. Don Bell's jet airplane, for one, and some other things about which you don't have the Need to Know.

"Frogger can be held there without anybody seeing him, and with virtually no chance of his getting away. There's no way to walk away, and his chances of getting away in a car are slim to none.

"One of your Lodestars is en route to that air base now, carrying a flight crew for the Constellation—men who know not to ask questions. You and Howard will fly the Lodestar back to Burbank, you having completed your pilot training.

"As soon as I hear from Allen Dulles, Frogger will be flown, with Fischer and two of my men, in the Constellation to Canoas Air Base in Brazil. It'll be up to you to get him from there to Argentina—any problems with that?"

Frade shook his head.

"And you will fly one of your SAA Lodestars to Argentina. Okay? The managing director of SAA having gotten his ATR first. Still with me?"

Frade nodded.

"By the time you're ready to move Frogger from Brazil, we'll get him into civilian clothing and get him a passport. Probably South African."

Graham looked between them.

"Any questions?"

Both Frade and Hughes shook their heads.

"Okay," Graham said, "then have a nice flight."

XVI

[ONE]
Aeropuerto El Alto
La Paz, Bolivia
1230 11 August 1943

The airfield at La Paz left a good deal to be desired. The single runway was short and paved with gravel. The customs officials who met the SAA Lodestar were in ill-fitting khaki uniforms and expected to receive—and did—a little gift in appreciation of their professional services.

The fuel truck was a 1935 Ford ton-and-a-half stake-bodied truck—not a tanker—sagging under the weight of a dozen fifty-five-gallon barrels of aviation fuel. The pump was hand-cranked.

There was a small silver lining to that, however. When Frade examined the barrels, he saw from the intact paint on the openings that they hadn't been opened since leaving the Howell Petroleum Refinery in Louisiana. The fuel would be safe to use.

Cletus Howell Frade did not mention to Gonzalo Delgano his connection with Howell Petroleum.

The weather station was "temporarily" out of communication with anybody else, which meant that they would have to rely on the weather report they'd gotten just before taking off from Guayaquil, Ecuador, not quite six hours before. That one had reported good weather all over the eastern half of South America, and from what they'd seen in the air, the report was valid.

They both were tired. It had been a very long flight. They'd left Burbank at six in the morning on August ninth and flown nonstop to Mexico City. They'd taken on fuel there and flown on to Guatemala City, whose airfield was downtown and surrounded by hills. The final approach was a dive at the threshold.

Frade and Delgano spent the night in Guatemala City in a charming old hotel, which apparently had not replaced the mattresses since they were first installed. But nevertheless both had overslept. They had planned to leave at six a.m., but it was a few minutes after eight before they broke ground on the next leg, to Guayaquil, Ecuador.

They didn't want to try to go any farther, so they spent the night there, just about on the equator, which meant tropical temperatures and hordes of biting insects—many of them mosquitoes—that the somewhat ragged mosquito nets did little to discourage.

The next morning, they were wide awake at five a.m. and took off for La Paz as intended, at six a.m., without availing themselves of anything more than coffee for breakfast.

It had been a nearly six-hour flight, and as soon as they could after landing they headed for the airport restaurant.

The tableware was dirty, the *papas fritas* limp and greasy, and the *lomo*—filet mignon—was thin and had the tenderness of a boot sole.

"I don't mean to be critical, Gonzo, but I have had better *lomo*," Frade said as he pushed his plate away and reached for another piece of bread.

"Patience is a virtue, as you may have heard. In just a matter of hours, Cletus, my friend, we will be in Argentina, where, as you have learned, the women are beautiful and the beef magnificent."

Delgano saw something in Frade's eyes.

"What?" he asked.

"Gonzo, we have to talk."

"I thought this would be coming."

"Truth time?" Frade asked.

"That's always useful. But one of the truths here is that I'm afraid we have different loyalties."

"Different isn't the same as opposing."

"Would your admitting that you are a serving officer—a major—of the U.S. Corps of Marines attached to the OSS be the kind of truth you're talking about?"

"Not really," Frade said. "Colonel Martín has known that for some time, and so have you, Major Gonzalo Delgano of the Ethical Standards Office of the Bureau of Internal Security."

Delgano considered that and nodded. He then said: "Colonel Martín also believes that you know a good deal more than you're admitting about the disappearance of the Froggers. Are you going to tell me the truth about that? Is that what this is all about?"

Frade nodded.

"You kidnapped them?" Delgano asked.

"No. They came to me. I didn't kidnap them."

"We wondered about that. Kidnapping a German diplomat and his wife would have been very dangerous, and we couldn't understand why you would do something so foolish."

"Frogger had been ordered back to Germany. He was afraid he was suspected of being a traitor."

"Colonel Martín considered that. He has a hard time believing Frogger is Galahad."

"He's not. And, yeah, Gonzo, I realize that when I say he's not, I'm admitting there is a Galahad. Truth time."

Delgano smiled wryly.

"Colonel Martín thinks Galahad is Major von Wachtstein," Delgano said.

"Does he?"

"I didn't really expect you to admit something like that," Delgano said. "Why did Frogger go to you?"

"He didn't. When he decided that he had to run, he went to somebody else, who brought the Froggers to me."

"Are you going to tell me who that 'somebody else' is?"

"No," Frade said simply.

"So why did you take them? Knowing how dangerous for you that would be?"

"I'd like to say because I'm a Good Samaritan, but I won't. I'm not, and you wouldn't believe it anyway. The truth is that my friend had no place to hide them and I couldn't let them go. The Germans would learn who brought them to me, for one thing. And, for another, I got word that the SS had decided that Frogger knew too much and had put out an order to kill him—both of them; the wife, too—wherever and whenever found."

"So what are you going to do with them?"

"This is where telling the truth gets uncomfortable."

"Do you have any choice?"

Frade shook his head. After a moment, he said, "Do you remember having breakfast with a man called Stevens, an assistant consular officer, when we were at Canoas?"

Delgano nodded.

"Well, he solved my problem of what to do with the Froggers. He's not an assistant consular officer at the embassy in Rio de Janeiro."

"I didn't think he was. Who is he?"

"A very senior OSS officer."

"Who works for Colonel Graham?"

"Who works *with* Colonel Graham."

"An important man," Delgano said.

Frade nodded. "When I told him about the Froggers . . . I have to go off on a tangent here, Gonzo. What do you know about Operation Phoenix?"

Delgano gestured with his hand toward Frade. "Why don't you tell me about Operation Phoenix?"

"I will if you tell me whether or not you've heard about it, Major Delgano."

Delgano shrugged. "Very well. I've heard about it."

"Okay. I'll tell you everything I know about it, and you can then tell me if it's what you've heard."

"Fair enough."

"Just about everybody in Hitler's circle but Hitler himself has realized that the war essentially is over, and that most of them are going to get hung. So Martin Bormann came up with a plan—Operation Phoenix—to buy a sanctuary in South America. Primarily in Argentina, but also in Brazil, Paraguay . . ."

"That's pretty much what we've heard," Delgano said when Frade had finished.

"What have you heard about the ransoming of Jews out of the concentration camps and arranging for them to get out of Germany and come to Argentina and Uruguay?"

Delgano didn't reply immediately.

"Nothing," he finally said. "But it would certainly explain something that's been bothering us."

"What do you mean?"

"Two things: Where all those pathetic 'Spanish and Portuguese' Jews are coming from—pathetic meaning undernourished, showing signs of abuse, and looking very frightened. And with numbers tattooed on their inner arms." He pointed to his own arm. "We checked their passports. They're valid."

"You said two things," Frade said.

"And the passage of large amounts of dollars and pounds sterling through Argentina and into Uruguay."

Frade smiled knowingly. He said, "The operation is run by Himmler's adjutant, SS-Brigadeführer Manfred von Deitzberg, who was recently in Argentina wearing the uniform of a Wehrmacht major general."

"We knew that—that he was really SS—but never quite understood what he was doing in Argentina."

"Looking for Galahad and protecting the ransoming operation."

"From you?"

Frade nodded, and said, "But he really has nothing to worry about for the moment. President Roosevelt has decided that my shutting it down would have the effect of sending more Jews to the ovens or being worked—or starved—to death. So the plan is that we'll deal with those bastards once the Germans have surrendered."

"One of the problems you—the United States and England—have in Argentina, Cletus, is that very few people are willing to believe the Germans are capable of cruelty—mass murder—on that scale."

"Yeah, I know," Frade said, and went on: "My orders are to keep track of both Operation Phoenix and the ransoming money."

"This is where you have to tell me about South American Airways. Alejandro Martín doesn't believe much—in fact, anything—about the story you've given about why the U.S. suddenly is willing to provide us airplanes that Brazil—and other of your allies—would very much like to have."

Delgano paused, chuckled, then went on: "But his philosophy is much like yours, Cletus: *Let the bastards get away with whatever it is for now. We'll deal with them later, and in the meantime we'll have the airplanes.*"

"And Gonzo Delgano is watching the bastards like a condor?"

Delgano smiled and nodded.

"The true story is pretty incredible," Frade said. "You want to hear it anyway?"

Delgano nodded.

"You know who Colonel Charles Lindbergh is?"

Delgano's face showed he found the question unnecessary to the point of being insulting.

"Well, Lindbergh went to Germany, where Göring gave him a medal, then Lindbergh came home and announced that the Luftwaffe was the most advanced . . ."

"You're right," Delgano said. "That story is so incredible that I don't think you could have made it up. Really?"

Frade nodded. "That's it. Believe it or not. Okay. Getting back to the Froggers."

"Okay."

"You want the short version or the long one?" Clete asked.

"Try the short one first."

"The Froggers had three sons. Two of them were killed. Lieutenant Colonel Wilhelm Frogger was captured with General von Arnim when the Afrikakorps surrendered, and was taken to America. When I was gone—ostensibly getting my ATR check ride in a Lodestar—I actually flew a Constellation to the POW cage in Mississippi. I showed Frogger pictures of his parents with me and Len Fischer. I told him why his parents—at least his father—had fled the German embassy—"

" 'At least his father'?"

"La Señora Frogger is a dedicated Nazi. And, as such, too much of a zealot to believe that the Nazis would kill her and her husband without blinking an eye."

Delgano's face showed surprise, but he said nothing.

"Anyway, I told Frogger about Operation Phoenix—"

"And he believed you?"

Frade nodded. "And he's willing to talk to his father about helping me keep track of the Operation Phoenix and ransoming money."

"Two questions about that. First, why would he do that? Second, how could he do that from a prisoner camp in . . . where did you say? Mississippi?"

"He's not in Mississippi," Frade said.

Delgano considered that a moment, then an eyebrow went up. "Canoas?"

Frade nodded again.

"How did he get there?"

"In a Constellation."

"The same one you flew to Mississippi to see him?"

"Yeah."

"It doesn't add up, Cletus. I don't think you're lying to me, but I'm sure you're not telling me everything."

Clete smiled. "I'm not and I'm not."

"You're going to have to tell me everything."

"Tell me what doesn't add up, and I'll try."

"Let's go back to SAA's insurance being canceled," Delgano said. "Martín doesn't believe that. He thinks it was arranged to give you a credible excuse to come to the United States. To see this Colonel Frogger?"

"It was."

Delgano squinted his eyes. He looked a little mad . . . or maybe hurt.

"Your anger was very convincing," he said. "I told Martín I believed you."

"I didn't know until we got to the Chateau Marmont. Graham was there."

Delgano considered that, then asked, "Who arranged the scenario?"

"The man you met in Canoas. His name is Allen Dulles. He does in Europe what Graham does in the Western Hemisphere."

"As important as keeping a track on the German money in Argentina may be to you, I don't think it's important enough for all of this. And I find it very hard to believe that a German lieutenant colonel is going to change sides simply because you have his parents."

Frade didn't reply for a long moment. Then he said, "Frogger had changed sides, to use your term, before I saw him. Before he was captured. I didn't know this when I went to see him, and he was everything you'd expect an officer to be. He wouldn't give me anything but his name and his rank and his service number."

"What happened?"

"I really don't want to tell you this, and after I do you will probably—almost certainly—wish I hadn't told you."

"We won't know that, will we, until you do? So tell me."

Frade made a grunt. "Okay. There is a plot involving a number of senior German officers to kill Hitler and end the war they know they have no chance of winning before more people are killed. Frogger has been part of it for some time. When it came out that we knew about it—"

"You told him?"

"It came out almost accidentally. He threw a name at me and saw on my face that I knew it."

"That tells me, you know, that the Germans you're working with in Buenos Aires—Galahad certainly, the ambassador maybe, and probably others—are involved in this assassination plot."

"I don't want to answer that, Gonzo."

Delgano looked Frade in the eyes a long moment.

"You don't have to, Cletus. And you're right, my friend. My life would be a lot more comfortable from now on if I didn't know about this."

"If it gets out, a lot of good, decent officers are going to wind up with piano wire around their necks and hanging from butcher hooks."

"And if it doesn't get out, Hitler is assassinated."

"That's what we're hoping for."

It was another long moment before Delgano went on: "The rest of the scenario is that we fly to Canoas, then smuggle Frogger into the country. And I tell no one. Is that it?"

"That's part of it. The other part is that we smuggle the Froggers out of Argentina into Brazil, where they will be seen boarding a British warship or airplane—that hasn't been worked out completely yet—then smuggle them back into Argentina."

"To call off the hunt for them in Argentina?"

Frade nodded.

"And you're asking me to help you with this?"

"Yes, I am."

"You realize that I am honor bound to tell Colonel Martín everything you've told me."

"That's the call you have to make, Gonzo. What does your honor demand of you?"

"Goddamn you, Cletus!"

Delgano stood up.

"If I walk out of here without giving you an answer, are you going to shoot me?"

"I should, but I couldn't, and I think you know that."

"I'm going to take a walk. I think better when I'm walking. And I also pray better while walking, rather than on my knees."

He walked quickly to the door, then turned back toward Frade.

"Don't come after me," he said. "And for Christ's sake, don't try to reason with me."

When Delgano had been gone for twenty minutes, Frade relit the cigar he had been holding unlit for most of that time and walked to the door. He spotted Delgano on the threshold of the runway, walking slowly back and forth across the markings. Delgano could have been talking to himself.

Finally, Delgano threw his hands up in what could have been a gesture of frustration—or one of decision—and started walking purposefully back toward the terminal building.

He walked up to Frade, who had stepped out of the building.

They locked eyes for a long moment.

"May God damn you, Cletus. And may God forgive me."

"What does that mean?"

"It means," Delgano said, his voice strained with emotion, "that if you promise to try to remember the Lodestar is not a fighter, I'll let you fly to Canoas."

Clete nodded. *"Muchas gracias, mi amigo."*

Then he saw tears in Delgano's eyes and felt them well up in his own. He grabbed Delgano and hugged him tightly.

[TWO]
Canoas Air Base
Pôrto Alegre, Brazil
2135 11 August 1943

Canoas ground control told them to turn off the runway onto Taxiway 6 and hold; a Follow-Me would meet them.

The checkerboard-painted truck appeared two minutes later and led them to a remote corner of the field, across the runway complex from Base Operations. A Constellation was parked there, and before they could bring the Lodestar to a stop next to it, a MP jeep—a red light on its fender flashing brightly in the night—came racing up, followed by a staff car on the bumper of which was the starred plate of a general officer.

United States Army Air Forces Brigadier General J. B. Wallace, his aide-de-camp, and two MPs, one of them a captain, were standing on the tarmac when Frade opened the passenger door and got out.

Frade resisted the Pavlovian impulse to salute.

"Welcome back to Canoas, Señor Frade," Wallace said.

"I didn't expect to be met by the base commander, sir," Frade said.

"Well, I would think the circumstances rather dictated that I should, wouldn't you?"

"Very kind of you, sir."

Delgano came out of the Lodestar somewhat awkwardly, carrying a canvas overnight bag in each hand.

Wallace eyed him warily, glanced at the Connie, then said, "The . . . others . . . arrived a few hours ago. May I ask who this gentleman is?"

"El Señor Delgano is South American Airways' chief pilot."

"And will he be going with us to meet . . . the others?"

"Oh, yes," Frade said.

General Wallace made a rather grand gesture toward the staff car.

Wallace's aide indicated that Frade and Delgano should get in the backseat. As the general got in the front passenger seat, the aide extended his hand for the overnight bags, then put them in the trunk and got in the car behind the wheel.

"Blow the horn at them," General Wallace ordered, then reached over and did it himself. "Let's get the show on the road!"

The siren on the MP jeep began to howl, and both vehicles took off.

General Wallace turned in his seat to face Frade. "May I speak with Mr. . . . Delgano, you said? . . . here?"

"Anything you have to say to me, sir, you can say to Captain Delgano."

"I had a personal message from General Arnold directing me to place all my facilities at the disposal of the OSS for this operation of yours."

"Did you?"

And General Arnold didn't mention that this operation of mine is sort of a secret, and that running us around the base behind a MP jeep with its siren and strobe going might not be such a good idea?

You didn't think that might make people wonder what the hell is going on?

"What I've done is put the crew of the Constellation in the visiting officers' BOQ. I've put you—and the others—in a senior officers' quarters—a rather nice little cottage that was, fortunately, vacant. I hope that's all right, Mr. Frade?"

"Fine. Thank you, sir."

"And put it under secure guard, of course," General Wallace concluded.

There was another MP jeep in the driveway of a red-tile-roofed cottage. It was parked nose out, and its headlights illuminated the lawn of the adjacent cottage, where two Brazilian women—obviously maids of some sort—stood with their arms folded, almost visibly wondering what all the activity was about. As the general's escort jeep pulled to a stop and its siren died, the MPs in the parked jeep jumped out, popped to attention, and saluted the staff car.

"Would you like me to come in with you, Mr. Frade?" General Wallace asked. He already had his front passenger door open.

"That won't be necessary, General, thank you. What I want you to do, if you'd be so kind, is to get us a car and driver to use while we're here. It's getting late, and we still have to go to the officers' club for dinner."

"I can arrange for the club to deliver your dinner, if you'd like. Security might be a problem there."

"We'd rather go to the club, if that would be all right. And speaking of security, you can send the MPs away, please."

"Is that wise?"

"I think so. I appreciate your concern, but we're all armed."

"Whatever you say, Mr. Frade. Can you give me some idea how long you'll be here?"

"We'll leave at first light. And as soon as we break ground, the Constellation will go back to the States. I presume that if I need anything, I can get in touch with you by asking the operator for the commanding general?"

Wallace nodded, then said rather formally, "I'll be available around the clock, Mr. Frade."

"I'll make sure General Arnold knows of my appreciation of all your efforts, General."

"That's kind of you, Mr. Frade. But unnecessary. I am just doing my duty."

"And doing it in an outstanding manner, in my opinion. Thank you again, General."

Frade reached across the seat, shook Wallace's hand, and got out of the staff car. Delgano followed him and they walked to the door of the cottage. There Frade turned and waved to General Wallace as he drove off.

He looked at Delgano and shook his head.

Delgano smiled. "We have officers like that in the Ejército Argentino, too. Many of them are colonels and generals."

"Shame on you, Major Delgano."

Frade lifted the knocker on the door and let it fall.

One of Howard Hughes's Saints pulled the door open a crack and, when he recognized Frade, opened it all the way.

"Be on your guard," Frade announced. "I sent the MPs away."

He intended it to be a joke. If it amused Howard's Saint, there was no sign of it on his face.

"They're in the kitchen," Howard's Saint said.

Len Fischer was still wearing major's leaves and MP insignia on his uniform, but the white leather accoutrements were gone. Oberstleutnant Wilhelm Frogger was wearing suit pants and a white shirt with the tie pulled down. Frade saw Frogger's suit jacket on the back of a chair.

Frade said, "What happened to your pistol, Len? And the fancy holster?"

"Good evening, sir. It's nice to see you again, sir. I'm fine, thank you."

"Don't let that major's leaf go to your head, Len," Frade said, then motioned toward Delgano. "You remember Captain Delgano, right?"

The two wordlessly shook hands.

Fischer turned around. He had a Model 1911-A1 Colt pistol in the small of his back.

"And who is this gentleman?" Frade asked about Frogger.

"My name is Wilhelm Fischer," Frogger said formally. "I am a South African."

"And presumably you have a passport to prove it?"

Frogger reached into an interior pocket of the suit jacket and came out with a passport, which he handed to Frade.

Frade studied it carefully for almost a minute, then handed it to Delgano.

"This is Mr. Fischer, of Durban, South Africa," Frade said. "He'll be flying to Buenos Aires with us."

Delgano examined the passport.

"According to this, Mr. Fischer is already in Argentina," he said.

"It also shows he's been all over South America in the last six months. And if you look carefully, Gonzo, you'll see that the immigration officer was a little sloppy with his stamp. You can't quite make out the date when he passed through immigration. Just that it was this month."

"Very good," Delgano said. "Why the name 'Fischer'?"

Len Fischer answered the question: "Colonel Graham said because Fischer, 'one who fishes,' is close to Frogger, 'one who spears frogs.' And easy to remember."

"Who are you?" Frogger asked Delgano somewhat arrogantly.

Frade said: "He's the chief pilot of South American Airways, Mr. Fischer. And if you don't exchange any more information than that, both of you will be able to truthfully tell anyone who asks that you don't know anything about the other one. I introduced you here. Leave it at that."

He let that sink it, then said: "Two questions, Len. One, is there any reason that we—the Lodestar and the Constellation—can't leave here at first light? And, two, do you know how to get in touch with the Connie crew?"

"Colonel Graham said it was your call how far I went?" Len Fischer said.

"I can't see any reason why you can't go back to the States on the Connie. So answer my questions."

"The crew is in the BOQ. I have a number."

"Call it. Tell them as soon as General Wallace sends a car, we're going to the club for dinner. Ask the pilot to meet me there."

[THREE]
Estancia San Pedro y San Pablo
Near Pila
Buenos Aires Province, Argentina
1105 12 August 1943

"How's your dead-reckoning navigation, Gonzo?" Frade had asked as they had begun the climb-out from Canoas, the sun still low on the horizon.

"I'm afraid to ask why we're going to need it."

"I don't want to fly across Uruguay or Argentina to Jorge Frade. Nobody's going to spot us if we fly fifty miles off the coast, then make a hard right to Estancia San Pedro y San Pablo at Samborombón Bay."

Delgano understood.

"And then go back out to sea, then up the River Plate to Jorge Frade, once we discharge our passenger?"

"You got it."

"And you're not going to call Jorge Frade with our ETA?"

Frade gestured at the instrument panel. "Our radios are out. Didn't you notice that I couldn't tell Canoas what our destination was when they asked?"

Delgano shook his head. He dug into his overnight bag and came out with an E6B flight computer, an unusual-looking slide rule.

"Where'd you get the Whiz Wheel?" Frade asked, surprised that Delgano had one.

"Courtesy of the Lockheed Aircraft Company. They gave everybody one."

"Not me."

"Well, they probably figured if Howard Hughes let you fly a Constellation, you probably already had one. Or they don't like you. One or the other."

"Compute time at three hundred twenty knots per hour to Punta del Este. I'll come in close enough to see it. If you're anywhere close, we can use that to plot where to turn for Samborombón Bay."

Delgano had nodded his understanding.

Punta del Este, Uruguay, a point jutting into the Atlantic Ocean and marking the northern end of the 120-mile-wide mouth of the River Plate, became visible ninety seconds before Delgano's calculations said it would.

And, about forty minutes later, so did Dolores, a village not far from the shore of Samborombón Bay. And, ten minutes after that, Frade made a pass over the runway at Estancia San Pedro y San Pablo.

There was now only one more problem, which Frade had first seriously thought of when taking off from Canoas. In the passenger compartment, in addition to Mr. Wilhelm Fischer and his two genuine if somewhat battered South African leather suitcases, there was an assortment of spare aircraft parts that included an engine and a propeller. It all brought the Lodestar to just about maximum gross takeoff weight.

The runway at Estancia San Pedro y San Pablo had not been constructed with an aircraft as large as a Lodestar in mind. Landing there had not been a problem so far, but never before had he attempted to land in such a heavily laden Lodestar.

Or tried to take off in one.

The worst scenario was that the wheels would sink into the runway during the landing roll, causing a crash. More probably, if they were going to sink through the macadam, they would do so when the aircraft had stopped, which wouldn't cause a crash but would keep him from getting the Lodestar back in the air until most of the weight was removed.

Whatever the risk, Frade had decided it had to be taken. The priority was to get Frogger safely off the airplane. He would have to deal with whatever happened after that had been done.

The direction of the windsock told Frade that the wind was from the south, which meant that he would have to land passing over the big house and end the landing roll at the southern end of the runway.

The landing itself went well, and if the weight was tearing up the runway, he couldn't tell it by feel. He braked carefully, and when the Lodestar had slowed until it was just moving, he immediately began to turn the airplane around. If it was going to sink into the ground, better that it do so near the hangar and the house. He had no trouble turning, and as he taxied toward the hangar, he could see no evidence of damage to the runway.

Frade first saw that his red Lodestar was parked in the hangar—but only as far in as its wider-than-the-hangar-doorway wings would permit. Then he saw Señora Dorotea Mallín de Frade standing in front of the hangar and waving.

As he drew closer, he could see the expression on her face. It was not that of the loving bride and mother-to-be joyously greeting her husband's return home.

Frade grew concerned.

Something's gone wrong.

From the look on her face, something terrible.

Then Clete saw Oscar Schultz, in his gaucho costume and a Thompson sub-machine gun hanging from his shoulder. Standing just inside the hangar were Technical Sergeant William Ferris and Captain Madison R. Sawyer III. Ferris had a self-loading shotgun cradled in his arms, and Sawyer another Thompson, plus a Model 1911-A1 in a holster.

What the hell is going on?

"Shut it down, Gonzo," Frade ordered. And then he changed his mind. "Leave Number Two running. We may have to get out of here."

He unfastened his harness and made his way quickly through the passenger compartment. Frogger was about to unfasten his seat belt.

"Stay there," Frade ordered as he wrestled with the door.

Dorotea ran to him and embraced him. He was conscious of the swell of her belly against him.

"What's with all the guns?" Clete asked, his mouth against her hair.

She exhaled audibly and pushed away from him.

"We couldn't be sure it was you in the plane," she said. "Where the hell have you been?"

"Sweetheart, what's happened?"

"Oscar and I went out to Casa Chica yesterday afternoon to take supplies. Oh, God, darling! There was nobody there, and bullet holes all over. And a lot of blood on the verandah and the stairs from the landing strip."

"The Froggers?"

She shook her head.

"Nobody was there. Not Enrico, not Rodolfo—he was out there, too—none of our gauchos, nobody."

"Jesus Christ!"

"Where the hell have you been? We didn't even know where to call you."

"I've been flying down here from Burbank. Delgano and me. And Oberst-leutnant Frogger."

Her face showed her confusion and surprise at that announcement. She said: "And Peter sent word—not much—telling me to be very careful."

Clete looked over her shoulder at Schultz as he approached.

"Chief?"

"It looks like somebody figured out where you stashed the Froggers, Major, and went and took them out." He held his hands out in front of him in a gesture of apology. "Christ, I'm sorry."

"Forget sorry," Frade said.

Delgano came out of the Lodestar, followed by Frogger, and walked up to them.

"We have a problem," Frade announced to them, then looked at Frogger. "Colonel, somebody—somebody, hell, who else could it be?—SS-Obersturmbannführer Cranz found out where we had your parents. Now we don't know where they are."

"Mein Gott!"

"It gets worse. According to Lieutenant Schultz"—he nodded at Schultz and Frogger's face showed surprise at that—"and my wife, they shot up the place pretty well. There was blood all over."

"The house is a fucking mess, Colonel," Schultz confirmed. "Looks like it's been in a war. We picked up some nine-millimeter Parabellum cases, which is interesting."

"You're saying my parents are dead?" Frogger asked evenly.

"We don't *know* that," Frade said.

Frogger's face showed that he was not in the mood for wishful thinking.

"But I think we have to accept that Obersturmbannführer Cranz's order that they be killed when and where found has been carried out. I'm very sorry, Colonel."

Frogger nodded just perceptibly.

"And now?" he asked.

"Now we have to keep the same thing from happening to you," Frade said, then turned to Delgano. "And we have to keep your ass out of a crack, Gonzo."

"Where did you have the Froggers?" Delgano asked.

"On a small estancia, Casa Chica, not that far from here."

"How could Cranz have heard about that?"

"I don't know. But it has to be him and the Germans. The Argentines would have just taken them and returned them to the embassy."

"Unless the Germans are somehow going to make it look as if you're responsible," Delgano said. "That would solve a lot of problems for them."

Frade looked at him as he considered that, then said, "The problem right now is to keep the colonel alive, and keep you out of trouble."

He waved for Captain Sawyer to come over. Sergeant Ferris came with him.

"This is Colonel Frogger," Frade said. Both saluted.

"Take him out on the estancia. Make him comfortable. He's very important. I can't tell you why, but we can't have him captured by either the Argentines or the Germans. We might have to take off for Uruguay—or Brazil—in a hurry, so be prepared for that. If he goes, everybody goes. Get my airplane out of the hangar and make it ready to take off in a hurry."

"Where are you going?"

"To Jorge Frade, where Gonzo and I will know nothing about any of this. I'll see what I can find out. The truth is we're going to have to play this by ear. The priority is to keep Colonel Frogger safe."

[FOUR]
Aeropuerto Coronel Jorge G. Frade
Morón, Buenos Aires Province, Argentina
1305 12 August 1943

They used up most of the runway getting the SAA Lodestar off the ground, but they made it.

"Write this down, Gonzo," Clete said as they were climbing out. "Don't try to take off from Estancia San Pedro y San Pablo in one of these at max gross takeoff weight."

Delgano didn't reply.

Frade said: "What you're going to do—what I hope you're going to do, because I wouldn't blame you if you went right to Colonel Martín—"

"I'm not going to do that. Did you really think I would?"

"Sorry. And thank you." He was quiet in thought a moment, then went on: "Since I don't think anybody saw us at Estancia San Pedro y San Pablo, maybe we can get away with acting as if we know nothing about what happened. We have just arrived from a very long flight from the States. I keep saying this, but keeping Frogger out of the hands of the Germans is the priority. He knows too much about the plot to take Hitler out."

"There's no way they can know we brought him with us," Delgano said. "If . . . you for some reason can't do it yourself, I'll take your Lodestar and fly him anywhere you say."

Frade looked at him. "That would be really putting your neck in the noose, you understand?"

"I understand."

Frade nodded. "Okay. If that becomes necessary, take Captain Ashton and the others with you. They'll—"

"Dorotea, too?"

Frade hesitated just perceptibly before saying, "Yeah, you'd better take her, too. She won't want to go, thinking she can somehow help me if she stays. Tell her I'm already in Canoas."

"I understand."

Frade spent most of the just-over-one-hour-flight to Morón thinking of the worst possible scenarios for what was going to happen next. There were at least a half-dozen of them—and they were all frightening.

They called the Jorge Frade tower as soon as they could pick up the radio direction finder signal. They were then just inside the mouth of the River Plate, from there a thirty-minute flight to Morón. But they were not more than twenty minutes out when the tower responded.

Clete Frade had an insane thought as he turned on final and ordered Delgano to put the gear down.

If we crash on landing, a lot of problems would be solved.

And as soon as the Lodestar touched down, Clete saw that the problems were about to begin: In civilian clothing, El Coronel Alejandro Bernardo Martín—the Chief of the Ethical Standards Office of the Bureau of Internal Security—was in front of one of the hangars, leaning on the fender of a 1939 Dodge sedan.

"I was afraid of that," Delgano said.

"Just remember: You know nothing."

"And what if someone did see us at Estancia San Pedro y San Pablo?"

Frade didn't reply.

As the Lodestar taxied past the closest hangar toward the second one, where Martín waited, Frade saw something he absolutely didn't expect to see: Sergeant Major Enrico Rodríguez, Cavalry, Retired. Enrico was sitting on the open tailgate of a 1941 Ford station wagon.

"Did you see what I saw, Gonzo?"

"Maybe things aren't as bad as they seem."

"That's known as pissing in the wind. But at least Enrico's alive."

Martín was waiting for them when they got out of the airplane.

"Well, I'm flattered to see you here, Colonel," Frade said. "But Delgano and I really expected a brass band."

Martín—not surprising Frade at all—did not seem amused.

"You look distressed," Frade said. "Is something wrong?"

"I'm afraid so."

"Are you going to tell me?"

"Colonel Perón made it quite clear that he would prefer to explain the situation to you personally."

"Well, I'm in no mood for him right now. It's been a very long flight, and I want to go home. I just saw that Enrico has brought a station wagon—"

"Going home," Martín interrupted, "will have to wait until you see Colonel Perón, I'm afraid, Señor Frade."

"That sounds awfully official, Colonel. Almost as if I said, 'I'm going home,' you'd put handcuffs on me and throw me in the back of your car."

"I hope it won't come to that, Señor Frade."

"Oh, Jesus Christ!" Frade said disgustedly. "Well, let me tell Enrico what's going on, then send him to my house in Buenos Aires."

Martín considered that for a long moment.

"All right," Martín said finally. "Please don't do anything impulsive like getting in your car and driving off."

"You want to come, Gonzo, and call your wife to let her know you're back?"

"I need a word with Señor Delgano," Martín said. "Please don't be long, Señor Frade."

"Señor Clete, when I saw you in the airplane, I knew that a merciful God had answered my prayers," Enrico said emotionally, and wrapped his arms around Frade.

He's actually crying.

But no time to get emotional.

"I have to know what happened, Enrico, and quickly."

Enrico nodded. "I have a dear friend in the mountain troops in San Martín de los Andes. He called me. We went to corporal's school together and to sergeant's school and—"

"What did he say when he called you?"

"That something strange was happening. He said the regiment had been quartering a half-dozen Nazis—the German Nazis, not Argentine, the ones who wear black uniforms and have a skull on their caps?"

Frade nodded his understanding.

"They came off a submarine?" Enrico asked.

Frade nodded again. "So I was told."

"Well, these Nazis were getting ready to—what he said was 'take care of some traitors'—and that they would be transported to Tandil in regimental trucks. And my friend said he knew that Casa Chica was near Tandil, and that I might want to tell you."

"So you were ready for them?"

"What is very sad, Don Cletus, it breaks my heart to tell you, is that this was done at the orders of El Coronel Perón."

"How do you know that?"

"I saw him with my own eyes, Don Cletus. I even took his picture when he was on the road."

"You did what?"

"I took his picture."

"I didn't know you had a camera," Clete said, thinking out loud.

"Doña Dorotea brought it to Casa Chica one day and then forgot it, and Señor Frogger showed me how to use it."

"Where is Señor Frogger now?"

"On Estancia San Pedro y San Pablo, of course. Safe, of course."

"What happened at Casa Chica, Enrico?"

"Well, when I knew that the Nazi bastards were up to something, Sergeant Stein and I took the Froggers back to Estancia San Pedro y San Pablo."

How the hell is that possible?

Dorotea knows nothing about that . . .

"Where's Stein?" Frade said.

"With the Froggers. If you keep interrupting, Don Cletus . . ."

"Sorry."

"I took them to the estancia, and picked up a few gauchos, all old soldiers, and took them back to Casa Chica."

"But you didn't say anything to Doña Dorotea?"

"Of course not. She is in the family way, thanks be to God, and I didn't want to worry her with this. I knew how to handle it."

That explains why she didn't know!

Frade discreetly looked back toward Delgano and Martín. They were deep in discussion. Frade turned to Enrico.

"And how did you handle it, Enrico?"

"Well, we drew the blinds and left the lights on, and the radio, and then we went and hid down by the road. That's where I saw El Coronel Perón. It was late in the afternoon . . ."

"And took his picture?"

"Yes. Him with the colonel of mountain troops and the Nazis in black uniforms."

"And?"

"What surprised me, Don Cletus, what shamed me and broke my heart, was that the mountain troops set up two machine guns, one behind the house and one in front, and fired maybe five hundred rounds, maybe a little more than that, at the house. They didn't try to arrest anybody. They just tried to kill whoever was in the house.

"Then the Nazis went in the house. And of course no one was there.

"So they went and told Colonel Perón and the colonel of mountain troops, and Colonel Perón told them they should stay—not in the house, but around it—in case somebody came back, and that he would send a truck back for them in the morning. So then he and the mountain troops left and the Nazis stayed."

"And then?"

I shouldn't be smiling; getting this story out of him is like pulling teeth.

"And then we waited until the trucks had gone far enough so that they couldn't hear the shots, and we killed the Nazi bastards. I personally killed two of them myself."

"What did you do with the bodies?"

"Left them there. I also took pictures of them, and took their identification papers and one of the hats with the skull on it."

"You think the photos came out?"

"I had them processed in Pilar the next morning—that would be yesterday morning. They came out very well."

"Why didn't you tell Doña Dorotea about any of this? Or at least El Jefe?"

"I tried. But when I came up to the house, I saw her and El Jefe had just driven off in the Horch. I couldn't catch them, as much as I would have liked to, to spare Doña Dorotea, in her delicate condition, what she would see when she got to Casa Chica. I was too late, I am sorry to say."

"Then why didn't you tell her when she came back?"

Sergeant Major Enrico Rodríguez, Cavalry, Retired, looked uncomfortable at being put on the spot. He broke eye contact, looked at his feet a long moment as he gathered his thoughts, then looked back at Clete.

"You know, Don Cletus, that I love you as if you were my own son," he began cautiously. "So I will tell you the truth: I was afraid she would not understand what I had done and would say something that she would later regret."

Clete forced back a smile.

"You can bet on that, Enrico."

"And then there was word that you would be coming back, so I thought I would come here and wait and tell you what had happened."

Now Clete did smile.

"Fess up, Enrico. You're afraid of Doña Dorotea."

"Do not be silly. She's a woman. A wonderful one, to be sure. . . . You will explain to her when we get back to Estancia San Pedro y San Pablo, Don Cletus?"

"I'll try, Enrico. I will try."

"We are going there now?"

"No, first I have to see El Coronel Perón. I'll be riding with Martín. You follow."

[FIVE]
4730 Avenida Libertador
Buenos Aires, Argentina
1515 12 August 1943

"Leave us, please, Colonel Martín," Colonel Juan Domingo Perón said.

"Would you like me to wait, sir?"

"That probably won't be necessary. But, yes, it might be a good idea."

They were in the library. Perón was seated in one of the red leather-upholstered chairs.

A clear memory came to Clete Frade of Hans-Peter von Wachtstein sitting in that chair, half in the bag and listening to Beethoven's Fifth Symphony, the night they first had met.

Seeing Perón in the chair angered him.

"How was the flight, Cletus?"

"Long and tiring, but everybody's going to get their airline transport rat-ings. That, however, is not what this is about, is it, Tío Juan?"

"No, it's not. Have you been to Estancia San Pedro y San Pablo? Talked to anyone there?"

"Is that any of your business?"

Perón's face tightened.

"To put a point on it, have you heard what happened in Tandil?"

"I heard you led some mountain troops there, along with the half-dozen SS troops who got off the U-405, and they shot up the house pretty badly."

"I have no idea where you got that. It's preposterous!"

"You were looking for the Froggers, Tío Juan. But you were a little late. Right about now they should be boarding a British cruiser in Rio de Janeiro. The Brits seem to think Frogger knows something about Operation Phoenix."

Perón's eyes bulged.

He blurted, "Do you have any idea what a dangerous position you're in, you damned fool?"

"Well, your Nazi friends tried to kill me once—in this very house—and that didn't work."

"That could happen again . . ."

"Oh, I don't think so. Now I've got you to protect me."

"What do you mean by that?"

"I mean that if anything should happen to me—or anyone around me—the photographs showing you on the road in Tandil with the colonel of moun-tain troops will surface. And the photos of the dead SS bleeding all over my verandah. That would be a little hard to explain."

Perón reached in his trousers pocket and came out with a small snub-nosed revolver.

Then suddenly there was the sound of the bolt slamming into place in a Remington Model 11 self-loading 12-gauge shotgun.

"What the hell do you think you're doing, Rodríguez?" Perón snapped. "How dare you aim a weapon at me, at an officer?"

You sonofabitch! Frade thought. *You're so drunk with power that you think you could get away with intimidating me—even killing me—in front of Enrico?*

You arrogant bastard. You'll never know such loyalty. . . .

"I suggest you put the pistol on the floor very carefully, Tío Juan," Frade said evenly. "I think Enrico would really like to shoot you. It would be a tragic accident, of course, witnessed by the son of your best friend in his library. Poor old Enrico didn't know it was loaded."

Perón complied.

"What's going to happen now, Tío Juan, is that we are going to forget we ever had this conversation—except, of course, for the part about you telling your Nazi pals that if anything happens to me, I'll make sure that not only are you exposed, but also that map of South America after the Anschluss."

He paused to let that sink in, then added: "And when we see each other again, we'll be pals."

Perón didn't respond.

"You understand me?" Frade demanded.

Perón nodded.

Frade turned and walked to the library door. There he stopped and turned. "One more thing, Tío Juan, you degenerate sonofabitch. You're going to have to find someplace else for your little girls. I want you out of here by tomorrow."

He turned again and walked into the foyer.

Sergeant Major (Retired) Enrico Rodríguez spit on the floor, then followed.

On 7 October 2004, the following story appeared in *The Buenos Aires Herald:*

PERÓN, THE NAZI EMPEROR?

Retired Brazilian Diplomat's Book Claims Perón Planned to Annex Neighboring Countries Had Hitler Won

A retired Brazilian diplomat who during the forties was a spy in Argentina claims that former three-term president Juan Domingo Perón was planning to annex several neighboring countries if the Nazis had won the Second World War, reports the Brazilian magazine *Veja* in its latest edition.

Sérgio Corrêa da Costa, who was the Brazilian ambassador in Washington and London, will reveal details of the plot in his upcoming book, *Chronicle of a Secret War,* scheduled to be launched in Brazil next week.

According to *Veja,* the book has all the ingredients "to become a solid reference for Nazi ideology dissemination research in South America during that period."

Apparently, Corrêa da Costa provides new information which helps to explain the Perónist regime's loyalty toward Adolf Hitler and concludes that this option followed the Argentine populist leader's intention to dominate South America in the event of an Axis victory.

The theory is based on a map which was found among the belongings of a German spy killed by British secret agents in 1941 in the city of Rio de Janeiro.

The map, "drawn by the German high command," showed South America split into five countries, half the current number.

According to the report, Argentina was shown annexing Uruguay, Paraguay, and, sharing with Brazil, other countries such as Peru and Bolivia.

Another document included in Corrêa da Costa's book is a manifesto from the Group of United Officers (GOU), a group of young Argentine army officers to which then-Colonel Perón belonged, who admired the achievements of fascism in Europe and who eventually supported the military coup which jump-started Perón in politics in June 1943.

Uruguay joined the Allies soon after the sinking in the River Plate of the Graf Spee in December 1939, and Brazil, under President Getúlio Vargas, following an agreement with U.S. President Franklin Roosevelt, joined the war effort, sending ground troops and air support to fight in Europe, mainly in the Italian theater of war.

Perón, who died in July 1974 while serving his third term, was the elected president of Argentina between 1946 and 1955. Argentina only declared war on Germany in the last days of the conflict, when it was evident the Axis would lose. (*Mercopress*)